2012年临沂大学"美国文学"精品课程建设成果；
2018年临沂大学"英国文学"精品课程建设成果；
2020年山东省社科规划项目"美国非理性小说叙事对文化认同的建构研究"（项目编号：20CWWJ10）阶段性成果；
2015年国家社科基金项目"美国梦视阈下幽默小说的历史书写"（项目编号：15CWW028）阶段性成果。

英美诗歌
——历史与文本

Anglo-Saxon Poetry: History and Text

唐 文 孟庆梅 马文霞 编著

·沈阳·

ⓒ 唐 文 孟庆梅 马文霞

图书在版编目（CIP）数据

英美诗歌：历史与文本 / 唐文，孟庆梅，马文霞编著. —— 沈阳：东北大学出版社，2020.11
ISBN 978-7-5517-2569-9

Ⅰ.①英… Ⅱ.①唐…②孟…③马… Ⅲ.①诗歌研究—英国②诗歌研究—美国 Ⅳ.①I561.072 ②I712.072

中国版本图书馆 CIP 数据核字（2020）第 237336 号

出 版 者：	东北大学出版社
	地址：沈阳市和平区文化路三号巷 11 号
	邮编：110819
	电话：024-83687331（市场部） 83680181（研发部）
	传真：024-83680180（市场部） 83687332（社务部）
	网址：http://www.neupress.com
	E-mail: neuph@neupress.com
印 刷 者：	广东虎彩云印刷有限公司
发 行 者：	东北大学出版社
幅面尺寸：	170 mm × 240 mm
印 张：	39
字 数：	559 千字
出版时间：	2020 年 11 月第 1 版
印刷时间：	2021 年 1 月第 1 次印刷
组稿编辑：	罗 鑫
责任编辑：	刘新宇 张德喜
封面设计：	汤 丽

ISBN 978-7-5517-2569-9 定 价：580.00 元

前　言

英美文学是世界文学的重要组成部分，也是了解世界文化的重要渠道。由于英美诗歌大多用英语写成，不但令不擅长英语的诗歌爱好者望而却步，连初步接触英语文学的本科学生也不敢涉猎。从本书编著者多年的教学经验可以看出，外国语高校大三学生在最初接触英语文学时一般都存在抵触情绪，而国内目前用学生的母语——汉语作为赏析媒介的教材和作品少之又少。此外，如何教好英文诗歌也是实现"完善校级精品课、争取建立省级精品课"目标的重要步骤之一。以上三个方面的原因促成了《英美诗歌——历史与文本》的编著。本书中的诗歌选文来自英文原著，赏析部分使用通俗易懂的汉语完成。所选的诗歌最大限度地展现了英国文学和美国文学的发展史，以诗歌为点，以文学史为线，并以"深度阅读"来扩充历史涵盖面，让学生在赏析诗歌的同时，对英美文学史有更深层次的了解。

学生对诗歌发怵，是促使我们动笔的主要原因。实际上，英语诗歌之所以让人望而却步，主要是因为其中的押韵格律以及修辞手法与汉语诗歌多有不同。只要稍微了解一些英语诗歌阅读技巧，再去读诗就会有豁然开朗的体会。英语诗歌有两个基本的概念，即押韵（rhyme）和音步（foot）。

所谓押韵，讲的是词汇与词汇之间的关系，指的是两个或两个以上的单词中包含相似的发音，韵文经常用在诗歌或歌曲中。例如，古诗《贝奥武甫之歌》中的一句诗"of men was the mildest and most beloved",辅音 /m/ 分别在三个单词 men、mildest 和 most 中出现,因此这三个词彼此押韵。在英语诗歌中,押韵又分为三种不同的类型:头韵(alliteration)、腹韵(assonance)和尾韵(consonance)。两个或两个以上的词语,如果读音的第一个辅音相同,就押头韵;如果读音中有相同或相似的元音,就押腹韵;如果读音中的最后一个辅音相同,而辅音前面的元音不同,就押尾韵。以托马斯·格雷《墓园挽歌》的第一个诗节为例。

The curfew tolls the knell of parting day,
The lowing herd wind slowly o'er the lea,
The plowman homeward plods his weary way,
And leaves the world to darkness and to me.

第 3 行中后面两个词"weary"和"way"以同一个辅音 /w/ 开始,因此押头韵;第 2 行中的两个词"slowly"和"o'er"读音中有一个共同的元音 /əu/,因此押腹韵;第 2 行中的"herd"和"wind"读音中最后一个辅音 /d/ 相同,因此押尾韵。

所谓音步,讲的是句与句之间的关系,指的是重读音节和非重读音节的组合,主要作用是衡量英文诗歌句子的格律。根据音步中重读音节和非重读音节的前后顺序,可以将音步分为抑扬格(iamb)、扬抑格(trochee)、抑抑扬格(anapaest)、扬抑抑格(dactyl)和扬扬格(spodee)五种。具体组合和例子如下:

非重读音节 + 重读音节 ⟶ 抑扬格

Shall 'I/ comp'are/ thee 'to/ a s'um/mer's d'ay

（莎士比亚《十四行诗》第 18 首）

重读音节 + 非重读音节 ⟶ 扬抑格
P'resent/ m'irth has/ p'resent/ l'aughter
（莎士比亚《第十二夜》）

非重读音节 + 非重读音节 + 重读音节 ⟶ 抑抑扬格
Of the m'id/ night ride o'f / Pau'l Rev'ere
（朗费罗《保罗·列维尔骑马来》）

重读音节 + 非重读音节 + 非重读音节 ⟶ 扬抑抑格
S'aying that now/ y'ou are not/ a's you were
（托马斯·哈代《卿轻呼唤》）

重读音节 + 重读音节 ⟶ 扬扬格
Th'ey di'ed/—n'or were/ th'ose flowers/ m'ore gay
（菲利普·弗瑞诺《野忍冬花》）

一般情况下，根据一行诗文中包含音步的个数，确定其为几音步。下面以最常见的抑扬格为例，来说明英文诗歌中使用频率最高的格律形式。弥尔顿在诗歌《悼亡妻》中使用了五步抑扬格（iambic pentameter），诗歌的第一句：

Meth'ought /I s'aw /my l'ate /esp'ous/ed s'aint
该诗使用了抑扬格的音步，该音步出现了五次，故称为五步抑扬格。以此类推，英语诗歌中比较常用的抑扬格格律形式有三步抑扬格（iambic

trimeter）、四步抑扬格（iambic tetrameter）、五步抑扬格、六步抑扬格（iambic hexameter）等。下面就抑扬格音步个数举例说明。

To j'oin/ the b'rim/ming r'iver（三步抑扬格；丁尼生《小溪》）

For m'en/ may c'ome/ and m'en/ may g'o（四步抑扬格；丁尼生《小溪》）

To s'well/ the g'ourd/ and pl'ump/ the h'a/zel sh'ells
（五步抑扬格；济慈《秋颂》）

The th'ings/ which' I/ have s'een/ I n'ow/ can s'ee/ no m'ore
（六步抑扬格；华兹华斯《颂诗——忆童年而悟不朽》）

诗歌格律的划分要求阅读者有一定的英语语音知识和语感，这对英语初学者来说确有难度。需要指出的是，近代特别是现代大多数诗人创作时不再拘泥于一种格律形式，甚至不再讲求格律，如美国自由派诗人狄更生和民主诗人惠特曼就是自由诗体的倡导者。

上文讲到的押韵涉及的是词汇之间的关系，音步探讨的是句子之间的关系，押韵格式（rhyme scheme）则展示了句子以及诗节之间的关系。顾名思义，押韵格式指的是诗歌中句子之间的押韵关系。通常情况下，判断押韵格式主要通过句子的尾韵，即每一行诗文最后一个单词的读音进行。根据习惯，用小写的英文字母来标示句与句之间的押韵。以莎士比亚的《十四行诗》（第20首）为例。

Sonnet 20

A woman's face with nature's own hand painted,
Hast thou, the master mistress of my passion;
A woman's gentle heart, but not acquainted
With shifting change, as is false women's fashion;

An eye more bright than theirs, less false in rolling,
Gilding the object whereupon it gazeth;
A man in hue all hues in his controlling,
Which steals men's eyes and women's souls amazeth.

And for a woman wert thou first created;
Till Nature, as she wrought thee, fell a-doting,
And by addition me of thee defeated,
By adding one thing to my purpose nothing.

But since she prick'd thee out for women's pleasure,
Mine be thy love and thy love's use their treasure.

根据每一行的最后一个发音，可以标示出诗歌的押韵格式为：abab cdcd efef gg。有些诗歌有固定的押韵格式，如上文中的莎士比亚《十四行诗》。综合看来，从押韵到音步，从音步到押韵格式，诗歌研究的视野从单词到诗节，十分清晰。和中文诗歌一样，修辞也是英文诗歌写作和赏析的重要组成部分。由于在修辞主题和手法方面和中文诗歌存在很多共同之处，不再一一赘述。

在调研时，我们发现有关英美诗歌的论著确实比较缺乏。由于涉及诗歌理论等专业知识，目前国内有关英美诗歌的论著比较少，而仅有的论著主要分为三类。其一，用英文编写的专业教材，如张剑、赵冬和王文丽编写的《英美诗歌选读》和郭嘉编写的《英美诗歌精品赏析》。其二，专门针对"英国诗歌"或"美国诗歌"的论著，其中大部分用英文编写。这类论著一般会包含同一作家的多个作品，并不会涉及太多的文学史，如陶洁编写的《美国诗歌选读》和李正栓、陈岩编写的《美国诗歌研究》。其三，主要用来普及英文诗歌理论和技巧的论著，这类作品所面对的读者群体是具有英语语言文学基础的专业人士，属于比较深层次的专业理论图书，如毕小君主编的《英美诗歌概论》。

在总结前人论著的基础上，我们在编写《英美诗歌——历史与文本》时，注重在以下几个方面有所创新。首先，论著力图做到以史为纲、以作家诗歌作品为点，点线结合，在学生脑海中构建一条清晰易懂的英国文学和美国文学发展史的同时，让其领略英文诗歌背后的独特魅力。其次，论著力求化复杂为简单，用朴素的语言讲述深奥的专业知识。论著中所选诗歌为原版的英文作品，而赏析部分用汉语写成，配以形象的图片文字，使其拥有更广大的读者群体。再次，论著中的赏析部分把诗人的创作理念以及诗歌包含的主题思想和同时代的政治因素、社会根源以及文化背景联系起来，而非就文学论文学。最后，论著主体后面加入"深度阅读"，扩大论著内容的含量，让读者更加清晰而深刻地了解诗歌的历史时代背景，更加全面地解读诗歌。

唐　文

2020年6月

目　录

英国诗歌部分

第一章　早期诗歌 ……………………………………………2
　一、Poem Reading ………………………………………………3
　二、Further Reading ……………………………………………6

第二章　中古时期诗歌 ……………………………………10
　一、Poem Reading ………………………………………………11
　　（一）Sir Gawain and the Green Knight ……………………11
　　（二）The Canterbury Tales …………………………………15
　二、Further Reading ……………………………………………19
　　（一）Cantus Troilus …………………………………………19
　　（二）A Rondel of Merciless Beauty ………………………22

第三章　文艺复兴时期诗歌 ………………………………25
　一、Poem Reading ………………………………………………26
　　（一）Sonnet 18 ………………………………………………26
　　（二）Sonnet 34 ………………………………………………29

二、Further Reading ··31
　　（一）True Love ··31
　　（二）Sonnet 29 ··33
　　（三）Sonnet 66 ··36
　　（四）Sonnet 73 ··38
　　（五）Spring（from *Love's Labor Lost*）···············40
　　（六）Hark！Hark! The Lark（from *Cymbeline*）········43
　　（七）To Be, or Not to Be（from *Hamlet*）·············45
　　（八）Sonnet 75 ··49

第四章　十七世纪革命与复辟时期诗歌 ····················52

一、Poem Reading ··53
　　（一）A Valediction: Forbidding Mourning ···············53
　　（二）Paradise Lost ·····································57

二、Further Reading ··64
　　（一）The Good-Morrow ·································64
　　（二）Song ··68
　　（三）The Flea ··71
　　（四）Song on May Morning ····························75
　　（五）On His Deceased Wife ···························77
　　（六）On His Blindness ································80
　　（七）On His Being Arrived to the Age of Twenty-Three ···83

第五章　十八世纪英国启蒙时期诗歌 ······················87

一、Poem Reading ··88
　　（一）The Rape of the Lock ·····························88
　　（二）Elegy Written in a Country Churchyard ············95

（三）The Chimney Sweeper ……………………………104
二、Further Reading ……………………………………………110
　　（一）An Essay on Criticism 1 ……………………………110
　　（二）An Essay on Criticism 2 ……………………………114
　　（三）An Essay on Man ……………………………………117
　　（四）Ode on Solitude ……………………………………120
　　（五）The Echoing Green …………………………………123
　　（六）The Tiger ……………………………………………127

第六章　浪漫主义时期诗歌 ………………………………132

一、Poem Reading ………………………………………………133
　　（一）I Wondered Lonely as a Cloud ……………………133
　　（二）Ode on a Grecian Urn ………………………………136
二、Further Reading ……………………………………………140
　　（一）She Dwelt Among the Untrodden Ways …………140
　　（二）The Solitary Reaper …………………………………142
　　（三）Composed Upon Westminster Bridge ……………147
　　（四）Lines Written in Early Spring ………………………150
　　（五）Lines Composed a Few Miles Above Tintern Abbey ……154
　　（六）Ode to a Nightingale ………………………………170
　　（七）To Autumn …………………………………………179
　　（八）The Human Seasons ………………………………184
　　（九）On the Grasshopper and Cricket …………………188

第七章　维多利亚时期诗歌 ………………………………191

一、Poem Reading ………………………………………………192
　　（一）Break, Break, Break …………………………………192

（二）My Last Duchess ··················195

　　（三）Goblin Market ····················200

二、Further Reading ·······················208

　　（一）Ulysses ···························208

　　（二）Crossing the Bar ···············216

　　（三）Eagle ·····························219

　　（四）In Memoriam A. H. H. ·······221

　　（五）Meeting at Night ···············224

　　（六）Parting at Morning ············226

　　（七）Home-Thoughts, From Abroad ···228

　　（八）Who Has Seen the Wind? ···230

　　（九）Paradise ··························232

　　（十）When I am Dead, My Dearest ···235

第八章 现当代诗歌 ·····················238

一、Poem Reading ························239

　　（一）The Second Coming ···········239

　　（二）The Love Song of J. Alfred Prufrock ···243

　　（三）Death of a Naturalist ·········253

二、Further Reading ·······················257

　　（一）The Wild Swans at Coole ···257

　　（二）When You Are Old ···········262

　　（三）Easter 1916 ······················264

　　（四）Byzantium ························273

　　（五）The Waste Land—The Burial of The Dead ···279

　　（六）From Preludes ··················284

　　（七）The Hollow Man ···············286

（八）Little Giddingo ……………………………………289
（九）Digging ………………………………………………299
（十）In Memoriam M.K.H., 1911—1984 ………………304

美国诗歌部分

第九章　殖民地时期诗歌 ………………………………308
一、Poem Reading ………………………………………309
（一）Verses Upon the Burning of Our House ………309
（二）Upon a Spider Catching a Fly …………………314
（三）The Indian Burying Ground ……………………320
二、Further Reading ……………………………………325
（一）To My Dear and Loving Husband ………………325
（二）The Author to Her Book …………………………326
（三）The Prologue ………………………………………329
（四）In Memory of My Dear Grandchild Elizabeth Bradstreet …336
（五）As Weary Pilgrim, now at Rest …………………338
（六）Huswifery …………………………………………342
（七）The Ebb and Flow …………………………………345
（八）Upon the Sweeping Flood ………………………347
（九）I Am the Living Bread: Meditation Eight: John 6:51 ……349
（十）The Wild Honey Suckle …………………………353
（十一）The Hurricane …………………………………356

第十章　浪漫主义时期诗歌 ……………………………362
一、Poem Reading ………………………………………364

- （一）Paul Revere's Ride ······364
- （二）Song of Myself ······373
- （三）A Narrow Fellow in the Grass ······383
- （四）The Raven ······388

二、Furthe Reading ······397
- （一）A Psalm of Life ······397
- （二）The Arrow and the Song ······401
- （三）The Tide Rises, the Tide Falls ······403
- （四）O Captain! My Captain! ······405
- （五）I Hear America Singing ······408
- （六）Out of the Cradle Endlessly Rocking ······410
- （七）Because I Could Not Stop for Death ······428
- （八）I Heard a Fly Buzz When— I Died ······432
- （九）I Died for Beauty ······434
- （十）Success ······436
- （十一）A bird Came Down the Walk ······438
- （十二）"Hope" Is the Thing With Feathers ······441
- （十三）"Why Do I Love" You, Sir? ······443
- （十四）The Soul Selects Her Own Society ······445
- （十五）Wild Nights! Wild Nights! ······447
- （十六）I'm Nobody! Who are you? ······449
- （十七）To Helen ······451
- （十八）Annabel Lee ······454
- （十九）A Dream Within a Dream ······459
- （二十）The City in the Sea ······461
- （二十一）To My Mother ······467

（二十二）Eldorado ·· 469

（二十三）Romance ·· 472

（二十四）Sonnet—To Science ···································· 475

（二十五）The Haunted Palace ···································· 477

（二十六）"Alone" ·· 482

第十一章 现代主义诗歌 ·· 485

一、Poem Reading ·· 486

（一）In a Station of the Metro ·································· 486

（二）Patterns ·· 489

（三）The Great Figure ·· 496

（四）The Road Not Taken ······································ 499

二、Further Reading ·· 503

（一）A Girl ·· 503

（二）A Pact ·· 505

（三）Salutation ·· 506

（四）Wind and Silver ·· 508

（五）Falling Snow ·· 510

（六）The Red Wheelbarrow ···································· 511

（七）Spring and All ·· 513

（八）This Is Just to Say ·· 517

（九）Mending Wall ·· 519

（十）Stopping by Woods on a Snowy Evening ·············· 524

（十一）Fire and Ice ·· 527

（十二）After Apple-Picking ···································· 528

（十三）Birches ·· 533

第十二章　当代诗歌 ·············539

一、Poem Reading ·············540
（一）Anecdote of the Jar ·············540
（二）Crusoe in England ·············543
（三）Howl—For Carl Solomon ·············554

二、Further Reading ·············564
（一）The Snow Man ·············564
（二）The Idea of Order at Key West ·············567
（三）The Emperor of Ice Cream ·············573
（四）The Fish ·············575
（五）Sestina ·············582
（六）The Armadillo ·············587
（七）At the Fish Houses ·············591
（八）A Supermarket in California ·············599

参考文献 ·············603

英国诗歌部分

第一章　早期诗歌

　　凯尔特人（Celts）是英国最早的土著居民。英国被罗马人占领后（公元前1世纪至公元410年），成为罗马帝国的一个行省，罗马帝国没落后，欧洲大陆的盎格鲁人（Angles）、撒克逊人（Saxons）和裘特人（Jutes）逐渐形成条顿人（Teutors），即日耳曼人，日耳曼人入侵该岛，把英国中部叫作安吉利（Anglia），或称为英格兰（England）。罗马帝国从不列颠撤军后，条顿人把当时的英国改名为盎格尔兰德（Angle-land），即现在的英格兰（England），使用的语言是盎格鲁撒克逊，也叫撒克逊语。

　　最初的古英语诗歌不是由土著人创作的，而是盎格鲁人、撒克逊人和裘特人以欧洲大陆为题材、背景创作而成的。该时期的异教徒诗歌主要以口头形式为特点；基督教诗歌主要特点是正式的书面语形式，由修道院的僧侣创作而成。基督文明的到来给英国带来了生活方式、社会制度和语言上的更新。

　　早期的英国诗人凯德姆（Caedmon）生活在7世纪下半期，塞里武甫（Cynewulf）生活在8世纪，两者都以宗教诗歌创作而出名。除此之外，还有四首非常出名的早期英语诗歌：《埃琳娜》（*Elinna*），《使徒们的命运》（*Disciples' Destiny*），《基督升天》（*The Messiah's Rising to Heaven*），

第一章　早期诗歌

《朱莉安娜》(*Juliana*)。英国早期诗歌还包括如《贝奥武甫之歌》(*The Song of Beowulf*)等在内的一些伟大史诗，著名的诗歌如《旅行者之歌》(*The Traveler's Song*)、《航海家》(*The Sea-farer*)中出现了旅行、航海等名词，诗歌主题丰富，表达了世事无常、失落感、分离、孤独、命运、死亡等主题，充分展现了日耳曼文化传统和基督教思想。

古英语诗歌主要以头韵体为特点。史诗《贝奥武甫之歌》共3182行，非常细腻地刻画了一位典型的民族英雄，史诗融故事与艺术于一体，对于当时整个欧洲来说，堪称一部不朽的杰作。

盎格鲁-撒克逊时期的诗歌强悍、忧郁。古英语诗人以非凡的想象力和高超的艺术手法表达了对于命运无常及人性的思索，同时也传递出他们对于美好生活的向往。

一、Poem Reading

Beowulf

1　Grendel snatched at the first Geat
　　He came to, ripped him apart, cut
　　His body to bits with powerful jaws,
　　Drank the blood from his veins and bolted
5　Him down, hands and feet; death
　　And Grendel's great teeth came together,
　　Snapping life shut. Then he stepped to another
　　Still body, clutched at Beowulf with his claws,
　　Grasped at a strong-hearted wakeful sleeper
10　And was instantly seized himself, claws
　　Bent back as Beowulf leaned up on one arm.

......

　　The high hall rang, its roof boards swayed,

　　And Danes shook with terror. Down

15　The aisles the battle swept, angry

　　And wild. Herot trembled, wonderfully

　　Built to withstand the blows, the struggling

　　Great bodies beating at its beautiful walls;

......

20　of men was the mildest and most beloved,

　　to his kin the kindest, keenest for praise.

　　Then the Goth's people reared a mighty pile

　　With shields and armour hung, as he had asked,

　　And in the midst the warriors laid their lord,

25　Lamenting. Then the warriors on the mound

　　Kindled a mighty bale fire; the smoke rose

　　Black from the Swedish pine, the sound of flame.

　　Mingled with sound of weeping; ... while smoke

　　Spreads over heaven. Then upon the hill

30　High, broad, and to be seen far out at sea.

　　In ten days they had built and walled in it

　　As the wise thought most worthy; placed in it

　　Rings, jewels, other treasures from the hoard.

　　They left the riches, golden joy of earls,

35　In dust, for earth to hold; where yet it lies,

　　Useless as ever. Then about the mound

　　The warriors rode, and raised a mournful song

第一章　早期诗歌

>   For their dead king; exalted his brave deeds,
>
>   Holding it fit men honour their liege lord,
>
> 40 Praise him and love him when his soul is fled.
>
>   Thus the （Geat's people）, sharers of his hearth,
>
>   Mourned their chief's fall, praised him of kings, of men
>
>   The mildest and the kindest, and to all
>
>   His people gentlest, yearning for their praise.

盎格鲁 - 撒克逊时期（449—1066），来自北欧的居民在移居英国大陆的时候，带来了自己的文明，其中著名的就有《贝奥武甫之歌》《旅行者之歌》《航海家》等。在北欧移民与当地居民融合的同时，北欧文明和当地的文化也出现了融合，代表作品便是《贝奥武甫之歌》。《贝奥武甫之歌》写作于八世纪到十一世纪，具体作家和年代已经无从考据。1731年，《贝奥武甫之歌》手稿遭遇大火，被严重损坏。而经历了几个世纪，现存的《贝奥武甫之歌》版本和最初的手稿已有所差别。

《贝奥武甫之歌》讲述的是济特族人贝奥武甫杀死怪兽的故事。诗歌共分为三个部分：第一部分和第二部分分别讲述了贝奥武甫远渡丹麦，帮助当地人杀死葛婪代及其母亲的情节；第三部分是贝奥武甫在自己国家统治五十年后，杀死了作恶的火龙的故事。故事叙述的过程，穿插着几段北欧历史故事，让读者感觉虚幻结合，更增加了贝奥武甫英雄故事的可信度。古诗深刻揭示了当时的社会文化背景。例如，虽然贝奥武甫是一个异教徒，诗人却多次提到了"上帝""统领者"等字眼，让读者感受到当时社会的基督教化。另外，面对葛婪代母子的暴行时丹麦人的不作为，以及面对火龙时济特族人的胆怯，从侧面揭露了盛行于中世纪英雄主义风尚的衰退。

《贝奥武甫之歌》原稿是用古英文创作而成的，如今读到的版本都是学者翻译过来的现代英文版本。诗歌的创作运用了大量的头韵，读起来朗

朗上口，例如选段中第 20 行和第 21 行就比较明显地使用了头韵，分别压 /m/ 和 /k/ 两个辅音。古诗还应用了大量的隐喻，例如"赏赐戒指的人"（ring-giver）指的是国王，而"天鹅的浴盆"（swan's bath）则意指大海。在选文的第 41 行"在壁炉前一同烤火的人"（sharers of his hearth）是与贝奥武甫一同作战的朋友。选文共分为两部分内容：第 1 行到第 19 行描写的是葛婪代吃人，以及贝奥武甫与葛婪代作战的精彩场面，刻画了葛婪代的贪婪可怕和贝奥武甫的勇敢无畏；第 20 行到第 44 行主要描写了贝奥武甫隆重的葬礼，贝奥武甫的死亡实际上预示着中世纪英雄主义的最终落幕。

二、Further Reading

Beowulf（L. 2792—2819）

1   The aged man in his pain—he gazed on the gold,

     "I utter in words my thanks to the Ruler of all,

     To the King of Glory, the everlasting lord,

     For the treasures which I here gaze upon,

5   In that I have been allowed to win

     Such things for my people before my day of death.

     Now that I have given my old life in barter

     For the hoard of treasure, do ye henceforth supply

     The people's needs! I may stay here no longer.

10   Bid ye war-veterans raise a conspicuous barrow

     After the funeral fire, on a projection by the sea,

     Which shall tower high on Hronesness

     As a memorial for my people,

     So that seafarers who urge their tall ships

15　Over the spray of ocean shall thereafter

　　　Call it Beowulf's barrow."

　　　The brave-souled prince undid from off his neck

　　　The golden collar, gave it to the thane,

　　　To the young spear-warrior, and his gold-mounted helmet,

20　Ring and corslet, —bad him use them well—:

　　　"Thou art the last of our race,

　　　The Waegmundings; fate has swept all

　　　My kinsfolk off, undaunted nobles, to their doom;

　　　I must go after them."

25　That was the veteran's last expression

　　　Of his spirit's thoughts before the bale-fire was his lot

　　　The hot destructive flames; his soul departed from his body

　　　To journey to the doom of righteous men.

【译文】

贝奥武甫（L.2792—2819）

1　年迈的国王忍着痛苦，望着财宝说：

　　"为了眼前这些瑰宝明珠，

　　我要感谢万物的统治者，

　　那光荣的王和永恒的主，

5　在我临死以前，能为我的人民

　　获得这么多的财富！

　　既然我用自己的生命换来这一切，

　　你务必拿它去供养百姓！

　　也许我的生命已经很有限，

10　请你在我火化之后吩咐士兵,
　　让他们在海岸上为我造一座墓,
　　好让我的人民前往悼念。
　　这墓要造得显眼,高过赫罗斯尼斯,
　　这样,当航海者迎着大海的浪花

15　驾驶他们高大的帆船航行,
　　就可称之为'贝奥武甫之墓'"。
　　勇敢的国王然后从脖子上摘下金项圈,
　　把它交给这位高尚的武士。
　　他还将饰金的头盔、戒指和胸甲

20　全部送给这位年轻人,并关照他
　　好好使用这些东西:
　　"你是我们威格蒙丁族最后一位勇士,
　　命运关乎全部宗亲,
　　无所畏惧的人未能逃脱死亡,
　　我现在就要去跟他们为伴。"

25　这就是老战士发自内心的最后声音,
　　不久那葬礼之火——毁灭生命的火焰
　　将吞没他,他的灵魂将脱离肉体
　　踏上正直者归宿的旅程。

（陈才宇　译）

【点评】

这是主人公杀死火龙后的一节（L. 2792—2819）。诗中刻画了国王为国家和臣民戎马一生、鞠躬尽瘁的君主形象,反映了英雄的国王在死亡面前对财富、对人生的思考:生命短暂,灵魂永恒。诗人采用超验的情怀,借助老国王这一角色表达了对上帝的感恩之情及基督教灵魂永生的观念。史诗融神话灵性思考与历史理性考量于一体,以明显的多元内容(上帝、生命、财富、名誉、死亡、灵魂、永生等)传达着日耳曼文化和基督教文明,两者的融合真实地反映了当时的社会风貌,传递了一定的社会文化信息。

第二章 中古时期诗歌

这一时期诗歌也称盎格鲁-诺曼底（Anglo-Normandy）诗歌。1066年，诺曼底公爵威廉（Duke William）率军登陆英国，英国被诺曼底人统治，法国语言和法国文化开始广泛影响此时的英国。

这一时期的文学特点是比较明快并充满浪漫色彩，以传奇故事为主，但也不乏男女间的爱情故事。在语言上，盎格鲁-撒克逊语不断简化，大量吸收法国词汇。英国文学创作也以法语和盎格鲁-撒克逊语为主。诺曼底的征服带来诺曼底文化，英国的中央集权制代替了以往盎格鲁-撒克逊的松散联合，新的语言文字在英国逐渐形成。

诺曼时期的故事主要取材于法国、希腊、罗马及不列颠。其中以14世纪头韵诗为特点的浪漫传奇故事《高文爵士和绿衣骑士》（*Sir Gawain and the Green Knight*）为代表，主要探讨人性基础上的行为标准和道德操守，揭示深刻且严肃的道德问题。

伟大的叙事诗人杰弗里·乔叟（Geoffrey Chaucer，1340—1400）的主要作品是《坎特伯雷故事集》（*The Canterbury Tales*），该作品反映了14世纪下半期英国文化的变迁。乔叟被称为"英国诗歌之父"，对英语语言的发展产生了一定的影响。

第二章　中古时期诗歌

中古时期，英格兰和苏格兰民谣较为兴盛，它是一种简短的叙事民间歌谣，语言质朴、节奏感强，用来表达对劳动群体的热爱之情。主要代表作品有《派屈克·司本斯爵士》（*Sir Patrick Spens*）和《罗宾汉》（*Robin Hood*）。

《坎特伯雷故事集》《高文爵士和绿衣骑士》为中古英国诗歌代表。以格律诗而论，以头韵体和双韵体为主要特征。

一、Poem Reading

（一）Sir Gawain and the Green Knight

Geoffrey Chaucer

1　Since the siege and the assault was ceased at Troy,
　　The walls breached and burnt down to brands and ashes,
　　The knight that had knotted the nets of deceit
　　Was impeached for his perfidy, proven most true,
5　It was high-born Aeneas and his haughty race
　　That since prevailed over provinces, and proudly reigned
　　Over well-nigh all the wealth of the West Isles.
　　……
　　While the New Year was new, but yesternight come,
10　This fair folk at feast two-fold was served,
　　When the king and his company were come in together,
　　The chanting in chapel achieved and ended.
　　Clerics and all the court acclaimed the glad season,
　　Cried Noel anew, good news to men;

15   Then gallants gather gaily, hand-gifts to make,

      Called them out clearly, claimed them by hand,

      Bickered long and busily about those gifts.

      Ladies laughed aloud, though losers they were,

      And he that won was not angered, as well you will know.

20   ……

      I shall give him as my gift this gisarme noble,

      This ax, that is heavy enough, to handle as he likes,

      And I shall bide the first blow, as bare as I sit.

      If there be one so willful my words to assay,

25   Let him leap hither lightly, lay hold of this weapon;

      I quitclaim it forever, keep it as his own,

      And I shall stand him a stroke, steady on this floor,

      So you grant me the guerdon to give him another.

                                   Sans blame.

30   In a twelvemonth and a day

      He shall have of me the same;

      Now be it seen straightway

      Who dares take up the game.

      ……

35   The Green Knight upon ground girds him with care:

      Bows a bit with his head, and bares his flesh:

      His long lovely locks he laid over his crown,

      Let the naked nape for the need be show.

      Gawain grips to his ax and gathers it aloft—

40   The left foot on the floor before him he set—

第二章　中古时期诗歌

  Brought it down deftly upon the bare neck,

  That the shock of the sharp blow shivered the bones

  And cut the flesh cleanly and clove it in twain,

  That the blade of bright steel bit into the ground.

45 The head was hewn off and fell to the floor;

  Many found it at their feet, as forth it rolled;

  The blood gushed from the body, bright on the green,

  Yet fell not the fellow, nor faltered a whit,

  But stoutly he starts forth upon stiff shanks,

50 And as all stood staring he stretched forth his hand,

  Laid hold of his head and heaved it aloft,

  Then goes to the green steed, grasps the bridle,

  Steps into the stirrup, bestrides his mount,

  And his head by the hair in his hand holds,

55 And as steady he sits in the stately saddle

  As he had met with no mishap, nor missing were

        his head.

  公元1066年，诺曼底公爵威廉带领军队打败了盎格鲁－撒克逊人，登陆英国大陆，开始了盎格鲁－诺曼时期（1066—1350）。诺曼人起初是一群居住在斯堪的纳维亚的流浪者，十世纪的时候，他们占领了法国北部的部分地区，并迅速接受了法国文明。所以，诺曼征服给英国带来了更多法国文化的影响。传奇（romance）是盎格鲁－诺曼时期主要的文学形式。传奇的行文一般比较长，有时用诗文写成，有时也会采用叙述文的形式。传奇的主角是出身高贵的英雄，传奇故事则围绕他们的生活和历险经历展开。按照内容划分，传奇有三种类别：法国查理曼大帝的故事、希腊罗马国王的故事（特别是特洛伊战争）以及亚瑟王和圆桌骑士的故事。《高文爵士和绿衣骑士》便属于第三类传奇故事。

　　新年夜里,当亚瑟王和圆桌骑士一起欢宴的时候,宫殿里来了一位不速之客,也就是选文里的绿衣骑士。绿衣骑士举起手中的巨斧,向亚瑟王和圆桌骑士提出挑战:是否有人敢用这把斧子砍下他的头颅,而且一年后敢于接受与他相同的命运?在大家害怕犹豫之际,亚瑟王的侄儿高文接受了挑战。被砍下头颅的绿衣骑士带着自己的头颅离开了宫殿,高文则踏上了寻找绿衣骑士的路途。经过将近一年,高文终于在他借宿的一座城堡里打听到绿衣骑士的住所。高文两次坦诚地告诉了堡主,城堡女主人试图诱惑他。但是他却偷偷保留了女主人送他的可以保命的魔力腰带。当最终的命运到来时,高文躲过了绿衣骑士的前两次攻击,却在第三次被砍伤了肩膀。高文谴责对方不遵守诺言,却被告知绿衣骑士其实就是城堡的主人。逃脱了前两次攻击是因为高文对堡主的坦诚,而第三次被砍中肩膀则是由于高文私藏了魔力腰带。羞愧的高文带着这个故事回到了亚瑟王宫,而佩戴绿色腰带则成为圆桌骑士的传统。

　　选文第1行便追根溯源到特洛伊战争,第5行又提出了战争中的英雄,也是希腊神话中的美神阿福狄德罗之子埃涅阿斯,故事讲述的又是亚瑟王朝圆桌骑士的故事,因此诗歌开门见山便把传奇的三种类别囊括在内,这也是《高文爵士和绿衣骑士》成为经典传奇的重要原因之一。不同于前一阶段盎格鲁-撒克逊时期文学的严肃和拘谨,盎格鲁-诺曼时期的文学则添加了一份活泼和洒脱,色彩变得鲜明跳跃,爱情的元素也不再被排除在外。选文中第9行到第19行描述了亚瑟王宫殿欢庆宴席的场面。第18行的行文中,参加宴席的女士似乎和骑士打了个赌,赌注是一个亲吻,而赌输了的女士不但不恼,反而大声笑了起来,这样开放热烈的氛围与盎格鲁-撒克逊时期阴暗压抑的气氛截然不同。虽然如此,选文的第35行到第57行描述的绿衣骑士被砍掉头颅的场景,斧子砍入地面,而骑士的头颅咕噜噜地在地上滚着,让读者回想起了盎格鲁-撒克逊时期《贝奥武甫之歌》

中的血腥场面。因此,《高文爵士和绿衣骑士》又不动声色地传承了前一时期文学的某些特点。

(二) The Canterbury Tales

Geoffrey Chaucer

1 As soon as April pierces to the root

  The drought of March, and bathes each bud and shoot

  Through every vein of sap with gentle showers

  From whose engendering liquor spring the flowers;

5 When zephyrs have breathed softly all about

  Inspiring every wood and field to sprout,

  And in the zodiac the youthful sun

  His journey halfway through the Ram has run;

  When little birds are busy with their song

10 Who sleep with open eyes the whole night long

  Life stirs their hearts and tingles in them so

  Then off as pilgrims people long to go,

  And palmers to set out for distant strands

  And foreign shrines renowned in many lands.

15 And specially in England people ride

  To Canterbury from every countryside

  To visit there the blessed martyred saint

  Who gave them strength when they were sick and faint.

  ……

20 A knight was with us, and an excellent man,

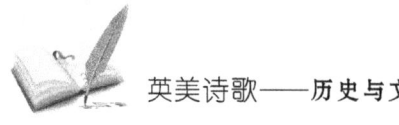

Who from the earliest moment he began

To follow his career loved chivalry.

Truth, openhandedness, and courtesy.

He was a stout man in the king's campaigns

25 Despite his prowess, honored in men's eyes,

Meek as a girl and gentle in his ways.

He had never spoken ignobly all his days

To any man by even a rude inflection.

He was knight in all things to perfection.

30 He rode a good horse, but his gear was plain.

For he had lately served on a campaign.

His tunic was still spattered by the rust

Left by his coat of mail, for he had just

Returned and set out on his pilgrimage.

35 There was also a Nun, a prioress,

Whose smile was gentle and full of guilelessness.

"By St. Loy!" was the worst oath she would say.

She sang mass well, in a becoming way,

Intoning through her nose the words divine,

40 And she was known as Madame Eglantine.

She spoke good French, as taught at Stratford-Bow

For the Parisian French she did not know.

She was schooled to eat so primly and so well

That from her lips no morsel ever fell.

45 She wet her fingers lightly in the dish

Of sauce, for courtesy was her first wish.

第二章　中古时期诗歌

　　　With every bite she did her skillful best
　　　To see that no drop fell upon her breast.
　　　She always wiped her upper lip so clean
50　That in her cup was never to be seen
　　　A hint of grease when she had drunk her share,
　　　She reached out for her meat with comely air.
　　　She was a great delight, always tried
　　　To imitate court ways, and had her pride,
55　Both amiable and gracious in her dealings.
　　　As for her charity and tender feelings,
　　　She melted at whatever was piteous.
　　　She would weep if she but came upon a mouse
　　　Caught in a trap, if it were dead of bleeding.
60　Some little dogs that she took pleasure feeding
　　　On roasted meat or milk or good wheat bread
　　　She had, but how she wept to find one dead
　　　Or yelping from a blow that made it smart,
　　　And all was sympathy and loving heart.
65　……
　　　She wore her cloak with dignity and charm,
　　　And had her rosary about her arm,
　　　The small beads coral and the larger green,
　　　And from them hung a brooch of golden sheen,
70　On it a large A and a crown above;
　　　Beneath, "All things are subject unto love."

杰弗里·乔叟是英国文学史上第一个真正做到声名远播、名垂青史的英国作家。被称为"英国诗歌之父"的乔叟主要活跃在英国 14 世纪后期，写作了《坎特伯雷故事集》、《特罗伊拉斯和克莱希德》（*Troilus and Criseyde*）、《声誉之屋》（*The House of Fame*）、《百鸟会议》（*The Parliament of Fowles*）等作品。其中，《坎特伯雷故事集》是乔叟最具代表性的一部作品。

故事发生在伦敦，诗人在塔巴德旅馆（Tabard Inn）碰到了一群前往坎特伯雷朝圣的人，并加入其中。旅馆主人哈瑞·贝利提议进行故事比赛，去朝圣的路上每人讲述两个故事，回来的路上再讲述两个故事，以此来打发路上的时光。这样，根据写作计划，乔叟将会完成 124 个故事。比赛由贝利做裁判，获胜者可以在塔巴德旅馆吃一顿免费的晚餐。遗憾的是，乔叟只写了 24 个故事便去世了，其中完整的故事是 23 个。虽然如此，《坎特伯雷故事集》所讲述的故事涉及 14 世纪的各个社会层面，描绘了不同人群的性格特征，反映了当时社会从中世纪跨越到封建社会的挣扎和动荡，是英国历史上第一部现实主义典范的作品。

故事集的"序诗"（general prologue）起到了提纲挈领的作用，对朝圣者的身份分别作了交代。选文是从"序诗"中选取的一部分，其中第 1 行到第 18 行交代了故事发生的时间，第 20 行到第 35 行描述了朝圣者中的领袖——骑士的身份，第 37 行到第 73 行则形象地展示了女修道院院长这一充满讽刺意味的人物。第一节选段描述的四月里春天的景象，让读者感觉心情澎湃：四月的汁液渗透到植物之中，百花绽放、万物复苏。20 世纪初，另一个英国诗人 T. S. 艾略特在《荒原》（*The Waste Land*）中对这一段精彩的描写进行了效仿：

"April is the cruellest month, breeding

"Lilacs out of the dead land, mixing

"Memory and desire, stirring

"Dull roots with spring rain"

第二章 中古时期诗歌

乔叟借用讽刺幽默的手法,刻画出骑士、乡绅、镇长、女修道院院长等风格迥异、形象鲜明的人物。选文中的骑士和女修道院院长形成了鲜明的对比,也衬托出14世纪英国社会所面临的巨大动荡。骑士是盎格鲁-诺曼时期的代表,他"追寻真理、慷慨大方而且彬彬有礼"(第23行),他"作战勇猛但心中充满了信仰,刚刚从战场回来便踏上了朝圣之路"(第35行)。道貌岸然的女修道院院长则与骑士形成了鲜明的对比。虽然同情流浪的猫狗(第60,61行),她却对受伤的人表现出强烈的厌恶。胸前"爱能融化一切"(第73行)的牌子却凸显出女修道院院长虚伪的性格。和盎格鲁-诺曼时期文学着重刻画经典英雄的写作倾向不同,《坎特伯雷故事集》除了刻画像骑士这样的英雄,也描绘了反映真实世态的女修道院院长。因此,从侧面让读者感受到英语文化对主流文化的冲击,而乔叟选用地道的伦敦英语写作作品也充分地说明了这一点。乔叟见过意大利作家皮特拉特和薄伽丘,并深深受到他们的影响。作为这种影响的表现之一,在《坎特伯雷故事集》中,他大量地应用了英雄双韵体(heroic couplets)。这种韵体形式是每两行押韵,而且每行都是五步抑扬格的韵律。例如,诗歌的前两行便是标准的英雄双韵体:

As s'oon as A'pril p'ierces t'o the r'oot

The d'rought of M'arch, and b'athes each bud and s'hoot

二、Further Reading

(一) Cantus Troilus

Geoffrey Chaucer

1　If no love is, O God, what fele I so?

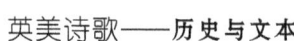

And if love is, what thing and whiche is he?

If love be good, from whennes cometh my wo?

If it be wikke, a wonder thinkenth me,

5   When every torment and adversitee

That cometh of him, may to me savory thinke;

For ay thurst I, the more that I it drinke.

And if that at myn owene lust I brenne,

Fro whennes cometh my wailing and my pleynte?

10 If harme agree me, wher-to pleyne I thenne?

I noot, ne why unwary that I faynte.

O quick deeth, o swete harm so queynte,

How many of thee in me swich quantitee,

But if that I consente that it be?

15 And if that I consente, I wrongfully

Compleyne, y-wis; thus possed to and fro,

A sterelees withinne a boot am I

Amid the sea, bytwixen windes two,

That in contrarie stonden eyermo.

20 Alias! what is this wonder maladye?

For hete of cold, for cold of hete, I dye.

【译文】

特罗勒斯的情歌

杰弗里·乔叟

1 假如没有爱，啊，我为何有如此感受？

第二章 中古时期诗歌

  假如真有爱，它究竟是个什么东西；
  假如爱是好的，又从何而来这哀愁？
  假如爱是坏的，我却感到有些离奇，
5 来自他的一切折磨和叛离，
  我却似乎有无比甜美之感：
  我喝得愈多，愈觉得口干。
  如果这是由于我自己情愿，
  又从哪里来这苦恼和怨恨？
10 如果灾害与我相容，何必抱怨？
  我既未疲劳，何以竟会发晕？
  啊，十足的死亡，甜蜜的祸根，
  你怎敢如此把我折磨，
  若不是我同意你那么做。
15 可要是我自己同意，我就不该
  如此抱怨；我终日来回飘荡，
  像一只无舵的船漂浮在大海，
  两股风从两个相反的方向
  朝着我吹打，使我永远飘荡。
20 啊，这是一种什么奇特的病，
  冷中发热，热中发冷，断我生命。

（何功杰　译）

【点评】

  《特罗勒斯的情歌》节选自《特罗伊拉斯和克莱希德》。《特罗伊拉斯和克莱希德》是乔叟于1372—1384年以薄伽丘的《爱的摧残》（*Filostrato*）为蓝本写成的，是一部现实主义作品。作品采用"宫廷诗体"——又译"君主诗体"（rhyme royal），也称为乔叟诗节（Chaucerian Stanza）——完成。

乔叟诗节是一种五步抑扬格的七行诗体,押韵格式为ababbcc,它也可看作一个三行体和两个双行体(aba bb cc)或一个四行体和一个三行体(abab bcc)。整首诗共分五卷,以特洛伊战争为背景,讲述了一对恋人的悲欢离合。战争、大灾难、性爱和死亡是这首长诗的主题。诗中的爱情伦理观、生命、死亡等主题充满了哲学和宗教的深刻含义,整个诗作字斟句酌,其对称美、优雅得体的文字、细腻的人物刻画及深刻的主题使得整部作品散发着迷人的光辉,具有极佳的审美价值。

这里所选的三节反映了特罗伊拉斯被执着的爱弄得无所适从的情景。爱使他悲哀、给他带来痛苦,爱给他带来折磨,但爱又会让他欣喜、让他思索。特罗伊拉斯这首爱的情歌一开始三行及第9,10,14,20行的问句表达了作者在现实生活中面对爱情时的矛盾心理和精神上的深思冥想。此诗的最后一行借用暗喻、反复、回环手法表达了爱如死之坚强。

(二)A Rondel of Merciless Beauty

Geoffrey Chaucer

1   Your two great eyes will slay me suddenly:
　　Their beauty shakes me who was once serene,
　　Straight through my heart the wound is quick and keen.

　　Only your word will heal the injury
5   To my hurt heart, while yet the wound is clean—
　　Your two great eyes will slay me suddenly;
　　Their beauty shakes me who was once serene.

　　Upon my word, I tell you faithfully

第二章　中古时期诗歌

　　　Through life and after death you are my queen,
10　For with my death the whole truth shall be seen.
　　　Your two great eyes will slay me suddenly;
　　　Their beauty shakes me who was once serene,
　　　Straight through my heart the wound is quick and keen.

【译文】
无情美人回旋曲

杰弗里·乔叟

1　你的两只大眼睛突然将我刺伤：
　　它们的美让我震撼，无法再安详，
　　直接而快速地穿透我的胸膛。

　　只有你的言语能治愈我的伤
5　趁现在它还没开始溃疡——
　　你的两只大眼睛突然将我刺伤
　　它们的美让我震撼，无法再安详。

　　我起誓，我真诚地向你表述衷肠
　　前生来世，你都是我的女王，
10　我以我的生命让您见证真相。
　　你的两只大眼睛突然将我刺伤
　　它们的美让我震撼，无法再安详，
　　直接而快速地穿透我的胸膛。

（郭嘉　译）

英美诗歌——历史与文本

【点评】

回旋曲源自法国，一般十四行左右，常采用反复手法，诗行之间形成平行互文。本诗主要采用拟人（personification）与夸张（hyperbole）的手法来赞颂诗中对方无法抵挡的美丽与魅力。第一行采用借代、拟人、夸张手法，强调诗中的"我"被对方美丽的眼睛折服，且对对方一见钟情，似乎是得了相思病。诗歌采用韵律格式为 abb。中间四行继续采用拟人和承上反复及夸张手法，突出对方的美，这美是无情的（merciless），因为"我"已经受伤（injury），且只有对方的言语能够治愈（heal）。后六行诗的韵式为 abb abb，承首三行诗反复，再次采用拟人、夸张手法赞叹对方的美丽，美到"无情"的境界，及我的不能自拔，病态憔悴。本诗是乔叟歌颂爱情的力作之一，语言形式唯美。诗歌表现了诗人正视现实、承认现实，也敢于总结现实的态度，即人类在爱情道路上无不经受着酸甜苦辣，为爱受伤，为爱着迷，体现了深刻的人文关怀。

第三章 文艺复兴时期诗歌

16世纪的英国资本主义制度逐渐确立。"羊吃人"的圈地运动促进了资产阶级和城市的发展,农民被迫成为城市中的劳动大军。英国国王亨利八世(1509—1549)即位后,自封为英国国教教主,加强了英国君主制度,政教合一成为国家政治政体。伊丽莎白女王统治时期(1558—1603),国家强盛,国力迅速增长。1558年英国打败西班牙无敌舰队,成为海上霸主。随之贸易在世界范围内开展,同时国内阶级分化严重,社会关系不断变化。

伊丽莎白女王时期是英国诗歌创新发展,百家争鸣、百花齐放的繁荣年代。这一时期,英国的文学文化艺术空前繁荣、蓬勃发展,进入了历史上的"文艺复兴"。大量的希腊、罗马经典作品被译介到英国。

16世纪最常见的诗歌形式是十四行诗,埃德姆·斯宾塞(Edmund Spenser,1552—1599)诗体(Spenserian Stanza)广为流传,其韵式结构为:abab bcbc cdcd ee。《仙后》(*Faerie Queene*)与《爱情小唱》(*Amoretti*)为其代表作。克里斯托弗·马洛(Christopher Marlowe,1564—1593)将无韵诗(blank verse)自如地运用于戏剧创作中,无韵诗表达性强,自由度高,可用于叙事、对话、独白等。

威廉·莎士比亚(William Shakespeare,1564—1616)是英国文学史

上最伟大的作家，是现实主义的奠基人。无论是其戏剧还是诗歌，称得上是对整个西方世界文化的缩影和概括。他的作品分为悲剧、喜剧和历史剧；在英国诗歌史上，莎翁开创了莎士比亚式的十四行诗（Shakespearean Sonnet）或称为英国十四行诗，通常韵式为 abab cdcd efef gg，其结构和语言艺术性极强，人文内涵深刻。

人文主义是这一时期最主要的特点。本时期著名的诗人还有托马斯·怀亚特（Thomas Wyatt，1503—1542）、菲利普·锡德尼（Philip Sidney，1554—1586）、托马斯·坎佩翁（Thomas Campion，1567—1620）、托马斯·纳什（Thomas Nashe）等。

一、Poem Reading

（一）Sonnet 18

William Shakespeare

1   Shall I compare thee to a summer's day?
    Thou art more lovely and more temperate:
    Rough winds do shake the darling buds of May,
    And summer's lease hath all to short a date:

5   Sometime too hot the eye of heaven shines
    And often is his gold complexion dimmed;
    And every fair from fair sometimes declines,
    By chance or nature's changing course untrimmed;

    But thy eternal summer shall not fade,

第三章　文艺复兴时期诗歌

10　Nor lose possession of that fair thou ow'st;
　　Nor shall death brag thou wander'st in his shade,
　　When in eternal lines to time thou grow'st:

　　So long as men can breathe, or eyes can see,
　　So long lives this, and this gives life to thee.

英语诗歌中的十四行诗来源于意大利诗人彼特拉克（Petrarch）。十四行诗有自己的押韵格式，行文一般分为两个部分：前八行诗一般描述或者探讨同一主题，后面六行诗文在内容上转向另一个主题。中世纪的意大利诗人十分喜爱使用十四行诗的形式进行创作，而这类诗歌一般都用来讲述或者讨论爱情。早在十六世纪，托马斯·怀亚特（Sir Thomas Wyatt）和萨里伯爵（the Earl of Surrey）就开始将意大利十四行诗介绍到英语诗歌的创作中来。尤其是托马斯·怀亚特，他写作的十四行诗 *Whoso List to Hunt*，隐喻了他对亨利八世的第二任妻子安妮·博林（Anne Boleyn）的爱慕，这首诗无论在形式上还是在内容上都遵循了意大利十四行诗的要求。十六世纪末期，十四行诗在英国诗歌创作中达到了顶峰，这时期出现了菲利普·锡德尼（Sir Philip Sidney），塞缪尔·丹尼尔（Samuel Daniel），埃德姆·斯宾塞（Edmund Spenser）等善用十四行诗的诗人。1609年，莎士比亚出版的《十四行诗》成为该种诗文在英国诗歌中发展成熟的重要标志。

莎士比亚的十四行诗大部分写作于16世纪末，直到1609年才得以发表。诗集在延续了彼特拉克十四行诗创作理念的同时，也进行了一系列创新的尝试。例如，*Sonnet* 99 有 15 行，*Sonnet* 126 只有六个对句，而 *Sonnet* 145 摒弃了五步抑扬格，使用了四步的抑扬格。诗集中，莎士比亚《十四行诗》严格遵守 abab cdcd efef gg 的押韵格式。但也有例外的情况，例如 *Sonnet* 29 的押韵格式就变为：abab cdcd ebeb gg。诗集共有 154 首十四行诗，除了诗人，出现了三个人物，分别是美少年（the fair youth）、黑夫人（the dark lady）和敌对诗人（the rival poet）。诗集从第1首到126首是写给美少年的，第127首到154首是写给黑夫人的，而敌对诗人的形象则出现在美少年的部分。

  Sonnet 18在整部诗集中处于重要的地位。严格按照十四行诗的行文规则，诗文的押韵格式为：abab cdcd efef gg，而且前面两个诗节通过和夏日的比较来呈现少年的美丽之后，第三个诗节笔锋一转谈到了艺术和永恒的问题：诗文赋予少年以永恒。在前17首诗中，诗人在描述少年美丽的同时，不断地督促少年赶快结婚，以便能够让他的美丽世代延续下去。这种情绪在Sonnet 18中得以急转，该诗中诗人开始将内心中的情感剖白给少年。他把少年比作夏日，却认为少年比夏日更加美丽、更加温柔，夏日转眼即逝，而少年的美丽却可以借助诗文得以永恒。Sonnet 20的第三个诗节中，诗人更加直白地向少年表达了自己的情感：

And for a woman wert thou first created;

Till Nature, as she wrought thee, fell a-doting,

And by addition me of thee defeated,

By adding one thing to my purpose nothing.

  因为母亲一时的疏忽，本来应为女人的少年变成了男人，而这也注定了诗人的情感永远得不到回馈。如果说诗人对少年的同性情感是精神恋爱，那么诗人与黑夫人之间的爱情则走向了身体恋爱的另一个极端。例如，在Sonnet 151中，第二个诗节就直白地提到"For, thou betraying me, I do betray/ My nobler part to my gross body's treason"。1609年出版的《十四行诗》的封皮注明，该诗集献给Mr. W. H.。Mr. W. H.很明显就是诗中的美少年，而对于这个人物在现实生活中具体指代谁，评论家莫衷一是。有的认为是莎士比亚的赞助者威廉·赫伯特（William Herbert），或者另一个支持者享利·里奥谢思利（Henry Wriothesley）。另有人认为 Mr. W. H. 是曾经在莎士比亚剧院工作的一个同事威廉姆·休斯（William Hughes），尤其是英国作家奥斯卡·王尔德（Oscar Wilde）专门写作了一篇中篇故事 *The Portrait of Mr. W. H.* 来支持这一观点。王尔德认为 *Sonnet* 20 中，第二个诗节的第 3 行 "A man in hue all hues in his controlling" 巧妙地将威廉姆·休斯的姓名隐含在内。然而，王尔德也承认，并没有具体的证据证明确有威廉姆·休斯其人。

（二）Sonnet 34

Edmund Spencer

1   Lyke as a ship that through the Ocean wyde,
     By conduct of some star doth make her way,
     Whenas a storme hath dimed her trusty guyde,
     Out of her course doth wander far astray:

5   So I whose star, that wont with her bright ray
     Me to direct, with cloudes is overcast,
     Doe wander now in darknesse and dismay,
     Through hidden perils round about me plast.
     Yet hope I well, that when this storme is past

10 My Helice the lodestar of my lyfe
     Will shine again, and looke on me at last,
     With lovely light to cleare my cloudy grief.
     Till then I wander carefully comfortlesse,
     In secret sorow and sad pensivenesse.

【译文】

爱情十四行诗第三十四首

爱德蒙德·斯宾塞

1 如同一只船驶在茫茫的海面，
  凭靠某一颗星辰来为它导航，
  一旦风暴把它可靠的向导遮暗，
  它就会远离自己的航道漂荡；
5 我的星辰也常常用它的亮光
  为我指路，现已被乌云笼罩，
  我在深深的黑暗和苦闷中彷徨，
  穿行于周围重重的险滩暗礁。
  但是我希望，经过这一场风暴，
10 我的北斗呵，我那生命的北极星，
  将重放光芒，最终把我来照耀，
  用明丽的光辉驱除我忧郁的阴云。
  在这以前，我忧心忡忡地徘徊，
  独自暗暗地悲伤，愁思满怀。

（胡家峦　译）

【点评】

　　这首诗采用五音步抑扬格，诗中包括三个四行组和一个两行组，韵式为 abab bcbc cdcd ee，这种韵式被称为"斯宾塞体"（Spenserian Sonnet）。诗中诗人一开始运用明喻（simile）手法"Lyke as a ship that through the Ocean wyde"将自己的生命比喻成一艘在茫茫大海上航行的船，需要"星辰"（star）——灯塔来为其导航，但有时也会遇到"风暴"（storme）而迷失方向。紧接着诗人用隐喻（metaphor）手法描写了自己正碰到生活

第三章 文艺复兴时期诗歌

中的"险滩暗礁"(hidden perils)并在黑暗中苦闷彷徨("Doe wander now in darknesse and dismay")。在第9行,诗人话锋一转,说出自己心中的盼望,指出生命中的北斗星——爱情,必将会重放光芒,驱散压在心里的忧伤"cleare my cloudy grief",将自己的生命照耀。最后两句诗歌作者又回到忧郁哀伤的状态中,与前8行诗歌的意境重合,这种结构的安排也传递了深刻的含义,亦即人生不如意有十之八九,但诗人总归是靠着9~12行传递着人生的盼望,表达了诗人乐观向上的人文情怀。诗人除了运用比喻外,也采用了象征手法,"star"指海上指示航行的灯塔,"lodestar"指代生命中美好的爱情,两者互相呼应,意象唯美,起到突出强调、深化主题的作用。另外,诗歌语言优美,除韵式外,诗行中大量的头韵"darknesse and dismay" "secret sorow and sad, lodestar of my lyfe" "cleare my cloudy" "carefully comfortlesse" "perils round about me plast"使得诗歌的节奏感强,突出了诗歌的音乐性。斯宾塞用诗歌表明:人生旅途如海上航行的船只,不会一帆风顺,但光明终会来临,驱走黑暗。诗歌表达了诗人勇于面对现实、对光明与美好生活的向往与追求。

二、Further Reading

(一) True Love

William Shakespeare

1 Let me not to the marriage of true minds
    Admit impediments. Love is not love
    Which alters when it alteration finds,
    Or bends with the remover to remove:
5 Oh, no! It is an ever-fixed mark,
    That looks on tempests and is never shaken;

It is the star to every wandering bark,

Whose worth's unknown, although his height be taken.

Love's not Time's fool, though rosy lips and cheeks

10 Within his bending sickle's compass come;

Love alters not with his brief hours and weeks,

But bears it out even to the edge of doom.

 If this be error, and upon me proved,

I never writ, nor no man ever loved.

【译文】
真正的爱

威廉·莎士比亚

1 请让我承认，真正的两心合一
   是不可阻挡的。那爱算不得真情，
   如果遇上变化，便随之而易，
   或者一旦迁流，便恋情别移；
5 哦，不！爱是恒久不变的标记，
   它凌驾于风暴之上，巍然屹立；
   对于迷舟，它是指引方向的星宿，
   他价值无量，尽管高度可求。
   爱不为时间愚弄，尽管朱唇和芳容
10 都将屈服于那一弯镰刀的席卷之中，
   爱不随光阴荏苒改变，
   它将延续到生命终点。
   如果这些话有误，并证明我确有错，

第三章 文艺复兴时期诗歌

就算我从未写过，也从未有人曾经真爱过。

【点评】

本诗是英国式十四行诗，是一首有关爱情的哲理诗。诗中采用抑扬格五音步，押韵格式为：abab cdcd efef gg。诗人一开始运用第一人称"Let me not"，宣告婚姻中的爱情应该是心心相印。第2行诗人采用同句首尾反复（epanalepsis）手法宣称"Love is not love"，并于第3，4行诗句举例说明。诗人第3，4行采用同源词（alters, alteration；remover, remove）指出如果爱情朝秦暮楚、移情别恋就不是真爱。第五诗行诗人借助形容词"ever-fixed"和意象词"mark"指出爱的特性：爱是恒久不变的标记。第6，7诗行中，诗人采用暗喻手法，运用意象词（tempests, star, wandering bark）形象生动地解释了爱的崇高价值——像狂暴大海上的灯塔，像黑夜中引航的星宿。第七行诗人采用人称代词"his"将"爱"拟人化，并指出"爱"价值无量。第8，9行运用拟人、隐喻手法指出时光容易消逝，紧接着第10行诗人指出，真爱永不改变，并将延续到生命终点。最后两行诗人以"就算我从未写过，也从未有人曾经真爱过"强烈表明"I"所说的真爱没有错误。

（二）Sonnet 29

William Shakespeare

1　When, in disgrace with Fortune and men's eyes,
　　I all alone beweep my outcast state,
　　And trouble deaf heaven with my bootless cries,
　　And look upon myself, and curse my fate,
5　Wishing me like to one more rich in hope,
　　Featur'd like him, like him with friends possess'd,

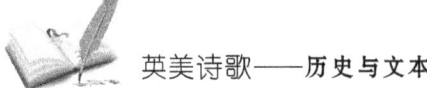

  Desiring this man's art, and that man's scope,

  With what I most enjoy contented least;

  Yet in these thoughts myself almost despising,

10 Haply I think on thee, and then my state,

  Like to the lark at break of day arising

  From sullen earth, sings hymns at heaven's gate;

  For thy sweet love remember'd such wealth brings

  That then I scorn to change my state with kings.

【译文】
十四行诗第二十九首
威廉·莎士比亚

1 我一旦失去了幸福,又遭人白眼,

  就独自哭泣,叹人家把我抛弃,

  白白地用哭喊来麻烦聋耳的苍天,

  又看看自己,只痛恨时运不济,

5 愿自己像人家那样:或前途远大,

  或一表人才,或胜友如云广交谊,

  想有这人的见识,那人的才华,

  于自己平素最得意的,倒最不满意,

  但在这几乎是自轻自贱的思绪里,

10 我偶尔想到了你呵,——我的心怀

  顿时像破晓的云雀从阴郁的大地

  冲上了天门,歌唱起赞美诗来;

  我怀着你的厚爱,如获至宝,

第三章　文艺复兴时期诗歌

教我不屑把处境跟帝王对调。

（屠　岸　译）

【点评】

莎士比亚的第29首十四行诗，是经典之作。第一行采用介词短语和名词性短语形式指出生活的困境，即失去幸福又遭人白眼。面对失意的生活，诗人号啕大哭，感叹命运的不公与无助（"And look upon myself, and curse my fate"）。诗中诗人借助想象力表达了自己的愿望：像人家那样：或前途远大，或一表人才，或胜友如云广交谊，想有这人的见识，那人的才华。诗人在自轻自贱、自我贬低中突然想到了"thee"，第10行诗成为整首诗的转折点，诗人的情绪突然高涨，一时间感觉自己像云雀，飞往天际，在天堂的门口唱起赞美的诗歌。最后两行诗表达了诗人在甜蜜的爱中感到无比幸福，对眼前的处境不屑一顾。整首诗在形而下与形而上的描绘中展示了世俗生活中有苦难、有挫折、有不公平，但是精神上爱的力量会战胜一切，而且使其如获至宝。诗歌前后对比强烈，第10行诗中的"thee"含义丰富，令人遐想。

整首诗押韵格式与以往不同，采用了abab cdcd ebeb gg格式。诗人两处运用了移就（transferred epithet）的修辞手法：第3行中的"deaf heaven"和第12行中的"sullen earth"，表达了"叫天天不灵，喊地地不应"的郁闷绝望心情。11行诗运用明喻（simile）"like to the lark at break of day arising"描写了自己突然像一只云雀，展翅飞翔。最后诗人在对比中直抒胸臆，"That then I scorn to change my state with kings"，因为有了"sweet love"，不屑于自己的失意。在"thy sweet love"中，精神得到升华。

—35—

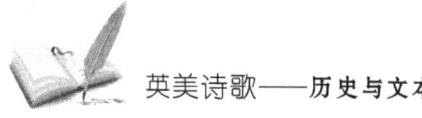

（三）Sonnet 66

William Shakespeare

1　Tired with all these, for restful death I cry,
　　As to behold desert a beggar born,
　　And needy nothing trimmed in jollity,
　　And purest faith unhappily forsworn,
5　And gilded honor shamefully misplaced,
　　And maiden virtue rudely strumpeted,
　　And rightful perfection wrongfully disgraced,
　　And strength by limping sway disabled,
　　And art made tongue-tied by authority,
10　And folly, doctor-like controlling skill,
　　And simple faith miscalled simplicity,
　　And captive Good attending captain Ill:
　　Tired with all these, from these would I be gone,
　　Save that, to die, I leave my love alone.

【译文】

十四行诗第六十六首

威廉·莎士比亚

1　难耐不平事，何如悄然去泉台
　　休说是天才，偏生做乞丐
　　人道是草包，偏把金银戴

第三章　文艺复兴时期诗歌

　　　说什么信与义，眼见无人睬
5　　道什么荣与辱，全是瞎安排
　　　少女童贞可怜遭横暴
　　　堂堂正义无端受掩埋
　　　跛腿权势反弄残了擂台汉
　　　墨客骚人官府门前口难开
10　　蠢驴们偏挂着指迷释惑教授招牌
　　　多少真心话错唤作愚鲁痴呆
　　　善恶易位，小人反受大人拜
　　　不平，难耐，所不如一死化尘埃
　　　待去也，又怎好让我爱人独守空阶

（辜正坤　译）

【点评】

　　此诗被认为是莎士比亚人文内涵最丰富、最深刻的一首十四行诗，无论其韵律、手法还是主旨内容，都有其独特之处。整首诗一反常态采用了 abab cccc adad ee 的韵式，反映了诗人内在交织的情感反复，表达了诗人厌恶假恶丑、向往真善美的崇高情怀。

　　诗中第一行"I"已厌倦这一切"tired with all these"，并呼唤死亡（restful death），创设悬念，吸引读者。紧接着诗人在第 2～12 行举例说明厌世的原因，诗行采用连词叠用（polysyndeton）的手法——"and"被重复使用十次，列举了种种社会的不公与邪恶：天才注定做叫花子，草包穿戴金银，信与义被搁置，荣与辱张冠李戴，少女贞操遭强暴，正义遭贬低，跛腿靠权势弄残擂台汉，艺术受压制，蠢驴们指手画脚，淳朴被看作是愚蠢，善恶易位，小人反受大人拜。透过一系列的描写不难看出，当时的社会矛盾重重，黑白颠倒，黑暗势力当道，邪恶压倒正义，百姓民不聊生。诗人除叠用"and"外，还使用了大量的抽象名词（nothing，faith， honor, virtue, perfection, authority, skill, simiplicity, Good, Ill）并赋予拟人（personification）、借喻或换喻（metonymy）的特征，生动而又讽刺地表达了诗人对社会、人生的思考，而这种思考的意义具有普适性，传递着极深的人文关怀。

最后两行诗意义丰富，诗人采用首尾呼应的语句"Tired with all these"，这种重复虽然悲凉，略显悲观消极，但却无情地鞭笞了当时权贵专横、道德堕落、正邪不分、百姓受压制的社会现实。诗歌最后一句"Save that, to die, I leave my love alone"似乎让读者看到曙光，当诗人悲观厌世，准备选择离开时，突然想到了"my love"，这似乎给予生命以希望。诗人最后点题，颂赞"爱"的价值及其赋予生命的意义。

（四）Sonnet 73

William Shakespeare

1   That time of year thou may'st in me behold
    When yellow leaves, or none, or few, do hang
    Upon those boughs which shake against the cold,
    Bare ruin'd choirs where late the sweet birds sang.
5   In me thou see'st the twilight of such day,
    As after sunset fadeth in the west;
    Which by and by black night doth take away,
    Death's second self, that seals up all in rest.
    In me thou see'st the glowing of such fire,
10 That on the ashes of his youth doth lie.
    As the deathbed whereon it must expire,
    Consumed with that which it was nourished by:

第三章 文艺复兴时期诗歌

This thou perceiv'st, which makes thy love more strong,
To love that well, which thou must leave ere long.

【译文】

十四行诗第七十三首
威廉·莎士比亚

1　那样的时令你可在我身上看到：
　　几片黄叶挂在枝头随风飘荡，
　　或枝头空空，只有寒风呼啸，
　　败落的唱诗坛，曾有鸟儿歌唱。
5　在我身上可以看见暮色沉沉，
　　宛如夕阳离去，退入了西天，
　　不久将进入黑夜——死神的化身，
　　连同世界万物，一起封进长眠。
　　你可在我身上看见这样的火焰：
10　躺在自己青春余烬上闪烁微光，
　　像躺在死床上一样，气息奄奄，
　　不久将同燃烧的物质一道消亡。
　　这一切你都看见，你更应把我爱，
　　真心地爱着我吧，我们就要分开。

（何功杰　译）

【点评】

　　此诗韵律为典型的五音步抑扬格的莎士比亚体（Shakespearean Sonnet），三个四行体诗节加一个双行体，韵式为：abab cdcd efef gg。整首诗结构清晰，语言唯美生动，意象丰富，从时间概念上体现了对生命的思索，意蕴深厚。

前三个诗节，诗人使用了三个反复叠句"That time of year thou may'st in me behold""In me thou see'st the twilight of such day""In me thou see'st the glowing of such fire"，使得整首诗歌结构紧凑、明晰。三个诗节中诗人都使用了隐喻，其中第一个诗节诗人将生命比喻成为一年中晚秋的景象。诗节中使用了意象词"yellow leaves"（or none, or few），"boughs"（shake against the cold），"birds"调动了读者的视觉，其中"against the cold"调动了触觉，拟声词"choirs"调动了听觉，不禁让人感到景象萧条、落败。第二个诗节将生命比喻成一天中的黄昏，随之，作者刻画了一幅黄昏图景，意象词"sunset""black night""Death's second self"，意旨生命渐渐老去时，连睡眠都被剥夺，描绘出严肃、凄凉、凋零、痛苦的生命景象。第三个诗节诗人将生命比喻成火焰，相较于前两个比喻意象，生命更加短暂，诗人看到火焰过后的余灰"ashes"，回忆起曾经的年轻时光(youth)，此诗节中，作者使用了一个明喻与委婉语"as the deadbed""expire"，指出生命短暂，很快如火燃烧完毕，在这个世界消失殆尽。前12行诗句作者借用比喻和丰富的意象栩栩如生地描绘了生命短暂及诗人生命将残的画面，哀婉、凄凉，语气似乎绝望。但最后两行诗意突然发生转变，诗中的"我"感到自己不久要永别尘世，由此号召他的爱友应当更好地去爱他，去珍惜他，否则来不及。

（五）Spring (from *Love's Labor Lost*)

William Shakespeare

1 When daisies pied and violets blue
    And ladysmocks all silver-white
    And cuckoobuds of yellow hue
    Do paint the meadows with delight,

第三章　文艺复兴时期诗歌

5　The cuckoo then, on every tree,
　　Mocks married men; for thus sings he:
　　Cuckoo!
　　Cuckoo, cuckoo! O word of fear,
　　Unpleasing to a married ear!"

10　When shepherds pipe on oaten straws,
　　And merry larks are plowmen's clocks,
　　When turtles tread, and rooks and daws,
　　And maidens bleach their summer smocks,
　　The cuckoo then, on every tree,
15　Mocks married men; for thus sings he:
　　Cuckoo !
　　Cuckoo, cuckoo! O word of fear,
　　Unpleasing to a married ear!

【译文】
春之歌（选自《爱的徒劳》）
　　　　威廉·莎士比亚

1　当杂色的雏菊开遍牧场,
　　蓝的紫罗兰,白的美人衫,
　　还有那杜鹃花吐蕾娇黄,
　　描出了一片广大的欣欢;
5　听杜鹃在每一株树上叫,
　　把那娶了妻的男人讥笑:

咯咕!

咯咕!咯咕!啊,可怕的声音!
害得做丈夫的肉跳心惊。

10　当无愁的牧童口吹麦笛,
　　清晨的云雀惊醒了农人,
　　斑鸠乌鸦都在觅侣求匹,
　　女郎们漂洗夏季的衣裙;
　　听杜鹃在每一棵树上叫,
15　把那娶了妻的男人讥笑:
　　咯咕!
　　咯咕!咯咕!啊,可怕的声音!
　　害得做丈夫的肉跳心惊。

(朱生豪　译)

【点评】

　　这是《爱的徒劳》落幕时的一支哲理抒情歌。此诗分为两个诗节,每个诗节9行,韵律为抑扬格四音步,韵式为:ababccdee fgfgccdee。

　　整首诗歌中,诗人使用了大量意象词(daisies, violets, ladysmocks, cuckoobuds, meadows, cuckoo, married men, shepherds, straws, larks, turtles, rooks and daws, maidens)来描写这首春之歌。这些意象词看似画面和谐,但细一察验就会发现里面的不一致,其中 cuckoo 和 married men 并置在一起,再加上"mocks""fear""unpleasing"等词很能说明问题,令人深思。人们都知道,杜鹃不孵卵哺雏,到了生殖季节,产卵在莺巢中,雌杜鹃还性喜易偶,两个诗节中的第5～9行采用反复重叠手法,突出杜鹃和结婚的男人,此反衬手法的使用意在提醒有妻室的男人得警醒,稍不留神妻子就会出轨,真爱需要付出努力。

第三章 文艺复兴时期诗歌

诗中多处使用修辞，使得诗歌生动形象，画面唯美，让读者如身临其境。第 3~6 行使用拟人手法"And cuckoobuds of yellow hue/Do paint the meadows with delight/The cuckoo then, on every tree/Mocks married men; for thus sings he"，第 7 行使用拟声修辞（onomatopoeia）"Cuckoo！"，模拟杜鹃的叫声；第 9 行使用部分带整体的提喻法（synecdoche）"a married ear"，用"耳朵"指代整个人；第 11 行使用隐喻手法"And merry larks are plowmen's clocks"将"云雀"比作"农夫的时钟"；诗歌中除尾韵外，诗行中的头韵（alliteration）"Mocks married men""turtles tread""summer smocks"及辅音韵（consonance）"larks are plowmen's clocks"亦增强了整首诗的节奏感，使之明快而忧郁；反复（repetition）修辞比较典型，即第 5~9 与第 14~18 行的反复，突出强调了诗的深刻性，隐含着给人启迪、令人警醒的智慧火花。

与莎士比亚同一时代的大学才子纳什的经典之作《春天》是一首田园抒情诗，极尽抒发春天大自然的美好之情，被广为传唱。

（六）Hark！Hark! The Lark （from *Cymbeline*）

William Shakespeare

1 Hark, hark！The lark at heaven's gate sings,
   And Phoebus' gins arise
   His steeds to water at those springs
   On chaliced flowers that lies;
5 And winking Mary-buds begin
   To ope their golden eyes:
   With every thing that pretty is,
   My lady sweet, arise:
   Arise, arise！

【译文】

听！听！云雀在天门歌唱（选自《辛白林》）

威廉·莎士比亚

1 听！听！云雀在天门歌唱，
   旭日早在空中高挂，
   天池的流水琮铮作响，
   日神在饮他的骏马；
5 瞧那万寿菊倦眼慵抬，
   睁开它金色的瞳睛：
   美丽的万物都已醒来，
   醒醒吧，亲爱的美人！
   醒醒，醒醒！

（朱生豪 译）

【点评】

这是《辛白林》第二幕第三场中乐工唱的一支歌。诗歌为九行一个诗节，韵律格式为 aaaabaaaa。作者采用反复、拟声、拟人、尾韵等文学手法，使得诗歌形象、生动、唯美。第一行诗歌，作者采用祈使句"Hark, hark!"，反复手法引起读者注意。诗句"The lark at heaven's gate sings"采用拟人手法，并与 Sonnet 29 诗中的 11 行呼应，其中意象"歌唱的云雀"与"天堂之门"给人愉快的感觉。第 2 行采用典故（allusion）——希腊神话中的太阳神"Phoebus"指代太阳升起，随后诗行中的意象"steeds, water, springs, flowers, Mary-buds, golden eyes"及拟人手法的使用，使得整首诗的画面清新美丽，用诗人的话说"With every thing that pretty is"，一切如此美好——天空、原野一片鸟语花香。如何不错过这美好并将之分享，诗人唯有叫醒还在睡觉的爱人（"My lady sweet, arise: Arise, arise！"），最后诗人采用三个"arise",唤醒美人,共享生命中的美好。

(七) To Be, or Not to Be (from *Hamlet*)

William Shakespeare

1 To be, or not to be, that is the question:
   Whether 'tis nobler in the mind to suffer
   The slings and arrows of outrageous fortune,
   Or to take arms against a sea of troubles,
5 And by opposing, end them. To die, to sleep—
   No more, and by a sleep to say we end
   The heart-ache and the thousand natural shocks
   That flesh is heir to: 'tis a consummation
   Devoutly to be wish'd. To die, to sleep—
10 To sleep, perchance to dream—ay, there's the rub;
   For in that sleep of death what dreams may come,
   When we have shuffled off this mortal coil,
   Must give us pause: there's the respect
   That makes calamity of so long life:
15 For who would bear the whips and scorns of time,
   Th' oppressor's wrong, the proud man's contumely,
   The pangs of despis'd love, the law's delay,
   The insolence of office, and the spurns
   That patient merit of th' unworthy takes,
20 When he himself might his quietus make
   With a bare bodkin; who would fardels bear,

To grunt and sweat under a weary life,

But that the dread of something after death,

The undiscover'd country, from whose bourn

25　No traveler returns, puzzles the will,

And makes us rather bear those ills we have,

Than fly to others that we know not of?

Thus conscience does make cowards [of us all],

And thus the native hue of resolution

30　Is sicklied o'er with the pale cast of thought,

And enterprises of great pitch and moment

With this regard their currents turn awry,

And lose the name of action.

【译文】
生存还是毁灭（选自《汉姆雷特》）
　　　　　　　　　　　　　威廉·莎士比亚

1　生存还是毁灭，这是个问题：

要做到高贵，究竟该忍气吞声

来容受狂暴命运的摧残呢，

还是该挺身反抗无边的苦恼？

5　扫它个干净？死，就是睡眠——

就这样；而如果睡眠能了结

心痛以及千百种身体要担受的

皮痛肉痛，那该是天大的好事，

正求之不得啊！死，就是睡眠；

10 睡眠也许要做梦，这就麻烦了！
   我们一旦摆脱了尘世的牵缠
   在死的睡眠里还会做些什么梦，
   一想到就不能不踌躇。这一点顾虑
   正好使灾难变成了长期的折磨。
15 谁甘心忍受人世的鞭挞和嘲弄，
   忍受压迫者虐待、傲慢者凌辱，
   忍受失恋的痛苦、法庭的拖延、
   衙门的横暴、做埋头苦干的大才
   受作威作福的小人一脚踢出去，
20 如果他只需要自己来使一下尖刀
   就可以得到解脱啊？谁甘心挑担子，
   拖着疲累的生命，呻吟，流汗，
   要不是怕一死就去了没有人回来的
   那个从未发现的国土，怕那边
25 还不知会怎样，因此意志动摇了，
   因此就宁愿忍受目前的灾殃，
   而不愿投奔另一些未知的苦难？
   这样子，顾虑使我们都成了懦夫，
   也就这样了，决断决行的本色
30 蒙上了惨白的一层思虑的病容；
   本可以轰轰烈烈地大作大为，
   由于这一点想不通，就出了别扭，
   失去了行动的名分。

（卞之琳　译）

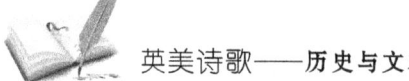

【点评】

此部分节选自《汉姆雷特》第三幕第一场。整个诗歌为汉姆雷特独白，主要围绕"不活"与"活"展开，大体结构为：不活—活—不活—活，在此过程中穿插对生、死、苦难、社会不公、灵魂等问题的思考。莎翁描绘了一幅在生死抉择中主人公踌躇矛盾、痛苦挣扎的画面，人物性格刻画细腻，跃然纸上。

独白诗一开始就提出问题并引人深思："To be, or not to be""Whether'tis nobler in the mind to suffer""Or to take arms against a sea of troubles"，"活"还是"不活"，要做到高贵该如何选择。接下来，汉姆雷特考虑"不活"的话该会怎样。如果不活就是死，就是睡眠，独白者对此种状态满意，因为可以了结肉体的麻烦，"The heart-ache and the thousand natural shocks/That flesh is heir to: 'tis a consummation"，但又想到死的睡眠里还会做梦，又开始犹豫。这里的"to die, to sleep"，在当时的英国文化中，应该仅仅指肉体死亡，因为基督教文化认为人的肉体回归尘土，灵魂不灭。诗中的"梦"应该是灵魂状态中的遭遇，灵魂会遭遇什么呢？汉姆雷特一想到这些就开始犹豫是否要"活"，一想到活下去，就得忍受现实社会中的种种苦难，"For who would bear the whips and scorns of time/Th'oppressor's wrong, the proud man's contumely/The pangs of despis'd love, the law's delay/The insolence of office, and the spurns/That patient merit of th'unworthy takes"，以上诗行表达了诗人对社会不公的鞭挞。随后诗人点出独白者生命的重担，应该也是每个活着的人所面对的，"To grunt and sweat under a weary life"，由于现实的灾殃，独白者想要了结这一切，但又怕"The undiscover'd country"，这里"那未知的国度"在基督教文化中应该不是指天堂就是地狱，如果独白者想要"自杀"离开这个世界的话，应该指的是地狱，因为基督教文化认为生命由上帝创造，人应当爱护生命而不能随意放弃。由于没有人知道灵魂离开肉体后会怎样，所以独白者犹犹豫豫，不

第三章 文艺复兴时期诗歌

能决断，不能行动。整首诗表达了对生、死、肉体、灵魂、现实、苦难、不公正等的思考，人文内涵极为深刻，发人深省。

诗人借助许多修辞手法使得诗歌唯美，感染力、艺术性极强。举例如下：① 隐喻（metaphor）："slings and arrows" "whips and scorns of time"使得诗歌生动形象；② 第 4 行中 "a sea of troubles" 使用了夸张（hyperbole）；③ 反复（repetition）：第 5，6，9，10，11，23 行中反复提到 "sleep" 和 "death"，突出对生命的思考，刻画人物性格；④ 第 17，28 行中运用拟人："the law's delay" "conscience does make cowards"；⑤ 第 18 行中运用借代："office"；⑥ 第 21，23 行中具有头韵与母韵 "bare bodkin, bear" "dread ... death" 等。

（八）Sonnet 75

Edmund Spenser

1　One day I wrote her name upon the strand,
　But came the waves and washed it away:
　Agayne I wrote it with a second hand,
　But came the tyde, and made my paynes his pray.
5　"Vayne man," sayd she, "that doest in vaine assay,
　A mortall thing so to immortalize,
　For I my selve shall lyke to this decay,
　And eek my name bee wyped out lykewise,"
　"Not so," quod I, "let baser things devize,
10　To dy in dust, but you shall live by fame:
　My verse your vertues rare shall eternize,
　And in the hevens wryte your glorious name.

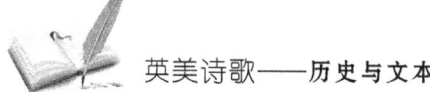

Where whenas death shall all the world subdew,
Our love shall live, and later life renew."

【译文】
爱情十四行诗第七十五首
   爱德蒙德·斯宾塞

1 一天,我把她的名字写在沙滩上,
   但海浪来了,把那个名字冲跑;
   我用手再一次把它写了一遍,
   但潮水来了,把我的辛苦又吞掉。
5 "自负的人啊,"她说,"你这是徒劳,
   妄想使世间凡俗的事物不朽;
   我本身就会像这样云散烟消,
   我的名字也同样会化为乌有。"
   "不,"我说,"让低贱的东西去筹谋
10 死亡之路,而你将靠美名而永活:
   我的诗将使你罕见的美德长留,
   并把你光辉的名字写在天国。
   死亡可以征服整个的世界,
   我们的爱将永存,生命永不绝。"

(胡家峦 译)

【点评】

诗作采用第一人称,对话叙事的方式书写,自然朴实,通俗易懂。韵式采用斯宾塞体:cbccdcdee。诗人借助本诗表达了文艺复兴时期普遍存在的人文理念:诗或文学永恒、爱情永恒、生命永恒。

第三章 文艺复兴时期诗歌

诗歌开始部分的意象"我"(I)、"沙滩"(strand)、"海浪"(waves)、"潮水"(tyde)构成了一幅人与自然的美好画面,唯美、动人、令人向往。第4行采用隐喻手法,将潮水比作野兽,将我写的名字吞掉"made my paynes his pray",其中"paynes""pray"使用了头韵,增加了潮涨潮落的动态感,使得诗歌节奏明快,读来优美,产生联想。诗歌中海水两次将名字冲刷掉,暗示了大自然有不可抗拒的一面,人只能顺应自然规律。紧接着第5~8行插入了女声部的话语,表达对人世间事物的看法:一切都是徒劳,一切都会过去。第5行中的两个形容词"Vayne, vaine"发音相似,意义几近相同,突出了人的徒劳。第6行"mortall, immortalize"两个词为同源辞格,但意义相反,形成对比。第5~8行对于尘世间短暂与死亡的思考表达了诗人深切的人文关怀。随后,第9~14行诗人说话,表示人世间一切虽然短暂,但诗歌作为载体,将把爱人的美德和他们之间的爱记录下来,从而永存,升华了主题。第10行中的"dy""live"形成对比,意指肉体虽然会归于尘土,但是爱人的美名将永活,诗句将永存,爱人光辉的名字将永存。最后两行中诗人重申两人之间的爱将永存,结婚后两人会衍生后代,或者灵魂进入天堂,为此生命将永不绝。整首诗歌画面唯美:自然美,爱人美,表达了诗人向往爱情婚姻的美好。

第四章　十七世纪革命与复辟时期诗歌

17世纪的英国处在动荡的时期，国内政治经济矛盾加深，宗教、科学、文化等社会各个方面都经历着巨变。资本主义的发展冲击着旧有的封建体制，新兴资产阶级与封建贵族不可调和的矛盾最终导致1642—1649年的资产阶级革命，查理士一世被送上断头台，克伦威尔领导的革命军获胜。当时英国资产阶级革命的一个显著特征是带有浓厚的宗教色彩，新兴资产阶级主要倡导清教主义信念，反对"君权神授"。克伦威尔为了维护大资产阶级的利益，实行独裁统治，引起人民的不满，他去世后，1660年，英国斯图亚特王朝复辟，恢复了君主专制制度。詹姆士二世统治时期，试图恢复天主教，导致新教派领导的1688年的"光荣革命"。最后各方力量妥协，君主立宪制确立，资产阶级控制的议会掌握了国家权力。

17世纪的诗歌包括两大派别：玄学派（metaphysical school）和骑士派（cavalier school）。诗人采用较为自由的创作态度，情感张扬，意象堆砌，风格夸张，复杂多变，给人类留下了宝贵的财富。玄学派诗人喜欢语出惊人，喜欢采用奇喻，使得互不相干的意象并置在一起，但也恰恰折射出动荡时代的历史现实。玄学派诗人约翰·多恩（John Donne），代表作有《歌与短歌》

第四章　十七世纪革命与复辟时期诗歌

（*Songs and Sonnets*）和《圣十四行诗》（*Holy Sonnets*）。此外，玄学派诗人还包括"玄学派诗圣"乔治·赫伯特（George Herbert）、亨利·沃恩（Henry Vaughn）与安德鲁·马维尔。骑士派诗人（the Cavalier poets）代表为本·琼生（Ben Jonson）还有"本的儿子们"（Sons of Ben）：赫里克、加莱、萨克林、勒夫莱斯等。

约翰·弥尔顿（John Milton）为英国17世纪最伟大的诗人。其代表作有史诗《失乐园》（*Paradise Lost*，1667），田园挽诗（*Lycidas*，1637），还有著名的《十四行诗》，弥尔顿是擅长使用素体诗（the blank verse）进行创作的大师。

一、Poem Reading

（一）A Valediction: Forbidding Mourning

John Donne

1　As virtuous men pass mildly away,
　　And whisper to their souls to go,
　　Whilst some of their sad friends do say
　　The breath goes now, and some say, No;

5　So let us melt, and make no noise,
　　No tear-floods, nor sigh tempests move,
　　'Twere profanation of our joys
　　To tell the laity our love.

　　Moving of th' earth brings harms and fears.

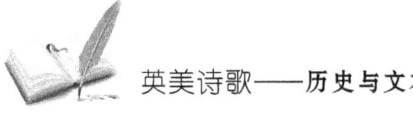

10 Men reckon what it did and meant;

But trepidation of the spheres,

Though greater far, is innocent.

Dull sublunary lovers' love

（Whose soul is sense） cannot admit

15 Absence, because it doth remove

Those things which elemented it.

But we by a love so much refined

That our selves know not what it is,

Inter-assured of the mind,

20 Careless, eyes, lips, and hands to miss.

Our two souls therefore, which are one,

Though I must go, endure not yet

A breach, but an expansion,

Like gold to airy thinness beat.

25 If they be two, they are two so

As stiff twin compasses are two;

Thy soul, the fixed foot, makes no show

To move, but doth, it th' other do.

And though it in the center sit,

30 Yet when the other far doth roam,

第四章　十七世纪革命与复辟时期诗歌

  It leans and hearkens after it,
  And grows erect, as that comes home.
  Such wilt thou be to me, who must
  Like th'other foot, obliquely run;
35 Thy firmness makes my circle just,
  And makes me end where I begun.

  17世纪的英国社会风云变幻，古老的中世纪逐渐让位于现代社会，科学推动着经济的迅速发展，在此前提下，商业也前所未有地繁荣起来。在思想意识领域，在科学发展撼动了对上帝绝对信仰根基的同时，个人意识也空前地发展起来。扑面而来的变化使17世纪上半期的英国诗坛涌现出风靡一时的玄学派诗人（metaphysical poets），而约翰·多恩（John Donne, 1572—1631）则是其中最有特点的代表诗人。

  "Metaphysical poets"一词是由另一位17世纪的诗人兼评论家约翰·德莱顿（John Dryden, 1631—1700）首次提出，而这个词正是用来描述约翰·多恩的。玄学派诗人是一批活跃于17世纪英国文坛的抒情诗人，他们尝试着用已有的世界观去认知这个日新月异的社会，所以玄学派诗歌多是对爱情、死亡、宗教等问题的思考。玄学派诗歌带有明显的巴洛克风格，形象鲜明、文体夸张，并大量地运用了奇喻（conceit）。所谓奇喻，是比喻的一种，但是这种比喻的不同之处在于将两个看似风马牛不相及的事物放在一起。例如，在 *A Flea* 中，约翰·多恩用一只叮咬了情人和自己的跳蚤的形象，暗喻两人之间的结合，想法大胆奇妙。除了多恩之外，其他被认为是玄学派的诗人包括乔治·赫伯特（George Herbert），安德鲁·马维尔（Andrew Marvell），亚伯拉罕考利（Abraham Cowley），安妮·布莱德斯翠特（Anne Bradstreet）等。

  A Valediction—Forbidding Mourning 写作于1611年。据多恩的传记作

者艾萨克·沃尔顿（Izaak Walton）描述，多恩在1611年远行法国和德国之前，为妻子安妮·莫尔（Anne More）写作此诗。该诗发表于1633年诗人的诗集 Songs and Sonnets，成为多恩的代表作品之一。诗歌共分为9个诗节，每个诗节都由4行诗组成，每行的格律均为五步抑扬格，每个诗节的押韵格式都是 abab。与 A Flea 和 Song 等诗歌大相径庭，该诗赞美了诗人与妻子之间的精神恋爱，对于情人之间肉体的缠绵表现出蔑视的态度。诗歌开篇的第1个诗节提到，品德高尚的人在离开人世的时候，往往都带走了灵魂。这就开门见山地提出了灵魂之间的爱情，或者精神恋爱的伟大之处。第2个诗节中，诗人认为分离的眼泪和聒噪是庸俗的情感，它们会玷污诗人和妻子之间的爱情。第4个诗节指出，情人一旦陷入对对方身体的眷恋，往往再也不能分离，因为身体是这种爱情的重要组成部分（"Those things which elemented it"）。在紧接的第5个诗节，诗人认为自己和妻子对彼此灵魂的依赖是更为高级的爱情，即使两人离开，爱情依旧存在（"Inter-assured of the mind/Careless, eyes, lips, and hands to miss"）。继而，诗人在第6个诗节中指出，在精神恋爱中，肉体的分离不是爱情的背叛，而是对感情的延伸（"Though I must go, endure not yet/ a breach, but an expansion"）。

　　奇喻作为玄学派诗歌的标志性修辞手法，也出现在了该诗中。第3个诗节中，诗人分别提到了地震（"moving of th' earth"）和天体的运动（"trepidation of the spheres"），并将前者比作带来伤害的身体恋爱，而将后者比作纯真的精神恋爱。第6个诗节中，诗人再次运用奇喻，将两人的分离比作了黄金（"gold"）。黄金无论被打造成何种形状，都是一个紧密相连的整体，诗人用这种意象来比喻两人无论分隔多远爱情永远不会改变。第7到第9个诗节给读者展示了多恩诗歌中最著名的奇喻——将妻子和自己比作圆规的两只脚，妻子是固定的那只脚，而诗人是可以活动的另一只（"Thy soul, the fixed foot" "Th' other do"）。当活动的另一只脚移动时，固定的那只脚虽然不动，却倾斜身体、时刻关注另一只脚的轨

第四章 十七世纪革命与复辟时期诗歌

迹。而这正像是诗人远行，妻子虽然没有跟随，却时刻关注丈夫的行为。当诗人归家时，两人也会像收起双脚的圆规一样（"And grows erect, as that comes home"）。诗歌的最后两句是该奇喻最精妙之处，像圆规两只脚的作用一样，妻子对于爱情的坚定使得诗人能完美地画出那个圆，而画过圆之后就可以再次和作为"固定的那只脚"的妻子团聚。圆的形象又让读者感受到诗人和妻子彼此的依赖以及爱情的最终圆满。

（二）Paradise Lost

John Milton

1 Nine times the space that measures day and night

  To mortal men, he with his horrid crew,

  Lay vanquished, rolling in the fiery gulf,

  Confounded though immortal. But his doom

5 Reserved him to more wrath; for now the thought

  Both of lost happiness and lasting pain

  Torments him; round he throws his baleful eyes,

  That witnessed huge affliction and dismay,

  Mixed with obdurate pride and steadfast hate.

10 At once, as far as angels ken, he views

  The dismal situation waste and wild;

  A dungeon horrible, on all sides round,

  As one great furnace flamed; yet from those flames

  No light, but rather darkness visible

15 Served only to discover sights of woe,

  Regions of sorrow, doleful shades, where peace

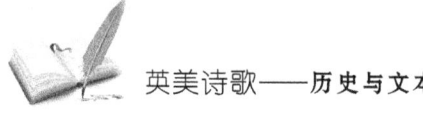

  And rest can never dwell, hope never comes

  That comes to all, but torture without end

  Still urges, and a fiery deluge, fed

20 With ever-burning sulphur unconsumed.

  Such place Eternal Justice had prepared

  For those rebellious; here their prison ordained

  In utter darkness, and their portion set,

  As far removed from God and light of Heaven

25 As from the center thrice to th'utmost pole.

  O how unlike the place from whence they fell!

  There the companions of his fall, o'erwhelmed

  With floods and whirlwinds of tempestuous fire,

  He soon discerns; and, weltering by his side,

30 One next himself in power, and next in crime,

  Long after known in Palestine, and named

  Beelzebub. To whom th'arch-enemy,

  And thence in Heaven called Satan, with bold words

  Breaking the horrid silence, thus began:

35 "If thou beest he—but O how fallen! How changed

  From him who, in the happy realms of light

  Clothed with transcendent brightness, didst outshine

  Myriads, though bright! If he whom mutual league,

  United thoughts and counsels, equal hope

40 And hazard in the glorious enterprise,

  Joined with me once, now misery hath joined

  In equal ruin; into what pit thou seest

第四章 十七世纪革命与复辟时期诗歌

From what height fallen, so much the stronger proved

He with his thunder; and till then who knew

45 The force of those dire arms? Yet not for those,

Nor what the potent Victor in his rage

Can else inflict, do I repent, or change,

Though changed in outward luster, that fixed mind,

And high disdain from sense of injured merit,

50 That with the mightiest raised me to contend,

And to the fierce contentions brought along

Innumberable force of spirits armed,

That durst dislike his reign, and me preferring,

His utmost power with adverse power opposed

55 In dubious battle on the plains of Heaven,

And shook his throne. What thought the field be lost?

All is not lost: the unconquerable will,

And study of revenge, immortal hate,

And courage never to submit or yield:

60 And what is else not to be overcome?

That glory never shall his wrath or might

Extort from me. To bow and sue for grace

With suppliant knee, and deify his power

Who, from the terror of this arm, so late

65 Doubted his empire—that were low indeed;

That were an ignominy and shame beneath

This downfall; since, by fate, the strength of gods

And this empyreal substance, cannot fail;

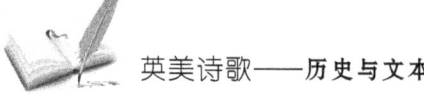

    Since, through experience of this great event,
70 In arms not worse, in foresight much advanced,
    We may with more successful hope resolve
    To wage by force or guile eternal war,
    Irreconcilable to our grand Foe,
    Who now triumphs, and in th'excess of joy
75 Sole reigning holds the tyranny of Heaven."
    So spake th'apostate angel, though in pain,
    Vaunting aloud, but racked with deep despair;
    ……

    "Is this the region, this the soil, the clime,"
80 Said then the lost archangel, "this the seat
    That we must change for Heaven? This mournful gloom
    For that celestial light? Be it so, since he
    Who now is sovereign can dispose and bid
    What shall be right: farthest from him is best,
85 Whom reason hath equaled, force hath made supreme
    Above his equals. Farewell, happy fields,
    Where joy forever dwells! Hail, horrors! hail,
    Infernal world! and thou, profoundest Hell,
    Receive thy new possessor, one who brings
90 A mind not to be changed by place or time.
    The mind is its own place, and in itself
    Can make a Heaven of Hell, a Hell of Heaven.
    What matter where, if I be still the same,
    And what I should be, all but less than he

第四章 十七世纪革命与复辟时期诗歌

95　Whom thunder hath made greater? Here at least
　　We shall be free; th'almighty hath not built
　　Here for his envy, will not drive us hence.
　　Here we may reign secure; and in my choice
　　To reign is worth ambition, though in Hell:
100　Better to reign in Hell than serve in Heaven.
　　But wherefore let we then our faithful friends,
　　Th'associates and copartners of our loss,
　　Lie thus astonished on th'oblivious pool,
　　And call them not to share with us their part
105　In this unhappy mansion, or once more
　　With rallied arms to try what may be yet
　　Regained in Heaven, or what more lost in Hell?"

17世纪的英国政治局面跌宕起伏，政治制度和主流宗教出现了更替和反复。由于许多文学家拥附主流政治势力，17世纪的英国文学创作缺乏一个固定的标准和模式，因而才有主观创作理念为上的"玄学派诗人"的出现。例如，约翰·德莱顿（John Dryden，1631—1700）在共和时期支持克伦威尔的统治，在查理士二世从法国席卷而来时又支持君主制复辟，而在詹姆士二世表现出明显的倾天主教态度后，又开始为天主教唱赞歌。在众多17世纪文学家中，最具风骨的应该是约翰·弥尔顿（John Milton，1608—1674）。他在风云变幻的政局中，始终站在资产阶级议会和清教徒一方，大声呼吁着共和制的建立。

1483—1603年，是英国都铎王朝时期。伊丽莎白女王去世之后，英国的托利党和辉格党邀请女王的表兄詹姆士入住英国，是为詹姆士一世。詹姆士一世即位后，一改与议会合作的态度，开始推行君主专制的制度，打

压议会的权力。之后的查理士一世更是明确地采用专制政府,完全无视议会权力。1642年,克伦威尔掀起了反对查理士一世统治的英国内战。他带领"铁骑军"和新模范军战胜了王党的军队,并建立了共和制的国家。此时,远在欧洲大陆旅行的弥尔顿听说了内战的消息立即返回英国。弥尔顿热情地支持克伦威尔的军队,并在其后成立的共和政府中担当外交大臣一职。弥尔顿除了承担本职的工作之外,还代替克伦威尔回答人民来信。由于工作艰辛,弥尔顿的双眼不久就出现问题,其后完全失明。查理士二世在1660年成功复辟了君主专制制度,并对弥尔顿等前朝的官员进行打压。此时的弥尔顿完全失明,作品被烧毁,并且最终只能隐居起来。《失乐园》等重要作品正是在这一时期写成。

《失乐园》于1667年问世,第一版中含有超过一万行诗文。1674年再版时,弥尔顿将《失乐园》分为十二本书,并进行了细微的改写。《失乐园》取材于《圣经·旧约》,主要讲述了撒旦反抗上帝权威的故事。作品属于史诗的范畴,由无韵体写成(不押韵的五步抑扬格)。因其行文多处用到倒置手法,加之受到拉丁文语法结构的影响,《失乐园》属于比较难读的诗歌。但是,弥尔顿在行文中注重音调的跌宕起伏和情感色彩的刻画,使得《失乐园》戴上了一层神圣庄严的光环,并被称为英国自《贝奥武甫之歌》之后最伟大的史诗作品。故事开始时,在天使之战中战败的撒旦和追随他的天使们被贬入地狱。面对地狱里恶劣的环境,撒旦们并没有放弃反抗上帝。之后的故事里,上帝创造了亚当和夏娃,将他们安置在伊甸园内,并嘱咐他们远离禁树上的禁果。得知上帝造人的消息后,撒旦历经重重考验冲出地狱,来到伊甸园诱惑夏娃吃下了禁果。得知夏娃触犯禁忌之后,亚当为了和夏娃承担共同的命运,也偷吃了禁果。上帝派大天使迈克尔将它们逐出伊甸园。迈克尔在亚当离开之前,向他展示了人类未来的发展,包括将要灭绝人类的大洪水。迈克尔提到了耶稣和救赎,并向亚当许诺将会得到一个更加幸福的伊甸园。

第四章 十七世纪革命与复辟时期诗歌

根据弥尔顿的自述，他创作《失乐园》的目的主要是"为上帝对待人类的方式辩护"。可是，在故事的行文中，撒旦这一角色却从上帝、天使、亚当和夏娃等中脱颖而出，正如雪莱所说，似乎他才是整个故事的主人公。联系当时查理士二世的复辟，在潜意识中弥尔顿是更倾向于撒旦这一角色的。《失乐园》中有三组人物角色，即上帝和天使、撒旦和恶魔以及亚当和夏娃，一组是神、一组是魔，而另一组是人。虽然从表面看来，《失乐园》讲的是亚当和夏娃失去伊甸园这一乐园的故事，可对于撒旦等角色，从天堂到地狱的贬罚，从外表光鲜的天使到丑陋灰暗的恶魔，这又何尝不是一出"失乐园"。如果上帝和天使代表了现实生活中的查理士二世和保皇派，撒旦和恶魔则是在现实生活中和王权对立的议会以及清教徒。撒旦对于自由和权力的追寻，正是代表了资产阶级议会和清教徒们对于权力的渴望和追寻。就像在故事中战败的撒旦和恶魔们一样，尽管议会权力被暂时压制，代表着资产阶级利益的阶层却不会因此而放弃对于民主和自由的向往以及追求。因此，尽管弥尔顿声称写作史诗是为了赞美上帝，他却在潜意识中将撒旦代表的资产阶级利益推到了闪亮的舞台中心。

上面的选文出自第二版的《失乐园》中的第一部篇首，描述了地狱的情景，包含了撒旦的两段独白。在坠落了九天九夜之后，撒旦们发现自己掉到了一个类似地窖的废弃而荒芜的洞穴之中（第 11 行，"waste and wild"）。弥尔顿在这里对地狱做了一个细节上的勾勒，它像个地窖一样，周边是圆的（第 12 行，"A dungeon horrible, on all sides round"），中间放着一个大火炉，由源源不断的硫磺供给的烈火熊熊燃烧着，火焰虽然炙热却不带一点光亮（第 12～13 行，"yet from those flames/No light, but rather darkness visible"），因此给撒旦们带来了更多的绝望和无助。面对这样的情形，撒旦第一个感触就是这里和天堂相差甚远（第 26 行，"O how unlike the place from whence they fell!"）。紧接着，撒旦对掉落在身边的别西卜开始了他的第一段独白。似乎由于经过长时间的坠落刚刚掉到地

狱，因此撒旦的思绪还不是很清晰，选文中的第35～42行，语法逻辑有些混乱，大概是感叹天堂和地狱之间的天壤之别。而后，撒旦整理好了自己的思绪，语言逻辑变得清晰起来。他讲到，失败所改变的只是外表的光鲜亮丽（第48行，"Though changed in outward luster"），坚定的意志和对上帝权力的蔑视却始终不会改变（第48～49行，"that fixed mind/And high disdain from sense of injured merit"）。在第一段独白的最后，撒旦表示了对上帝权力挑战的决心：经过天使之战，撒旦们得到了战斗的经验，武器更加精良、战术更加先进，（第70行，"In arms not worse, in foresight much advance"），因此永远不会向上帝妥协（第73行，"Irreconcilable to our grand Foe"）。第二段独白中，撒旦勇敢接受了坠入地狱的惩罚，并自诩为地狱的主人（第86～87行，"Farewell, happy fields, /Where joy forever dwells! Hail, horrors!"）。选文的第90～92行，Milton让撒旦说出了17世纪革命者的热情宣言：意志不会由于时间和地点的改变而改变，只要拥有坚强的意志，地狱也可以变成天堂。难怪在 *The Marriage of Heaven and Hell* 中，威廉·布莱克（William Blake）认为，弥尔顿在描写上帝和天使的时候束手束脚，而在描写撒旦和恶魔的时候却自由奔放，是因为他站在了恶魔的一方却并不自知（"of the devil's party without knowing it"）。

二、Further Reading

（一）The Good-Morrow

John Donne

1 I wonder by my troth what thou, and I
   Did, till we loved? Were we not weaned till then,
   But sucked on country pleasures, childishly?

第四章　十七世纪革命与复辟时期诗歌

  Or snorted we in the seven sleepers'den?

5 'Twas so; but this, all pleasures fancies be.

  If ever any beauty l did see,

  Which I desired and got,'twas but a dream of thee.

  And now good-morrow to our waking souls,

  Which watch not one another out of fear;

10 For love all love of other sights controls

  And makes one little room an everywhere.

  Let sea-discoverers to new worlds have gone,

  Let maps to others, worlds on worlds have shown:

  Let us possess one world; each hath one, and is one.

15 My face in thine eye, thine in mine appears,

  And true plain hearts do in the faces rest;

  Where can we find two better hemispheres,

  Without sharp North, without declining West?

  Whatever dies was not mixed equally;

20 If our two loves be one, or, thou and I

  Love so alike that none do slacken, none can die.

【译文】

早安

约翰·多恩

1 说真的，不知你我相爱之前

  是个什么样，像未断乳的小孩

　　只是吮吸着乡村里欢乐之奶？
　　或者像在洞里沉睡的七教士一样？
5　是的；除此，一切欢乐只是幻想。
　　如果有什么美人曾经使我向往，
　　并让我如愿，只是与你相见在梦乡。

　　现在我们向醒来的灵魂道声早安，
　　相互凝视着，彼此都不恐慌；
10　因为爱控制了我们对万物的爱，
　　爱使这斗室成了天下万方。
　　让海洋探险家去发现新的世界吧，
　　让地图向他人展示一个个新世界吧：
　　让我们占有一个；一人一个，合而为一。

15　我们俩的脸在彼此的眼中出现，
　　真诚而坦率的心驻留在两张脸上；
　　哪里可以找到两个更好的半球，
　　既无冰冻的北极，也无落日的西天？
　　万物消亡都是因为组合不当；
20　如果我们俩的爱始终如一，爱得一样，
　　谁都不会松劲，谁都不会消亡。

（何功杰　译）

【点评】

　　本诗共有三个诗节，第1～7行为第一诗节、第8行～14行为第二诗节、第15～21行为第三诗节。每个诗节按 abab ccc 押韵，诗人采用独白的形式向"我"的爱人倾诉何为永恒的爱情。

第四章　十七世纪革命与复辟时期诗歌

第一诗节中，诗人采用过去时态，隐喻（奇喻）手法，利用"未断乳的小孩"、"洞里沉睡的七教士"（历史典故）、"梦乡"的意象"Were we not weaned till then/But sucked on country pleasures, childishly?" "Or snorted we in the seven sleepers' den?"比喻"我"与恋人过去的爱情就像没断奶的婴孩，像在洞穴中沉睡的七位圣徒，意在表明过去的所谓爱情只是沉溺于感官上的，是幼稚的，即使有所谓美好，也好像是在梦乡，"If ever any beauty l did see/Which I desired and got, 'twas but a dream of thee"，是肉体而不是精神的。

第二诗节中诗人采用现在时态，将笔锋转向现在。第1～3行诗人采用拟人的手法，"And now good-morrow to our waking souls/Which watch not one another out of fear/For love all love of other sights controls"指出现在已经截然不同，因为灵魂已经醒来，与第一诗节最后两行所提到的美（肉体上的）形成对比。伴随着灵魂上的醒来彼此间有了"爱"。第二节第3～4行诗人采用拟人、反复与夸张的手法强调了"爱"力量的强大。"For love all love of other sights controls/And makes one little room an everywhere"诗句中的第一个"love"指的是精神上（灵魂）的爱，第二个对万物的"love"指的是世俗的爱，诗人在这里强调精神上的爱胜过一切世俗之爱（包括肉体），因为柏拉图的观点认为，精神乃为实质或本质，世俗乃为幻象。紧接着，诗人采用连词叠用的手法，连续使用三个反复、排比并用的祈使句"Let sea-discoverers to new worlds have gone/Let maps to others, worlds on worlds have shown/Let us possess one world; each hath one, and is one"强调由灵魂渗入所产生的真爱使得恋人们不再羡慕世俗杂念，而是拥有一个崭新的世界：一人一个且合二为一。

第三个诗节诗人又回到恋人们"对视"的镜头，"My face in thine eye, thine in mine appears"，各自的脸都映在对方眼中，像两个"半球"，且从脸上能够读出对方真诚朴实的情感。"And true plain hearts do in the faces rest",这里"heart"采用换喻手法,指代情感,意味着恋人间坚贞不渝的爱情,随后诗人采用反意疑问句"Where can we find two better hemispheres/ Without sharp North, without declining West?"表征恋人间精神上的合一不同于地球,已经成为一个新世界、新的天体。因为地球上有冰冻的北极(象征冷酷无情),有落日的西天(象征背叛),在这里,诗人再次强调精神上合二为一的爱情的伟大。最后,诗人指出如果恋人的合二为一的爱始终如一,谁都不会减弱的话,这样的爱将会永恒不朽,"If our two loves be one, or, thou and I/Love so alike that none do slacken, none can die"。

在整首诗中,诗人借助多样的修辞技巧、不同的意象与时态的转换向读者描绘了一个美好新世界。在那里,爱唤醒沉睡的灵魂,爱将永恒,只有精神渗入的爱才能将人带入新世界。

(二) Song

John Donne

1 Go and catch a falling star,
    Get with child a mandrake root,
    Tell me where all past years are,
    Or who cleft the Devil's foot,
5 Teach me to hear mermaids singing,
    Or to keep off envy's stinging,
    And find
    What wind
    Serves to advance an honest mind.

10 If thou be'st born to strange sights,

第四章　十七世纪革命与复辟时期诗歌

    Things invisible to see,

    Ride ten thousand days and nights,

    Till age snow white hairs on thee,

    Thou, when thou return'st, wilt tell me

15 All strange wonders that befell thee,

    And swear

    No where

    Lives a woman true, and fair.

    If thou find'st one, let me know,

20 Such a pilgrimage were sweet;

    Yet do not, I would not go,

    Though at next door we might meet;

    Though she were true when you met her,

    And last till you write your letter,

25 Yet she

    Will be

    False, ere I come, to two, or three.

【译文】

歌

约翰·多恩

1 去，把落下的流星抓住，

    叫曼德拉草根怀孕生孩，

    告诉我逝去的岁月在何处，

是谁把魔鬼的双蹄分开，
5　教我听美人鱼如何歌唱，
或怎样能避免妒忌刺伤，
去找找看
什么风向
有助于促进诚实思想的形成。

10　假如你天生喜欢奇景异象，
喜欢那些难以看到的景象，
你就骑马走一万个日夜去寻访，
直到岁月在你头上落满白霜，
你回来时再告诉我，
15　一切奇异的事物都见过，
但你发誓
无论哪里
找不到一个女人既忠诚又美丽。

假如你找到了，请告诉我，
20　这样的朝拜或许会称心如意，
然而，我不会去，也别对我说，
尽管我们可以相见在隔壁；
你见到她时，她会对你表示忠心，
不过不会长久，你求爱的信
25　还未写好
我还未到
她已经把两三个男人欺骗了。

第四章　十七世纪革命与复辟时期诗歌

（何功杰　译）

【点评】

此诗除第7～8行外，主要为四音步抑扬格，共分为三个诗节，每个诗节9行，押韵格式为：ababcc ddd。整首诗歌表达了对女人的否定，对爱情的否定。

多恩在此诗歌中一开始使用了祈使语气，"Go and catch a falling star/ Get with child a mandrake root/Tell me where all past years are,/ Or who cleft the Devil's foot/Teach me to hear mermaids singing,...And find"，并在第一节诗中将"falling star, mermaids, Devil's foot, mandrake root"（流星、美人鱼、魔鬼的双蹄、曼德拉草根等）互不相干的意象并置在一起，看似杂乱无章，但是结合语境才能辨别出：抓住陨落的星星，让曼德拉草根怀孕，劈开魔鬼的脚，找寻逝去的岁月，躲开嫉妒的刺伤，诗人的目的在于证明这些事情不可能实现，反衬了后两节诗中所表示出的对女人的歧视与爱情的否定，带有明显的性别偏见。整首诗中诗人采用奇喻和夸张的手法，描绘了女性的极端形象："No where Lives a woman true, and fair/If thou find'st one, let me know/ Such a pilgrimage were sweet/Yet do not, I would not go/ Though at next door we might meet/Though she were true when you met her/And last till you write your letter/Yet she/Will be/False, ere I come, to two, or three"。女性水性杨花，多变不忠。诗歌中女性是沉默的，话语权握在男性诗人手中且语气愤懑激昂。难道只有女人多变、背叛与不忠诚吗？很明显，诗歌传递了多恩的男权思想，同时也反映了那个时代男权至上的社会现实。

（三）The Flea

John Donne

1　Mark but this flea, and mark in this,

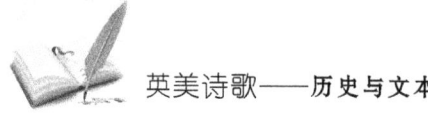

How little that which thou deniest me is;

Me it sucked first, and now sucks thee,

And in this flea our two bloods mingled be;

5   Thou know'st that this cannot be said

A sin, or shame, or loss of maindenhead,

Yet this enjoys before it woo,

And pampered swells with one blood made of two,

And this, alas, is more than we would do.

10   Oh stay, three lives in one flea spare,

Where we almost, nay more than married, are.

This flea is you and I, and this

Our marriage bed and marriage temple is;

Though parents grudge, and you, we are met,

15   And cloistered in these living walls of jet,

Though use make you apt to kill me

Let not to that, self-murder added be,

And sacrilege, three sins in killing three.

Cruel and sudden, hast thou since

20   Purpled thy nail, in blood of innocence?

Wherein could this flea guilty be,

Except in that drop which it sucked from thee?

Yet thou triumph'st, and say'st that thou

Find'st not thy self nor me the weaker now;

25   'Tis true, then learn how false fears be;

第四章　十七世纪革命与复辟时期诗歌

　　Just so much honor, when thou yield'st to me,

　　Will waste, as this flea's death took life from thee.

【译文】

跳蚤

约翰·多恩

1　你看吧，看看这跳蚤，

　　你否认我的成分能有多少？

　　它先咬了我，此刻又咬了你，

　　我俩的血已在它里边融为一体；

5　要承认，这件事不能被说成是羞耻

　　或罪过，也算不上你贞操的损失，

　　而它却未求婚就先得快意，

　　合我俩的血为一体，涨大它的腹肌，

　　唉，它做得远远超过我们自己。

10　啊，住手，饶过这跳蚤里的三个生命。

　　在它体内，我们不止是结了婚，

　　它是你是我，是我们的花烛温床，

　　是我们婚姻的殿堂；

　　尽管父母和你都不愿意，我们还是聚在一起。

15　同居于这乌黑的活墙里。

　　尽管习俗使你轻易杀我，

　　但不要把三个生命剥夺，

　　不要再加上自杀和渎圣的罪过。

你突然狠心地把毒手下，
20　用无辜者的血染紫了你的指甲？
这跳蚤只吸过你一口血，
这怎能算作一种罪过？
而你却得意洋洋地说，
你和我都不比从前弱；
25　不错，我因此全知：说你害怕是多么虚假！
你此时同意我，但跳蚤之死已把你生命夺下。
多少的道义全都浪费、白搭。

（李正栓　译）

【点评】

诗作分为三个诗节，每个诗节9行，韵式为：aabbccddd。诗人采用奇喻及戏剧性独白的手法，描摹了一幅生动、滑稽的求爱画面。

诗人一开始借用意象"flea"（跳蚤）来说理"Mark but this flea, and mark in this,/How little that which thou deniest me is;"（看这跳蚤，你否认我的成分能有多少），跳蚤的意象虽无美感，但设置了悬念，吸引着读者。跳蚤如何呢？再读发现"Me it sucked first, and now sucks thee/And in this flea our two bloods mingled be/Thou know'st that this cannot be said/A sin, or shame, or loss of maindenhead/ Yet this enjoys before it woo/ And pampered swells with one blood made of two/And this, alas, is more than we would do"，跳蚤咬了我又咬了你……，"我"的推理滑稽有趣。因其羡慕跳蚤"未求婚"就先得快意，此处使用拟人手法，自叹不如一只跳蚤——"它做得远远超过我们自己"。此外，诗人将跳蚤吸了两人的血（跳蚤本能）和"羞耻、罪过、贞操"这样严肃的抽象词语并置在一起，使得说理意趣盎然，荒诞滑稽。

第二个诗节中诗人采用夸张语气，说到跳蚤吸血后竟然已经孕育生命，两人还在跳蚤里结了婚，跳蚤是他们的花烛温床，是他们婚姻的殿堂。（"This

第四章 十七世纪革命与复辟时期诗歌

flea is you and I, and this/Our marriage bed and marriage temple is"）诗人同时继续使用跳蚤这一隐喻意象，将跳蚤与"婚姻、花烛温床、婚姻殿堂"等高雅词汇结合使用，继续说理，指出如果对方碍于习俗杀了跳蚤就如同把三个生命剥夺，是自杀和渎圣（"Let not to that, self-murder added be,/ And sacrilege, three sins in killing three."）。

第三个诗节中，诗人继续使用夸张手法，诗中的"我"小题大做，当对方把跳蚤杀死，"我"戏谑地称对方为"Cruel and sudden, hast thou since/Purpled thy nail in blood of innocence?"（你突然狠心地把毒手下，用无辜者的血染紫了你的指甲？）对方则回应道"Yet thou triumphst, and sayst that thou Findst not thy self nor me the weaker now"（而你却得意洋洋地说，你和我都不比从前弱），"我"赶紧应答"Tis true ; then learn how false fears be/Just so much honor , when thou yieldst to me/Will waste , as this fleas death took life from thee"。不错，"我"因此全知："说你害怕是多么虚假！你此时同意我，……"读到这里才明白，诗中的"我"借助跳蚤说了一大堆道理，原来是向对方求爱。诗人在奇思妙想中的推理张扬、滑稽、怪诞，但不乏理性。整首诗构思巧妙，堪称经典之作。

（四）Song on May Morning

John Milton

1 Now the bright morning star, day's harbinger,
   Comes dancing from the east, and leads with her
   The flowery May, who from her green lap throws
   The yellow cowslip and the pale primrose.
5 Hail, bounteous May, that dost inspire
   Mirth and youth and warm desire!

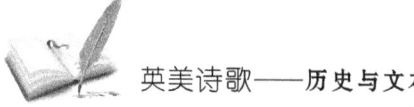

Woods and groves are of thy dressing;

Hill and dale doth boast thy blessing.

Thus we salute thee with our early song,

10　And welcome thee, and wish thee long.

【译文】

五月晨歌

约翰·弥尔顿

1　晶莹的晨星，白日的先驱，

　　她舞蹈着从东方带来娇侣，

　　百花的五月，从绿色的怀中撒下

　　金黄色的九轮花和淡红的樱草花。

5　欢迎，富丽的五月啊，你激扬了

　　欢乐、青春和热切的希望；

　　林木、树丛是你的装束，

　　山陵、溪谷夸说你的幸福。

　　我们也用清晨的歌曲向你礼赞，

10　欢迎你，并且祝福你永恒无边！

（朱维之　译）

【点评】

　　这是一首抒情赞美诗，语言典雅，感情崇高，韵式为：aabbccddee。诗人在第1行诗歌中提到"the bright morning star, day's harbinger"（晶莹的晨星，白日的先驱），典故（allusion）意象"the bright morning star"与圣经新约《启示录》22章16节下半句对应"the bright morning star"指的是上帝。第二行诗歌 "Comes dancing from the east, and leads with her"（她舞蹈着从

第四章 十七世纪革命与复辟时期诗歌

东方带来娇侣)中,"dancing""leads""her"采用拟人手法,生动形象。"leads"一词赋予晨星以领导权力,这正好与旧约圣经的《约伯记》38章12节对应,"你自生以来,曾命定晨光,使清晨的日光知道本位"。第3~4行诗"The flowery May, who from her green lap throws/The yellow cowslip and the pale primrose"(百花的五月,从绿色的怀中撒下/金黄色的九轮花和淡红的樱草花)中的意象词"flowery""her green lap""yellow cowslip""pale primrose"构建了一幅唯美生动的自然景观画像,美不胜收。

诗人在第5~6行诗中不禁高呼"Hail, bounteous May, that dost inspire/Mirth and youth and warm desire!"(欢迎,富丽的五月啊,你激扬/欢乐、青春和热情的希望),6行诗中采用了连词"and"叠用和尾部辅音押韵(mirth, youth)的手法,抒发了诗人的感受和激动心情。接下来7~8行诗中采用拟人手法,继续赞美五月的祝福"Woods and groves are of thy dressing;/Hill and dale doth boast thy blessing"。其中"woods, groves""hill, dale"尾部为辅音韵,音韵和谐悦耳。第6行诗中的抽象词"Mirth, youth, warm desire"同上下诗行中的意象词并置,情景交融,再加上多种修辞手法的使用,使得诗歌意境优美,感染力极强。

最后两句诗"Thus we salute thee with our early song/And welcome thee, and wish thee long"中的"salute"(致敬),"welcome"(欢迎),"wish"(祝愿)采用连词"and"叠用,直接抒发对"thee"(你)的赞美。诗中的"你"字面意义上为"晨光率领下的五月",但结合典故与文化背景来看实则指的乃是上帝,整首诗洋溢着对造物主的赞美之情。

(五)On His Deceased Wife

John Milton

1　Methought I saw my late espous'ed saint

Brought to me like Alcestis from the grave,

Whom Jove's great son to her glad husband gave,

Rescued from Death by force, though pale and faint.

5 Mine, as whom washed from spot of child-bed taint

Purification in the Old Law did save,

And such as yet once more I trust to have

Full sight of her in Heaven without restraint,

Came vested all in white, pure as her mind.

10 Her face was veiled; yet to my fancied sight

Love, sweetness, goodness, in her person shined

So clear as in no face with more delight.

But, oh! as to embrace me she inclined,

I waked, she fled, and day brought back my night.

【译文】
梦亡妻

约翰·弥尔顿

1 我仿佛看见婚后不久便进入天堂的妻

回到了我身边，像阿尔塞斯蒂从坟墓

被朱庇特伟大的儿子由死亡中抢救出，

交还她欣喜的丈夫，虽然她苍白无力。

5 我的妻，如同古戒律规定的净身礼

拯救的女子，洗净了产褥上的血污，

这样的她，我相信我必能再度

在天堂里无拘无束地细细瞻视，

她穿着和她心灵一样洁白的衣袍，

第四章 十七世纪革命与复辟时期诗歌

10　脸上蒙着面纱，但我好像看得真切，

　　爱、温柔、善良在她身上闪耀，

　　任何人脸上显不出这样的喜悦。

　　但是，唉，正当她俯身要和我拥抱，

　　我醒了，她逃了，白昼带回了我的黑夜。

（胡家峦　译）

【点评】

这是弥尔顿的一首悼念诗，以叙梦方式缅怀逝去妻子的一首表达爱情的诗，诗歌感情真挚、感人肺腑。全诗共 14 行，诗歌韵式为：abababab cdcdcd。

诗歌一开始，"Methought I saw my late espous'ed saint/ Brought to me like Alcestis from the grave/ Whom Jove's great son to her glad husband gave/ Rescued from Death by force, though pale and faint"，诗人看到自己刚刚去世不久的妻子，来到了自己的身边，就如同古希腊美女阿尔塞斯蒂"Alcestis"从坟墓被朱庇特伟大的儿子由死亡中抢救出，这里诗人运用典故与明喻，将已故美妻在梦中带进复活的样式。接下来第 5～8 行诗"Mine, as whom washed from spot of child-bed taint/Purification in the Old Law did save,/And such as yet once more I trust to have/Full sight of her in Heaven without restraint"表明爱妻死于产褥热，（在旧约中，妇女生产因流血被认为不洁净）但"我的妻，如同古戒律规定的净身礼拯救的女子，洗净了产褥上的血污"，诗人借用了旧约圣经典故，其中的"Old Law"指代摩西律法。随即诗人赞美自己的妻子"Came vested all in white, pure as her mind/Her face was veiled; yet to my fancied sight/Love, sweetness, goodness, in her person shined/ So clear as in no face with more delight"，其中"pure as her mind"运用明喻手法，赞美亡妻的心灵洁白无瑕。"Love, sweetness, goodness, in her person shined"，在此诗句中，诗人使用连词省略（asyndeton）与拟人手法，列举了妻子种种美德：

爱、温柔、善良在她身上闪耀,任何人脸上显不出这样的喜悦。但当妻子俯身要和诗人拥抱时,梦醒了("I waked, she fled, and day brought back my night"),我又回到黑暗中,陷入无边的痛苦与惆怅,表达了诗人对亡妻的深切怀念之情。但是梦境中的相遇传递出希望,说明诗人与爱妻分离只是短暂的,终究还会在天堂相遇,爱将永恒。

整首诗歌对比鲜明,意象丰富,例如:天堂("Heaven")、地狱("Death")、希腊神话("Alcestis")、旧约圣经("Purification in the Old Law")、穿戴("vested all in white")等传递了深厚的西方文化内涵及对生命的思索。

(六)On His Blindness

John Milton

1　When I consider how my light is spent
　　Ere half my days in this dark world and wide,
　　And that one talent which is death to hide
　　Lodged with me useless, though my soul more bent
5　To serve therewith my Maker, and present
　　My true account, lest He, returning, chide,
　　"Doth God exact day-labour, light denied?"
　　I fondly ask. But Patience, to prevent
　　That murmur, soon replies, "God doth not need
10　Either man's work or his own gifts. Who best
　　Bear his mild yoke, they serve him best. His state
　　Is kingly: thousands at his bidding speed
　　And post o'er land and ocean without rest;
　　They also serve who only stand and wait."

第四章　十七世纪革命与复辟时期诗歌

【译文】

哀失明

约翰·弥尔顿

1　想到自己未到半生就双目失明，
　　眼前的世界是一片茫茫的黑暗，
　　想到那被埋没的才干
　　于我而言已毫无用处，尽管
5　我的灵魂更愿意侍奉我的造主
　　并献上真心，免得算账时遭斥；
　　"神要人白天做工，竟不给光明？"
　　我愚蠢自问。但忍耐阻止抱怨
　　抢先做了应答："神既不要人的
10　工作也不收回他的礼物；谁最
　　能轻松地背稳神轭，谁就最能
　　侍奉。他君临天下，差遣千万
　　万天使，越疆跨海，忙碌不停：
　　那些只站立等候的，也在侍奉。"

（黄宗英　译）

【点评】

　　此诗为弥尔顿的一首十四行诗，此诗一改英国诗体结构，而采用传统的意大利体：前八行提问（octave），后六行作答（sestet），但诗人做了小小改动，在第 7 行发问，而不是传统的第 8 行。诗歌采用对话体叙事。全诗采用抑扬格五音步格律，韵式为：abbaabba cdecde。此诗表达了诗人强调精神、追求生命的清教主义人文思想。

　　一开始诗人在思忖该如何让自己的生命发光 "I consider how my light is

spent",因为人生未过半就双目失明,接下来的人生要在茫茫的黑夜中度过,"Ere half my days in this dark world and wide"其中"days""dark"构成头韵(alliteration),"world""wide"两词押头韵,发音上还押尾部辅音韵,构成了修辞学上的"Pararhyme",意指诗人失明后黑夜茫茫而又漫长,表达了极深的痛苦。1行诗中的"light"一词与第2行中的"dark"形成对比,具有多重含义,表面看指的是"视力",对于清教主义诗人的弥尔顿来说,这里的光应该也指上帝赋予的才干(《约翰福音》第1章第4节"生命在他里头,这生命就是人的光",《马太福音》第5章第14节"你们是世上的光")。接下来"And that one talent which is death to hide/Lodged with me useless",诗人感叹失明后自己的才干会被埋没,将无用武之地。此处的"talent"与上文中的"light"构成同义反复,都是指上帝赋予的才能。这里与《马太福音》25章第14～30节耶稣论才干的比喻相呼应,其中一位仆人将上帝赋予的一千两银子埋起来,未能好好使用,结果被上帝训斥并拿走。对于满是宗教情怀的诗人来说,苦难岂能阻挡服侍上帝的热情?"though my soul more bent/To serve therewith my Maker, and present/My true account, lest He, returning, chide",诗人的灵魂更愿意侍奉上帝并献上真心,免得下场如那位圣经上所提的懒惰的仆人。

在第7行"Doth God exact day-labour, light denied?"诗人发问,上帝让人在白天做工,岂不赐下光明吗?这里"light"有多重含义,指代"视力"、"光明"与"才能"。这句诗歌的语气明显有抱怨在里面,失明的诗人想说"上帝啊,我想服侍你,请给我光明"。"fondly"一词表示诗人自认这样的发问是天真的、愚蠢的,因为上帝是全能的。诗人借助"Patience"并将之拟人化来阻止我的抱怨。诗人在患难中,忍耐来劝慰,这与《圣经·罗马书》5章第3～5节相呼应"……因为知道患难生忍耐,忍耐生老练"。Patience回答我说"God doth not need/Either man's work or his own gifts. Who best/Bear his mild yoke, they serve him best. His state/Is kingly: thousands at his bidding speed/ And post

第四章 十七世纪革命与复辟时期诗歌

o'er land and ocean without rest/They also serve who only stand and wait"上帝不需要人的工作，也不收回他的礼物。"gift"与前面提到的"light""talent"同义，都指代上帝的恩赐。那人怎样服侍上帝呢？第11行诗说到只要背负好自己的"yoke"（上帝给予人类的负担）就是最好的服侍上帝。第12～14行诗解释上帝不需要人的工作的原因：因为上帝君临天下，调动万有，差遣千万万天使，他们越疆跨海，忙碌不停，即使那些只站立等候的，也在侍奉上帝。

整首诗中"serve"（侍奉）反复出现三次，强化了诗歌的主题。清教主义诗人弥尔顿面对失明的苦难，虽有软弱，但还在思考该如何让造物主所赋予自己的生命才华更好地发光以侍奉上帝，同时亦表达了对上帝大能的赞美，传递了诗人积极乐观的宗教人文情怀。

（七）On His Being Arrived to the Age of Twenty-Three

John Milton

1 How soon hath Time, the subtle thief of youth,
   Stolen on his wing my three-and-twentieth year!
   My hasting days fly on with full career,
   But my late spring no bud or blossom shew'th.
5 Perhaps my semblance might deceive the truth
   That I to manhood am arrived so near;
   And inward ripeness doth much less appear,
   That some more timely-happy spirits endu'th.
   Yet, be it less or more or soon or slow,
10 It shall be still in strictest measure even
   To that same lot, however mean or high,

Toward which Time leads me, and the will of Heaven;

All is, if I have grace to use it so,

As ever in my great Task-Master-s eye.

【译文】
时光匆匆

约翰·弥尔顿

1 时光飞逝，带着我的青春私奔，

   它的双翼，载走我那二十三年的光阴。

   岁月如梭，眨眼间，不知溜走了多少青春，

   可是我迟到的春天还不曾把花蕾吐出。

5 也许我有着年轻的外表，

   然而我的年龄已接近成年。

   稚嫩的内心从没有遭受历练，

   实在不及那些时间的宠儿。

   不管才华来得是多是少，是快是慢，

10 它都严格遵守着规律，

   始终是同样的命运，无论或卑或贵

   这是时间与上帝的旨意。

   如果善加利用，一切仍宛如

   上帝眼中的风景画般美丽。

（毕小君 译）

【点评】

　　这首十四行诗是弥尔顿 23 岁生日时写给自己的。诗歌采用五音步抑扬格，韵式为：abbaabbacdedce。

第四章　十七世纪革命与复辟时期诗歌

诗歌一开始，诗人运用感叹句"How soon hath Time, the subtle thief of youth/ Stolen on his wing my three-and-twentieth year!"同时采用了隐喻手法，指出时间如盗贼，感叹时光飞逝，转眼已经23岁了。3行诗"My hasting days fly on with full career"中"hasting days"押母韵，"fly... full"押头韵，使得诗行读起来朗朗上口，节奏感强，同时强调时间飞逝如梭。诗人在第四行诗"But my late spring no bud or blossom shew'th"中运用了比喻（metaphor），将生命比作迟到的春天，其中"bud... blossom"押头韵，且为同义反复，比喻生命中的"成功或成就"。

第5～6行诗"Perhaps my semblance might deceive the truth/ That I to manhood am arrived so near"采用了拟人手法，指出我的外表掩盖了事实，实际上，我已经接近成年。第7～8行诗人提到自己内心的成熟（"And inward ripeness doth much less appear"）没有与外表一致（暗指23岁了，才情还未显露，还未取得成功）。不像有些人，内心与外表一致（"That some more timely-happy spirits endu'th"），这里的"ripeness"和前文所提的比喻"bud or blossom"互文，"spirits"使用换喻手法指代那些才华横溢且取得成就的同龄人。前8行诗提出问题，时光飞逝，23岁还一事无成，自己外表和内心看起来不那么相称（年龄和成就不相符）。

第9～12行中诗人对此提出自己的看法：不管才华来得是多是少，是快是慢，它都严格遵守着规律，始终是同样的命运，无论或卑或贵，这是时间与上帝的旨意（"Yet, be it less or more or soon or slow/It shall be still in strictest measure even/To that same lot, however mean or high/Toward which Time leads me, and the will of Heaven"）。第9行中诗人采用连词"or"叠用，强调无论什么情况，都是遵循着一定的规律。第10行诗中"measure"一词指的是尺寸，这里引申为规律。第11行诗中的"mean or high"形成对比，意指无论高低贵贱，都在上帝的意志下由时间来引导。第12行诗中，诗人采用拟人手法，将时间的首字母大写并赋予生命，表达了对时间和上

帝的敬畏之情。最后两行"All is, if I have grace to use it so/As ever in my great Task-Master-s eye"强调：所有一切，都是上帝恩典，要好好珍惜并加以利用，其中"the great Task-Master"指上帝。

　　一开始诗人把时间比作盗贼，但随后诗人对时间有了新的认识("Toward which Time leads me")；一开始诗人对自己怀才不遇也颇有微词，但在诗歌的后半部分，诗人也渐渐廓清了自己的看法，无论怎样，都是上帝的旨意，应当以感恩的心来看待（"if I have grace to use it so"），整首诗传递了诗人坚定的信仰情怀。

第五章　十八世纪英国启蒙时期诗歌

18世纪，英国爆发了启蒙运动，开启了启蒙主义时期。启蒙主义者崇尚理性、平等与科学。理性成为衡量人类行为与关系的尺度，"永久的真理""永久的公正""天赋的平等"成为人们衡量一切事物的标准。启蒙主义者倡导全民教育，他们认为教育可以使人臻于理智，民主平等的人类社会只有依靠教育，才能实现并趋向完美。

18世纪初，在文学领域，新古典主义（Neoclassicism）成为文学时尚。新古典主义者推崇理性，强调明晰、对称、节制、优雅，追求艺术形式的完美与和谐，努力使作品喜闻乐见并富于教义。这一时期诗体丰富，各有其创作原则。主要诗歌有：嘲弄式英雄史诗、骑士抒情诗、讽喻诗及讽刺短诗。诗歌的古典气质与技巧对后世文学诗歌创作产生了深远影响。

新古典主义的代表人物约翰·德莱顿（John Dryden）主要运用英雄双韵体技巧进行创作，气势阳刚。亚历山大·蒲柏（Alexander Pope）深受德莱顿的影响，将英雄双韵体诗歌进一步发展，其成名作为《论批评》（*On Criticism*）。

在18世纪后期田园诗兴起，与感伤主义（Sentimentalism）融合。这一时期英国资本主义加速发展，社会矛盾日益加剧，感伤情绪日渐浓厚。托马斯·格雷（Thomas Gray）的《墓地挽歌》（*Elegy Written in a Country Churchyard*）表达了浓浓的伤感之情，成为感伤主义代表作。到18世纪下半期，英国文学前浪漫主义（Pre-Romanticism）随着1798年华兹华斯和柯勒律治的《抒情歌谣集》（*Lyrical Ballads*）的发表兴起。代表人物还有威廉·布莱克（William Blake），其作品有著名的《经验之歌》（*Songs of Experience*）和《天真之歌》（*Songs of Innocence*）；苏格兰民族诗人罗伯特·彭斯（Robert Burns）的作品主要有《友谊地久天长》（*Auld Lang Syne*）、《我的心在高原》（*My Heat's in the Highlands*）等。

一、Poem Reading

（一）The Rape of the Lock

Alexander Pope

Part III

1   Close by those Meads for ever crown'd with Flow'rs,
    Where Thames with Pride surveys his rising Tow'rs,
    There stands a Structure of Majestick Frame,
    Which from the neighb'ring Hampton takes its Name.
5   Here Britain's Statesmen oft the Fall foredoom
    Of Foreign Tyrants, and of Nymphs at home;
    Here Thou, great Anna! whom three Realms obey,
    Dost sometimes Counsel take—and sometimes Tea.
    Hither the Heroes and the Nymphs resort,
10 To taste awhile the Pleasures of a Court;

第五章 十八世纪英国启蒙时期诗歌

In various Talk th'instructive hours they past,
Who gave the Ball, or paid the Visit last:
One speaks the Glory of the British Queen,
And one describes a charming Indian Screen.
15　A third interprets Motions, Looks, and Eyes;
At ev'ry Word a Reputation dies.
Snuff, or the Fan, supply each Pause of Chat,
With singing, laughing, ogling, and all that.
Mean while declining from the Noon of Day,
20　The Sun obliquely shoots his burning Ray;
The hungry Judges soon the Sentence sign,
And Wretches hang that Jury-men may Dine;
The Merchant from th'exchange returns in Peace,
And the long Labours of the Toilette cease
25　Belinda now, whom Thirst of Fame invites,
Burns to encounter two adventrous Knights,
At Ombre singly to decide their Doom;
And swells her Breast with Conquests yet to come.
Strait the three Bands prepare in Arms to join,
30　Each Band the number of the Sacred Nine.
Soon as she spreads her Hand, th'Aerial Guard
Descend, and sit on each important Card,
First Ariel perch'd upon a Matadore,
Then each, according to the Rank they bore;
35　For Sylphs, yet mindful of their ancient Race,
Are, as when Women, wondrous fond of place.

......

But when to Mischief Mortals bend their Will,

How soon they find fit Instruments of Ill!

40   Just then, Clarissa drew with tempting Grace

A two-edg'd Weapon from her shining Case;

So Ladies in Romance assist their Knight,

Present the Spear, and arm him for the Fight.

He takes the Gift with rev'rence, and extends

45   The little Engine on his Finger's Ends:

This just behind Belinda's Neck he spread,

As o'er the fragrant Steams she bends her Head:

Swift to the Lock a thousand Sprights repair,

A thousand Wings, by turns, blow back the Hair,

50   And thrice they twitch'd the Diamond in her Ear,

Thrice she look'd back, and thrice the Foe drew near.

Just in that instant, anxious Ariel sought

The close Recesses of the Virgin's Thought;

As on the Nosegay in her Breast reclin'd,

55   He watch'd th' Ideas rising in her Mind,

Sudden he view'd, in spite of all her Art,

An Earthly Lover lurking at her Heart.

Amaz'd, confus'd, he found his Pow'r expir'd,

Resign'd to Fate, and with a Sigh retir'd.

60   The Peer now spreads the glitt'ring Forfex wide,

T'inclose the Lock; now joins it, to divide.

Ev'n then, before the fatal Engine clos'd,

第五章　十八世纪英国启蒙时期诗歌

  A wretched Sylph too fondly interpos'd;

  Fate ur'd the Sheers, and cut the Sylph in twain,

65　（But Airy Substance soon unites again）

  The meeting Points that sacred Hair dissever

  From the fair Head, for ever and for ever!

  Then flash'd the living Lightnings from her Eyes,

  And Screams of Horror rend th'affrighted Skies.

70　Not louder Shrieks to pitying Heav'n are cast,

  When Husbands or when Lap-dogs breath their last,

  Or when rich China Vessels, fal'n from high,

  In glittring Dust and painted Fragments lie!

  Let Wreaths of Triumph now my Temples twine,

75　（The Victor cry'd）the glorious Prize is mine!

  While Fish in Streams, or Birds delight in Air,

  Or in a Coach and Six the British Fair,

  As long as Atalantis shall be read,

  Or the small Pillow grace a Lady's Bed,

80　While Visits shall be paid on solemn Days,

  When numerous Wax-lights in bright Order blaze,

  While Nymphs take Treats, or Assignations give,

  So long my Honour, Name, and Praise shall live!

  What Time wou'd spare, from Steel receives its date,

85　And Monuments, like Men, submit to Fate!

  Steel cou'd the Labour of the Gods destroy,

  And strike to Dust th'Imperial Tow'rs of Troy.

  Steel cou'd the Works of mortal Pride confound,

And hew Triumphal Arches to the Ground.
90　What Wonder then, fair Nymph! thy Hairs shou'd feel
　　The conqu'ring Force of unresisted Steel?

　　经历了17世纪资产阶级革命的洗涤之后，18世纪的英国社会政局逐渐稳定下来。国王权力和议会权力之间的主要矛盾逐渐转移，在议会权力稳固的同时，议会和民众之间，以及资产阶级权力内部的矛盾逐渐突显。托利党和辉格党早在17世纪后半期就开始活跃在英国的政坛，他们之间的权利纷争一直处于一个平衡的状态，两党轮流执政、互相制衡。这一时期，英国政权还推出了第一任首相罗伯特·沃波尔（Robert Walpole，1676—1745），一种崭新的资产阶级政权体制逐渐代替了原有的封建君主专制制度。随着国内政局的稳定，英国的经济也得到了进一步的发展，特别是商务贸易的发展更是突出。由此看来，尽管不像大革命时期那样大刀阔斧地进行政体改革，18世纪的英国社会却也暗流涌动，一股股新鲜的血液冲击着社会古老的静脉，引起了各个阶层社会人士的阵痛。面对这种情形，这一时期的英国文学家也开始在作品中探索一个均衡点，以期在旧的理念和新的改变之间达到一种平衡，王历山大·蒲柏（Alexander Pope，1688—1744）就是其中的一个代表人物。蒲柏是18世纪上半期最有代表性的英国诗人。据统计，在所有的英国作家之中，蒲柏的诗歌引用率仅次于莎士比亚和丁尼生，排在第三位。蒲柏的代表作品有《夺发记》（*The Rape of the Lock*）、《论批评》和《人论》等。

　　《夺发记》最初匿名发表于1712年，包含了两个诗篇，共334行诗文。第2版发表于1714年，蒲柏的名字首次出现在作者的位置，他将诗歌扩展到了5个诗篇，共794行。1717年的第3版中，蒲柏再次加入了诗歌中的人物Clarissa的一段言论。《夺发记》的故事有它的现实版本。贵族彼特（Petre）偷偷剪断了阿拉贝拉·弗莫尔（Arabella Fermor）的一缕

第五章　十八世纪英国启蒙时期诗歌

卷发，从而引发了两个贵族家庭之间的矛盾。蒲柏的朋友约翰·卡莱尔（John Caryll）提议让他将这个真实的故事写下来，通过讽刺两家拿着鸡毛当令箭小题大做的行为，最终达到使两家和好的目的。

再版的《夺发记》由五个诗篇组成。第一个诗篇重点描绘美貌的女主角贝琳达（Belinda），她的守护者是莎士比亚戏剧中的精灵亚里尔（Ariel）。诗篇的最后对于晨起打扮的贝琳达做了一个详细的描写。第二个诗篇提到了故事中的男主角男爵（the Baron），他深深爱慕着贝琳达，并暗自策划着一场阴谋来夺取贝琳达的卷发。对此，亚里尔有所预感，但却不能确定将要发生的悲剧，因此安排众多小精灵小心防备着。第三个诗篇的开始，贝琳达在泰晤士河坐船来到汉普顿宫苑，并在这里和男爵等两人打起了奥伯尔牌（ombre）。之后在餐桌上，男爵的爱慕者克拉丽莎（Clarissa）递给他一把剪刀，他用这把剪刀剪下了贝琳达的一缕卷发。第四个篇章集中描写贝琳达的悲伤，她的朋友们天卫二（Umbriel）、泰利斯（Thalestris）和普莱姆（Sir Plume）试图安慰贝琳达，但最终只换来了贝琳达愤怒的爆发。第五个篇章通过希腊神话中诸神之间的战争，来影射贝琳达情绪爆发后引起的骚乱。她愤懑地冲向男爵，将普莱姆的鼻烟扔向他。但在骚乱平息以后，大家却发现贝琳达被剪掉的那缕卷发已然升天、得到永生。选段为第三个篇章中男爵偷剪贝琳达卷发的情节，是为整个诗歌的最高潮。尽管亚里尔等精灵们给了贝琳达三次警告，可是她却仍然丝毫没有察觉男爵的动机（第 50 和 51 行，"And thrice they twitch'd the Diamond in her Ear/ Thrice she look'd back, and thrice the Foe drew near"）。被男爵突然袭击剪了头发之后，贝琳达眼里喷出怒火，并大声尖叫了起来（第 68 和 69 行，"Then flash'd the living Lightnings from her Eyes,/And Screams of Horror rend th'affrighted Skies"）。

蒲柏善用英雄双韵体。所谓英雄双韵体，指的是两行用五步抑扬格写成的押韵的诗文。例如，选文中的 82 和 83 行就是一对英雄双韵体：

While 'Nymphs take 'Treats, or 'Assignations 'give,

'So long my 'Honour, 'Name, and 'Praise shall 'live!

  《夺发记》不仅通篇使用英雄双韵体写成，而且还是英国文学史上著名的英雄滑稽体诗歌（mock-epic）。所谓英雄滑稽诗，一般是讽刺文或者是滑稽的模仿文。虽然采用的是古典的英雄史诗的形式，但是英雄滑稽诗非但不描写英雄，反而将小人物放到了英雄史诗中原有的英雄的位置，通过夸张等手法以期达到反讽的目的。在《夺发记》中，蒲柏使用英雄叙述史诗的形式记叙了一个微不足道的小故事。蒲柏模仿荷马的《伊利亚特》等史诗，用了诸多希腊神话中的神祇和特洛伊战争的传说，并把这些元素穿插到了故事中。例如，选文中的第一个诗节，描写了贝琳达在泰晤士河乘船来到汉普顿宫苑。这段描写极具夸张的元素："Close by those Meads for ever crown'd with Flow'rs/ Where Thames with Pride surveys his rising Tow'rs"，将贝琳达和历任君主进行了比较，让读者联想到史诗《奥德赛》中，奥德修斯冲破重重障碍渡过特洛伊和希腊之间海域的故事。史诗的形式和琐碎的主题之间的组合，可以达到两种效果。一方面，阳春白雪的史诗形式和琐碎的儿女情长的故事之间的不和谐，暗含了英国原有社会体系的古老观念和当时社会看似琐碎的改变之间的矛盾；另一方面，通过这种大材小用的方式，蒲柏讽刺了英国上层社会生活的不切实际、小题大做的风气。

  需要指出的是，尽管蒲柏尝试用诗歌来审时度势地观察这个社会的种种变化，并希望用自己的方式来诠释这些新的事物，但其写作视角和当时社会的主流是一致的。因此，在蒲柏的诗歌作品中，可是看到一个矛盾的存在体：他在努力接纳社会变革的同时，却表现出一种"排他"的倾向。例如，在《夺发记》中，蒲柏就毫不掩饰他对女性的贬低和嘲笑。像是选文的第70行，作者讽刺地夸大了贝琳达被剪掉头发后的反应，说她的喊叫声震天响（"Not louder Shrieks to pitying Heav'n are cast"），从而丑化

第五章　十八世纪英国启蒙时期诗歌

了女性的形象。

（二）Elegy Written in a Country Churchyard

Thomas Gray

1　The curfew tolls the knell of parting day,
　　The lowing herd wind slowly o'er the lea,
　　The plowman homeward plods his weary way,
　　And leaves the world to darkness and to me.

5　Now fades the glimmering landscape on the sight,
　　And all the air a solemn stillness holds,
　　Save where the beetle wheels droning fight,
　　And drowsy tinkling lull the distant folds;

　　Save that from yonder ivy-mantled tower
10　The moping owl does to the moon complain
　　Of such, as wandering near her secret bower,
　　Molest her ancient solitary reign.

　　Beneath those rugged elms, that yew tree's shade,
　　Where heaves the turf in many a moldering heap,
15　Each in his narrow cell forever laid,
　　The rude forefathers of the hamlet sleep.

　　The breezy call of incense-breathing Morn,

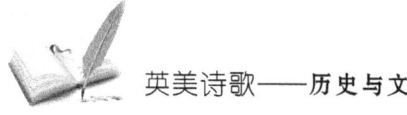

The swallow twittering from the straw-built shed,
The cock's shrill clarion, or the echoing horn,
20 No more shall rouse them from their lowly bed.

For them no more the blazing hearth shall burn,
Or busy housewife ply her evening care;
No children run to lisp their sire's return,
Or climb his knees the envied kiss to share.

25 Oft did the harvest to their sickle yield,
Their furrow oft the stubborn glebe has broke;
How jocund did they drive their team afield!
How bowed the woods beneath their sturdy stroke!

Let not Ambition mock their useful toil,
30 Their homely joys, and destiny obscure;
Nor Grandeur hear with a disdainful smile
The short and simple annals of the poor.

The boast of heraldry, the pomp of power,
And all that beauty, all that wealth e'er gave,
35 Awaits alike the inevitable hour.
The paths of glory lead but to the grave.

Nor you, ye proud, impute to these the fault,
If Memory o'er their tomb no trophies raise,

第五章 十八世纪英国启蒙时期诗歌

    Where through the long-drawn aisle and freted vault
40 The pealing anthem swells the note of praise.
    Can storied urn or animated bust
    Back to its mansion call the fleeting breath?
    Can Honor's voice provoke the silent dust,
    Or Flattery soothe the dull cold ear of Death?

45 Perhaps in this neglected spot is laid
    Some heart once pregnant with celestial fire;
    Hands that the rod of empire might have swayed,
    Or waked to ecstasy the ling lyre.

    But Knowledge to their eyes her ample page
50 Rich with the spoils of time did ne'er unroll;
    Chill Penury repressed their noble rage,
    And froze the genial current of the soul.

    Full many a gem of purest ray serene,
    The dark unfathomed caves of ocean bear:
55 Full many a flower is born to blush unseen,
    And waste its sweetness on the desert air.

    Some village Hampden, that with dauntless breast
    The little tyrant of his fields withstood;
    Some mute inglorious Milton here may rest,
60 Some Cromwell guiltless of his country's blood.

The applause of listening senates to command,

The threats of pain and ruin to despise,

To scatter plenty o'er a smiling land,

And read their history in a nation's eyes.

65　Their lot forbade: nor circumscribed alone

Their growing virtues, but their crimes confined;

For bade to wade through slaughter to a throne,

And shut the gates of mercy on mankind,

The struggling pangs of conscious truth to hide,

70　To quench the blushes of ingenuous shame,

Or heap the shrine of Luxury and Pride

With incense kindled at the Muse's flame.

Far from the madding crowd's ignoble strife,

Their sober wishes never learned to stray;

75　Along the cool sequestered vale of life

They kept the noiseless tenor of their way.

Yes even these bones from insult to protect

Some frail memorial still erected nigh,

With uncouth rhymes and shapeless sculpture decked,

80　Implores the passing tribute of a sigh.

Their name, their years, spelt by the unlettered Muse,

第五章 十八世纪英国启蒙时期诗歌

  The place of fame and elegy supply:

  And many a holy text around she strews,

  That teach the rustic moralist to die.

85 For who to dumb Forgetfulness a prey,

  This pleasing anxious being e'er resigned,

  Left the warm precincts of the cheerful day,

  Nor cast one longing linger look behind?

  On some breast the parting soul relies,

90 Some pious drops the closing eye requires;

  Even from the tomb the voice of Nature cries,

  Even in our ashes live their wonted fires.

  For thee, who mindful of the unhonored dead

  Dost in these lines their artless tale relate:

95 If chance, by lonely contemplation led,

  Some kindred spirit shall inquire thy fate,

  Haply some hoary-headed swain may say,

  "Oft have we seen him at the peep of dawn

  Brushing with hasty steps the dews away

100 To meet the sun upon the upland lawn.

  "There at the foot of yonder nodding beech

  That wreathes its old fantastic rots so high,

His listless length at noontide would he stretch,
And pore upon the brook that babbles by.

105 "Hard by on wood, now smiling as in scorn,
Muttering his wayward fancies he would rove,
Now drooping, woeful wan, like one forlorn,
Or crazed with care, or crossed in hopeless love.

"One morn I missed him on the customed hill,
110 Along the heath and near his favorite tree;
Another came; nor yet beside the rill,
Nor up the lawn, nor at the wood was he;

"The next with dirges due in sad array
Slow through the churchway path we saw him borne.
115 Approach and read (for thou canst read) the lay,
Graved on the stone beneath yon aged thorn.

The Epitaph
Here rests his head upon the lap of Earth
A youth to Fortune and to Fame unknown.
120 Fair Science frowned not on his humble birth,
And Melancholy marked him for her own.

Large was his bounty, and his soul sincere,
Heaven did a recompense as largely send:

第五章　十八世纪英国启蒙时期诗歌

　　He gave to Misery all he had, a tear,
125　He gained from heaven ('twas all he wished) a friend.

　　No farther seek his merits to disclose,
　　Or draw his frailties from their dread abode.
　　(There they alike in trembling hope repose),
　　The bosom of his Father and his God.

　　17世纪兴起的古典主义，将文学经典奉为模仿的对象，从主题和形式两个方面对其进行模仿。18世纪，英国的古典主义文学中发展出了"奥古斯丁时代"(the Augusten Age)，代表作家为亚历山大·蒲柏（1688—1744），丹尼尔·斯威夫特(Daniel Swift, 1667—1745)和约瑟夫·艾迪生(Joseph Addison, 1672—1719)。这些作家模仿罗马时期的文学形式，强调作品的社会关注度，竭力模仿罗马时代作品所宣扬的自我节制、优雅、得体端庄等主题。与18世纪古典主义文学发展相对应的是，这一时期出现了浪漫主义文学的创作倾向，被称为前浪漫主义(pre-Romanticism)，代表作家是托马斯·格雷（1716—1771）和威廉·布莱克（1757—1827）。与古典主义作家追求经典文学的做法不同，托马斯·格雷在游览了约克郡、德贝郡和苏格兰的自然风貌和名胜古迹之后，将他见到的这些元素都融入到了自己的作品之中，并把哥特因素也注入其中，从而写作了不少早期的浪漫主义作品，其中最著名的就是选文中的 *Elegy Written in a Country Churchyard*（以下简称"*Elegy*"）。值得指出的是，除了浪漫主义元素之外，这首诗在诗歌的韵律上非常讲究，却沿袭了古典主义诗作的传统。因此，这是一首包含了古典主义创作理念和浪漫主义诗歌元素的作品。

　　托马斯·格雷的好朋友理查德·韦斯特(Richard West)在1742年去世，这成为诗人创作诗歌的重要原因之一。而后，格雷的姑姑在1749年去世，他的好朋友霍勒斯·沃尔波尔（Horace Walpole，1717—1797）遭遇意外差点身亡。这一系列的事件促使诗人对于人生和死亡进行了深入的思考，从而于1750年写作完成了 Elegy。由此看来，死亡是诗歌的重要主题之一。最初诗人并没有看好自己的作品，将诗作随意邮寄给了沃尔波尔，没想到这首诗在伦敦广受好评。伦敦的出版商威廉·欧文（William Owen）在未经得格雷同意的情况下想出版 Elegy，得悉这一消息之后，格雷在沃尔波尔的帮助之下提前让诗歌问世。虽然诗歌采用的是"挽歌"（elegy）的形式，却又区别于传统的挽歌。首先，虽然整体看来带有悲伤的基调，但它没有一个固定的被哀悼者；其次，它没有传统挽歌的一些固定元素，如哀悼者、鲜花、牧童、向神灵的祈祷等；最后，区别于传统挽歌将墓地作为诗歌背景的做法，Elegy 应用了自然事物作为背景，从而让诗文有了更深层次的含义。

诗文总共129行，包含着若干的诗节，每个诗节包含4行诗文，押韵格式为：abab，每行诗文均用五步抑扬格写成。诗歌写作处处可见诗人的别具匠心，精美之处时有闪现。前三个诗节描绘出了一幅伤感而优美的动态自然风景：夕阳西下（"the knell of parting day" "the glimmering landscape"），牧人往家赶着牲口；很快夜幕降临，猫头鹰对着月亮不停地叫着。第四个诗节指出了诗歌的主角——在榆树下、紫杉树下，静静躺着的已然逝去的村野莽夫。从第21行开始的诗节回忆了逝者去世之前温馨的家庭生活，后面的一个诗节则在怀念他劳动时的情景，再后面的四个诗节则是感叹尽管这些村野莽夫活得卑微，但是在死亡面前无论高低贵贱大家一律平等。第45～72行的诗节，感叹了已逝者曾经失去的扬名立万的好时机，其中第53～56行，是为感叹机遇不经意流失的经典名句。第73～92行的诗节对已经逝去的无名者曾经安于乡村生活的行为进行了感叹和赞美。其中，第73行中的 Far from the madding crowd（远离尘嚣）成为20世纪英国小说家托马斯·哈代（Thomas Hardy）一部重要小说作品的题目。从第93行开始一直到文末，诗人开始感叹自己的命运，颇有"侬今葬花人

第五章 十八世纪英国启蒙时期诗歌

笑痴，他年葬侬知是谁"的意味。当有人问起自己时，可能某一位头发花白的乡村老人会忆起，他曾经奔跑在山坡上、睡在山毛榉树的阴凉处、休憩在小溪旁边，时而漫步、时而低吟、时而丧气、时而忧心忡忡。而有一天，当自己再次出现时，却是躺在了行进的棺木之中："The next with dirges due in sad array/Slow through the churchway path we saw him borne"（第113～114行）。诗歌最后附着的是诗人为自己写的墓志铭，韵律和前文保持一致，但是对于死亡的态度却有了较大的变化。墓志铭的第一个诗节提到诗人生性敏感，虽然接受过教育，却一生无权无势，下面的诗节总结了他慷慨的个性和深怀信仰的一生，而最后的一个诗节则提到了永生的问题。

从诗歌的整体结构看来，该诗主要包含了三个主题。首先，诗人在字里行间透露出了对于乡村自然风光的喜爱和对农村田园生活的赞美和向往。诗歌创作的年代恰在英国工业革命如火如荼地进行之前，诗人在感受到工业化对农村生活的冲击后，表现出了对田园生活的眷恋。诗文的第73行"Far from the madding crowd's ignoble strife"，更是直截了当地指出了诗人对城市喧嚣生活的厌恶。诗中的教堂指的大概是英国美丽的托克波吉斯小镇（Stoke Poges）中的圣贾尔斯教堂（St. Giles），诗人死后就被埋在了这一独具乡村风光特色的教堂。其次，诗歌的大量篇幅都用来感叹人生不经意间而丧失的机遇。由于教育的缺失和生活的贫穷（第49～52行），本来可以扬名立万的人却变成了村野莽夫，这些乡村"汉普顿"（第57行）、无名的"弥尔顿"（第18行）和清白的"克伦威尔"只能默默地逝去，对此诗人表现出无限的遗憾和感慨。从另一个角度看，更是表达了诗人认为人无论高低贵贱生性平等的观点。而这种忧伤和遗憾的情绪也是"Elegy"和传统挽歌最大的共同点。最后，对于死亡主题的思考是诗歌最重要的主题。虽然有别于传统的挽歌，但是死亡的基调同样也贯穿于整首诗。诗歌最初版本的结尾包含这些诗文：

"In still small Accents whisp'ring from the Ground

"A grateful Earnest of eternal Peace

"No more with Reason & thyself at strife;

"Give anxious Cares & endless Wishes room

"But thro' the cool sequester'd Vale of Life

"Pursue the silent Tenour of thy Doom."

很明显，作者认为对于死亡要持有一种隐忍的态度，接受它并最终默默走向它。但是，在诗歌后来的版本中，诗人除了改动了结尾，又加上了自己的墓志铭，其中的最后两句 There they alike in trembling hope repose / the bosom of his Father and his God" 却表现出了诗人对于来生来世的渴求，表现出与原来诗歌中对死亡隐忍态度的不同。

诗人在 *Elegy* 细节处的用心，使得每一行诗文都精巧别致，像头韵、首语重复法（anaphora）、隐喻、拟人等手法随处可见。例如，诗歌的第一个诗节就包含三种行中韵（internal rhyme），像头韵 "weary way"、腹韵（"lowing"、"slowly" 和 "o'er"），以及尾韵 "herd wind" 等。第34行的 "all that" 两次重复，以及第91～92行开头的 "even"，都属于首语重复的用法。第53～56行中，沉浸在深海中无人发现的珠宝（gem）和隐藏在沙漠之中悄悄绽放的花朵（many a flower），隐喻了一生默默无闻而死后也无人知晓的村野莽夫。而拟人的手法更比比皆是，例如，第29行中的 "Ambition"，第31行中的 "Grandeur"，第49行中的 "Knowledge"，第51行中的 "Chill Penury"，第119行中的 "Science"，第120行中的 "Melancholy" 等，都作为行动的主体而成为主动者。

（三）The Chimney Sweeper

William Blake

1　When my mother died I was very young,

第五章　十八世纪英国启蒙时期诗歌

  And my father sold me while yet my tongue

  Could scarcely cry 'weep! 'weep! 'weep! 'weep!

  So your chimneys I sweep, and in soot I sleep.

5 There's little Tom Dacre, who cried when his head,

  That curled like a lamb's back, was shaved: so I said,

  "Hush, Tom! never mind it, for when your head's bare,

  You know that the soot cannot spoil your white hair."

  And so he was quiet; and that very night,

10 As Tom was a-sleeping, he had such a sight,

  That thousands of sweepers, Dick, Joe, Ned, and Jack,

  Were all of them locked up in coffins of black.

  And by came an angel who had a bright key,

  And he opened the coffins and set them all free;

15 Then down a green plain leaping, laughing, they run,

  And wash in a river, and shine in the sun.

  Then naked and white, all their bags left behind,

  They rise upon clouds and sport in the wind;

  And the angel told Tom, if he'd be a good boy,

20 He'd have God for his father, and never want joy.

  And so Tom awoke; and we rose in the dark,

  And got with our bags and our brushes to work.

  Though the morning was cold, Tom was happy and warm;

So if all do their duty they need not fear harm.
——*Songs of Innocence*

1 A little black thing among the snow
   Crying "'weep, 'weep," in notes of woe!
   "Where are thy father & mother? Say?"
   "They are both gone up to the church to pray.

5 "Because I was happy upon the heath,
   And smil'd among the winter's snow;
   They clothes me in the clothes of death,
   And taught me to sing the notes of woe.

   "And because I am happy and dance and sing,
10 They think they have done me no injury,
   And are gone to praise God and his priest & King,
   Who make up a heaven of our misery."
   ——*Songs of Experience*

威廉·布莱克（1757—1827）是英国另一位重要的早期浪漫主义诗人，他被认为是英国文学史上最有原创性的诗人之一。出身卑微的布莱克尽管没有受过很正式的教育，却是一位极具天赋的诗人。布莱克热情地支持法国大革命，并将这种浪漫主义热情注入到自己的作品中；他反对任何形式的绝对权威，因而表现出对政治独裁和宗教专制的强烈反感；他独爱想象，运用自己的想象力，他甚至创造了一个崭新的神话世界。虽然诗人在世的时候并没有受读者追捧，其作品却在他去世之后赢得了越来越多的关注。

第五章　十八世纪英国启蒙时期诗歌

美国皇后大学的文学教授爱德华·拉里西（Edward Larrisy）认为，布莱克是对20世纪产生影响最大的一位浪漫主义诗人。

因为曾经跟随一位知名的雕刻师詹姆斯·巴西尔（James Basire）做学徒，因此布莱克擅长蚀刻版画（relief etching）和雕版画（engraving），他不仅将自己的诗作用版画的方式呈现出来，还为其他作家的作品做版画，其中一位就是17世纪的诗人约翰·弥尔顿（John Milton）。尽管两位诗人作品的主题相似，都是追寻自由、反对任何专制和权威，但是整体看来，两位诗人的作品却又大相径庭。对于17世纪的作家来讲，他们的思维很难摆脱上帝中心论，即任何问题都得围绕自己的宗教信仰进行思考。所以《失乐园》中的撒旦敢于挑战上帝的权威追寻自由，不难看出在作者弥尔顿的眼中，撒旦就如如来佛手心中的猴子一样，根本摆脱不了上帝的束缚。而布莱克的创作理念则完全不同，他的艺术世界已经摆脱了上帝中心论，取而代之的是个人，或者说是想象力，而这也是19世纪浪漫主义文学的核心思想。浪漫主义者认为，主观想象力（subjective imagination）完全可以改变生活现实，因此个人和主观世界被推到了前台，而以前的上帝中心论则被置后。这也是将布莱克定性为浪漫主义诗人的重要因素之一，也是他被公认为"非正统的基督徒"（unorthodox Christian）的原因。他的许多代表诗作，如《伦敦》（London）和《虎》（The Tyger）等就表现出了比较明显的浪漫主义创作倾向。选文中的两首《扫烟囱的小男孩》（The Chimney Sweeper）分别选自布莱克的两部代表诗集《纯真之歌》（Songs of Innocence，1789）和《经验之歌》（Songs of Experience，1794）。

《纯真之歌》《经验之歌》是布莱克重要的诗集，包含了诗人许多重要的诗作。发表于1789年的《纯真之歌》似乎专为儿童而作，诗集中的诗歌使用的语言大多通俗易懂、朗朗上口，诗歌多从儿童的角度出发观察世界，因此淳朴的主题和快乐的基调是《纯真之歌》中诗歌的主要特点。在《纯真之歌》中，诗人将自己比作一个坐在云端大声欢笑的儿童（a laughing child upon a cloud）。与《纯真之歌》不同的是，《经验之歌》中的诗歌用成年人历经沧桑的双眼去观察这个世界，集中描写了人生的不幸、贫穷、悲痛等消极的方面，而诗人认为唯一的救赎就是激烈的抗争。在《经验之歌》中，诗人将自己比作一个在晚露中哭泣的堕落的灵魂（the lapsed soul weeping in the evening dew）。两部诗集分别从孩子和成人两个角度出发，对同一事物进行不同的观察，因而两部诗集中分别包含了许多对应的诗歌，选文中两首 The Chimney Sweeper 就是这样对应的两首诗。18世纪的英国社会普遍存在着雇佣童工的现象，其中就有许多儿童由于家庭贫穷而被卖去扫烟囱。这些孩子的遭遇十分悲惨，除了缺吃少穿，他们整日生活在烟灰中，晚上也睡在装满烟灰的袋子上面。为了节省开支，雇主们甚至不给孩子们衣服穿。这样的境遇使得许多孩子生病甚至死去。由于长时间攀爬在烟囱中，他们的脚踝和脊柱往往生长畸形，很多孩子或者死于火灾，或者死于呼吸道疾病。就是这样一群卑微的孩子，成为诗人笔下的主角。

《纯真之歌》中的 The Chimney Sweeper 由六节四行诗组成，押韵格式是 abab。诗歌以扫烟囱的孩子为第一人称进行叙述，母亲早逝，父亲将他卖给了人家扫烟囱。第二个诗节中提到了他的朋友汤姆·戴克（Tom Dacre）。为了清扫烟囱便利，汤姆浓密的头发被剪掉了，并为此伤心不已。在汤姆的梦中，许多扫烟囱的孩子被关在黑色的棺木中（第12行，"coffin of black"），就在这时一位天使从天而降并将孩子们释放。得到自由的孩子们愉快地嬉戏玩耍，并得到许诺：只要他听话，上帝就会作为父亲庇护他，使之再也不缺少欢乐（第19～20行，"if he'd be a good boy/He'd have God for his father, and never want joy"）。梦醒之后，汤姆和故事的叙述者起床扫烟囱。尽管天气寒冷，他们却感到无比的幸福和温暖（第23行，"happy and warm"），因为他们坚信，只要好好扫烟囱就不会受到任何伤害。《经验之歌》中的 The Chimney Sweeper 由三个四行诗节组成，押韵格式为：aabb cdcd efef。三个诗节描述的内容不断地升华，批判的角度直指宗教的

第五章　十八世纪英国启蒙时期诗歌

最高权威者——上帝和政治的最高权威者——国王。与《纯真之歌》不同的是，《经验之歌》中扫烟囱的孩子早早地意识到自己悲惨的命运。第二个诗节运用了隐喻的手法，指出孩子的天真善良被父母所利用。"在荒地仍然感到幸福，在雪地里仍然保持微笑"（第5～6行），暗示了孩子出生时的纯真，而"父母给我穿上死亡的衣裳，叫我去唱悲伤的格调"，则指出父母不顾孩子的死活将其卖去扫烟囱的事实。这个诗节中描写的内容突出了"纯真"和"经验"之间的对立，这一对立延续到了第三个诗节中："因为我愉快地唱歌跳舞，他们以为不会伤害到我，因此跑去赞美上帝、教士和国王，而这些人其实是我们灾难的源头。"

《纯真之歌》《经验之歌》中的 The Chimney Sweeper 分别从孩子纯真的角度和成年人经验的角度进行描写，所以尽管叙述者都是扫烟囱的孩子，但是所包含的主题思想是大相径庭的。一方面，尽管《纯真之歌》中扫烟囱的孩子生活境遇非常悲惨，但却对未来的生活充满了希望，这一点可以从汤姆的梦看出来。黑色的棺木暗示着孩子们黑暗的生活境遇，也预示了他们大多将会面临早早夭折的命运。天使在梦中出现，带来了希望，不但将孩子们从棺木中放出，而且还许诺给他们未来。天使的诺言使得一觉醒来的汤姆和故事的叙述者对生活充满了信心和希望。而《经验之歌》中的孩子谈到了父母给他穿着"死亡的外衣"（第7行），这表明他感到自己的生活毫无希望可言，等待他的只有死亡而已。因此，就在"希望"这一主题上，《纯真之歌》《经验之歌》是相对立的。另一方面，两首诗歌表达了不同的宗教思想。《纯真之歌》中，天使告诉汤姆只要他听话，上帝就会作为父亲庇护他，使之再也不缺少欢乐（第19～20行），其中包含着"今生受苦，来世将被救赎"的基督教思想。但《经验之歌》中的上帝和教士则是以压迫者的形象出现，扫烟囱的孩子更是将其归类为万恶的源头之一。由此看来，《经验之歌》包含了比较锋利的批判矛头，诗中的孩子清楚地看到了自己处在层层压迫的最底层：

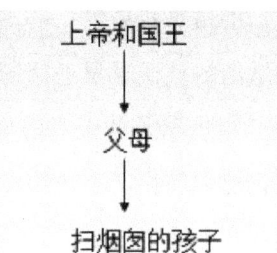

在这个权利体系中,孩子处于最底层,而父母不顾孩子的感受将其卖去扫烟囱,因而形成了对孩子的第一层压迫。最顶层的上帝和国王在压迫父母的同时,也成为孩子们受苦受难的最终原因。

从两首描写对象相同、主题思想却截然不同的 *The Chimney Sweeper* 可以看出,诗人认为对待"纯真"和"经验"不是两者取一,而是在两者之间寻求一种平衡。一方面,"纯真"虽然能使人们在极端困窘的情况下仍然感受到幸福和希望,但却阻碍了他们看到真实的情况,甚至像《纯真之歌》中的孩子一样认识不到自己是层层压迫制度的受害者。另一方面,诗人通过《经验之歌》的叙述者阐述了一个事实,即"经验"能够使人们更加真实地看清楚自己的境遇,更具有反叛的思想,但是完全信赖"经验"却只能让人们感受到无尽的痛苦和黑暗。因此,只有在两者之中寻求一种平衡,才是诗人眼中最好的生存状态。

二、Further Reading

(一) An Essay on Criticism 1

(Excerpts)

Alexander Pope

1　True ease in writing comes from art, not chance,
　　As those move easiest who have learn'd to dance.

第五章　十八世纪英国启蒙时期诗歌

'Tis not enough no harshness gives offence,

The sound must seem an echo to the sense.

5　Soft is the strain when Zephyr gently blows,

　　And the smooth stream in smoother numbers flows;

　　But when loud surges lash the sounding shore,

　　The hoarse, rough verse should like the torrent roar.

　　When Ajax strives some rock's vast weight to throw,

10　The line too labours, and the words move slow;

　　Not so, when swift Camilla scours the plain,

　　Flies o'er th'unbending corn, and skims along the main.

　　Hear how Timotheus' varied lays surprise,

　　And bid alternate passions fall and rise!

【译文】
论批评

（节选）

亚历山大·蒲柏

1　笔下的飘逸凭技艺不凭灵机，

　　正如学过舞蹈者舞姿才飘逸。

　　只是无令人不快的粗糙不成，

　　得让音韵听来像意义的回声。

5　微风习习轻吹出柔软的声音，

　　溪水潺潺却是如此流畅动听。

　　当汹涌的波涛拍打着海岸，

　　诗行也应该像怒吼的狂澜。

埃杰斯用力抛出沉重的磐石,
10 诗行缓移,词句读来也吃力。
当飞毛腿卡米拉飞过原野禾不弯,
滑过海面不沾水,诗行也应改变。
蒂莫修变化的歌声令听者惊奇,
听者的感情会随之降落或升起。

(潘 莉 译,何功杰 校译)

【点评】

《论批评》是蒲柏的成名之作。《论批评》共744行,分三个部分。前200行为第一部分,指出文学批评的重要性和如何成为一名好的批评家。蒲柏指出,鉴赏力(Taste)乃为一个批评家基本的品质,鉴赏力需要遵循自然(Nature)规律,因为自然规律是一切真理的体现,遵循自然带来真正的智慧(wit)。第201~559行为第二部分,重点探讨了影响阻碍做出正确判断的十大因素(骄傲、浅学、枝节、挑剔或奉承、崇古或厚今、偏颇、怪僻、易变、党见、妒忌)。第三部分从第560行至最后,论述文学批评的准则,回顾了文学批评历史及批评家的角色。蒲柏的《论批评》是在吸取古人思想精华的基础上通过以诗论诗的手法写成,彰显了他非凡的才华。

此节为第362~375行,诗人采用英雄双韵体,即每两行押韵的五音部抑扬格写成。一开始,诗人采用类比(analogy)手法点题,指出诗歌创作要达到真正的飘逸需要有技艺,而不是靠灵感,而这种技艺可以后天习得,如同舞蹈者的舞姿飘逸是靠学习而得一样,"True ease in writing comes from art, not chance/ As those move easiest who have learn'd to dance"。头两句尾部韵"[ɑːns]",第二行诗压行内韵"/t/, /d/"读起来朗朗上口,与诗人写作的意象吻合,飘逸优美。诗人在第3~4诗行中采用隐喻手法,指出诗歌的形式应同诗歌的内容一致:"'Tis not enough no harshness gives

第五章 十八世纪英国启蒙时期诗歌

offence/The sound must seem an echo to the sense"。其中第 3 行诗中采用低调陈述（litotes）法，运用双重否定表达肯定：诗句中的粗糙令人满足。第 4 行诗指出，诗歌的音韵应同诗的意义一致，听起来像诗意的回响。其中头韵词为"sound, seem, sense"，音韵和谐，强调突出了重点。第 5～6 行诗，诗人举例说明微风习习轻吹出的声音是柔软的，溪水潺潺的声音是流畅动听的，"Soft is the strain when Zephyr gently blows/And the smooth stream in smoother numbers flows"。其中第五行诗中运用了倒装（inversion）表示强调，头韵"Soft ... strain"中的 /s/ 音与微风吹过的轻柔声融为一体，第 6 行诗中的头韵 /s/ 音同样传递出优美动听的溪水潺潺音。这两句末尾词"blows, flows"都与微风、溪水意象结合，形成美好的意境。第 7～8 行诗诗人运用隐喻继续举例说明诗歌的创作技巧，指出如果诗歌所写是关于汹涌的波涛拍打着海岸，那么诗行应该像怒吼的狂澜予以呼应，"But when loud surges lash the sounding shore/The hoarse, rough verse should like the torrent roar"。第 7 行诗中运用了行内韵：头韵"loud, lash" "surges, sounding, shore"及辅音韵"lash, shore"中的 /ʃ/ 音，第 8 行中的头韵"rough, roar"及行内的母韵 /ɔːs/ "hoarse, roar"这些音韵与隐喻及拟声手法（onomatopoeia）的使用，将汹涌的波涛拍打海岸的画面刻画得惟妙惟肖，淋漓尽致。第 9～14 行诗中诗人运用典故（allusion）继续阐明声音必须是意义的回响这一诗歌创作技巧。其中埃杰斯（Ajiax）是荷马史诗《伊利亚特》（Iliad）中的希腊英雄、大力士，以掷巨石闻名。卡米拉（Camilla）是维吉尔史诗《埃涅阿斯纪》（Aeneid）中快捷如飞的女英雄，行于水面，鞋不湿；行于麦田，麦不倒，犹如神行太保。蒂莫修（Timotheus）是英国 17 世纪诗人德莱顿所写诗篇《亚历山大的盛宴》（Alexander's Feast）中的乐师，音乐多变，令听众情感随其变化。

蒲柏在点评诗歌创作技艺时，自己以诗论诗，很好地示范表达了诗歌创作的技巧与艺术。其中的音韵、比喻、意象、典故等修辞手法使用显示

了蒲柏的博学及高超的诗歌创作才华。"得让音韵听来像意义的回声"(The sound must seem an echo to the sense)成为诗歌文学界的至理名言。

(二) An Essay on Criticism 2

(excerpt)

Alexander Pope

1 A little learning is a dangerous thing;
    Drink deep, or taste not the Pierian spring.
    There shallow draughts intoxicate the brain,
    And drinking largely sobers us again.
5 Fired at first sight with what the Muse imparts,
    In fearless youth we tempt the heights of arts,
    While from the bounded level of our mind
    Short views we take, nor see the lengths behind;
    But more advanced, behold with strange surprise
10 New distant scenes of endless science rise!
    So pleased at first the towering Alps we try,
    Mount o'er the vales, and seem to tread the sky,
    The eternal snows appear already past,
    And the first clouds and mountains seem the last;
15 But, those attained, we tremble to survey
    The growing labors of the lengthened way,
    The increasing prospect tires our wandering eyes,
    Hills o'er hills, and Alps on Alps arise!

第五章　十八世纪英国启蒙时期诗歌

【译文】

论批评

（节选）

亚历山大·蒲柏

1　学识浅薄是一件危险的事情；
　　派利亚泉水要深吸，否则别饮。
　　浅浅喝几口是大脑不清，
　　大量畅饮反会使我们清醒。

5　缪斯让第一个情景激发我们的灵感，
　　无畏的青年就企图攀登艺术顶端，
　　但是，我们的眼界所见事物有限，
　　前瞻既看不远，后顾也看不见；
　　但是再前进，我们会惊奇地发现，

10　远处胜景层出，那里新知无限！
　　我们初登阿尔卑斯山多么高兴，
　　越谷登山，仿佛踩着天底旅行，
　　永恒的积雪似乎早就过去，不再出现，
　　初见的云彩和群山好像是最后的景点；

15　然而，当爬到山顶，我们颤抖着俯瞰
　　绵延的路还需要更大的努力去登攀，
　　前面不断出现的景色使我们目眩惊叹，
　　群山与群山相望，高山之外还有高山！

（何功杰　译）

【点评】

此部分选自《论批评》第 215 ~ 232 行，采用英雄双韵体。第一行诗

英美诗歌——历史与文本

乃为大家熟知经典名句"A little learning is a dangerous thing",道出了一知半解、学识浅薄在求学问上是一件可怕的事情,作者采用行内押韵"learning, thing"的手法,使得诗歌读起来明快,有节奏感。第二句诗歌借用典故"Pierian spring"阐述传说派利亚泉水因为缪斯女神的缘故而成了神水,任何人只要饮此处泉水即可获得文艺和诗歌上的灵感,Pierian spring 指产生诗歌灵感的源泉、知识的源泉。随后,诗人继续使用此典故并用嘲讽语气(ironical tone)指出浅尝辄止还不如不喝,大量畅饮会让大脑清醒("There shallow draughts intoxicate the brain/And drinking largely sobers us again")。其中"intoxicate"与"sobers"形成对比。

第5~6诗行诗人使用典故指出,当缪斯让第一个情景激发我们的灵感,无畏的青年就企图攀登艺术顶端("Fired at first sight with what the Muse imparts/In fearless youth we tempt the heights of arts")。其中在西方的希腊罗马神话中缪斯是诗人的保护神,并掌管文艺,是诗和一切艺术的化身,Muse 表示"灵感、诗才"。紧接着诗人指出即使我们尝到了灵感的滋味,但我们的眼界所见事物有限,前瞻既看不远,后顾也看不见,这里诗人强调眼界与知识的重要性。紧接着诗人继续鼓励前行,因为你会惊奇地发现,远处胜景和新知无限("But more advanced, behold with strange surprise/New distant scenes of endless science rise!"),其中采用头韵手法"strange surprise""scenes ... science"),使得诗行画面感强烈,读起来朗朗上口,更加生动。诗中第11~18行诗人采用登山的隐喻将攀登艺术的高山的过程想象成攀登阿尔卑斯山的过程,道明学海无涯、学无止境的道理。

第11~12行"So pleased at first the towering Alps we try/ Mount o'er the vales, and seem to tread the sky"运用明喻与夸张手法,"towering ... try""seem ... sky"使用头韵,第14行诗中的"first, last"两词形成对比,第16行中"labors"与"lengthened"形成头韵,最后一行诗"Hills o'er hills, and Alps on Alps

第五章　十八世纪英国启蒙时期诗歌

arise!"诗人采用反复手法，突出主题，与开头呼应。指出学海无涯，学无止境，山外有山，人外有人，学识浅薄是一件危险的事情，人不能因为有了点知识就浅尝辄止，骄傲自满，应该不断努力，勇于攀登。蒲柏的诗，充满理性思考，给人启示，令人回味。

（三）An Essay on Man

Alexander Pope

1　Know then thyself, presume not God to scan;
　　The proper study of mankind is Man.
　　Placed on this isthmus of a middle state,
　　A being darkly wise, and rudely great:
5　With too much knowledge for the skeptic side,
　　With too much weakness for the Scotic's pride,
　　He hangs between; in doubt to act, or rest,
　　In doubt to deem himself a god, or beast;
　　In doubt his mind or body to prefer,
10　Born but to die: and reasoning but to err;
　　Alike in ignorance, his reason such,
　　Whether he thinks too little, or too much:
　　Chaos of thought and passion, all confused;
　　Still by himself abused, or disabused;
15　Created half to rise, and half to fall;
　　Great lord of all things, yet a prey to all:
　　Sole judge of truth, in endless error hurled:
　　The glory, jest, and riddle of the world!

【译文】

人论

亚历山大·蒲柏

1　先了解自己吧，且莫狂妄地窥测上帝，
　　人的研究对象应该是人类自己。
　　他愚昧的聪明，拙劣的伟大，
　　位于中间状态的狭窄地岬。

5　他要怀疑一切，可是又知识过多，
　　他要坚毅奋发，可是又意志薄弱，
　　他悬持中间，出处行藏，犹豫不定，
　　犹豫不定，是自视为神灵，还是畜生，
　　犹豫不定，是要灵魂，还是要肉体，

10　生来要死，依靠理性反而错误不已，
　　想得过多，想得过少，结果相同，
　　思想的道理都是同样的愚昧荒懵，
　　思想和感情，一切都庞杂混乱，
　　他仍放纵滥用，或先放纵而后收敛。

15　他生就的半要升天，半要入地，
　　既是万物之主，又受万物奴役，
　　他是真理的唯一裁判，又不断错误迷离，
　　他是世上的荣耀、世上的笑柄、世上的谜！

（吕千飞　译）

【点评】

《人论》是蒲柏采用新古典主义的文学创作原则，用英雄双韵诗体写

第五章　十八世纪英国启蒙时期诗歌

的一篇哲理诗,阐述了人性、人与社会、人与宇宙、人的幸福等伦理关系问题。《人论》共有四章:第一章说我们的幸福来自两个方面;第二章讨论了作为个人的人的本性与处境;第三章探讨了人在社会的作用;第四章评论了人与幸福的关系。

蒲柏在诗歌创作中讲究音韵和谐,结构整齐,他追求理智、平衡和秩序的伦理思想。

蒲柏在诗歌一开始使用祈使句来表明主题:人要认识自己,要研究人类,不要妄论上帝("Know then thyself, presume not God to scan/The proper study of mankind is Man")。第三句点出人类位于中间状态的狭窄地岬,这在西方文化中应该是指在天堂与地狱之间。紧接着诗人采用悖论(paradox)手法指出人的两种性质"A being darkly wise, and rudely great":人聪明伟大,但也卑微和愚昧。紧接着"With too much knowledge for the sceptic side/With too much weakness for the stoic's pride",诗人采用悖论手法指出人总是怀疑一切,但又知识渊博,总是固守人的骄傲但又软弱无力,其中"With too much"是诗人采用的首语反复(anaphora)手法,带有强烈的讽刺意味。"He hangs between; in doubt to act, or rest/In doubt to deem himself a god, or beast/In doubt his mind or body to prefer/Born but to die: and reasoning but to err",诗人继续以悖论的方式阐述人的本性,其中"in doubt"被反复使用三次,指出人的局限性:生来要死,依靠理性反而不断犯错。接下来,诗人继续指出人的两面性:想得过多,想得过少,结果相同,思想的道理都是同样的愚昧荒悖/思想和感情,一切都庞杂混乱,他仍放纵滥用,或先放纵而后收敛/他生就的半要升天,半要入地/既是万物之主,又受万物奴役,他是真理的唯一裁判,又不断错误迷离/他是世上的荣耀、世上的笑柄、世上的谜!

整个《人论》第二章,诗人采用悖论、讽刺、对比、音韵等多种修辞手法,辩证理性地指出人性的矛盾和复杂性。诗歌的创作非常完美地诠释了蒲柏

所提出的写诗应该考虑技艺和智慧，音韵应为意义的回响。诗人在诗歌中表达了对上帝权威的敬畏，同时强调人要能够认识自己。

（四）Ode on Solitude

Alexander Pope

1　Happy the man, whose wish and care
　　A few paternal acres bound,
　　Content to breathe his native air
　　In his own ground.

5　Whose herds with milk, whose fields with bread,
　　Whose flocks supply him with attire;
　　Whose trees in summer yield him shade,
　　In winter fire.

　　Blest, who can unconcern'dly find
10　Hours, days, and years slide soft away
　　In health of body, peace of mind,
　　Quiet by day.

　　Sound sleep by night; study and ease
　　Together mix'd; sweet recreation,
15　And innocence, which most does please
　　With meditation.

第五章 十八世纪英国启蒙时期诗歌

  Thus let me live, unseen, unknown;

  Thus unlamented let me die;

  Steal from the world, and not a stone

20 Tell where I lie.

【译文】
孤寂颂

亚历山大·蒲柏

1 一个人能将愿望和牵挂限制在祖传的几顷土地上,

  他就算是幸福的,

  他满足于在他自己的土壤上

  呼吸他乡土的空气。

5 他有牧群供奶,他有田地供粮,

  他有羊群供他衣着,

  他的树木在夏季给他阴凉,

  在冬季为他供火。

  他幸福,能无忧无虑地感受到

10 时日和岁月轻松地溜过,

  心情平安,身体健好,

  白昼宁静祥和;

  夜间熟睡:学习与闲情

  互相调和;甜美的娱乐,

15　又有最讨人喜欢的天真
　　与沉思默想结合。

　　因此，让我生活，不为人见，不为人知，
　　因此让我死去，不要为我哀伤；
　　从这世界上偷偷离去，不要为我树立碑石
20　宣告我躺卧的地方。

（秦希廉　译）

【点评】

　　蒲柏的这首诗《孤寂颂》共分五个诗节，每节押韵格式为abab。众所周知，蒲柏生于一个天主教家庭，成名很早，但一生受病魔困扰，身体驼背，身材矮小。这首诗歌表达了诗人对渴望过上正常生活的美好心愿。

　　诗歌一开始诗人点题，指出什么样的人才是幸福的，幸福的条件是什么：一个人能将愿望和牵挂限制在祖传的几顷土地上，满足于在自己的土地上呼吸着乡土的空气。第二个诗节"Whose herds with milk, whose fields with bread/Whose flocks supply him with attire/Whose trees in summer yield him shade/In winter fire"中诗人采用排比（parallelism）和反复（其中whose乃为首语反复）手法，描绘了一幅田园生活的画面：有牧群供奶，有田地供粮，有羊群供他衣着，有树木在夏季给他阴凉，在冬季为他供火。意象丰富，生动形象。第三、四诗节诗人继续描绘幸福人的生活的画面，指出人幸福是因为他能无忧无虑地感受到时日和岁月轻松地溜过，身体健康，心灵上宁静，身心统一，白昼宁静祥和 "Blest, who can unconcern'dly find/Hours, days, and years slide soft away/In health of body, peace of mind/Quiet by day"。其中"Hours, days, and years"诗人运用语义递增（climax）手法，"slide soft"采用头韵。第三诗节最后一句起到承上启下的作用，"day"与下一个诗节中的"night"形成对比与连接，第四个诗节中诗人强调幸福的人之

第五章 十八世纪英国启蒙时期诗歌

所以幸福还因为夜间能够熟睡,学习与闲情互相调和,在愉悦的天真中冥想。诗人借助前四个诗节描绘了一幅人幸福生活的画面,接下来诗人用第五个诗节来为自己向上帝祈愿,希望自己默默生活,静静离开。"因此,让我生活,不为人见,不为人知,/因此让我死去,不要为我哀伤;/从这世界上偷偷离去,不要为我树立碑石/宣告我躺卧的地方。""Thus let me live, unseen, unknown/Thus unlamented let me die/Steal from the world, and not a stone/Tell where I lie"其中"thus"为首语反复,"unseen""unknown""unlamented"为句内与句间头韵,"let me live""let me die"运用反复与对比(antithesis)手法。不难看出,诗歌技艺与智慧融合在一起,凸显了诗人非凡的才华与真知灼见。

(五)The Echoing Green

William Blake

```
1   The sun does arise,
    And make happy the skies;
    The merry bells ring
    To welcome the Spring;
5   The skylark and thrush,
    The birds of the bush,
    Sing louder around.
    To the bells' cheerful sound,
    While our sport shall be seen
10  On the Echoing Green.

    Old John, with white hair,
```

  Does laugh away care,

  Sitting under the oak,

  Among the old folk,

15 They laugh at our play,

  And soon they shall say,

   "Such, such were the joys,

  When we all—girls and boys—

  In our youth-time were seen

20 On the Echoing Green."

  Till the little ones, weary,

  No one can be merry:

  The sun does descend,

  And our sports have an end.

25 Round the laps of their mothers

  Many sisters and brothers,

  Like birds in their nest,

  Are ready for rest,

  And sport no more be seen

30 On the darkening Green.

【译文】

回荡的绿草地

威廉·布莱克

1 东方升起了太阳,

第五章　十八世纪英国启蒙时期诗歌

　　天空一片喜气洋洋；
　　欢乐的钟声响起，
　　欢迎春天来到大地；
5　云雀和画眉，
　　林中的各种鸟类，
　　他们和着钟声高唱，
　　欢乐的歌声响彻四方；
　　孩子们就要开始做游戏，
10　就在这块回荡的绿草地。

　　老约翰，白发满头，
　　笑得开心忘了烦忧。
　　乡亲们坐在栎树下方，
　　欢声笑语在空中荡漾，
15　他们看着我们尽情玩耍，
　　没多久就有人开口说话：
　　"我们当年也这般开怀，
　　那时我们男孩女孩一块——
　　我们小时候常来到这里
20　就在这块回荡的绿草地。"

　　小朋友玩到筋疲力尽，
　　再也没有人感到开心：
　　太阳从西边慢慢落下，
　　我们结束游戏回家。
25　许多小弟弟小妹妹，

爬到母亲膝上打瞌睡，
像鸟儿回到了巢里，
夜幕降临准备休息，
再也不见有人游玩，
30 草地变得漆黑一团。

（何功杰 译）

【点评】

　　这首《回荡的绿草地》取自布莱克的《经验之歌》。全诗分三节，每节十行，押韵格式为：aabbccddee，其中每一节最后的两行韵式相同。诗人在诗歌中描绘了一天中从太阳升起至夜幕降临，青草地上孩子们玩耍欢乐、大人们在旁边欢笑的场景。第一诗节诗人运用意象词"太阳、天空、云雀、画眉、钟声、树林、绿草地"（The sun, skies, skylark, thrush, bells, bush, Green）和拟人、夸张手法描绘了一幅大自然春天生机盎然，孩子们户外玩耍的景象。天空一片喜气洋洋，欢乐的钟声响起，欢迎春天来到大地；云雀和画眉，林中的各种鸟类，他们和着钟声高唱，欢乐的歌声响彻四方。第二诗节中，诗人主要描绘了忘记忧伤的老约翰和坐在栎树下面的欢声笑语的乡亲们看着孩子们玩耍的画面，其中诗人采用插叙手法，让大人们回忆了自己小时候在绿草地玩耍的情形，意指生命飞逝，一代过去，一代又来，暗含诗人对生命的哲思。第三诗节中，诗人叙述了天色已晚，孩子们已经尽兴玩耍，且玩得精疲力竭，围坐在妈妈身边，如倦鸟归林"Like birds in their nest"，此处运用的修辞手法是明喻（simile）。夜幕降临，曲终人散，草地又回归宁静。诗歌最后"rest" "no more be seen" "darkening"几个词所指的含义与前面描写孩子们欢欣、大人们快乐回忆的场景形成鲜明对比，深藏着诗人对生命的深深思索。

　　诗歌虽然语言简单，但是意象丰富，外加拟人等修辞手法的使用，使得整首诗歌画面生动、形象、唯美。诗人在描写人类原始欢乐的同时，隐

第五章　十八世纪英国启蒙时期诗歌

藏着对人生的哲思。

（六）The Tiger

William Blake

1　Tiger! Tiger! burning bright
　　In the forests of the night,
　　What immortal hand or eye
　　Could frame thy fearful symmetry?

5　In what distant deeps or skies
　　Burnt the fire of thine eyes?
　　On what wings dare he aspire?
　　What the hand dare seize the fire?

　　And what shoulder, and what art,
10　Could twist the sinews of thy heart?
　　And when thy heart began to beat,
　　What dread hand? and what dread feet?

　　What the hammer? What the chain?
　　In what furnace was thy brain?
15　What the anvil? What dread grasp
　　Dare its deadly terrors clasp?

　　When the stars threw down their spears,

And watered heaven with their tears.

Did he smile his work to see?

20　Did he who made the lamb make thee?

　　Tiger! Tiger! burning bright

　　In the forests of the night,

　　What immortal hand or eye,

　　Dare frame thy fearful symmetry?

【译文】
老虎

威廉·布莱克

1　老虎！老虎！光焰闪耀，

　　在黑夜的林中熊熊燃烧，

　　什么样的不朽之眼和手

　　能把你那可怕的匀称建构？

5　你眼中的烈火熊熊

　　来自多远的深处或高空？

　　他凭什么翅膀敢飞到九天？

　　什么样的手敢去抓那火焰？

　　什么样的臂力，什么样的技艺

10　才能拧成你那心脏的腱肌？

　　当你的心脏开始弹跳，

第五章　十八世纪英国启蒙时期诗歌

什么样的手造成你那可怕的脚？

用什么样的锤子？什么样的链条？
在什么样的炉里炼成了你的大脑？
15　在什么样的铁砧上？用什么样的臂力
敢抓住这可以致命的可怕东西？

当星星投下他们的矛枪，
用他们的泪水浇灌穹苍，
他见到自己的作品时可微笑？
20　难道是他造了你也造了羊羔？

老虎！老虎！光焰闪耀，
在黑夜的林中熊熊燃烧，
什么样的不朽之眼和手
敢把你那可怕的匀称建构？

（何功杰　译）

【点评】

此诗选自布莱克的《经验之歌》，三步扬抑格另加一重读音节的韵律，aabb 的押韵格式，使得整首诗歌听起来庄严、凝重，深化了诗的象征意义与神秘感。1992 年，哥伦比亚大学出版社出版了《名诗五百首》，《老虎》排名第一，是布莱克《经验之歌》中最好的一首。整首诗结构整齐、匀称，语言简洁、铿锵有力。

第一诗节一开始，诗人运用反复、隐喻、象征手法与感叹句呼唤老虎出场："Tiger! Tiger! burning bright/In the forests of the night"，其中"Tiger! Tiger!"为反复，"tiger，bright"为母韵，"burning bright"为头韵，这

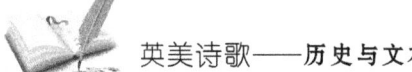

种反复与行内韵交叉的形式创设了一种凝重的氛围。老虎像是光焰在闪耀，在黑夜的林中熊熊燃烧。老虎象征黑夜中的光明，象征力量，由于布莱克创作这首诗歌时法国革命爆发，有学者亦提出老虎还象征法国革命。"the night"应该暗指当时的社会现实，因为当时随着资产阶级的发展，阶级矛盾深化，人民生活困苦，社会急需变革，诗人借助诗歌，借助老虎呼唤正义。紧接着诗人采用问句发问，实则发出赞叹：什么样的不朽之眼和手，能把你那可怕的匀称建构？"What immortal hand or eye/Could frame thy fearful symmetry?"其中"immortal"（不朽的，永恒的），"fearful"，增加了老虎形象的神圣性。"frame, fearful"为头韵，"hand, eye"采用提喻(synecdoche)手法，指代伟大的造物主，诗人赞叹老虎形象完美的同时，亦表达对造物主的赞美之情。

第二个诗节中诗人连用三个"what"感叹以疑问句的形式对老虎发出赞美（"In what distant deeps or skies" "Burnt the fire of thine eyes?" "On what wings dare he aspire?What the hand dare seize the fire?"），其中意象词"fire"与旧约《圣经·耶利米书》第21章第12～14节呼应："大卫家啊，耶和华如此说：你们每早晨要施行公平，拯救被抢夺的脱离欺压人的手，恐怕我的忿怒因你们的恶性发作，如火着起，甚至无人能以熄灭。……我必按你们做事的结果刑罚你们；我也必使火在耶路撒冷的林中着起，将他四围所有的尽行烧灭。"这里的意象"火"代表力量，公义和惩罚。

其中翅膀"On what wings dare, What the hand dare"明则赞美老虎，但结合圣经意象不难明白，这里暗指如果上帝公义愤怒的惩罚临到，没有什么可以阻挡。

第三个诗节诗人以四个反复的"what"感叹外加只问不答的句式及隐喻的修辞强调需要完美的力量和艺术才能把老虎创造完美，实则赞美上帝的伟大（"And what shoulder, and what art,/Could twist the sinews of thy heart?/And when thy heart began to beat/What dread hand? and what dread feet?"）。

第五章 十八世纪英国启蒙时期诗歌

第四个诗节中诗人反复运用五个"what"和问句并借助铁匠打铁的意象("hammer""chain""furnace""anvil")描绘了老虎完美地被创造及老虎所象征的力量、光明、公义等的不可阻挡,诗人再次赞美造物主创造的伟大,暗示一切都在上帝的手中,惩罚必快来到。

第五个诗节中,诗人使用拟人、夸张、象征手法和只问不答的句式描绘了一幅上帝施行公义审判,恶人受到惩治的画面:当星星投下他们的矛枪,用他们的泪水浇灌穹苍,他见到自己的作品时可微笑?难道是他造了你也造了羊羔?("When the stars threw down their spears""And watered heaven with their tears""Did he smile his work to see?""Did he who made the lamb make thee?")。"当星星投下他们的矛枪,用他们的泪水浇灌穹苍",这里诗人遥想了一幅反动势力被革命的人民打败的画面。后两句诗中的"他"指代造物主,是上帝造了老虎也造了羔羊。这里羔羊乃为圣经意象,指代替人类担当罪性的救世主"耶稣基督"。"老虎"与"羔羊"形成对比,构成了上帝的两个属性:公义与爱。结合圣经意象不难看出诗中的"老虎"指代上帝愤怒的惩罚,代表公义的形象。众所周知"羔羊"是和平的君主,是代表上帝"爱"的形象。在这一节中,诗人借助这两个意象表达了对上帝的敬畏之情,同时也传递了自己的民主革命精神。

最后一个诗节,诗人除了将"could"替换为"dare"外,重复了第一个诗节,首尾呼应,再次呼唤老虎出场,呼唤上帝的公义来临。诗人借助老虎被创作的过程,表达了对上帝的敬畏与信靠之情,同时暗讽当时社会的黑暗与不公,但诗人相信上帝的公义一定会来到。布莱克把对革命的热望同宗教信仰结合起来,使整首诗歌呈现出一种神秘、庄重之感。

最后需要说明的是诗中"老虎"的象征意义丰富,不同学者有不同观点,有人认为老虎象征法国大革命;有人认为象征启蒙精神;也有人觉得它只是浪漫主义的想象力。笔者通过分析认为,黑暗中的老虎象征上帝的公义及其愤怒的惩罚。

第六章 浪漫主义时期诗歌

18世纪末、19世纪初,欧洲文学进入了"浪漫主义时期"(Romanticism)。英国浪漫主义作家深受德国唯心主义古典哲学的影响,重新去认识"自我"、审视"自我"、追求"自我"价值的实现。

《抒情歌谣集》的《序言》(*The Prelude*)里,诗人华兹华斯指出:"一切好的诗歌都是强烈感情的自然流露"(All good poetry is the spontaneous overflow of powerful feeling);诗人们主张诗歌语言不必追求高雅精致,注重想象力、热爱自然、强调个性是英国浪漫主义文学的三大突出特征。

英国浪漫主义时期的文学主要表现在诗歌上,深受广大读者的喜爱。其主题往往是人们所关注的自然、工业文明早期的社会矛盾、对自由的讴歌、对民主和平等的热爱。代表诗人有华兹华斯、科勒律治、拜伦、雪莱及济慈。丰富的意象是浪漫主义诗人创造性想象的产物,具有独特的作用和魅力,浪漫主义诗人崇尚自然,主张返璞归真,将自然界作为创作的素材。

但同为浪漫主义作家,他们彼此很少唱和追随,从政治信仰到文学理念,他们往往大相径庭,彼此悖驳。华兹华斯是最亲近自然的诗人,他把自然视为灵感的源泉。《丁登寺赋》中,华兹华斯指出大自然是"我最纯净的思想的寄托,我心灵的保姆、向导和守护人,我所有善良的本质的精

第六章 浪漫主义时期诗歌

魂。"在他眼中,大自然具有支配人类情感的力量,能给人愉悦,具有疗效作用,是连接人类与上帝的云梯。柯勒律治则赋予自然神奇色彩,擅长描绘瑰丽的超自然幻境。拜伦自我表现意识强烈,而雪莱则深受柏拉图哲学影响,憧憬美好的理想和理念。济慈的诗歌以美为追求,主张"美即是真,真即是美",是一位创造艺术美的天才诗人。

一、Poem Reading

(一) I Wondered Lonely as a Cloud

William Wordsworth

1　I wondered lonely as a cloud
　　That floats on high o'er vales and hills,
　　When all at once I saw a crowd,
　　A host, of golden daffodils;
5　Beside the lake, beneath the trees,
　　Fluttering and dancing in the breeze.

　　Continuous as the stars that shine
　　And twinkle on the milky way,
　　They stretched in the never-ending line
10　Along the margin of a bay:
　　Ten thousand saw I at a glance,
　　Tossing their heads in sprightly dance.

　　The waves beside them danced; but they

    Out-did the sparkling waves in glee:
15 A poet could not but be gay,
    In such a jocund company:
    I gazed—and gazed—but little thought
    What wealth the show to me had brought:

    For oft, when on my couch I lie
20 In vacant or in pensive mood,
    They flash upon that inward eye
    Which is the bliss of solitude;
    And then my heart with pleasure fills,
    And dances with the daffodils.

  法国大革命的浪潮引起了英国社会各个层面的不同响应,在文学圈里出现了19世纪浪漫主义诗歌的高潮期,英国浪漫主义诗人歌颂自由、赞美自然,运用想象的力量将自然刻画得充满人性,认为个人是世界的中心,将人的能量提升到了极致。英国浪漫主义诗人被划分为两代,而威廉·华兹华斯(William Wordsworth,1770—1850)则是第一代的三位代表诗人之一(其他两个是威廉·布莱克和塞缪尔·泰勒·柯尔律)。写作于1804年到1807年之间的 *I Wondered Lonely as a Cloud*(也被称为 *Daffodils*)是华兹华斯最重要的代表作品。

  在《抒情歌谣集》的序言中,华兹华斯谈到了诗歌创作的技巧。他认为,诗歌的功能应该是赋予日常事物以意想不到的光环,而诗人进行创作的必要条件是静思(tranquil contemplation)。所谓静思,指的是诗人产生创作冲动到诗歌写成之间的艺术思考和沉淀。该诗正是华兹华斯这一文学创作理论的重要实践之一。1802年4月15日,华兹华斯和妹妹多萝西(Dorothy)漫步在英格兰西北部的湖泊地区(the Lake District),发现了一片美丽的

第六章　浪漫主义时期诗歌

黄水仙，诗人当时就产生了艺术创作的冲动。经过艺术的沉淀，华兹华斯在1807年写成了该诗，并发表于他当年出版的诗集《两卷诗》（*Poems in Two Volumes*）。从最初见到黄水仙到后来写成诗歌，前后经历了五年的时间，充分说明了诗人对艺术沉淀"静思"的重视程度，而该诗后来的成功也正说明了这一创作理念的合理性。

由四步抑扬格（iambic tetrameter）写成的诗歌共分为四个诗节，每个诗节都由六行诗文组成，包括一个四行诗和两行对句，押韵格式为：ababcc。诗文运用了大量的修辞手法，例如比喻（as a cloud, as the stars）、对比（out-did the sparkling waves）、和拟人（tossing their head, dancing）等。前三个诗节主要是写景：诗人把自己比喻成一朵白云，偶遇在山谷中、河畔边成千上万的水仙花，它们如银河里的繁星，在微风吹拂下此起彼伏的花海比起旁边波光粼粼的湖水更引人注目，这样的美景让诗人沉醉不已。最后一个诗节主要是寓情：诗人常有空虚无聊或者情绪低落的时候，而每次想到了随风起舞的水仙花，诗人总能感到无比的欣喜和快乐。

华兹华斯诗歌的一个重要主题就是探讨人与自然之间的和谐共存，而这也是本诗的核心所在。通过观察、欣赏、沉思自然，得到启发的诗人不断地总结着生活中的经验，得出人类与自然和谐生存的哲理。本诗的前三个诗节中，诗人只是沉醉于自然之美，而在最后一个诗节中则到了一种"物我合一"的状态：诗人将自己想象成那一片快乐的水仙花，通过自然的净化力量摆脱了原本低落的情绪，内心又再次充满了对生活的热情。正因如此，华兹华斯认为妻子玛丽·哈钦森（Mary Hutchinson）写成的两行诗文"They flash upon that inward eye/Which is the bliss of solitude"是全诗的精华所在。在华兹华斯看来，独处（solitude）是诗人常有的状态之一。一方面，诗歌创作本身就是个人情绪的艺术升华，只有在独处的状态下才能创作出好的诗歌；另一方面，独处时诗人才能对自然进行深度的思考，才能对人生进行反思从而写作诗歌。而正是因为自然的陪伴，独处的诗人才不会感到孤独。

(二) Ode on a Grecian Urn

John Keats

1 Thou still unravish'd bride of quietness,
　Thou foster-child of silence and slow time,
　Sylvan historian, who canst thus express
　A flowery tale more sweetly than our rhyme:
5 What leaf-fring'd legend haunts about thy shape
　Of deities or mortals, or of both,
　In Tempe or the dales of Arcadey?
　What men or gods are these? What maidens loth?
　What mad pursuit? What struggle to escape?
10 What pipes and timbrels? What wild ecstasy?
　Heard melodies are sweet, but those unheard
　Are sweeter; therefore, ye soft pipes, play on;
　Not to the sensual ear, but, more endear'd,
　Pipe to the spirit ditties of no tone:
15 Fair youth, beneath the trees, thou canst not leave
　Thy song, nor ever can those trees be bare;
　Bold lover, never, never canst thou kiss,
　Though winning near the goal—yet, do not grieve;
　She cannot fade, though thou hast not thy bliss;
20 For ever wilt thou love, and she be fair!

　Ah, happy, happy boughs! that cannot shed

第六章 浪漫主义时期诗歌

　　　Your leaves, nor ever bid the spring adieu;
　　　And, happy melodist, unwearied,
　　　For ever piping songs for ever new;
25　More happy love! more happy, happy love!
　　　For ever warm and still to be enjoy'd,
　　　For ever panting, and for ever young:
　　　All breathing human passion far above,
　　　That leaves a heart high-sorrowful and cloy'd,
30　A burning forehead, and a parching tongue.
　　　Who are these coming to the sacrifice?
　　　To what green altar, O mysterious priest,
　　　Lead'st thou that heifer lowing at the skies,
　　　And all her silken flanks with garlands drest?
35　What little town by river or sea shore,
　　　Or mountain-built with peaceful citadel,
　　　Is empties of this folk, this pious morn?
　　　And, little town, thy streets for evermore
　　　Will silent be; and not a soul to tell
40　Why thous art desolate, can e'er return.
　　　O Attic shape! Fair attitude! With brede
　　　Of marble men and maidens overwrought,
　　　With forest branches and the trodden weed;
　　　Thou, silent form, dost tease us out of thought
45　As doth eternity: Cold Pastoral!
　　　When old age shall this generation waste,
　　　Thou shalt remain, in midst of other woe

> Than ours, a friend to man, to who thou say'st,
> "Beauty is truth, truth beauty," —that is all
> 50　Ye know on earth, and al ye need to know.

　　以威廉·华兹华斯为代表的第一代英国浪漫主义诗人，注重描写自然、寓情于景，但是第一代诗人对于世事的变革、新思潮的冲击主要持一种保守的态度。不同于他们，第二代浪漫主义诗人，以乔治·拜伦（George Byron）、珀西·雪莱（Percy Shelley）、约翰·济慈（John Keats）为代表，不但大胆革新了诗歌的写作技巧，使之更加切合诗人抒情的需要，而且对社会变革和新事物的出现主要表现出积极的态度。虽然没有拜伦的理想主义热情和雪莱的革命主义激情，济慈歌颂人的自由和情感、描述个人和社会的关系等方面写作的诗歌也是可圈可点的。特别是济慈的"颂歌系列"（*Ode on Indolence*，*Ode on a Grecian Urn*，*Ode on Melancholy*，*Ode to a Nightingale*，*Ode to Psyche*），较之前的颂歌创作模式，在诗歌内容和写作技巧上都有所创新。"颂歌系列"中，*Ode on a Grecian Urn* 既表现出了与其他颂歌的一致性，也体现了自己鲜明的艺术特点，是济慈作品中较受争议的一部。

　　《*Ode on a Grecian Urn*》共分为五个诗节，描述的是存在于诗人想象世界中的一个希腊古瓮上的图画。在第一个诗节中，诗人先是将古瓮比作一个安静的新娘和一个博学的历史学家，而后描述了瓮上一个火热的追逐场面：一群男人在疯狂地追逐一群女人。第二个诗节中有三个出场的事物：无声的吹笛人、常青的大树和永远碰触不到却永远相爱的情侣。在第三个诗节中，诗人借助对三个事物的深入论述，用"for ever"凸显了艺术和现实、永生和死亡的强烈对比。第四个诗节描写了一个祭祀小母牛的场景，其后诗人谈到了祭祀者们居住的小城镇，再次突出了艺术和现实的主题。诗人在最后一个诗节的开始赞美了古瓮的精致和美丽，而后明确提到了永恒和艺术的主题：人会年华老去，而古瓮却会永远存在下去。诗歌最后"Beauty

第六章 浪漫主义时期诗歌

is truth, truth beauty"涉及的对话双方及其具体的意思,是20世纪评论家争议的热点。如果这句诗文是诗人对古瓮讲的,那么诗人便指出了代表艺术的古瓮的缺陷所在;而如果是古瓮对读者所讲,那么这里古瓮一方面是在讲述一个普遍的永恒真理,另一方面又再次谈到了艺术、现实以及审美的美学关系。

该诗最重要的一个主题是探讨艺术和现实之间的关系。开篇伊始,诗人便把古瓮比作一位"安静的新娘",又在后面的行文中重点描述了树下的一对情侣,所以"美丽"(beauty)和"爱情"(love)的标签下,古瓮成为艺术的代表。文中出现了多处疑问句式,分别用到了"what"和"who",诗人似乎是想再次追寻古瓮画面的真实性,或者说,想要探究艺术和现实的关系。而第四个诗节中诗人提到祭祀画面之外真实的城镇时,再次提到了艺术是否起源于现实的问题。古瓮上,树下的恋人永远不能亲吻("never, never canst thou kiss"),永远体验不到爱情的欢愉("hast not thy bliss"),这两句诗文点明了现实高于艺术。但是,不能亲吻的恋人却能永久地相爱、远离世俗情感带来的悲痛("a heart high-sorrowful and cloy's" "a burning forehead, and a parching tongue"),这又说明了艺术的魅力远远高于现实。诗人的观点看似矛盾,这也是诗歌备受争议的原因之一,但不可否认的是,通过两种不同观点的呈现,诗人在这里做了一次让读者参与到艺术赏析过程中的大胆尝试。读济慈的诗歌,读者会有享受了一顿感官盛宴的体验。如果说 *Ode to a Nightingale* 让读者体验到了诗歌的音符之美,该诗的行文则展示了一幅看似无声、却胜似有声的希腊古瓮的精美画面。静止的追逐、常青的大树、无声的笛音、亲吻不到的恋人、没有归处的祭祀者,这一幕一幕视觉盛宴让读者充分体会到了艺术的永恒之美。

在结构上,诗歌共有五个诗节,每个诗节由10行诗文组成。每个诗节中,前四行的押韵格式严格按照莎士比亚四行诗写作:abab,主要用来

指明内容;后面的六行诗则参照了弥尔顿的行文特点,不拘一格,主要进行深入讨论。在写作颂歌时,济慈发觉传统的颂歌体根本不能满足他对灵魂、艺术、自然和永生等问题的探讨。这样的押韵格式,在表面上遵循古典诗歌创作理念的同时,也让诗人能够深入浅出地谈论诗歌的主题。在韵脚的应用方面,诗人却完全摒弃了传统的抑扬格。在全诗的 250 对音节中,有 37 对使用了扬扬格(spondee)。第二个诗节中,诗人为了强调个别词汇反复使用 /p/(pipe, play, spirit)、/v/(ever, never, lover)、/b/(beneath, bare, bold, bliss)三个辅音。另外,诗人还大胆启用了英文诗歌中不多见的半谐音(assonance),充分体现了诗歌的精妙之处。例如,第二个诗节中的第 1 行诗文"Heard melodies are sweet, but those unheard...","ea"在"heard"和"unheard"中构成半谐音,而"o"在"melodies"和"those"中构成半谐音。

二、Further Reading

(一) She Dwelt Among the Untrodden Ways

William Wordsworth

1   She dwelt among the untrodden ways
    Beside the springs of Dove,
    A Maid whom there were none to praise
    And very few to love.

5   A violet by a mossy stone
    Half hidden from the eye!
    —Fair as a star, when only one

第六章 浪漫主义时期诗歌

　　is shining in the sky.

　　She lived unknown, and few could know
10　When Lucy ceased to be;
　　But she is in her grave, and, oh,
　　The difference to me!

【译文】
她居住在杳无人烟的地方
威廉·华兹华斯

1　结庐鸽泉边，
　　野径少人攀。
　　平生无知己，
　　红颜堪自怜。

5　罗兰傍青石，
　　苔藓半遮颜。
　　丽质赛星斗，
　　一点闪长天。

　　生时无人识，
10　死时无吊唁。
　　凄然眠冷墓，
　　我独碎心肝！

（辜正坤 译）

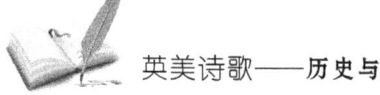

【点评】

这是华兹华斯写给妹妹多萝西的悼亡诗。多萝西终身未嫁,一直在身边照顾他的生活,直至去世。全诗共分三节,每节奇数行采用五音步抑扬格,偶数行为三音步抑扬格,每节押韵格式为 abab。

诗人以第一行诗作为标题,第一节中的词 "untroden" "none" "few" 创设出一种非常凄凉的感觉。第二诗节中诗人运用暗喻将 "she" 比喻为苔藓石旁的一株紫罗兰 "A violet by a mossy stone/Half hidden from the eye",紧跟着诗人采用明喻将其比喻成天空中一颗美丽耀眼的星 "—Fair as a star, when only one/is shining in the sky",这两个比喻的共同之处在于 "美" 与 "孤独",既暗示了她的美,又符合冷色、孤独的整体氛围,给人以无限凄美之感。第三诗节中诗人回顾了 "Lucy" 孤独的一生:生时无人识,死时无吊唁("She lived unknown, and few could know/When Lucy ceased to be")。最后一句道出了诗人的心声,虽然 "she" 一生默默无闻,如今躺在坟墓里,却是令我肝肠寸断。

华兹华斯塑造的露西几乎没有与社会来往,她生长和消失于大自然中。诗歌语言朴实,丰富的意象 "springs of Dove" "violet" "mossy stone" "star" "sky" "grave",将露西和大自然融为一体,表现了诗人丰富的想象力。诗歌中,诗人将自己的感情融入,表达了对逝去的亲人无限的哀思。整首诗意境优美,语气凄凉哀婉。

(二)The Solitary Reaper

William Wordsworth

1   Behold her, single in the field,
      Yon solitary Highland Lass!
      Reaping and singing by herself;

第六章　浪漫主义时期诗歌

  Stop here or gently pass!
5 Alone she cuts and binds the grain,
  And sings a melancholy strain;
  O Listen! For the vale profound
  Is overflowing with the sound.

  No Nightingale did ever chant
10 More welcome notes to weary bands
  Of travellers in some shady haunt
  Among Arabian sands;
  A voice so thrilling ne'er was heard
  In spring-time from the cuckoo-bird,
15 Breaking the silence of the seas
  Among the farthest Hebrides.

  Will no one tell me what she sings?—
   Perhaps the plaintive numbers flow
  For old, unhappy; far-off things,
20 And battles long ago;
  Or is it some more humble lay,
  Familiar matter of to day?
  Some natural sorrow, loss, or pain,
  That has been, and may be again?

25 What'er the theme, the maiden sang
  As if her song could have no ending;

  I saw her singing at her work,

  And o'er the sickle bending;

  I listen'd, motionless and still,

30 And, as I mounted up the hill,

  The music in my heart I bore,

  Long after it was heard no more.

【译文】
孤独的收割者
威廉·华兹华斯

1 瞧那孤独的苏格兰少女,

  一个人在田地里割禾,

  一边收割一边唱歌;

  有时在这边停步,或者轻轻走过!

5 她独自收割并捆扎谷禾,

  一面唱着一支忧郁之歌;

  听啊!这歌声嘹亮,

  正在那幽深的山谷中泛滥。

  在阿拉伯的沙漠上,

10 从不曾有夜莺给困乏的旅客群

  在阴凉憩息的地方,

  鸣唱得如此悦耳动听;

  在遥远的赫布里底也从未听到

  春季的杜鹃鸟

第六章 浪漫主义时期诗歌

15　有如此动人的歌声,
　　打破大海的寂静。
　　有人能告诉我她唱些什么吗?
　　这凄婉的歌曲
　　也许是咏叹古老、不幸的遥远事物,
20　以及往昔的战役;
　　要么就是较平凡的小曲一支,
　　唱的是今日熟知的寻常事?
　　某些已有的,今后也会再有的
　　自然忧伤、失落或苦痛?

25　不论这少女唱的主题是什么,
　　她似乎唱得没完没了;
　　我看到她一边干活一边唱,
　　弯着腰按动镰刀;——
　　我静静地倾听着,伫立不动晃;
30　当我登上山冈,
　　那音乐我不再能欣赏,
　　我把它长久珍藏在我的心坎上。

(秦希廉　译)

【点评】

《孤独的收割者》是一首抒情诗,诗歌描绘了一幅苏格兰少女边收割边唱歌的画面,展示了其丰富的内心世界。表达了诗人对自然、人性的美与艺术的热爱,同时展示了诗人对历史与生命的深刻思考。整首诗歌共分四节,每节八行,为四音步抑扬格,第一节与第四节押韵格式为:abcbddee,中间两节为:ababccdd,变化的韵式结合跳跃的意象使得诗歌节奏轻快活泼,穿越感强。其结构形式为:偶遇——景或物与诗人主体相交、相感——回忆的愉悦。

诗歌一开始,诗人采用呼语(apostrophe)调动听众的视觉和听觉,向读者展示了一幅在广袤的苏格兰高地上,一位孤独的苏格兰少女独自一人在田间边歌唱边收割谷物的田园画面。"Behold her, single in the field" "Yon solitary Highland Lass" "Reaping and singing by herself" "Stop here or gently pass!"其中"solitary Highland Lass"为一语双叙(syllepsis),亦即"solitary Highland"和"solitary Lass",简洁生动的语言突出了苏格兰高地的空旷及苏格兰少女的孤寂。"Alone she cuts and binds the grain/And sings a melancholy strain/O Listen! For the vale profound/Is overflowing with the sound",诗人运用细腻、夸张手法,描绘了一幅苏格兰少女勤劳、乐观、善思的画面。少女的歌喉嘹亮动听,响彻山谷。整个画面将人、劳动、歌声与自然融合为一体,传递了诗人有机世界的整体观念。第一个诗节中的词汇"single" "solitary" "alone" "melancholy"给动态的画面蒙上了一层荒凉的感觉,寓意深刻。

第二个诗节诗人采用对比手法,将苏格兰少女忧郁的歌声与夜莺的歌唱、春天杜鹃鸟的歌声进行比较,对比指出少女的歌声更加悦耳动听,而且有消除游人疲惫的功效,诗人将少女与夜莺、杜鹃并置,突出了诗人更看重"人"生命的宝贵,人乃为万物之灵长,这正好契合了诗人华兹华斯的基督教信仰观念。其中丰富的意象词"夜莺、游人、阿拉伯沙漠、杜鹃鸟、大海、赫布里底岛"(nightingale, travellers, Arabian sands, cuckoo-bird, seas, Hebrides)勾画出一幅辽阔悠远的画面,拉长了空间的立体感,唯美生动。其中采用了头韵"welcome, weary" "silence, seas",拟人与夸张"Breaking the silence of the seas"更显诗人的创作魅力。

第三个诗节诗人猜测少女凄婉歌声的内涵:也许是咏叹古老、不幸的遥远事物,往昔的战役,也许是较平凡的小曲一支,只不过是今日熟知

第六章 浪漫主义时期诗歌

的寻常事或某些已有的,今后也会再有的自然忧伤、失落或苦痛,其中诗句"Some natural sorrow, loss, or pain/That has been, and may be again?"对应圣经《传道书》第一章第 9~10 行"已有的事后必再有;已行的事后必再行。日光之下并无新事。岂有一件事人能指着说这是新的?哪知,在我们以前的世代早已有了。"《传道书》第一章第 13 行"applied my mind to seek and to search out by wisdom all that is done under heaven; it is an unhappy business that God has given to human beings to bu busy with"(我专心用智慧寻求、查究天下所做的一切事,乃知上帝叫世人所经练的是极重的劳苦),圣经诗句中的"unhappy"与诗人所描述的歌声"melancholy"一致,其内涵不得而知,诗人由眼前的景象——苏格兰少女独自一人在旷野中干着繁重的收割工作想到了圣经中的诗句,圣经意象与眼前景象的融合表达了诗人融情于景,在信仰中展开诗人对历史与生命苦难的思索,展示了诗人对人类尤其是女性命运的深切同情。

第四诗节诗人用平和的语言表达了苏格兰少女美妙的歌声吸引着"我",令我驻足,流连忘返,为继续生命旅程,诗人将歌声珍藏在自己的心坎上("The music in my heart l bore"),苏格兰少女余音绕梁的歌声,增添了诗歌绵延悠长的意境。

这首诗语言简朴而清新,意象优美,勤劳女性边劳动边歌唱的画面,传递着诗人对女性、生态的关心,表达了诗人眷恋自然、热爱生命的旷世情怀。

(三)Composed Upon Westminster Bridge

William Wordsworth

1   Earth has not anything to show more fair:
    Dull would he be of soul who could pass by

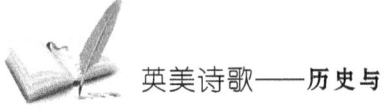

A sight so touching in its majesty;
This City now doth, like a garment, wear
5 The beauty of the morning: silent, bare,
Ships, towers, domes, theaters, and temples lie
Open unto the fields, and to the sky;
All bright and glittering in the smokeless air.
Never did sun more beautifully steep
10 In his flrst splendor, valley, rock, or hill;
Ne'er saw I, never felt, a calm so deep!
The river glideth at his own sweet will:
Dear God! the very houses seem asleep;
And all that mighty heart is lying still!

【译文】
威斯敏斯特桥上

威廉·华兹华斯

1 大地再没有比这儿更美的风貌：
  若有谁，对如此壮丽动人的景物
  竟无动于衷，那才是灵魂麻木；
  瞧这座城市，像披上一领新袍，
5 披上了明艳的晨光；环顾周遭：
  船舶、尖塔、剧院、教堂、华屋，
  都寂然、坦然，向郊野、向天穹赤露；
  在烟尘未染的大气里粲然闪耀。
  旭日金辉洒布于峡谷山陵，

第六章 浪漫主义时期诗歌

10　也不比这片晨光更为奇丽；
　　我何尝见过、感受过这深沉的宁静！
　　河上徐流，由着自己的心意；
　　上帝呵！千门万户都沉睡未醒，
　　这整个宏大的心脏仍然在歇息！

(杨德豫　译)

【点评】

这是华兹华斯的一首十四行诗，诗歌描绘了初秋之际从泰晤士河上的威斯敏斯特大桥远眺清晨的伦敦城的情景。整首诗节奏徐缓，感情真实细腻，语言凝练，音韵和谐、庄重而恬静，押韵格式为：abbaabbacdcdcd。

诗人一开始采用低调陈述(understatement)中的反叙(litotes)手法点出在整个地球上这里的风景最美，只有灵魂麻木的人才对此无动于衷，以此引起读者的注意，创设了悬念 "Earth has not anything to show more fair/Dull would he be of soul who could pass by"，随后诗人采用"总—分"法，整体上运用明喻("like a garment")与拟人手法["This City now doth, ... wear/The beauty of the morning: silent, bare"("beauty"和"bare"为头韵)]描绘这座城市在明艳的晨光中，像披上一领新袍，宁静、坦然。接着是具体描绘：船舶、尖塔、剧院、教堂、华屋向郊野、向天穹赤露，在烟尘未染的大气里粲然闪耀("Ships, towers, domes, theaters, and temples lie/Open unto the fields, and to the sky/ All bright and glittering in the smokeless air")，在此，诗人将静态的伦敦城和大自然融为一体，体现了诗人有机的自然整体观。随后，诗人采用对比(contrast)手法指出融入自然的伦敦城在晨光中更为奇丽，即使旭日金辉洒布于峡谷山陵，也不比这片晨光，诗人自己说从未见过、感受过这深沉的宁静！一般来说，工业文明中的城市总是喧嚣繁杂，因此浪漫主义时期的诗人们往往去大自然寻求心灵的宁静，但是华兹华斯一改常态，来描写伦敦赞美伦敦，当然这里的赞美是宏观的、外在的、有条件的，是清晨沉睡中的伦敦城，是诗人在泰晤士河上的威斯敏斯特桥上所看到的与自然融为一体的伦敦城。"Never did sun more beautifully steep/In his first splendor, valley, rock, or hill/Ne'er saw I, never felt, a calm so deep!" 句中诗人重复使用三个"never"，两个倒装句"Never did""Ne'er saw I"强调这里晨光美丽，这里的宁静深沉，这里的河水由着自己的心意缓缓流淌。在最后两句诗歌中，诗人借用拟人（personification）和隐喻（metaphor）由衷地向造物主发出感叹：千门万户都沉睡未醒，这整个宏大的心脏仍然在歇息！（"Dear God! the very houses seem asleep/And all that mighty heart is lying still!"）

整首诗歌意象丰富：城市意象如"ships, towers, domes, theatres, temples, house, mighty heart（借指伦敦城）"、自然意象如"the fields, the sky, the smokeless air, sun, valley, rock, hill, river"。这两组意象并置在一起且交互融合，表现了诗人融情于景，运用充满感情色彩的语言（fair, majesty, splendor, mighty 等）描绘了一幅在大自然怀抱中的伦敦城清晨的景象，再现了历史悠久、文化底蕴丰富的伦敦城壮观的风貌。

（四）Lines Written in Early Spring

William Wordsworth

1   I heard a thousand blended notes,
    While in a grove I sate reclined,
    In that sweet mood when pleasant thoughts
    Bring sad thoughts to the mind.

5   To her fair works did Nature link
    The human soul that through me ran;
    And much it grieved my heart to think

第六章　浪漫主义时期诗歌

What man has made of man.

Through primrose tufts, in that green bower,

10　The periwinkle trailed its wreaths;

And 'tis my faith that every flower

Enjoys the air it breathes.

The birds around me hopped and played,

Their thoughts I cannot measure—

15　But the least motion which they made

It seemed a thrill of pleasure,

The budding twigs spread out their fan,

To catch the breezy air;

And I must think, do all I can,

20　That there was pleasure there.

If this belief from heaven be sent,

If such be Nature's holy plan,

Have I not reason to lament

What man has made of man?

【译文】
写于早春

　　　　　威廉·华兹华斯

1　我躺卧在树林之中，

听着融谐的千万声音，
闲适的情绪，愉快的思想，
却带来忧心忡忡。

5　大自然把她的美好事物
通过我联系人的灵魂，
而我痛心万分，想起了
人怎样对待着人。
那边绿荫中的樱草花丛，
10　有长春花在把花圈编制，
我深信每朵花不论大小，
都能享受它呼吸的空气。

四周的鸟儿跳了又耍，
我不知道他们想些什么，
15　但他们每个细微的动作，
似乎都激起心头的欢乐。

萌芽的嫩枝张臂如扇，
捕捉那阵阵的清风，
使我没法不深切地感受到，
20　它们也自有欢欣。

如果上天叫我这样相信，
如果这是大自然的用心，
难道我没有理由悲叹

第六章 浪漫主义时期诗歌

人怎样对待着人?

(王佐良 译)

【点评】

该诗歌写于1798年,是华兹华斯经历法国大革命后创作的,同年刊载于《抒情歌谣集》中。全诗共分六节,采用四音步抑扬格,每节押韵格式为abab。诗人在诗歌中用情感真挚的笔墨,描绘了一幅生机盎然、充满灵性与欢乐的大自然景象,同时饱含了诗人对人性的思考。

诗歌第一诗节中的"我"躺卧在树林中,倾听大自然中千万和谐的声音,此处诗人用夸张(overstatement)手法将自然比喻(metaphor)为一个音乐大师("I heard a thousand blended notes/ While in a grove I sate reclined"),给"我"带来愉悦的心情,同时带给"我"悲伤的思绪("In that sweet mood when pleasant thoughts/Bring sad thoughts to the mind")。诗歌中处在自然中的"我"愉快而又忧伤,这种矛盾的心理突出了诗歌的张力。第一行内的单词"heard""thousand""blended"押辅音韵 /d/,第三行内单词"that""sweet""pleasant"押辅音韵 /t/,第四行内韵"sad""mind"为 /d/。第一诗节中清音、浊音的交替使用与诗中第一行"blended notes"(混响、混合音符)相呼应,如万马奔腾,烘托出自然的包罗万象与伟大。最后两行诗中"sweet""pleasant""sad"采用悖论(paradox)手法,其中"thoughts"被反复使用,突出了具有"理性"的"我"所代表的人类与大自然的不相和谐,这与第二、六诗节中的"What man has made of man"(人是如何改变了人)互文。

第二个诗节中,诗人采用拟人手法指出大自然把我体内流淌的灵魂和她的精妙杰作熔铸一体,此时的"我"也是大自然的一个部分。这里的"Nature"一词首字母大写,在上下文的语境中指代造物主,诗人借此暗指人与自然一起乃为造物主所创造的作品,原本和谐,但是诗人接着说"And much it grieved my heart to think/ What man has made of man","我"在将自己融入自然感到欣喜时,突然乐极生悲,产生疑问,人如何改变了自己!

意指人已经与大自然格格不入,暗讽了英国当时在"理性"主导下的工业文明给人类带来的痛苦与信仰的坠落。

在第三、四、五个诗节中,诗人运用拟人手法描绘了一幅和谐的充满灵性的大自然画面:绿荫中的樱草花丛,有长春花在把花圈编制,长春花缀出了花环,鲜花喜欢它呼吸的空气;鸟雀似乎和诗人成了好朋友,在与诗人嬉戏玩耍,而且鸟雀心头渗透着快乐和欢欣;柔叶嫩枝如巨扇般展开,去招惹那阵阵轻风,而那快乐永恒、画面唯美充满和谐与生命的律动,暗藏诗人对造物主的赞美与大自然的热爱。

诗人论证完大自然的和谐之后在最后一个诗节中表达自己的观点:倘若这信念确为上苍所赐,若这确是大自然(上帝)的神圣旨意,我岂不更有理由去叹息,人如何改变了自己!整个诗节指出,造物主所造的一切(包括人)原本和谐,但是,人在当时的时代文化背景中已经偏离正道,与自然格格不入,由此诗人焦虑叹息"What man has made of man?"通过诗歌结尾部分能充分体味到诗人的忧伤和感慨。

整首诗歌首尾呼应,意象丰富,语言朴实无华。每一个诗节中的"我"存在于思考,契合了浪漫主义所倡导的个性重要的理念。需要指出的是,诗中的自然(Nature)与汉语中的自然界(环境)不同,诗歌中的自然在上下文的环境中充满了灵性与神圣性,更确切地指向造物主,意境更加高远,表达了诗人对上帝的赞美敬畏之情,体现了诗人对于人类工业文明带来痛苦与堕落现状的思索,传递了诗人深切的人文关怀。

(五) Lines Composed a Few Miles Above Tintern Abbey

On Revisiting the Banks of the Wye During a Tour.

July 13, 1798

William Wordsworth

1　Five years have past; five summers, with the length

第六章 浪漫主义时期诗歌

  Of five long winters! and again I hear

  These waters, rolling from their mountain-springs

  With a soft inland murmur. Once again

5 Do I behold these steep and lofty cliffs,

  That on a wild secluded scene impress

  Thoughts of more deep seclusion; and connect

  The landscape with the quiet of the sky.

  The day is come when I again repose

10 Here, under this dark sycamore, and view

  These plots of cottage ground, these orchard tufts,

  Which at this season, with their unripe fruits,

  Are clad in one green hue, and lose themselves

  'Mid groves and copses. Once again I see

15 These hedgerows, hardly hedgerows, little lines

  Of sportive wood run wild: these pastoral farms,

  Green to the very door; and wreaths of smoke

  Sent up, in silence, from among the trees!

  With some uncertain notice, as might seem

20 Of vagrant dwellers in the houseless woods,

  Or of some Hermit's cave, where by his fire

  The Hermit sits alone.

  These beauteous forms,

  Through a long absence, have not been to me

25 As is a landscape to a blind man's eye;

  But oft, in lonely rooms, and 'mid the din

  Of towns and cities, I have owed to them

In hours of weariness, sensations sweet,

Felt in the blood, and felt along the heart;

30   And passing even into my purer mind,

With tranquil restoration;—feelings too

Of unremembered pleasure; such, perhaps,

As have no slight or trivial influence

On that best portion of a good man's life,

35   His little, nameless, unremembered, acts

Of kindness and of love. Nor less, I trust,

To them I may have owed another gift,

Of aspect more sublime; that blessed mood,

In which the burthen of the mystery,

40   In which the heavy and the weary weight

Of all this unintelligible world,

Is lightened—that serene and blessed mood,

In which the affections gently lead us on—

Until, the breath of this corporeal frame

45   And even the motion of our human blood

Almost suspended, we are laid asleep

In body, and become a living soul;

While with an eye made quiet by the power

Of harmony, and the deep power of joy,

50   We see into the life of things.

If this

Be but a vain belief, yet, oh! how oft—

In darkness and amid the many shapes

Of joyless daylight; when the fretful stir
55　Unprofitable, and the fever of the world,
　　Have hung upon the beatings of my heart—
　　How oft, in spirit, have I turned to thee,
　　O sylvan Wye! thou wanderer thro' the woods,
　　How often has my spirit turned to thee!
60　And now, with gleams of half-extinguished thought,
　　With many recognitions dim and faint,
　　And somewhat of a sad perplexity,
　　The picture of the mind revives again;
　　While here I stand, not only with the sense
65　Of present pleasure, but with pleasing thoughts
　　That in this moment there is life and food
　　For future years. And so I dare to hope,
　　Though changed, no doubt, from what I was when first
　　I came among these hills; when like a roe
70　I bounded o'er the mountains, by the sides
　　Of the deep rivers, and the lonely streams,
　　Wherever nature led—more like a man
　　Flying from something that he dreads than one
　　Who sought the thing he loved. For nature then
75　(The coarser pleasures of my boyish days,
　　And their glad animal movements all gone by)
　　To me was all in all. —I cannot paint
　　What then I was. The sounding cataract
　　Haunted me like a passion the tall rock,

80   The mountain, and the deep and gloomy wood,

Their colours and their forms, were then to me

An appetite; a feeling and a love,

That had no need of a remoter charm,

By thought supplied, nor any interest

85   Unborrowed from the eye.—That time is past,

And all its aching joys are now no more,

And all its dizzy raptures. Not for this

Faint I, nor mourn nor murmur, other gifts

Have followed; for such loss, I would believe,

90   Abundant recompence. For I have learned

To look on nature, not as in the hour

Of thoughtless youth; but hearing oftentimes

The still, sad music of humanity,

Nor harsh nor grating, though of ample power

95   To chasten and subdue. And I have felt

A presence that disturbs me with the joy

Of elevated thoughts; a sense sublime

Of something far more deeply interfused,

Whose dwelling is the light of setting suns,

100   And the round ocean and the living air,

And the blue sky, and in the mind of man:

A motion and a spirit, that impels

All thinking things, all objects of all thought,

And rolls through all things. Therefore am I still

105   A lover of the meadows and the woods,

第六章　浪漫主义时期诗歌

  And mountains; and of all that we behold

  From this green earth; of all the mighty world

  Of eye, and ear,—both what they half create,

  And what perceive; well pleased to recognise

110 In nature and the language of the sense,

  The anchor of my purest thoughts, the nurse,

  The guide, the guardian of my heart, and soul

  Of all my moral being.

   Nor perchance,

115 If I were not thus taught, should I the more

  Suffer my genial spirits to decay:

  For thou art with me here upon the banks

  Of this fair river; thou my dearest Friend,

  My dear, dear Friend; and in thy voice I catch

120 The language of my former heart, and read

  My former pleasures in the shooting lights

  Of thy wild eyes. Oh! yet a little while

  May I behold in thee what I was once,

  My dear, dear Sister! and this prayer I make,

125 Knowing that Nature never did betray

  The heart that loved her;'tis her privilege,

  Through all the years of this our life, to lead

  From joy to joy: for she can so inform

  The mind that is within us, so impress

130 With quietness and beauty, and so feed

  With lofty thoughts, that neither evil tongues,

Rash judgments, nor the sneers of selfish men,
Nor greetings where no kindness is, nor all
The dreary intercourse of daily life,
135　Shall e'er prevail against us, or disturb
Our cheerful faith, that all which we behold
Is full of blessings. Therefore let the moon
Shine on thee in thy solitary walk;
And let the misty mountain winds be free
140　To blow against thee: and, in after years,
When these wild ecstasies shall be matured
Into a sober pleasure; when thy mind
Shall be a mansion for all lovely forms,
Thy memory be as a dwelling place
145　For all sweet sounds and harmonies; oh! then,
If solitude, or fear, or pain, or grief,
Should be thy portion, with what healing thoughts
Of tender joy wilt thou remember me,
And these my exhortations! Nor, perchance—
150　If I should be where I no more can hear
Thy voice, nor catch from thy wild eyes these gleams
Of past existence—wilt thou then forget
That on the banks of this delightful stream
We stood together; and that I, so long
155　A worshipper of Nature, hither came
Unwearied in that service; rather say with warmer love
—oh! with far deeper zeal

第六章 浪漫主义时期诗歌

    Of holier love. Nor wilt thou then forget,

    That after many wanderings, many years

160 Of absence, these steep woods and lofty cliffs,

    And this green pastoral landscape, were to me

    More dear, both for themselves and for thy sake!

【译文】
丁登寺赋

重游怀河河谷后赋于丁登寺旁数英里处

1798 年 7 月 13 日

威廉·华兹华斯

1   五年过去了;五个夏天,连同

    五个漫长的冬季!我又听到

    这流水,从山泉中滚滚而来,

    带着内河的潺潺细语。——我又一次

5   看到这陡峭的山岩,

    在一片野外幽静的背景中,

    使人产生更加幽远的思绪;并使这

    景色与苍穹的静穆融为一体。

    这一天终于来临,我又在

10 这棵苍郁的槭树下憩息,并眺望

    一块块的村地和一簇簇的果树,

    树上的果实尚未成熟,

    果林披着一片青绿,与别的灌木

    相溶成一种颜色。我又看到

15 这些树篱,哪里是树篱——倒不如说是
恣意蔓生的枝条:这些绿色一直铺到
田庐的门边;这些在寂静里
从树林中升起的袅袅炊烟!
它们的来源飘忽难辨,恍惚是
20 浪游者在没有屋舍的林中点燃,
或来自隐士幽居的洞穴,他正
独自坐在炉火边。
这些美景
虽然并不常见,对我却并非
25 像一片风景之于盲人的眼睛:
在我蛰居喧闹的都市,感到
孤寂无聊时,正是这些美景呵
常常给我带来愉悦的心境,
它流淌在血液里,跳跃在心头;
30 并流入我被净化的脑海中,
使我恢复恬静的心绪——重新
感受到已淡忘的往日的快乐:这快乐
也许能产生不可忽视的影响,
在无形中培育善良者最美好的品德,
35 使他做出虽非轰轰烈烈、令人缅怀,
但却充满善意和爱的举动。同样,
我还要感谢它给我的另一个赐予,
一个更高尚的赐予;在这幸福的心绪中,
那心灵上神秘的负担,
40 那不可理解的人世所带来的

第六章　浪漫主义时期诗歌

　　使人厌倦的沉重的负荷

　　也为之减轻了——在这恬静的心绪中，

　　那高尚的情感引导着我们，

　　使我们仿佛暂时停止了呼吸，

45　甚至连血液也不再流动，

　　我们的肉体已陷入酣睡。

　　我们变成了一种纯粹的精神：

　　和谐的力量，欢乐的深远的力量。

　　使我们能带着平静的眼光

50　去洞察事物的真谛。

　　假如这一切

　　只是虚妄的信念，呵不！曾有过多少次——

　　在黑暗中，在郁郁寡欢的白昼的

　　纷繁事务中，当无益的烦恼

55　和人世的热病都一股脑儿

　　压抑着我跳荡的心灵——

　　曾有多少次呵，我的精神转向你，

　　噢怀河！你穿越丛林的浪游者，

　　曾有多少次呵，我的精神转向你！

60　如今，带着半灭的思绪的微光，

　　带着许多朦胧暗淡的记忆，

　　并掺着某种难言的怅惘，

　　脑海中的景象重又复活了：

　　当我站在这里时，我不仅感受着

65　眼前的欢乐，而且欣喜地想到

　　这一刻也为未来的岁月孕育着

生命和精神的食粮。以昔视今
也正是如此,尽管与我第一次来这山谷
漫游时相比,我无疑已有所改变;

70 那时,我像一头小鹿蹦跳在山冈上,
在幽深的河滨和寂寞的溪畔,
一切随心所至:那时我疾步如飞,
与其说像寻觅心爱的景色,倒不如说
像要躲避什么可怕的景象。那时

75 (我幼年时代的天真的游戏
和单纯的欢乐都已成为过去)
大自然对于我就是一切——我实难描摹
我当时的情状。那喧响的瀑布
常引起我热烈的追求;那峭岩,

80 那山冈,那幽深的树林,
它们的雄姿秀色对于我曾是
一种享受;是一种感情和爱,
它无须从沉思冥想中得来,
也不必靠视觉以外的探求。

85 但如今,那个时代已经消逝了,
连同使人隐隐生悲的欢乐
和使人销魂的狂喜。然而我并不为此
感到沮丧,也不悲吟怨诉;
因为有新的馈赠相随而来,

90 足以补偿以上的损失。因为我已能
以新的方式观察自然,已不同于
往日天真的青年;我常常听见

第六章　浪漫主义时期诗歌

人生低沉而哀伤的音乐，

尽管它具有使人压抑的威力，

95　却并不显得粗粝嘈杂。我还在自然中

感到一种存在——它以高尚思想的喜悦

以及对某种深深交织

在一起的事物的崇高感激荡我的心灵，

它寄寓在落日的余晖中，

100　在滚圆的海洋和流动的大气中，

在蔚蓝的天空和人的头脑中：

它是一种运动和精神，推动着

一切有思之物和一切思维的对象

在宇宙万汇中运行。因此我仍然

105　钟爱我们从这绿色的大地上

所能看到的一切；

这由眼、耳所感受到的

整个美妙的世界——既包括它们的观察，

也有它们的半创造；我欣喜地在自然

110　和感觉的语言中看到了

我最纯净的思想的寄托，我心灵的

保姆、向导和守护人，我所有善良的

本质的精魂。

　或许，

115　即使我未能得此顿悟，我天性中的

快乐精神也不致消殒：

因为你正如和我一起在这美丽的

河岸上；你，我最亲爱的朋友。

我亲爱的、亲爱的朋友；我从你声音里
120　可以听到我过去心灵的语言，从你
　　　狂野的闪烁的目光中看到
　　　我过去的欢乐。呵！且让我在片刻中，
　　　从你身上看到我往日的形象，
　　　我亲爱的、亲爱的妹妹！我作此祈求，
125　因我知道自然永远不会辜负
　　　热爱它的心灵；它有一种力量
　　　能使我们的一生从欢乐
　　　走向欢乐：它能如此丰富地启发
　　　我们内在的心灵，给它留下
130　如此的美和恬静，给它灌输
　　　如此崇高的思想，无论是邪恶的语言、
　　　鲁莽的判断，还是利己者的讥嘲、
　　　缺乏善意的问候，或日常生活中
　　　一切枯燥沉闷的交往，
135　都不能压倒我们，或动摇
　　　这样一个愉悦的信念：我们看到的
　　　一切都是出于恩惠。那么就让月亮
　　　照耀着你孤寂地漫步吧；
　　　让山野的带雾的风自由地
140　向你吹拂吧：在今后的岁月里，
　　　当这些粗犷的欢乐终于沉淀为
　　　平静的喜悦；当你的心灵
　　　成为储藏千种美景的广厦，
　　　当你的记忆成为寄寓万曲音乐

第六章 浪漫主义时期诗歌

145　的庐舍；呵！到那时呵，
　　如果你偶尔感到寂寞、惶恐、痛苦
　　或悲伤，这温和的欢乐将带来
　　多少慰藉，并使你想起了我，
　　和我的这些诗句！或许——

150　即使当我不再听到你的
　　声音，不再能从你狂野的眼睛中
　　看到如今的目光——你也不会忘记
　　我们曾一起站在这可爱的
　　河畔，不会忘记我这自然的永恒的

155　崇拜者，曾不知疲倦地
　　来此膜拜；或不如说奉献热烈的爱
　　——噢！奉献由更神圣的爱所产生的
　　更深沉的激情。你也不会忘记
　　经过四方浪游，经过多年

160　阔别，这些陡峭的森林和峥嵘的山崖，
　　以及这苍翠的田园，由于它们自己，
　　也由于你，对我变得更为亲切可爱！

（顾子欣　译）

【点评】

1798年7月，华兹华斯在妹妹多萝西的陪同下故地重游，写下了《丁登寺赋》这首诗。《丁登寺赋》收录在《抒情歌谣集》中，成为压轴作，表达了大自然和谐秩序的主题。诗歌用内心独白的形式，以五音步抑扬格为主，采用无韵诗（blank verse）的格律写成。

全诗大致分为五段，第一段第1～22行前半行，主要描写诗人五年后故地重游时的所见所闻，诗人采用丰富的意象来描绘怀河河谷与丁登

寺的景色，优美而又宁静。诗人在诗的开篇处，发出了这样的感叹："Five years have passed; five summers, with the length/Of five long winters"。诗人采用反复手法，"five"被三次重复，意蕴深厚，表达了诗人对时光飞逝的感慨，对故地重游的喜悦，对五年来所经历的无法用言语表达的内心感受。

第22行后半行至第49行前半行为第二段，诗人回顾五年前与妹妹初次游历怀河河谷和丁登寺时所留下的深刻印象及其对诗人心灵的冲击和净化。诗人采用对比手法主要描写了这美景赋予"我"甜美的感觉，融入血液，荡漾心底，流进我纯净的心灵，唤起我对昔日欢乐的记忆。诗人想到自己独居一室，置身于城镇的喧嚣中，对那来自不可理喻的世界强加于人们的令人厌倦的神秘重负深感疲惫。而这种甜美的感觉使"我"在恬静中恢复活力，而且还使诗人道德升华，饱含着善意与友爱，另外美好的自然还赋予诗人"一种满足的惬意"，惬意中诗人感到爱心引导着向前，灵魂似乎离开肉体，诗人感到和谐和喜悦的力量与他一起，目光因而变得宁静安详，借此洞察人间万象。此段中，诗人使用抽象词如"blessed, sublime, mystery"使得眼前的景象、诗人内心灵魂深处的感受与造物主的神性融为一体，意境更加柔美、庄严而神圣。自然对诗人而言已经是精神上的导师，心灵的慰藉，烦恼的解除者，神秘重负的解惑者，和谐、宁静、愉悦的源泉。

第三段从第49行的后半句至第57行，从诗句中不难看出，诗人对第二段的信念与感受予以肯定，因为就是自然帮助诗人从无益的烦闷和世界热病的沉重压迫中解脱出来。其中"the fever of the world"为隐喻手法，"How oft""spirit""turned to thee"等被反复使用，抒发了诗人强烈的情感，强调了自然对诗人来说并非一种虚妄的信念。

第四段从58至111行的前半句，诗人采用对比手法及大量的意象词来描绘儿时的大自然，强调故地重游的不同感受。第一次游历时，诗人像

第六章　浪漫主义时期诗歌

是一头小鹿["when like a roe"（明喻）]蹦跳在山岗上，在幽深的河滨和寂寞的河畔。那时诗人疾步如飞，大自然对他来说就是一切，是一种享受，是一种感情和爱["The sounding cataract/Haunted me like a passion the tall rock/The mountain, and the deep and gloomy wood"（明喻、拟人、移就）]，无须沉思冥想。但如今，过去的一切虽有不同，诗人感到新的馈赠足以补偿，诗人已经以新的"存在"方式观察自然，高尚而又崇高，诗人感到自然就是他心灵的保姆、向导和守护人，是他所有善良的本质的精魂。"The anchor of my purest thoughts, the nurse/The guide, the guardian of my heart, and soul/Of all my moral being"中诗人运用拟人和比喻手法，使得诗歌更加形象生动。

第五段从第111行后半句至第159行，主要为诗人融会前面所有因素的一种狂喜的结尾。诗人将妹妹融入诗歌中，从她身上看到过去的自我。诗人在妹妹的陪伴下发出自己的祈愿，因为自然永远不会辜负热爱它的心灵；它有一种力量能使我们一生从欢乐走向欢乐。"Our cheerful faith, that all which we behold/Is full of blessings"强调这一切都是"恩惠"，诗人将这一切都归结为造物主的祝福。诗人指出，"With warmer love —oh! with far deeper zeal/Of holier love"表达了对大自然的爱源于神圣的爱，这与《圣经·约翰一书》第四章第7节后半句"因为爱是从上帝来的"有异曲同工之妙。不难看出，诗人眼前的喜乐是自然与天人合一的结果。诗歌最后又将亲情融入这一切，"More dear, both for themselves and for thy sake!"指出因为有妹妹在身边，这一切具有了更加崇高的意义。

华兹华斯在《丁登寺赋》中阐明了自己的自然观及自然与人的关系。大自然给人的财富不仅有美丽的自然风光，更有精神上的抚慰和滋养，它能给人带来愉悦、欢欣，治愈人类的创伤，给人以心灵、道德的启迪。人只有回归自然、顺应自然规律才能避免一切痛苦惆怅。

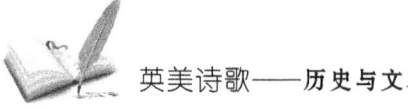

（六）Ode to a Nightingale

John Keats

1   My heart aches, and a drowsy numbness pains
     My sense, as though of hemlock I had drunk,
     Or emptied some dull opiate to the drains
     One minute past, and Lethe-wards o had sunk
5   'Tis not through envy of thy happy lot,
     But being too happy in thy happiness,
     That thou, light-winged Dryad of the trees,
     In some melodious plot
     Of beechen tree, and shadows numberless,
10   Singest of summer in full-throated ease.

     O, for a draught of vintage! That hath been
     Cool'd a long age in the deep-delved earth,
     Tasting of Flora and the country green,
     Dance, and Provencal song, and sunburnt mirth!
15   O for a beaker full of the warm South,
     Full of the true, the blushful Hippocrene,
     With beaded bubbles winking at the brim,
     And purple-stained mouth;
     That I might drink, and leave the world unseen,
20   And with thee fade away into the forest dim:

第六章　浪漫主义时期诗歌

  Fade away, dissolve, and quite forget

  What thou among the leaves hast never known,

  The weariness, the fever, and the fret

  Here, where men sit and hear each other groan;

25 Where palsy shakes a few, sad, last gray hairs,

  Where youth grows pale, and spectre-thin, and dies;

  Where but to think is to be full of sorrow

  And leaden-eyed despairs,

  There Beauty cannot keep her lustrous eyes,

30 Or new Love pine at them beyond tomorrow.

  Away! away! for I will fly to thee,

  Not charioted by Bacchus and his pards,

  But on the viewless wings of Poesy,

  Though the dull brain perplexes and retards:

35 Already with thee! tender is the night,

  And haply the Queen-Moon is on her throne,

  Cluster'd around by all her starry Fays;

  But here there is no light,

  Save what from heaven is with the breezes blown

40 Through verdurous glooms and winding mossy ways.

  I cannot see what flowers are at my feet,

  Nor what soft incense hangs upon the boughs,

  But, in embalmed darkness, guess each sweet

  Wherewith the seasonable month endows

45 The grass, the thicket, and the fruit-tree wild;

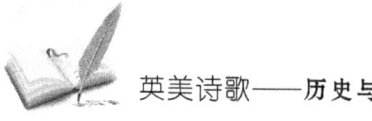

White hawthorn, and the pastoral eglantine;

Fast fading violets cover'd up in leaves;

And mid-May's eldest child,

The coming musk-rose, full of dewy wine,

50 The murmurous haunt of flies on summer eves.

Darkling I listen; and, for many a time

I have been half in love with easeful Death,

Call'd him soft names in many a mused rhyme,

To take into the air my quiet breath;

55 Now more than ever seems it rich to die,

To cease upon the midnight with no pain,

While thou art pouring forth thy soul abroad

In such an ecstasy!

Still wouldst thou sing, and I have ears in vain—

60 To thy high requiem become a sod.

Thou wast not born for death, immortal Bird!

No hungry generations tread thee down;

The voice I hear this passing night was heard

In ancient days by emperor and clown:

65 Perhaps the self-same song that found a path

Through the sad heart of Ruth, when, sick for home,

She stood in tears amid the alien corn;

The same that oft-times hath

Charm'd magic casements, opening on the foam

70　　Of perilous seas, in faery lands forlorn.

　　　　Forlorn! the very word is like a bell
　　　　To toll me back from thee to my sole self!
　　　　Adieu! the fancy cannot cheat so well
　　　　As she is fam'd to do, deceiving elf.
75　　Adieu! adieu! thy plaintive anthem fades
　　　　Past the near meadows, over the still stream,
　　　　Up the hill-side; and now 'tis buried deep
　　　　In the next valley-glades:
　　　　Was it a vision, or a waking dream?
80　　Fled is that music — Do I wake or sleep?

【译文】
夜莺颂
约翰·济慈

1　　我的心疼痛啊，似有一种昏昏欲睡
　　　感官麻木的痛苦，仿佛饮了毒芹，
　　　或吞服了大量的鸦片使全身麻醉，
　　　顷刻之间就向着列斯忘川下沉。
5　　这并非我羡慕你的幸福命运，
　　　而是你的欢乐使我太欢欣，
　　　你呀，如同森林中羽翼轻盈的仙女，
　　　在长满山毛榉的
　　　欢悦之地，在无数的树影里，

10 你放声自由歌唱夏季。

　　哦！我多么想饮一杯葡萄佳酿，
　　它在深掘的地窖里冷藏的年代很久，
　　有乡村的花香和绿野的风光，
　　普罗旺斯的阳光、舞蹈和歌声悠悠。
15 哦！要是能饮上一杯真正的灵泉，
　　来自南国，充溢着殷红和温暖，
　　珍珠般的泡沫在杯沿眨眼，
　　染成紫色的嘴唇闪灿，
　　一杯过肠就悄然离开这个世界，
20 和你一道遁隐到那幽暗的林间。
　　远远地退隐，消融，完全忘却
　　你在枝叶间从不知道的事情，
　　那劳累，那烧热，和那烦忧；
　　这儿，人们坐听着彼此的呻吟；
25 瘫痪老人最后几根悲哀白发在摇晃，
　　年轻人变得苍白、消瘦，最后死亡；
　　这儿，你只要想一想就满腹悲伤，
　　双眼沉重，完全失望；
　　这儿，美难以保持她的双眸发亮，
30 新欢在憔悴，待不到明天。
　　去吧！去吧！因为我将要飞向你，
　　不乘酒神之车，不要群豹驾辕，
　　只乘那无形的诗神羽翼，
　　虽然迟钝的大脑使我困惑、迟缓；

第六章　浪漫主义时期诗歌

35　我早已和你在一起！夜如此温柔，
　　月后也正好登上了她的宝座，
　　四周有璀璨的星仙侍候：
　　但这儿没有亮光，
　　除了从天上吹来的微风，
40　穿过葱绿的幽暗和苔藓曲径。
　　我看不清脚下是什么花草，
　　也辨不清枝头上飘溢的是什么清香，
　　但是，在芬芳的黑暗里我可以猜到
　　五月时节赋予的是什么芬芳
45　给野果树、丛林和绿草；
　　田园里的野蔷薇、白山楂；
　　叶丛下那些易谢的紫罗兰；
　　五月中旬最先开放的宠儿，
　　以及露珠晶莹即将绽放的麝香玫瑰，
50　夏夜蚊蝇，嗡嗡造访的地方。
　　我在黑暗中倾听；曾有多少次
　　我几乎爱上了安逸的"死亡"，
　　多少次在诗中轻轻呼唤你的名字，
　　请你把我的气息带到空中。
55　此刻死去似更富情味，
　　半夜里停止呼吸，没有痛苦，
　　而你仍在倾吐你的心声，
　　如此神醉，如此狂喜！
　　你将一直歌唱，我有耳也听不见——
60　你的安魂曲，如草泥一片。

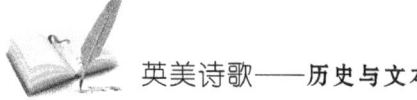

永生的鸟儿啊，你天生不会死去！

没有任何饥饿的一代能把你蹂躏；

我在这消逝的夜晚听到的歌声

古代的帝王和村民也曾聆听；

65　或许就是这同样的一首歌曲

曾使露丝心碎，当她思念家乡，

在异乡的麦地里泪水汪汪；

这同样的歌曲

常把魔窗深深吸引，开着窗扉，

70　在凄凉的仙境，把汹涌的大海眺望。

凄凉啊！这个词的本身犹如钟鸣

把我从你处唤回，回到孤独的自己！

再见！幻想虽有欺骗的名声，但决不能

欺骗得如此巧妙竟能欺骗她自己。

75　再见！再见！你那哀怨的圣歌

飞过附近草地，飘过静谧小溪，

爬上了山坡，此刻它已深藏

在下个山谷的林间空地：

这是幻觉，抑或是醒着做梦？

80　那乐曲消失了：我是醒着还是在睡乡？

（何功杰　译）

【点评】

《夜莺颂》写于1819年。该年5月，济慈住在伦敦汉普斯特德（Hampstead）的一位朋友家里，朋友家门前的一棵李子树上面有个夜莺筑的巢。一天早上，济慈离开餐桌，搬了一把椅子在树下坐了两三个小时，在几张纸上写了一些诗行，后经过朋友整理成为这首名篇佳作。全诗共分

第六章　浪漫主义时期诗歌

八节,每节10行,每节除第8行为三音步抑扬格外,其余均为五音步抑扬格,韵式为 ababcdecde。诗歌运用对比手法,在每一节中诗人的痛苦与幸福自由的夜莺并置,表达了现实世界充满痛苦,但诗人最后选择生活在现实中,表达了诗人热爱生命、积极乐观的人生态度。

济慈八岁丧父,14岁丧母,弟弟因疾病死于他的怀中,由于疾病,济慈被迫与相爱的恋人分手。26岁时因肺痨不治而死于罗马。诗歌一开始诗人描绘自己如"死"一般的痛苦:我的心疼痛啊,似有一种昏昏欲睡感官麻木的痛苦,仿佛饮了毒芹,或吞服了大量的鸦片使全身麻醉,顷刻之间就向着列斯忘川下沉。其中"as though"为明喻标记,诗人连续使用三个比喻(sustained simile),"Lethe"是希腊神话中冥府的一条河流,死者的灵魂喝了这条河的水就忘记生前的一切。在极度痛苦中诗人对夜莺的歌唱做出告白:"'Tis not through envy of thy happy lot/But being too happy in thy happiness"(这并非我羡慕你的幸福命运,而是你的欢乐使我太欢欣),其中"happy"一词被反复使用,在此,诗人运用联觉(synesthesia)手法强调夜莺幸福的歌唱给自己带来幸福的感觉,这与前面的"死"一般的感觉形成对比。接下来诗人采用拟人、隐喻手法赞美夜莺:你呀,如同森林中羽翼轻盈的仙女,在长满山毛榉的欢悦之地,在无数的树影里,放声自由歌唱夏季,其中"Dryad"为希腊神话中的森林女神,这里指代夜莺。

在第二节诗歌中,诗人使用反复的句法结构构成平行:"O, for a draught of vintage!""O for a beaker full of the warm South",表达了希望借美酒的力量进入梦幻世界的强烈愿望,诗人展开想象,夜莺的歌唱让其想到了美酒,只有美酒能让诗人忘记痛苦。它"有乡村的花香和绿野的风光,普罗旺斯的阳光、舞蹈和歌声悠悠。哦!要是能饮上一杯真正的灵泉,来自南国,充溢着殷红和温暖,一杯过肠就悄然离开这个世界,和你一道遁隐到那幽暗的林间。"其中"Flora"为罗马神话中的花神,此处指花香。"Provencal song"指12世纪普鲁旺斯地方行吟诗人的爱情诗歌,第4行诗中运用连词叠用手法列举了酒带来的美好（"Dance, and Provencal song, and sunburnt mirth!"），第5行中的"warm South"指欧洲南部温暖气候下酿出的美酒。第6行的"the blushful Hippocrene"（红色的灵泉）中"Hippocrene"是希腊神话中阿波罗和缪斯的圣地赫利孔山（Helicon）上的灵感的泉源，这里用灵泉的水指代美酒。夜莺美好的歌声让诗人如同饮用了灵泉之水，如痴如醉，忘记了现实中的痛苦，进入夜莺的国度。

在第三诗节里，他又回到了现实世界，这里充满"疲劳、热病和焦躁"。诗人运用五个由"where"引导的平行句式来强调现实世界的苦痛：人们坐听着彼此的呻吟；瘫痪老人最后几根悲哀白发在摇晃，年轻人变得苍白、消瘦，最后死亡；这儿，你只要想一想就满腹悲伤、双眼沉重、完全失望；这儿，美难以保持她的双眸发亮，新欢在憔悴，待不到明天。该诗节于"where"处所使用的反复手法，于第1行诗中的"fade far … forget"和第3行诗中"fever…forget"处使用的头韵，还有拟声词"groan"，连词叠用（"Where youth grows pale, and spectre thin, and dies"）强烈地唱出了诗人在现实世界中苦痛的悲歌。

第四诗节中，诗人一开始运用反复手法，通过"Away! away!"发出号令向夜莺飞去，不是靠酒神和豹子拉拽的车子，而是靠"viewless wings of Poesy"（无形羽翼的诗歌），其中"Bacchus"为希腊神话中的酒神巴克斯，"his pards"是用豹子指代为酒神拉车的老虎或山猫。意象词"Bacchus pards""viewless wings of Poesy""starry Fays""throne""Queen-Moon"（典故、拟人）勾勒出一幅神仙世界的画面。读者不难看到，诗人的卓越的诗才可与夜莺那美妙的歌声媲美，正是这浪漫主义的诗歌让诗人同夜莺一起遨游仙境。

第五诗节里在充满意象的诗行中，诗人陶醉在"温馨的幽暗"的夏夜里。"五月时节赋予的是什么芬芳，给野果树、丛林和绿草；田园里的野蔷薇、白山楂；叶丛下那些易谢的紫罗兰；五月中旬最先开放的宠花，以及露珠晶莹即将绽放的麝香玫瑰，夏夜蚊蝇，嗡嗡造访的地方。"其中"the seasonable month endows"运用拟人修辞，"mid-May's eldest child""dewy

第六章 浪漫主义时期诗歌

wine"运用隐喻修辞,"murmurous haunt"为拟声词。

第六诗节中,诗人就死亡与永恒展开思索,"我"会死去,夜莺仍将歌唱,但没有了"我"同在,夜莺的歌唱将失去意义。第七诗节中,诗人采用大量的意象,借用历史("Thou wast not born for death, immortal Bird""No hungry generations tread thee down""The voice I hear this passing night was heard""In ancient days by emperor and clown")中世纪神话("Charm'd magic casements, opening on the foam/ Of perilous seas, in faery lands forlorn")、圣经典故("Through the sad heart of Ruth, when, sick for home/She stood in tears amid the alien corn/The same that oft-times hath")指出流浪人的心总是向往回归,诗人借类比说明,虽然随着夜莺美妙的歌声来到仙界,但心总归要回到现实世界。第八诗节中诗人运用明喻("Forlorn! the very word is like a bell/To toll me back from thee to my sole self!")结束心灵的幻想之旅,回归现实中的自己。诗人连用三个"别了!"(adieu!)告诉自己,这是个幻觉,其中"那歌声去了"指歌唱的夜莺飞远,诗人的心灵也不再翱翔,这一切像是一场梦。

诗歌中意象丰富,三界(现实世界、冥界、仙界)的空间感使得诗歌富有张力,深化了诗歌的内涵,令人回味。诗人采用大量修辞手法——尾韵、头韵、明喻、隐喻、典故、拟人、反复、排比、对比等,使得诗歌语言精美,意境典雅、哀婉,展现了诗人对理想与现实、短暂与永恒、幸福与痛苦及生命与死亡的深刻思索。

(七)To Autumn

John Keats

1 Season of mists and mellow fruitfulness,
　　Close bosom-friend of the maturing sun;

Conspiring with him how to load and bless

With fruit the vines that round the thatch-eaves run;

5 To bend with apples the moss'd cottage-trees,

And fill all fruit with ripeness to the core;

To swell the gourd, and plump the hazel shells

With a sweet kernel; to set budding more,

And still more, later flowers for the bees,

10 Until they think warm days will never cease,

For summer has o'er-brimm'd their clammy cells.

Who hath not seen thee oft amid thy store?

Sometimes whoever seeks abroad may find

Thee sitting careless on a granary floor,

15 Thy hair soft-lifted by the winnowing wind;

Or on a half-reap'd furrow sound asleep,

Drows'd with the fume of poppies, while thy hook

Spares the next swath and all its twined flowers;

And sometimes like a gleaner thou dost keep;

20 Steady thy laden head across a brook;

Or by a cider-press, with patient look,

Thou Watchest the last oozings hours by hours.

Where are the songs of Spring? Ay, where are they?

Think not of them, thou hast thy music too,—

25 While barred clouds bloom the soft-dying day,

And touch the stubble-plains with rosy hue;

第六章　浪漫主义时期诗歌

　　Then in a wailful choir the small gnats mourn
　　Among the river-sallows, borne aloft
　　Or sinking as the light wind lives or dies;
30　And full-grown lambs loud bleat from hilly bourn;
　　Hedge-crickets sing; and now with treble soft
　　The red-breast whistles from a garden-croft;
　　And gathering swallows twitter in the skies.

【译文】
秋颂
约翰·济慈

1　迷雾浓浓的季节，甘果累累的金秋！
　　成熟的太阳，亲密而衷心的朋友；
　　你和太阳默默祝福，秘密筹谋
　　如何叫屋檐下四周的藤蔓挂满硕果；
5　如何把屋旁长满苔藓的苹果树压弯，
　　用熟透的果汁把所有果实装满；
　　让葫芦膨胀，用甜蜜的果仁把榛果
　　鼓得圆圆；让蓓蕾越来越多，
　　叫迟开的花朵为蜜蜂开放，
10　直到他们以为日子会永远温暖；
　　因为夏日填满了他们黏糊的蜂房。

　　谁没看见你常在丰收的谷仓中间？
　　有时人们外出时会发现

你坐在打谷场上，快活悠闲，
15 你的头发被扬谷的风轻轻吹起；
或者在收割完一半的垄沟里沉睡，
那是罂粟花香使你昏睡，搁下镰刀，
留下了下一畦庄稼和缠结的花草；
有时，你像一位拾谷穗的小孩，
20 头上稳稳顶着一筐谷穗从小溪走过，
或者连续几小时站在榨果机旁
耐心观看，直到流尽最后一滴果浆。

春天的歌在哪里，啊，在哪里？
你也有自己的歌，何必把他们缅怀——
25 当彩云叫慢慢逝去的一天花开天际，
把满是残梗的田野染成玫瑰色彩，
各种小昆虫就会出现在河畔的柳林里
举行大合唱，音调哀婉，
声音随风起落，时高时低；
30 完全成熟的羊羔在山头上咩咩叫唤，
蟋蟀在篱边歌唱，知更鸟
在园林里啾啾，柔和而高亢，
成群的燕子在空中鸣啭呢喃。

(何功杰　译)

【点评】

《秋颂》是济慈的名作之一，全诗共三节，每节 11 行，采用五音部抑扬格。第一节韵式为 ababcdedcce，第二、三节为 ababcdecdde。诗人调动人们的视觉、触觉、听觉等几个方面，分别写了秋天的色彩、秋天的人

第六章　浪漫主义时期诗歌

及秋天的声音，描绘出一幅美好的秋日画面。

一开始诗人运用拟人手法，将雾气霭霭、硕果累累的秋天拟化为太阳的密友（"Season of mists and mellow fruitfulness/Close bosom-friend of the maturing sun"），诗中的抽象名词"fruitfulness"指代（metonymy）具体的果实，前两行中的"mists""maturing""mellow"为行内与行间头韵，"maturing""mellow"为同义反复（tautology），其中"maturing sun"乃为移就修辞。不难看出，一开始诗人就借用多种修辞格来描摹秋天，语言华丽，意境美好。接下来诗人继续勾画："你和太阳默默祝福，秘密筹谋如何叫屋檐下的葡萄藤挂上硕果；如何把屋旁长满苔藓的苹果树压弯，用熟透的果汁把所有果实装满；让葫芦膨胀，用甜蜜的果仁把榛果鼓得圆圆；让蓓蕾越来越多，叫迟开的花朵为蜜蜂开放，直到他们以为日子会永远温暖。"第一诗节中诗人采用大量修辞手法，运用丰富的意象词描绘出一幅植物与唯一动物——"蜜蜂"都硕果累累的动态的大自然秋季画面，此时，济慈笔下，一切都散发着生机。

在第二诗节中，诗人描绘出一幅丰收的景象。将"秋"拟人，采用了英国乡村劳动者各种常见的形象："你常在丰收的谷仓中间""你坐在打谷场上""或者在收割完一半的垄沟里沉睡""有时，你像一位拾谷穗的小孩，头上稳稳顶着一筐谷穗从小溪走过；或者连续几小时站在榨果机旁耐心观看，直到流尽最后一滴果浆。"诗人提到"那是罂粟花香使你昏睡，搁下镰刀，留下了下一畦庄稼和缠结的花草"，罂粟花让人想到鸦片，有麻醉作用，这是否和诗人平时吃的药物相关？另外，虽然丰收，但沉重的收割对劳动者来说是极其疲惫的，躺在地里就睡着了（"sound asleep"），这里的沉睡是否还让诗人想到不久以后，自己也会沉睡于这块大地上？这里"睡"的含义丰富，人文内涵深厚。诗中的"拾穗人"与圣经《路得记》中的路得形象吻合，同时与《夜莺颂》中的圣经典故互文。最后的两句"Or by a cider-press, with patient look/Thou Watchest the last

-183-

oozings hours by hours"意象"cider-press"和"oozings hours by hours"与圣经《启示录》第22章第一段互文〔"天使又指示我在城内街道当中一道生命水的河,明亮如水晶,从上帝和羔羊的宝座流出来。"("榨汁机"对应宝座,"流出的果酱汁"对应生命水的河)〕。此时诗人是否在自己的灵魂里已经进入另一个世界,满了生命的新天地。另外,"the last oozings hours by hours"也暗指诗人意识到自己不久将离开人世。此画面中,秋天、劳动者、果实、大地与诗人的幻想融为一体,展现了诗人整体性的生态意识及对造物主的赞美及新生命的期盼。

第三个诗节中,诗歌一开始呼唤春天("Where are the songs of Spring? Ay, where are they?"),诗人运用春天与秋天对比的手法,突出秋天也有自己的色彩。"While barred clouds bloom the soft-dying day/And touch the stubble-plains with rosy hue"此两句诗描绘了天空的彩云和落日下玫瑰色的田野。诗人又描绘了一幅动态的秋天的动物景象:"各种小昆虫就会出现在河畔的柳林里举行大合唱,音调哀婉,声音随风起落,时高时低;完全成熟的羊羔在山头上咩咩叫唤,蟋蟀在篱边歌唱,知更鸟在园林里啾啾,柔和而高亢,成群的燕子在空中鸣啭呢喃。"整个诗节的画面丰满,虽透露着悲秋的语气,但也带有期盼。蟋蟀只在秋天呢喃,其歌唱短暂,但是成群的燕子虽在冬天飞往南方,但在生机盎然的春天还会再回来。

《秋颂》是诗人在生命晚期谱写的一首生命交响曲,是用他对生命和自然的挚爱谱写出的华丽而又朴素的天地合一、生态和谐的乐章。

(八) The Human Seasons

John Keats

1　Four Seasons fill the measure of the year;
　　There are four seasons in the mind of man

第六章　浪漫主义时期诗歌

　　He has his lusty Spring, when fancy clear
　　Takes in all beauty with an easy span:
5　He has his Summer, when luxuriously
　　Spring's honey'd cud of youthful thought he loves
　　To ruminate, and by such dreaming high
　　His nearest unto heaven: quiet coves

　　His soul has in its Autumn, when his wings
10　He furleth close; contented so to look
　　On mists in idleness——to let fair things
　　Pass by unheeded as a threshold brook:

　　He has his Winter too of pale misfeature,
　　Or else he would forego his mortal nature.

【译文】
人生四季
约翰·济慈

1　春夏秋冬把一年的时间填满，
　　人的心灵也拥有四个季节。
　　在朝气蓬勃的春天，清晰的幻想
　　一瞬间就把所有的美轻易包揽。

5　在他的夏天，他喜欢用年轻思想
　　把春天里采的花蜜反复酝酿，

细细品味蜜汁的甘甜芳香,
　　乘着这高远的梦想冲天而飞。

　　在他心灵丰盈的秋天,
10　他心满意足地收拢翅膀,
　　悠闲地凝视着朦胧般美好的事物
　　犹如门前的小溪轻轻淌过。

　　他也有满目苍凉的冬天,
　　除非他走在命定的劫数之前。

（郭　嘉　译）

【点评】

　　本诗为十四行诗,全诗共分四个诗节,前三个诗节为四行,最后一节为两行,整个诗歌结构蕴含着作者对人生四季的理解。如果前三个诗节代表春夏秋,那么其生命是饱满的;最后一个诗节如果代表冬天,那么它是萧条的、生命力欠缺的。整首诗韵式为:abab cdcd efef gg。

　　一开始诗人采用类比（analogy）手法指出,一年有春夏秋冬四个季节,同样,人生亦有四季。人有朝气蓬勃的春天,在这个季节,人的想象力丰富,可以瞬间将所有的美一览无余。第1～2行诗中"measure""mind""man"为行间与行内头韵,"Spring"一词为隐喻手法。第3,4行诗"He has his lusty Spring, when fancy clear/Takes in all beauty with an easy span"中"lusty""fancy"为尾部元音韵,"beauty""easy"为元音韵。

　　第二个诗节以反复"He has his"及隐喻手法进入夏季（"Summer"）,在人生的夏季,人进入青年期,喜欢思考,喜欢把春天的花蜜反复酝酿,细细品味蜜汁的甘甜芳香,乘着梦想的翅膀冲天而飞。第2行诗中的

第六章 浪漫主义时期诗歌

"Spring"与第一节的春季呼应，两节诗歌的衔接性强，体现了生命的连续性。第 1 行中"Summer""luxuriously"为母韵，第 2 行中的"honey'd cud""loves"与第 3 行中的"ruminate"、第 4 行中的"coves"为行内及行间母韵，整个第二诗节中 /ʌ/ 音的重复，彰显了夏季人生的生命力与活力。

第三个诗节中诗人采用隐喻手法进入秋季（"Autumn"），突出了人生进入秋季的不同，这个季节主要指心智上的成熟，亦即内在灵魂生命的提升。在心灵丰盈的秋天，他心满意足，悠闲地凝视着朦胧般美好的事物，犹如门前的小溪轻轻淌过。第 1～2 行中的收拢自己的翅膀（"when his wings/He furleth close"）与第二诗节中的"乘着这高远的梦想冲天而飞"互为衔接，第 1 行"soul"与第 3～4 行中的"close""so, to, look""On""to""threshold""brook"一起为母韵 /əu/、/u/。其中"close""contented"为头韵，第 3～4 行的"mists""unheede"押母韵，第 4 行中"as a threshold brook"为明喻，诗人将灵魂生命成熟的季节——"Autumn"——与意象——"门前小溪"——并置在一起，这与圣经《启示录》第二十二章第 1 段的意象互文，"天使又指示我在城内街道当中一道生命水的河" 象征诗人对生命超验的一种较为成熟的理解，表达了诗人对造物主的赞美之情，切合了济慈生死哲学的理念，亦即死亡仅仅是重生的开始，符合其基督教信仰的核心，即"出死入生"。

最后两句诗诗人一笔勾过了人生的冬季（"Winter"）：满目苍凉。隐含着诗人对生命的哲思，即尘世的人生短暂，肉体终将逝去，只有一种情况除外，那就是"除非他走在命定的劫数之前"。这两行诗透露出凄凉的氛围，但好在前三个季节中，有"春"的幻想，"夏"的思想与梦的飞翔，"秋"丰盈的灵魂生命。从济慈出死入生的哲学观看，"秋"似乎更具生命的希望，这与作者的《秋颂》不谋而合。

(九) On the Grasshopper and Cricket

John Keats

1 The poetry of earth is never dead:
  When all the birds are faint with the hot sun,
  And hide in cooling trees, a voice will run
  From hedge to hedge about the new-mown mead;
5 That is the Grasshopper's—he takes the lead
  In summer luxury , —he has never done
  With his delights; for when tired out with fun
  He rests at ease beneath some pleasant weed.
  The poetry of earth is ceasing never:
10 On a lone winter evening, when the frost
  Has wrought a silence, from the stove there shrills
  The Cricket's song, in warmth increasing ever,
  And seems to one in drowsiness half lost,
  The Grasshopper's among some grassy hills.

【译文】

蝈蝈与蛐蛐

    约翰·济慈

1 大地的诗歌绵绵不息,
  当小鸟在烈日中露出倦容,

第六章 浪漫主义时期诗歌

　　躲进绿荫中小憩，一阵歌声

　　沿着树篱，从新刈的草地传出，

5　那是蝈蝈的歌，它领唱于

　　仲夏的华筵；它欢快地唱着，

　　总也唱不完，兴尽曲罢，

　　便悠然歇息于芳草丛中。

　　大地的诗歌此起彼伏，

10　在凄冷的冬晨，当严霜织出一片静谧，

　　炉边传出蛐蛐的细声歌唱，

　　它们在炉火的温煦中越唱越欢，

　　使人坠入梦境，幻觉不断，

　　仿佛那蝈蝈鸣唱于青翠的山峦。

（刘守兰　译）

【点评】

　　本诗为十四行诗，押韵格式为：abba abba cde ecd。诗歌借小鸟、蝈蝈与蛐蛐三个动物意象谱写了一曲大自然生命的赞歌。

　　一开始，诗人运用隐喻点出：大地的诗歌绵绵不息（"The poetry of earth is never dead"），通过下文可知"poetry"指的是大自然动物的歌唱，显然诗人运用拟人手法，首先描写了大家熟知并擅长歌唱的鸟儿（"When all the birds are faint with the hot sun/ And hide in cooling trees"），但诗人只在时间状语中描绘了一幅倦鸟归林的画面，整个主句归给了"Grasshopper"，在树篱、草地中，他领唱于仲夏的华筵，欢快地唱着，总也唱不完，兴尽曲罢，便悠然歇息于芳草丛中。三个平行加反复的句式"he takes the lead" "he has never done" "He rests at ease"强调突出了"Grasshopper"在夏天大自然的主体地位。第9行诗与第1行诗为反复手法（"The poetry

of earth is ceasing never"），诗人只是改变了一个单词（"ceasing"），起到了强调和突出主题及引领下文的作用。接下来诗人又描写了冬天的诗歌（"The Cricket's song"）。在凄冷的冬晨，当严霜织出一片静谧，炉边传出蛐蛐的细声歌唱（"On a lone winter evening, when the frost/Has wrought a silence, from the stove there shrills"），诗人运用移就、拟人及拟声手法渲染了冬天的氛围、内心的感受及大自然的声音。最后，诗人运用明喻手法指出蛐蛐欢欣的歌唱让人温暖，幻觉不断，仿佛听到了夏天在清脆的山峦中歌唱的"Grasshopper"（"The Cricket's song, in warmth increasing ever/And seems to one in drowsiness half lost/The Grasshopper's among some grassy hills"）。

　　整首诗歌首尾呼应，衔接性强。诗人象征性地运用两个微不足道的生灵（"Grasshopper"和"Cricket"）、两个季节（夏天与冬天）的交叉描绘出一幅大自然生命万象与生命不息的画面。诗人借助丰富的想象力，将人、自然和谐地勾画在一起，"never dead"与"ceasing never"传递出永恒的意蕴，表面上看似是对大自然生态和谐的赞美，实则洋溢着诗人对造物主的歌颂。

第七章　维多利亚时期诗歌

第七章　维多利亚时期诗歌

　　维多利亚女王（1819—1901）执政期间，英国国力昌盛。这一时期，随着大工业革命的到来，各种科技发明与技术创新为英国经济带来繁荣。人们面对经济发展和科学进步却存在着社会心理上浓重的悲观主义和焦躁不安的情绪。在繁荣与财富的掩盖下，阶级矛盾日益尖锐，1836—1848年，发起了英国历史上著名的宪章运动。

　　维多利亚时代追求自尊、谦逊、爱国的民族精神，是一个重视伦理道德的时代，因此，对于伦理道德问题的关注成为这一时期文学创作的一个基本特征。作家关注社会发展中面临的问题，在作品中针砭时弊，惩恶扬善。在19世纪后30年中，大英帝国与维多利亚价值观都逐渐走向衰落，世纪末伤感主义盛行，以王尔德为代表的唯美主义文学家都极力推崇"为了艺术而艺术"（Art for art's sake）的观点。这一时期科学的发展与各个领域的新发现与传统的宗教信仰产生摩擦，精神道德信仰日渐式微。这个时期的诗歌以阿尔弗雷德·丁尼生（Alfred Tennyson）和罗伯特·勃朗宁（Robert Browning）为代表，表现出典雅、凝重的诗风。

　　阿尔弗雷德·丁尼生是英国维多利亚时代最具代表性的诗人，继华兹

华斯之后被封为桂冠诗人。他十分注重诗歌的思想性、艺术性和音乐感召力。诗歌内容健康、语言高雅，注重语言形式和音韵之美，代表作有《尤利西斯》（*Ulysses*），《悼念集》（*In Memoriam A. H. H*，1850）。

诗人罗伯特·勃朗宁对英国诗歌的最大贡献是发展和完善了戏剧独白诗（Dramatic monologue）。勃朗宁夫人伊丽莎白·巴雷特·勃朗宁（Elizabeth Barrett Browning）学识渊博，善于思考。他们夫妻合著的作品是《葡语十四行诗集》（*Sonnets from the Portuguese*）。这一时期还出现了"前拉斐尔派诗人"，主要代表人物有丹蒂·加布里埃尔·罗塞蒂（Dante Gabriel Rossetti，1828—1882）及其天才妹妹克里斯蒂娜·罗塞蒂（Christina Rossett，1830—1894）。克里斯蒂娜是英国文学史上最有才华的女诗人之一，与勃朗宁夫人齐名，她的诗用词清纯、简练、情感真挚，宗教与爱情是贯穿克里斯蒂娜一生的两条精神主线。

一、Poem Reading

（一）Break, Break, Break

Alfred Lord Tennyson

1　Break, break, break,
　　On thy cold gray stones, O Sea!
　　And I would that my tongue could utter
　　The thoughts that arise in me.

5　O, well for the fisherman's boy,
　　That he shouts with his sister at play!
　　O, well for the sailor lad,

第七章 维多利亚时期诗歌

That he sings in his boat on the bay!

And the stately ships go on

10　To their haven under the hill;

But O for the touch of a vanished hand,

And the sound of a voice that is still!

Break, break, break,

At the foot of thy crags, O Sea!

15　But the tender grace of a day that is dead

Will never come back to me.

1837 年,维多利亚女王继承了叔叔威廉四世的王位,开始了历史上的维多利亚时期。维多利亚统治时期,英国加快了由农业国家转变为工业强国的进程。统计结果显示,到 1851 年,英国城镇的居民数量就已经超过了农业人口。工业化和城市化催生了一个普遍的社会问题:在农业社会转向工业社会的环境中该如何定位个人、确定个人和社会的关系?而这也成为维多利亚时期的文学所探讨的主要问题之一。因此,孤独感、隔离感和边缘化成为这一时期诗歌的重要主题,而着重探讨人精神领域的活动也成为这一时期诗歌与浪漫主义时期的重要区别。这正是阿尔弗雷德·丁尼生(1809—1892)写作的背景。

Break, break, break 这首诗写作于 1835 年,出版于 1842 年。1834 年圣诞节期间,诗人满心期待地来到林肯郡(Lincolnshire)和朋友共度节日,然而却受到了朋友的冷落。强烈的孤独感促使他写成了该诗。诗歌开篇便呈现了冰冷的海水猛烈拍击灰色岩石的场景,让读者感受到了无限的悲凉。此时的诗人是心有千头万绪,张口却难道其一("And I would(wish)that my tongue could utter/The thoughts that arise in me")。在第二个诗节中,

诗人描写了两个鲜明活泼的形象——和姐姐嬉戏玩耍的渔夫的儿子,以及小船上引吭高歌的年轻水手。他们的欢愉和诗人的悲伤形成强烈的对比,突显了诗人的孤独感。

除了表达孤独的情绪,该诗还饱含了对已故亡友亚瑟亨利哈勒姆(Arthur Henry Hallam)的悼念。哈勒姆是诗人早年在剑桥读书时的同学,他的才华和气度深深吸引着丁尼生,两人很快建立了深厚的友谊。哈勒姆后来和丁尼生的妹妹埃米莉(Emily)订婚。然而,在1833年,哈勒姆在维也纳游玩时突发脑溢血,去世的时候只有22岁。诗人在极度悲伤的情绪下,写作了诗集 *In Memoriam*,用以寄托哀思。*Break, break, break* 也有明显的哀歌色彩。在第三个诗节中,和前两行描写的安全进入港湾的航船形成对比,诗人笔锋一转描写了丧友之痛:再也碰触不到那双手、再也听不到他的声音!("But O for the touch of a vanished hand/And the sound of a voice that is still!")

诗人往往借助诗中描写的景物抒发情感,该诗中的主要景物是在第一个诗节和最后一个诗节中提到的海浪猛烈拍击岩石的场景。然而,这一场景并未随着诗人悲伤情绪的升华而有所改变,开篇的海浪和结尾的海浪一样,机械地、冷漠地敲击着岩石。由此看来,该诗的另一个主题是自然界对个人情感和命运的冷漠和无情。该主题是对前文中叙述的个人和社会之间关系的一种折射,冷漠的自然和冷酷的工业社会化为一体,将个人的悲伤和孤独感推到了顶点。难怪诗人在诗歌结尾处会感叹:那美好的日子一去再不复返!("But the tender grace of a day that is dead/Will never come back to me.")

整首诗分为四个诗节,每个诗节中第2行和第4行压尾韵,诗中韵脚的运用并不规律,不过大量抑抑扬格(anapaest)的应用使诗歌读起来节奏感很强,营造出类似海浪拍击声的效果。例如:

iambic   anapaest   anapaest   anapaest

第七章 维多利亚时期诗歌

But O / for the touch / of a van / （n）ished hand,

anapaest　　　anapaest　　anapaest

And the sound / of a voice / that is still!

同样为了音律美，诗人还在行文中应用了大量的头韵（alliteration）。例如，第三个诗节中"stately"和"ships"、"haven"和"hill"、"sound"和"still"都为头韵，读起来朗朗上口。另外，诗歌还运用了其他的修辞手法，像是顿呼（apostrophe）、拟人、对比等。例如，在诗歌的第一行"Break, break, break"中，诗人就将海浪拟人化，对其大声疾呼。所以，诗歌虽然短小，但就其写作技巧和主题来说，诗人别具匠心、对每一个细节都考虑地<u>丝丝</u>入扣。

（二）My Last Duchess

Robert Browning

Ferrara

1　That's my last Duchess painted on the wall,

　　Looking as if she were alive. I call

　　That piece a wonder, now: Fra Pandolf's hands

　　Worked busily a day, and there she stands.

5　Will't please you sit and look at her? I said

　　"Fra Pandolf" by design, for never read

　　Strangers like you that pictured countenance,

　　The depth and passion of its earnest glance,

　　But to myself they turned（since none puts by

10　The curtain I have drawn for you, but I）

　　And seemed as they would ask me, if they durst,

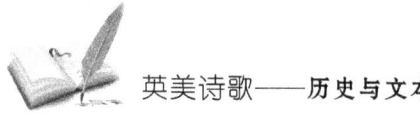

How such a glance came there; so, not the first

Are you to turn and ask thus. Sir, 'twas not

Her husband's presence only, called that spot

15　Of joy into the Duchess' cheek: perhaps

Fra Pandolf chanced to say "Her mantle laps

Over my lady's wrist too much", or "Paint

Must never hope to reproduce the faint

Half-flush that dies along her throat": such stuff

20　Was courtesy, she thought, and cause enough

For calling up that spot of joy. She had

A heart—how shall I say?—too soon made glad,

Too easily impressed; she liked whate'er

She looked on, and her looks went everywhere.

25　Sir, 'twas all one! My favor at here breast.

The dropping of daylight in the West,

The bough of cherries some officious fool

Broke in the orchard for her, the white mule

She rode with round the terrace—all and each

30　Would draw from her alike the approving speech,

Or blush, at least. She thanked men—good! But thanked

Somehow—I know not how—as if she ranked

My gift of a nine-hundred-years-old name

With anybody's gift. Who'd stoop to blame

35　This sort of trifling? Even had you skill

In speech—(which I have not)—to make your will

Quite clear to such an one, and say, "Just this

第七章　维多利亚时期诗歌

Or that in you disgusts me; here you miss,

Or there exceed the mark" —and if she let

40　Herself be lessoned so, nor plainly set

Her wits to yours, forsooth, and made excuse

—E'en then would be some stooping; and I choose

Never to stoop. Oh sir, she smiled, no doubt,

Whene'er I passed her; but who passed without

45　Much the same smile? This grew; I gave commands;

Then all smiles stopped together. There she stands

As if alive. Will't please you rise? We'll meet

The company below, then. I repeat,

The Count your master's known munificence

50　Is ample warrant that no just pretense

Of min for dowry will be disallowed;

Though his fair daughter's self, as I avowed

At starting, is my object. Nay, we'll go

Together down, sir. Notice Neptune, though,

55　Taming a sea horse, thought a rarity,

Which Claus of Innsbruck cast in bronze for me!

罗伯特·勃朗宁（1812—1889）是和丁尼生齐名的维多利亚诗人。与丁尼生不同的是，勃朗宁写作更加注重内容的呈现，从而在一定程度上忽略诗歌形式的细节问题。另外，勃朗宁的诗歌更多地探讨了人性以及人的思维活动。随着丁尼生后期诗歌创作力不足，勃朗宁的名气更是跃居这位桂冠诗人之上。勃朗宁在诗歌中对人性黑暗面的描写（*Pippa Passes, The Ring and the Book, My Last Duchess* 等），以及他的妻子伊丽莎白·芭蕾特·勃

朗宁（Elizabeth Barrett Browning）写作的《爱情十四行诗》（*Sonnets from the Portuguese*）成为维多利亚诗歌里两道独特的风景线。在诗歌写作技巧上，勃朗宁所做的最大贡献是将戏剧独白（dramatic monologue）的形式引入了诗歌的创作之中，*My Last Duchess* 就是诗人将戏剧独白和诗歌进行完美结合的典范之一。诗文韵律简单统一，是由28对押韵的对句组成，每行诗文均为五步抑扬格（iambic pentameter）。

1842年，该诗初次发表于诗人的诗集《戏剧抒情诗》（*Dramatic Lyrics*）之中。诗文前面的"费拉拉共和国"（Ferrara）点明了故事中公爵的现实身份。据推测，公爵真实姓名为阿方索·德埃斯特二世（Alfonso II d'Este），是意大利费拉拉共和国第五代公爵。他于25岁时迎娶了14岁的新娘卢克雷齐娅（Lucrezia）。卢克雷齐娅的家庭出身并不显赫，婚后被丈夫冷落，并在结婚不到三年的时候去世了。外界推测卢克雷齐娅是被公爵下毒害死。随后，公爵又娶了一位出身显赫的伯爵的女儿。该诗完全由公爵的独白组成，假想的听众是为公爵第二桩婚姻牵线的媒人。诗文开始时，公爵正带着媒人参观城堡中的艺术品，包括隐藏在窗帘之后的已故公爵夫人的画像。从行文的第21～23行可以明确看出，他认为公爵夫人生性十分轻浮（"She had/A heart—how shall I say?—too soon made glad /Too easily impressed"），而且轻视自己的家族荣誉（第32～33行："as if she ranked/My gift of a nine-hundred-years-old name/With anybody's gift"）。公爵最终不能容忍已故夫人的行径，而派人杀死她（第45～46行："I gave commands/Then all smiles stopped together）。讲完这个故事之后，公爵邀请媒人起身继续欣赏另一艺术青铜雕塑——海神驯服一匹海马。

从故事的表层来看，诗人讲述的是一个谋杀案：控制欲极强、疑心重重的公爵杀死了年轻美丽无辜的妻子。无论是诗人崇尚的复兴时期的意大利社会，还是维多利亚社会，它们都是男权占主导地位的，女性只能处于被动的、受欺压的地位，而这似乎是诗人所不齿的。从公爵的自述能够判

第七章 维多利亚时期诗歌

断出,妻子轻薄的性格完全是他想象出来的。行文的第43～45行,公爵讲到:"she smiled, no doubt/Whene'er I passed her; but who passed without/ Much the same smile? This grew",公爵夫人的笑容是他判断的主要根据。所谓男性自尊心又让公爵拒绝为妻子提醒(第42～43行:"and I choose/ Never to Stoop")。由此看来,公爵不仅疑心重、控制欲强,而且坚信男性的地位是高于女性的,而这正是悲剧发生的直接原因。如果深层解读,不难发现诗人其实是在隐喻当时社会对个人发展的压抑。工业的发展和科学的进步,给当时的人带来了生活和信仰上的巨大冲击,他们竭力调整自己的意识形态以适应当时的变革。而为了维护统治而故步自封的维多利亚王朝对这种调整持否定,甚至打击的态度。所以,如果公爵和其家族荣誉隐喻了维多利亚王庭,被杀死的公爵夫人则成为难以突破旧我的维多利亚时期的个人。正因如此,为了扩大讽刺面、使诗歌具有时代性,诗人在使用真实故事的同时,编造了两个艺术家Fra Pandolf(第3行)和Claus of lnnsbruck(第56行)。

戏剧独白的诗歌有三个条件:独白者不是诗人,有一个不出场的听众,独白能够彰显独白者的性格特征。正是因为诗人从第三人称的角度呈现戏剧独白的诗文,便要求读者能够将独白中的信息串联起来,推断出故事的来龙去脉和独白者的性格特征。从这个角度看,戏剧独白式的诗歌的确能够使读者更主动地参与到诗文的赏析之中。这样,在赏析诗文的同时,读者就更有可能意识到诗歌的深层含义和讽刺意味。该诗还为读者提出了一个问题:艺术是否含有任何道德因素?这和与勃朗宁同时代的夏尔·波德莱尔(Charles Baudelaire)以及英国20世纪的作家奥斯卡·王尔德所宣扬的唯美主义(aestheticism)又有不谋而合之处。需要指出的是,诗歌的行文中大量使用了诗句的跨行连续(enjambment),加之其涉及的公爵阴暗心理的描写,已经颇有即将流行于20世纪的意识流的写作特点。

英美诗歌——历史与文本

（三）Goblin Market

Christina Georgina Rossetti

1 Morning and evening

  Maids heard the goblins cry:

  "Come buy our orchard fruits,

  Come buy, come buy:

5 Apples and quinces,

  Lemons and oranges,

  Plump unpeck'd cherries,

  Melons and raspberries,

  Bloom-down-cheek'd peaches,

10 Swart-headed mulberries,

  Wild free-born cranberries,

  Crab-apples, dewberries,

  Pine-apples, blackberries,

  Apricots, strawberries;—

15 All ripe together

  In summer weather,—

  Morns that pass by,

  Fair eves that fly;

  Come buy, come buy:

20 Our grapes fresh from the vine,

  Pomegranates full and fine,

  Dates and sharp bullaces,

第七章　维多利亚时期诗歌

　　Rare pears and greengages,

　　Damsons and bilberries,

25　Taste them and try:

　　Currants and gooseberries,

　　Bright-fire-like barberries,

　　Figs to fill your mouth,

　　Citrons from the South,

30　Sweet to tongue and sound to eye;

　　Come buy, come buy."

　　Evening by evening

　　Among the brookside rushes,

　　Laura bow'd her head to hear,

35　Lizzie veil'd her blushes:

　　Crouching close together

　　In the cooling weather,

　　With clasping arms and cautioning lips,

　　With tingling cheeks and finger tips.

40　"Lie close," Laura said,

　　Pricking up her golden head:

　　"We must not look at goblin men,

　　We must not buy their fruits:

　　Who knows upon what soil they fed

45　Their hungry thirsty roots?"

　　"Come buy," call the goblins

　　Hobbling down the glen.

......

But sweet-tooth Laura spoke in haste:
50 "Good folk, I have no coin;
To take were to purloin:
I have no copper in my purse,
I have no silver either,
And all my gold is on the furze
55 That shakes in windy weather
Above the rusty heather."
"You have much gold upon your head,"
They answer'd all together:
"Buy from us with a golden curl."
60 She clipp'd a precious golden lock,
She dropp'd a tear more rare than pearl,
Then suck'd their fruit globes fair or red:
Sweeter than honey from the rock,
Stronger than man-rejoicing wine,
65 Clearer than water flow'd that juice;
She never tasted such before,
How should it cloy with length of use?
She suck'd and suck'd and suck'd the more
Fruits which that unknown orchard bore;
70 She suck'd until her lips were sore;
Then flung the emptied rinds away
But gather'd up one kernel stone,
And knew not was it night or day

As she turn'd home alone.

75 ......

Tender Lizzie could not bear

To watch her sister's cankerous care

Yet not to share.

She night and morning

80 Caught the goblins' cry:

"Come buy our orchard fruits,

Come buy, come buy;" —

Beside the brook, along the glen,

She heard the tramp of goblin men,

85 The yoke and stir

Poor Laura could not hear;

Long'd to buy fruit to comfort her,

But fear'd to pay too dear.

She thought of Jeanie in her grave,

90 Who should have been a bride;

But who for joys brides hope to have

Fell sick and died

In her gay prime,

In earliest winter time

95 With the first glazing rime,

With the first snow-fall of crisp winter time.

......

One may lead a horse to water,

Twenty cannot make him drink.

100　Though the goblins cuff'd and caught her,

　　　Coax'd and fought her,

　　　Bullied and besought her,

　　　Scratch'd her, pinch'd her black as ink,

　　　Kick'd and knock'd her,

105　Maul'd and mock'd her,

　　　Lizzie utter'd not a word;

　　　Would not open lip from lip

　　　Lest they should cram a mouthful in:

　　　But laugh'd in heart to feel the drip

110　Of juice that syrupp'd all her face,

　　　And lodg'd in dimples of her chin,

　　　And streak'd her neck which quaked like curd.

　　　……

　　　Days, weeks, months, years

115　Afterwards, when both were wives

　　　With children of their own;

　　　Their mother-hearts beset with fears,

　　　Their lives bound up in tender lives;

　　　Laura would call the little ones

120　And tell them of her early prime,

　　　Those pleasant days long gone

　　　Of not-returning time:

　　　Would talk about the haunted glen,

　　　The wicked, quaint fruit-merchant men,

125　Their fruits like honey to the throat

第七章 维多利亚时期诗歌

> But poison in the blood;
> (Men sell not such in any town):
> Would tell them how her sister stood
> In deadly peril to do her good,
> 130 And win the fiery antidote:
> Then joining hands to little hands
> Would bid them cling together,
> "For there is no friend like a sister
> In calm or stormy weather;
> 135 To cheer one on the tedious way,
> To fetch one if one goes astray,
> To lift one if one totters down,
> To strengthen whilst one stands."

维多利亚中期，随着科技和工业的继续发展，宗教信仰失去了原有的魔力，社会各个层面都出现了动荡。古老的认知方式已经不适应科技视角下的社会，新的叙述方式呼之欲出。正是在这种背景下，维多利亚中期给世人呈现了三个大师级的叙述高手：查尔斯·达尔文（Charles Darwin），卡尔·马克思（Karl Marx）和西格蒙德·弗洛伊德（Sigmund Freud），他们分别从生物进化论、政治学和心理学领域试图把即将破碎的认知领域重新拼贴起来。这也是维多利亚中期小说的主旨之一：竭力将中产阶级的价值观作为主线，恢复社会的和谐秩序。然而，这一时期也有一些逆文化主流的作者，他们的作品对社会认知方式的支离破碎起到了推波助澜的作用。其中，克里斯蒂娜·罗塞蒂（Christina Georgina Rossetti，1830—1894）的 *Goblin Market* 就是这样一首诗歌。

罗塞蒂是另一位英国诗人丹蒂·加布里埃尔·罗塞蒂（1828—1882）

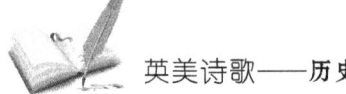

的妹妹,她和伊丽莎白·勃朗宁并称为英国最伟大的女诗人。罗塞蒂是一位虔诚的圣公会教徒,因为宗教信仰她一生过着安静、隐居的生活,终身未婚。可是,在女诗人平静的外表下面有一颗不平静的心。罗塞蒂极富诗歌创作天赋,善于借用小诗对人生进行思考,例如她的诗歌 When I am dead, my dearest 就集中了她对死亡的思考。1862年,罗塞蒂出版了她的第一部诗集 Goblin Market and Other Poems,其中的 Goblin Market 是她最具代表性的作品。

Goblin Market 的故事围绕着利兹(Lizzie)和劳拉(Laura)姐妹俩展开。黄昏来临,一群精灵会在山谷中叫卖看起来香甜可口的水果。曾经的朋友珍妮(Jeanie)因为吃了他们的水果而病死,死后坟墓上寸草不生。想起这些利兹就劝说劳拉不要随便品尝水果。然而,劳拉没有抵制住精灵们的诱惑,用自己的一缕头发和一滴眼泪换取了吃水果的机会。渴望再次品尝到水果的劳拉却再也听不到精灵们的叫卖声,她的身体日渐衰弱,并且濒临死亡。为了拯救劳拉,利兹跑去找精灵买水果。而当精灵得知利兹是为别人买水果时愤怒异常,它们不但殴打利兹,还将水果疯狂地投向她。利兹回到家里让劳拉舔食自己身上的果汁,通过这样方式救活了劳拉。两个姐妹成年后各自成立了家庭,她们经常向孩子讲述精灵的故事,让他们引以为戒。在形式上,该诗没有固定的押韵格式。很多四行诗文都运用了 abab 的押韵格式(例如第1~4行),对句在诗歌中也常常用到(例如第15~16行),而且很多诗行都是压同一尾韵的(例如第5~14行)。另外,诗人在格律形式上也不拘一格,比较典型的是一行中有4~5个重音。

不可否定,Goblin Market 是一部儿童文学,讲述的是姐妹俩和坏精灵的故事,赞扬了姐妹之间的感情和友谊,特别是诗歌最后的第133~138行强化了这一主题:"For there is no friend like a sister/In calm or stormy weather/To cheer one on the tedious way/To fetch one if one goes astray/To lift one if one totters down/To strengthen whilst one stands"。

第七章　维多利亚时期诗歌

然而，自20世纪70年代开始，评论家指出，和1865年刘易斯·卡罗尔（Lewis Carroll）写作的 *Alice's Adventures in Wonderland* 一样，两位作者都是利用儿童文学的形式，避开了当时流行的维多利亚小说体，从而得以表达主流文学中不能表达的边缘意识和小众思想。

从诗歌中"水果"的象征入手，可以看出其隐含的早期女性主义思想。在《圣经》中，由于受到撒旦的诱惑，亚当和夏娃违背了上帝的旨意吃了禁果，因此被逐出伊甸园。该诗中出现了大量有关水果的词汇，诗中的第125～126行中，诗人指出：水果吃起来可口，咽下去却变成了毒药（"Their fruits like honey to the throat/But poison in the blood"），这就明确了禁果和诗中水果之间的关联性。如果利兹和劳拉是诗中的被诱惑者，精灵则是扮演了撒旦的角色。不同的是，利兹抵制住了诱惑，而劳拉再次犯了亚当的错误，对诱惑做出了妥协。从禁果的含义出发，可以看出诗中含有女性欲望的主题。

维多利亚时期的道德观严格束缚女性的自由，对那些所谓不守妇道的女人冠以"堕落女人"（fallen women）的称呼，并将她们监禁起来。在写作诗歌之前的1859年，罗塞蒂就曾经在囚禁"堕落女人"的监狱中工作过。尽管诗人对劳拉向诱惑妥协表现出否定的态度，但该诗中出现了大量暗喻性爱的隐晦描写。例如，当劳拉出卖了自己的头发和眼泪之后，沉浸在水果的香甜之中，作者在第62～66行写道：

"Then suck'd their fruit globes fair or red/Sweeter than honey from the rock/Stronger than man-rejoicing wine/Clearer than water flow'd that juice/She never tasted such before"。

在第89～92行，利兹回想起死去的珍妮时（"Who should have been a bride/But who for joys brides hope to have/Fell sick and died"），就比较大胆地指出了女性的身体欲望。更有评论家指出，该诗中还暗含有女性同性恋的情节。对于女性欲望的描写和阐释，是作者对其所处的维多利亚时期限

制女性自由的一种含蓄但却有力的控诉，难怪她会借助儿童文学这种题材进行创作。罗塞蒂在该诗中所表达的女性自由和肉体欲望的主题，是早期的女性意识萌芽的表现，和后期的女性主义运动遥相呼应。

二、Further Reading

（一）Ulysses

Alfred Lord Tennyson

1   It little profits that an idle king,
    By the still hearth, among these barren crags,
    Matched with an aged wife, I mete and dole
    Unequal laws unto a savage race,
5   That hoard, and sleep, and feed, and know not me.

    I cannot rest from travel; I will drink
    Life to the lees. All times I have enjoyed
    Greatly, have suffered greatly, both with those
    That loved me, and alone; on shore, and when
10 Through scudding drifts the rainy Hyades
    Vexed the dim sea. I am become a name;
    For always roaming with a hungry heart
    Much have I seen and known—cities of men
    And manners, climates, councils, governments,
15 Myself not least, but honored of them all—
    And drunk delight of battle with my peers,

第七章 维多利亚时期诗歌

Far on the ringing plains of windy Troy,

I am a part of all that I have met.

Yet all experience is an arch wherethrough

20　Gleams that untraveled world whose margin fades

Forever and forever when I move,

How dull it is to pause, to make an end,

To rust unburnished, not to shine in use!

As though to breathe were life! Life piled on life

25　Were all too little, and of one to me

Little remains; but every hour is saved

From that eternal silence, something more,

A bringer of new things; and vile it were

For some three suns to store and hoard myself,

30　And this gray spirit yearning in desire

To follow knowledge like a sinking star,

Beyond the utmost bound of human thought.

This is my son, mine own Telemachus,

To whom I leave the scepter and the isle—

35　Well-loved of me, discerning to fulfil

This labor, by slow prudence to make mild

A rugged people, and through soft degrees

Subdued them to the useful and the good.

Most blameless is he, centered in the sphere

40　Of common duties, decent not to fail

In offices of tenderness, and pay

Meet adoration to my household gods,

When I am gone. He works his work, I mine.

There lies the port; the vessel puffs her sail;

45　There gloom the dark, broad seas. My mariners,

Souls that have toiled, and wrought, and thought with me—

That ever with a frolic welcome took

The thunder and the sunshine, and opposed

Free hearts, free foreheads—You and I are old,

50　Old age hath yet his honor and his toil.

Death closes all; but something ere the end,

Some work of noble note, may yet be done,

Not unbecoming men that strove with Gods.

The lights begin to twinkle from the rocks,

55　The long day wanes; the slow moon climbs; the deep

Moans round with many voices. Come, my friends,

'Tis not too late to seek a newer world.

Push off, and sitting well in order smite

The sounding furrows; for my purpose holds

60　To sail beyond the sunset, and the baths

Of all the western stars, until I die.

It may be that the gulfs will wash us down;

It may be we shall touch the Happy Isles,

And see the great Achilles, whom we knew.

65　Though much is taken, much abides; and though

We are not now that strength which in old days

第七章 维多利亚时期诗歌

Moved earth and heaven, that which we are, we are—

One equal temper of heroic hearts,

Made weak by time and fate, but strong in will

70　To strive, to seek, to find and not to yield.

【译文】
尤利西斯

阿尔弗雷德·丁尼生

1　当个空头国王无所得益，

　　深居巉岩之中，坐在静静的炉旁，

　　由一位老妻相伴，向一个野蛮民族

　　发布各种不同奖惩法令，他们只知

5　屯积储藏，吃吃睡睡，却不知我是谁。

　　我不能居安而不出；我要喝干

　　人生这杯酒。我享受过莫大欢乐，

　　也吃过大苦头，和爱我的人一起，

　　或独自一个；或在岸上，或穿过

10　暴雨阵阵，毕宿星团使大海

　　掀起滚滚波涛。如今我只是一个虚名。

　　因为我总是如饥似渴地四处漫游，

　　见得多，知道的也多——城市里的

　　人物风情，各种天气，各国议员和政府，

15　我本人并非不重要，而是受到大家尊重，——

　　我和我的同僚们共享战斗的欢欣，

英美诗歌——历史与文本

在那遥远的风起云涌的特洛伊旷野上，
我是所有经历中的一部分；
然而，一切经历只是一座拱门，拱门外
20 还有未游历的世界在闪光，它的
边界随着我们前移永远退向前方。
停滞不前，就此终结，不磨砺而任其生锈，
不使用也不发光，这是何等枯燥乏味！
仿佛生命只是呼吸而已！几次生命相加
25 还嫌太少，我的生命只有一次
而且所剩无几；但是从那永恒的静寂中
省下的每个小时都会增加一些东西，
带来新的事物；可耻的是
三年来我把自己封存和储藏起来，
30 可这斑白的心灵却迫切地向往
去追随知识，像那西沉的星星，
到那人类思想极限以外的地方。

这是我的儿子，我的忒勒玛科斯，
我要把这君权和岛国留给他掌管——
35 我很爱他，他也有眼力，能够完成
这项艰辛的任务，会慢慢而谨慎地
把这粗野民族驯化。用温和的方法
征服他们，使他们成为良民百姓。
他专心于公众事务，无可指责，
40 我离开以后，他会妥善的
处理好那些需要谨慎应付的事务，

第七章　维多利亚时期诗歌

也会对祖宗表示恰如其分的敬奉，
他做他的事，我走我的路。

海港就在前方；船上的风帆飘扬；
45　大海沉沉，朦胧一片。我的水手们，
曾经和我同劳、同作、同思想，——
他们总是高高兴兴地去迎接雷霆和阳光，
用自由的心、自由的头脑去与之抗争——
你们和我现在都老了；但是老年人
50　也还有他的荣誉感，还有他的用场。
死亡将终止一切；但是，在结束之前，
还可以有所作为，可以做点高尚事情，
我辈与神抗争也并非不适宜。
那礁石上的灯光已开始闪亮；
55　长昼快要结束，月亮爬上了天边；
海洋的呻吟和各种声音在四周回荡。
来吧，朋友们，去发现新世界为时不晚。
开船出发吧，大家坐好坐稳，
让我们破浪前进；我们要驶向
60　落日的彼岸，驶向群星沐浴的
西方，直到我死后方休。
也许，大海会把我们吞没，
也许，我们会抵达"幸福岛"，
会见伟大的阿喀琉斯，我们熟悉的朋友。
65　虽然我们被夺走了很多，剩下的也不少，
虽然我们已经没有从前那样的精力

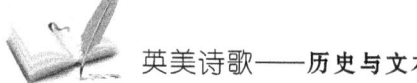

去战天斗地，但我们还是和以前一样——
有一样的勇气，有一样的雄心，
虽被时光和命运摧弱，但仍有坚强意志
70　去斗争，去求索，去发现，不屈服。

（何功杰　译）

【点评】

《尤利西斯》是丁尼生在他的大学好友亚瑟·哈莱姆突然逝世之后（1833）创作的，发表于1842年。《尤利西斯》源于希腊神话中的著名英雄奥德修斯（希腊名为Odysseus，拉丁名为Ulysses）的传奇故事。在荷马史诗的影响下，尤利西斯成为西方文化中家喻户晓的英雄形象。尤利西斯在但丁的《神曲》中攻克特洛伊之后，没有回到家乡，而是继续向西挺进以寻求新的人生经历。丁尼生借鉴了尤利西斯这一经典题材，以戏剧独白的形式，通过年迈英雄尤利西斯之口，塑造了一位勇敢、坚毅、坦然、果断的暮年壮士形象。

这首诗语言优美，思想内容积极。整首诗歌采用无韵体（Blank verse）写成，基本格律是五音步抑扬格，但其中有变化，整首诗音、义、节奏结合紧密。全诗共70行，可分三个部分。第一部分为第1～32行，尤利西斯表示对当前生活的不满、回顾了充满各种经历的过去及对未来充满展望。第二部分为第33～43行，尤利西斯决定将王权授给有能力又能胜任的儿子"Telemachus"。第三部分为第44～70行，一切准备就绪，尤利西斯召集部下准备出海，探索新的世界。

诗歌一开始，尤利西斯表达了对眼前生活的不满（"It little profits"），生活好像变得无趣：深居巘岩之中，坐在静静的炉旁，由一位老妻相伴，向一个野蛮民族发布各种不同奖惩法令，他们只知屯积储藏，吃吃睡睡，却不知我是谁。"That hoard, and sleep, and feed, and know not

第七章 维多利亚时期诗歌

me"中的连词叠用表达了尤利西斯对野蛮民族的鄙视。尤利西斯决定要改变眼前的生活["I cannot rest from travel; I will drink Life to the lees"(我不能居安而不出;我要喝干人生这杯酒)],"travel"与"drink"为隐喻。在第7~18行,尤利西斯回顾了自己人生征途上充满欢乐也充满痛苦的各种经历——在充满暴风雨的海上、在城市里、在旷野的战场上。随即诗人运用隐喻手法将人生的经历贴切地比喻为"拱门"("all experience is an arch"),拱门外还有未游历的世界在闪光,它的边界随着前移永远退向前方,意指生命将永远前行才有意义。尤利西斯渴望通过前行、不断游历来充实自己的生命:从那永恒的静寂中省下的每个小时都会增加一些东西,带来新的事物。第31~32行["To follow knowledge like a sinking star/Beyond the utmost bound of human thought"(像那西沉的星星,到那人类思想极限以外的地方)]诗人运用明喻表达了尤利西斯灵魂深处渴求对永恒知识与生命的探索。第二部分中,尤利西斯把王权传位给自己的儿子,因为儿子有能力治理国家,他也有眼力,会慢慢而谨慎地把这粗野民族驯化,会用温和的方法征服他们,他专心于公众事务,无可指责("blameless")。

第三部分一开始尤利西斯已准备好一切,准备起航远行。其中"There lies the port; the vessel puffs her sail"运用拟人手法,然后诗人运用连词叠用("My mariners/Souls that have toiled, and wrought, and thought with me""The thunder and the sunshine, and opposed/Free hearts, free foreheads—You and I are old")表达了对忠心于自己的水手们的赞美:曾经和我同劳、同作、同思想,他们总是高高兴兴地去迎接雷霆和阳光,用自由的心、自由的头脑去与之抗争。其中"took/The thunder and the sunshine ... Free hearts, free foreheads"使用了一语双叙手法。尤利西斯感叹自己已老,已接近死亡,但是在结束之前,还可以有所作为,可以做点高尚事情,去发现新世界为时不晚。"我们要驶向落日的彼岸,驶向群星沐浴的西方"("To sail beyond the sunset, and the baths/Of all the western stars, until I die")。尤利西斯决定探索未知

新世界,直到生命终结。诗人运用两个平行结构指出此次航行可能发生的情况,"It may be that the gulfs will wash us down/It may be we shall touch the Happy Isles"其中之一就是可能会抵达"幸福岛"("Happy Isles"),意指寻求到生命的意义所在。不管如何,重要的是要有坚强意志,去斗争、去求索、去发现。

最后诗中豪迈的言辞形象地刻画了一位生命不息、奋斗不止、追求无止境的老年英雄形象,与汉语古诗中的"老骥伏枥,志在千里"不谋而合,催人奋进、励人前行。

(二) Crossing the Bar

Alfred Lord Tennyson

1 Sunset and evening star,

   And one clear call for me!

   And may there be no moaning of the bar,

   When I put out to sea.

5 But such a tide as moving seems asleep.

   Too full for sound and foam

   When that which drew from out the boundless deep

   Turns again home.

   Twilight and evening bell.

10 And after that the dark!

   And may there be no sadness of farewell,

   When I embark.

第七章 维多利亚时期诗歌

>   For though from out our bourne of Time and Place
>   The flood may bear me far,
> 15 I hope to see my pilot face to face
>   When I have crossed the bar.

【译文】
过沙洲
阿尔弗雷德·丁尼生

1   落日，晚星，
    一个清晰的声音把我呼喊！
    但愿那沙洲没有呻吟，
    当我登船出海远航。

5   如此流动的海潮宛如入睡，
    潮水太满反无声息也无浪花，
    那来自无限海洋之外的灵魂，
    今日又要转程回家。

    黄昏，晚钟，
10 随后是黑夜茫茫！
    但愿告别时没有悲痛，
    当我登船出航。

    虽然潮水会把我带到

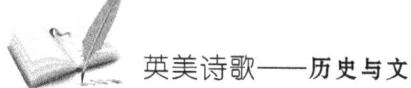

　　　　幽幽时空之外去远游，
15　我希望当面见到"舵手"，
　　　　当我越过了沙洲。

（何功杰　译）

【点评】

　　《过沙洲》是丁尼生最著名的诗歌之一，写于他80岁高龄时。全诗共分四个小节，每个诗节押韵格式为abab。整首诗歌的主题为死亡，但却充满着平静与盼望。

　　诗人一开始运用隐喻意象"落日，晚星"（夜晚即将来临），来形容自己年事已高，已到垂暮之年，一个清晰的声音把我呼喊！（"Sunset and evening star/And one clear call for me!"）其中"sunset"和"star"、"clear"和"call"为头韵，"one clear call"指代死亡。诗人用沙洲指代"生与死的边界"，一句"但愿那沙洲没有呻吟"表达了诗人想要安详而没有痛苦地离开这个世界的愿望。诗人将踏上死亡的路程比喻为登船出海远航，亦即另一个行程，这与作者基督教信仰中的出死入生不无关联。其中"may"和"moaning"、"be"和"bar"为头韵。第二个诗节诗人笔下的大海没有暴风，一片平静，如同沉睡，潮水太满，反无声息也无浪花。"But such a tide as moving seems asleep/Too full for sound and foam/ When that which drew from out the boundless deep/Turns again home"诗人使用头韵、拟人、比喻将大海看作人类灵魂的安息之地，是回家，诗人在这里表达了乐观的生死态度。他以其正统的基督教信仰表达了一个八旬老人在告别这个世界前的宁静与安详。

　　第三个诗节中，诗人以同义反复的手法（"黄昏""晚钟"与第1行诗"落日""晚星"相呼应），再次强调自己不久要离开这个世界，诗人只是希望当自己开启另一段旅程前的告别没有悲痛。再次显示了80岁的诗人面对死亡时的安静与乐观。第四个诗节中，诗人强调如果离开这个世界，只

第七章　维多利亚时期诗歌

不过是到幽幽时空之外去远游。只是希望自己在越过沙洲（离开世界）后，能见到"舵手"（上帝），最后诗人将生命与远游及与造物主连接在一起，表明了基督教信仰中"出死入生"的永恒生命价值观念。

诗中大量头韵及尾部 abab 的韵式，使得整首诗歌韵律感强。丰富的意象、比喻、拟人等修辞手法的使用使得整首诗歌意境鲜明，诗人虽在言说死亡，但却不曾留下悲伤。

（三）Eagle

Alfred Lord Tennyson

1　He clasps the crag with crooked hands;
　　Close to the sun in lonely lands,
　　Ringed with the azure world, he stands.

　　The wrinkled sea beneath him crawls;
5　He watches from his mountain walls,
　　and like a thunderbolt he falls.

【译文】
鹰

阿尔弗雷德·丁尼生

1　它用弯曲的爪子抓住峭壁，
　　紧靠太阳却独居孤寂之地，
　　它屹立着，与苍茫的宇宙齐鸣。

　　汹涌的大海在它脚下蠕动，

5　峭壁上它双目炯炯，
　　如雷鸣闪电一样向下冲。

（刘守兰　译）

【点评】

全诗是由两个诗节六行组成的短诗。每行有8个音节，4个音步，非重读音节和重读音节交替出现，先强后弱，构成四音步抑扬格的格律。每一诗节尾韵格式为aaa，这首短诗意象完整，特色鲜明。诗行简洁明快，很好地传达了雄鹰矫健的神韵。

诗人在第一节诗中描绘了一幅静态的画面。鹰用弯曲的爪子抓住峭壁，紧靠太阳却独居孤寂之地，它屹立着，与苍茫的宇宙齐鸣（"He clasps the crag with crooked hands/Close to the sun in lonely lands/Ringed with the azure world, he stands"）诗中意象细腻丰富：老鹰（He）、爪子（hands）、峭壁（crag）、太阳（sun）、大地（land）、宇宙（azure world），意象由小到大，由具体到抽象，为读者提供了丰富的想象空间。诗人运用大量修辞：拟人（He，hands）、夸张（Close to the sun）、移就（lonely lands）、拟声（ringed）、头韵（clasps the crag with crooked，lonely lands）、尾韵（hands，stand，lands），修辞技巧的使用使得诗歌更加形象生动、韵律感强、更加传神。第二个诗节中，诗人描绘了一幅动态的画面。汹涌的大海在它脚下蠕动，峭壁上它双目炯炯，如雷鸣闪电一样向下冲。"The wrinkled sea beneath him crawls/He watches from his mountain walls/and like a thunderbolt he falls"中描写的意象包括：大海（sea）、鹰（him，he，his）、峭壁（mountain walls）、雷电（thunderbolt），两个诗节中的意象结合在一起，使得整首诗歌的空间层次感丰富，感染力强。修辞如移就（wrinkled sea）、拟人（He watches）、明喻（like a thunderbolt）渲染了诗歌的氛围，将鹰展翅翱翔的雄姿描绘得惟妙惟肖，具有极佳的审美价值。诗中的音韵修辞达到了蒲柏所强调的"语音乃语义的回响"，增强了诗歌的节奏感与美感。

第七章 维多利亚时期诗歌

"鹰"是一种独自在长空翱翔的动物,在圣经文化意象中具有救赎、力量、保护等积极意义。如:《出埃及记》(*Exodus*)19:4 "……且看见我如鹰将你们背在翅膀上,带来归我"("... and how I bore you on eagles' wings and brought you to myself");《诗篇》(*Psalms*)103:5 "他用美物使你所愿得以知足,以致你如鹰返老还童"("Who satisfies you with good as long as you live/so that your youth is renewed like the eagle's");《以赛亚书》(*Isaiah*)40:31 "但那等候耶和华的,必从新得力,他们必如鹰展翅上腾……"("but those who wait for the Lord shall renew their strength, they shall mount up with wings like eagles, ...")。丁尼生以短短6行诗文所描绘的鹰透露出几分苍劲、孤傲、雄健、力量与超越的感觉,"它屹立着,与苍茫的宇宙齐鸣""汹涌的大海在它脚下蠕动,峭壁上它双目炯炯"诗歌里面宏大的意象与细微的描写展示了诗人精神上超验的追求与内心的矛盾、纠结与思索。整个"鹰"的意象带有浓厚的象征主义与浪漫主义色彩。

(四)In Memoriam A. H. H.

Alfred Lord Tennyson

1 I held it truth, with him who sings
  To one clear harp in diverse tones,
  That men may rise on stepping stones
  Of their dead selves to higher things.

5 But who shall so forecast the years
  And find in loss a gain to match?
  Or reach a hand through time to catch
  The far-off interest of tears?

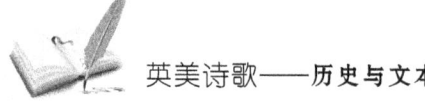

Let Love clasp Grief lest both be drowned,
10   Let darkness keep her raven gloss.
Ah, sweeter to be drunk with loss,
To dance Death, to beat the ground,

Than that the victor Hours should scorn
The long result of love, and boast,
15   "Behold the man that loved and lost,
But all he was is overworn."

【译文】
悼念 A. H. H

    阿尔弗雷德·丁尼生

1   和着一支嘹亮的竖琴唱出种种曲调
对于他,我认为这是真理:
人可以沿着用他们死去的自己
铺成的石阶达成更高的目标。

5   但是谁能预见那些岁月
并在消失中发现与之相当的得益?
或者伸出一只手穿过时日
去抓住那泪水感兴趣的遥远事业?

让"爱"抱住"悲",以免二者都被湮没,
10   让黑暗的光泽保持乌黑。

第七章　维多利亚时期诗歌

啊，陶醉于消失，这样更美，

拍打着地面，与死神跳舞。

免得让"时间"这个胜利者嘲笑

爱的长期结果，并吹嘘，

15　"瞧，他曾经爱过又失去，

他过去拥有的一切现在全都没有了。"

（毕小君　译）

【点评】

《悼念》是由131首抒情诗所组成。这首诗写于1833年，但直到1850年才得以出版。全诗可分为四部分：第1～27首记述了诗人得知好友哈勒姆死讯时的悲痛心情；第28～77首则是把痛失好友的悲哀与对"生与死"的哲学思考联系起来；第78～103首诗人由缅怀亡友上升为对上帝与人类灵魂的哲学和宗教思考；第104～131首，主要是对当时主要社会问题的思考。本诗共四个小节，韵式为abba。在当时工业文明、新兴科学正试图吞并信仰的大背景下，该诗充满着诗人对死亡和永生、怀疑与信仰的哲学思考。

一开始，"他"和着一支嘹亮的竖琴唱出种种曲调，"我"认为这是真理，接着诗人解释人可以沿着用他们死去的自己铺成的石阶达成更高的目标。其中"diverse tones"（各种曲调）指代复杂的人生经历，人只有经历过才能唱出令人回味的曲调。下文中的"dead selves"（死去的自己）与基督教信仰中的耶稣替人类钉十字架，将人从罪的辖制中拯救出来，亦即与靠着信仰耶稣基督得以重生，生命在基督中得以变化的信仰相一致。"higher things"与前面的各种曲调互文，指代历经风雨，生命才更加丰盈。第一诗节，诗人采用类比手法认为人只有经历过重生，经过苦难，新的生命才能不断变化成长，更像上帝基督的样式。第一诗节中，真理、信仰、死亡与

-223-

永生并置，增加了诗歌的张力。诗人在第二个诗节中连续运用两个问句，展示了诗人在信仰中对人生命定的苦难难以把握的心理，无论是摆在前面的或是已经发生过的。其中"loss"与"gain"为对比，"tears"指代苦难。第三个诗节中，诗人采用拟人手法给出建议：让"爱"抱住"悲"，以免二者都被淹没。这里"爱"指代信仰、上帝《圣经·约翰一书》第四章第八节"……因为上帝就是爱"），"悲"指代苦难或者死亡。既然人不能摆脱死亡的威胁，就是要坚定对上帝的信仰，坚持光明与黑暗的二元对立，在对上帝的信仰中面对并超越死亡，这样会更美。第四个诗节中诗人运用拟人指出，如果放弃传统、放弃信仰（爱），一切将归于虚无。对于时间来说——"Hours"指代时间，也暗含着人生的短暂之意,将是一个笑柄（"瞧，他曾经爱过又失去，他过去拥有的一切现在全都没有了"）。

本诗中许多冲突的意象，如生与死、爱与悲、短暂与永恒，它们被完美地糅合在一起，强烈地冲击着读者的感官，呈现出一种张力美，展示了诗人在生命、死亡、传统、信仰、与现实中的沉思，体现了诗人深刻的终极人文关怀情结。

（五）Meeting at Night

Robert Browning

1 The gray sea and the long black land;
  And the yellow half-moon large and low;
  And the startled little waves that leap
  In fiery ringlets from their sleep,
5 As I gain the cove with pushing prow,
  And quench its speed i' the slushy sand.
  Then a mile of warm sea-scented beach;

第七章 维多利亚时期诗歌

  Three fields to cross till a farm appears;
  A tap at the pane, the quick sharp scratch
10 And blue spurt of a lighted match,
  And a voice less loud, thro' its joys and fears,
  Than the two hearts beating each to each!

【译文】
夜中幽会
    罗伯特·勃朗宁

1 灰蒙蒙的大海，黑黝黝的大地，
  黄灿灿的新月又大又低；
  受惊的细浪卷起一个个火环，
  在沉睡中跳得好不欢畅。
5 我推着小船进入海湾，
  把船停泊在泥泞的沙地上。
  然后沿海水飘香的沙滩行走一英里，
  再跨过三块麦地，一个农庄便在眼底；
  窗玻璃上轻轻一磕，随即迅速一擦，
10 点燃的火柴喷吐火苗，呈一片蓝色；
  又惊又喜中发出一声轻轻的呼叫，
  那声音比两颗心的撞击还微小。

        （陈才宇　译）

【点评】

全诗共两节，每节韵式为abccba，主要采用三音步抑扬格。诗歌主要描绘了主人公在深夜海陆兼程赶去与恋人幽会的情景。

一开始诗人描写了一幅夜空下在大海上航行的画面。意象词丰富：大海（sea）、陆地（land）、月亮（moon）、海浪（wave）、小船（cove）和沙地（sand）。诗中的"long, land""large, low""little, leap""pushing, prow""slushy, sand"为行内头韵，配合尾韵abccba，将行驶在海上的愉快心情与归心似箭的氛围表现得淋漓尽致，节奏明快、音韵和谐。"And the startled little waves that leap/In fiery ringlets from their sleep"中使用了拟人修辞，使得画面更加生动形象，感染力强。

第二节诗人描绘了一幅恋人幽会的画面。诗中的主人公沿海水飘香的沙滩行走了一英里，又跨过三块麦地，才到达恋人居住的地方，与恋人相会。其中"sea-scented"（海水飘香的沙滩）的 /s/ 音为海浪敲击海滩的声音，此处诗人调动嗅觉与听觉表达轻快的心情。主人公来到恋人窗前轻轻一磕（"A tap at the pane"），等待的恋人点燃了火柴，又惊又喜中发出一声轻轻的呼叫，那声音比两颗心撞击的声音还微小。最后两句（"And a voice less loud, thro' its joys and fears/Than the two hearts beating each to each!"）表面上是写两人说话声音的轻微，实际上强调的是心跳的剧烈。

整首诗意象优美，音韵和谐，很好地描绘了一幅月光下以大海、麦田为背景，相隔千里的恋人幽会的美好画面。

（六）Parting at Morning

Robert Browning

1 Round the cape of a sudden came the sea,
And the sun looked over the mountain's rim:

第七章 维多利亚时期诗歌

And straight was a path of gold for him,

And the need of a world of men for me.

【译文】

晨别

罗伯特·勃朗宁

1　大海突然从海岬旁闪出，

　　太阳从山脊上展出面容，

　　笔直的金光之道在他面前延伸，

　　那正是我所期盼的男人世界。

（郭　嘉　译）

【点评】

《晨别》是《夜中幽会》的续篇。描绘了在甜蜜的夜间幽会后，次日清晨离别的情景。四行诗采用四音步抑抑扬格、abba 的韵式。第一行诗"Round the cape of a sudden came the sea"（大海突然从海岬旁闪出）的意象词包括：大海、海岬，将读者拉到了大海边。这里主人公披着一身霞光，带着自己在这社会上的责任和义务与情人话别。头韵词"cape, came""sudden, sea"音韵和谐、节奏明快。接下来诗人三个"and"连词叠用描写了眼前的景象：太阳从山脊上展出面容，笔直的金光之道在他面前延伸。诗人用阳光铺陈画面，"sun""path of gold"象征此次主人公的这次远行将会是鹏程万里。最后一句"And the need of a world of men for me"主人公道出了自己作为男性，应该负起自己的责任，回到男人世界。

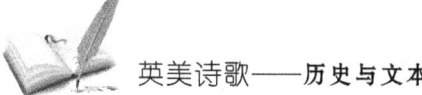
英美诗歌——历史与文本

(七) Home-Thoughts, From Abroad

Robert Browning

1   Oh, to be in England,
    Now that April's there,
    And whoever wakes in England
    Sees, some morning, unaware,
5   That the lowest boughs and the brushwood sheaf
    Round the elm-tree bole are in tiny leaf,
    While the chaffinch sings on the orchard bough
    In England-now!

    And after April, when May follows,
10 And the whitethroat builds, and all the swallows!
    Hark, where my blossom'd pear-tree in the hedge
    Leans to the field and scatters on the clover
    Blossoms and dewdrops—at the bent spray's edge—
    That's the wise thrush; he sings each song twice over,
15 Lest you should think he never could recapture
    The first fine careless rapture!
    And though the fields look rough with hoary dew,
    All will be gay when noontide wakes anew
    The buttercups, the little children's dower
20 —Far brighter than this gaudy melon-flower!

第七章　维多利亚时期诗歌

【译文】
海外思乡
罗伯特·勃朗宁

1　啊，但愿此刻身在英格兰，
　　在这人间四月天，
　　清晨从梦中醒来，
　　悄然不知中发现，
5　榆树四周低矮的枝条和灌木丛中，
　　小小的嫩叶已初显葱茏，
　　听金燕雀在果园枝头唱歌，
　　身在英格兰啊，就在此刻！

　　四月过去，五月来临，
10　燕子都在衔泥，白喉鸟在筑巢！
　　家中园里篱笆外的梨树
　　把如雨的花瓣和露珠
　　洒满了树枝之下的田野；
　　聪明的画眉鸟把每支歌都唱上两遍，
15　免得你猜想，它不可能重新捕获
　　第一遍即兴唱出的美妙欢乐！
　　尽管田野还笼罩着露水，显得有些灰暗，
　　到中午一切又将喜气盎然，
　　苏醒的金凤花是孩子们的"嫁妆"，
20　——这华而俗的甜瓜花哪儿比得上它漂亮那般！

（郭　嘉译）

【点评】

这首诗是勃朗宁最著名的短诗之一,写于他和妻子伊丽莎白在意大利侨居期间。诗人用记忆中家乡的春之美景,来抒写思念故乡、眷恋祖国之情。全诗分为两节,第一节描写英格兰的四月万物复苏,共有 8 行,押韵格式为 ababccdd;第二节主要描写欣欣向荣的英格兰五月天,共 12 行,押韵格式为 eefgfghhiijj。

一开始诗人运用一个感叹句"Oh, to be in England,/Now that April's there"表达了希望回到英格兰,打开了一幅英格兰四月天的画卷。你会看见并听见"That the lowest boughs and the brushwood sheaf/ Round the elm-tree bole are in tiny leaf/While the chaffinch sings on the orchard bough"(榆树四周低矮的枝条和灌木丛中,小小的嫩叶已初显葱茏,听金燕雀在果园枝头唱歌),最后诗人喊出"In England-now!"(身在英格兰啊,就在此刻!)表达了难以抑制的思乡之情。第二节诗人诉诸读者的听觉来描绘春意盎然的五月。燕子都在衔泥,白喉鸟在筑巢!家中园里篱笆外的梨树把如雨的花瓣和露珠洒满了树枝之下的田野;聪明的画眉鸟把每支歌都唱上两遍,诗人还想到了英格兰的金凤花(buttercups)与孩子们,与眼前的甜瓜花作了对比,指出家乡的更美、更漂亮,再次表达了诗人的思乡与爱国之情。

诗人借景抒情,寓情于景,情景交融。丰富的意象、拟人等的修辞手法及欢快的回忆使得整首思乡的诗歌没有过多的哀愁和惆怅,反倒让读者沉浸在英格兰美丽的春天中。

(八) Who Has Seen the Wind?

Christina Georgina Rossetti

1 Who has seen the wind?

第七章　维多利亚时期诗歌

　　Neither I nor you;

　　But when the leaves hang trembling,

　　The wind is passing through.

5　Who has seen the wind?

　　Neither you nor I;

　　But when the trees bow down their heads,

　　The wind is passing by.

【译文】
谁曾经见过风?
克里斯蒂娜·罗塞蒂

1　谁曾经见过风?

　　不是我也不是你;

　　但当树叶儿抖动,

　　这时风正吹起。

5　谁曾经见过风?

　　不是你也不是我;

　　但当树木俯首鞠躬,

　　这时风正吹过。

(陈才宇　译)

【点评】

全诗共两个诗节,尾韵格式为 abcb。两节诗中诗人都是采用"问句—回答"的方式["Who has seen the wind""Neither I nor you"(谁曾经见过风?

不是我也不是你）]，指出没有人能用肉眼看见风的样式。随后诗人采用转折（"but"）提出"But when the leaves hang trembling"（但当树叶儿抖动）、"But when the trees bow down their heads"（但当树木俯首鞠躬），只有在上述的条件下，人们才相信风的存在。两节诗歌结构整齐，诗人采用三行反复的手法：第1~2行完全重复，第3行"But when"反复，第4行除"through，by"外，其余单词反复。反复手法强调了"风"的意象，丰富了其语义功能。诗中"wind"与"pass by"结合在一起，难免让人想到生命与死亡，诗人是否在感受到风的同时，联想到生命的短暂呢！风与《圣经》中的意象连在一起，又赋予这首诗歌新的意义。在《圣经·传道书》第一章第六节（*Ecclesiastes*, Chapter1, Verse 6）关于风的描写有这样的诗句——"The wind blows to the south, and goes around to the north; round and round goes the wind, and on its circuits the wind returns"（风往南刮，又向北转，不住地旋转，而且返回转行原道），本诗句用来赞美造物主的神奇与伟大，突出人智慧的有限与无奈。结合圣经意象来分析思考，不难推测出诗人是借用自然之风颂赞上帝的伟大、神秘与奇妙。

（九）Paradise

Christina Georgina Rossetti

1   Once in a dream I saw the flowers
    That bud and bloom in Paradise;
    More fair they are than waking eyes
    Have seen in all this world of ours.
5   And faint the perfume-bearing rose
    And faint the lily on its stem,
    And faint the perfect violet,

第七章 维多利亚时期诗歌

Compared with them.

I heard the songs of Paradise:
10   Each bird sat singing in his place,
   A tender song so full of grace,
   It soared like incense to the skies.
   Each bird sat singing to his mate
   Soft cooing notes among the trees:
15   The nightingale herself were cold
   To such as these.

【译文】
天堂

克里斯蒂娜·罗塞蒂

1 我曾在梦中见过许多鲜花,
   它们在天堂上萌芽开放,
   肉眼在这世上所见的花朵,
   全没这般娇媚烂漫。
5 与那里的鲜花相比,
   玫瑰的芬芳显得平淡,
   百合花说不上亭亭玉立,
   紫罗兰称不得绮丽无双。

   我听见天堂上歌声嘹亮,
10 鸟儿都在自己的处所啼鸣,

悦耳的歌声优美而典雅，
像缭绕的香烟直升蓝天。
每只鸟都把歌献给伴侣，
沁人心脾的音符回荡林间：
15　与这样优美的乐音相比，
夜莺的歌显得索然无味。

（陈才宇　译）

【点评】

　　著名作家弗吉尼亚·伍尔芙曾这样评价：在英国女诗人中，克里斯蒂娜·罗塞蒂名列第一位，她的歌唱得好像知更鸟，有时又像夜莺。全诗共分两节，每节8行，尾韵格式为abbacded。全诗采用对比手法向读者描绘了一个天堂梦境：那里的花、那里的歌声无比美丽，唤起人们对天堂的向往之情。

　　一开始诗人引起读者的视觉联想，梦中的"I"看到天堂中萌芽开放的鲜花娇媚烂漫（"More fair"）。诗人运用对比指出，天堂里充满生命力的鲜花是世上所有的鲜花，包括玫瑰（rose）、百合花（lily）、紫罗兰（violet）所无法比拟的。"bud, bloom"为头韵，"waking eyes"为移就，第5～7行中使用平行反复（"faint"）强调世界上肉眼看到的美景在天堂鲜花的美丽衬托下，显得暗淡无光。第二个诗节中诗人调动了读者的听觉（"I heard the songs of Paradise"）来描写天堂的歌声。那歌声优美典雅，如同缭绕的香烟直升蓝天（"A tender song so full of grace, / It soared like incense to the skies"）。其中"like incense to the skies"为明喻，"song, so, soared, skies"为行内、行间韵。最后，诗人采用对比手法指出那歌声沁人心脾，与这样优美的乐音相比，夜莺的歌显得索然无味（"Soft cooing notes among the trees/ The nightingale herself were cold/To such as these"）。

　　克里斯蒂娜的诗歌唯美、忧郁，充满着灵动的生命感。《天堂》一诗

第七章 维多利亚时期诗歌

充满着美与神秘性,诗人将天堂描绘得惟妙惟肖,蕴含了诗人灵魂深处对美的追求,整首诗歌唤起读者心中对美的意识及对天堂的向往,从而回归上帝。

(十) When I am Dead, My Dearest

Christina Georgina Rossetti

1   When I am Dead, my dearest,
    Sing no sad songs for me;
    Plant thou no roses at my head,
    Nor shady cypress tree;
5   Be the green grass above me
    With showers and dewdrops wet;
    And if thou wilt, remember,
    And if thou wilt, forget.

    I shall not see the shadows,
10 I shall not feel the rain;
    I shall not hear the nightingale
    Sing on, as if in pain:
    And dreaming through the twilight
    That doth not rise nor set,
15 Haply I may remember,
    And haply may forget.

英美诗歌——历史与文本

【译文】

当我离开人世，我最亲爱的

克里斯蒂娜·罗塞蒂

1　当我离开人世，我最亲爱的，
　　不要为我把悲歌惋唱，
　　不用在我的头边种下玫瑰，
　　也不用栽种成荫的柏树：
5　成为我头顶青青的绿草吧，
　　让那晶莹的露水沾湿我的身
　　如果你愿意，就记在心里，
　　如果你愿意，就把它忘记

　　我看不见那绿荫，
10　我感受不到那雨露；
　　我听不到那夜莺
　　在苦痛中的低吟泣诉：
　　我在熹微的晨光中沉迷，
　　那晨光不升也不落，
15　也许我将会记住，
　　也许我将会忘记。

（郭　嘉　译）

【点评】

《当我离开人世，我最亲爱的》表达了诗人对生命与死亡的探索。全诗共分二节，每节8行。第1，5，7，9，13，15行均为三音步抑扬格；第2，4，6，8，10，12，14，16行为三音步抑扬格；第3，11行为四音步抑扬格，

第七章 维多利亚时期诗歌

韵脚为 abcbbadaefgfaada。

第一诗节中"我"假设自己已死("Dead"),诗人连用三个"不"〔"Sing no sad songs for me/Plant thou no roses at my head/ Nor shady cypress tree"(不要为我把悲歌惋唱,不用在我的头边种下玫瑰,也不用栽种成荫的柏树)〕叮嘱自己所挚爱的"my dearest",让坟墓上长出青青的绿草,可以有晶莹的露水沾湿"我"的身。最后两句如同祈祷词〔"And if thou wilt, remember/And if thou wilt, forget"(如果你愿意,就记在心里,如果你愿意,就把它忘记)〕,诗人运用反复手法和强烈对比表达诗人对待死亡的一种态度:让一切都顺其自然。

第二个诗节中,诗人以第一人称连用三个反复排比〔"I shall not see the shadows/I shall not feel the rain/I shall not hear the nightingale/Sing on, as if in pain"(我看不见那绿荫,我感受不到那雨露;我听不到那夜莺在苦痛中的低吟泣诉)〕描写死亡后的景象,但是诗人在悲伤的语调中告知读者"And dreaming through the twilight/That doth not rise nor set"(我在熹微的晨光中沉迷,那晨光不升也不落),自己只是在梦中("dreaming"),其中"twilight"具有一定的象征意义,诗中的"我"在不升不落的晨光中表明进入了一个永恒的状态,这与基督教"出死入生"永恒的生命信仰观相一致。最后诗人再次用反复与对比手法("Haply I may remember/And haply may forget")表达了一种超然的生命态度。无论是形式上还是语义上,都与第一诗节的最后两句遥相呼应,结构整齐,突出了无论"你"还是"我"对待发生的一切应该有一种超脱的态度,因为世界上的生命短暂,但会"出死入生",所以对待死亡应顺其自然并处之泰然。

整首诗歌中还运用了大量头韵如:"dead, dearest""sing, sad, songs""green grass"等,语言节奏感强、淳朴自然、感情细腻、哀婉动人、形式完美,表达了诗人乐观的生死观念,同时蕴含了诗人生命永恒的精神信仰观。

第八章 现当代诗歌

1901年维多利亚女王去世，爱德华七世继位，新的历史条件下，传统受到质疑，各种矛盾涌现。随着帝国主义的发展，英联邦到处扩张、矛盾升级、战争不断，冲击着英国社会的各个层面。1914—1918年，第一次世界大战爆发，战争灾难在物质、精神文化等方面给人类造成巨大冲击，英国海上霸主的地位开始动摇。20世纪30年代，全球经济危机爆发，英国亦未能幸免，往日的帝国风雨飘摇、每况愈下。接着规模更大的第二次世界大战也跟着爆发。各帝国主义国家在对外扩张的同时，也加强了内部的社会变革，他们采取急功近利的改革方式，导致了反叛与绝望的情绪在国内弥漫。第二次世界大战后，英国面临的国际形势发生了根本性变化，一些前殖民国家纷纷宣布独立。20世纪50年代末，英国出兵苏伊士运河以失败告终，虽然往日的帝国雄风不再，但是英国在政治、经济、文化等方面对前殖民国家仍存在重大影响。

英国的文学发展与时代的变迁密切相关。具有现代意识的作家开始质疑、抨击维多利亚时代中产阶级的价值传统。19世纪末，资本主义发展到帝国主义时期的文化危机导致了反现实主义文学和艺术的兴盛。托马斯·哈代（Thomas Hardy, 1840—1928）是维多利亚时期最后一位著名的小说家、诗人，其诗歌主题主要为爱情与死亡。R. 吉卜林（Rudyard Kipling, 1865—1936）

第八章　现当代诗歌

是英国小说家、诗人，是颂扬帝国主义的英雄主义的狂热分子。毛姆的小说《人性的枷锁》强调挣脱精神上的枷锁才能成为无所依恋、无所追求的自由人。英国现代主义文学主要体现在小说和诗歌上。以乔伊斯(Joyce)、伍尔夫(Woolf)为代表的意识流小说家刻意表现普通人的内心活动，展示现代人丰富复杂的内心世界。在诗歌方面，威廉·巴特勒·叶芝（William Buttler Yeats，1865—1939）作为爱尔兰诗人、评论家和剧作家，致力于建立神秘主义象征体系，探讨深刻的人生哲学问题，叶芝在1923年获得了诺贝尔文学奖。T.S.艾略特（Eliot）采用神话、象征描绘战后西方世界精神的荒原，传递出人类救赎须回归基督文明的呐喊，其《荒原》是公认的现代主义诗歌的最高成就。

英国诗歌在20世纪的发展呈现多元化的趋势，超现实主义、表现主义、运动派、集团派、贝尔法斯特派、极微派、苏格兰派、利物浦派、火星派等在40年代后逐渐涌现。诗人创作个性更加突出，女性诗人、少数族裔诗人崛起，北爱尔兰诗歌是20世纪末英国诗歌中最重要的组成部分。20世纪从20年代到70年代著名的诗人有T.S.艾略特，W.H.奥登(Oden)、狄兰·托玛斯(Dylan Thomas)，菲利普·拉金(Philip Larkin)，泰德·休斯(Ted Hughes)和谢默斯·希尼(Seamus Heaney)。其中希尼于1995年因其作品"具有抒情诗般的美和伦理深度，使日常生活中的奇迹和活生生的往事得以升华"荣获诺贝尔文学奖。其诗歌在描写北爱尔兰乡村生活的同时，探索着物质与精神、传统与文化、民族与身份的交流与融会。语言淳朴、意象丰富、民族色彩鲜明。

一、Poem Reading

（一）The Second Coming

William Butler Yeats

1　Turning and turning in the widening gyre

The falcon cannot hear the falconer;
Things fall apart; the centre cannot hold;
Mere anarchy is loosed upon the world,
5　The blood-dimmed tide is loosed, and everywhere
The ceremony of innocence is drowned;
The best lack all conviction, while the worst
Are full of passionate intensity.

Surely some revelation is at hand;
10　Surely the Second Coming is at hand.
The Second Coming! Hardly are those words out
When a vast image out of Spiritus Mundi
Troubles my sight: somewhere in sands of the desert
A shape with lion body and the head of a man,
15　A gaze blank and pitiless as the sun,
Is moving its slow thighs, while all about it
Reel shadows of the indignant desert birds.
The darkness drops again; but now I know
That twenty centuries of stony sleep
20　Were vexed to nightmare by a rocking cradle,
And what rough beast, its hour come round at last,
Slouches towards Bethlehem to be born?

20世纪初，第一次世界大战等战事使得欧洲大陆满目疮痍，人们第一次真正意识到战争具有迅速毁灭世界的能力，所谓文明和进步在战争面前显得不堪一击。原有的世界观和价值观崩塌，而一种新的世界秩序亟待产

第八章 现当代诗歌

生。因此，战争给整个欧洲大陆蒙上了一层灰暗的薄纱，而战争也使得欧洲社会进入了标新立异的现代主义时期。其实，英国作家约瑟夫·康拉德Joseph Conrad，1857—1924）早在第一次世界大战爆发前，就在《黑暗的心》等作品中表现出了对现代文明秩序不堪一击的担忧。在英国的文坛，这种忧虑随着第一次世界大战的进行和结束愈演愈烈。作为英国现代主义早期的代表诗人之一，威廉·巴特勒·叶芝（William Butler Yeats，1865—1939）在其诗歌作品中形象地刻画了一幅幅旧有世界分崩离析、新生世纪不期而至的景象。*The Second Coming* 就是这样一首充满了末世论基调的诗歌。

叶芝出生在爱尔兰的首都都柏林，在诗歌创作早期便表现出了对爱尔兰的民间传说以及凯尔特神话的关注，他主要活跃于都柏林和伦敦两个地方。24岁以后，由于对毛德·岗（Maud Gonne）的爱恋，他自愿转变成了一位民族主义分子，和格雷戈里夫人（Lady Gregory）共同经营了一家剧院（the Abbey Theatre），后来这家剧院成为爱尔兰复兴运动的中心。第一次世界大战之前，叶芝主要的诗歌作品都带有浪漫主义的色调。例如，*The Wanderings of Orisin*（1889）便集合了浪漫主义、民族理想主义、爱尔兰神话和神秘主义等元素的诗歌，而在 *The Lake Isle of Innisfree*（1888）中，诗人则表现出消极浪漫主义诗人的远离世事烦扰、逃离到理想主义王国（Innisfree）的愿望。经历了第一次世界大战之后，叶芝的创作倾向有了一个较大的转折，从原来的浪漫主义转向了现代主义，他的诗歌更多地去思考战后的政治形势和社会变革。面对战争后社会各个方面的重新整合，诗人表现出消极的末世论基调，其中的代表作品便是 *The Second Coming*。

该诗写作于1919年，在1920年首次出版在美国杂志 *The Dial* 上面。1921年，叶芝出版了一部诗歌集 *Michael Robartes and the Dancer*，里面就包含了 *The Second Coming*。该诗共有两个诗节，第一个诗节是从第1～8行，而第二个诗节则从第9～22行。诗人主要从诗文的内容上着手划分诗节，并没有过多地考虑诗歌的形式。另外，*The Second Coming* 没有固定的韵律形式，虽然大量地使用了抑扬格，但是却在行文中不断突破这种格律的限制。除了前面的4行诗文（"gyre" "falconer"，"hold" "world"）和第14～15行诗文（"man" "sun"）押韵之外，并没有规律的押韵格式。这种虽然出现韵律，却在行文中不断被突破的写作手法，与虽然表面平静如往常，但却即将分崩离析的文明秩序相呼应，使诗歌形式和主题达到了内在的统一，表现出诗人明确的现代主义创作理念。

该诗借用了基督教中的世界末日，描述了欧洲大陆岌岌可危的文明秩序，预言了欧洲大陆未来的发展局势。第一个诗节通过第2行中的"falcon"和"falconer"以及第5～6行中的"the blood-dimmed tide"和"the ceremony of innocence"两个对比鲜明的形象，刻画了文明秩序被打破、世界末日即将到来的情景：猎鹰越飞越高脱离了养鹰者的束缚，腥风血雨的暗涌吞噬了无辜的人群。如果养鹰者和无辜的人群代表了现代社会井然有序的秩序，猎鹰和暗涌则是涌动在表面秩序之下、具有极强破坏力的现代元素。第3～4行明确指出了秩序的中心失去了操控力，世界即将分崩离析，而第7～8行则对即将到来的新世纪有了一个大概的描绘——那即将是一个恶者（"the worst"）战胜善者（"the best"）的黑暗时代。第二个诗节集中在狮身人面怪兽上。第9～10行直接引用了《圣经》中的"启示"（"revelation"）和"基督再临"（"the second coming"），暗示世界末日的来临。从第11行开始，狮身人面的怪兽出现。第12行中的"Spiritus Mundi"（"the spirit of the world"）是产生怪兽的源泉，其中暗含着荣格心理学中"集体无意识"（"the collective unconsciousness"）的内涵。诗文的第13～17行描写了狮身人面兽的形象：沙漠中的怪兽目光呆滞、笨重而冷漠，看似还没有完全恢复生命的活力，身后围绕着一群义愤的沙漠鸟。第18～22行中，诗人再次用到了两处《圣经》中有关"基督再临"的典故 ["twenty centuries of stony sleep"（第19行）和"towards Bethlehem to be born"（第22行）]。

第八章 现当代诗歌

虽然借用了"基督再临"的典故，但是诗人在诗文中的"再临"和《圣经》中的有很大的区别。首先，《圣经》认为，两千年后的世界末日，耶稣基督将会再次降临人间对人类进行审判，因此世界末日也被称为审判日；而在 The Second Coming 中，虽然同是世界末日，再次降临地球的却是狮身人面的黑暗怪兽。其次，《圣经》认为人类的历史是线性发展的，并没有反复性；而 The Second Coming 中的历史则是重复的、轮回的，这和作者叶芝的历史观相吻合。叶芝认为，人类整个历史发展有一定的模式。这个模式由两个圆锥体组成，每个圆锥体是一个历史发展的过程，呈螺旋上升的状态，当历史发展到顶点，即到了世界末日。在下一个轮回中，历史重新开始，再次由圆锥体的地段螺旋上升直到顶点。两个圆锥体完全不同，因此当世界末日来临之际，世界秩序将会被颠倒发展。在 The Second Coming 中，狮身人面兽代表着下一个历史圆锥中的主导因素，下一个轮回即是颠倒是非、否定现有价值观的黑暗世界，因此其中带有强烈的悲观主义色彩。

（二）The Love Song of J. Alfred Prufrock

T. S. Eliot

S' io credesse che mia risposta fosse
A persona che mai tornasse al mondo,
Questa fiamma staria senza piu scosse.
Ma perciocche giammai di questo fondo
Non torno vivo alcun, s' i' odo il vero,
Senza tema d' infamia ti rispondo.

1　Let us go then, you and I,

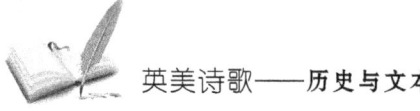

When the evening is spread out against the sky

Like a patient etherized upon a table;

Let us go, through certain half-deserted streets,

5   The muttering retreats

Of restless nights in one-night cheap hotels

And sawdust restaurants with oyster-shells:

Streets that follow like a tedious argument

Of insidious intent

10   To lead you to an overwhelming question ...

Oh, do not ask, "What is it?"

Let us go and make our visit.

In the room the women come and go

Talking of Michelangelo.

15   The yellow fog that rubs its back upon the window-panes,

The yellow smoke that rubs its muzzle on the window-panes

Licked its tongue into the corners of the evening,

Lingered upon the pools that stand in drains,

Let fall upon its back the soot that falls from chimneys,

20   Slipped by the terrace, made a sudden leap,

And seeing that it was a soft October night,

Curled once about the house, and fell asleep.

And indeed there will be time

For the yellow smoke that slides along the street,

25　Rubbing its back upon the window panes;
　　There will be time, there will be time
　　To prepare a face to meet the faces that you meet;
　　There will be time to murder and create,
　　And time for all the works and days of hands
30　That lift and drop a question on your plate;
　　Time for you and time for me,
　　And time yet for a hundred indecisions,
　　And for a hundred visions and revisions,
　　Before the taking of a toast and tea.

35　In the room the women come and go
　　Talking of Michelangelo.

　　And indeed there will be time
　　To wonder, "Do I dare?" and, "Do I dare?"
　　Time to turn back and descend the stair,
40　With a bald spot in the middle of my hair—
　　　（They will say: "How his hair is growing thin!"）
　　My morning coat, my collar mounting firmly to the chin,
　　My necktie rich and modest, but asserted by a simple pin—
　　　（They will say: "But how his arms and legs are thin!"）
45　Do I dare
　　Disturb the universe?
　　In a minute there is time
　　For decisions and revisions which a minute will reverse.

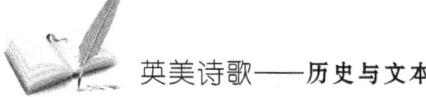

For I have known them all already, known them all:
50 Have known the evenings, mornings, afternoons,
I have measured out my life with coffee spoons;
I know the voices dying with a dying fall
Beneath the music from a farther room.
So how should I presume?

55 And I have known the eyes already, known them all—
The eyes that fix you in a formulated phrase,
And when I am formulated, sprawling on a pin,
When I am pinned and wriggling on the wall,
Then how should I begin
60 To spit out all the butt-ends of my days and ways?
And how should I presume?

And I have known the arms already, known them all—
Arms that are braceleted and white and bare
（But in the lamplight, downed with light brown hair!）
65 Is it perfume from a dress
That makes me so digress?
Arms that lie along a table, or wrap about a shawl.
And should I then presume?
And how should I begin?

Shall I say, I have gone at dusk through narrow streets
70 And watched the smoke that rises from the pipes

第八章 现当代诗歌

Of lonely men in shirt-sleeves, leaning out of windows? ...

I should have been a pair of ragged claws

Scuttling across the floors of silent seas.

And the afternoon, the evening, sleeps so peacefully!

75　Smoothed by long fingers,

Asleep ... tired ... or it malingers,

Stretched on the floor, here beside you and me.

Should I, after tea and cakes and ices,

Have the strength to force the moment to its crisis?

80　But though I have wept and fasted, wept and prayed,

Though I have seen my head（grown slightly bald）brought in upon a platter,

I am no prophet—and here's no great matter;

I have seen the moment of my greatness flicker,

And I have seen the eternal Footman hold my coat, and snicker,

85　And in short, I was afraid.

And would it have been worth it, after all,

After the cups, the marmalade, the tea,

Among the porcelain, among some talk of you and me,

Would it have been worth while,

90　To have bitten off the matter with a smile,

To have squeezed the universe into a ball

To roll it toward some overwhelming question,

To say, "I am Lazarus, come from the dead,

Come back to tell you all, I shall tell you all" —

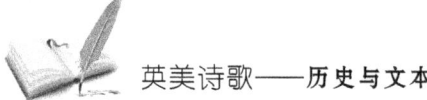

95   If one, settling a pillow by her head,

        Should say, "That is not what I meant at all;

        That is not it, at all."

        And would it have been worth it, after all,

        Would it have been worth while,

100 After the sunsets and the dooryards and the sprinkled streets,

        After the novels, after the teacups, after the skirts that trail along the floor—

        And this, and so much more?—

        It is impossible to say just what I mean!

        But as if a magic lantern threw the nerves in patterns on a screen:

105 Would it have been worth while

        If one, settling a pillow or throwing off a shawl,

        And turning toward the window, should say:

          "That is not it at all,

        That is not what I meant, at all."

110 No! I am not Prince Hamlet, nor was meant to be;

        Am an attendant lord, one that will do

        To swell a progress, start a scene or two,

        Advise the prince; no doubt, an easy tool,

        Deferential, glad to be of use,

115 Politic, cautious, and meticulous;

        Full of high sentence, but a bit obtuse;

        At times, indeed, almost ridiculous—

        Almost, at times, the Fool.

第八章　现当代诗歌

  I grow old ... I grow old ...
120　I shall wear the bottoms of my trousers rolled.

  Shall I part my hair behind? Do I dare to eat a peach?
  I shall wear white flannel trousers, and walk upon the beach.
  I have heard the mermaids singing, each to each.

  I do not think that they will sing to me.

125　I have seen them riding seaward on the waves
  Combing the white hair of the waves blown back
  When the wind blows the water white and black.

  We have lingered in the chambers of the sea
  By sea-girls wreathed with seaweed red and brown
  Till human voices wake us, and we drown.

  第一次世界大战之后的英国社会尽管在竭力维持自己超级大国的形象，其世界霸主地位却逐渐被美国所取代。当时的人们感到英国好像是一只没有头的苍蝇，不知道未来的走向到底如何。而对社会整体丧失信心的直接后果就是人们对自身生存意义的思考和怀疑，这就是在20世纪流行于英国的"荒诞派戏剧"（the Theatre of Absurd）所竭力表述的"荒诞"。所谓荒诞，指的是个人的主观期盼和客观世界的冷漠之间的强烈对比，以及由此产生的个人对生活的挫败感。这种荒诞的情绪在现代诗歌里得到了惟妙惟肖的表达，而 *The Love Song of J. Alfred Prufrock* 就是这样一首描述现代人生活荒诞性的诗歌。

艾略特（1888—1965）是英国现代史上具有代表性的诗人，他同时也是戏剧作家和文学评论家。艾略特出生于美国，自1915年开始定居英国，于1927年加入了英国国籍，并获得了1948年的诺贝尔文学奖。艾略特在诗歌中大量地实践自己的文学批评理论，采用诸如意识流（stream of consciousness）、戏剧独白（dramatic monologue）、早期的新批评主义（New Criticism）等写作手法和理念，并将现代文学中的中心主题——荒诞——作为其诗歌创作的重点，因此当之无愧为现代文学的先驱者之一。1922年，除了被标榜为现代文学经典之作的《尤利西斯》的出版，更有艾略特的《荒原》（The Waste Land）问世，而这一年则被评论家普遍认为是标识现代主义文学创作理念定型的最关键的一年。尽管《荒原》被认为是艾略特最有代表性的作品，作者在其中广泛地运用了创新的诗歌写作技巧，但由于其中含有大量的文学引用，并且整首诗歌缺乏明确的主题，因此也备受争议。相比较看，诗人早期的作品 The Love Song of J. Alfred Prufrock 虽然也含有很多现代主义元素，所受争议却并不多，而这首诗也包含了诗人后期创作的主要理念。

该诗创作完成于1911年，并在埃兹拉·庞德（Ezra Pound）的推荐下，于1915年发表在杂志 Poetry: A Magazine of Verse 上。在最初的草稿上，该诗本来有一个副标题 Prufrock among the Women，尽管最终的版本上艾略特并没有采用这个副标题，它却明白无误地指明了诗歌的主要内容。整首诗歌都是普鲁弗洛克（Prufrock）的内心戏剧独白，诗中的普鲁弗洛克似乎在焦急地等待一个约会的到来。虽然非常盼望向喜爱的女士表达爱意，由于年老体衰而缺乏信心的普鲁弗洛克在诗歌的结尾处也没有迈出约会的第一步。

诗歌的序诗取自但丁《神曲·地狱篇》，其中但丁见到了智者吉多（guido da montefeltro）。普林斯顿大学"但丁项目"（"Dante Project"）对这6行诗文的翻译如下：

第八章 现当代诗歌

If I but thought that my response were made

to one perhaps returning to the world,

this tongue of flame would cease to flicker.

But since, up from these depths, no one has yet

returned alive, if what I hear is true,

I answer without fear of being shamed.

大概的意思是：如果我知道你将会返回那个世界，我不会对你诉说；但是，既然我听说没有人从这个黑暗的王国里活着回去，我将要大胆地向你诉说。综合下文看来，艾略特引用这段诗文的主要宗旨是指出诗歌的形式为内心独白，而这首内心独白并不想让旁人听到。因此，从字面意思去看，诗文的第1行"Let us go then, you and I"中，独白者普鲁弗洛克化身成了但丁，而其中的"you"表面指的是吉多，实际上可以是任何一位读者。诗歌的前三个诗节（前23行）主要描写了窗外的景色：时间是十月的一个黄昏，半荒废的街道（第4行："half-deserted streets"）和下等的旅馆和饭店（第6～7行："cheap hotels/And sawdust restaurants"），空气中弥漫着让人窒息的黄色的雾（第三个诗节）。第四到第六个诗节中，普鲁弗洛克反复强调了一个问题——"there will be time"，似乎在为自己的犹豫拖沓找借口。从第54～69行，普鲁弗洛克一方面承认自己已经熟知想要与之交流的女性，另一方面却十分苦恼于一个问题——"我该怎么开始？"（"How should I presume?"）诗文的第70～121行诗节里，普鲁弗洛克展开了自己的想象力，设想在和女士见面的整个过程中，如何开始、如何应答、如果遭到羞辱该有什么反应，等等，他在这一部分的最后承认了自己已经年老没有吸引力，从根本上否定了自己（第118行："ridiculous"；第119行："Fool"）。在最后一部分诗文中，普鲁弗洛克想象自己见到了美人鱼，在惊叹于她们的美丽之余，他听到了人的声音，美梦破碎，他又回到了残酷的现实世界。

"荒诞"是现代文学的一个重要主题，它源自个人主观期盼和冷漠的

外在世界之间的落差，在该诗中"荒诞"仍然是作者刻画的重点。诗文中，普鲁弗洛克期盼向自己心仪的女性表达爱意，可是他却发现由于自己并不属于心仪女性所属的世界，这种爱意始终难以启齿。诗文的第三个诗节中，读者通过普鲁弗洛克的双眼看到了弥漫大街小巷的黄色的雾气。黄雾敲打着窗格子（第15～16行），舔食着黄昏的每一个角落（第17行），让读者感觉到沉闷而压抑。这个弥漫四周的雾气十分形象地刻画了一个荒诞的氛围，为普鲁弗洛克的爱情悲剧做好了铺垫。作者在行文中刻画了两个对比鲜明的事物：一个是年老力衰、毫无自信的普鲁弗洛克，另一个是养尊处优的女性世界。他们之间鲜明的对比，更是说明了普鲁弗洛克的爱情期盼将是无果的。在第二和第五个诗节呈现了同一幕场景：女士在客厅走来走去，谈论着米开朗琪罗。女士们的行为和言谈将她们的世界打上了"优雅""高贵"的标签。与此同时，普鲁弗洛克也认识到自己已经开始变老，甚至头发也开始掉落。内心敏感的普鲁弗洛克想要缩短自己和女性世界的差距，为了显得年轻一些，他甚至想是否该像年轻人一样把裤脚卷起来（第121行）。普鲁弗洛克在行文中反复地提出了一些问题，例如"我敢吗？"（"Do I dare?"），"我该怎么开始？"（"How should I presume？"）等，这些问题更使他显得笨拙而毫无自信。在第45～46行中，当他再一次问自己："我有勇气去打扰这个世界（"the universe"）吗"，普鲁弗洛克明确地提出了卑微的自己和冷漠的女性世界之间的对立。结尾处，普鲁弗洛克意识到自己的爱情期盼根本不可能有结果，开始想象大海中的美人鱼。虽然美人鱼不愿意向他歌唱，但是他却自认为可以默默地欣赏她们的美丽。然而，即使在想象世界中，普鲁弗洛克的爱情期望也难以实现——他不久便被人声拉回现实。因此，*The Love Song of J. Alfred Prufrock* 是主人公普鲁弗洛克为自己的爱情悲剧所唱的一首挽歌，其中读者看到的是一个生活在荒诞压抑氛围下的卑微的普通人。

在写作技巧上，该诗突破了传统诗歌格律的束缚，不拘一格地使用了许

第八章 现当代诗歌

多具有现代色彩的手法,例如内心戏剧独白(inner dramatic monologue)和互文性(intertexuality)等。首先,该诗采用了内心戏剧独白的形式,一方面突显了独白者普鲁弗洛克怯于将自己的内心暴露给别人的卑微的心态,另一方面这种形式方便了作者艾略特使用意识流的叙述方式。意识流是现代文学中一个标志性的叙述方式,读者通过普鲁弗洛克的意识流可以察觉到,其实主人公自始至终并没有迈出一步前去赴约;可是,身虽未动,却达到了神游千里的目的。诗文的后面,普鲁弗洛克的思维更具有跳跃性,他展开想象力,描述了一幅幅自己在高贵女士面前露怯的情景,使得诗歌带有一种自嘲而心酸的语调。其次,该诗互文性特点的重要标志之一,是艾略特在其中穿插了大量的文学典故。除了序诗来自但丁的《神曲》,文学经典的影子处处闪现,如第52行"I know the voices dying with a dying fall"源自莎士比亚戏剧《第十二夜》中的对白,而第81～82行的典故则出自奥斯卡王尔德的戏剧作品《萨洛米》。艾略特强调对文本的研究,为后来的新批评主义奠定了一定的理论基础,而诗文中的互文性则成为他针对这一文学理论的重要实践。

(三) Death of a Naturalist

Saemus Heaney

1 All year the flax-dam festered in the heart

  Of the townland; green and heavy headed

  Flax had rotted there, weighed down by huge sods.

  Daily it sweltered in the punishing sun.

5 Bubbles gargled delicately, bluebottles

  Wove a strong gauze of sound around the smell.

  There were dragon-flies, spotted butterflies,

  But the best of all was the warm thick slobber

Of frogspawn that grew like clotted water
10　In the spade of the bank. Here, every spring
I would fill jampotsfuls of the jellied
Specks to range on window-sills at home,
On shelves at school, and wait and watch until
The fattening dots burst into nimble
15　Swimming tadpoles. Miss Walls would tell us how
The daddy frog was called a bullfrog
And how he croaked and how the mammy frog
Laid hundreds of little eggs and this was
Frogspawn. You could tell the weather by the frogs too
20　For they were yellow in the sun and brown
In rain.
Then one hot day when fields were rank
With cowdung in the grass the angry frogs
Invaded the flax-dam; I ducked through hedges
25　To a coarse croaking that I had not heard
Before. The air was thick with a bass chorus.
Right down the dam gross-bellied frog were cocked
On sods; their loose necks pulsed like sails. Some hopped:
The slap and plop were obscene threats. Some sat
30　Poised like mud grenades, their blunt heads farting.
I sickened, turned and ran. The great slime kings
Were gathered there for vengeance and I knew
That if I dipped my hand the spawn would clutch it.

昔日辉煌历史的映照下，进入现代纪元的英国社会呈现出一种迷失的

第八章 现当代诗歌

状态,对于未来发展的何去何从缺乏一个固定的方向。在这种大背景下的英国文学领域里,那些并不是处于主流文化中心的"旁观者"往往更能深刻地剖析社会的深层问题。因此,在英国现代文学中,很多苏格兰、威尔士、爱尔兰等作家异军突起,取得了主流文学望尘莫及的成就。例如,在20世纪末的诗歌领域里,三位北爱尔兰诗人独领风骚,成为英国文学中一道独特的风景线:谢默斯·希尼(Seamus Heaney,1939—2013),德里克·马洪(Derek Mahon,1941—)和保罗·穆尔顿(Paul Muldoon,1951—)。其中,谢默斯·希尼在1995年以其"具有美好抒情和道德深度的作品"获得了诺贝尔文学奖,他的作品既讴歌了日常生活中的点滴逸事,也赞美了记忆之中活灵活现的过去。

虽然希尼的作品在英国市场的销售榜上始终位列前茅,但作为北爱尔兰的一名民族主义者,他却始终否认自己的创作属于英国主流文化的中心。1982年出版的一部英国诗歌集里面,未经希尼同意便收录了他的作品。对此,作家表示出强烈的不满,他强调自己是爱尔兰人,而非英国人。希尼将自己定性为一名英国主流文化的"旁观者",将英国文学传统和爱尔兰文学传统结合起来,通过对传统和历史的审慎,对英国的现代社会进行了形象的刻画和深刻的揭露。1999年,希尼出版发行了他翻译的《贝奥武甫之歌》,这部译作将现代英语的行文方式和古英语的韵律很好地结合在一起,真正将过去和现在做到了比较完美的整合。《博物学家之死》(*Death of a Naturalist*)选自诗歌集 *Death of a Naturalist*,虽然出版时间较早,却也包含了希尼主要的文学创作理念,在写作技巧上别具匠心。

希尼的第二部诗集 *Death of a Naturalist* 出版于1966年,其中包含了34首短诗。大部分的诗歌都涉及了对童年的回忆,谈及了家庭成员之间的关系、乡村生活的美好等问题,在讲述其成人过程的同时,表现了作者对于童年的怀念。*Death of a Naturalist* 是该诗集的第二首短诗,也是希尼具有代表性的一首诗歌。该诗分为两个看似并不对称的诗节,第一个诗节有21行诗文，第二个诗节有12行诗文。第一个诗节主要是对童年里去洼边捞蛙卵的回忆。为了制作亚麻布，必须将亚麻放在水洼里沤一段时间，充满了发酵味和腐败味的水洼成为青蛙产卵的地方。每每这个时候，童年时代的诗人便会用果酱瓶子装满蛙卵，放置在家里的窗台上或者学校的书架上以便观看蛙卵变成蝌蚪的整个过程。学校里的老师沃尔斯小姐（Miss Walls）也会绘声绘色地向学生讲述青蛙如何产卵的过程，以及根据青蛙的皮肤判断天气的变化等常识。第二个诗节是诗人对于童年回忆的一个反思，本来充满童趣的经历在成年人的眼中改变了内涵。青蛙变成了入侵者：它的声音聒噪，脉搏鼓动的脖子好像风帆，蠢笨的头颅不停地释放着气体，连姿势都像是一颗土手榴弹。诗人看到青蛙这令人作呕的样子，不禁转身逃跑了。他的心中确信，青蛙是为了报他少年时偷走蛙卵的仇而来，而如果诗人再次将手放到水洼里，蛙卵定会紧紧钳住他的手。

诗文用无韵体（不押韵的五步抑扬格）写成，为了描写童年时代诗人眼中充满童趣的景象和凸显成年后诗人眼中荒诞的景象，诗人用了腹韵、头韵等押韵形式和明喻、拟人等修辞方式，还大量地使用了诗句的跨行连续。例如，在第一个诗节中，"flax-dam festered"（第1行），"heavy headed"（第2行），和"jampotsfuls of the jellied"（第11行）都使用了腹韵和头韵的押韵方式，使诗节整体读起来有很强的韵律感，从侧面衬托出儿童眼中美好而神奇的世界。"the punishing sun"（第4行）使用了拟人的修辞手法，"Bubbles gargled delicately"（第5行）则含有拟声的运用，而用"bluebottles"借喻苍蝇，并把蛙卵比作一块块凝固的水域（"clotted water"，第9行），都充分说明了童年的诗人充满想象力的双眼。因此，诗文的前10行，通过押韵、拟人、拟声等手法表现了一个儿童眼中色彩斑驳的世界。第15～21行中，诗人使用了像是"daddy""mammy""and"等儿童用语，更是强化了童年的纯真可爱。如果第一个诗节中的"跨行连续"让读者看到了儿童眼中被想象力冲碎的景象，在第二个诗节中的"跨

第八章 现当代诗歌

行连续"则有了更深层次的含义。例如：第 23～24 行的"跨行连续"，通过凸显"Invaded"一词更是明确了青蛙在入侵的事实。而像"coarse croaking"（第 25 行）和"slap and plop"（第 29 行）等拟声词的运用，则表现了一个聒噪荒诞的青蛙世界。

正像是威廉·布莱克的《纯真之歌》和《经验之歌》将童年和成年划分开一样，该诗的两个诗节分别描述了童年和成年后诗人眼中不同的世界。在第一个诗节的最后，诗人讲到青蛙在太阳底下是黄色的，而到了雨中则变成了黄褐色的。这种变色暗喻了诗人的成长和世界观的改变，而第二个诗节的第 1 行"Then one hot day"中时间的改变也呼应了诗人的成长。成年的诗人用自己已经获得的知识再次审视童年时自己眼中的世界时，却发现早年的乐趣已不复存在，剩下的只是尔虞我诈的成人世界的解读。由此看来，哀悼童年纯真和乐趣的丧失是该诗的重要主题之一。因而，题目《博物学家之死》中，"死亡"的真正内涵并不是博物学家的死亡，而是指热爱自然和生活的童年纯真的失去。通过该诗，希尼再次将过去和现在进行整合，通过现在了解到了过去，而与此同时却表达了对"逝去"的怀念。另外，通过童年和成年两个不同的视角，作者在诗中展现了自然的双面性：她既是美丽而充满神秘色彩的，同时又是荒诞的人类的敌人，而这也是诗歌另外一个重要的主题。

二、Further Reading

（一）The Wild Swans at Coole

William Butler Yeats

1　The trees are in their autumn beauty,
　　The woodland paths are dry,

Under the October twilight the water
Mirrors a still sky;
5   Upon the brimming water among the stones
Are nine-and-fifty swans.

The nineteenth autumn has come upon me
Since I first made my count;
I saw, before I had well finished,
10 All suddenly mount
And scatter wheeling in great broken rings
Upon their clamorous wings.

I have looked upon those brilliant creatures,
And now my heart is sore.
15 All's changed since I, hearing at twilight,
The first time on this shore,
The bell-beat of their wings above my head,
 Trod with a lighter tread.

Unwearied still, lover by lover,
20 They paddle in the cold
Companionable streams or climb the air;
Their hearts have not grown old;
Passion or conquest, wander where they will,
Attend upon them still.

25 But now they drift on the still water,

第八章 现当代诗歌

Mysterious, beautiful;

Among what rushes will they build,

By what lake's edge or pool

Delight men's eyes when I awake some day

30　To find they have flown away?

【译文】
库尔的野天鹅

威廉·巴特勒·叶芝

1　树木披上绚烂的秋装，

　　林中的小径晒得干爽。

　　十月的微曦朦胧，

　　一片静空铺水中。

5　一湖秋水，满池卵石，

　　五十九只天鹅在悠游。

　　自我第一次来此数天鹅，

　　至今已是第十九个秋天。

　　正当我数着，我看见，

10　天鹅突然成群冲向蓝天

　　然后散开，绕着残缺的围圆飞行，

　　喧闹地扑棱着翅膀。

　　看着这灿烂的生灵，

　　我感到痛苦忧伤。

15　沧桑巨变，自从我乘着日色苍茫
　　在湖畔第一次听到
　　它们在我头顶盘旋时钟摆似的飞翔，
　　那时我的步伐多么轻盈。

　　它们比翼双飞，永不厌倦，
20　荡桨于多情的湖面，
　　时而双翮凌空，一举千里，
　　活力永不衰减。
　　不论游往何地，激情和志向，
　　将伴随它们，日久天长。

25　如今，它们悠游于幽静的水面，
　　神秘而又美妍。
　　它们将沿着怎样的湖边，
　　在怎样的蒲苇中筑起家园，
　　让人们把喜悦写入眼帘，
30　当某天早晨我突然起身，
　　发现它们早已杳无踪痕？

（刘守兰　译）

【点评】

《库尔的野天鹅》写于1916年10月，于1917年6月发表。这是一首表面上描写白天鹅，实则抒发自己心中失望、悲观、忧虑的孤独之情的诗作。诗歌共五个诗节，每节诗韵式为abcbdd。

一开始，诗人交代了时间（秋天）、地点和周围的环境，意象丰富（trees, woodland paths, twilight, water, sky, stones, swans），比喻生动（"The

第八章　现当代诗歌

trees are in their autumn beauty" "Under the October twilight the water/Mirrors a still sky"），句式整齐（两个主谓句，然后两个倒装句），描绘了一幅秋天净空高远、生态和谐的唯美画面。第二个诗节中诗人回忆了19年前第一次在湖边数天鹅的情景：正当我数着，我看见，天鹅突然成群冲向蓝天然后散开，绕着残缺的围圆飞行，喧闹地扑棱着翅膀。（"I saw, before I had well finished/All suddenly mount/And scatter wheeling in great broken rings/Upon their clamorous wings"）。其中诗人使用隐喻手法及其中两个形容词"broken rings""clamorous wings"与尾韵的使用，暗示当时失恋的状态及悲观的心情。第三个诗节中灿烂的生灵与诗人痛苦忧伤的心形成对比，一晃19年过去，过去的自己步伐轻盈，暗示自己已经远不如当年，感慨生命飞逝。"The bell-beat of their wings above my head,/ Trod with a lighter tread"中的"bell-beat"为拟声与头韵，"Trod"与"tread"为相似韵，增强了诗歌的节奏感与美感，感染力强。第四个诗节中，诗人惟妙惟肖地描绘了一幅天鹅比翼双飞的画面，和谐温馨：它们比翼双飞，永不厌倦，荡桨于多情的湖面，时而双翮凌空，一举千里，活力永不衰减。不论游往何地，激情和志向，将伴随它们，日久天长。水上的天鹅悠然自得，双宿双飞，形影不离，永不厌倦。暗示自己与恋人不能长久相伴，失恋、孤独、疲惫的心境。诗句"They paddle in the cold/Companionable streams or climb the air"中的"cold""Companionable""climb"为行内、行间韵，"Companionable streams"为移就修辞，艺术手法的使用增强了诗歌的美感与感染力。第五诗节中诗人采用"Mysterious""beautiful"来描写天鹅给人带来的超验感觉，神秘而又美妍。最后诗人运用问句想象着洁白的天鹅说不定哪天早上醒来会不辞而别，离开库尔庄园，"当某天早晨我突然起身，发现它们早已杳无踪痕？"展示了诗人焦虑惆怅的内心。

整首诗歌中，诗人借用对比手法将白天鹅的永恒之美与自己的生命短暂及痛苦内心进行对比，抒发了诗人失恋的惆怅与苦闷。诗歌描写唯美、

哀婉，内涵丰富，令人回味。

（二）When You Are Old

William Butler Yeats

1 When you are old and gray and full of sleep,
   And nodding by the fire, take down this book,
   And slowly read, and dream of the soft look
   Your eyes had once, and of their shadows deep;

5 How many loved your moments of glad grace,
   And loved your beauty with love false or true,
   But one man loved the pilgrim soul in you,
   And loved the sorrows of your changing face;

   And bending down beside the glowing bars,
10 Murmur, a little sadly, how Love fled
   And paced upon the mountains overhead
   And hid his face amid a crowd of stars.

【译文】
当你老了

威廉·巴特勒·叶芝

1 当你老了，白发苍苍，睡意蒙眬，
   在炉前打盹，请取下这本诗篇，

第八章 现当代诗歌

　　慢慢吟诵，梦见你当年的双眼
　　那柔美的光芒与青幽的晕影；

5　多少人真情假意，爱过你的美丽，
　　爱过你欢乐而迷人的青春，
　　唯独一人爱你朝圣者的心，
　　爱你日益凋谢的脸上的哀戚；

　　当你佝偻着，在灼热的炉栅边，
10　你将轻轻诉说，带着一丝伤感：
　　逝去的爱，如今已步上高山，
　　在密密星群里埋藏它的赧颜。

（飞　白　译）

【点评】

本诗写于1891年，是诗人采用假设想象的艺术手法，为心中恋人毛德·岗所写的情诗。叶芝长期苦恋爱尔兰著名美女毛德·岗，曾为她写下许多美丽而略带忧伤的情诗。叶芝赞美她无与伦比的美貌，甚至把她比作希腊美人海伦。叶芝在本诗中以深沉的感情和优美的诗句表达了他对毛德·岗的深深爱慕。全诗共三节，每节押韵方式为：abba cddc effe。诗行在遵循五音步抑扬格、重轻音节规律的基础上，略带节奏的变化，起到了很好的强调作用。

第一诗节中诗人运用连词叠用手法，描绘了一幅恋人年老时的样子：当你老了，白发苍苍，睡意蒙眬，在炉前打盹（"When you are old and gray and full of sleep/And nodding by the fire"）。随后诗人在想象中想到恋人会取下这本诗篇，慢慢吟诵，并借着恋人的回忆赞美其美丽的双眼中那柔美的光芒与青幽的晕影。第二个诗节中诗人采用对比手法渲染了恋人不仅仅

是外在美,其内在更美。有些人虚情假意,只爱慕恋人的外在美丽["How many loved your moments of glad grace/And loved your beauty with love false or true"("glad,grace"为头韵,"false or true"为对比)],但是诗人更爱其朝圣者的心,爱其日益凋谢的脸上的哀戚("But one man loved the pilgrim soul in you/And loved the sorrows of your changing face"),其中"soul"与"sorrows"乃为行间头韵,强调诗人对恋人的爱之坚定。第三个诗节中的炉火意象"glowing bars"与第一诗节中的"the fire"呼应,给人以温暖,更易引起人们的回忆。最后两句诗行"And paced upon the mountains overhead/And hid his face amid a crowd of stars"中的"mountains"与"stars"乃为象征手法,强调诗人对恋人的爱如同大山一般坚毅,如同星辰一般永恒。

整首诗歌意象优美,韵律节奏明快,诗人运用连词"and"叠用,反复使用"love",行内、行间头韵,对比及象征等手法使得诗歌艺术感强烈,意蕴突出。诗歌华丽、柔美而朦胧,充分体现出叶芝早期诗歌的特点。

(三)Easter 1916

William Butler Yeats

1 I have met them at close of day
   Coming with vivid faces
   From counter or desk among grey
   Eighteenth-century houses.
5 I have passed with a nod of the head
   Or polite meaningless words,
   Or have lingered awhile and said
   Polite meaningless words,
   And thought before I had done

第八章　现当代诗歌

10　Of a mocking tale or a gibe

　　To please a companion

　　Around the fire at the club,

　　Being certain that they and I

　　But lived where motley is worn:

15　All changed, changed utterly:

　　A terrible beauty is born.

　　That woman's days were spent

　　In ignorant good-will,

　　Her nights in argument

20　Until her voice grew shrill.

　　What voice more sweet than hers

　　When, young and beautiful,

　　She rode to harriers?

　　This man had kept a school

25　And rode our winged horse;

　　This other his helper and friend

　　Was coming into his force;

　　He might have won fame in the end,

　　So sensitive his nature seemed,

30　So daring and sweet his thought.

　　This other man I had dreamed

　　A drunken, vainglorious lout.

　　He had done most bitter wrong

　　To some who are near my heart,

35　Yet I number him in the song;
　　He, too, has resigned his part
　　In the casual comedy;
　　He, too, has been changed in his turn,
　　Transformed utterly:
40　A terrible beauty is born.

　　Hearts with one purpose alone
　　Through summer and winter seem
　　Enchanted to a stone
　　To trouble the living stream.
45　The horse that comes from the road,
　　The rider, the birds that range
　　From cloud to tumbling cloud,
　　Minute by minute they change;
　　A shadow of cloud on the stream
50　Changes minute by minute;
　　A horse-hoof slides on the brim,
　　And a horse plashes within it;
　　The long-legged moor-hens dive,
　　And hens to moor-cocks call;
55　Minute by minute they live:
　　The stone's in the midst of all.

　　Too long a sacrifice
　　Can make a stone of the heart.

O when may it suffice?
60   That is Heaven's part, our part
     To murmur name upon name,
     As a mother names her child
     When sleep at last has come
     On limbs that had run wild.
65   What is it but nightfall?
     No, no, not night but death;
     Was it needless death after all?
     For England may keep faith
     For all that is done and said.
70   We know their dream; enough
     To know they dreamed and are dead;
     And what if excess of love
     Bewildered them till they died?
     I write it out in a verse——
75   MacDonagh and MacBride
     And Connolly and Pearse
     Now and in time to be,
     Wherever green is worn,
     Are changed, changed utterly:
80   A terrible beauty is born.

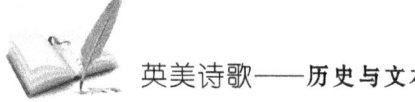

【译文】
1916年复活节

威廉·巴特勒·叶芝

1　我曾在黄昏时候见过他们
　　带着生气勃勃的面孔
　　从18世纪灰房子里的
　　柜台或写字台之中走来。
5　我走过他们时点点头
　　或说些无意义的客套话，
　　或停留片刻，作一些
　　有礼貌但无意义的交谈；
　　谈话结束前就想到讲一个
10　冷嘲的故事或热讽的笑话
　　让坐在俱乐部炉火旁的
　　伙伴们开心欢乐一番，
　　因为我觉得他们和我不过是
　　生活在一个小丑居住的世界：
15　但一切都变了，彻底地变了：
　　一种可怕的美已经诞生。

　　那位女士把白天花费在
　　天真无知的善意上，
　　夜晚则去参加争论
20　直争得她声嘶力竭。
　　哪有声音比她的更甜美

当她年轻美丽的时候
纵马外出逐兔打猎？
这个人曾经拥有一所学校
25 驾驭着我们的飞马；
这另一个是他的助手与朋友
也参加了他的战斗；
他本可以最终赢得盛名，
因为他有如此敏感的天性，
30 思想如此大胆又如此温情。
还有这个人，我原认为
是个酒鬼，是个自负粗俗之徒。
他曾经狠毒地伤害过
我心坎上的那个人，
35 但我也要为他而歌；
他也从这个荒诞的喜剧里
退出了他扮演的角色；
他，也改变了，
彻底地改变了：
40 一种可怕的美已经诞生。

心中只有一个目的
任凭夏去冬来，似乎
变成了一块着魔的石头
扰乱生命之溪流。
45 路过的马，马上的
骑手，从云层飞向

翻滚云层的鸟儿,
他们分分秒秒在改变;
溪水中的云影
50 　分分秒秒在改变;
一只马蹄在溪边滑落,
一只马在水中拍打;
长腿的母松鸡俯冲而下,
母松鸡对着公松鸡叫唤;
55 　他们分分秒秒地活着:
石头却在一切的中间。

太长时间的牺牲
能把人心变成石头。
噢,何时才能了结?
60 　那是老天的事情,我们
只是念叨一个一个的名字,
像母亲轻唤着孩子的名字
当睡眠终于降临
野跑的四肢终于安歇。
65 　难道这不是夜幕降临?
不,这不是夜幕而是死亡;
难道这不是无谓的牺牲?
因为英格兰或许会信守诺言
无论它做过什么,说过什么。
70 　我们知道他们的梦想;知道他们
梦想过并且死了,这已足够;

第八章 现当代诗歌

知道他们因过度的爱

困扰他们直至死亡有什么用?

我把他们用诗句写出——

75 麦克唐纳和麦布莱德

还有康纳利和皮尔斯

现在和以后的岁月里,

只要有绿色的地方,

一切都会改变,彻底地改变:

80 一种可怕的美从此诞生。

（李　璐　原译，何功杰　改译）

【点评】

  1916年4月24日,爱尔兰共和兄弟会举行反抗英国政府的起义,遭到英军的残酷镇压,时隔五日,爱尔兰民族主义者的复活节起义宣告失败,起义领袖中有15人被处死,而其中大多是叶芝当年的友人。整首诗歌在赞扬起义者的英勇壮烈行为中展示了诗人对民族、社会、历史的文学性思考。全诗共分四个诗节,一、三诗节为16行,每节韵式为 ababcdcdefefghgh,二、四诗节为24行,每节韵式为 ababcdcdefefghghijijklkl。

  第一个诗节中诗人以平和的笔调回忆了自己和这些参加起义人的关系：我曾在黄昏时候见过他们/带着生气勃勃的面孔/从18世纪灰房子里的/柜台或写字台之中走来/我走过他们时点点头/或说些无意义的客套话/或停留片刻/一些有礼貌但无意义的交谈/谈话结束前就想到讲一个/冷嘲的故事或热讽的笑话/让坐在俱乐部炉火旁的/伙伴们开心欢乐一番。第6行和第8行中诗人重复"meaningless"（无意义的）强调平时的交往只不过是泛泛之交,见面就是打个招呼,寒暄几句,没什么价值可言。因为我觉得他们和我不过是生活在一个小丑居住的世界（"Being certain that they and I/But lived where motley is worn"）,在诗人眼中,人们平时的交

往只不过是都戴着面具。但是最后两句诗"All changed, changed utterly/A terrible beauty is born"(但一切都变了/彻底地变了/一种可怕的美已经诞生)采用反复(句间与段落间)手法强调这些人的不同。"terrible beauty"为矛盾修饰法,其中"terrible"用来描写流血暴力革命的可怕,"beauty"指代起义为爱尔兰带来美好独立自主铺陈了道路,由此可见诗人对于这次起义的矛盾心理。"terrible beauty"的反复凸显了整首诗歌的主题。

  第二个诗节中诗人具体描写了不同领导人的不同性格,刻画了不同的人物形象。那位女士把白天花费在/天真无知的善意上/夜晚则去参加争论/直争得她声嘶力竭/哪有声音比她的更甜美/当她年轻美丽的时候/纵马外出逐兔打猎?/这个人曾经拥有一所学校/驾驭着我们的飞马/这另一个是他的助手与朋友/也参加了他的战斗/他本可以最终赢得盛名/因为他有如此敏感的天性/思想如此大胆又如此温情/还有这个人/原认为是个酒鬼/是个自负粗俗之徒/他曾经狠毒地伤害过/我心坎上的那个人/但我也要为他而歌/他也从这个荒诞的喜剧里/退出了他扮演的角色。第一诗节中,诗人貌似与这些人的交往平平,但在这里却描写得如此细腻,说明平时的交集比较多,了解也较深。两个诗节的对比增强了诗歌的张力,凸显了不同的叙述声音——有诗歌内部的,也有外部的,诗人在平静的语调中表明其对这些人的复杂感情。最后一句"A terrible beauty is born"与第一个诗节、第二诗节末后一行重复,凸显了主题。

  第三个诗节中诗人运用丰富的意象对于执着于不成熟的起义争取民族独立自主发出感慨(心中只有一个目的/任凭夏去冬来,似乎/变成了一块着魔的石头/扰乱生命之溪流)。诗人强调一切都在改变:马,马上的骑手,翻滚云层的鸟儿,溪水中的云影,长腿的母松鸡、公松鸡。诗人采用反复手法强调"一切都在改变",蕴含着诗人不赞成革命取得独立,而是对英国政府抱有幻想,希望和平解决独立问题。这一诗节中的石头("stone")象征僵化的起义。

第八章　现当代诗歌

第四个诗节中诗人怀疑起义的必要性：太长时间的牺牲／能把人心变成石头／噢，何时才能了结？／那是老天的事情。但是诗人把为起义献身的人的名字呼唤：只是念叨一个一个的名字／像母亲轻唤着孩子的名字／当睡眠终于降临／野跑的四肢终于安歇。在此表达了诗人对起义者的纪念和赞美之情。接下来，诗人感叹如果不贸然起义，也许英国政府会信守诺言。但无论如何事情已经发生，起义者已经献出生命，应该值得纪念：我把他们用诗句写出：麦克唐纳和麦布莱德／还有康纳利和皮尔斯／现在和以后的岁月里／只要有绿色的地方／一切都会改变，彻底地改变。最后一句"一种可怕的美从此诞生"与第一诗节和第二个诗节的末行呼应，突出这次起义的重要性及其价值。

诗歌主题是纪念为民族大业在起义中牺牲的领导者们，题目"1916年复活节"赋予此事件以崇高的宗教含义。人们都知道圣经中耶稣被钉十字架，然后死而复活，升天并赐下圣灵，具有了永恒的生命价值。诗人以复活节为衬托，暗示在起义中牺牲的生命将永垂不朽，从而肯定了起义的意义和价值。

（四）Byzantium

William Butler Yeats

1　The unpurged images of day recede;
　　The emperor's drunken soldiery are abed;
　　Night resonance recedes, night-walker's song
　　After great cathedral gong;
5　A starlit or a moonlit dome disdains
　　All that man is,
　　All mere complexities,

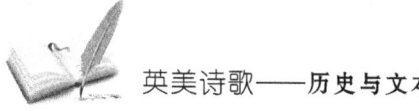

The fury and the mire of human veins.

Before me floats an image, man or shade,
10　Shade more than man, more image than a shade;
For Hades' bobbin bound in mummy-cloth
May unwind the winding path,
A mouth that has no moisture and no breath
Breathless mouths may summon;
15　I hail the superman;
I call it death-in-life and life-in-death.

Miracle, bird or golden handiwork,
More miracle than bird or handiwork,
Planted on the star-lit golden bough,
20　Can like the cocks of Hades crow,
Or, by the moon embittered, scorn aloud
In glory of changeless metal
Common bird or petal
And all complexities of mire and blood.

25　At midnight on the emperor's pavement flit
Flames that no faggot feeds, nor steel has lit,
Nor storm disturbs, flames begotten of flame,
Where blood-begotten spirits come
And all complexities of fury leave,
30　Dying into a dance,

第八章 现当代诗歌

  An agony of trance,

  An agony of flame that cannot singe a sleeve.

  Astraddle on the dolphin's mire and blood,

  Spirit after spirit! The smithies break the flood,

35 The golden smithies of the Emperor!

  Marbles of the dancing floor

  Break bitter furies of complexity.

  Those images that yet

  Fresh images beget,

40 That dolphin-torn, that gong-tormented sea.

【译文】
拜占庭

威廉·巴特勒·叶芝

1 白昼退隐了他不洁的形象；
  皇帝的近卫兵醉卧在床上；
  夜籁沉寂，夜行者的歌声
  伴随着大教堂的锣鸣；
5 星辉或月光下的圆屋顶
  蔑视人类的一切，
  一切不过是混杂的聚合，
  是狂暴和人类情绪的淤泥。

  我眼前浮动一个影像，鬼或人，

10 是人更像鬼，是鬼更像影；
　　因为哈得斯裹在尸布中的线轴
　　会解开缠绕的道路；
　　一张口没有气息也没有水分
　　会把众多喘息的口召集；
15 我向那超人欢呼致意：
　　我称它为生中之死，死中之生。

　　奇迹，金鸟或金制的玩意，
　　说鸟和玩意不如说是奇迹，
　　栖止在星光灿烂的金枝，
20 能像哈得斯的晨鸡一样鸣啼，
　　或在怨怼的明月之下，闪烁着
　　不朽金属的光芒，大声轻贱
　　平庸的飞鸟或花瓣
　　和一切淤泥和血浆的混杂聚合。

25 夜半，皇帝的甬道上飘闪
　　不假柴薪和钢镰燃点的火焰，
　　狂风不扰，火自相生，
　　浴血的精魂来到其中，
　　一切狂暴的聚合于是逃遁，
30 长逝在一个乐舞，
　　一个恍惚的痛苦，
　　一个烧不焦衣袖的火焰的痛苦中。

第八章 现当代诗歌

跨骑着海豚的泥血之体,

精魂队队!锻造坊截断洪水,

35 那皇帝御用的金作坊!

那舞场铺地的大理石方

粉碎了聚合的狂暴怒气,

那些依然在化生

新影像的虚影,

40 那海豚撕裂的,锣声折磨的大海。

(傅 浩 译)

【点评】

拜占庭城址位于当今土耳其的伊斯坦布尔,历史上曾是东罗马帝国的都城和东正教的圣地,以灿烂的文化历史著称。叶芝一生中写了两首关于拜占庭的诗歌。一首为《驶向拜占庭》,写于 1923 年;另一首是这首《拜占庭》,写于 1930 年。据记载,叶芝没去过拜占庭,但在诗中把拜占庭看作艺术和智慧永恒的国度。在这首诗歌中,诗人生动地描绘了灵魂在超脱前的最后一次净化过程。全诗共五节,每个诗节韵式为 aabbcddc。

第一个诗节中,诗人首先描述了白昼退去夜色即将主宰大地的景象:白昼退隐了他不洁的形象 / 皇帝的近卫兵醉卧在床上 / 夜籁沉寂,夜行者的歌声 / 伴随着大教堂的锣鸣。随后诗人运用拟人手法采用嘲讽的语气定义了人的本相:一切不过是混杂的聚合 / 是狂暴和人类情绪的淤泥。其中"recede"为反复,"resonance""song""gong"为拟声,"dome disdains"为拟人与头韵,第 6~7 行中的"all"为反复,表示强调,"The fury and the mire of human veins"中诗人运用讽刺和隐喻,其中"veins"为提喻。

第二个诗节诗人描述了他眼中所见的幽灵世界以及获得最后净化前鬼魂飘荡、聚集的景象。第 1~2 行诗中的词"image""man""shade"

反复使用，加上最后一行中的"death-in-life and life-in-death"（生中之死，死中之生）强调了凡俗世界与冥界、生与死的不可分性。第2行"Shade more than man, more image than a shade"为首尾反复，第3行"Hades"（哈得斯）是希腊神话中的冥王，诗人希望它解开缠绕着它的裹尸布，"unwind""winding"为同源辞格法，"Breathless mouths"指的是鬼魂，为提喻手法。

第三个诗节描述了象征永恒与艺术的金鸟对普通的鸟及人类的嘲笑。第1~2行中诗人反复使用"Miracle""bird""handiwork"强调艺术的超然之美，"Can like the cocks of Hades crow"使用了明喻，此节第5~6行的"Or, by the moon embittered, scorn aloud"为拟人手法，与第一诗节的第6行互文，"Common bird or petal"指凡俗世界的鸟与花，"And all complexities of mire and blood"与第一诗节最后一行互文，指代人类。

第四个诗节描绘了众多鬼魂经过艺术而得到净化的过程：不假柴薪和钢镰燃点的火焰／狂风不扰，火自相生／浴血的精魂来到其中／一切狂暴的聚合于是逃遁／长逝在一个乐舞／一个恍惚的痛苦／一个烧不焦衣袖的火焰的痛苦中。这一诗节中，诗人描绘了一幅肉体与灵魂脱离的画面。其中"flame"反复使用，强调永恒圣火的净化力量，此节中最后两行中的"agony"则强调灵魂超脱需要付出的代价，在痛苦中历练、净化。

第五个诗节中众多驮着灵魂的海豚形成了一幅壮丽的图画。大海中的海豚将人类的灵魂超度并使之进入永恒，远离肉体痛苦。这里的画面具有宗教与神秘主义色彩。此节中的意象：海豚、泥血之体、精魂队队、锻造坊、洪水、金作坊、大理石方、大海等具有很强的象征意义，令人揣摩，但都在灵魂净化中起到了一定的作用。

整首诗歌描绘的是夜晚的情形，意象丰富，画面鬼魅而又超然，灵与肉的分离、肉体的痛苦与灵魂的净化、短暂与永恒在诗人笔下显示出无限的张力。另外，各种修辞技巧及象征手法的使用更加增强了诗歌的魅力。

第八章　现当代诗歌

严谨的写作风格充满着诗人对人生的哲学思考，诗意含蓄而悠远。

（五）The Waste Land—The Burial of The Dead

（Excerpts）

T.S. Eliot

1 　APRIL is the cruellest month, breeding
　　Lilacs out of the dead land, mixing
　　Memory and desire, stirring
　　Dull roots with spring rain.
5 　Winter kept us warm, covering
　　Earth in forgetful snow, feeding
　　A little life with dried tubers.
　　Summer surprised us, coming over the Starnbergersee
　　With a shower of rain; we stopped in the colonnade,
10 　And went on in sunlight, into the Hofgarten,
　　And drank coffee, and talked for an hour.
　　Bin gar keine Russin, stamm' aus Litauen, echt deutsch.
　　And when we were children, staying at the archduke's,
　　My cousin's, he took me out on a sled,
15 　And I was frightened. He said, Marie,
　　Marie, hold on tight. And down we went.
　　In the mountains, there you feel free.
　　I read, much of the night, and go south in the winter.

　　What are the roots that clutch, what branches grow

20   Out of this stony rubbish? Son of man,

You cannot say, or guess, for you know only

A heap of broken images, where the sun beats,

And the dead tree gives no shelter, the cricket no relief,

And the dry stone no sound of water. Only

25   There is shadow under this red rock,

（Come in under the shadow of this red rock）,

And I will show you something different from either

Your shadow at morning striding behind you

Or your shadow at evening rising to meet you;

30   I will show you fear in a handful of dust.

Frisch weht der Wind

Der Heimat zu.

Mein Irisch Kind,

Wo weilest du?

35   "You gave me hyacinths first a year ago;

They called me the hyacinth girl."

—Yet when we came back, late, from the Hyacinth garden,

Your arms full, and your hair wet, I could not

Speak, and my eyes failed, I was neither

40   Living nor dead, and I knew nothing,

Looking into the heart of light, the silence.

Od' und leer das Meer.

第八章 现当代诗歌

【译文】
荒原——死者的葬礼（节选）
T.S. 艾略特

1　四月最残忍，从死了的
　　土地滋生丁香，混杂着
　　回忆和欲望，让春雨
　　挑动着呆钝的根。

5　冬天保我们温暖，把大地
　　埋在忘怀的雪里，使干了的
　　球茎得一点点生命。
　　夏天来得意外，随着一阵骤雨
　　到了斯坦伯吉西；我们躲在廊下，

10　等太阳出来，便到郝夫加登
　　去喝咖啡，又闲谈了一点钟。
　　我不是俄国人，原籍立陶宛，是纯德国种。
　　我们小时候，在大公家做客，
　　那是我表兄，他带我出去滑雪橇，

15　我害怕死了。他说，玛丽，玛丽，
　　抓紧了呵。于是我们冲下去。
　　在山中，你会感到舒畅。
　　我大半夜看书，冬天去到南方。

　　这是什么根在抓着，是什么树杈
20　从这片乱石里长出来？人子呵，
　　你说不出，也猜不着，因为你只知道

　　一堆破碎的形象，受着太阳拍击，
　　而枯树没有阴凉，蟋蟀不使人轻松，
　　干石头发不出流水的声音。只有
25　一片阴影在这红色的岩石下，
　　（来吧，请走进这红岩石下的阴影）
　　我要指给你一件事，它不同于
　　你早晨的影子，跟在你后面走
　　也不像你黄昏的影子，起来迎你，
30　我要指给你恐惧是在一撮尘土里。
　　风儿吹得清爽，
　　吹向我的家乡，
　　我的爱尔兰孩子，
　　如今你在何方？
35　"一年前你初次给了我风信子，
　　他们都叫我风信子女郎。"
　　——可是当我们从风信子花园走回，天晚了，
　　你的两臂抱满，你的头发是湿的，
　　我说不出话来，两眼看不见，我
40　不生也不死，什么也不知道，
　　看进光的中心，那一片沉寂。
　　荒凉而空虚是那大海。

（查良铮　译）

【点评】

　　《荒原》（1922）是艾略特的代表作，是西方文学中一部划时代的作品。《荒原》写出了整整一代人的精神状态，是对战后西方文明走向迷惘和式微的高度概括。《荒原》的主题是要恢复人们的信仰，强调的是基督教的救赎。

第八章 现当代诗歌

全诗分为5章,这是《荒原》第一章《死者的葬礼》中的第一、第二段。第1章《死者的葬礼》,概括了第一次世界大战后西欧万物凋零的景象。现实生活充满了虚伪和邪恶的欲望。第2章《对弈》是对社会不同阶层的扫描。第3章《火诫》,镜头对准伦敦的过去和现在。昔日充满诗意的泰晤士河,如今冷风袭人,阴森恐怖。伦敦人的生活卑琐庸俗。诗人认为,火能够烧去情欲,使人再生,重返自然。第4章《水里的死亡》仅10行,告诫人们,虽然人们渴望水,但是水同样可以使人们死亡。最后一章《雷霆的话》,表达的是欧洲是一片荒原的主题。诗人宣扬"施舍、慈悲和克制",诗人认为,人类只有通过古老的宗教信仰和东西方的智慧才能重新获得精神的新生。

诗歌一开始套用了乔叟《坎特伯雷故事》中《序言》开篇的春天场景。但诗人没有赞美象征春天的四月,没有像乔叟那样赞美"当四月的甘霖渗透了三月枯萎的根须",而是这里的四月最残忍,从死了的/土地滋生丁香,混杂着/回忆和欲望,让春雨/挑动着呆钝的根。此诗歌中的四月充满着死亡和欲望,诗人更喜欢冬天,因为冬天保我们温暖,把大地/埋在忘怀的雪里,使干了的/球茎得一点点生命。一开始诗人采用悖论手法,展开对于两个季节所代表的死亡与生命的描绘,展现了诗人对于生命的哲思,死亡的冬天孕育着生命,欣欣向荣的春天蕴含着死亡。诗人寻求的是从不合理中表现出合理,他认为荒谬之中自有真理存在。这与基督教的复活教义一致,即基督死后能够复活并非个例,万物死后都能够复活,这就是艾略特的意象中所包含的新义。描述完两个季节后,独白者在意识流中思考:夏天来得意外,随着一阵骤雨/到了斯坦伯吉西;我们躲在廊下/等太阳出来,便到郝夫加登/去喝咖啡,又闲谈了一点钟/我不是俄国人,原籍立陶宛,是纯德国种/我们小时候,在大公家做客/那是我表兄,他带我出去滑雪橇/我害怕死了。他说,玛丽,玛丽/抓紧了呵/于是我们冲下去/在山中,你会感到舒畅/我大半夜看书,冬天去到南方。这一段描写来自马丽公爵夫人于1916年出版的她个人的《回忆录》(*MY PAST*)中叙述的

事情。这一个意象群涉及一连串的死亡,有死于火、有死于水。很明显,诗人通过这一段的穿插意在突出"死亡"这个话题。但是隐含的水与火的意象即代表死亡,也代表灵魂的重生。显示了诗人对生命的基督教哲思。

  接下来,诗人以上帝的口吻说:人子呵/你说不出,也猜不着,因为你只知道/一堆破碎的形象,受着太阳拍击/而枯树没有阴凉,蟋蟀不使人轻松/干石头发不出流水的声音。"一堆破碎的形象"实为荒原的景象。在圣经中基督(人子)被比喻为流出活水(生命)的磐石,这里"干石头发不出流水的声音"指出人们信仰的失落、灵魂里的干枯,叙述者以上帝的口吻道出了荒原人缺乏信仰的精神现实。诗歌中的石头("stone""rock")指代基督。"我要指给你恐惧是在一撮尘土里"中的"尘土"指代的是没有对上帝存敬畏之心的人类,因为《圣经》上说,人来源于尘土,回归尘土。但诗人在诗句"不生也不死,什么也不知道,看进光的中心,那一片沉寂。荒凉而空虚是那大海"中指出可怕的一面在于"不生也不死",一种永远的荒凉景象。因为在《圣经》中指出,死可以带来复活。这里的不生不死表达了诗人对人类现实世界的一种绝望心情。

(六) From Preludes

(Excerpts)

T. S. Eliot

1 The winter evening settles down
   With smell of steaks in passageways.
   Six o'clock.
   The burnt-out ends of smoky days.
5 And now a gusty shower wraps
   The grimy scraps

Of withered leaves about your feet

And newspapers from vacant lots;

The showers beat

10　On broken blinds and chimney-pots,

And at the corner of the street

A lonely cab-horse steams and stamps.

And then the lighting of the lamps.

【译文】
序曲（节选）

T.S. 艾略特

1　冬天的黄昏带着牛排气味

　　停留在过道里

　　六点钟

　　烟气弥漫的白天烧剩的烟蒂

5　一阵骤雨裹起

　　枯叶污秽的渣滓

　　在你脚底

　　还有从空地上吹来的旧报纸

　　阵雨敲击

10　破烂的百叶窗和烟囱

　　街道拐角

　　一匹寂寞的马喷着热气刨着蹄

　　然后灯光亮起

（区　铻　译）

【点评】

《序曲》写于1915年，诗歌所描绘的是一个杂乱无序的世界景象：杂乱的意识、杂乱的生活。此部分主要写了傍晚杂乱与肮脏的冬天的伦敦景象。诗人以碎片化的意象组成诗体，表达了诗人对精神空虚的现代世界的厌恶、忧虑之情。

"The winter evening settles down/With smell of steaks in passageways/Six o'clock/The burnt-out ends of smoky days"（冬天的黄昏带着牛排气味/停留在过道里/六点钟/烟气弥漫的白天烧剩的烟蒂），诗人借用冬天黄昏反映出死气沉沉的荒原景象。下午六点中过道里飘出的牛排味反映了些许生活气息。然而烟雾弥漫和狂风暴雨的意象把读者带到一幅象征现代文明的破败景象中：一阵骤雨裹起/枯叶污秽的渣滓/在你脚底/还有从空地上吹来的旧报纸/阵雨敲击/破烂的百叶窗和烟囱。除了这些碎片式的景象，诗人还描写了一匹马，一匹有生气但孤独的马（"A lonely cab-horse steams and stamps"），更加衬托出冬日黄昏伦敦街头的寂寥与冷落。诗人寥寥几笔，纷呈迭出的意象将现代人的孤独寂寥描绘得淋漓尽致，诗人以一种超脱的心态来表现他对现代文明的复杂情感。

（七）The Hollow Man

（Excerpts）

T. S. Eliot

1   We are the hollow men
    We are the stuffed men
    Leaning together
    Headpiece filled with straw. Alas!
5   Our dried voices, when

第八章 现当代诗歌

  We whisper together
  Are quiet and meaningless
  As wind in dry grass
  Or rats' feet over broken glass
10 In our dry cellar.

  Shape without form, shade without colour,
  Paralyzed force, gesture without motion;

  Those who have crossed
  With direct eyes, to death's other Kingdom
15 Remember us—if at all—not as lost
  Violent souls, but only
  As the hollow men
  The stuffed men.

【译文】
空心人（节选）
T. S. 艾略特

1 我们是空心人
  我们是填塞起来的人
  彼此倚靠着
  头颅装满了稻草。可叹啊！
5 我们干枯的嗓音，在
  我们说悄悄话时

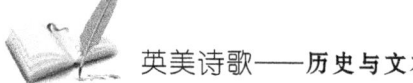

寂静而无意义

像干草地中的风

或碎玻璃堆上的老鼠脚

10　在我们那干燥的地窖里

有态而无形，有影而无色

麻木了的力度，没有动作的手势；

那些已经亲眼目睹

跨进了死亡这另一个国度时

15　只要记得我们——不是

丢魂失魄的野人，而只是

空心人

填塞起来的人。

（赵罗蕤　译）

【点评】

  本诗与名篇《荒原》的创作手法与所揭示的主题相一致。《空心人》沿袭了《荒原》的思想模式，进一步批判了现代人的精神贫乏和混乱无序。诗人以更深入细致的笔触展示了现代文明下人精神崩溃、空虚、无望的死一般的生存状态。

  诗人在诗歌一开始就定义了人这一群体，当然包括诗人自己在内："We are the hollow men/We are the stuffed men/Leaning together/Headpiece filled with straw."（我们是空心人 / 我们是填塞起来的人 / 彼此倚靠着 / 头颅装满了稻草）。"hollow"（没有灵魂）与"stuffed"（肉体）相对，里面装满了草，意指没有内涵、没有灵魂、没有信仰，如死活人，声音干枯、寂静而无意义。"Our dried voices, when/We whisper together/Are quiet and meaningless/As

第八章　现当代诗歌

wind in dry grass/Or rats' feet over broken glass/In our dry cellar"（我们干枯的嗓音，在 / 我们说悄悄话时 / 寂静而无意义 / 像干草地中的风 / 或碎玻璃堆上的老鼠脚 / 在我们那干燥的地窖里）中诗人采用复合明喻（"As wind in dry grass /Or rats' feet over broken glass"），明喻意象毫无生气且令人厌恶。通过"Shape without form, shade without colour/Paralyzed force, gesture without motion"，诗人继续描绘毫无生气的人类样式：有态而无形，有影而无色 / 麻木了的力度，没有动作的手势。其中"Shape"与"shade"押头韵，与"Paralyzed""without motion"呼应强调了灵魂失落的堕落人类的样子。接下来的诗文中诗人提到了"Kingdom"（国度），这与基督教的基督再临带来的国度相一致。其中"Violent souls"与"hollow men"和"The stuffed men"对应，再次强调"Soul"的缺失，讽刺当今社会的人类只是充满了欲望的空心人而已。

整首诗歌意象奇特，充分体现了艾略特对现实社会的深刻洞察及对人性的了解，展示了诗人对精神生活的向往和追求以及他对社会现实的失望与批判。

（八）Little Giddingo

T. S. Eliot

1　Ash on an old man's sleeve

　　Is all the ash the burnt roses leave.

　　Dust in the air suspended

　　Marks the place where a story ended.

5　Dust inbreathed was a house—

　　The wall, the wainscot and the mouse.

　　The death of hope and despair,

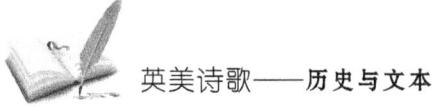

This is the death of air.

There are flood and drouth

10 Over the eyes and in the mouth,

Dead water and dead sand

Contending for the upper hand.

The parched eviscerate soil,

Gapes at the vanity of toil,

15 Laughs without mirth.

This is the death of earth.

Water and fire succeed

The town, the pasture and the weed.

Water and fire deride

20 The sacrifice that we denied.

Water and fire shall rot

The marred foundations we forgot,

Of sanctuary and choir.

This is the death of water and fire.

25 In the uncertain hour before the morning,

Near the ending of interminable night

At the recurrent end of the unending

After the dark dove with the flickering tongue.

Had passed below the horizon of his homing

30 While the dead leaves still rattled on like tin

Over the asphalt where no other sound was

第八章 现当代诗歌

      Between three districts whence the smoke arose

      I met one walking, loitering and hurried

      As if blown towards me like the metal leaves

35 Before the urban dawn wind unresisting.

      And as I fixed upon the down-turned face

      That pointed scrutiny with which we challenge

      The first-met stranger in the waning dusk

      I caught the sudden look of some dead master

40 Whom I had known, forgotten, half recalled.

      Both one and many; in the brown baked features

      The eyes of a familiar compound ghost

      Both intimate and unidentifiable.

      So I assumed a double part, and cried

45 And heard another's voice cry: "What! are you here?"

      Although we were not, I was still the same,

      Knowing myself yet being someone other—

      And he a face still forming; yet the words sufficed

      To compel the recognition they preceded

50 And so, compliant to the common wind,

      Too strange to each other for misunderstanding,

      In concord at this intersection time

      Of meeting nowhere, no before and after,

      We trod the pavement in a dead patrol.

55 I said: "The wonder that I feel is easy,

      Yet ease is cause of wonder. Therefore speak:

      I may not comprehend, may not remember."

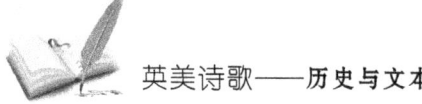

And he: "I am not eager to rehearse

My thought and theory which you have forgotten.

60　These things have served their purpose: let them be.

So with your own, and pray they be forgiven

By others, as I pray you to forgive

Both bad and good. Last season's fruit is eaten,

And the fullfed beast shall kick the empty pail.

65　For last year's words belong to last year's language

And next year's words await another voice.

But, as the passage now presents no hindrance

To the spirit unappeased and peregrine

Between two worlds become much like each other,

70　So I find words I never thought to speak

In streets I never thought I should revisit

When I left my body on a distant shore.

Since our concern was speech, and speech impelled us

To purify the dialect of the tribe

75　And urge the mind to aftersight and foresight,

Let me disclose the gifts reserved for age

To set a crown upon your lifetime's effort.

First, the cold friction of expiring sense

Without enchantment, offering no promise

80　But bitter tastelessness of shadow fruit

As body and soul begin to fall asunder.

Second, the conscious impotence of rage

At human folly, and the laceration

第八章　现当代诗歌

       Of laughter at what ceases to amuse.
85   And last, the rending pain of re-enactment
       Of all that you have done, and been, the shame
       Of motives late revealed, and the awareness
       Of things ill done and done ro others' harm
       Which once you took for exercise of virtue
90   Then fools' approval stings, and honour stains.
       From wrong to wrong the exasperated spirit
       Proceeds, unless restored by that refining fire
       Where you must move in measure, like a dancer."
       The day was breaking. In the disfigured street
95   He left me, with a kind of valediction,
       And faded on the blowing of the horn.

【译文】
小吉丁
　　　　T.S. 艾略特

1   一个老人衣袖上的灰
     是燃尽的玫瑰留下的一切的灰。
     悬在半空中的尘土
     标志着一个故事的终结之处。
5   吸入的尘土曾是一幢房子——
     墙、护壁板还有耗子。
     希望和绝望的死亡，

这是空气的死亡。

在眼前在嘴中

10 有着水灾和干旱，

死水和死沙

争着要占上风。

干燥龟裂，再无生气的土壤

瞪视着劳动的虚空，

15 没有快意的笑声。

这是土地的死亡。

水和火继承

城镇、牧场和青草。

水和火嘲笑

20 我们拒不作出的牺牲。

水和火将会锈去

我们忘却了的

圣殿和唱诗班高坛破损的地基。

这是水和火的死亡。

25 在黎明前的那一不能肯定的时刻

接近那漫无止境的长夜的终结

在漫无终结中重现的终结

当黑色的鸽子吐着闪亮的舌头

在他归途的地平线下经过

30 而枯叶仍像罐头一般砰砰作响

在听不到其他声音的沥青路上

在浓烟升起的那些区域中

我遇到一个人漫步缓缓而又匆匆

就仿佛金属的树叶一般向我飘来

35　叶子飘零一任城市拂晓时的风。

当我凝视着那张低垂的脸

用我们在暮色中向第一次遇到的陌生人

所作的挑战似的打量凝视着他

我看到某个逝去的大师的意外的眼光

40　我曾认识他，后来忘却了，又回忆起一半

一个和许多个：在晒成棕色的容貌中

一个熟悉的混合的鬼魂的眼睛

既是亲密无间，又是难以区分。

于是我用一种双重身份来呼喊

45　听到另一个声音高喊着："什么！你在这里？"

虽然我们不曾在这里，我过去也是一模一样，

知道我是自己但同时又是另一个人——

而他一张脸正形成；但这些话足够

促进他们已开始了的相认。

50　这样，顺着共同的风，

相互太为陌生，因而不会误解，

与空前绝后、无处相遇中相遇的

时间的交叉点上一致

在死一般寂静的巡逻中我们走在人行道上。

55　我说："奇怪的是我感到的是轻松，

但轻松正是惊讶的原因。所以你说吧：

我或许不能理解，或许记不住。"

他说:"我不急于背诵

你已忘了的我的思想和理论。

60 这些东西已达到了目的:就让它们去吧。

你自己的也是如此,祈祷它们能被其他人

宽恕,就像我请你宽恕我的

好的和坏的。上个季节的水果已被吃净,

吃饱了的野兽就要踢开空桶。

65 因为去年的话属于去年的语言,

而明年的话等待另外一个声音。

但是,就像这条通道现时并未呈现任何障碍,

妨害没有满足的以及到处流浪的精神

在两个变得彼此很像的世界之中,

70 于是我找到了我从未想过要说的话,

在我从未想到要重访的街道上,

那时我将躯体留于一个遥远的海岸。

既然我们的关注是言语,言语逼迫我们

使部落的方言纯净,

75 使头脑去思前瞻后;

让我打开为老年保留的礼品,

给你终身的努力戴上一顶皇冠。

首先,缺乏魅力的,不能给人希望的,

只有水果影子的苦涩无味的,

80 熄灭中感性的冰冷摩擦声

就像身体和灵魂开始分解。

其次,对人类的愚蠢的狂怒:

意识到狂怒的无能以及对

第八章　现当代诗歌

　　那不再可笑的东西揪心地笑。

85　最后，对你所做、所是的一切
　　重新立法的剧烈痛苦，动机的
　　可耻性后来才被披露，关于事情
　　做得不好，还有做得有损别人的感觉，
　　而你曾将此当作德行的运用。

90　然后傻瓜的赞同隐隐作痛，荣誉成了污点。
　　从错到错，那激怒的灵魂继续
　　向前冲，除非从净化的火中恢复过来，
　　火里你必须按着拍子移动，像个舞蹈者。"
　　天色破晓。在毁坏的街衢中

95　他离开了我，说着告别词，
　　在号角鸣响时渐渐隐去身形。

（裘小龙　译）

【点评】

　　《四个四重奏》是艾略特的最后一部长诗，这部诗作标志着艾略特诗歌创作生涯中的最高成就。《四个四重奏》是一部现代主义经典作品，是由四首诗构成的，分别是发表于1935年的《燃毁的诺顿》，1940年的《东库克》，1941年的《干塞维奇斯》和1942年的《小吉丁》。整部作品围绕着时间与空间、生与死、短暂与永恒、过去与未来、有限与无限展开叙述和讨论，引发人们进行哲理性的思考，亦即人应该怎样看待自己，该如何活着才有意义以及该怎样过一个有意义的人生。人类在有限的时空内如羊走迷，忘记了来时的路，忘记了出发的目的，不知道从哪里来到哪里去。艾略特的意图是思索解决二元矛盾的途径，从而为拯救人类的时间找到方法。《小吉丁》是《四个四重奏》整部作品的最后一部分，是整部作品思想的升华，最后一首诗完成之后，艾略特便封笔不再写诗，使得《小吉丁》

这首诗成为艾略特诗歌创作生涯中永恒的绝唱。

《小吉丁》可以看成整篇组诗的总结。标题中的"小吉丁"是亨廷顿郡（Hungtingdonshire）的一个村庄。1625 年，尼古拉斯·费拉尔（Nicholas Farrar, 1592—1637）在此建造了教堂，成立了英国圣公会宗教社区。1647 年，在内战（查理一世与议会的战争）结束后，清教徒解散了这个宗教社区并摧毁了教堂。该教堂在 19 世纪得以重修，至今仍在。这首诗写于 1942 年，当时正值第二次世界大战期间，英国处于历史的关键时刻，艾略特在伦敦作为防火巡警，德国飞机狂轰滥炸的残酷现实使他感慨万千。他在诗中以小吉丁为背景，对历史和现实进行了深刻的思考。

《小吉丁》是由五个乐章组成，这里所选的是本"重奏"中的第二乐章。这一章的主题内容基本包括两部分：开始的三小节是第一部分，最后的一长节是第二部分。在第一部分的三小节中，每一小节包括 8 个诗行，韵式为 aabbccdd。诗人总结了前面三个四重奏中提及的几种死亡。第一节诗人总结了空气之死（"This is the death of air"），第二节总结了土之死（"This is the death of earth"），第三节总结了水与火之死（"This is the death of water and fire"）。诚然，这"死亡"是德国轰炸机带来的，但诗人把它与这构成物质世界的四大元素联系在一起，与古希腊哲学家赫拉克利特（Heraclitus, 前 504—前 470）提出的四元素相亡相生的理论相似："气亡生火，土亡生水，水亡生土"（"Fire lives in the death of air; water lives in the death of earth; and earth lives in the death of water"）。四大物质元素之"死"象征着天地万物和精神之死。在这里，死与生虽然并不相交，但死亡意味着超越时间，暗示着复活的希望, 与下面一节有着内在的联系。在第二部分，诗人以一位已故大师的告诫为线索揭示了自己对死与生的感悟。诗人从基督教的思想出发，描述了灵魂从困境走上解脱的过程。"吐着火舌的黑色鸽子"（"After the dark dove with the flickering tongue"）既象征德国轰炸机，又象征着《圣经》中多舌火焰的圣灵；既是死亡的象征，又是复活再

第八章　现当代诗歌

生的象征。诗人借另外的意象——"混合鬼魂"（compound ghost）——告诫：从错到错，那激怒的灵魂继续 / 向前冲，除非从净化的火中恢复过来 / 火里你必须按着拍子移动，像个舞蹈者。

全诗语言简洁，富有音乐性，与早期大量用典、晦涩费解的诗风迥异；整首诗意象丰富，象征性强，抒发了诗人对死亡与重生、短暂与永恒的深切思索，虽然带有宗教色彩，但却没有给人留下说教之感。从本节选来看，虽然《小吉丁》造就了一个虚无缥缈的迷幻世界，但是艾略特的伟大之处便是运用感官的领会带领读者领悟精妙的奥秘，以一种新的语言形式和新的思想创作出新的诗歌体裁，对当时诗坛的影响意义深远。

（九）Digging

Saemus Heaney

1 Between my finger and my thumb
  The squat pen rests; as snug as a gun.

  Under my window a clean rasping sound
  When the spade sinks into gravelly ground:
5 My father, digging. I look down
  Till his straining rump among the flowerbeds
  Bends low, comes up twenty years away
  Stooping in rhythm through potato drills
  Where he was digging.

10 The coarse boot nestled on the lug, the shaft
  Against the inside knee was levered firmly.

He rooted out tall tops, buried the bright edge deep
To scatter new potatoes that we picked
Loving their cool hardness in our hands.

15 By God, the old man could handle a spade.
Just like his old man.

My grandfather could cut more turf in a day
Than any other man on Toner's bog.
Once I carried him milk in a bottle
20 Corked sloppily with paper. He straightened up
To drink it, then fell to right away
Nicking and slicing neatly, heaving sods
Over his shoulder, digging down and down
For the good turf. Digging.

25 The cold smell of potato mold, the squelch and slap
Of soggy peat, the curt cuts of an edge
Through living roots awaken in my head.
But I've no spade to follow men like them.

Between my finger and my thumb
30 The squat pen rests.
I'll dig with it.

第八章 现当代诗歌

【译文】
挖掘

谢默斯·希尼

1 在我大拇指和其他手指中间
   一支粗壮的笔躺着,舒适自在像一支枪。

   我的窗下,一个清晰而粗粝的响声
   铁铲切进了砾石累累的土地:
5 我爹在挖土。我向下望
   看到花坪间他正使劲的臀部
   弯下去,伸上来,二十年来
   穿过白薯垄有节奏地俯仰着,
   他在挖土。

10 粗劣的靴子踩在铁铲上,长柄
   贴着膝头的内侧有力地撬动,
   他把表面一层厚土连根掀起,
   把铁铲发亮的一边深深埋下去,
   使新薯四散,我们捡在手中,
   爱它们又凉又硬的味儿。

15 说真的,这老头子使铁铲的巧劲
   就像他那老头子一样。

   我爷爷的土纳的泥沼地

一天挖的泥炭比谁个都多。

有一次我给他送去一瓶牛奶,

20　用纸团松松地塞住瓶口。

他直起腰喝了,马上又干开了,

利索地把泥炭截短、切开,把土

撩过肩,为找好泥炭,

一直向下,向下挖掘。

25　白薯地的冷气,潮湿泥炭地的

咯吱声、咕咕声,铁铲切进活薯根的短促声响

在我头脑中回荡。

但我可没有铁铲像他们那样去干。

在我大拇指和其他手指中间

30　那支粗壮的笔躺着。

我要用它去挖掘。

（袁可嘉　译）

【点评】

　　希尼的《挖掘》中涌动着祖辈父辈的血液,洋溢着故乡土地的芳香。该诗借用笔和铁铲的类比,反映出希尼传承本族文化、寻求民族精神、找寻自我、回归文化自我的内心诉求。

　　诗人一开始介绍手中的笔,舒适自在像一支枪（"Between my finger and my thumb/The squat pen rests; as snug as a gun"）。很明显,诗人采用明喻手法,将笔比作"枪",这两个意象带有很强的象征意义,暗示用笔创作就如同战场上用枪作战。一开始诗人就为本诗埋下了伏笔。在下两个诗节中,诗人描写了劳动中挖土豆的父亲形象,具体刻画了父亲娴熟使用铁铲,利用其挖土

第八章 现当代诗歌

豆时的情景：我的窗下，一个清晰而粗糙的响声/铁铲切进了砾石累累的土地：/我爹在挖土。我向下望/看到花坪间他正使劲的臀部/弯下去，伸上来，二十年来/穿过白薯垄有节奏地俯仰着/他在挖土/粗劣的靴子踩在铁铲上，长柄/贴着膝头的内侧有力地撬动/他把表面一层厚土连根掀起/把铁铲发亮的一边深深埋下去/使新薯四散，我们捡在手中/爱它们又凉又硬的味儿。这两节诗中诗人除了使用了大量动作词，如"sinks""digging""Stooping""comes up"，还运用了尾韵（"sound""ground"）、头韵（"spade sinks""gravelly ground"）等音韵及拟声（"rasping sound"）、拟人（"The coarse boot nestled on the lug"）等手法，形象具体生动地刻画了父亲劳动的画面。这一幅劳动场景中的父亲、泥土、土豆等意象与时间（"二十多年来"）结合，强调了诗人对家乡与土地的眷恋之情。尤其是诗文中透过父亲的挖掘想到爷爷的挖掘场景（"说真的，这老头子使铁铲的巧劲/就像他那老头子一样"），生命与土地结合，祖祖辈辈在这块土地上劳作、休养生息的历史画面，延长了诗歌的历史，丰富了文化内涵，增强了诗歌的民族生存内涵（"我爷爷的土纳的泥沼地/一天挖的泥炭比谁个都多/有一次我给他送去一瓶牛奶/用纸团松松地塞住瓶口。他直起腰喝了，马上又干开了/利索地把泥炭截短、切开，把土/撩过肩，为找好泥炭/一直向下，向下挖掘"）。诗人笔下的父亲、爷爷都是淳朴、勤劳的劳动者。他们都是在土地上用铁铲挖掘："白薯地的冷气，潮湿泥炭地的咯吱声、咕咕声，铁铲切进活薯根的短促声响"。但诗人不同于他们，诗人是用笔在"挖掘"（"But I've no spade to follow men like them/Between my finger and my thumb/The squat pen rests/I'll dig with it"）诗人运用隐喻暗示，相对于父辈们，诗人已受过良好教育，他不需要用铁铲去守护家园，他要用"笔"去挖掘、去战斗、去守护、去传承。

整首诗歌意象丰富，用词鲜明生动，诗人巧妙的用词、大量修辞手法的使用、各种感官的配合给予读者美的享受，形象地展示了作者爱尔兰民族的历史文化情结。诗人把田园风光与童年记忆相融合并加以提炼，创作出了一幅意境深远、节奏铿锵、历史文化浓厚并带有沧桑感的壮丽诗篇。

(十) In Memoriam M.K.H., 1911—1984

(From Clearances—5)

Seamus Heaney

1　The cool that came off the sheets just off the line
　　Made me think the damp must still be in them
　　But when I took my corners of the linen
　　And pulled against her, first straight down the hem
5　And then diagonally, then flapped and shook
　　The fabric like a sail in a cross-wind,
　　They made a dried-out undulating thwack.
　　So we'd stretch and fold and end up hand to hand
　　For a split second as if nothing had happened
10　For nothing had that had riot always happened
　　Beforehand, day by day, just touch and go,
　　Coming close again by holding back
　　In moves where I was x and she was o
　　Inscribed in sheets she'd sewn from ripped-out flour sacks.

【译文】

纪念 M.K.H.，1911—1984

谢默斯·希尼

1　刚从晒衣绳上取下的床单透着一丝凉气，

第八章 现当代诗歌

让我觉得里面还带着几分潮气
但是当我提起亚麻布床单的两角,
和她相对站着把床单拉开,先把四边拉直
5 然后又沿对角叠起,接着又拍打、抖搂
那床单却一如逆风中鼓涌的船帆,
发出干爽的波浪拍岸般的啪啪声
我们就这样拉开、折起,最后手对手地
在那一瞬间,似乎什么事也没发生过,
10 因为在此之前,这样的事也不断重演,
一天又一天,双手相触又快速分开,
向后退去又再次接近
在移动中我是 X 她是 O
那字母镌刻在她用撕开的面粉袋缝制的床单上。

(刘守兰 译)

【点评】

纪念 M.K.H. 是诗人写的一首悼念母亲的十四行诗,《出空》(*Clearances*)是一组专门悼念母亲的诗,收入诗集《山楂灯笼》(*The Haw Lantern*)中。本诗所描述的是诗人幼年时和母亲一起叠床单的情景。全诗的押韵格式为 ababcdcdeefgfg。

一开始,诗人描述了"我"收床单的情景("The cool that came off the sheets just off the line/Made me think the damp must still be in them")。其中"cool"与"came"为头韵,第 2 行中的 /m/ 音反复使用,传递了"我"怀疑床单是否晾干的心理。第 4 行诗中才出现"her"(母亲),母子俩叠床单的情景跃然纸上"But when I took my corners of the linen/And pulled against her, first straight down the hem/And then diagonally, then flapped and shook"(但是当我提起亚麻布床单的两角 / 和她相对站

着把床单拉开，先把四边拉直/然后又沿对角叠起，接着又拍打、抖搂），诗中的动作描写具体入微，展示了诗人善于观察的天性及描写的功底。

"The fabric like a sail in a cross-wind/They made a dried-out undulating thwack"两句诗中，诗人运用明喻与拟声修辞，增添了诗歌的艺术感染力与审美意识。"So we'd stretch and fold and end up hand to hand/For a split second as if nothing had happened"诗句中使用连词叠用，表明与母亲一起叠床单，面对面，最后是手对手，又好像在那一瞬间，似乎什么事也没发生过（"For a split second as if nothing had happened"），因为在此之前，这样的事也不断重演，一天又一天，双手相触又快速分开，向后退去又再次接近（"Beforehand, day by day, just touch and go/Coming close again by holding back"）。以上诗句表明，诗人常常和母亲一起干家务，是母亲的好帮手。最后两句点题，强调母亲的勤劳与持家的能力："In moves where I was x and she was o/Inscribed in sheets she'd sewn from ripped-out flour sacks"（在移动中我是 X 她是 O/那字母镌刻在她用撕开的面粉袋缝制的床单上）。其中的字母 X 象征在叠床单时，"我"是围绕母亲移动，再次肯定了母亲在家中的中心地位。

全诗写得情真意切，感人至深。诗人怀念已故的母亲，他回忆童年时代和母亲一起叠床单的点滴时光。诗人在整首诗歌中塑造了一位勤劳节俭、灵巧能干又喜爱洁净的爱尔兰农村贫苦人家的母亲形象，画面真实、细腻、唯美，隽义深刻。

美国诗歌部分

第九章 殖民地时期诗歌

殖民地时期的美洲大陆居住、生活条件十分艰苦，人们忙于生计，无暇吟诗作赋，文学水平层次也较低。这时期的统治者控制殖民地思想意识的主要手段就是宗教，出版的图书也大都是关于神学方面的研究。诗歌是当时最流行的文学形式，且内容也大多与宗教相关，其次是随笔、散文和游记类。总的来说，无论是从内容上还是从形式上，这些作品都不成熟，是美国文学的雏形。

1650年，安妮·布莱德斯翠特（Anne Bradstreet）的诗集《近来在美洲出现的第十个缪斯》在英国出版，大受英美两地追捧。这位女诗人的诗歌具有英国诗歌的传统形式，但内容却涉及了宗教、政治，反映了殖民者在美洲大陆创业时的艰苦和心态。布莱德斯翠特的诗歌感染力强、感情真挚，突破了当时的保守观念，为女性鼓与呼，是殖民地时期较有成就的诗人之一。爱德华·泰勒（Edward Taylor）是一位宗教诗人，深受保守派的推崇。他的诗歌鼓吹原罪和基督教教义教化，人类只有苦行度日才能得到救赎，否则就会受到永世惩罚。泰勒的诗歌创作体现了他作为牧师的职业特点，其内容也和他的布道密切相关。泰勒去世后，他的作品直到20世纪30年代才被整理出版。总体而言，泰勒的诗歌哲理性强、情感细腻、

第九章　殖民地时期诗歌

清新优美，这些诗歌使他在殖民地时期的美国文学史上留下了厚重的一笔。

1760—1790年是美国历史上的黑暗时期之一。这段时期英国在殖民地大肆开采矿山，开发种植园，建立纺织、冶炼等多种工业形式，经济形势较好。英国政府为了增加国内财政收入，对殖民地人民进行野蛮压榨，税收名目繁多，这点燃了北美大陆人民独立、自由的战火，无数的革命诗歌也应运而生，造就了独立战争舆论，也鼓舞了美利坚民族的斗志。资产阶级革命诗人菲利普·弗瑞诺（Philip Freneau）是当时最杰出的一位。在《英国囚船》（*The British Prison Ship*）中，弗瑞诺讽刺地表达出了对英军虐待俘虏罪行的愤慨之情。这是美国文学史上第一位将诗歌和战斗结合起来的诗人，被誉为"美国独立革命的诗人"。作为一名诗人，弗瑞诺的诗歌预示着美国文学的独立。他的诗作分前后两个时期，前期作品主要涉及民族、国家命运等重大历史题材，后期作品已初具浪漫主义的萌芽，语言风格清新自然，又被称为"美国诗歌之父"。

一、Poem Reading

（一）Verses Upon the Burning of Our House

Anne Bradstreet

1　In silent night when rest I took,
　　For sorrow ne'er I did not look,
　　I waken'd was with thundering nois
　　And piteous shrieks of dreadfull voice.
5　That fearfull sound of fire and fire,
　　Let no man know is my Desire.

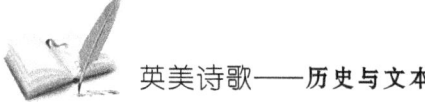

```
        I, starting up, the light did spye,
        And to my God my heart did cry
        To strengthen me in my Distresse
   10   Then coming out beheld a space,
        The flame consume my dwelling place.
        And, when I could no longer look,
        I blest his Name that gave and took,
        That layd my goods now in the dust:
   15   Yea so it was, and so 'twas just.
        It was his own: it was not mine;
        Far be it that I should repine.

        He might of All justly bereft,
        But yet sufficient for us left.
   20   When by the Ruines oft I past,
        My sorrowing eyes aside did cast,
        And here and there the places spye
        Where oft I sate, and long did lye.

        Here stood that Trunk, and there that chest;
   25   There lay that store I counted best:
        My pleasant things in ashes lye,
        And them behold no more shall I.
        Under thy roof no guest shall sitt,
        Nor at thy Table eat a bitt.
```

第九章 殖民地时期诗歌

30   No pleasant tale shall'ere be told,
      Nor things recounted done of old.
      No Candle'ere shall shine in Thee,
      Nor bridegroom's voice ere heard shall bee.
      In silence ever shalt thou lye;
35   Adieu, Adeiu; All's vanity.

      Then streight I gin my heart to chide,
      And didst thy wealth on earth abide?
      Didst fix thy hope on mouldring dust,
      The arm of flesh didst make thy trust?
40   Raise up thy thoughts above the skye
      That dunghill mists away may flie.

      Thou hast an house on high erect
      Fram'd by that mighty Architect,
      With glory richly furnished,
45   Stands permanent tho'this bee fled.
      It's purchased, and paid for too
      By him who hath enough to doe.

      A Prise so vast as is unknown,
      Yet, by his Gift, is made thine own.
50   Ther's wealth enough, I need no more;
      Farewell my Pelf, farewell my Store.
      The world no longer let me Love,

My hope and Treasure lyes Above.

清教思想始于17世纪的英国社会。随着英国国教（the church of England）的发展，清教徒认为它已经偏离了正统的基督教思想。清教徒分为两种，即改革派（conformist）和激进派（non-conformist）。改革派认为，尽管英国国教存在问题，这些问题可以通过改革加以纠正；而激进派则主张完全推翻英国国教，再建立一个符合正统基督教思想的国教。在伊丽莎白女王的绥靖政策之后，詹姆士一世和查理士一世使用铁腕手段镇压清教徒。在这种情况下，许多清教徒，特别是激进派的清教徒，离开了英国，乘船前往他们的梦想之地——美国。在他们的眼中，美国就是上帝曾经给他们许诺的迦南之地，在此他们可以建立自己的王国和教会。阿拉贝拉号（"Arabella"）就是运送清教徒前往美洲大陆的船只之一，她于1630年到达美国的马萨诸塞湾，女诗人安妮·布莱德斯翠特（1612—1672）就是乘坐阿拉贝拉号来到了美国。

布莱德斯翠特于1612年出生于英国的诺桑普顿，她在18岁随家人来到美国，父亲和丈夫都是殖民地的官员。布莱德斯翠特的诗作极具代表性，她是在美洲大陆出版发行作品的第一位女诗人，被世人称为"第十个缪斯女神"。一方面，布莱德斯翠特的将大量的清教思想渗透在自己的作品中。清教徒认为命由天定（predestination），将上帝放置于自己信仰的中心加以膜拜。面对美洲大陆荒芜但却美丽的自然风光，女诗人将其和自己的清教思想结合，创作了不少经典的作品，《沉思录》（Contemplations）就是其中重要的代表作品。另一方面，诗人的许多作品涉及了反叛和个人欲望等与清教思想格格不入的主题。生性敏感的布莱德斯翠特虽然也是怀揣着宗教的梦想，但在踏上了荒芜的美洲土地之后，她也不得不面对生活的艰辛和困顿。因此，她的作品中也暗含了对上帝的疑惑和质疑。其实，由于清教思想中对家庭观念的重视和对女性地位的轻视，布莱德斯翠特写作诗歌这件事本身就是对上帝的不敬。布莱德斯翠特作品中隐含的矛盾，预示着后期乔纳森·爱德华兹（Jonathan Edwards, 1703—1758）领导的"大觉

第九章　殖民地时期诗歌

醒运动"和本杰明·富兰克林（Benjamin Franklin, 1706—1790）支持的"自然神论"之间的冲突，而这也为美国人将理想主义和实用主义融合在一起的性格埋下了伏笔。选文中的诗歌就是布莱德斯翠特写作的一首宗教理想和现实需求之间冲突的作品。

1666 年，布莱德斯翠特的家中发生了火灾，所有的财产都付之一炬。面对天灾，诗人写作了 *Verses Upon the Burning of Our House*，原文的题目为 *Here follow Some Verses Upon the Burning of Our House*。诗歌共由九个诗节组成，按照内容可以划分为三个部分，诗节中每两行押韵。诗歌中使用了大量的隐喻（metaphor），诗人用这些隐喻阐述自己的宗教思想，探讨上帝和自己的关系。需要指出的是，美国文学的一个重要特点就是象征（symbolism）手法的运用，而这和殖民地时期像布莱德斯翠特这样的清教作家大量使用隐喻的写作手法是紧密相关的。例如，在第 3 行中（"thundering nois"）将火灾现场的噪音隐喻成巨大的雷声，表达了这一事故对诗人内心冲击力之大。而第 34 行之后，诗人摒弃了对世俗事物的眷恋，而将天堂比喻成一个装修得富丽堂皇的房屋，从精神层面得到了升华。第 41 行中，诗人将世俗物质比喻成粪堆（"dunghill"），将自己的注意力转向了精神方面的追求。第 43 行中的"mighty Architect"隐喻了上帝，指出上帝才是自己精神追求目标的最高引领者，很符合清教徒对上帝绝对权威的崇敬。第 42～47 行的倒数第二个诗节中，诗人使用了耶稣基督被钉在十字架上的典故（"It's purchased, and paid for too/By him who hath enough to doe"），并再次用到了隐喻，将由上帝构思、耶稣建造的精神支柱比作精致装修过的房屋。从这些隐喻的使用，可以看出诗人深埋在内心中的清教思想，与此同时，由于房屋这个形象贯穿于诗歌的始终，让读者感受到了她对世俗事物的眷恋。

根据诗歌的主题思想，可以将其划分为三个部分，每三个诗节为一个部分。在第一部分中，诗人描述了火灾的现场以及由于财产丧失而导致的伤心和难过，虽然在第三个诗节中她提出了"命由天定"的思想（第 13 行，

"I blest his Name that gave and took"),但这却难以平息诗人内心情感的涌动。第6,9行中大写首字母的"Desire"和"Distresse"凸显了诗人内心的绝望和悲痛,而像是"my Desire"和"my dwelling place"中强调"我的",以及第8行中"内心在哭泣"("my heart did cry")等也表达了诗人对烧毁事物的眷恋和不舍。诗人在诗歌的第二部分中将这种眷恋和不舍扩大化,更多地体现出自己物质性的一面。第四个诗节中,诗人谈到当自己经过废墟之时,不禁想到了曾经在房子中的欢愉,从而不忍继续看下去。第五和第六个诗节中,诗人用到了首语重复法(第24,25行,"there that chest/there lay that store";第30～33行使用了四个以"No"开头的句子),除了表现出一个妇人喃喃抱怨的样子之外,更让读者感同身受,不禁潸然泪下。第35行是该诗的一个重要转折,在承认"一切都是虚浮"("All's vanity")之后,诗人转向了内心对精神和信仰层面的追求。第三部分中的第七个诗节,诗人通过几个反问句对自己在诗歌前面所表现出来的物质欲进行了斥责。在之后的第八个诗节中,诗人描述了上帝在天堂中为自己构造的精美房屋,最终将信仰的精神力量放置于物质欲望之上。在最后一个诗节的终结中,诗人再次重申了对世俗事物欲望的摒弃("Farewell my Pelf, farewell my Store")和对精神信仰层面的执着。综观全诗,从开始的"普通人"到后来的"宗教人",这首诗歌整体表现出了诗人对于上帝信仰执着的清教思想,但是诗中反复出现的"房屋"这一字眼和形象,以及诗人在诗歌前半部分表现出来对烧毁房屋的眷恋,则体现了她没有因为盲目信仰而泯灭基本的物质欲望。

(二)Upon a Spider Catching a Fly

Edward Taylor

1　Thou sorrow, venom Elfe:

第九章 殖民地时期诗歌

  Is this thy play,

  To spin a web out of thy selfe

  To Catch a Fly?

5 For Why?

  I saw a pettish wasp

  Fall foule therein:

  Whom yet thy Whorle pins did not clasp

  Lest he should fling

10 His sting.

  But as affraid, remote

  Didst stand hereat,

  And with thy little fingers stroke

  And gently tap

15 His back.

  Thus gently him didst treate

  Lest he should pet,

  And in a froppish, aspish heate

  Should greatly fret

20 Thy net.

  Whereas the silly Fly,

  Caught by its leg

  Thou by the throate tookst hastily

  And 'hinde the head

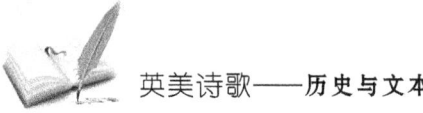

25 Bite Dead.

      This goes to pot, that not

      Nature doth call.

      Strive not above what strength hath got,

      Lest in the brawle

30 Thou fall.

      This Frey seems thus to us.

      Hell's Spider gets

      His intrails spun to whip Cords thus

      And wove to nets

35 And sets.

      To tangle Adams race

      In's stratigems

      To their Destructions, spoil'd, made base

      By venom things,

40 Damn'd Sins.

      But mighty, Gracious Lord

      Communicate

      Thy Grace to breake the Cord, afford

      Us Glorys Gate

45 And State.

第九章 殖民地时期诗歌

We'll Nightingaile sing like

When pearcht on high

In Glories Cage, thy glory, bright,

And thankfully,

50 For joy.

爱德华·泰勒（1642—1729）是美国殖民地时期另一位具有代表性的清教诗人。泰勒是一位激进派的清教徒，在英国期间受到了"玄学派诗人"的影响，因而在作品中运用了大量的明喻。查理士二世于1660年复辟了封建制度，并用铁腕手段镇压清教徒，促使一大批新教徒离开英国前往美洲大陆，其中就包括了泰勒。诗人于1668年到达美国，随后进入哈佛大学进行学习。毕业之后，他接受任命前往边缘的韦斯特菲尔德（Westfield）做牧师。在韦斯特菲尔德，泰勒不只是一名牧师，他还兼做医生和公务员，赢得了当地居民的一致认可。诗人认为，诗歌创作是与上帝进行沟通的方式，是属于个人行为。因此，诗人不但生前没有正式出版自己的作品，他还在遗嘱中禁止后人出版他的诗歌作品。所以，一直到1937年托马斯·约翰逊（Thomas H. Johnson）和1960年唐纳德·斯坦福（Donald E. Stanford）出版发行了诗人的两部诗集，泰勒作为诗人的身份才被读者知晓。泰勒诗歌的发表具有重要的意义，因为它为读者提供了审视清教思想和艺术的一个新角度。诗人流传至今的诗歌分成三个部分：一组抒情诗、长诗 *God Determinations* 和一组冥想诗歌 *Preparatory Meditations*。

泰勒是冥想派（the meditative poetry）的代表诗人。作为一名公理教会的清教徒（Congregational Puritan），泰勒的作品十分关注上帝在日常生活中透露的点点滴滴的神迹和救赎思想。他在清教诗歌和玄学诗歌中间寻找到了一个平衡点，即通过"明喻"的介入，赋予生活中的普通事物以深层次的意义，这也是他留下的217首冥想诗歌的中心思想。因此，尽管同为清教诗人,与接受了英国文学主流创作手法的布莱德斯翠特不同,泰勒在自己的冥想诗歌中加入了玄学派诗歌的因素,一方面使得他的诗歌区别于同时代其他的清教作品,另一方面这些诗歌却因为大量形而上的宗教冥想而变得晦涩难懂。需要指出的是,早在17世纪后半期,玄学派诗歌便开始被清教作家所厌弃,而泰勒也是美洲大陆唯一一位重要的玄学派诗人。玄学派的诗歌创作方式一直到19世纪才再次受到美国超验主义作家的青睐。虽然泰勒的作品大部分到了20世纪才问世,但是由其创作的时间段来看,他在作品中表现出来的对精神信仰世界和对"自省"(self-scrutiny)的关注,延续到了艾默生、惠特曼、狄更生甚至艾略特等美国后世几代作家的作品中。

  选文 *Upon a Spider Catching a Fly* 是泰勒重要的冥想诗歌之一,也是所有冥想诗歌中比较通俗易懂的一首。诗歌一共包含了十个诗节,每个诗节由5行诗文组成,所有诗节中对应的诗文都有固定的音节组成:6,4,8,4,2。每个诗节中的每行诗文长度参差不齐,从形式上看类似蜘蛛网的一部分,而十个诗节共同组成了一面完整的蜘蛛网,等待猎物的到来。第一个诗节将蜘蛛描述为小精灵,诗人紧接着问了它两个问题:"蜘蛛网是不是用来捕捉苍蝇?"以及"为什么费力织出网来捕捉苍蝇?"。第二到第六个诗节中,诗人描写了蜘蛛网上的两个访客:黄蜂和苍蝇。一方面害怕黄蜂的毒刺(第9,10行,"Lest he should fling/His sting"),另一方面也担心易怒的黄蜂会损坏网子(第19,20行,"should greatly fret/Thy net"),蜘蛛不但不敢轻举妄动,反而采取了"绥靖"的政策:它用小手指轻轻抚摸敲击黄蜂的背部(第13~15行,"And with thy little fingers stroke/And gently tap/His back")。第五个诗节的第一个单词"Whereas",凸显了另一个"访客"苍蝇和黄蜂的不同。和"易怒"(第6行,"pettish")的黄蜂不同,苍蝇被冠以"愚蠢"的形容词(第21行,"silly")。当苍蝇不小心被蜘蛛网缠住双脚之后,蜘蛛

第九章 殖民地时期诗歌

毫不犹豫地一口咬住苍蝇的喉咙并将其咬死。第六个诗节对这一部分做出了简要的评论：不要做超出自己力量之外的事情（第28行，"Strive not above what strength hath got"）。正是因为清楚自己的实力，蜘蛛才会做出对两位"访客"不同的反应。第七到第十个诗节里，诗人就蜘蛛捕食的问题进行了深入讨论。在诗人眼中，蜘蛛变成了撒旦（第32行，"Hell's Spider"），而它的猎物才是曾经在伊甸园中失落的亚当和夏娃（第36行，"Adams race"）。人类为了防止跌落如蜘蛛网的危险，唯有相信上帝（第43行，"Thy Grace to breake the Cord"）。诗歌最终的落脚点在对上帝的崇仰，由于对上帝的崇敬，人类再也不是苍蝇或者黄蜂之类的被诱惑者，反而变成了唱着欢快歌曲的夜莺。

和泰勒的其他诗歌一样，*Upon a Spider Catching a Fly* 也是围绕着与《圣经》有关的"失乐园"（paradise lost）和"复乐园"（paradise regained）展开。其中，诗人再次使用了玄学派人士善用的明喻，将蜘蛛比喻成诱惑者撒旦，而将黄蜂和苍蝇比作亚当一样的被诱惑者。黄蜂和苍蝇是两类不同的被诱惑者，前者具有较强的个性和判断力，因而不会轻易被蜘蛛所捕获，而后者因为其薄弱的意志力和战斗力，只能成为蜘蛛嘴下的牺牲品。面对两类不同的被诱惑者，撒旦蜘蛛使出了不同的招数。诗歌在结尾处指出，抵御蜘蛛或者撒旦威胁的最好办法就是坚定对上帝的信仰，从而比较清晰地勾勒出了诗人在诗中贯穿的清教思想。另外，这首诗歌是一首宗教内涵丰富的冥想诗。例如，从第一个诗节中诗人的两个问题，可以看出他对于上帝允许人世间存在不公允现象的疑问。而第六个诗节中，诗人又直接表达了对蜘蛛"量力而行"的捕食策略的赞同，从而表达出了对它的象征事物——撒旦的复杂的情感。但是，和其他大部分清教徒一样，尽管有着些许疑问，但却对上帝至高无上的地位毫无疑义。泰勒将诗歌的落脚点定在对上帝的赞美之上，充分表达了其坚定的宗教信仰。

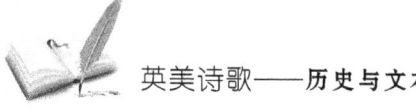

（三）The Indian Burying Ground

Philip Freneau

1   In spite of all the learn'd have said,
     I still my old opinion keep;
     The posture, that we give the dead,
     Points out the souls eternal sleep.

5   Not so the ancients of these lands,
     The Indian, when from life releas'd,
     Again is seated with his friends,
     And shares again the joyous feast.

     His imaged birds, and painted bowl,
10 And venison, for a journey dressed,
     Bespeak the nature of the soul,
     Activity, that knows no rest.

     His bow, for action ready bent,
     And arrows, with a head of stone,
15 Can only mean that life is spent,
     And not the finer essence gone.

     Thou, stranger, that shalt come this way.
     No fraud upon the dead commit—
     Observe the swelling turf, and say

第九章 殖民地时期诗歌

20　They do not lie, but here they sit.

　　Here still a lofty rock remains,
　　On which the curious eye may trace,
　　　（Now wasted, half, by wearing rains）
　　The fancies of a ruder race.

25　Here still an aged elm aspires,
　　Beneath whose far—projecting shade,
　　　（And which the shepherd still admires）
　　The Children of the forest play'd!

　　There oft a restless Indian queen,
30　　（Pale Shebah, with her braided hair）
　　And many a barbarous form is seen,
　　To chide the man that lingers there.

　　By midnight moons, o'er moistening dews,
　　In habit for the chase array'd,
35　The hunter still the deer purses,
　　The hunter and the deer, a shade!

　　And long shall timorous fancy,
　　The painted chief, and pointed spear,
　　And Reason's self shall bow the knee,
40　To shadows and delusions here.

美国殖民地时期文学的最大特点是模仿英国文学的写作模式和作品主题。像布莱德斯翠特和泰勒这样的作家，他们都是从英国移民到美国的，早在到达美国之前便已经潜移默化地接受了英国文学的影响。因而，大多数殖民地时期的文学作品都在忠实地模仿英国的文学形式和题材。菲利普·弗瑞诺（1752—1832）算是历史上第一位真正写作"美国"主题的诗人。弗瑞诺出生在纽约市，毕业于普林斯顿大学，后来参加了美国独立战争。由于注重描写美国的本土风光，弗瑞诺被公认为"美国诗歌之父"（the father of American poetry）和"美国独立战争的诗人"（the poet of American Revolution），是美国18世纪最重要的诗人。他的作品一般被分为两类，一类描写美国自然风光和当地印第安土著文明，如 The Wild Honey Suckle 和 The Indian Burying Ground；另一类则与美国独立战争有关，代表诗作是 The British Prison Ship 和 The Rising Glory of America。

弗瑞诺的诗歌作品有两个主要的特点，即同时具备新古典主义（neoclassicism）特点和浪漫主义元素。一方面，虽然诗人主要写作"美国"主题，描写美国本土美丽的自然风光和当地的土著文明，反对英国对美国内政的干涉，并热情地支持美国独立革命，但是，不可否认的是，他的作品中也包含了大量英国传统诗歌的元素。例如，诗人非常注重诗歌的押韵和节奏，并且在诗歌中引入了许多经典文学的故事和传说，而这也是他的作品被认为是具有新古典主义特质的原因。另一方面，处于18世纪晚期19世纪初期，即美国文学从殖民地时期到浪漫主义时期的过渡阶段，弗瑞诺作品中包含了许多浪漫主义元素。例如，他在 The Wild Honey Suckle 中通过对忍冬花的描写来赞叹美洲的自然风光，直接影响到了几乎同一时期的超验主义作家。他笔下自然呈现出一种"高贵的野性"（noble savage），而这样的自然延续到了后世几代作家的作品之中。另外，弗瑞诺作品中的哥特因素也影响到了另一位重要的浪漫主义作家——埃德加·爱伦·坡（Edgar Allen Poe，1809—1849）。

第九章 殖民地时期诗歌

　　The Indian Burying Ground 发表在诗人于 1788 年出版的诗集 *Miscellaneous Works* 中，后来成为诗人最具代表性的诗作之一。据说，1787 年的某一天，诗人曾亲眼目睹了印第安人埋葬逝者的场景，并为他们葬礼的习俗所震撼，于是发挥自己的想象力写作了该诗。诗歌共由十个诗节组成，押韵格式为 abab，韵律使用的是四步抑扬格（iambic tetrameter）。从诗歌写作严谨的格式可以看出弗瑞诺受到了新古典主义的影响。根据诗歌的内容可以将其分成两个部分，前四个诗节描写了印第安人坟墓；后六个诗节中，诗人展开想象力，再现了曾经鲜活的印第安文明。诗歌的前两句提到了"我"和"学者"（"the learn'd"）观点的不同，直接明了地宣告了和已经被广泛接受了的欧洲文明的决裂，暗喻了一个新的国邦的独立。在第一个部分中，前两个诗节将欧洲文明中的埋葬方式和印第安文明的埋葬方式进行了比较：前者中逝者是躺在坟墓中的，暗示了灵魂的永远安息；而后者则是以坐姿安葬，似乎随时准备和朋友一起享用一顿盛宴。第三和第四个诗节描述了坟墓内的装饰品，鸟的画像、画钵、鹿肉以及箭在弦上的弓箭，这些装饰品隐喻了生命的延续。在第二个部分中，诗人想象出了一幅印第安土著人的生活画卷。具有土著特色高耸的岩石（第 21 行，"lofty rock"）旁边，古老的榆树下面（第 25 行，"aged elm"），多少印第安人曾经停留过。曾经有一位像《圣经》中示巴女王一样美丽的女孩在这里停留过，和其他的印第安人一起斥责徘徊在此的异乡人。夜半时分，追逐鹿群的印第安猎人盛装出行，这一场景在光与影的交织中变成永恒（第八个诗节）。最后一个诗节（第九个诗节）中，诗人提到了理性（reason）和想象力的较量：在想象力面前，理性败下阵来，沉醉在诗人想象世界中的印第安文明之中。

　　虽然该诗描写的对象是印第安人埋葬地，但是却包含了不同的主题。首先，作者在诗中对死亡的主题进行了探讨。在印第安殡葬文化中，死亡

-323-

只是生命历程中的一站,并不是生命的终结,所以死亡之后的生命可能更加精彩(第16行,"And not the finer essence gone")。正因如此,下面的诗文中,读者看到了不同人物的鬼魂——天真的印第安牧羊人、美丽的印第安女孩、充满活力的印第安猎人,尽管他们早已逝去,但却仍然守护在古老的榆树下面,守护着这片古老的土地。从这个角度看,老榆树正是象征了古老的印第安文明。其次,诗人在该诗中将欧洲文明和印第安文明进行了比较。诗歌伊始,两种埋葬方式的比较便开门见山地指出了两种文明的区别。而贯穿诗歌始终的陌生人(第17行,"stranger";第22行,"the curious eye";第32行,"the man that lingers there";第37行,"timorous fancy"),很明显是欧洲文明的代言人。面对印第安古老文明,陌生人除了震撼,更是对其产生了好奇和疑惑。尽管诗人在回忆和赞美印第安文明,但是读者却可以看出整个文明画卷的展开却是在他的想象之中。因而可以断定,印第安文明虽然具有神秘感和魅力,却是一种即将、或者已然消亡的文明。而弗瑞诺在写作的时候,也不自觉地用了"一个更加野蛮的种族"(第24行,"a ruder race")和"粗野的人群"(第31行,"many a barbarous form")等字眼,表现出了其内心盎格鲁-撒克逊文明的优越感。最后,诗歌中对印第安文明的描写都是在诗人的想象世界中展开,诗中的哥特元素,以及对于古老文明的向往等主题,都充分说明了诗歌的浪漫主义特质。诗歌具有挽歌的特点,行文中也出现了不少模仿托马斯·格雷 *Elegy Written in a Country Churchyar* 的信息。例如,第19行的"the swelling turf"以及第25行的"elm"都是 *Elegy Written in a Country Churchyar* 中提到的重要景物,两者在主题上也多有重合。如果说格雷的 *Elegy Written in a Country Churchyar* 具有浪漫主义特点的话,该诗也不应该被划出浪漫主义诗歌的范畴。

二、Further Reading

（一）To My Dear and Loving Husband

Anne Bradstreet

1   If ever two were one, then surely we.
     If ever man were lov'd by wife, then thee.
     If ever wife was happy in a man,
     Compare with me ye women if you can.
5   I prize thy love more than whole mines of gold,
     Or all the riches that the East doth hold.
     My love is such that rivers cannot quench,
     Nor ought but love from thee give recompense.
     Thy love is such I can no way repay;
10 The heavens reward thee manifold, I pray.
     Then while we live, in love let's so preserves,
     That when we live no more we may live ever.

【译文】

致我亲爱的丈夫

安妮·布莱德斯翠特

1   如果曾有两人合二为一，是我俩无疑。
     如果曾有男人被女人爱，那必是你；
     如果曾有妻子在男人怀里陶醉，
     跟我比比吧，女人们，如果你们无愧。

  5 你的爱比整座金矿更珍贵，
    胜过整个东部所有的翡翠。
    我对你的爱像江河永不干涸，
    唯你也爱我，是我一生所求。
    你一往情深，我无法全部回报，
  10 唯祈愿上苍给你加倍的犒劳。
    有生之年，让我们相爱以恒；
    离世之后，我们仍在爱中永生。

（周建新　译）

【点评】

  《致我亲爱的丈夫》先用四个重复的 if 句式，凸显布莱德斯翠特对丈夫纯真、炙热的夫妻之爱。接着布莱德斯翠特用夸张的比喻表现了她对丈夫的爱之深及对爱的珍视，在她心目中，爱高于世间一切。诗人用金矿、东部财富、江河等意象来比喻夫妻之爱的无与伦比和矢志不渝。在尘世中肉体的不分你我也寓意着在天堂中精神的合二为一。她认为尘世之爱是一种精神救赎，但对怎样才能使尘世之爱永恒充满疑惑。结尾的四行诗强调了爱情的不朽与奉献，珍惜世俗之爱，并超越世俗世界，以期达到永恒，这也是清教有关来世信仰的一种写照。这首诗的韵律为五步抑扬格，全诗由六组各自押韵的两行诗组成，韵脚是 aabbccddeeff，双行押韵格式。格律工整，主题兼容宗教思想、自然感悟以及对永恒价值的憧憬和吟诵是布莱德斯翠特诗歌最突出的特征。

（二）The Author to Her Book

Anne Bradstreet

  1 Thou ill-formed offspring of my feeble brain,

第九章 殖民地时期诗歌

Who after birth didst by my side remain,

Till snatched from thence by friends, less wise than true,

Who thee abroad, exposed to public view,

5 Made thee in rags, halting to th' press to trudge,

Where errors were not lessened （all may judge）.

At thy return my blushing was not small,

My rambling brat （in print） should mother call,

I cast thee by as one unfit for light,

10 Thy visage was so irksome in my sight;

Yet being mine own, at length affection would

Thy blemishes amend, if so I could:

I washed thy face, but more defects I saw,

And rubbing off a spot still made a flaw.

15 I stretcht thy joints to make thee even feet,

Yet still thou run'st more hobbling than is meet;

In better dress to trim thee was my mind,

But nought save homespun cloth I'th'house I find.

In this array 'mongst vulgars may'st thou roam,

20 In critic's hands beware thou dost not come;

And take thy way where yet thou art not known;

If for thy father asked, say thou hadst none;

And for thy mother, she alas is poor,

Which caused her thus to send thee out of door.

【译文】
作者致其书

安妮·布莱德斯翠特

1　你是我贫乏大脑的畸形产物,
　　自从出生便不曾在我的左右,
　　直至被忠诚而愚钝的友朋
　　拉到国外,暴露于大庭广众,
5　让你衣衫褴褛,步履蹒跚,
　　错误未减(人人皆可判断)。
　　你的归来令我羞红了脸颊:
　　报端闲逛的淘气小儿称我妈,
　　我推开你,想你不宜抛头露面,
10　依我看你的脸蛋有些令人烦;
　　但你终究是我所出,如果我能,
　　亲情终将会修正你的毛病:
　　我为你洗脸,却看到更多瑕疵,
　　揩去一处斑点,竟成一种缺陷。
15　我活动关节让你双脚不走样,
　　你倒好,脚步反而更踉跄;
　　我本想为你穿体面的衣服,
　　四处收罗,只找到家织土布;
　　这样穿着,你尽可在平民中游荡;
20　只是当心别撞到批评家的手上;
　　走路应选沿途人多没交道,
　　若问你的父亲,就说未曾有过;

第九章 殖民地时期诗歌

问起你的母亲 只说他潦倒贫困,

别无他法 只得把你赶出家门。

(张跃军 译)

【点评】

布莱德斯翠特生于英国,嫁给了曾经两度担任马萨诸塞总督的丈夫西蒙,相夫教子之余布莱德斯翠特开始写诗,记载生活经历,宣泄情感,但仅限于亲朋好友间的传阅。她的姐夫在未经布莱德斯翠特允许的情况下将她的 15 首诗带到英国出版,题名为 *The Tenth Muse Lately Spring Up in America*。随着诗集的印刷出版,作者不打算与人分享的情感被公之于众,这给她带来了苦恼,也让世人很难理解,诗集能让她名利双收,为何烦恼?《著者和她的书》正反映了当时复杂的情感。在诗中,布莱德斯翠特不便把这种感情直白地表达出来,只能采取比喻的方式,用浓浓的母子情来描述她对书的态度。对待诗集,布莱德斯翠特就像一位溺爱孩子的母亲,虽然看到了孩子的诸多缺点错误,但并不以为耻,也并不打算矫正,谁又是完美的呢?此诗流露出诗集被别人冒昧出版的不快,也表现出布莱德斯翠特对自己作品的欣赏和怜爱。此诗典型的修辞格是拟人和双关,格律为英雄双韵体,每两行押韵,每个诗行为五音步抑扬格。

(三) The Prologue

Anne Bradstreet

1   To sing of Wars, of Captains, and of Kings,

    Of Cities founded, Commonwealths begun,

    For my mean Pen are too superior things:

    Or how they all, or each their dates have run

5   Let Poets and historians set these forth,

My obscure lines shall not so dim their worth.

But when my wond'ring eyes and envious heart
Great Bartas sugared lines do but read o'er,
Fool I do grudge the Muses did not part
10 Twixt him and me that overfluent store;
A Bartas can do what a Bartas will
But simple I according to my skill.

From Schoolboy's tongue no Rhetoric we expect,
Nor yet a sweet Consort from broken strings,
15 Nor perfect beauty where's a main defect;
My foolish, broken, blemished Muse so sings,
And this to men, alas, no Art is able,
'Cause Nature made it so irreparable.

Nor can I, like that fluent sweet-tongued Greek
20 Who lisped at first, in future times speak plain.
By Art he gladly found what he did seek,
A full requital of his striving pain.
Art can do much, but this maxim's most sure:
A weak or wounded brain admits no cure.

25 I am obnoxious to each carping tongue
Who says my hand a needle better fits,
A poet's pen all scorn I should thus wrong,

第九章　殖民地时期诗歌

  For such despite they cast on female wits.
  If what I do prove well, it won't advance,
30 They'll say it's stol'n, or else it was by chance.

  But sure the antique Greeks were far more mild
  Else of our Sex, why feigned they those nine
  And poesy made Calliope's own child?
  So' mongst the rest they placed the Arts divine.
35 But this weak knot they will full soon untie,
  The Greeks did nought but play the fools and lie.

  Let Greeks be Greeks, and Women what they are.
  Men can have precedency and still excel,
  It is but vain unjustly to wage war.
40 Men can do best, and women know it well.
  Preeminence in all and each is yours;
  Yet grant some small acknowledgement of ours.

  And oh ye high flown quills that soar the skies,
  And ever with your prey still catch your praise,
45 If e'er you deign these lowly lines your eyes,
  Give thyme or Parsley wreath, I ask no Bays;
  This mean and unrefined ore of mine
  Will make your glist'ring gold but more to shine.

【译文】
序诗

安妮·布莱德斯翠特

1　纵情歌唱战争、船长和国王，
　　赞美新建之城、初始之国，
　　我这卑微的笔怎敢奢望；
　　岁月的迁延，诸事的始末
5　自有诗人与史家去评判，
　　其辉煌这无名诗行难以表现。

　　但当我寻觅的目光和欣羡的心
　　扫过伟大巴特斯华美的诗行，
　　我像傻瓜般抱怨缪斯不曾赐予我
10　他那无与伦比的酣畅的笔墨；
　　巴特斯可以文采飞扬，
　　不才如我只能写下平凡的词章。

　　学童口中不能指望华丽的词句，
　　折断的琴弦弹不出优美的乐章，
15　显明的缺陷成就不了旷世佳丽；
　　我笨拙、断弦的琴弦却来献唱，
　　老天，补救的技艺都帮不上忙：
　　先天的不足使修补成了奢望。

　　我也无法，如那声音甜润的希腊人，

第九章　殖民地时期诗歌

20　起先笨口拙舌，后变得口齿清晰。
　　凭技艺他欣喜地发现了己心所寻，
　　那是对他艰苦付出的最好奖励。
　　技艺虽万能如许，也终有所短：
　　疗治虚弱、受伤的大脑便难如愿。

25　我易受世人口舌之箭所伤，
　　他们称我的双手握针倒能用得上，
　　若说诗笔鄙薄一切我难免矫枉，
　　纵然人们如此看低女性的睿智：
　　即便我妙笔生花，作用也不多，
30　他们会说那是偷来，或纯属巧合。

　　古希腊人远比我们朴素单纯，
　　他们为何创造异于人的九缪斯，
　　并使诗歌成为卡利俄铂的后人；
　　万物中他们独尊艺术为神祇，
35　这松垮的结，他们本可轻易解开，
　　但希腊人只是取笑别人或者乱说。

　　就让希腊人和女人如期所是
　　男人占了先机且遥遥领先，
　　不合理地宣战完全无用；
40　男人可以做到最佳，女人却可以心照不宣，
　　你们的优势遍布每个角落；
　　但对我们的些许优势也得认可。

-333-

啊，你这天上高高飞舞的彩笔，
永远以战利品的姿态收获着礼赞，
45 若屈尊惠顾简陋如许的诗句
赏我百里香、欧芹做的花篮，
我这低微、未经提炼的矿藏
会使你耀眼的金块更加闪亮。

（张跃军　译）

【点评】

《序诗》是一首四十八行诗，共分八个诗节，每节6行，采用抑扬格五音步，韵律节奏为ababcc。诗风平实、沉稳、不卑不亢，表达观点貌似低调、谦逊，却又柔中带刚、以理服人。作为美国殖民地时期的第一位女诗人，布莱德斯翠特出版的诗集 The Tenth Muse Lately Spring Up in America 给她带来巨大荣誉的同时，也伴有对女性诗人诗歌的质疑。在这首诗中，布莱德斯翠特道出了自己对女性诗人这一角色的探讨和思索，以及对当时女性社会地位低下、受到不公正待遇的强烈不满。诗人辩解的语气能让我们深切体会到她当时面临的压力和无奈。女性事业的发展受到当时社会条件的制约，尤其是美国的女诗人，在身份、创作空间、创作理念上遭遇种种非议，得不到应有的评价。

《序诗》为诗人的史诗集 The Four Monarchies 的序言。一方面，本诗作为诗集的开篇，本意在于为读者接下来的阅读做好准备，态度谦逊沉稳：对于庞大的史诗类题材，诗人在诗的前半部分将自己的诗作成果指称为"无名诗行"（obscure lines），并声明它们只是在创作中"资质平平"（according to my skill），的自然结果，并不打算与男性诗人及历史学家般那样去触及战争、国王、联邦等宏大的话题。另一方面，本诗最为人所关注之处与诗人独特的女性身份息息相关：在全诗谦逊的基调中，一种强烈的情感在后半部分得到充分表露，即对女性诗人饱受偏见的抨击与女性诗人对诗歌艺

第九章 殖民地时期诗歌

术的热爱追求。

在诗歌的前半部分，诗人表达了对文学巨匠才华的仰慕，谦称自己的才华不足以讴歌堂皇、宏伟的主题，自己的诗歌创作也只是一种技艺而已，如"学童之口""断弦"，但这些缺陷又难以补救，因为我"虚弱、受伤的大脑"。言下之意是尽管我在诗歌方面资质平平，但我热衷于诗歌创作之心绝不因此停息。

诗人由一般的诗人立场至特别的女性诗人的转变起始于第五小节。她一改前面谦卑地表达自己思想和观点的语气，转而谴责那些诋毁女性诗人之人，即便是貌似尊崇女人的希腊人也不例外。"我易受世人口舌之箭所伤／他们称我的双手握针倒能用得上……即便我妙笔生花，作用也不多／他们会说那是偷来，或纯出巧合"。在这里她为自己创作能力辩护的同时，也为自己的性别身份进行辩驳。诗人竭力维护女性诗人角色的完全合理性，谴责世人对女性的不公预设和对待，尽管她追求的并不是男女平等，而只是一点点认可。在诗歌的后半部分，对于女性诗人所遭受到的偏见和不公现象，以及渴求社会对女性诗人身份地位的认可，在布莱德斯翠特的淡定、从容中得以表达，增强了文字的说服力和感染力，既表达了作者对于诗歌的热爱、执着之心，又表达了对所谓流言蜚语的无所畏惧，字里行间透露出的幽默着实讽刺了那些对她作品的诋毁者。在诗的结尾部分，作者又一次显露出对待自己作品无比谦逊的态度，同时强调了对女性诗人地位的肯定和对诗歌艺术的热忱。总体看来，诗人对于女性诗人定位的坚定宣言与其卑微谦抑的写作风格形成了有机的统一：看似谦和低微的语言因坚定决绝的情感而愈发饱含张力，内核炽热坚决的情感因沉静平和的语言而显得更加庄重深沉。

(四) In Memory of My Dear Grandchild Elizabeth Bradstreet
Who Deceased August, 1665 Being a Year and a Half Old
Anne Bradstreet

1   Farewell dear babe, my heart's too much content,
    Farewell sweet babe, the pleasure of mine eye,
    Farewell fair flower that for a space was lent,
    Then ta'en away unto eternity.
5   Blest babe why should I once bewail thy fate,
    Or sigh the days so soon were terminate;
    Sith thou art settled in an everlasting state.
    By nature trees do rot when they are grown,
    And plums and apples throughly ripe do fall,
10 And corn and grass are in their season mown,
    And time brings down what is both strong and tall.
    But plants new set to be eradicate,
    And buds new blown to have so short a date,
    Is by his hand alone that guides nature and fate.

【译文】

纪念我亲爱的孙女　伊丽莎白·布莱德斯翠特

安妮·布莱德斯翠特

她殁于1665年8月，年仅1岁半

1　再见亲爱的孩子，我满心欢喜，

第九章　殖民地时期诗歌

再见乖孩子,你让我喜在眼中,
再见宁馨儿,你先被借往异地,
之后更是前往远方走向永恒。
5 　神佑的孩子,我何须一度悲切
你的命运,或哀叹你生命将终结;
你实安居于永不衰竭的天国。
按自然规律树木长成后会腐朽,
李子苹果熟透了便跌落于地,
10 庄稼和田里的草一到季节便要收,
时间会让一度强健挺拔者衰颓。
然而鲜嫩的植物终究会终止,
新长的嫩苗只能短暂地维持,
自然与命运皆由造化之手操持。

（张跃军　译）

【点评】

布莱德斯翠特一生育有八个子女,诗集中反映出她既是一位贤良淑德的妻子,又是一位称职的母亲、慈爱的祖母。由于布莱德斯翠特所处时代医疗水平的限制,布莱德斯翠特去世时,八名子女中仅剩一人。面对亲人去世,为表达心中的哀思和无助,布莱德斯翠特写有不少挽诗,悼念亲人的离世,祝愿死后必去天国,死亡之行也演变成天国之旅,以此来排解心中的苦痛与悲凉。挽诗在布莱德斯翠特诗歌中占不小的比重,有写给婴孩的,也有写给成年人的。

这首诗是诗人为悼念自己年仅一岁半夭折的孙女所作的一首十四行诗,采用五步抑扬格格律,韵律节奏为ababccc。诗人在诗中呈现出两重情感:一方面,作为一位慈爱的祖母,她为失去爱孙而感到深切的哀恸;另一方面,作为一个虔诚的清教徒,她努力将此结果视为上帝的意旨,即自然更替的

必然现象。

　　于一个上了年纪的人而言，孙辈的夭折难免会让人歇斯底里、怨天尤人，在本诗的开始，诗人对孙女的深情和对其逝去的悲恸流露无疑，但本诗又表现出了诗人对待此事异乎寻常的冷静和淡定。诗人是一名清教徒，宗教情感与体验是解读她诗歌的关键。人有今生来世，今生是短暂的、犹如昙花一现，来世却是永恒的、与上帝同在。基于此清教主义思想背景，诗歌前半部分主要描述她与孩子道别、依依不舍，强忍悲痛之情，将其永远离去视为走向人生永恒的天国之旅，以此来宽慰自己的内心。诗人的信仰引导其由对孙女纯粹的深爱与对其逝去的悲痛转向对自己的警示，即自己应该牢记孙女已离开尘世去往天堂与上帝同在；随后，诗人纵观寰宇万千，于诸多自然现象的更迭中感叹时光吞噬万物的流变；诗歌的后半部分将人之死亡解读为如同花开花落般的自然现象，虽如此，孩子夭折如同蓓蕾凋零，万般可惜，也道出了对掌控万物的主的怨言。最后，诗人总结道，尽管孙女在自然规律中只享受了极为短暂的一段生命时光，但作者得以从自己的信仰中寻得慰藉，即其个人的丧孙之痛均出于上帝的安排，而孙女则得以在阴世中享受与上帝永恒的欢乐。

（五）As Weary Pilgrim, now at Rest

Anne Bradstreet

1　As weary pilgrim, now at rest,

　　Hugs with delight his silent nest

　　His wasted limbes, now lye full soft

　　That myrie steps, haue troden oft

5　Blesses himself, to think vpon

　　his dangers past, and travailes done

　　The burning sun no more shall heat

第九章　殖民地时期诗歌

  Nor stormy raines, on him shall beat.

  The bryars and thornes no more shall scratch

10 nor hungry wolues at him shall catch

  He erring pathes no more shall tread

  nor wild fruits eate, in stead of bread,

  for waters cold he doth not long

  for thirst no more shall parch his tongue

15 No rugged stones his feet shall gaule

  nor stumps nor rocks cause him to fall

  All cares and feares, he bids farwell

  and meanes in safity now to dwell.

  A pilgrim I, on earth, perplext

20 wth sinns wth cares and sorrows vext

  By age and paines brought to decay

  and my Clay house mouldring away

  Oh how I long to be at rest

  and soare on high among the blest.

25 This body shall in silence sleep

  Mine eyes no more shall ever weep

  No fainting fits shall me assaile

  nor grinding paines my body fraile

  Wth cares and fears ne'r cumbred be

30 Nor losses know, nor sorrowes see

  What tho my flesh shall there consume

  it is the bed Christ did perfume

  And when a few yeares shall be gone

　　　　this mortall shall be cloth'd vpon
35　A Corrupt Carcasse downe it lyes
　　　a glorious body it shall rise
　　　In weaknes and dishonour sowne
　　　in power 'tis rais'd by Christ alone
　　　Then soule and body shall vnite
40　and of their maker haue the sight
　　　Such lasting ioyes shall there behold
　　　as eare ne'r heard nor tongue e'er told
　　　Lord make me ready for that day
　　　then Come deare bridgrome Come away.

【译文】
疲惫的朝圣者

安妮·布莱德斯翠特

1　疲惫的朝圣者正在休憩，
　　欣喜地蜷缩在静谧的小巢里
　　他疲惫的四肢松软地伸展
　　它们曾跋涉泥泞的荒原
5　他祝福自己，当他想起
　　工作已完成，危险已过去
　　灼热的太阳不再暴晒着他
　　暴风骤雨不再将他鞭挞。
　　不再怕荆棘丛刺伤手臂
10　不需要担心饿狼的追击

第九章 殖民地时期诗歌

　　不会迷失方向重入歧途
　　不再野果代面包暂且果腹，
　　对凉水他不再满怀期望
　　因干渴再难将他舌头灼伤
15　粗粝碎石不再磨破他双脚
　　树桩和石块再难将他绊倒
　　对烦恼与恐惧，他挥手再见
　　他眼下感受到的只有安全。
　　作为地上的朝圣者，我困惑
20　因那忧虑和悲伤缠绕的罪恶
　　因岁月和病痛侵蚀而衰垮
　　我这泥塑之躯日渐坍塌
　　啊，我多么盼望得到安眠
　　在上帝的保佑中高居云天。
25　身体将会静静地睡去
　　眼睛也不会再度哭泣
　　头脑不会一阵阵地眩晕
　　钻心的疼痛不再将我陪伴
　　不复受制于烦恼与恐惧
30　不知何为损失，何为忧虑
　　纵使我身体消损又有何妨
　　它像床榻散发出主的芬芳
　　而当若干年相继度过
　　这具血肉之躯将被包裹
35　入土时尸骨已然衰颓腐烂
　　它终将成为荣耀之身而升天

在虚弱和耻辱中播下种子
而拯救的力量来自基督
灵魂和肉体将会合二为一
40 并亲眼见到自己的造物主
这份快乐将持久绵长地存在着
仿佛耳朵不曾听、双目未曾见过
主啊,请让我为那天做好安排
然后来吧,新郎,快过来。

(张跃军　译)

【点评】

在诗歌的前半部分,布莱德斯翠特讲述了自己所见信徒的一生:当他们的生命到达终点时,他们"欣喜地蜷缩在静谧的小巢里",现在的他们已不再为"烈日""暴雨""狼群""饥渴"等人生旅途中的艰难困苦而烦恼,而是在天国找到了自己的安息地,得以放松疲惫的身心,得到前所未有的安全感。在诗歌的后半部分,布莱德斯翠特表达了自己渴望成为朝圣者的夙愿:"我多么盼望得到安眠/在上帝的保佑中高居云天"。但这并非意指"我"现在就想死去,而是当"我"完成人生旅途的艰难困苦时,"我"期待着能沉浸在永恒的安息之所。作为世人的"我",年老体弱又罪孽深重,已做好了"离开"的准备,血肉之躯的消亡又何妨?因为"我"的灵魂已升往天堂,与上帝同在。末句中的"新郎"指耶稣基督,这来源于基督教的教义,据说人类的灵魂嫁给了耶稣。

(六) Huswifery

Edward Taylor

1　Make me, O Lord, thy Spinning Wheele compleat;

第九章 殖民地时期诗歌

    Thy Holy Worde my Distaff make for mee.

    Make mine Affections thy Swift Flyers neate,

    And make my Soule thy holy Spoole to bee.

5 My Conversation make to be thy Reele,

    And reele the yarn thereon spun of thy Wheele.

    Make me thy Loome then, knit therein this Twine:

    And make thy Holy Spirit, Lord, winde quills:

    Then weave the Web thyselfe. The yarn is fine.

10 Thine Ordinances make my Fulling Mills.

    Then dy the same in Heavenly Colours Choice,

    All pinkt with Varnish't Flowers of Paradise.

    Then cloath therewith mine Understanding,

    Will, Affections, Judgment, Conscience, Memory;

15 My Words and Actions, that their shine may fill

    My wayes with glory and thee glorify.

    Then mine apparell shall display before yee

    That I am Cloathd in Holy robes for glory.

【译文】
家务

爱德华·泰勒

1 主啊，把我变成完美纺机，

    恳求您把您圣言做成线杆，

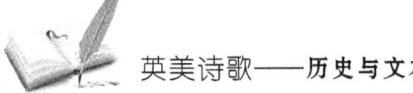

祈求您把我激情做成梭子，
但愿您把我灵魂做成圣管，
5 一定要让我祈祷做成卷盘，
从而把纺出的线做成线圈。

把我做成织布机编织股线，
再让圣灵，主，把线卷上，
然后编织成布，绝妙空前，
10 把您旨意做成万能的染坊，
用天国颜色染成纯色布料，
让天国鲜艳花朵打扮闪耀。

穿于我身显我领悟，意志，
倾心，判断，良心，记忆，
15 我的言行，这一切会普照
我荣耀的前程，和颂扬您。
穿着我的衣装，跪您面前，
神圣服装在身，光辉无限。

（胥少先　译）

【点评】

《家务》写于1685年，这首诗讲述的是把自己的一生献给上帝的人的故事。诗人记录了他和圣灵精神、肉体合二为一，整个人得到升华的过程，最终成为一个与以前不同的自己。诗的第1～6行讲述了"我""上帝"和"纺车"各部件之间的关系。第7～12行表述了在纺纱、织布、染色的过程中，我和圣灵已经融为一体。第13～18行进一步强调了我和上帝精神、肉体的合二为一，我已不是原来的"我"。美国学者唐纳德·斯坦福也认

第九章　殖民地时期诗歌

为 Taylor 最好的诗作来自"他那些神秘的日记、灵修体验以及与上帝的交流"。本诗很好地体现了这一点。在诗歌的起始部分，借助奇喻修辞格，诗人巧妙地把自己比喻成一台纺车，并深入细致地分析了纺纱过程。奇喻是 20 世纪玄学派诗歌的中心，它将两个貌似毫无交集、怪诞不经的事物，以明喻或暗喻为桥梁作比较，能给人耳目一新、恍然大悟之感。在诗的结尾，他不再是一部纺车，而是穿着由纺车纺出的布料做成衣服的人。泰勒认为，一些普通的日常小事，就像纺纱，也有它的玄学意义。世界上的一切事物因为有了上帝的旨意而有了更深层次的意义。此诗也印证了"诗人神学家"的诗作特点："精巧的艺术构思之中显出深邃而新颖的思想要素"。

（七）The Ebb and Flow

Edward Taylor

1　When first thou on me, Lord, wrought'st Thy sweet print
　　My heart was made Thy tinder box.
　　My affections were Thy tinder in't,
　　Where fell Thy sparks by drops.
5　Those holy sparks of heavenly fire that came
　　Did ever catch and often out would flame.

　　But now my heart is made Thy censer trim,
　　Full of Thy golden altar's fire,
　　To offer up sweet incense in
10　Unto Thyself entire:
　　I find my tinder scarce Thy sparks can feel
　　That drop out from Thy holy flint and steel.

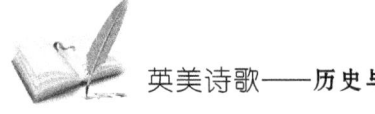

      Hence doubts out bud for fear Thy fire in me

      's a mocking ignis fatuus,

15 Or lest Thine altars fire out be,

      It's hid in ashes thus.

      Yet when the bellows of Thy spirit blow

      Away mine ashes, then Thy fire doth glow.

【译文】

潮涨潮落

爱德华·泰勒

1 当你，主啊，最初以你美好的形象为模

    造出一个我

    我的心就成为你的火绒盒。

    而我的热情是其中的火绒，

5 承接你的火星点点坠落。

    那来自天堂的圣火

    将我的心点燃，火焰熊熊。

    可是现在当我的心变作你整洁的香炉，

    盛满你那金色的祭坛之火，

10 为你献上甜蜜的熏香，

    我却发现我的火绒再难感受到你的火星

    坠落自你那神圣的打火石和铁。

    所以怀疑开始萌发：难道我心里的圣火

第九章 殖民地时期诗歌

其实只是一簇鬼火?
15 或者是为了不让你的祭坛之火熄灭,
才把它藏在灰烬中?
一旦你圣灵的风箱开始鼓动,
我的灰烬就会被吹走,而你的火又将燃烧。

(王文丽 译)

【点评】

中国学者认为泰勒的诗歌既体现了宗教精神,又结合了诗歌艺术。在泰勒看来,上帝就是他的一切,他创作诗歌的目的不是为了发表,而是通过描述与上帝的交流和那些神秘的灵修体验,更好地为上帝服务,教化子民。本诗采用了五步抑扬格格律,诗人作为一位牧师,用海水的潮起潮落比拟自己在不同人生时期对于上帝信仰的程度流变。在诗的第一小节,诗人表明自己在年轻之际最初信仰上帝时,其强烈程度堪比燃烧的烈火;在诗的第二小节,诗人信仰情感的强烈程度大大降低,进而将其比作香炉中的灰烬,难以再感知火焰的高温;在诗的最后一小节,诗人又转言尽管他当下的信仰已如火灰般不再热烈,但其内心深处仍留有点点火星的余热,仅需一点点上帝的进一步指引和激励便可再燃成熊熊烈焰。此诗从侧面表达了上帝的子民渴望得到无所不能的上帝的救赎,上帝的恩典和大爱能给子民带来无限希望。

(八) Upon the Sweeping Flood

Edward Taylor

1 Oh! That I'd had a tear to've quenched that flame
   Which did dissolve the heavens above

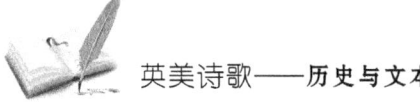

  Into those liquid drops that came

  To drown our carnal love.

5 Our cheeks were dry and eyes refused to weep.

  Tears bursting out ran down the sky's dark cheek.

  Were th' heavens sick? Must we their doctors be

  And physic them with pills, our sin?

  To make them purge and vomit, see,

10 And excrements out fling?

  We've grieved them by such physic that they shed

  Their excrements upon our lofty heads.

【译文】
有感于滔滔雨势
     爱德华·泰勒

1 啊！但愿我先前有这样一种泪，
  能够浇灭云霄里那种火——
  它把天熔成一滴滴的水，
  来将肉体的爱淹没。

5 但眼睛不肯哭，我们的脸很干。
  天迸出了泪，淌下它暗淡的脸。

  难道天病了？我们得做它大夫？
  拿我们罪孽给它做泻药？
  瞧，不是要使它下泻上吐，

第九章 殖民地时期诗歌

10　把该排泄的都排掉？
　　我们的泻药已经使天空悲伤，
　　使它排泄在我们高傲的头上。

（黄杲炘　译）

【点评】

此诗是泰勒最具宗教精神和清教徒风格意蕴的作品之一。泰勒受英国玄学派诗人邓恩影响颇深，他们善用奇思妙喻，认为人生意义在于服务上帝和自我反省。诗中的一个奇特意象，浩瀚的天空变作了人的内脏，滂沱大雨就是他的排泄物，读来感觉古怪、粗糙和过分夸张。在诗中，天空即上帝，因他们犯下的罪孽，他欲拯救芸芸众生，而他的子民并未意识到，"但眼睛不肯哭，我们的脸很干"，不得已，上帝只能靠自己的眼泪来冲刷人类的罪孽，彰显了上帝博大的胸襟、慈悲的情怀。而有余罪的我们，是否有资格医治天空，"拿我们罪孽给它做泻药？"引人深思。在本诗中作为"诗人神学家"、虔诚清教徒的泰勒借用"天""泪""水""泻药"的联想将对冥顽不化的人的救赎和上帝的博爱悲悯联系在一起。

（九）I Am the Living Bread: Meditation Eight: John 6:51

Edward Taylor

1　I kening through Astronomy Divine
　　The Worlds bright Battlement, wherein I spy
　　A Golden Path my Pensill cannot line,
　　From that bright Throne unto my Threshold ly.
5　And while my puzzled thoughts about it pore
　　I finde the Bread of Life in't at my doore.

When that this Bird of Paradise put in

This Wicker Cage (my Corps) to tweedle praise

Had peckt the Fruite forbad: and so did fling

10 Away its Food; and lost its golden dayes;

It fell into Celestiall Famine sore:

And never could attain a morsell more.

Alas! alas! Poore Bird, what wilt thou doe?

The Creatures field no food for Souls e're gave.

15 And if thou knock at Angells dores they show

An Empty Barrell: they no soul bread have.

Alas! Poore Bird, the Worlds White Loafe is done

And cannot yield thee here the smallest Crumb.

In this sad state, Gods Tender Bowells run

20 Out streams of Grace: And he to end all strife

The Purest Wheate in Heaven, his deare-dear Son

Grinds, and kneads up into this Bread of Life.

Which Bread of Life from Heaven down came and stands

Disht on thy Table up by Angells Hands.

25 Did God mould up this Bread in Heaven, and bake,

Which from his Table came, and to thine goeth?

Doth he bespeake thee thus, this Soule Bread take.

Come Eate thy fill of this thy Gods White Loafe?

Its Food too fine for Angells, yet come, take

30 And Eate thy fill. Its Heavens Sugar Cake.

What Grace is this knead in this Loafe? This thing

Souls are but petty things it to admire.

Yee Angells, help: This fill would to the brim

Heav'ns whelm'd-down Chrystall meele Bowle, yea and higher.

35 This Bread of Life dropt in thy mouth, doth Cry.

Eate, Eate me, Soul, and thou shalt never dy.

【译文】
我是生命之粮：沉思录之八：约翰福音 第六章五十一节
爱德华·泰勒

1　凭借神圣的天文学，我忽然间看到了
　　那个明亮的世界雉堞，并从中窥见了
　　一条我无法用诗笔来描绘的金色道路，
　　从金光闪烁的天国宝座直通我的门前。
5　正当我苦苦沉思，百思不得其解之时，
　　我突然发现生命的粮已摆在我的门前。

　　天国乐园的灵魂之鸟被关进了
　　这个柳条笼子（我的躯体）颂歌啼
　　啄食了园中的禁果，就这样丢失了
10　它的食物；辉煌的日子也一去不复还；
　　一个跟头栽进天国饥荒痛苦的深渊，
　　而且从此吃不上一口天国乐园的食粮。

　　哎呀呀！这可怜的鸟儿，你要做什么？

英美诗歌——历史与文本

　　　　生物世界是永远无法为灵魂提供食粮。
15　假如你敲响天使的天门,她们会给你
　　　　一个空桶:他们无法提供灵魂的食粮。
　　　　可怜的鸟呀!世间的白面包已经用完,
　　　　哪怕是小小的一口,也无法提供给你。

　　　　悲伤之时,上帝柔软的肠子里留出了
20　恩典;为了结束纠结,他碾碎了天堂里
　　　　最纯净的小麦———他亲生的儿子,
　　　　并把自己亲爱的儿子揉成生命的粮食。
　　　　这生命之粮从天儿降,是上帝借天使
　　　　之手把他的亲生儿子摆上了我的餐桌。

25　上帝做面包,并在天堂里烘烤,
　　　　面包来自他的桌子上,而后献给你?
　　　　这样他定会说:来吃这人间面包。
　　　　来把您上帝做的这块白白的面包吃?
　　　　这食品对天使实在好,可是来吃吧,
30　吃下您做的面包。这是您的甜点呀。

　　　　上帝揉成的这生命之粮是何等的恩赐?我们
　　　　这些人只不过是赞美您的小人物。
　　　　您的天使帮帮忙,这面包大得很,
　　　　装满天堂闪光的碗,碗中高高竖。
35　这生命之粮掉进了你的口中,并喊道:
　　　　吃了,吃了我,灵魂,你将永生不死。

　　　　　　　　　　　　　　(黄宗英　高黎平　译)

第九章 殖民地时期诗歌

【点评】

这是《沉思录》之八,以耶稣宣言——"我是生命之粮"来命名的一首诗歌,主题是赞美上帝爱子民,他不惜以血肉之躯喂食世间罪人,满足他们饥渴的灵魂,从而得到救赎,获得永生,以此彰显上帝的恩典和特殊的人格魅力。此诗是诗人最具代表性的宗教诗歌之一。全诗分六个诗节,每节六行,采用五音步抑扬格格律,韵脚为 ababcc。作为一名虔诚、博学的清教徒,爱德华·泰勒十分重视主持圣餐仪式,在组织每次圣餐前都会陷入冥思。在他看来,圣餐仪式不仅为神与人提供了沟通交流的机会,也是耶稣灵魂真实再现的神圣场所。

在本诗中,泰勒探讨了耶稣"我是生命之粮"这一宣言所蕴含的隐喻深度,在第一节中,泰勒描述了一幅一条大路从世界的边界起始、延伸,直指天堂的宝座的景象,并指出生命之粮正在沿着这条道路神秘地传递着。在接下来的诗节中,通过面包这种意象,诗人极富想象力地描述了救赎的情节。诗人把世人的灵魂描绘成一只笼中鸟,因人类的灵魂之鸟啄食禁果被逐出乐园,丢失了它的食物,陷入了饥荒的境地。然而,上帝在恩典中把"天堂里最纯净的麦子",即他自己的儿子,研磨、揉捏来烘烤灵魂可以吃的面包。这种面包被称为"白白的面包"和"甜点",维持着灵魂永恒的生命。泰勒在描述制作生命之粮时那些貌似粗粝的画面:"碾压""揉捏""塑形""烘焙"无不唤起人们对上帝的敬畏和感恩之情。

(十)The Wild Honey Suckle

Philip Freneau

1   Fair flower, that dost so comely grow,
    Hid in this silent, dull retreat,

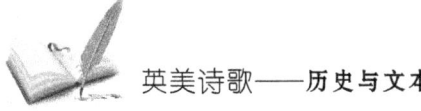

Untouched thy honeyed blossoms blow,

Unseen thy little branches greet:

5 No roving foot shall crush thee here,

No busy hand provoke a tear.

By Nature's self in white arrayed,

She bade thee shun the vulger eye,

10 And planted here the guardian shade,

And sent soft waters murmuring by;

Thus quietly thy summer goes,

Thy days declining to repose.

Smit with those chams, that must decay,

I grieve to see your future doom;

15 They died—nor were those flowers more gay,

The flowers that did in Eden bloom;

Unpitying frosts, and Autumn's power

Shall leave no vestige of this flower.

From morning suns and evening dews

20 At first thy little being came:

If nothing once, you nothing lose,

For when you die you are the same;

The space between, is but an hour,

The frail duration of flower.

第九章 殖民地时期诗歌

【译文】
野金银花

菲利普·弗瑞诺

1　美好的花呀，你长得这么秀丽，
　　却藏身在这僻静沉闷的地方——
　　甜美的花儿开了却没人亲昵，
　　招展的小小枝梢也没人观赏；
5　没游来荡去的脚来把你踩碎，
　　没东攀西摘的手来催你落泪。

　　大自然把你打扮得一身洁白，
　　她叫你避开庸俗粗鄙的目光，
　　她布置下树荫把你护卫起来，
10　又让潺潺的柔波淌过你身旁；
　　你的夏天就这样静静地消逝，
　　这时候你日见萎蔫终将安息。

　　那些难免消逝的美使我销魂，
　　想起你未来的结局我就心疼，
15　别的那些花儿也不比你幸运——
　　虽开放在伊甸园中也已凋零，
　　无情的寒霜再加秋风的威力，
　　会叫这花朵消失得一无踪迹。

　　朝阳和晚露曾把你养育，

20　让你这小小的生命来到世上，
　　原来若乌有，就没什么可失去，
　　因为你的死让你同先前一样；
　　这来去之间不过是一个钟点——
　　这就是脆弱的花享有的天年。

（黄杲炘　译）

【点评】

　　本诗写于1786年，据说是诗人在南卡罗来纳州的查尔斯顿看到一簇簇花丛之后有感而作。弗瑞诺赞赏金银花之优美，由此讴歌了他对这片土地、对国家的深厚感情。诗中，诗人以其敏锐的感受力意识到自然界的秀美动人和倏忽即逝。万物有生有死、有荣有枯。花开花落、四季转换乃自然界的规律，它标示着生与死是无法逃避的自然法则。这首诗共分两大部分，前两诗节写景，后两诗节抒情。从诗的前两节，读者很容易感受到诗人心中涌动着的对大自然无限的崇拜之情、对生命的赞叹。但从第三诗节，弗瑞诺笔锋一转，感叹生命的短暂和大自然的冷酷，开始了对生命本质的探讨，使本诗在清新亮丽、乡土气息浓郁的意境中又多了一层哲理的思考。金银花不会因为最终的凋零而拒绝开放，人类也是如此，不能因为生命的结局是死亡而放弃对生命的珍爱。诗歌采用传统的英诗格律，共四小节，每小节六行，四音步，采用ababcc式句末押韵形式，抑扬顿挫，富有节奏感和音乐美，阅读起来朗朗上口。

（十一）The Hurricane

Philip Freneau

1　HAPPY the man who, safe on shore,
　　Now trims, at home, his evening fire;

第九章 殖民地时期诗歌

Unmov'd, he hears the tempests roar,

That on the tufted groves expire:

5   Alas! on us they doubly fall,

Our feeble bark must bear them all.

Now to their haunts the birds retreat,

The squirrel seeks his hollow tree,

Wolves in their shaded caverns meet,

10 All, all are blest but wretched we—

Foredoom'd a stranger to repose,

No rest the unsettled ocean knows.

While o'er the dark abyss we roam,

Perhaps, with last departing gleam.

15 We saw the sun descend in gloom,

No more to see his morning beam,

But buried low, by far too deep,

On coral beds, unpitied, sleep!

But what a strange, uncoasted strand

20 Is that, where fate permits no day —

No charts have we to mark that land,

No compass to direct that way

What pilot shall explore that realm,

What new Columbus take the helm?

25　While death and darkness both surround,
　　And tempests rage with lawless power,
　　Of friendship's voice I hear no sound,
　　No comfort in this dreadful hour—
　　What friendship can in tempests be,
30　What comfort on this troubled sea?

　　The barque, auustomed to obey,
　　No more the trembling pilots guide:
　　Alone she gropes her trackless way,
　　While mountains burst on either side—
35　Thus, skill and science both must fall;
　　And ruin is the lot of all.

【译文】
飓风

菲利普·弗瑞诺

1　人们在安全的岸上多幸福,
　　这黄昏时在家中拨旺炉火;
　　无动于衷地听暴风雨狂呼,
　　一丛丛树已使之大为减弱:
5　风雨呀却把我们加倍猛抽,
　　这脆弱的三桅船全得承受。

　　现在鸟儿都飞回了生息地,

第九章 殖民地时期诗歌

　　松鼠也寻找着自己的树洞，
　　野狼在黑森森的穴中聚集，
10　谁都有福分，除了我们——
　　海洋早注定了会变幻莫测，
　　休憩安息它永远也不懂得。

　　我们漂流在幽暗的深海上，
　　也许见过了这昏沉的落日，
15　见过它离去时最后一道光，
　　就再也见不到次日的晨曦；
　　在最深最深的珊瑚礁葬身，
　　沉眠在那里没谁来伤心！

　　可那没岸沿的地方多古怪，
20　在那里命定了永没有阳光——
　　没一份海图把那儿标出来，
　　没一台罗盘能指明那航向——
　　有哪位领航可探索那王国，
　　有哪位新哥伦布可来掌舵？
25　当周围是一片死亡和黑暗，
　　是暴风雨恣意地肆虐逞威，
　　在这可怕的时刻我听不见
　　友情的声音和任何的抚慰——
　　暴风雨中能有怎样的友谊，
30　肆虐的海上又有什么慰藉？

习惯于听任摆布的三桅船，
颤抖的舵手已不再能操纵，
拔地而出的山在左右两舷，
孤独的船却摸索在茫茫中——
35 技能和知识这两者既无效，
我们都只有毁灭的路一条。

（黄杲炘　译）

【点评】

本诗是弗瑞诺根据本人的一次海上经历写成，1784年，他在去牙买加的航行中遇上了飓风。弗瑞诺对大自然有着敏锐的洞察力，他的诗歌因为关注自然与社会，探讨生与死的自然法则，被称为"书写大自然的抒情诗人"。他的浪漫主义诗歌艺术特质在被认为是"弗瑞诺的风格"的《野金银花》中得到了充分体现。弗瑞诺的诗歌不仅擅长描述大自然中柔弱、寂寥的花花草草，也展示了大自然冷酷、无情的另一面，传达出这样的信息：自然界万物的生生息息乃大自然的神力所致，不能为人类所左右。

船漂流在幽深、黑暗、狂风肆虐的海面之上，面对具有吞噬一切力量的飓风，人类感受到的只是自己的渺小、无助，对生活的留恋、对死亡的恐惧以及毁灭到来之时的绝望。在诗歌的前半部分，诗人先是用"脆弱的三桅船""幽暗深海上""暴风雨狂呼"写出了船上之人在风雨飘摇的海面之上，生命危在旦夕的困顿；接着描述了岸上人的闲适、惬意："安全的岸上多幸福""在家中拨旺炉火""无动于衷地听暴风雨狂呼"，甚至羡慕起岸上的动物都有属于自己的温暖的家："谁都有福分，除了我们"。通过对比"船上的人"和"岸上的万物"的生存状况，更加突出显示了"船上人"在面对大自然的威力时一筹莫展的状态，他们犹如世界的弃儿般惶恐不安，只能在凄风苦雨中苦苦煎熬，任凭命运的摆布。在诗歌的后半部分，诗人转而责怪无情、肆虐的海洋："海洋早注定了会变幻莫测，休憩安息

第九章　殖民地时期诗歌

它永远也不懂得";并感叹世事难料,人生无常:"见过它离去时最后一道光,就再也见不到次日的晨曦";面对即将到来的毁灭,充斥诗人内心的不仅仅是伤感,更多的是对未知世界的恐惧:"可那没岸沿的地方多古怪,在那里命定了永没有阳光"。面对人生厄运,当"我"一切的羡慕、责怪、反思、祈求、恐惧等心理消失后,摆在面前的依旧是死亡的威胁,"我"只能"习惯于听任摆布的三桅船""我们都只有毁灭的路一条",绝望之情可想而知。

第十章 浪漫主义时期诗歌

盛行于19世纪的英国浪漫主义文学思潮对美国浪漫主义文学产生了深远的影响，浓厚的民族主义色彩又让美国浪漫主义有别于英国浪漫主义。否定欧洲文化传统、憧憬西部大开发的宏伟蓝图使得美国浪漫主义极具民族特色。以小说和诗歌为主要形式的浪漫主义文学既是美国文学发展的第一个高潮、又是美国文学跻身世界文学的标志。以华盛顿·欧文（Washington Lrving）、爱伦·坡（Allan Poe）的作品为代表的前期浪漫主义文学多具有美国独特的民族风格。脱离了对欧洲文化，尤其对英国文化的附庸，这些作家也成为美国民族文学的先驱人物。爱伦·坡认为诗歌之精髓就是美，好的诗歌必须具备三方面的特征——模糊性、音乐性和象征性，他也是美国第一位主张"为艺术而艺术"的作家。坡的作品主题充斥着这些元素：异国情调的背景、遥远的年代、梦魇般的气氛、阴暗的心理和美人之死。他十分重视节奏、音韵、象征手段以及情节结构和手法技巧所产生的效果。

美国东北部的新英格兰地区既是美国的文化中心，又是最早的工业区。19世纪30年代以后，美国的经济开始繁荣起来，此时的文学摒弃了以往的宗教和独立自由的政治主题，主要围绕个人情怀、人性善恶、人与自然的关系展开。作品采用各式创作形式，表现手法也多种多样，注重心理分析，

第十章 浪漫主义时期诗歌

细腻的情感描写直击人心灵深处。超验主义是这个时期文学作品的主要表现形式,这标志着小说、诗歌、散文的发展到达了一个新高度。美国浪漫主义运动的中心位于新英格兰地区,它不仅是一场声势浩大的文学运动,也是一场人文主义的思想解放运动。它强调以人为本、崇尚直觉,主张个性解放,反对盲目崇拜。以爱默生(Emerson)、梭罗(Thoreau)为代表的超验主义作家解放了美国思想,强调了人的价值和审美标准,开创了美国的文艺复兴运动。朗费罗(Longfellow)、洛威尔(Lowell)等是这一时期诗歌方面比较有成就的诗人。他们大都来自文化中心——新英格兰地区,家世显赫,又是知识界的上层人物,但思想守旧、缺乏创新。虽然出于民主主义和人道主义之心,这些诗人反对南方蓄奴制,主张自由、解放,同情土著印第安人,批评一些社会弊端,但他们的观点一般较为温和,措辞委婉,被称为"绅士派诗人"。朗费罗一生写作了大量诗歌,多以抒情诗为主。他的《海华沙之歌》是美国文学史上的一篇巨著,也是美国第一部关于印第安人的史诗,诗中一些关于印第安人的神话传说既表达了诗人对印第安人生活土地的热爱,也赞扬了他们的勇敢、智慧和坚韧。

美国诗歌从一开始就具有多样性和反叛性的特点。这两者在19世纪浪漫主义诗歌中表现得更为突出。所谓多样性,不仅仅指诗人是由各种民族和不同种族组成,更重要的是他们在诗歌的风格技巧和主题内容等方面都各具特色,极少雷同。惠特曼(Whitman)和迪金森(Dickinson)是两位最富有革新精神的诗人代表。惠特曼的诗歌糅合演讲术、新闻报道和歌剧等各种技巧,用散文式的日常口语成功地创造了充满重复、排列、长句、头韵等富有音律节奏感的自由体诗歌。惠特曼开创了美国诗歌试验革新之先风,对20世纪甚至当今美国和世界诗歌都有深刻影响。迪金森在创新方面的成就不亚于惠特曼,她经常采用4行一节并且押韵的传统赞美诗形式、奇怪的破折号或大写字母等手法使她的诗歌具有神秘的色彩。她无视一切语法规则,但这一切又显得十分自然贴切。她的意象和比喻别出心裁,

加上她简练而精确的刻画，常常产生超乎寻常的效果。她对生与死、爱情和苦难、上帝和神灵等问题所持的怀疑而又执着探讨的精神使她超越了时代，成为 20 世纪现代主义诗歌的先驱。

一、Poem Reading

（一）Paul Revere's Ride

Henry Wadsworth Longfellow

1 Listen, my children, and you shall hear
   Of the midnight ride of Paul Revere,
   On the eighteenth of April, in Seventy-five;
   Hardly a man is now alive
5 Who remembers that famous day and year.
   He said to his friend, "If the British march
   By land or sea from the town to-night,
   Hang a lantern aloft in the belfry arch
   Of the North Church tower as a signal light,—
10 One, if by land, and two, if by sea;
   And I on the opposite shore will be,
   Ready to ride and spread the alarm
   Through every Middlesex village and farm,
   For the country folk to be up and to arm."

15 Then he said, "Good-night!" and with muffled oar
   Silently rowed to the Charlestown shore,

第十章 浪漫主义时期诗歌

  Just as the moon rose over the bay,

  Where swinging wide at her moorings lay

  The Somerset, British man-of-war;

20 A phantom ship, with each mast and spar

  Across the moon like a prison bar,

  And a huge black hulk, that was magnified

  By its own reflection in the tide.

  Meanwhile, his friend, through alley and street,

25 Wanders and watches with eager ears,

  Till in the silence around him he hears

  The muster of men at the barrack door,

  The sound of arms, and the tramp of feet,

  And the measured tread of the grenadiers,

30 Marching down to their boats on the shore.

  Then he climbed the tower of the Old North Church,

  By the wooden stairs, with stealthy tread,

  To the belfry-chamber overhead,

  And startled the pigeons from their perch

35 On the sombre rafters, that round him made

  Masses and moving shapes of shade,—

  By the trembling ladder, steep and tall,

  To the highest window in the wall,

  Where he paused to listen and look down

40 A moment on the roofs of the town,

And the moonlight flowing over all.
Beneath, in the churchyard, lay the dead,
In their night-encampment on the hill,
Wrapped in silence so deep and still
45   That he could hear, like a sentinel's tread,
The watchful night-wind, as it went
Creeping along from tent to tent,
And seeming to whisper, "All is well!"
A moment only he feels the spell
50   Of the place and the hour, and the secret dread
Of the lonely belfry and the dead;
For suddenly all his thoughts are bent
On a shadowy something far away,
Where the river widens to meet the bay,—
55   A line of black that bends and floats
On the rising tide, like a bridge of boats.

Meanwhile, impatient to mount and ride,
Booted and spurred, with a heavy stride
On the opposite shore walked Paul Revere.
60   Now he patted his horse's side,
Now gazed at the landscape far and near,
Then, impetuous, stamped the earth,
And turned and tightened his saddle-girth;
But mostly he watched with eager search
65   The belfry-tower of the Old North Church,

第十章　浪漫主义时期诗歌

　　As it rose above the graves on the hill,

　　Lonely and spectral and sombre and still.

　　And lo! as he looks, on the belfry's height

　　A glimmer, and then a gleam of light!

70　He springs to the saddle, the bridle he turns,

　　But lingers and gazes, till full on his sight

　　A second lamp in the belfry burns!

　　A hurry of hoofs in a village street,

　　A shape in the moonlight, a bulk in the dark,

75　And beneath, from the pebbles, in passing, a spark

　　Struck out by a steed flying fearless and fleet;

　　That was all! And yet, through the gloom and the light,

　　The fate of a nation was riding that night;

　　And the spark struck out by that steed, in his flight,

80　Kindled the land into flame with its heat.

　　He has left the village and mounted the steep,

　　And beneath him, tranquil and broad and deep,

　　Is the Mystic, meeting the ocean tides;

　　And under the alders that skirt its edge,

85　Now soft on the sand, now loud on the ledge,

　　Is heard the tramp of his steed as he rides.

　　It was twelve by the village clock,

　　When he crossed the bridge into Medford town.

       He heard the crowing of the cock,
90 And the barking of the farmer's dog,
       And felt the damp of the river fog,
       That rises after the sun goes down.

       It was one by the village clock,
       When he galloped into Lexington.
95 He saw the gilded weathercock
       Swim in the moonlight as he passed,
       And the meeting-house windows, blank and bare,
       Gaze at him with a spectral glare,
       As if they already stood aghast
100 At the bloody work they would look upon.

       It was two by the village clock,
       When he came to the bridge in Concord town.
       He heard the bleating of the flock,
       And the twitter of birds among the trees,
105 And felt the breath of the morning breeze
       Blowing over the meadows brown.
       And one was safe and asleep in his bed.
       Who at the bridge would be first to fall,
       Who that day would be lying dead,
110 Pierced by a British musket-ball.

       You know the rest. In the books you have read,

第十章　浪漫主义时期诗歌

How the British Regulars fired and fled,—
How the farmers gave them ball for ball,
From behind each fence and farm-yard wall,
115　Chasing the red-coats down the lane,
Then crossing the fields to emerge again
Under the trees at the turn of the road,
And only pausing to fire and load.

So through the night rode Paul Revere;
120　And so through the night went his cry of alarm
To every Middlesex village and farm,—
A cry of defiance and not of fear,
A voice in the darkness, a knock at the door
And a word that shall echo forevermore!
125　For, borne on the night-wind of the Past,
Through all our history, to the last,
In the hour of darkness and peril and need,
The people will waken and listen to hear
The hurrying hoof-beats of that steed,
And the midnight message of Paul Revere.

享利·沃兹沃思·朗费罗（Henry Wadsworth Longfellow，1807—1882）在19世纪的美国享有盛名，他是第一个让世界认可的美国诗人，很多评论家甚至将他的地位放于同时代的英国诗人阿尔弗雷德·丁尼生（Alfred Tennyson）之上。"炉边诗人"（The Fireside Poets）是19世纪重要的诗人群体，包括朗费罗，威廉·柯伦·布赖恩特（William Cullen Bryant），约翰·格

林里夫·惠蒂埃(John Greenlead Whittier),詹姆斯·罗素·洛厄尔(James Russel Loweel)和奥利弗·温德尔·霍姆斯(Oliver Wendel Holmes)。这些诗人以普通读者为艺术创作对象,注重诗歌的押韵节奏和整体结构,写出的诗歌一般都便于朗诵和记忆,而朗读和背诵他们的诗歌成为家庭朋友聚会在壁炉边烤火时的娱乐方式之一。朗费罗是"炉边诗人"重要的成员,而从他所属的这个群体可以看出他的诗歌的特点——注重诗歌的形式和节奏美。

朗费罗虽然曾经在19世纪享有盛誉,之后却逐渐淡出了评论家的视野,除了他的某些抒情短诗,大多诗集中已经不见他的踪影,而朗费罗这一名字也从美国各部教材中被隐去。究其原因,大部分评论家认为,诗人似乎在整个美国文学发展史的过程中并没有特别重要的地位和作用。一方面,和弗瑞诺等具有强烈"美国性"的作家不同,朗费罗并不单纯地追求"美国主题",而是将大量的欧洲文学主题和形式引介入美国文学。爱德加·爱伦·坡(Edgar Allan Poe, 1809—1849)曾经将朗费罗称作美国最好的诗人("the best poet in America"),但之后却毫不留情地发动了所谓"朗费罗战争"(The Longfellow War),认为朗费罗是一个不知廉耻的剽窃者。坡之所以认定朗费罗是"剽窃者",是因为朗费罗在主题和形式都对欧洲文学著作进行了模仿。另一方面,和后期具有强烈现代主义特点的诗人,如艾米莉·迪金森(Emily Dickinson, 1830—1886)和沃尔特·惠特曼(Walt Whitman, 1819—1892)不同,朗费罗在诗歌作品中注重传统的主题和格式,特别是诗歌的节奏韵律美,似乎看来又脱离了现代主义文学史发展的必然轨道。因此,无论是"承上",还是"启下",从美国文学发展史纵向的角度来看,朗费罗逐渐淡出文学历史舞台似乎是必然的。然而,无论是从"美国性"还是从"现代性"的角度,上述的观点都是有失偏颇的。首先,尽管模仿欧洲文学的模式,注重诗歌的节奏和韵律,但是和弗瑞诺等诗人创作理念的目的一样,朗费罗是想通过模仿为美国文学寻求一种独立的身

第十章　浪漫主义时期诗歌

份。换句话说,尽管目的不同,但是朗费罗却通过另一种方式为美国文学的独立,甚至是美国的独立寻求方法。而像是选文 *Paul Revere's Ride* 更是通过美国独立战争时期的民间故事为当时美国的局势指点迷津。其次,现代文学的一个重要特点是讲故事,而既然朗费罗是公认的大师级的讲故事的人(the masterly storyteller),就不能将他的作品完全划归于现代文学之外。朗费罗尽量避免作品中出现自传因素,并着力模仿欧洲文学的模式,这虽然与现代文学的创作理念有所不同,但不可否认的是他是美国第一位享有名气的史诗作家。*Paul Revere's Ride* 就是朗费罗最有代表性的史诗作品之一。

Paul Revere's Ride 是朗费罗根据美国爱国主义者保罗·里维尔(Paul Revere)的真实故事改编而成。诗歌最初于1861年发表于《大西洋月刊》(*The Atlantic Monthly*),之后改名为 *The Landlord's Tale* 并被收藏在朗费罗的长篇诗集 *Tale of a Wayside Inn*(1863)中。*Paul Revere's Ride* 共包含了131行诗文,分布在十三个诗节中。诗歌没有固定的押韵格式和节律,每个诗节都有独特的押韵格式。需要指出的是,诗文大部分为四音步(tetrameter),韵律多为抑扬格(iamb)和抑抑扬格(anapest)。如诗歌的第2行:

Of the 'midnight ride 'of Paul Rev'ere

第2行诗文包括了前面的一个抑抑扬格和后面的三个抑扬格,是诗歌比较典型的节奏分配。再如诗歌的第3行:

On the eigh'teenth of 'April, in 'Seventy-five

第4行同样也是四音步诗文,与第2行不同的是,它包含了四个抑抑扬格的节律。这种抑扬格和抑抑扬格结合的四音步节律,给读者和听者的

感觉像是飞奔的马蹄声，而这正和诗歌所要讲述的内容相符合。

故事发生的背景是英国人入侵美洲大陆，讲述的是得知英国人入侵消息后，故事主角保罗·里维尔骑马飞奔通知临近的美国人的故事。从诗歌的前4行判断，作者是通过一个年老的叙事者在讲述一个发生在1775年的故事，这和"炉边诗人"创作目的是相符合的。按照故事内容可以将诗歌分为两个部分，前五个诗节是第一部分，后面八个诗节是第二部分。第一部分中，里维尔和朋友约定，一旦英国人入侵，朋友就在教堂的塔楼上悬挂灯笼，而里维尔则负责将消息告知大家。如果英国人通过陆路，朋友悬挂一盏灯笼，而如果他们通过水路则悬挂两盏灯笼。看到通过水路入侵的英国人，朋友急忙挂上了两盏灯笼。第二部分主要讲述了看到两盏灯笼的里维尔快马加鞭地将消息传播到了周边。午夜十二点到达了梅德福，凌晨一点到达了列克星敦，凌晨两点他便把消息传播到了康科德。第十二个诗节中，故事的讲述者提到了战争最终以美国人的胜利结束，而这段故事其实早已是大家所熟悉的。最后一个诗节再次赞扬了里维尔的勇敢，认为那次响彻午夜的马蹄声始终会激荡在美国人民的心中。

有些评论者因为朗费罗诗歌行文的简单和节奏的讲究而把诗人归类为"儿童文学家"。其实，正是因为诗歌的通俗易懂，才使得朗费罗拥有更为广大的读者群，从而扩大了他爱国主义诗歌的影响力。从这个角度去看，朗费罗不失为一位讲故事的高手。有人指出，保罗·里维尔的真实故事并不是像朗费罗在诗中指出的那样。当晚有三个人跑去送信，里维尔并没有成功地将消息送抵目的地。实际上，所谓不准确（inaccuracies）也是诗人讲故事的一个砝码。Paul Revere's Ride 写作于1860年美国内战前夕，在发表之前，南卡罗来纳州已经宣布脱离美利坚合众国。在这种情形下，朗费罗改编并发表 Paul Revere's Ride 的实际目的是惊醒美国人，让其认识到当时情形的严重性。所以，从以史实为基础改编出符合时局的故事来看，朗费罗是一位真正的故事大师。另外，无论从故事的主题，还是从写作技巧

第十章 浪漫主义时期诗歌

来看，该诗具有明显的浪漫主义倾向。诗人在诗中赞美了里维尔的勇敢和担当，在他策马前行的瞬间，更是从马蹄之下迸发出耀眼的火花（第75，76行，"And beneath, from the pebbles, in passing, a spark/Struck out by a steed flying fearless and fleet"），这火花最终将形成燎原之势，将革命的情怀灌输到每个美国人的心中。在行文中诗人还运用了大量的哥特因素，像是第五个诗节中，里维尔的朋友从教堂往下看到的墓地的场景（第42～44行，"Beneath, in the churchyard, lay the dead,/In their night-encampment on the hill/Wrapped in silence so deep and still"）。

（二）Song of Myself

Walt Whitman

1　I CELEBRATE myself, and sing myself,
　　And what I assume you shall assume,
　　For every atom belonging to me as good belongs to you.
　　I loafe and invite my soul,
5　I lean and loafe at my ease observing a spear of summer grass.
　　My tongue, every atom of my blood, form'd from this soil, this air,
　　Born here of parents born here from parents the same, and their parents the same,
　　I, now thirty-seven years old in perfect health begin,
10　Hoping to cease not till death.
　　Creeds and schools in abeyance,
　　Retiring back a while sufficed at what they are, but never forgotten,
　　I harbor for good or bad, I permit to speak at every hazard,
　　Nature without check with original energy.

15 Houses and rooms are full of perfumes, the shelves are crowded with perfumes,

I breathe the fragrance myself and know it and like it,

The distillation would intoxicate me also, but I shall not let it.

The atmosphere is not a perfume, it has no taste of the

20 distillation, it is odorless,

It is for my mouth forever, I am in love with it,

I will go to the bank by the wood and become undisguised and naked,

I am mad for it to be in contact with me.

The smoke of my own breath,

25 Echoes, ripples, buzz'd whispers, love-root, silk-thread, crotch and vine,

My respiration and inspiration, the beating of my heart, the passing of blood and air through my lungs,

The sniff of green leaves and dry leaves, and of the shore and

30 dark-color'd sea-rocks, and of hay in the barn,

The sound of the belch'd words of my voice loos'd to the eddies of the wind,

A few light kisses, a few embraces, a reaching around of arms,

The play of shine and shade on the trees as the supple boughs wag,

35 The delight alone or in the rush of the streets, or along the fields and hill-sides,

The feeling of health, the full-noon trill, the song of me rising from bed and meeting the sun.

Have you reckon'd a thousand acres much? have you reckon'd the

40 earth much?

第十章　浪漫主义时期诗歌

Have you practis'd so long to learn to read?
Have you felt so proud to get at the meaning of poems?
Stop this day and night with me and you shall possess the origin of all poems,

45 You shall possess the good of the earth and sun, (there are millions of suns left,)
You shall no longer take things at second or third hand, nor look through the eyes of the dead, nor feed on the spectres in books,
You shall not look through my eyes either, nor take things from me,

50 You shall listen to all sides and filter them from your self.
I have heard what the talkers were talking, the talk of the beginning and the end,
But I do not talk of the beginning or the end.
There was never any more inception than there is now,

55 Nor any more youth or age than there is now,
And will never be any more perfection than there is now,
Nor any more heaven or hell than there is now.
Urge and urge and urge,
Always the procreant urge of the world.

60 Out of the dimness opposite equals advance, always substance and increase, always sex,
Always a knit of identity, always distinction, always a breed of life.
To elaborate is no avail, learn'd and unlearn'd feel that it is so.
Sure as the most certain sure, plumb in the uprights, well

65 entretied, braced in the beams,
Stout as a horse, affectionate, haughty, electrical,

I and this mystery here we stand.

Clear and sweet is my soul, and clear and sweet is all that is not my soul.

70　Lack one lacks both, and the unseen is proved by the seen,

Till that becomes unseen and receives proof in its turn.

Showing the best and dividing it from the worst age vexes age,

Knowing the perfect fitness and equanimity of things, while they discuss I am silent, and go bathe and admire myself.

75　Welcome is every organ and attribute of me, and of any man hearty and clean,

Not an inch nor a particle of an inch is vile, and none shall be less familiar than the rest.

I am satisfied—I see, dance, laugh, sing;

80　As the hugging and loving bed-fellow sleeps at my side through the night, and withdraws at the peep of the day with stealthy tread,

Leaving me baskets cover'd with white towels swelling the house with their plenty,

Shall I postpone my acceptation and realization and scream at my

85　eyes,

That they turn from gazing after and down the road,

And forthwith cipher and show me to a cent,

Exactly the value of one and exactly the value of two, and which is ahead?

90　Trippers and askers surround me,

People I meet, the effect upon me of my early life or the ward and city I live in, or the nation,

第十章　浪漫主义时期诗歌

The latest dates, discoveries, inventions, societies, authors old and new,

95　My dinner, dress, associates, looks, compliments, dues,

The real or fancied indifference of some man or woman I love,

The sickness of one of my folks or of myself, or ill-doing or loss or lack of money, or depressions or exaltations,

Battles, the horrors of fratricidal war, the fever of doubtful news,

100　the fitful events;

These come to me days and nights and go from me again,

But they are not the Me myself.

Apart from the pulling and hauling stands what I am,

Stands amused, complacent, compassionating, idle, unitary,

105　Looks down, is erect, or bends an arm on an impalpable certain rest,

Looking with side-curved head curious what will come next,

Both in and out of the game and watching and wondering at it.

Backward I see in my own days where I sweated through fog with linguists and contenders,

110　I have no mockings or arguments, I witness and wait.

I believe in you my soul, the other I am must not abase itself to you,

And you must not be abased to the other.

Loafe with me on the grass, loose the stop from your throat,

115　Not words, not music or rhyme I want, not custom or lecture, not even the best,

Only the lull I like, the hum of your valved voice.

I mind how once we lay such a transparent summer morning,

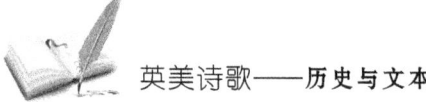

120　How you settled your head athwart my hips and gently turn'd over upon me,

And parted the shirt from my bosom-bone, and plunged your tongue to my bare-stript heart,

And reach'd till you felt my beard, and reach'd till you held my feet.

Swiftly arose and spread around me the peace and knowledge that

125　pass all the argument of the earth,

And I know that the hand of God is the promise of my own,

And I know that the spirit of God is the brother of my own,

And that all the men ever born are also my brothers, and the women my sisters and lovers,

130　And that a kelson of the creation is love,

And limitless are leaves stiff or drooping in the fields,

And brown ants in the little wells beneath them,

And mossy scabs of the worm fence, heap'd stones, elder, mullein and poke-weed.

135　A child said What is the grass? fetching it to me with full hands;

How could I answer the child? I do not know what it is any more than he.

I guess it must be the flag of my disposition, out of hopeful green stuff woven.

140　Or I guess it is the handkerchief of the Lord,

A scented gift and remembrancer designedly dropt,

Bearing the owner's name someway in the corners, that we may see and remark, and say Whose?

Or I guess the grass is itself a child, the produced babe of the

第十章 浪漫主义时期诗歌

145 vegetation.

Or I guess it is a uniform hieroglyphic,

And it means, Sprouting alike in broad zones and narrow zones,

Growing among black folks as among white,

Kanuck, Tuckahoe, Congressman, Cuff, I give them the same, I

150 receive them the same.

And now it seems to me the beautiful uncut hair of graves.

Tenderly will I use you curling grass,

It may be you transpire from the breasts of young men,

It may be if I had known them I would have loved them,

155 It may be you are from old people, or from offspring taken soon out of their mothers' laps,

And here you are the mothers' laps.

This grass is very dark to be from the white heads of old mothers,

Darker than the colorless beards of old men,

160 Dark to come from under the faint red roofs of mouths.

O I perceive after all so many uttering tongues,

And I perceive they do not come from the roofs of mouths for nothing.

I wish I could translate the hints about the dead young men and

165 women,

And the hints about old men and mothers, and the offspring taken soon out of their laps.

What do you think has become of the young and old men?

And what do you think has become of the women and children?

170 They are alive and well somewhere,

The smallest sprout shows there is really no death,

And if ever there was it led forward life, and does not wait at the end to arrest it,

And ceas'd the moment life appear'd.

175　All goes onward and outward, nothing collapses,

And to die is different from what any one supposed, and luckier.

　　伴随着美国独立战争的结束，浪漫主义文学逐渐兴起并发展开来。在意识领域里，美国人认识到了民主的重要性，在要求政治权力平等的同时，经济也得到了长足的发展，从而为文化的繁荣发展奠定了基础。在社会领域中，工业化的发展、移民的大量涌入以及西进运动等，种种社会变革和发展呼唤着一种新的文学表达形式。而在宗教领域里，原有清教思想的保守性和落后性已经暴露无遗，清教徒所倡导的绝对理性和节制逐渐为人所不齿，而这也为浪漫主义文学在美国的发展铺垫了道路。美国的浪漫主义时期涌现出众多优秀的诗人，沃尔特·惠特曼（1819—1892）就是其中最具有代表性的一位。

　　惠特曼被称为美国的第一位"民主诗人"（poet of democracy），他被学者比喻成美国文学史上的一座大山——你可以绕行，但是你却不能否认大山的存在。尽管褒贬不一，他的《草叶集》（*Leaves of Grass*）自1855年之后陆续出版了九个版本。除了歌颂美国政治的独立和民主，惠特曼的诗歌中包含了大量的超验主义思想，并表现出现实主义创作的倾向。作为一位具有"美国性"的民主诗人，也为了体现作品中"自由"等主题，惠特曼在诗作中不拘泥于传统诗歌的押韵格式和韵律安排而大量地使用了"自由诗体"（free verse），真正做到了诗歌内容和诗歌形式的统一。惠特曼在《草叶集》中将自由诗体的作用发挥到了极致，所以尽管他不是文学史上第一个运用自由诗体的诗人，但却被学者公认为"自由诗体之父"。除了自由

第十章 浪漫主义时期诗歌

诗体的运用,惠特曼还在其诗歌作品中尝试了很多实验派的诗歌写作技巧。例如,语音重复(phonetic repetition)就是诗人重要的也是成功的试验技巧之一。《草叶集》是诗人思想和艺术创作的集大成者,而选文《自我之歌》(*Song of Myself*)则是其中最具代表性的一首诗歌。

评论家以斯拉·格林斯潘(Ezra Greenspan)认为,《自我之歌》代表了惠特曼诗歌创作理念的精华所在。这首长诗包含了惠特曼诗歌创作的大部分主题,如歌颂美国的独立和自由、阐释自己的超验主义思想、勾勒写实的现实主义元素、歌颂标新立异的"身体主义"、思考生死循环的永生问题等。《自我之歌》最初发表于1855年的第一版《草叶集》,是其中十二首未命名的诗歌之一。在1856年第二个版本中,惠特曼将这首长诗命名为 *Poem of Walt Whitman, an American*,而后在第三个版本(1860)中将题目缩短为 *Walt Whitman*。1867年出版的第四版《草叶集》中,该诗被惠特曼分为52个长短不一的诗篇,而在1882年版本的诗集中,该诗最终被命名为《自我之歌》。从诗歌题目的演绎过程可以看出,《自我之歌》在强调"自我"和"民族性"的同时,包含了许多其他的主题。选文节选了《自我之歌》的前六个诗篇,从节选的片段就可以看出整首诗歌的内涵之丰富。诗人情之所至、言之所到,通过自由诗体的运用,在诗歌行与行之间不受任何拘束地表达着自己。

在第一个诗篇中,诗人便开门见山地提出了贯穿于整首诗的多个主题。首先,诗人在第1行中便说到:"I CELEBRATE myself, and sing myself",将"自我"的身份推至前台,为整首诗歌颂自我的浪漫主义情怀铺垫了道路。有学者指出,惠特曼的"自我"包含了三个不同的层次,分别是作为诗人的独特自我、作为美国人的泛自我以及美利坚合众国这个带有"民族性"的自我。第二,诗人在第2个诗节中提出了身体和精神的分离("I loafe and invite my soul/I lean and loafe at my ease observing a spear of summer grass"),这里的"I"很明显指的是肉体,而肉体邀请去一共观赏夏日草丛的正是精神。由此可以看出，诗人在接受超验主义思想影响的同时，却别具一格地提出了肉体的伟大所在，这在他另一首诗《带电的肉体》（*I Sing the Body Electric*）中有更深层次的体现。第三，第3个诗节中的诗人提出了有关个人和集体互相渗透的思想。惠特曼的诗歌中，肉体具有将个人和集体融合在一起的作用。所以在此，他从一个历史纵向的角度提出，他身上的每一个细胞都是世世代代生活在美国的祖先们所赐予的，而正是因为这种生理遗传关系，个人在某种意义上就是代表了整体。最后，诗人在第一个诗篇的最后一个诗节中提出了写作该诗的主要理念：在不违背传统的信条和规范的同时，自由自在地书写自己最本真的思想。这种创作理念与以拉尔夫·艾默生（Ralph Emerson，1803—1882）为代表的超验主义思想有着重要的联系。

　　第二个诗篇同样也是主要体现了诗人的超验主义思想。开篇提到了"perfume"和"atmosphere"的区别，尽管香水的味道充斥着四周，但诗人却意识到那并不是本真的味道。他要做的是赤身裸体、毫无掩饰地来到丛林旁边的河岸（第22行，"I will go to the bank by the wood and become undisguised and naked"），即将自己沉浸到自然之中去体会真正的自我。这自然会让读者联想到亨利·大卫·梭罗（Henry David Thoreau，1817—1862）为实践超验主义的思想来到瓦尔登湖畔独居两年的行为。因此，诗人在这里想要申明的是，自己愿意沉浸于自然，体味个人和"超灵"之间的融合，寻求真正的自我。与此同时，他也向读者发出了邀请："Stop this day and night with me and you shall possess the origin of/all poems"（第43，44行），抛开日常琐碎生活的烦扰，随同诗人一起去体味真正的艺术源泉。第三个诗篇通过批判空谈者（"talkers"），诗人表达了自己注重实践和体验的一面。诗歌的第68～71行中，诗人提出了肉体和精神尽管是分离的，但却同时是"纯净和甜美的"（"Clear and sweet"），两者缺一不可，一方的存在以另一方的存在为前提。同时，诗人还在第三个诗篇中提到了自

第十章 浪漫主义时期诗歌

已独有的历史观(第54～57行)和性爱观(第58～62行)。第四个诗篇带有明显的现实主义倾向。开始的"trippers and askers"代表了诗人在生活中碰到的难题和疑惑,随后诗人描写了世间发生的一系列不行事件,而他自己则作为一个旁观者("observer")慢慢观察和了解着这一切。第五个诗篇中,肉体再次邀请精神一同观赏草叶,随后诗人描写了肉体和精神之间类似同性性行为的一幕。除了通过肉体个体和整体得以整合的主题之外(第128～129行),在这个诗篇中诗人还提出超验主义中个人和"上帝"融合的思想(第126～127行)。第六个诗节中利用孩子的问题谈到了永生的问题。一个孩子问诗人:"什么是草叶"(第135行),诗人做了一系列的猜测之后(第138～151),提到了长在坟墓上的草叶。在诗人眼中,世上并没有死亡("there is really no death",第171行),今生结束之后会通往来生("it led forward life",第172行)。有关死亡和永生的问题,惠特曼在他的另一首诗歌 Out of the Cradle Endlessly Rocking 中有进一步的阐释。

(三) A Narrow Fellow in the Grass

Emily Dickinson

1 A narrow Fellow in the Grass
   Occasionally rides —
   You may have met Him — did you not
   His notice sudden is —

5 The Grass divides as with a Comb —
   A spotted shaft is seen —
   And then it closes at your feet

And opens further on —

He likes a Boggy Acre
10   A Floor too cool for Corn —
Yet when a Boy, and Barefoot —
I more than once at Noon

Have passed, I thought, a Whip lash
Unbraiding in the Sun
15   When stooping to secure it
It wrinkled and was gone —

Several of Nature's People
I know, and they know me —
I feel for them a transport
20   Of cordiality —

But never met this Fellow,
Attended, or alone
Without a tighter breathing
And Zero at the Bone —

19世纪初期主要发生在美国的超验主义运动虽然影响深远，但是发展到后来却逐渐显示出自己的弊端。艾默生所倡导的"人性本善"以及"人即是上帝"等观点逐渐被学者所质疑，"黑色浪漫主义"（Dark Romanticism）运动就是在这种背景下发起的。所谓"黑色"，是和超验

第十章 浪漫主义时期诗歌

主义者表现出的积极乐观的态度相对立的,指的是一种相对消极、被动的世界观。黑色浪漫主义者主要有三种观点:其一,他们认为人并不是完美的,人的内心总有对罪恶和毁灭趋之若鹜的心态;其二,虽然和超验主义一样认为自然拥有超验的力量,不断为人类揭示真理,但是在黑色浪漫主义者眼中,自然所揭示的真理可以是邪恶的,甚至威胁到人类的生存;其三,黑色浪漫主义者认为,人类想要改变自己命运的许多努力是徒劳无益的,人只能是命运被动的牺牲品。最具有代表性的黑色浪漫主义小说家有纳撒尼尔·霍桑(Nathaniel Hawthorne,1804—1864)和赫尔曼·梅尔维尔(Herman Melville,1819—1891),最具代表性的黑色浪漫主义诗人则是爱德加·爱伦·坡(Edgar Allan Poe,1809—1849)和艾米莉·迪金森(Emily Dickinson,1830—1886)。

迪金森是美国文学史上最著名的女诗人之一。她一共写作了将近1800首诗歌,尽管生前发表的作品并不多,诗人却垂名于身后,她的诗作得到了越来越多学者的认同和赞美。女权主义运动者称之为"英语语言中最伟大的女诗人"(the "greatest woman poet in English language"),而美国的现实主义文学之父威廉·迪安·霍威尔斯(William Dean Howells)虽然将迪金森的诗歌标注为"奇怪的诗作"("strange poetry"),却也不否认她的诗歌为世界文学做出了巨大的贡献,而这在美国文学之中是很少见的。尽管诗人生性羞涩、不善与人交往,但是在诗歌创作的领域里却做出了许多大胆的试验。首先,诗人在创作中突破了传统对文学语言和形象的束缚,进行了大胆的尝试。例如,在诗歌行文中不断出现不合语法的大写字母和让传统诗人费解的破折号。诗人对于诗歌形象的创新也成为后来意象派诗人模仿的对象。其次,迪金森善于使用简单、通俗、简短的文字塑造独特鲜明的形象。虽然她的诗歌看来与众不同,但行文使用的却是最常见的文字。最后,诗人不受传统诗歌创作习惯的限制,精于运用自由诗体。迪金森尽量避免使用最为常见的五步抑扬格,而大量地使用三步、四步抑扬格,有时甚至启用两步抑扬格，足见她想要突破传统的创作倾向。*A Narrow Fellow in the Grass* 是诗人生前发表的诗歌之一，也集中体现了她的艺术创作理念和价值观。

A Narrow Fellow in the Grass 在未经诗人同意的情况下发表于 1866 年 2 月 14 日的 *Springfield Daily Republican*，并被冠以题目 *The Snake*。和所有迪金森的其他诗歌一样，诗人在创作该诗的时候并没有为它设定题目。虽然整首诗歌好像是诗人为读者设定的一个谜语，但是加上题目之后，反而降低了整首诗歌的艺术高度。诗歌一共包含了六个诗节，每个诗节由四行诗文组成。第一个诗节中提到的"narrow fellow"很明显指的就是蛇，但是在整首诗的行文中并没有直接出现"snake"这个词。根据诗人的描述，它经常在草丛上"骑行"（"ride"），而且会突然出现在人的面前。第二个诗节描述了一幅动态的蛇行图，巨大的草丛中好像有什么穿行而过，隐约可见带着斑点的条状物。诗人用简单几个词语便勾勒出一幅"草蛇灰线，伏延千里"的景象。诗人在第三和第四个诗节中回忆起童年经常发生的一幕。正午时分，还是"男孩"的诗人光着脚走在湿滑的草丛上，突然看到了在阳光中摊开的鞭绳（"a Whip lash/Unbraiding in the Sun"，第 13，14 行）。当男孩弯腰去捡拾"鞭绳"的时候，它却化作蛇身转而不见了。这两个诗节凸显了蛇狡猾的一面，"wrinkle"这个词本身就含有"鬼点子"的意思。第五和第六个诗节将蛇和诗人所熟识的其他动物（"Several of Nature's People"，第 17 行）作了一个比较。虽然诗人可以和其他动物和谐相处，但是每每见到蛇的时候，却会禁不住害怕到呼吸急促、冰冷沁骨。这两个诗节突出了蛇令人恐惧、毛骨悚然的一面。

和其他的黑色浪漫主义作家一样，迪金森在看到自然美好一面的同时，也体会到了其中所蕴含的邪恶力量。在赞美自然的同时，她也写过像 *Apparently with no Surprise* 这样谴责自然无情的诗歌。同样的，*A Narrow Fellow in the Grass* 中蛇的形象也代表了自然中神秘不可知、令人敬畏和恐

第十章　浪漫主义时期诗歌

惧的力量。除此之外，还有两个重要的主题贯穿于诗歌之中，即"现实"和"表现"之间的区别以及"恐惧"的主题。首先，诗人开篇提到蛇的时候用了"伙计"（"narrow fellow"）这样的字眼，让读者感觉到了蛇与人之间的亲切。而且，由于蛇经常出没于草丛之中，诗人通过一个随意的反问（"did you not"，第3行）更加显得蛇的形象普通而亲切。但是随着诗文的进一步展开，诗人也将蛇狡诈和令人恐惧的一面展现了出来，从而使得读者推翻了开篇时对蛇的第一印象。所以，"表现"不等于"现实"，诗人似乎通过该诗思考了这一问题。其次，诗人通过蛇的形象表达了对未知世界的恐惧。和超验主义先行者的乐观精神不同，迪金森等黑色浪漫主义者在作品中主要表达了对未知世界的疑惑和恐惧。正如评论家巴巴拉·英戈尔（Barbara Ingold）所说，正是由于无知，人类才会有许多非理性的恐惧。蛇这一形象带来的神秘感正是人类对其产生恐惧的根源。和主题相比较，该诗的形式真正体现出诗人的别具匠心。

该诗一共包含了六个诗节，每个诗节都是由4行诗文组成，诗人在行文中运用了"民谣诗节"（ballad stanza）。"民谣诗节"在民歌中被广泛运用，它包含了4行诗文，第1，3行一般有4个重读音节（tetrameter），第2，4行一般有3个重读音节（trimeter），押韵格式为abcb。其中，押韵的第1，3行也不是完整的押韵模式，而被称为"半押韵"（压尾韵）。例如，第一个诗节中第2行和第4行就是压尾韵 /z/。使用朗朗上口的"民谣诗节"来描述蛇的形象，符合诗人的创作理念。整首诗中还出现了大量的"行间韵"（internal rhyme），像是头韵（"spotted"和"shaft"，第6行；"attended"和"alone"，第22行）和腹韵（"narrow"和"fellow"，第1行；第10行"A Floor too cool for Corn"中的"floor"和"corn"以及"too"和"cool"）。除了韵律，诗人在用词酌句上也大费心思。表面上突兀的大写字母其实蕴含了诗人的别具匠心。例如，第5行的"The Grass divides as with as Comb"，大写的"Grass"和"Comb"鲜明地勾勒出了蛇在深草

之中闪身而过的景象。另外，像"narrow Fellow"这样的词组，给读者呈现的就是一条绵延不断前进的蛇的形象。整首诗虽然没有"snake"的字眼出现，但诗人却通过一个大写的"Z"（"Zero"）在最后一行诗文中巧妙地安插了一条吐着信子、活灵活现的蛇。而贯穿于整首诗的破折号，除了使整首诗表现出活泼灵动的文风，更是凸显了蛇出没时毫无预兆的狡诈和给人带来的恐惧。由此看来，诗人在形式上的创新很好地服务了诗文的主题。

（四）The Raven

Edgar Allen Poe

1 Once upon a midnight dreary, while I pondered weak and weary,
Over many a quaint and curious volume of forgotten lore,
While I nodded, nearly napping, suddenly there came a tapping,
As of some one gently rapping, rapping at my chamber door.
5 "Tis some visitor," I muttered, "tapping at my chamber door—
Only this, and nothing more."

Ah, distinctly I remember it was in the bleak December,
And each separate dying ember wrought its ghost upon the floor.
Eagerly I wished the morrow; — vainly I had sought to borrow
10 From my books surcease of sorrow—sorrow for the lost Lenore—
For the rare and radiant maiden whom the angels named Lenore—
Nameless here for evermore.

And the silken sad uncertain rustling of each purple curtain
Thrilled me—filled me with fantastic terrors never felt before;

第十章　浪漫主义时期诗歌

15　So that now, to still the beating of my heart, I stood repeating
　　"Tis some visitor entreating entrance at my chamber door—
　　Some late visitor entreating entrance at my chamber door;—
　　This it is, and nothing more,"

　　Presently my soul grew stronger; hesitating then no longer,
20　"Sir," said I, "or Madam, truly your forgiveness I implore;
　　But the fact is I was napping, and so gently you came rapping,
　　And so faintly you came tapping, tapping at my chamber door,
　　That I scarce was sure I heard you" —here I opened wide the door; —
　　Darkness there, and nothing more.

25　Deep into that darkness peering, long I stood there wondering, fearing,
　　Doubting, dreaming dreams no mortal ever dared to dream before
　　But the silence was unbroken, and the darkness gave no token,
　　And the only word there spoken was the whispered word, "Lenore!"
　　This I whispered, and an echo murmured back the word, "Lenore!"
30　Merely this and nothing more.

　　Back into the chamber turning, all my soul within me burning,
　　Soon again I heard a tapping somewhat louder than before.
　　"Surely," said I, "surely that is something at my window lattice;
　　Let me see then, what thereat is, and this mystery explore—
35　Let my heart be still a moment and this mystery explore;—
　　'Tis the wind and nothing more!"

Open here I flung the shutter, when, with many a flirt and flutter,
In there stepped a stately raven of the saintly days of yore.
Not the least obeisance made he; not a minute stopped or stayed he;
40 But, with mien of lord or lady, perched above my chamber door —
Perched upon a bust of Pallas just above my chamber door—
Perched, and sat, and nothing more.

Then this ebony bird beguiling my sad fancy into smiling,
By the grave and stern decorum of the countenance it wore,
45 "Though thy crest be shorn and shaven, thou," I said, "art sure no craven.
Ghastly grim and ancient raven wandering from the nightly shore—
Tell me what thy lordly name is on the Night's Plutonian shore!"
Quoth the raven, "Nevermore."

Much I marvelled this ungainly fowl to hear discourse so plainly,
50 Though its answer little meaning—little relevancy bore;
For we cannot help agreeing that no living human being
Ever yet was blessed with seeing bird above his chamber door—
Bird or beast above the sculptured bust above his chamber door,
With such name as "Nevermore."

55 But the raven, sitting lonely on the placid bust, spoke only,
That one word, as if his soul in that one word he did outpour.
Nothing further then he uttered—not a feather then he fluttered—
Till I scarcely more than muttered "Other friends have flown before—
On the morrow he will leave me, as my hopes have flown before."

60 Then the bird said, "Nevermore."

　　Startled at the stillness broken by reply so aptly spoken,
　　"Doubtless," said I, "what it utters is its only stock and store,
　　Caught from some unhappy master whom unmerciful disaster
　　Followed fast and followed faster till his songs one burden bore—
65 Till the dirges of his hope that melancholy burden bore
　　Of 'Never-nevermore'."

　　But the raven still beguiling all my sad soul into smiling,
　　Straight I wheeled a cushioned seat in front of bird and bust and door;
　　Then, upon the velvet sinking, I betook myself to linking
70 Fancy unto fancy, thinking what this ominous bird of yore—
　　What this grim, ungainly, ghastly, gaunt, and ominous bird of yore
　　Meant in croaking "Nevermore."

　　This I sat engaged in guessing, but no syllable expressing
　　To the fowl whose fiery eyes now burned into my bosom's core;
75 This and more I sat divining, with my head at ease reclining
　　On the cushion's velvet lining that the lamp-light gloated o'er,
　　But whose velvet violet lining with the lamp-light gloating o'er,
　　She shall press, ah, nevermore!

　　Then, methought, the air grew denser, perfumed from an unseen censer
80 Swung by Seraphim whose foot-falls tinkled on the tufted floor.
　　"Wretch," I cried, "thy God hath lent thee-by these angels he has sent thee

Respite—respite and nepenthe from thy memories of Lenore!
Quaff, oh quaff this kind nepenthe, and forget this lost Lenore!"
Quoth the raven, "Nevermore."

85 "Prophet!" said I, "thing of evil!—prophet still, if bird or devil!—
Whether tempter sent, or whether tempest tossed thee here ashore,
Desolate yet all undaunted, on this desert land enchanted—
On this home by horror haunted—tell me truly, I implore—
Is there—is there balm in Gilead? —tell me – tell me, I implore!"
90 Quoth the raven, "Nevermore."

"Prophet!" said I, "thing of evil!—prophet still, if bird or devil!
By that Heaven that bends above us—by that God we both adore—
Tell this soul with sorrow laden if, within the distant Aidenn,
It shall clasp a sainted maiden whom the angels named Lenore—
95 Clasp a rare and radiant maiden, whom the angels named Lenore?"
Quoth the raven, "Nevermore."

"Be that word our sign of parting, bird or fiend!" I shrieked upstarting—
"Get thee back into the tempest and the Night's Plutonian shore!
Leave no black plume as a token of that lie thy soul hath spoken!
100 Leave my loneliness unbroken! —quit the bust above my door!
Take thy beak from out my heart, and take thy form from off my door!"
Quoth the raven, "Nevermore."

And the raven, never flitting, still is sitting, still is sitting

第十章 浪漫主义时期诗歌

> On the pallid bust of Pallas just above my chamber door;
> 105　And his eyes have all the seeming of a demon's that is dreaming,
> 　　And the lamp—light o'er him streaming throws his shadow on the floor;
> 　　And my soul from out that shadow that lies floating on the floor
> 　　Shall be lifted—nevermore!

爱德加·爱伦·坡是美国浪漫主义时期最重要的作家之一，他的创作属于黑色浪漫主义的范畴，探讨了人类心理阴暗的一面。如果说迪金森只是对"人性本善"提出了质疑，在坡的眼中，由于人类心理生来就存在对邪恶的渴望，罪恶可能发生在每一个人的身上。坡不但是一流的诗人和短篇小说家，还是一位见解犀利的评论家。他是侦探小说的和心理分析批判学说的鼻祖，他的作品还预见了科幻小说的出现。坡的创作理念影响了法国的象征主义者和"为了艺术而艺术"的唯美主义者。由于作品中备受争议的黑暗元素，坡被称为最受争议的、也是最受学者误解的作家之一。

作为一个文学评论家，坡在形成自己文学理论体系的同时，将这些理论——实践于他的文学创作之中。坡的文学评论代表作品有两部，即 *The Philosophy of Composition* 和 *The Poetic Principle*。对于诗歌创作，坡提出并实践了一套他自己认为行之有效的理论。首先，在长度上，诗歌应该控制篇幅的长度，最好是能让读者一次读完的长度；其次，在创作动机上，坡认为诗歌作品应该能够激发读者内心的一种美感；再次，在作品基调上，坡认为忧郁（melancholy）是所有诗歌基调中最合情合理的；最后，在形式上，坡强调诗歌的节奏美，认为只有具有乐感美的"纯诗歌"（"pure poetry"）才是好的诗歌，因为作家应该"为了艺术而艺术"（"art for art's sake"）。坡曾经总结了自己的艺术观点，认为："毫无疑问，一个美丽女人的死亡是这个世界上最具有诗性的主题"。诗人提出，他的代表作品 *The Raven* 无疑是诗歌创作理论的最好实践。实际上，*The Philosophy* of Composition 正是为了总结 The Raven 的创作理念而写成的。

The Raven 是坡的成名作品,也是他最具代表性的诗歌之一。该诗以其节奏上的乐感美、程式化的诗歌语言以及超自然的故事氛围而著称。诗人最初将 The Raven 给了格雷厄姆杂志的编辑,但却不幸被对方退稿。之后坡将该诗卖给了 The American Review,但只得到了 9 美元的稿费。1845 年 2 月,The American Review 第一次出版了 The Raven,但署名作者却是"Quarles",暗示其可能是英国诗人弗朗西斯·夸尔斯(Francis Quales)的作品。出版之后,The Raven 立刻吸引了学者们的注意,变得炙手可热。New York Tribune,Broadway Journal,Southern Literary Messenger 等杂志分别刊登了 The Raven,而该诗也成为许多诗集的必选诗歌之一。坡在谈起诗歌创作的对象时,认为它的读者群体包括学者也包括普通大众读者,而该诗的成功似乎正验证了诗人的观点。

The Raven 是一首长篇叙事诗,讲述了一只乌鸦前来造访刚刚丧失伴侣勒诺尔(Lenore)的年轻诗人的故事。该诗一共包含了 108 行诗文,分为十八个诗节,每个诗节包含了 6 行诗文。根据故事的进程,可以将诗歌分成三个部分。第一个部分是前七个诗节,讲述了乌鸦如何进屋的过程:一个萧条的十二月的午夜,新进丧偶的年轻诗人正在书房读书,希望借助图书能够忘记丧偶之痛,但所有的努力似乎都冲不淡心中对勒诺尔的思念。就在这时,他听到了敲门的声音,可是开门之后,除了无尽的黑暗根本没有人的踪影。面对黑暗,诗人既害怕又渴望("wondering, fearing/Doubting,第 25,26 行"),因为他在隐隐期盼着勒诺尔鬼魂的回归。然而当他向黑暗深处呼喊勒诺尔的名字时,回应他的只是细微的回声而已。重新回到书房的诗人再次听到了敲击声,这次他打开了窗户,从窗户外面大步迈进了一只乌鸦。第二部分是第八到第十二五个诗节,乌鸦飞进书房之后,直接落到了房门上面的雅典娜半身像上,而诗人与乌鸦有了第一次"交锋"。诗人和乌鸦的首次交流氛围比较融洽,

第十章 浪漫主义时期诗歌

因为在第八和第十二个诗节的开头,诗人都不禁露出了笑容("beguiling my sad fancy into smiling",第 43 行;"beguiling all my sad soul into smiling",第 67 行)。面对种种疑问和猜测,乌鸦都能适时地回答"永不复焉"("Nevermore"),诗人猜度这只乌鸦的主人肯定遭遇到了什么麻烦,因而每天重复这个词语,而乌鸦正是从主人那里学到了该词。第三部分为剩下的六个诗节,在与乌鸦的交流之中,诗人加入了有关勒诺尔的信息。诗人在不知不觉中将头枕到了椅背上,感受到了紫色天鹅绒布料的质感,由此突然想起已经死去的勒诺尔曾经也坐在这把椅子上。诗人针对死去的勒诺尔问了乌鸦三个问题:"乌鸦是不是上帝派来让我忘却勒诺尔的?""在遥远的吉利德(Gilead)是否真的有忘忧膏?""天堂里是否有一位叫勒诺尔的天使?"。三个问题乌鸦都给出了否定的回答——"Nevermore"。诗人由此被乌鸦激怒,他大声驱赶乌鸦,可是乌鸦却坐在雅典娜神像上一动不动,似乎成为诗人永远摆脱不了的魔咒。

坡在写作诗歌时,十分注重音节的押韵和行文的节奏感。诗人曾经就伊丽莎白·巴雷特(Elizabeth Barrett)的诗歌 *Lady Geraldine's Courtship* 写过评论文章,而 *The Raven* 就是基于 Barrett 的这首诗中复杂的节奏和韵律写成的。学者沃纳(W. L. Werner)仔细计算过,全诗一共包含了 719 个完全音步,705 个完全扬抑格(trochee)和 10 个不完全扬抑格,其中只有四个音节是长短格(dactyl)。总体说来,该诗一共包含了十八个诗节,每个诗节 6 行诗文,一般用八音步扬抑格写成。例如,第一句诗文

'O'nce 'u'pon a 'm'idnight 'd'reary, while I 'p'ondered 'w'eak and 'w'eary,

根据诗人自己的介绍,诗中除了八音步,还包含了七音步和四音步,以及它们的省略音步(catalectic)。诗歌每个音节的押韵格式是 abcbbb 或者 aabcccbbb,每个诗节中的"b"和单词"nevermore"押韵,而由于"nevermore"本身就是省略音步(缺少一个弱读),所以一方面起到了强调的作用,另

一方面也突出了诗歌的音律感。诗人为了凸显节奏美,在行文中大量使用了头韵。例如:第1行中的"weak and weary",第3行中的"nodded, nearly napping"和第26行中的"Doubting, dreaming dreams"。该诗无论是在音节押韵还是在顿挫的节奏感上,处处都显示出诗人的用心。

坡极力反对作品带有任何形式的教化意味,认为艺术作品要保有自己的纯洁度,即"为了艺术而艺术"。*The Raven* 中的年轻诗人虽然表面上想要尽快忘记勒诺尔,但是在与乌鸦的交流中却处处透露出寻找已逝爱人的讯息。打开门之后,面对午夜的黑暗,他发自内心地呼喊着自己恋人的名字。而当意识到乌鸦可能是上帝派来的,他更是急切地向其询问勒诺尔的消息。诗人摇摆在这种理性上想要忘却、感性上却始终难以忘怀之间,痛苦着却又难以自拔。难怪诗歌的最后当乌鸦否定了勒诺尔在天堂之后,诗人会变得恼羞成怒,更是陷入疯狂的边缘。因此,*The Raven* 不但没有带有任何现实的教化意味,反而更像是诗人在对"纯粹艺术"的玩味。另外,诗歌的另一亮点是其中所包含的哥特艺术元素。故事发生的背景是午夜幽闭的书房,而乌鸦本身就带有不祥的意味,贯穿故事始终的又是年轻人对美丽的已逝恋人的怀念,因此它和坡的短篇哥特小说"Ligeia"一样,似乎在描述一种黑暗的力量,一种可以使死者复苏的力量。围绕乌鸦这一形象,诗人暗指多处文学引喻。实际上,这一形象最初来源于Charles Dickson(1746—1796)的小说 *Barnaby Rudge*。而诗文中,年轻诗人认为乌鸦来自冥河岸边("the Night's Plutonian shore",第47行),显然指的是罗马神话中冥王普鲁托。北欧神话中,主神奥丁就拥有两只乌鸦,分别代表了思想(thought)和记忆(memory)。而在圣经文化中,诺亚在方舟上放飞了一只白色的乌鸦,让其探查洪水消退的情况,这只贪玩的乌鸦没有完成使命,最终受到了严厉的惩罚——变为黑色羽毛,并且只能吃动物的腐尸。这些文学引喻赋予了诗歌的中心形象乌鸦以丰富的文学内涵和象征,而这些也成为诗歌最大的魅力之一。

第十章 浪漫主义时期诗歌

二、Furthe Reading

(一) A Psalm of Life

Henry Wadsworth Longfellow

1　Tell me not in mournful numbers,
　　Life is but an empty dream!
　　For the soul is dead that slumbers,
　　And things are not what they seem.

5　Life is real! Life is earnest!
　　And the grave is not its goal;
　　Dust thou art, to dust returnest,
　　Was not spoken of the soul.

　　Not enjoyment, and not sorrow,
10　Is our destined end or way;
　　But to act, that each to-morrow
　　Find us farther than to-day.
　　Art is long, and Time is fleeting,
　　And our hearts, though stout and brave,
15　Still, like muffled drums, are beating.
　　Funeral marches to the grave.

　　In the world's broad field of battle,
　　In the bivouac of Life,

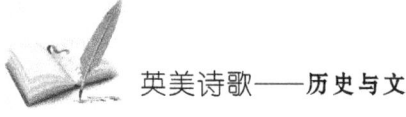

```
        Be not like dumb, driven cattlte!
20      Be a hero in the strife!


        Trust no future, howe'er pleasant!
        Let the dead Past bury its dead!
        Act, —act in the living Present!
        Heart within, and God o'erhead!


25      Lives of great men all remind us,
        We can make our lives sublime,
        And, departing, leave behind us
        Footprints on the sands of time;


        Footprints that perhaps another,
30      Sailing o'er life's solemn main,
        A forlorn and shipwrecked brother,
        Seeing, shall take heart again.


        Let us, then, be up and doing,
        With a heart for any fate;
35      Still achieving, still pursuing,
        Learn to labour and to wait.
```

第十章　浪漫主义时期诗歌

【译文】
人生颂

享利·沃兹沃思·朗费罗

1 别用悲切的诗句对我唱：
　　"人生只是虚幻的梦一场！"
　因为昏睡的灵魂已死亡，
　而事物不是看来那模样。

5 人生多真切！它绝非虚度！
　　一抔黄土哪里会是它归宿；
　　"你来自泥尘，得重归泥尘。"
　这话所指的并不是灵魂。

　我们命定的终点和道路，
10 既不是享乐，也不是悲苦；
　行动吧，要让每一个明天
　看我们比今天走得更远。

　学艺费光阴，时日去匆忙，
　任我们的心勇敢又坚强，
15 却依然像那蒙住的丧鼓
　敲打着哀乐走向那坟墓。
　在风云世界的广阔战场，
　在人生征途的野宿营帐，
　别像默默的牛羊任驱赶！

-399-

20　要争做英雄，能征善战！

　　将来再美好也别空指望！
　　让死的过去把死的埋葬！
　　干吧，在活着的此刻就干！
　　胸内有红心，头顶有上苍！

25　伟人的生平向我们指出：
　　我们能使此生超群脱俗，
　　一朝逝去，时间的沙滩上
　　将留下我们的脚印行行。

　　在庄严的生活之海航行，
30　也许有兄弟会遭遇不幸，
　　会因为航船沉没而绝望，
　　但见那脚印，又变得顽强。

　　就让我们振奋、行动起来，
　　凭着对付任何命运的胸怀；
35　不断去收获，不断去追求，
　　学会劳动，也要学会等候。

（黄杲炘　译）

【点评】

　　1848 年，此时的朗费罗正遭遇人生的低谷，妻子去世，追求心仪的女子又遇到诸多波折，这反而让朗费罗悟出来一些人生道理，写了《人生颂》来勉励自己。此诗共九节，每节 4 行，以四步扬抑格写成，韵脚为 abab。

第十章 浪漫主义时期诗歌

这是一首哲理诗,在诗中,诗人感叹生活的辛苦、不易,面对如此困境,人们不应自暴自弃,要积极进取、奋发向上。在诗的第一节,诗人驳斥了"人生不过梦一场!"的虚无主义论调,接着阐述自己的观点:"人生是真切的!人生是严肃的!",如醍醐灌顶,惊醒了迷途中的旅人。诗人将诗的核心聚焦在最能体现人类生命力与希望的年轻人身上,以"年轻人的心"作为叙事者,阐释了自己对人生和死亡这一永恒主题的理解。人生苦短,时光飞逝,人们应该行动起来,直面现实,只有如此,我们的人生才有意义。诗中断然否定人生如梦的悲观论调,突出地强调现实行动的、战斗不止的人生观,反映了美国开拓时期的时代气氛和民族精神。最后一节与第一节呼应,与读者互勉("要学会劳作,学会等待")。此诗是一首励志诗,犹如人生旅程中的清流,涤荡心灵,指点迷津,激励了一代又一代的人。

(二)The Arrow and the Song

Henry Wadsworth Longfellow

1　I shot an arrow into the air;
　　It fell to earth, I knew not where;
　　For, so swiftly it flew, the sight
　　Could not follow it in its flight.

5　I breathed a song into the air;
　　It fell to earth, I knew not where;
　　For who has sight so keen and strong,
　　That it can follow the flight of song?

　　Long, long afterward, in an oak
10　I found the arrow, still unbroke;

And the song, from beginning to end,
I found again in the heart of a friend.

【译文】
箭与歌

亨利·沃兹沃思·朗费罗

1　我把一支箭向空中射出，
　　它落下地来，不知在何处；
　　那么急，那么快，
　　眼睛怎能跟得上它一去如飞的踪影？

5　我把一支歌向空中吐出，
　　它落下地来，不知在何处；
　　有谁的眼力这么尖，这么强，
　　竟能追上歌声的飞扬？

　　很久以后，我找到那支箭，
10　插在橡树上，还不曾折断；
　　也找到那支歌，首尾俱全，
　　一直藏在朋友的心间。

（杨德豫　译）

【点评】

《箭与歌》是朗费罗歌颂友谊的一首抒情短诗，作者用"箭"来象征"友谊"，因为"友谊"就像"箭"一样，可以跨越遥远的距离。这首诗语言平实，貌似浅显，却内涵深刻，拥有一股清澈透明的诗意，深深地打动着读者的

第十章　浪漫主义时期诗歌

心。在这首诗中，射向空中的箭和响彻空中的歌表达了作者对友情的渴望。人与人之间的友情，如同飞翔的箭射到橡树身上，随日月而日渐加深浓厚。友情的歌，始终唱响、萦绕在朋友心中。作者通过丰富的联想，用箭、歌声、橡树来比喻友情之珍贵、深厚，不受时空限制，历久弥坚，日渐醇厚。

（三）The Tide Rises, the Tide Falls

Henry Wadsworth Longfellow

1　The tide rises, the tide falls,
　　The twilight darkens, the curlew calls;
　　Along the sea-sands damp and brown
　　The traveler hastens toward the town,
5　And the tide rises, the tide falls.

　　Darkness settles on roofs and walls,
　　But the sea, the sea in the darkness calls;
　　The little waves, with their soft, white hands,
　　Efface the footprints in the sands,
10　And the tide rises, the tide falls.

　　The morning breaks; the steeds in their stalls
　　Stamp and neigh, as the hostler calls;
　　The day returns, but never more
　　Returns the traveler to the shore,
　　And the tide rises, the tide falls.

【译文】
潮水升,潮水落

亨利·沃兹沃思·朗费罗

1 潮水升了,潮水落了,
  天色已晚,鹬鸟啼鸣;
  踏着暗黄的湿润海沙,
  行人赶路,前往小城。
5 潮水升,潮水落。

  屋顶、墙垣都沉入黑暗里,
  黑暗里,大海呼号不息;
  细浪用又软又白的手儿
  抹去沙上行人的脚迹。
10 潮水升,潮水落。

  厩里的驿马跺蹄长嘶,
  天亮了,它听见马夫呼唤;
  白天回来了,那位行人呢,
  他却永远不再回海岸。
15 潮水升,潮水落。

(杨德豫 译)

【点评】
　　此诗写于1879年,于次年发表,是诗人又一篇探讨人生意义的哲理诗。何为永恒?何为重要?在时间的历史长河中,人类只是沧海一粟。诗歌从

第十章 浪漫主义时期诗歌

描述傍晚的景象开始，一位旅人正匆匆赶往城镇。最后一节描述了次日清晨的场景，旅人不知所终，暗示着人生如过客，代表大自然的大海和沙滩才是永恒。朗费罗反复五次吟诵"潮涨潮落"，表明时间的周而复始，循环往复，象征大自然的永恒运动；相比而言，人生犹如过客，匆匆而来，又匆匆离去，受制于时间而无能为力。这首诗蕴含的哲理是：时光无限，生命有限，珍爱生命。此诗共有三个小节，每小节5行，采用四音步抑扬格诗行，韵律为：aabba aacca aadda，其中最后一行为叠句。

（四）O Captain! My Captain!

1 O Captain! my Captain! our fearful trip is done,

   The ship has weather'd every rack, the prize we sought is won,

   The port is near, the bells I hear, the people all exulting,

   While follow eyes the steady keel, the vessel grim and daring;

5 But O heart! heart! heart!

  O the bleeding drops of red,

   Where on the deck my Captain lies,

    Fallen cold and dead.

   O Captain! my Captain! rise up and hear the bells;

10 Rise up—for you the flag is flung—for you the bugle trills,

   For you bouquets and ribbon'd wreaths—for you the shores a-crowding,

   For you they call, the swaying mass, their eager faces turning;

   Here Captain! dear father!

   This arm beneath your head!

15 It is some dream that on the deck,

You've fallen cold and dead.

My Captain does not answer, his lips are pale and still,

My father does not feel my arm, he has no pulse nor will,

The ship is anchor'd safe and sound, its voyage closed and done,

20 From fearful trip the victor ship comes in with object won;

Exult O shores, and ring O bells!

But I with mournful tread,

Walk the deck my Captain lies,

Fallen cold and dead.

【译文】
哦．船长，我的船长！

沃尔特·惠特曼

1　哦，船长，我的船长！我们险恶的航程已经告终，

　　我们的船安渡过惊涛骇浪，我们寻求的奖赏已赢得手中，

　　港口已经不远，钟声我已听见，万千人众在欢呼呐喊，

　　目迎着我们的船从容返航，我们的船威严而勇敢。

5　可是，心啊！心啊！心啊！

　　哦，殷红的血滴流淌，

　　在甲板上，那里躺着我的船长，

　　他已倒下，已死去，已冷却。

　　哦，船长，我的船长！起来吧，请听听这钟声，

10　起来，——旌旗，为你招展——号角，为你长鸣。

　　为你，岸上挤满了人群——为你，无数花束、彩带、花环。

第十章　浪漫主义时期诗歌

为你，熙攘的群众在呼唤，转动着多少殷切的脸。

这里，船长！亲爱的父亲！

你头颅下边是我的手臂！

15　这是甲板上的一场梦啊，

你已倒下，已死去，已冷却。

我们的船长不作回答，他的双唇惨白、寂静，

我的父亲不能感觉我的手臂，他已没有脉搏、没有生命，

我们的船已安全抛锚停泊，航行已完成，已告终，

20　胜利的船从险恶的旅途归来，我们寻求的已赢得手中。

欢呼，哦，海岸！轰鸣，哦，洪钟！

可是，我却轻移悲伤的步履，

在甲板上，那里躺着我的船长，

他已倒下，已死去，已冷却。

（江　枫　译）

【点评】

　　这首诗是为纪念林肯总统而作。1865年，南北战争结束，废除了奴隶制，正当全国欢庆之时，林肯总统却遇刺身亡，举国悲哀。惠特曼悲痛至极，怀着对总统深深的敬意，写下《哦，船长！我的船长！》。"船长"在这里指代"林肯"，美国就是这艘"大船"。该诗使用短促的呼语作为标题，表达了诗人强烈的悲愤之情，也是诗人心灵深处对"船长"的深切呼唤，他不能相信也不愿接受敬爱的船长已经离去的事实。该诗韵律整齐，共三个诗节，每个诗节貌似一艘船的形状，这是诗人有意为之。"captain"在诗节的最前端，暗含着林肯是美国这艘大航船的引领者。每节前四行大体上是七个音步，后四行是四音步与三音步相间，韵体为aabbcded，朗朗上口。

该诗的第一节讲述了船长在引领着航船经历了险恶的航程,到达胜利的彼岸时却牺牲了的场景。第二节讲述的是诗人的反应,面对如此结局,诗人悲伤不已,不愿相信船长已去的事实,宁愿它是一场梦。最后一节表达了诗人的无奈,不得不接受这个船长离去的事实。与此同时,诗人也表达了对美国这艘大船未来航程的担忧。在每一节中,诗人都极力描写群众欢迎航船的盛大场面,这与甲板上躺着的死去的船长形成了鲜明的对照,让读者深切感受到此次航程的悲壮气氛。诗中长短句交替使用,每段的结尾反复使用同一句子,更加渲染了悲愤之情,加强了表达效果。由于诗人的感情非常真挚、深沉,再加上比喻、象征等手法的运用,增加了诗歌的感染力。

(五) I Hear America Singing

Walt Whitman

1   I hear America singing, the varied carols I hear,

    Those of mechanics, each one singing his as it should be blithe and strong,

    The carpenter singing his as he measures his plank or beam,

    The mason singing his as he makes ready for work, or leaves off work,

5   The boatman singing what belongs to him in his boat, the deck-hand singing on the steamboat deck,

    The shoemaker singing as he sits on his bench, the hatter singing as he stands,

    The wood-cutter's song, the ploughboy's, on his way in the morning, or at noon intermission, or at sundown,

    The delicious singing of the mother, or of the young wife at work, or of the girl sewing or washing,

第十章 浪漫主义时期诗歌

　　Each singing what belongs to her, and to none else,

10　The day what belongs to the day—at night, the party of young fellows, robust, friendly,

　　Singing with open mouths, their strong melodious songs.

【译文】

我听见美利坚在歌唱

沃尔特·惠特曼

1　我听见美利坚在歌唱，我听见各种不同的欢歌，

　　机工在欢歌，各自唱着自己的歌，歌声快乐而高亢，

　　木工在裁量他的木板和横梁时唱着他的歌，

　　石工在准备上工或歇工时唱着他的歌，

5　船夫唱着他船上自己拥有的一切，水手在轮船的甲板上歌唱，

　　鞋匠坐在板凳上歌唱，帽匠站着唱歌，

　　伐木工在唱歌，农家子在早晨上工、中午休息、太阳西下时唱着歌，

　　母亲的甜润歌声，年轻的妻子在工作室、少女在缝补或浆洗时的歌声，

　　每个人唱着属于他自己或她个人而非属于旁人的歌，

10　白天唱着白天的事情——晚上是成群的小伙子，健康，友善，

　　放开喉咙唱着他们铿锵而优美的歌。

（赵萝蕤　译）

【点评】

　　作为一名诗人，惠特曼的伟大之处在于两个方面：第一，之所以被称为美国民族文化的代表，是因为他能充分表达美国普通劳动者的思想感情。第二，他的诗不论在内容上还是形式上，都开创了一种让后人不断效仿的

新风格。可以说是美国诗人当中最具世界影响力的。"我听见美利坚在歌唱"很充分地体现了以上两个特点。这是一首对劳动和劳动者的颂歌,大而言之,也是对美洲的颂歌。这首诗向读者展现出这样一幅画面:惠特曼环游美国,沿途听到同胞们在歌唱。诗人所描绘的来自各行各业的劳动人民的歌唱让读者感受到一种人民富足、安居乐业的景象。这也体现了惠特曼诗中最常用的一种排比手法。对大体相同的词句展开一幅又一幅画面,有气势恢宏之感。惠特曼歌颂劳动、歌颂劳动者的理想形象、歌颂这个欣欣向荣的国家和她的人民,他的歌颂渗透了对人类的广博的爱,并以博大、包罗万象的气魄反映了广大劳动群众在创造一个新世界的过程中乐观、积极向上的精神。在诗中,惠特曼特意提到母亲、妻子和少女的劳动之歌,也反映了他进步的、男女平等的民主思想。这首诗的艺术风格和传统的诗体大不相同,诗行长短不一,没有韵,也没有规则的轻重音节奏,这种自由体诗为美国诗歌开拓了一条崭新的道路。

(六) Out of the Cradle Endlessly Rocking

Walt Whitman

1   Out of the cradle endlessly rocking,

Out of the mocking-bird's throat, the musical shuttle,

Out of the Ninth-month midnight,

Over the sterile sands and the fields beyond, where the child leaving his bed, wander'd alone, bareheaded, barefoot,

5   Down from the shower'd halo,

Up from the mystic play of shadows, twining and twisting as if they were alive,

Out from the patches of briers and blackberries,

第十章 浪漫主义时期诗歌

From the memories of the bird that chanted to me,

From your memories sad brother, from the fitful risings and fallings I heard,

10　From under that yellow half-moon, late-risen, and swollen as if with tears,

From those beginning notes of yearning and love, there in the mist,

From the thousand responses of my heart, never to cease,

From the myriad thence-arous'd words,

From the word stronger and more delicious than any,

15　From such, as now they start, the scene revisiting,

As a flock, twittering, rising, or overhead passing,

Borne hither, ere all eludes me, hurriedly,

A man, yet by these tears a little boy again,

Throwing myself on the sand, confronting the waves,

20　I, chanter of pains and joys, uniter of here and hereafter,

Taking all hints to use them, but swiftly leaping beyond them,

A reminiscence sing.

Once Paumanok,

When the lilac-scent was in the air and Fifth-month grass was growing,

25　Up this seashore, in some briers,

Two feather'd guests from Alabama, two together,

And their nest, and four light-green eggs spotted with brown,

And every day the he-bird, to and fro, near at hand,

And every day the she-bird, crouch'd on her nest, silent, with bright eyes,

30　And every day I, a curious boy, never too close, never disturbing them,

Cautiously peering, absorbing, translating.

Shine! shine! shine!

Pour down your warmth, great sun!

While we bask, we two together.

35　Two together!

Winds blow South, or winds blow North,

Day come white, or niqht come black,

Home, or rivers and mountains from home,

Singing all time, minding no time,

40　While we two keep together.

Till of a sudden,

May-be kill'd, unknown to her mate,

One forenoon the she-bird crouch'd not on the nest,

Nor return'd that afternoon, nor the next,

45　Nor ever appear'd again.

And thenceforward all summer, in the sound of the sea,

And at night, under the full of the moon, in calmer weather,

Over the hoarse surging of the sea,

Or flitting from brier to brier by day,

50　I saw, I heard at intervals, the remaining one, the he-bird,

The solitary guest from Alabama.

Blow! blow! blow!

第十章 浪漫主义时期诗歌

Blow up, sea-winds, along Paumanok's shore;

I wait and I wait, till you blow my mate to me.

55 Yes, when the stars glisten'd,

All night long, on the prong of a moss-scallop'd stake,

Down, almost amid the slapping waves,

Sat the lone singer, wonderful, causing tears.

He call'd on his mate;

60 He pour'd forth the meanings which I, of all men, know.

Yes, my brother, I know,

The rest might not, but I have treasur'd every note;

For more than once, dimly, down to the beach gliding,

Silent, avoiding the moonbeams, blending myself with the shadows,

65 Recalling now the obscure shapes, the echoes, the sounds and sights after their sorts,

The white arms out in the breakers tirelessly tossing,

I, with bare feet, a child, the wind wafting my hair,

Listen'd long and long.

Listen'd to keep, to sing, now translating the notes,

70 Following you, my brother.

Soothe! soothe! soothe!

Close on its wave soothes the wave behind,

And again another behind, embracing and lapping, every one close,

But my love soothes not me, not me.

75   Low hangs the moon, it rose late;

O It is lagging—O I think it is heavy with love, with love.

O madly the sea pushes upon the land,

With love, with love.

O night! do I not see my love fluttering out among the breakers?

80   What is that little black thing I see there in the white?

Loud! loud! loud!

Loud I call to you, my love!

High and clear I shoot my voice over the waves;

Surely you must know who is here, is here;

85   You must know who I am, my love.

Low-hanging moon!

What is that dusky spot in your brown yellow?

O it is the shape, the shape of my mate!

O moon, do not keep her from me any longer.

90   Land! land! O land!

Whichever way I turn, O I think you could give me my mate back again, if you only would;

For I am almost sure I see her dimly whichever way I look.

O rising stars!

Perhaps the one I want so much will rise, will rise with some of you.

第十章　浪漫主义时期诗歌

95　O throat! O trembling throat!

Sound clearer through the atmosphere!

Pierce the woods, the earth;

Somewhere listening to catch you, must be the one I want.

Shake out, carols!

100　Solitary here, the night's carols!

Carols of lonesome love! Death's carols!

Carols under that lagging, yellow, waning moon!

O, under that moon, where she droops almost down into the sea!

O reckless, despairing carols.

105　But soft! sink low;

Soft! let me just murmur;

And do you wait a moment, you husky-noised sea;

For somewhere I believe I heard my mate responding to me,

So faint, I must be still, be still to listen;

110　But not altogether still, for then she miqht not come immediately to me.

Hither, my love!

Here I am! here!

With this just-sustain'd note I announce myself to you;

This gentle call is for you, my love, for you.

115　Do not be decoy'd elsewhere!

That is the whistle of the wind, it is not my voice;

That is the fluttering, the fluttering of the spray;

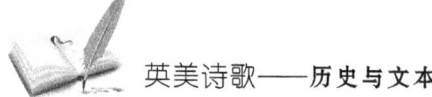

Those are the shadows of leaves.

O darkness! O in vain!

120 O I am very sick and sorrowful.

O brown halo in the sky, near the moon, drooping upon the sea!

O troubled reflection in the sea!

O throat! O throbbing heart!

And I singing uselessly, uselessly all the night.

125 O past! O happy life! O songs of joy!

In the air, in the woods, over fields;

Loved! loved! loved! loved! loved!

But my mate no more, no more with me!

We two together no more.

130 The aria sinking,

All else continuing, the stars shining,

The winds blowing, the notes of the bird continuous echoing,

With angry moans the fierce old mother incessantly moaning,

On the sands of Paumanok's shore, gray and rustling;

135 The yellow half-moon enlarged, sagging down, drooping, the face of the sea almost touching;

The boy ecstatic, with his bare feet the waves, with his hair the atmosphere dallying,

The love in the heart long pent, now loose, now at last tumultuously bursting,

The aria's meaning, the ears, the Soul, swiftly depositing,

The strange tears down the cheeks coursing,
140　The colloquy there, the trio, each uttering,
The undertone, the savage old mother, incessantly crying,
To the boy's Soul's questions sullenly timing, some drown'd secret hissing,
To the outsetting bard of love.

Demon or bird! (said the boy's soul,)
145　Is it indeed toward your mate you sing? or is it really to me?
For I, that was a child, my tongue's use sleeping, now I have heard you,
Now in a moment I know what I am for, I awake,
And already a thousand singers, a thousand songs, clearer, louder and more sorrowful than yours,
A thousand warbling echoes have started to life within me, never to die.

150　O you singer solitary, singing by yourself, projecting me,
O solitary me listening, never more shall I cease perpetuating you;
Never more shall I escape, never more the reverberations,
Never more the cries of unsatisfied love be absent from me,
Never again leave me to be the peaceful child I was before what there, in the night,
155　By the sea, under the yellow and sagging moon,
The messenger there arous'd, the fire, the sweet hell within,
The unknown want, the destiny of me.

O give me the clew! (it lurks in the night here somewhere,)

O if I am to have so much, let me have more!

160 A word then, (for I will conquer it,)

The word final, superior to all,

Subtle, sent up—what is it？—I listen；

Are you whispering it, and have been all the time, you sea-waves？

Is it from your liquid rims and wet sands？

165 Whereto answering, the sea,

Delaying not, hurrying not,

Whisper'd me through the night, and very plainly before daybreak,

Lisp'd to me the low and delicious word DEATH,

And again death, death, death, death,

170 Hissing melodious, neither like the bird, nor like my arous'd child's heart,

But edging near, as privately for me, rustling at my feet,

Creeping thence steadily up to my ears, and laving me softly all over,

Death, death, death, death, death.

Which I do not forget,

175 But fuse the song of my dusky demon and brother,

That he sang to me in the moonlight on Paumanok's gray beach,

With the thousand responsive songs, at random,

My own songs, awaked from that hour;

And with them the key, the word up from the waves,

180 The word of the sweetest song, and all songs,

That strong and delicious word which, creeping to my feet,

第十章 浪漫主义时期诗歌

（Or like some old crone rocking the cradle, swathed in sweet garments, bending aside,）

The sea whisper'd me.

【译文】
从那永远摇荡着的摇篮里

沃尔特·惠特曼

1　从那永远摇荡着的摇篮里，
　　从反舌鸟那婉转如簧的歌喉，
　　从九月的午夜，
　　在荒瘠的沙洲和远处的田野上，那儿有个从床上爬起的孩子光着头赤着脚在独自漫游，
5　在阵雨般洒落的月光下面，
　　在黑影像活物般相互缠绕的神秘游戏的上方，
　　从一片片长满荆棘和乌莓的土地，
　　从那只向我歌唱的鸟儿的记忆之乡，
　　从你的回忆里呀，忧伤的兄弟，从我听到的那忽高忽低的阵阵歌声中，
10　从那迟迟升起、好像饱含泪水的黄澄澄的半轮明月下，
　　从那在迷雾中唱出的渴慕与爱恋的最初几个音符中，
　　从我心脏的永不停息的千百次反应中，
　　从那由此而引起的无数的言语中，
　　从那个比任何言语都更加强烈、更加甜美的单词中，
15　从那个如它们现在开始重访的那样的场景，
　　像一群啁啾着、升腾着或在上空经过的飞鸟，
　　在一切都逃避我之前，匆忙地将一个男人负载着，

将一个从这些眼泪看又成了小孩的男人负载到这里，

我，把自己抛在沙洲上，面对海涛，

20　我这痛苦与欢乐的歌手，现今与今后的连接者，

领会着一切的暗示并利用它们，但又立即把它们超过了，

我唱一支回忆的歌。

从前，在巴曼诺克，

当紫丁香的芬芳在空中缭绕、五月的草在生长的时候，

25　在这海岸上某处的荆棘丛里，

有两位来自阿拉巴马的羽衣客人，双宿双飞，

还有小巢和四枚浅绿色带棕色斑点的小蛋，

每天雄鸟在近处来回飞翔，

每天雌鸟伏在她的窝里，悄悄地，眨着晶亮的双眼，

30　每天我——一个好奇的男孩，从不过于接近，从不打扰它们，

小心地窥伺着，吸收着，解释着这些情景。

照耀吧！照耀吧！照耀吧！

把你的温暖泼下，伟大的太阳！

让我们一起暴晒，我们俩。

35　我们俩在一起呀！

风吹向南方，风吹向北方，

白天白了，黑夜黑了，

故乡，从故乡来的河流与山冈

一直在歌唱，忘记了时光，

40　而我们总是在一起，我们俩。

第十章　浪漫主义时期诗歌

　　直到突然之间，
　　她大概被杀害了，但她的伴侣不知道，
　　有天上午那雌鸟没伏在窝里，
　　下午也没有回来，第二天仍没有，
45　并且永远不再出现了。

　　以后的整个夏天，在海涛声中，
　　晚上天气平静时，在皎洁的月光下，
　　在海面波翻浪涌，
　　或者白天，从一个荆棘丛飞向另一个荆棘丛，
50　我不时看到和听到那剩下的一只，那只雄鸟，
　　那个来自阿拉巴马的孤独的客人。

　　吹吧！吹吧！吹吧！
　　海风啊，沿着巴曼诺克河岸；
　　我等着，等着，直到你把我的伴侣吹回到我身边！
55　是的，当星星闪闪发亮的时候，
　　整个夜晚，在那长满苔藓的木桩上头，
　　几乎就在砰砰拍击的浪涛中，
　　停栖着那个孤独而奇妙的催人泪下的歌手。

　　他呼叫他的伴侣，
60　他倾诉着只有我才能了解的心绪。

　　是的，我的兄弟，我了解，
　　别的人可能不会，而我一直珍藏着每个音响，

因为我不止一次在昏暗中溜到海岸上,
悄悄地避开月光,让我自己与黑影融合在一起,
65　这时回想那些模糊的形体,那回声,那各种的声音和景象,
巨浪永不疲倦地甩出雪白的臂膀,
我,一个孩子,光着双脚,头发在海风里漂游,
在这里谛听,很久很久。

听后要记住,要歌唱,现在我就把曲调翻译在这里,
70　按照你的意思,我的兄弟。

抚爱着,抚爱着,抚爱着!
紧跟着的后浪抚爱着前浪,
后面又一个浪头出现了,拥抱着,拍打着,一个紧跟着一个,
但是我的爱人不来抚爱我,不抚爱我了。

75　月亮低低地悬着,它起得晚了,
它姗姗地慢走哦,我想它是背着爱的重荷,爱的重荷。

哦,海浪疯狂地向陆地冲来,
满怀着爱,满怀着爱。

啊,黑夜,莫非我看见了我的爱人在海涛中翻飞?
80　我看见的白浪中那小小的黑色的东西是什么呢?

大声些!大声些!大声些!
我大声叫唤你,我的爱侣!

第十章　浪漫主义时期诗歌

　　我高高地清晰地把我的声音投入海空；
　　你一定会知道是谁在这里，在这里；
85　你必然知道我是谁，我的爱侣。

　　低悬的月亮啊！
　　你那棕黄色中的黑点是什么呢？
　　啊，它是那形体，我的伴侣的形体！
　　啊，月亮，请别阻拦她，使她不能回到我这里。

90　陆地！陆地！啊，陆地！
　　无论我转向哪里，啊，我想你能够把我的伴侣送还我，只要你愿意，
　　因为我几乎确信我依稀看见了她，无论我朝哪个方向望去。

　　啊，正在上升的星星！
　　也许我渴望的那一颗会上升，会同你们中的几颗上升到天空。
95　啊，歌喉！颤抖的歌喉呀！
　　请在大气中唱得更响亮吧！
　　穿透树林，响遍大地，
　　在某个地方谛听着你的必定是我心之所系的那一位。

　　扬起歌声吧，
100　在寂寞的这儿，黑夜的歌声！
　　孤独的爱的歌声！死亡的歌声！
　　在那缓步慢行的黄色残月下的歌声！
　　啊，在那个月亮下，她几乎要落到海里去了！
　　啊，不顾一切的绝望的歌声。

105　沙哑的海涛啊，请停一停，
　　　请你柔和些，放低声音，
　　　好让我只细语喁喁，
　　　因为我相信我听见我的伴侣在某处回答我，
　　　那么轻微，我必须安静，必须谛听，
110　可是又不能完全静寂，因为那样她就不可能立即来临。

　　　到这里来吧，我的爱人！
　　　我在这里，在这里！
　　　以这个刚好能维持的声音向你宣布我自己，
　　　这个轻柔的呼唤是给你的，我的爱人啊，给你。

115　不要被误引到别的地方去啊，
　　　那是风的呼啸，不是我的声音，
　　　那是浪花在飞扑，在飞扑呀，
　　　那些都是树叶的阴影。

　　　啊，黑暗！啊，空想！
120　啊，我是多么痛苦而悲伤！

　　　啊，天空月亮的褐色晕轮，快要坠落到海上！
　　　啊，海中那凌乱的映像！
　　　啊，歌喉！啊，急跳的心！
　　　而我在徒然地歌唱，整夜徒然地歌唱。

125　啊，从前！啊，愉快的生活！啊，欢乐的歌！

第十章　浪漫主义时期诗歌

　　在空气中，在树林里，在田野上，
　　曾经爱呀！爱呀！爱呀！爱呀！
　　可是我的伴侣没了，不再同我一起了！
　　我们俩不再一起了，我们俩。

130　歌声沉寂了，
　　别的都在继续，星星在闪耀，
　　海风吹着，鸟的歌在不断地引起回声，
　　暴躁的老母亲愤怒地呻吟，不停地呻吟，
　　在巴曼诺克灰色的沙沙作响的河滩上，
135　那黄色的半圆月胀大了，在倾斜，在坠落，快要接触到海浪，
　　那神情恍惚的孩子，海涛在戏弄他的脚，海风在吹拂他的头发，
　　那禁锢在心中的爱情已经开放，现在终于哄乱地爆发了，
　　那歌的含义、耳朵、灵魂正在迅速地贮藏，
　　奇怪的眼泪在两颊流淌，
140　那里的对话，三方面都发出各自的声音，
　　那低沉的声调，凶暴的老母亲不停地哼哼，
　　阴沉地配合孩子的灵魂所提的问题，咝咝地吐露某个被淹没的秘密，
　　向那刚刚出发的诗人。
　　鸟啊，或者精灵！（孩子的灵魂说，）
145　你真的是在向你的伴侣歌唱吗？或者其实是对我？
　　因为我，那时还是个孩子，我的舌头的功能还在睡觉，但现在我听
　　　见你了，

　　如今霎时间我明白了我生来是为了什么，我醒了，
　　于是有了一千名歌手，一千支歌，比你的更清亮、更高亢也更忧愁

的歌,

一千种悠扬的回声,已在我心里活起来,永远不会沉没。

150　啊,你这孤独的歌手,你独自歌唱,影射着我,

啊,孤独的我,我听着,我将永不停息地使你永生;

我永远不再逃避,永不逃避这震颤的余音,

这未曾满足的爱的呼叫将永不离开我心头,

我也永远不再是那天晚上以前的孩子,那么平静,

155　那天晚上在海边,在昏黄低垂的月亮下,

信使唤醒了那烈火,那内心深处甜蜜的魔影,

那无名的欲望,我的命运。

啊,给我那个线索吧!(它在这里黑夜中的某个地方躲着;)

啊,我既然会得到这么多,就给我更多些吧!

160　要不,就给一个词,(因为我要掌握它,)

一个最后的词,超越一切的词,

微妙的,已经传出那是什么?我听着!

你在细声说着它,而且一直是这样吗,你们这些海波?

它是从你们晶莹的水面和潮湿的沙砾中来的吗?

165　大海朝这里回答,

不迟延,也不匆促,

整夜向我低语,黎明前十分清楚,

低低地向我说出"死"这个美妙的词,

接着又说死,死,死,

170　悦耳的咝咝声,既不像那只鸟,也不像我这唤醒了的孩子的心,

只是偷偷地靠近我,在我脚边发出沙沙的声音,

第十章　浪漫主义时期诗歌

又从那里一步步爬到我耳边，并温柔地沐浴着我的整个身子，

死，死，死，死，死。

这我不会忘记，

175　但要把我那兄弟、那阴暗的精灵的歌，

他在巴曼诺克灰暗河滩上的月光下向我唱出的歌，

同一千支信口唱出的回答之歌，

同我自己的从那个时刻醒来的歌相融合，

还要把它们同那个关键的词，那个来自水波上的词，

180　那个属于最美的歌曲和一切歌曲的词，

那个由爬到我脚边的，

（或者像一个裹着漂亮长袍、低着头站在一旁摇着摇篮的老妇人的，）

大海向我低语的强大而美妙的词相融合。

（李野光　译）

【点评】

午夜时分，一个小男孩赤脚来到海边，孩子感受着小鸟的幸福、大海的涛声。诗中的互动包括四方面：小鸟、大海、男孩和男孩成年后的诗人。随着男孩的思想日趋成熟，最终达到了对生命、爱情、生离死别和重生意义的领悟。惠特曼在此诗中非常巧妙地探讨了死亡和爱情主题。整首诗分为三部分：第 1～40 行歌唱的是鸟的幸福，一种理想中的爱情；第 41～129 行吟唱的是一种孤寂之爱；第 130～182 行描述的是对肉体之爱的超越，一种永失我爱后的精神上的自我救赎。

死亡并不代表着一切的终结，而是昭示了新生活的开始。"摇篮"在此诗中出现次数虽然不多，却承载了重要的象征意义。在开篇，不断摇摆的摇篮很容易让我们联想到循环往复的海浪和熟睡中的婴儿。婴儿

的成长代表着从纯真走向成熟，也是诗中的小男孩所经历的成长过程。最后，无休无止的摇篮象征着大自然的周而复始。生固然是生命的开端，死亡又何尝不是另外一种新生活的序曲？暗示着从肉体到精神的一种浴火重生。

本诗写得极为精致，借助诗歌语言，人类生命的有限和短暂升华到了精神世界的无限和永恒，人类死亡的自然规律也相应地诗化成了另类的重生。"打破旧传统，创立新世界"的观念也影响了本世纪初中国的一代文人。其中郭沫若的"凤凰涅槃"和此诗有着异曲同工之妙。

诗歌叙事构思精巧，叙事者以男孩和成年诗人的身份交替叙述，男孩用他纯真、圣洁之心在海边"倾听""翻译"，而成年诗人依赖对过去的记忆，穿越了"今世"和"来生"。诗中排比句的使用也像波涛汹涌的大海般气势磅礴、一浪追逐一浪，翻滚着、震撼着读者。

（七）Because I Could Not Stop for Death

Emily Dickinson

1 Because I could not stop for Death—
  He kindly stopped for me—
  The Carriage held but just Ourselves—
  And Immortality.

5 We slowly drove — He knew no haste
  And I had put away
  My labor and my leisure too,
  For His Civility —

第十章 浪漫主义时期诗歌

　　　We passed the School, where Children strove

10　At Recess — in the Ring —

　　　We passed the Fields of Gazing Grain ,

　　　We passed the Setting Sun.

　　　Or rather, He passed Us;

　　　The Dews drew quivering and chill—

15　For only Gossamer my Gown,

　　　My Tippet— only Tulle —

　　　We paused before a House that seemed

　　　A Swelling of the Ground —

　　　The Roof was scarcely visible—

20　The Cornice — in the Ground —

　　　Since then —Tis Centuries—and yet

　　　Feels shorter than the Day

　　　I first surmised the Horses' Heads

　　　Were toward Eternity.

【译文】
因为我不能停步等候死神
艾米莉·迪金森

1　因我不能停步等候死神——

　　他殷勤停车接我——

车厢里只有我们俩——
还有"永生"同座。

5 我们缓缓而行，他知道无须急促——
他也抛开劳作
和闲暇，以回报
他的礼貌——

我们经过学校，恰逢课间休息——
10 孩子们正喧闹，在操场上——
我们经过注目凝视的稻谷的田地——
我们经过沉落的太阳——

也许该说，是他经过我们而去——
露水使我颤抖而发凉——
15 因为我的衣裳，只是薄纱——
我的披肩——，只是绢网——

我们停在一幢屋前，这屋子
仿佛是隆起的地面——
屋顶，勉强可见——
20 屋檐，低于地平面——

从那时算起，已有几个世纪——
却似乎短过那一天的光阴——
那一天，我初次猜出

第十章 浪漫主义时期诗歌

马头,朝向永恒——

(江枫 译)

【点评】

此诗是迪金森关于死亡主题的最具有代表性的诗篇。诗人以轻松的语调、豁达的态度来谈论"死亡"这个沉重的话题。她不视"死神"为灾祸,可怕的死神在她眼中是一位风度翩翩、温文尔雅的绅士,是一位期待已久的贵客。她之所以放弃工作、放弃闲暇,甚至放弃生命追随死神而去是因为她知道死亡是通向"永恒"和"不朽"的必经之路。

在第一诗节,诗人平静地等待死神的来临,此时的死神被拟人化成一位魅力十足的绅士,足以让诗人欣然与之同行,另外一个重要人物是"永生"。诗人、死神、永生"同座",暗示了人的肉体必死,但灵魂会得到永生。诗人这里采用具体的意象来表达抽象概念,深化了主题。考虑到"carriage"的乘客,这里应该是指"灵柩"。灵车通向坟墓的路途应该也是一场人生的巡礼。他们的车首先经过的是学校,孩子们在操场嬉戏;然后是举目凝望的稻田,稻田此时被拟人化了,暗含着茁壮的生命力;最后经过的是落日,代表着衰落。孩童、稻田、夕阳这三个意象分别代表了人生的3个阶段:幼年、青年或壮年、暮年。夕阳西下,夜幕降临,一天的行程结束,也暗含了人一生的终结,诗歌所描述的衣袂飘飘的丧服和冰冷彻骨的肌肤,让人不由得对死神心生敬畏。面对自己最后的归宿,诗人称之为"房子",并且饶有趣味地打量起来,也传递着诗人内心的轻松和解脱。于她而言,"死亡就是永生的开始"。

迪金森诗作的一个特点就是善用破折号,本诗就是一个很好的例子。诗中频繁使用的破折号貌似把原来的句子随意断开,把互不相干的词汇组合在一起,却让读者感受到了诗人汹涌的思绪和澎湃的情感。

（八）I Heard a Fly Buzz When— I Died

Emily Dickinson

1 I heard a Fly buzz—when I died;
   The stillness in the Room
   Was like the Stillness in the Air—
   Between the Heaves of Storm —

5 The Eyes around — had wrung when them dry —
   And Breaths were gathering firm
   For that last Onset — when the King
   Be witnessed — in the Room —

   I willed my Keepsakes —Signed away
10 What portion of me be
   Assignable — and then it was
   There interposed a Fly —

   With Blue — uncertain stumbling Buzz —
   Between the light — and— me
15 And then the Windows failed —and then
   I could not see to see —

第十章 浪漫主义时期诗歌

【译文】

我听到苍蝇的嗡嗡声 —— 当我死时

艾米莉·迪金森

1 我听到苍蝇的嗡嗡声 —— 当我死时
　房间里，一片沉寂
　就像空气突然平静下来 ——
　在风暴的间隙

5 注视我的眼睛 ——泪水已经流尽——
　我的呼吸正渐渐变紧
　等待最后的时刻——上帝在房间里
　现身的时刻——降临
　我已经分掉了——关于我的

10 所有可以分掉的
　东西——然后我就看见了
　一只苍蝇——

　蓝色的——微妙起伏的嗡嗡声
　在我——和光——之间
15 然后窗户关闭——然后
　我眼前漆黑一片——

（灵　石　译）

【点评】

此诗是迪金森从另类角度写的关于死亡主题的一首诗。诗人正在观察、

记录死亡的过程:她如何订立遗嘱、分发纪念品;苍蝇如何遮住了光线;她的视力和听觉又是如何消失。对人而言,死亡是很自然、再平常不过的事情。对旁观者而言,死亡又是充满苦痛和令人恐惧的。一些评论家认为,此诗中苍蝇遮挡了光线寓意着诗人不能看见来自天堂的光,因此担心死后无缘永生。诗人游走在生与死的边缘,飞进来的苍蝇不仅打破了房间的寂静,也成了连接生与死的纽带。诗人用苍蝇来象征她最后一次触摸人世间,也暗含了人奄奄一息,即将走到生命的尽头。此外,"fly"用意巧妙,可以指"一种昆虫";另外还可做"free flying",指人死后,没有了物质的羁绊,一切得到解脱,可以自由飞翔,无拘无束。迪金森诗歌特点:通过大写字母和运用大量的破折号来表示语气的停顿和强化诗意。

(九) I Died for Beauty

Emily Dickinson

1   I died for Beauty—but was scarce

    Adjusted in the Tomb,

    When One who died for Truth, was lain

    In an adjoining room—

5   He questioned softly "Why I failed"?

    "For Beauty," I replied—

    "And I— for Truth— Themself are One—

    We Brethren, are," He said—

    And so, as Kinsmen, met a Night—

10 We talked between the Rooms——

第十章 浪漫主义时期诗歌

Until the Moss had reached our lips —

And covered up — our names —

【译文】
我为美而死

　　　　艾米莉·迪金森

1　我为美而死——然而
　　很难适应这座坟墓
　　一个为真理献身的人
　　这时躺在我的邻屋——

5　他轻柔地问"我为何而亡"？
　　"为了美"，我回答——
　　他却说"我——为了真理——
　　美真是一体，我们是兄弟"——

　　于是像亲人夜里相逢——
10　我们隔墙侃侃而谈——
　　直到青苔蔓延到唇际——
　　并把我们的姓名——遮掩——

（蒲　隆　译）

【点评】

　　此诗表达了迪金森关于美与真理密不可分的美学主题。两个人在墓地相逢，一个为美而死，一个为真理而亡，但他们死后却成为邻居，诗歌反映了诗人追求本真的性情。迪金森遇见过风度翩翩的死神，如"Because I could not Stop for Death"所述；也谈到过临死前的情景，如"I Heard a Fly

Buzz—when I Died"；此次谈到了死亡原因是为真而死、为美而死，美与真等同，不论哪个，都值得付出毕生的精力去追求。

（十）Success

Emily Dickinson

1 Success is counted sweetest
By those who ne'er succeed.
To comprehend a nectar
Requires sorest need.

5 Not one of all the purple Host
Who took the Flag today
Can tell the definition
So clear of Victory

As he defeated—dying—
10 On whose forbidden ear
The distant strains of triumph
Burst agonized and clear!

【译文】
成功

艾米莉·迪金森

1 从未成功的人们

第十章　浪漫主义时期诗歌

　　认为成功最甜蜜。
　　要领略仙酒的滋味，
　　须经最痛楚的寻觅。

5　紫袍华裘的诸公
　　如今执掌着大旗，
　　他们谁也说不清
　　胜利的确切含义——

　　只有垂死的战败者
10　失去听觉的耳朵里
　　才迸出遥远的凯旋歌
　　如此痛彻而清晰！

（屠　岸　译）

【点评】

这是一首富有哲理的、励志型的小诗。无论人们隶属于何种行业，每个人都渴望成功。究竟谁才能品尝到成功的甘甜？谁才能真正懂得成功的内涵？对那些失败者而言，成功可望而不可即，它的甜美滋味只能靠臆想而已；成功同样也不属于那些出身显赫、位高权重之人：对他们而言，成功能够唾手可得，太轻而易举，也失去了成功应有的价值；而那些有着坚定信念和进取精神，为理想目标而努力奋斗，直至"垂死"的"战败者"们才有可能真正领悟成功的真谛，听到嘹亮的凯歌。诗人貌似在评判"成功"，笔锋斗转，真正的"成功"却是它的对立面——"失败"，于"失败"中品尝成功的苦涩与甘甜。依诗人看来，战场上濒死的战败者才是真正的成功者，这与世人眼中的成功者形象大相径庭。这种对成功者形象的解读既是对世俗观念的一种嘲讽，同时也告诫大家，不要因失败而丧失前

行的动力与追求,只有经历过失败的煎熬与伤痛,才更能体会到成功的甜美与愉悦。诗人喜欢独处,过着几乎幽居般的生活,在诗坛也是籍籍无名,对于自己钟爱的事业,谁不渴盼成功?此诗对于成功的辩证性思考既反映了诗人对自己事业孜孜不倦、永不言弃的追求,也反映了诗人强大的内省力和思辨力。

(十一) A bird Came Down the Walk

Emily Dickinson

1 A bird came down the walk,

  He did not know I saw;

  He bit an angle-worm in halves

  And ate the fellow, raw.

5 And then he drank a dew

  From a convenient grass,

  And then hopped sidewise to the wall

  To let a beetle pass.

  He glanced with rapid eyes

10 That hurried all abroad,

  They looked like frightened beads, I thought;

  Like one in danger; cautious.

  He stirred his velvet head,

  I offered him a crumb,

第十章　浪漫主义时期诗歌

15　And he unrolled his feathers

　　And rowed him softer home.

　　Than oars divide the ocean,

　　Too silver for a seam,

　　Or butterflies, off banks of noon,

20　Leap, splashless, as they swim.

【译文】
一只小鸟沿小径走来
艾米莉·迪金森

1　一只小鸟沿小径走来,

　　它不知道我在瞧:

　　它把一条蚯蚓啄成两段

　　再把这家伙生着吃掉。

5　然后从近旁的草叶上,

　　吞饮下一颗露水珠,

　　又向墙根,侧身一跳

　　给一只甲虫让路。

　　它用受惊吓的珠子般

10　滴溜溜转的眼睛,

　　急促地看了看前后左右;

　　像个遇险的人,小心。

抖了抖它天鹅绒的头,

我给它点面包屑,

15 它却张开翅膀,划动着

飞了回去,轻捷。

胜过在海上划桨,

银光里不见缝隙,

胜过蝴蝶午时从岸边跃起

20 游泳,却没有浪花溅激。

(江　枫　译)

【点评】

　　迪金森的生活圈子狭窄,孤独单调的生活使得她对大自然的观察细致入微。她写了500多首关于大自然的诗歌,竭力表达自己亲近大自然,想把自己融入大自然的生态思想。通过这首诗歌,迪金森向读者展现了一幅跃动流畅的大自然画卷,既体现了诗人敏锐的观察力和对大自然的亲和力,也是诗人探索自然与人性的一个佐证。诗歌的第一、二诗节描述了小鸟一些自由自在的活动,这时的它还没有意识到人类的存在或是"觊觎"吧。啄蚯蚓—饮露珠—侧身跳,读来情趣盎然、跃然纸上。后面三个诗节描述了小鸟发现人类后的一些反应:受惊的眼神、忐忑的张望、优雅的离去。诗中的"我"看到可爱小鸟的一举一动,心生欢喜,满怀柔情地想用手中的食物引诱它、亲近它,然而它却振振翅膀、不留痕迹地飞走了。"我"对小鸟的亲近和欢喜,换来的只是小鸟的恐惧和逃避,一方面展示了以自我为中心的人类在大自然之中的渺小和无奈,另一方面也暗示了大自然对人类的冷酷和漠然。动物与人、还有大自然的其他生命形式一样,都是大自然的一份子,有其自身的发展、消亡规律。它们都是生而平等的,为自身的存在而存在,无关乎人类的福祉和利益。人类只有了解生命、敬畏自然,

第十章 浪漫主义时期诗歌

才能和谐共处，其乐融融。

（十二）"Hope" Is the Thing With Feathers

Emily Dickinson

1　"Hope" is the thing with feathers—
　　That perches in the soul—
　　And sings the tune without the words—
　　And never stops—at all—

5　And sweetest—in the Gale—is heard—
　　And sore must be the storm—
　　That could abash the little Bird
　　That kept so many warm—

　　I've heard it in the chillest land—
10　And on the strangest Sea—
　　Yet, never, in Extremity,
　　It asked a crumb—of Me.

【译文】

"希望"是个有羽毛的东西

艾米莉·迪金森

1　"希望"是个有羽毛的东西——
　　它栖息在灵魂里——

唱没有歌词的歌曲——

永远，不会停息——

5　在暴风中，听来，最美——

令人痛心的是这样的风暴——

它甚至能窘困那温暖着

多少人的小鸟——

我曾在最陌生的海上——

10　在最寒冷的陆地，听到——

它却从不向我索取

些微的，面包。

（江　枫　译）

【点评】

　　本首诗歌中的"希望"是迪金森讴歌的主题。诗人采用比喻和拟人手法，将抽象的"希望"物化为长着羽毛的"小鸟"。这只小鸟栖息在人类灵魂深处，唱着无词之曲，永不停息。即使环境再艰苦恶劣（"the Gale" "the storm" "in the chillest land" "on the strangest sea"），它也不曾退缩、停止歌唱，一次次战胜绝望，带来温暖人心的希望。狂风暴雨面前的鸟儿是窘迫的，但这时的它也是最美的。鸟儿虽历经磨难，但它总能给人以面对困境时的信心和安慰、且又是无欲无求的（"Yet, never, in Extremity / It asked a crumb—of Me"）。此处凸显鸟儿的无私、无畏、无欲，它是人们生活中不可或缺的精神支柱，是鞭策人类前行的动力。本诗中破折号的重复出现也是迪金森诗歌的一大特色：它既是语音、语义上的一种停顿、过渡，也标志着情感的一种迁移和转变，令读者沉思、回味。

第十章 浪漫主义时期诗歌

（十三）"Why Do I Love" You, Sir?

Emily Dickinson

1 "Why Do I Love" You, Sir?

　　Because—

　　The Wind does not require the Grass

　　To answer—Wherefore when He pass

5　She cannot keep Her place.

　　Because He knows—and

　　Do not You—

　　And We know not—

　　Enough for Us

10　The Wisdom it be so—

　　The Lightning—never asked an Eye

　　Wherefore it shut—when He was by—

　　Because He knows it cannot speak—

　　And reasons not contained—

15　—Of Talk—

　　There be—preferred by Daintier Folk—

　　The Sunrise—Sire—compelleth Me—

　　Because He's Sunrise—and I see—

　　Therefore—Then—

英美诗歌——历史与文本

20 I love Thee—

【译文】

"为什么我爱"你,先生?

艾米莉·迪金森

1　"为什么我爱"你,先生?
　　因为——
　　风,从不要求小草
　　回答,为什么他经过
5　她就不得不动摇。

　　因为他知道,而你,
　　你不知道——
　　我们不知道——
　　我们有这样的智慧
10　也就够了。

　　闪电,从不询问眼睛,
　　为什么,他经过时,要闭上——
　　因为他知道,它说不出——
　　有些道理——
15　难以言传——
　　高雅的人宁愿,会意——

　　日出,先生,使我不能自已——

第十章　浪漫主义时期诗歌

因为他是日出,我看见了——

所以,于是——

20　我爱你——

（江　枫　译）

【点评】

对于处在恋爱中的男女而言,"为什么会爱"总是被反复提及。本诗以此为题,阐释了爱情是真实情感的自然流露,是自然而然发生的、不需要原因和理由的,更深层次的爱情体验皆是无法言说的。虽然是老生常谈的爱情话题,此诗读来却清新自然,别具一格。恋爱中的"我"是一名女性,"我"被比喻成"小草""眼睛""观赏日出的人"。而男人如同"大风""闪电""日出"。在男人面前,我"摇摆""眨眼""情难自已",全是因为这"难以言传"的爱情。"我"对"你"的爱恋近似疯狂,如同风对草、闪电对眼睛、日出对观赏者,全因为你有着一种不可抗拒的魅力,才让我这么永远爱你。

（十四）The Soul Selects Her Own Society

Emily Dickinson

1　The Soul selects her own Society—

　　Then—shuts the Door—

　　To her divine Majority—

　　Present no more—

5　Unmoved — she notes the Chariots — pausing —

　　At her low Gate —

　　Unmoved — an Emperor be kneeling

Upon her Mat —

I've known her — from an ample nation —
10   Choose One —
Then — close the Valves of her attention —
Like Stone —

【译文】
灵魂选择自己的伴侣
艾米莉·迪金森

1   灵魂选择自己的伴侣，
然后，把门紧闭——
她神圣的决定——
再不容干预——

5   发现车辇，停在，她低矮的门前——
不为所动——
一位皇帝，跪在她的席垫——
不为所动

我知道她，从人口众多的整个民族——
10   选中了一个——
从此，封闭关心的阀门——
像一块石头——

（江 枫 译）

第十章 浪漫主义时期诗歌

【点评】

《灵魂选择自己的伴侣》写于1862年，正处于1861—1865年迪金森创作的高峰期。短短五年时间，迪金森就创作了800多首诗歌。本诗发表于1955年由托马斯·约翰逊（Thomas. H. Johnson）编辑出版的《狄金森诗歌全集》中，共收录诗歌1775首，本诗排名303。"灵魂"此处被喻为一名"女性"，在她找寻到自己的伴侣后，便钟情于"它"，不为外界所利诱。即便代表权势和利禄的皇帝屈尊向她传递爱意，她也不为所动，对自己的伴侣矢志不渝。"我"对这位"灵魂女神"仰慕已久，便决心效仿她，外面的花花世界和凡尘俗世与"我"何干。"我"只需遵从自己的内心，选择适合自己的"灵魂伴侣"，断绝与尘世间的一切往来，自"我"封闭即可。对此诗中暗指的我的"灵魂伴侣"，一说是迪金森为之倾注一生的诗歌事业；另外一说是因为经历过几次恋爱的坎坷，使得迪金森心灰意冷，开始了她独身幽居的生活模式。总而言之，这是一首迪金森选择诗歌创作和隐居生活的宣言诗。

（十五）Wild Nights! Wild Nights!

Emily Dickinson

1   Wild Nights! —Wild Nights!

    Were I with thee,

    Wild Nights should be

    Our luxury!

5   Futile — the Winds—

    To a heart in port, —

    Done with the Compass—

    Done with the Chart!

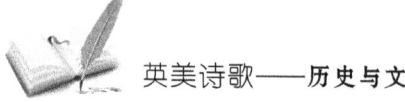

>   Rowing in Eden—
> 10 Ah! the Sea!
>   Might I but moor—To-night—
>   in Thee!

【译文】
暴风雨夜！ 暴风雨夜！

　　　　　　艾米莉·迪金森

> 1 暴风雨夜！ 暴风雨夜！
>   我若和你在一起，
>   暴风雨夜就是
>   豪奢的喜悦！

> 5 风，无能为力——
>   心，已在港内——
>   罗盘，不必！
>   海图，不必！

>   泛舟在伊甸园——
> 10 啊，海！
>   但愿我能，今夜——
>   泊在你的水域！

（江　枫　译）

【点评】

迪金森在隐居之前，有两段刻骨铭心的感情。此诗写于 1861 年，距

第十章　浪漫主义时期诗歌

迪金森深居简出已过去了六年，但从字里行间透露出的对爱情的渴望与痴狂以及拥有爱情时的满足与甜蜜，都可窥见迪金森当时的苦痛与煎熬、幸福与痴狂。此诗也被认为是迪金森爱情诗的代表作。本诗同样包含了迪金森诗歌的一些特点：没有固定的音步、格律，抑扬格、扬抑格兼有，诗的自由度比较高。另外，大量使用破折号和单词的不规则大写，既表达了诗歌场景的连续性和情感的变化过程，增加了诗歌的节奏感，也让读者感受到了"我"对心上人的浓浓爱意和为爱披荆斩棘的勇气和决心。在这首诗中，诗人通过大海、小船、狂风、海港、罗盘、海图等隐喻，给读者营造出这样一个场景：狂风暴雨之夜，一只小船在海面上颠簸，几番挣扎，欲停泊在宁静的海湾。在本诗中，大海辽阔、无边无际，既能负船而行，又能提供避风的港湾，象征了胸怀宽广、包容性强、能够给予"我"庇护的男性恋人。而"我"是航行在茫茫大海中的一只小船。风雨飘摇之夜，随时都有倾覆的危险，"我"是多么渴望能够停泊在爱的港湾，得到"大海"的呵护和爱恋啊。在第一诗节，"我"向恋人吐露深情，表达了"我"想和"他"相依相伴的急迫心情：假如能和你在一起，即便狂风骤雨，于我而言，是何等的喜悦，为了爱情，我愿历尽千辛万苦。第二诗节写到了"我"得到爱情之后的满足感和男女之间爱情的真谛，就是心与心之间的交流和碰撞，对栖息在爱的港湾的小船而言，狂风暴雨也无能为力。第三诗节写泛舟在爱情的伊甸园，渴望在温暖的大海怀抱中停泊，如同真爱找到归属之地。通过一连串的隐喻，诗人淋漓尽致地描述了男女恋人之间炽热的爱情。

（十六）I'm Nobody! Who are you?

Emily Dickinson

1　I'm nobody! Who are you?
　　Are you nobody, too?

Then there's a pair of us—don't tell!
　　They'd banish us, you know.
5　How dreary to be somebody!
　　How public, like a frog
　　To tell your name the livelong day
　　To an admiring bog!

【译文】
我是一个小人物，你呢？
艾米莉·迪金森

1　我是一个小人物，你呢？
　　也是一个小人物，对吗？
　　这就成了一双。别出声！
　　你知道，他们会赶我们。

5　做个大人物多么要命！
　　多么张扬，就好似青蛙
　　成天价唠叨你的姓名——
　　向仰慕你的泥沼絮聒！

（黄杲炘　译）

【点评】
　　迪金森虽出身名门、接受过良好的教育，但终身未嫁，过着隐士般的生活，创作出来的诗歌数量惊人，这些都引起了人们对她独特生活方式的关注，此诗在一定程度上阐释了迪金森为何选择这么一种平静安宁的低调生活模式。在第一诗节，采用戏剧独白的方式，诗人寻觅与"我"一样同

第十章 浪漫主义时期诗歌

是无名之辈的朋友。见到志同道合之人,不免惊喜,又略带担忧地告诫"别出声!""他们会赶我们"。喜忧之间,也暗示出貌似与社会格格不入的生活,于"我"而言,却是一种自信、一种幸福、一种难以割舍的情怀。在第二诗节,诗人道出了不愿成为名人的原因。出身显赫或许洞悉了各式社交场合觥筹交错中的浮华喧嚣,诗人对所谓名人有更清醒的认识:名人为名利所累,为引起公众的关注,不厌其烦地介绍自己的名字、推介自己。他们自吹自擂的受众只不过是一些因为各种利益关系去迎合他们的、庸俗的无脑之辈而已。诗人认为,名人的这些行为与沼泽地里无聊叫嚣的青蛙无异,徒增聒噪而已。这种将名人喻为青蛙的名利观也暗示了诗人生活中的淡泊名利、超凡脱俗。

(十七) To Helen

Edgar Allan Poe

1 HELEN, thy beauty is to me
    Like those Nicean barks of yore,
    That gently, o'er a perfumed sea,
    The weary, way-worn wanderer bore
5 To his own native shore.

    On desperate seas long wont to roam,
    Thy hyacinth hair, thy classic face.
    Thy Naiad airs have brought me home
    To the glory that was Greece,
10 And the grandeur that was Rome.

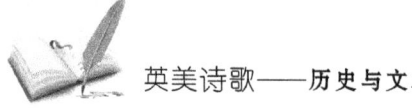

```
       Lo! in yon brilliant window niche,
       How statue—like I see thee stand,
       The agate lamp within thy hand!
       Ah, Psyche, from the regions which
15     Are Holy Land！
```

【译文】
致海伦

爱德加·爱伦·坡

```
1   海伦，对于我，你的美
    正像古时奈西亚帆船，
    载着疲惫的旅人
    悠悠飘过芳香的海域，
5   驶向他故乡的海岸。

    在长久习于汹涌的海面，
    你那卷发及典雅的脸，
    你海仙女的风姿使我熟记
    古希腊的荣耀、
10  古罗马的庄严。

    瞧！我见你玉立亭亭，
    在光彩的壁龛里，
    如玉雕神女，
```

第十章 浪漫主义时期诗歌

手里还握着玛瑙油灯!

15　呵,你是赛琪,来自天国的圣地。

(李正栓 译)

【点评】

坡的诗有两大特点:一是内容上追求新奇怪诞,充满神秘诡异的想象,有时则流露出对世俗的叛逆和反抗;二是诗的音乐性强,音律上刻意工整,词语华丽而富有节奏感,有时给人以过分雕琢之感。《致海伦》是坡的抒情诗代表作,据说此诗为坡少年时代所做,被一位同学的母亲——简·斯蒂奇·斯坦达德(Mrs. Jane Stith Stanard)的美所震撼,坡写诗表达了他对美的感受,诗中充满了联想和暗示,简·斯蒂奇·斯坦达德在此诗中被比作希腊神话中的美女海伦。

在第一诗节,诗人提到希腊美神海伦,海伦之美犹如尼西亚的帆船,这种经典联想增添了诗中的古雅气氛。诗人把自己比喻成奥德赛,奥德赛在海上流浪了十年才乘船回到故乡。海伦之美犹如他执着于追求艺术的真谛——真、美恒久不变。古时战船载英雄回故乡,他心中的美神海伦带他来到了艺术的梦想之地。所有艺术的发源地只有一个,那就是美,而希腊、罗马又是美的故乡、艺术的神圣殿堂。第二诗节中"desperate seas"是一种移就修辞格,既写出了大海的波涛汹涌,又描绘了诗人追求艺术之美的澎湃激情。在第三诗节,海伦直接被比作来自圣地的女神赛琪,站立在神龛里,圣洁无瑕,暗示出海伦的灵魂之美,而灵魂之美又是至纯至真之爱的根源,再一次表达了诗人对美的孜孜不倦的追求,以及他心目中的理想、神圣之爱。正如坡所说:这是"我在热情洋溢的青少年时代,写给我心灵中第一次纯理想之爱的诗行"。全诗共三节,每节5行,多为四音步抑扬格诗行,韵式为:ababb ababa abbab。

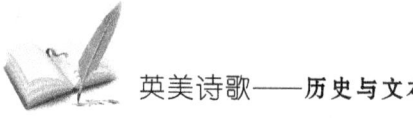

(十八) Annabel Lee

Edagr Allan Poe

1 It was many and many a year ago,
In a kingdom by the sea,
That a maiden there lived whom you may know
By the name of ANNABEL LEE; —
5 And this maiden she lived with no other thought
Than to love and be loved by me.

I was a child and she was a child,
In this kingdom by the sea,
But we loved with a love that was more than love—
10 I and my ANNABEL LEE—
With a love that the winged seraphs of heaven
Coveted her and me.

And this was the reason that, long ago,
In this kingdom by the sea,
15 A wind blew out of a cloud by night
Chilling my ANNABEL LEE;
So that her highborn kinsman came
And bore her away from me,
To shut her up in a sepulchre
20 In this kindom by the sea.

The angels, not half so happy in the heaven,

Went evnying her and me:—

Yes! That was the reason (as all men know,

In this kingdom by the sea)

25 That the wind came out of a cloud, chilling

And killing my ANNABEL LEE.

But our love it was stronger by far than the love

Of those who were older than we—

Of many far wiser than we—

30 And neither the angels in Heaven above,

Nor the demons down under the sea,

Can ever dissever my soul from the soul

35 Of the beautiful ANNABEL LEE:—

For the moon never beams without bringing me dreams

Of the beautiful Annalbel Lee;

And the stars never rise, but I see the bright eyes

Of the beautiful ANNABEL LEE;

And so, all the night-tide, I lie down by the side

Of my darling—my darling—my life and my bride,

40 In the sepulchre there by the sea—

In her tomb by the side of the sea.

【译文】
安娜贝尔·李

爱德加·爱伦·坡

1 很多很多年以前,
   海边一个王国里,
   居住着一少女,
   名叫安娜贝尔·李
5 她在世上无杂念,
   唯知与我相爱怜。

   我们两人皆孩童,
   住在海边王国里;
   相爱程度比爱浓,
10 我和安娜贝尔·李;
   天上六翼众天使,
   垂涎我和我的李。

   正是因为我们爱,
   就在海边王国里,
15 云中吹出寒风来,
   冻死我的漂亮李;
   于是高贵亲属来,
   从我手中掠她去,
   墓穴把她关起来,
20 就在海边王国里。

第十章　浪漫主义时期诗歌

  天上天使并不悦，
  开始妒忌她和我——
  的确此因人人解，
  （就在海边这王国。）
25 寒风乘夜云端起，
  冻杀我的安娜·李。

  但是我们爱更浓，
  胜比我们年长者——
  胜比几许智多星——
30 天上众多神天使，
  海里无数怪妖精，
  妄想拆散灵与魂！
  我们生死不分离！

  因为月辉带我梦，
35 梦见漂亮安娜·李；
  除非见她明亮眸，
  否则星辰难升起；
  所以长夜邀我睡，
  伴我生命伴新娘，
40 就在海边墓穴内，
  滔滔海边她墓内。

（李正栓　译）

【点评】

《安娜贝尔·李》发表于1849年10月，是坡死后发表的，也是他创作的最后一首诗。坡的妻子弗吉尼亚病逝于1847年,年仅24岁,两年后,坡也离开人世。坡十分爱他的妻子,据说这首诗就是为纪念爱妻所作。

在《安娜贝尔·李》中,坡没有用妻子的真实姓名,而是杜撰了一个假名,生活场景也不是真实的,而是虚构的一个"海边王国",这反而让"我"和"少女"的爱情故事蒙上了一层神秘色彩。另一方面也向读者暗示出这样至纯至真的爱只能存在于古时的一个神秘王国,表达了坡对现实的不满。

诗中描绘的一对纯真的少年男女自幼青梅竹马、无视门第高低,相亲相爱。他们爱得热烈、深沉,却招来了天使的嫉妒。于是阴风刮来,姑娘因病突然离世。少年十分伤心,但他坚信,他们的爱情是任何人也阻挡不了的。死亡并不能隔断"我"的爱恋,伴着月亮、星星,在海边,"我"守护我的新娘直到永远。诗人将他的忠贞爱情在诗中表现得淋漓尽致,让人唏嘘不已。

这首诗被评论家们推崇为坡的顶峰之作。坡的诗歌创作美学就是展现美,就是在读者心中产生美的感受,其最高形式就是让读者的心灵产生震撼、共鸣,其中悲情主题最能产生作者与读者之间心灵的震颤、发人深思。因此,对年轻美貌少女的离世的悲痛便成了坡经常采用的诗歌创作主题。本诗在很多方面契合坡的诗学理论:诗不是太长,41行,能够一口气读完;悲伤、忧郁的主基调充斥着整个诗篇;故事讲述的是一个美丽女人的消亡。可以说,《安娜贝尔·李》是坡创作美学的最佳实践。

本诗是歌谣体,让诗读起来舒缓流畅,具有较高的音乐美。抑抑扬格的音步又能够抒发诗人抑郁悲哀的情绪,追忆过去的美好,表达对逝者的思念。音韵低缓,句尾不断重复"Annabel Lee",像诗人一遍又一遍地呼唤她的名字,期待她归来,抒发了诗人对她的无限眷恋,传达出凄婉哀怨的情绪;以|'i:'|音为韵脚,特别是最后两行重复"sea",让诗读起来缠绵悱恻、情真意切,有一种悲怆之感,充分表达了诗人对爱人之死的悲痛之情。

第十章 浪漫主义时期诗歌

（十九）A Dream Within a Dream

Edagr Allan Poe

1 Take this kiss upon the brow!
   And, in parting from you now,
   Thus much let me avow
   You are not wrong, who deem
5 That my days have been a dream;
   Yet if hope has flown away
   In a night, or in a day,
   In a vision, or in none,
   Is it therefore the less gone?
10 All that we see or seem
   Is but a dream within a dream.

   I stand amid the roar
   Of a surf-tormented shore,
   And I hold within my hand
15 Grains of the golden sand
   How few! yet how they creep
   Through my fingers to the deep,
   While I weep, while I weep!
   O God! can I not grasp
20 Them with a tighter clasp?
   O God! can I not save

One from the pitiless wave?
Is all that we see or seem
But a dream within a dream?

【译文】
梦中之梦

爱德加·爱伦·坡

1   请你的眉间接受这一吻！
    在这我与你分手的时分，
    到此为止让我向你承认——
    你并没有错，当你认定
5   我这一生一直是一场梦；
    但若是希望已付诸东流
    在一个夜晚，或在白昼，
    在幻想之中，或在虚渺，
    它难道因此失去得更少？
10 我们所见或似见的一切
    都不过是一场梦中之梦。

    我站在咆哮轰鸣的海边，
    我站在波涛汹涌的海岸，
    我紧紧地握在我的手里
15 一粒粒金光灿灿的沙粒——
    真少！可它们仍然溜走，
    悄悄钻过我紧握的指头，

第十章　浪漫主义时期诗歌

当我在哭问，当我哭吼！
哦，上帝！我难道不能
20　把这些沙粒儿抓得更紧？
哦，上帝！我难道不可
留下这无情的浪花一朵？
我们所见或似见的一切
难道只是一场梦中之梦？

（曹明伦　译）

【点评】

这首诗表达了诗人与心爱的人分别时绝望的心情，共24行，可以分成两个部分。第一部分表达了诗人对已逝过去的遗憾、追悔之心。逝去不可追，没有把握住过去的美好、荒废了生命，宁愿此时的分离也是梦幻一场，那样就无须伤悲。第二部分写诗人的痛苦和无奈，如同流沙离开手掌，他再也不能掌控任何东西。此时的他，虽已意识到了感情的珍贵，但终究不能力挽狂澜。他想留住生活中的美好，但是留不住，就像他站在汹涌的大海里紧握沙粒一样，无论捏得多紧，终究要被海浪冲得干干净净，此时诗人将绝望和无助之情表现得淋漓尽致。最后的问题更加表明坡宁愿生活在梦中，但事实上梦也不能给他安宁，他就是这样成为一个生活在噩梦中的诗人。

（二十）The City in the Sea

Edagr Allan Poe

1　Lo! Death has reared himself a throne
　　In a strange city lying alone
　　Far down within the dim West,

      Where the good and the bad and the worst and the best

5   Have gone to their eternal rest.

      There shrines and palaces and towers

        (Time-eaten towers and tremble not!)

      Resemble nothing that is ours.

      Around, by lifting winds forgot,

10   Resignedly beneath the sky

      The melancholy waters lie.

      No rays from the holy Heaven come down

      On the long night-time of that town;

      But light from out the lurid sea

15   Streams up the turrets silently—

      Gleams up the pinnacles far and free—

      Up domes—up spires—up kingly halls—

      Up fanes—up Babylon-like walls—

      Up shadowy long-forgotten bowers

20   Of sculptured ivy and stone flowers—

      Up many and many a marvellous shrine

      Whose wreathed friezes intertwine

      The viol, the violet, and the vine.

      Resignedly beneath the sky

25   The melancholy waters lie.

      So blend the turrets and shadows there

      That all seem pendulous in air,

      While from a proud tower in the town

第十章 浪漫主义时期诗歌

  Death looks gigantically down.

30 There open fanes and gaping graves
  Yawn level with the luminous waves;
  But not the riches there that lie
  In each idol's diamond eye—
  Not the gaily-jewelled dead
35 Tempt the waters from their bed;
  For no ripples curl, alas!
  Along that wilderness of glass—
  No swellings tell that winds may be
  Upon some far-off happier sea—
40 No heavings hint that winds have been
  On seas less hideously serene.
  But lo, a stir is in the air!
  The wave—there is a movement there!
  As if the towers had thrust aside,
45 In slightly sinking, the dull tide—
  As if their tops had feebly given
  A void within the filmy Heaven.
  The waves have now a redder glow—
  The hours are breathing faint and low—
50 And when, amid no earthly moans,
  Down, down that town shall settle hence,
  Hell, rising from a thousand thrones,
  Shall do it reverence.

【译文】
海中之城

爱德加·爱伦·坡

1 瞧! 死神为他自己竖起了宝座,
  在一座奇妙的城市,萧森寥落,
  就在那遥远而迷蒙的西方,
  那儿,欢乐与痛苦、邪恶与善良
5 都早已坠入永恒的梦乡。
  那些神龛、宫殿和塔楼
  (时间侵蚀的塔楼不再摇晃!)
  看起来都不像我们所有。
  四周,被消散的风儿遗忘
10 在苍昊之下如槁木死灰
  是一汪忧郁凄清的海水。

  从冥冥穹天没有星光月色
  洒向这座荒城的漫漫长夜;
  只有微光来自苍白的海面
15 悄然无声地映在角楼塔尖——
  映在塔尖,把四方映遍——
  映在圆顶、尖顶、帝王的厅堂——
  映在圣殿——巴比伦式的粉墙——
  映在早就被遗忘的空濛的凉亭,
20 凉亭有石雕的鲜花和青藤——
  映在许多叹为观止的神庙,

第十章 浪漫主义时期诗歌

其萧墙照壁有石刻玉雕
古琴、藤蔓和紫罗兰互相缠绕。
在苍昊之下如槁木死灰
25 是那汪忧郁凄清的海水。
塔楼和阴影在水中汇融
仿佛一切都悬浮于空中,
而在城中的一座高塔之上
死神正巍然地朝下眺望。

30 下面,裂开的坟墓和神庙
与微微发光的海面齐高;
但那儿并没有金银财富
在每一尊神像面前展露——
也没有珠光宝气的死者
35 想从海底把波涛诱惑;
因为,唉!没有漪澜
泛起在茫茫如镜的海面——
没有鳞波显示风儿也许
吹拂在远方更幸运的海域——
40 没有浪花暗示风儿吹在
静得不那么可怕的大海。

但瞧,天空出现了一阵骚动!
这海——这海也有了一阵汹涌!
仿佛那些塔楼正微微下坠
45 倾泻着插入阴郁的潮水——

-465-

仿佛那些塔尖已经放弃

它们在朦胧天空的位置。

这海此刻有了更红的颜色——

时间在呼吸,气息微弱——

50　而这时,那座城将下沉,下沉,

从此再听不见人世的呻吟。

地狱,从一千个王位上升起,

将对它表示深深的敬意。

(曹明伦　译)

【点评】

　　坡的诗歌和小说以怪诞、阴森恐怖著称。此诗作于1845年,是一首充满神秘奇特和梦幻色彩的浪漫主义诗歌。全诗53行,围绕死亡主题,诡异鬼魅的氛围笼罩其中,让读者有一种身临其境之感。"海中之城"象征意味明显,意指像纽约这样的大都市,充斥着罪恶和奢靡之气,终有一天将遭受上帝的惩罚,摆脱不了沉沦、毁灭的悲惨命运。此诗也是对人类社会发展前景的警示:在工业化进程加快和科技进步的当时,人们心生恐慌、精神危机加重,坡认为人类文明如那"萧森寥落的城市",被死神之手攫取,而诗人内心的隐忧也如那"一汪忧郁凄清的海水",既表现了诗人的无奈,也体现了诗人对处于文化危机时代社会的忧思。在诗歌的第一节,诗人就道出了象征终极权利的死神成为城市的主宰者,使得城市"萧森寥落",一切善恶是非烟消云散,人也无影无踪,沉浸在海水中的死寂城市充满迷幻、怪异色彩,是鬼魅般的存在,令人毛骨悚然("那些神龛、宫殿和塔楼/看起来都不像我们所有")。第二诗节描述了笼罩在死神之手的城市如漫漫长夜,黑黢黢一片,只有来自海面的微光映照在幽灵般的建筑物上。"塔楼和阴影在水中汇融/仿佛一切都悬浮于空中"描绘出城市中的建筑物与它的海面倒影交融,悬挂在死寂的黑暗之中;"死神位于高塔之上，巍然朝下眺望"，这种奇特意象更加突出了这座如噩梦般存在的被死神笼罩之城的沉寂、恐怖、幽深、冰冷。第三诗节主要讲述了如镜般的海面，貌似风平浪静、没有涟漪、也没有浪花，但被它所吞噬的神庙、坟墓、死者述说着海水曾经的疯狂。最后的诗节提到随着海水的骚动、变色，城市进一步下沉，红色的海水如同地狱之门的烈焰，将要吞噬整座城市。

（二十一）To My Mother

Edagr Allan Poe

1　Because I feel that, in the Heavens above,
　　The angels, whispering to one another,
　　Can find, among their burning terms of love,
　　None so devotional as that of "Mother,"
5　Therefore by that dear name I long have called you—
　　You who are more than mother unto me,
　　And fill my heart of hearts, where Death installed you
　　In setting my Virginia's spirit free.

　　My mother—my own mother, who died early,
10　Was but the mother of myself; but you
　　Are mother to the one I loved so dearly,
　　And thus are dearer than the mother I knew
　　By that infinity with which my wife
　　Was dearer to my soul than its soul-life.

【译文】

致我的母亲

爱德加·爱伦·坡

1　因为我感到：我们头上的天堂里，
　　彼此间轻声交谈的天使，在他们
　　充满爱的炽热词汇中，找不到词
　　具有"母亲"一词的这种献身精神，
5　所以我一直以这亲切的词叫你——
　　对我来说，现在你比母亲还要亲，
　　而在解放我弗吉尼娅的灵魂时，
　　死神把你深深埋进了我的内心。
　　我的母亲，我很早就去世的母亲，
10　只不过是我本人的母亲，可是你，
　　你却生下了我曾如此热爱的人，
　　所以我的先母远不能同你相比，
　　有如对我灵魂而言，灵魂的生命
　　远不能同我的妻子比一比谁亲。

（黄杲炘　译）

【点评】

坡的生母于 1811 年去世，当时的坡才两岁，父亲此前已离家出走，养父母抚养坡长大成人。本首诗中的母亲指坡的岳母——玛丽亚·爱伦坡·克莱姆（Maria Poe Clemm），即他的妻子弗吉尼娅的母亲；玛丽亚·爱伦坡·克莱姆的另一个身份是坡的姑姑。坡娶了表妹弗吉尼娅，他们于 1836 年完婚，弗吉尼娅在 1847 年去世，此诗写于妻子去世后的 1849 年。在第一诗节，坡就表达了对"母亲"这一称呼的敬意，因为它代表了"奉献"。

第十章　浪漫主义时期诗歌

"我"爱我自己的母亲,但更爱你,因为你是我挚爱之人的母亲。第二诗节仍是对岳母爱意的表白。我的母亲虽然生下了我,但你生下了我的灵魂伴侣,让我怎能不心存感激,你比母亲还要亲。诗的主题貌似致意岳母、感恩岳母,实际上流露出的更多的是对妻子弗吉尼娅的深深怀念,妻子去世带给坡巨大的心理创伤,诗中对妻子的眷恋和浓浓的爱意让人不禁悲从中来。

(二十二) Eldorado

Edagr Allan Poe

1　Gaily bedight,
　　A gallant knight,
　　In sunshine and in shadow,
　　Had journeyed long,
5　Singing a song,
　　In search of Eldorado.

　　But he grew old—
　　This knight so bold—
　　And o'er his heart a shadow—
10　Fell as he found
　　No spot of ground
　　That looked like Eldorado.

　　And, as his strength
　　Failed him at length,

15　He met a pilgrim shadow—

　　"Shadow," said he,

　　"Where can it be—

　　This land of Eldorado?"

20　"Over the Mountains

　　Of the Moon,

　　Down the Valley of the Shadow,

　　Ride, boldly ride,"

　　The shade replied,—

　　"If you seek for Eldorado!"

【译文】
爱尔多拉多

爱德加·爱伦·坡

1　华美的服饰，

　　豪侠的骑士，

　　在阳光下或在阴影里，

　　长途跋涉，

5　他一路唱歌——

　　要把爱尔多拉多寻觅。

　　他虽是英豪，

　　却变得衰老，

　　一个阴影落在他心上——

第十章 浪漫主义时期诗歌

10 因为他发现:

没一个地点

同那爱尔多拉多相像。

到得临了时,

力尽又筋疲,

15 他遇见个漂泊的幽魂——

"幽魂,"我问你,

"到底在哪里——

这爱尔多拉多?"他发问。

20 "翻过月亮里

一座座山岳,

走过那阴影中的幽壑,

骑马大胆找,"

幽魂回答道,

25 "要是想寻爱尔多拉多。"

（黄杲炘　译）

【点评】

"Eldorado"源自西班牙语,指传说中的一位印第安首领。据说此人喜欢在湖水中洗去身上因仪式涂抹的黄金粉,他的下属也因而往湖中抛洒金银珠宝,久而久之,此词成了"富庶之地"的代名词,也指早期的西班牙殖民者在南美洲竭力找寻但徒劳未果的"黄金国"。从结构上而言,Eldorado由四个诗节组成,每节6行。第一诗节用明快的语调描述了一个身着华服的豪侠骑士乐观地、坚定不移地认为会找寻到心目中的"Eldorado"。第二诗节的语调略显低沉,多了几丝忧虑,因为骑士已走向老年并开始质疑自己的人生目标能否实现。接下来的诗节讲述了直到骑

士的生命终了之时，他的意愿都未达成，于是半希冀半失望地要求幽魂解读他生命中的困惑。在最后一个诗节中，幽魂建议人生的追寻直至死亡也不能停歇。骑士的追寻从出生走向死亡，完成了人类的一个生命周期。在该诗中，诗人借用西班牙征服者苦苦追寻的黄金国指代自己毕生所追求的一种文学艺术上的难以企及的理想境界，抒发了自己终身追寻却毫无所获的失望之情。

（二十三）Romance

Edagr Allan Poe

1 Romance, who loves to nod and sing,
  With drowsy head and folded wing,
  Among the green leaves as they shake
  Far down within some shadowy lake,
5 To me a painted paroquet
  Hath been—a most familiar bird—
  Taught me my alphabet to say—
  To lisp my very earliest word
  While in the wild wood I did lie,
10 A child—with a most knowing eye.

  Of late, eternal Condor years
  So shake the very Heaven on high
  With tumult as they thunder by,
  I have no time for idle cares
15 Through gazing on the unquiet sky.

第十章　浪漫主义时期诗歌

  And when an hour with calmer wings
  Its down upon my spirit flings—
  That little time with lyre and rhyme
  To while away—forbidden things!
20 My heart would feel to be a crime
  Unless it trembled with the strings.

【译文】
罗曼司
爱德加·爱伦·坡

1　罗曼司总爱收拢了翅膀
  瞌着睡意蒙眬的头歌唱，
  还远在某个幽暗的湖底，
  在颤动着的碧绿繁叶里，
5　对我而言，它曾经是一只
  绚丽鹦鹉（对这鸟我很熟），
  它教我念出字母一连串，
  把我最早的话牙牙说出——
  那时我躺在莽莽荒林中，
10 是长着机灵眼睛的儿童。
  后来，永远是秃鹰的岁月，
  飞过时发出的轰响骚乱
  把高高的天庭猛烈震撼，
  我没时间操心一些闲事——
15 不能光凝视不安宁的天。

片刻间便轻柔些的翅膀
把其绒羽拂在我心灵上,
要我犯禁地用诗琴和韵
把那么一点时间消磨光,
20　我的心会感到犯了罪行,
除非它同琴弦一起震荡!

（黄杲炘　译）

【点评】

"Romance"一词在此处译为"罗曼司",并非特指爱情中的浪漫故事。该词原指12世纪以来的西欧关于中世纪骑士的传奇故事,后泛指某些带有传奇或浪漫色彩的或虚构、或真实的奇闻逸事等。在本首诗歌中,诗人描述了人生的两个主要阶段对romance的不同领悟。童年时期的romance如同一只漂亮的鹦鹉,而壮年时期的romance则变成了雄鹰。不同的人生阶段,romance被比喻成两个不同物种的鸟。这两种鸟分别象征年少时期的激情澎湃、无忧无虑和成年后的生活艰辛、瞻前顾后。在孩提时代,romance被拟人化成"喜欢点头和唱歌"的一只绚丽的鹦鹉。这只美丽的、色彩缤纷的小鸟代表了童年的不谙世事和那个时代所拥有的幸福快乐时光。成年后世事纷繁芜杂,心灵得不到片刻安宁,再也不能与世无争、不谙世事,奔波成了生活的主题。这时的romance如同一只在天地间翱翔的大鸟——秃鹰,为了生存,在天地间搏击。这种感情的抒发也和坡的生活、文学诗歌创作经历有关。坡认为诗歌创作的目的就是创造美,这种美能够触及读者的灵魂深处并带来愉悦之感,理智和逻辑不属于诗人的考虑范畴,这有别于当时比较流行的诗歌理论。本诗的韵律格式为aabbcdcdee和deedeffgfgf,为抑扬格四音步,这种音韵美于不知不觉中加深了诗人的情感表达。

（二十四）Sonnet—To Science

Edagr Allan Poe

1   Science! true daughter of Old Time thou art!
      Who alterest all things with thy peering eyes.
      Why preyest thou thus upon the poet's heart,
      Vulture, whose wings are dull realities?
5   How should he love thee? or how deem thee wise,
      Who wouldst not leave him in his wandering
      To seek for treasure in the jewelled skies,
      Albeit he soared with an undaunted wing?
      Hast thou not dragged Diana from her car,
10 And driven the Hamadryad from the wood
      To seek a shelter in some happier star?
      Hast thou not torn the Naiad from her flood,
      The Elfin from the green grass, and from me
      The summer dream beneath the tamarind tree?

【译文】

十四行诗——致科学

爱德加·爱伦·坡

1   科学哟！你是古代忠实的女儿！
      你变更一切，用你眼睛的凝视。
      为何要这样蹂躏诗人的心坎儿，

兀鹰，你的翅膀是阴暗的现实？
5 他何以爱你？何以认为你深奥，
你总是不愿任凭他去漂泊游荡，
不愿他去镶满钻石的天空觅宝，
纵令他展开无畏的翅翼去翱翔？
你不是已把狄安娜拖下了马车？
10 不是已把山林仙子逐离了森林，
让她去某颗幸运的星躲灾避祸？
你不是已从水中攥走水泽女神，
把小精灵赶出绿茵，然后又从
凤眼果树下驱散我夏日的美梦？

（曹明伦 译）

【点评】

　　科学虽然促进了社会的发展，给我们的生活带来日新月异的变化，但并未受到诗人们的青睐，反而备受指责。究其原因：正是科学扼杀了诗人创作灵感的源泉，摧毁了诗人丰富的想象力，从而破坏了诗歌的意境。在本诗中，科学被比喻成兀鹰的翅膀，代表了赤裸裸的、残酷的现实世界。科学限制了诗人的想象力和创造力，阻滞了诗人诗歌的创作，正如同兀鹰的翅膀阻碍了他在更为广阔的天地之间翱翔一样。因为科学讲究实事求是，科学的发展使得人们对大自然的认识更为深入、客观，不再像人类文明初期那样，出于对大自然的敬畏，产生出各类神话故事。从诗人的角度来看，科学撕破了坡蒙在这些神话故事上的美丽面纱，使其露出了本来面目，失去了它应有的诗意。这如同古代神话故事中的一些人物，像"狄安娜""山林仙子""水泽女神""小精灵"被逐出大自然一般。对此状况，诗人感到既愤懑又无奈。

第十章 浪漫主义时期诗歌

（二十五）The Haunted Palace

Edagr Allan Poe

1 In the greenest of our valleys
  By good angels tenanted,
  Once a fair and stately palace—
  Radiant palace—reared its head.
  In the monarch Thought's dominion,
5 It stood there!
  Never seraph spread a pinion
  Over fabric half so fair!

  Banners yellow, glorious, golden,
  On its roof did float and flow
10 (This—all this—was in the olden
  Time long ago)
  And every gentle air that dallied,
  In that sweet day,
  Along the ramparts plumed and pallid,
15 A winged odor went away.

  Wanderers in that happy valley,
  Through two luminous windows, saw
  Spirits moving musically
20 To a lute's well-tuned law,

Round about a throne where, sitting,

Porphyrogene!

In state his glory well befitting,

The ruler of the realm was seen.

25　And all with pearl and ruby glowing

Was the fair palace door,

Through which came flowing, flowing, flowing

And sparkling evermore,

A troop of Echoes, whose sweet duty

30　Was but to sing,

In voices of surpassing beauty,

The wit and wisdom of their king.

But evil things, in robes of sorrow,

Assailed the monarch's high estate;

35　(Ah, let us mourn!—for never morrow

Shall dawn upon him, desolate!)

And round about his home the glory

That blushed and bloomed

Is but a dim-remembered story

40　Of the old time entombed.

And travellers, now, within that valley,

Through the red-litten windows see

Vast forms that move fantastically

　　　　To a discordant melody;
45　While, like a ghostly rapid river,
　　　　Through the pale door
　　　　A hideous throng rush out forever,
　　　　And laugh—but smile no more.

【译文】
闹鬼的宫殿

爱德加·爱伦·坡

1　在我们最绿的山谷之间
　　那儿曾住有善良的天使，
　　曾有座美丽庄严的宫殿——
　　金碧辉煌，巍然屹立。
5　在思想国王的统辖之内——
　　那宫阙岩岩直插天宇！
　　就连长着翅膀的撒拉弗
　　也没见过宫殿如此美丽！

　　金黄色的旗幡光彩夺目，
10　在宫殿的屋顶漫卷飘扬——
　　（这一切——都踪影全无，
　　已是很久以前的时光）
　　那时连微风也爱嬉戏，
　　在那甜蜜美好的年岁，
15　沿着宫殿的粉墙白壁，

带翅的芳香隐隐飘飞。

　　当年流浪者来到这山谷，
　　能透过两扇明亮的窗口，
　　看见仙女们翩翩起舞，
20　伴和着诗琴的旋律悠悠，
　　婆娑曼舞围绕一个王位，
　　上坐降生于紫气的国君，
　　堂堂皇皇，他的荣耀光辉
　　与所见的帝王完全相称。

25　珍珠和红宝石熠熠闪光
　　装点着宫殿美丽的大门，
　　从宫门终日飘荡，飘荡，
　　总是飘来一阵阵回声，
　　一对对厄科穿门而出，
30　她们的任务就是赞美，
　　用优美的声音反反复复
　　赞美国王的英明智慧。

　　但是邪恶，身披魔袍，
　　侵入了国王高贵的领地。
35　（呜呼哀哉！——让我们哀悼，
　　不幸的君王没有了翌日！）
　　过去御园的融融春色，
　　昔日王家的万千气象，

第十章 浪漫主义时期诗歌

现在不过是依稀的传说,
40 早已被悠悠岁月淡忘。
而今旅游者走进山谷,
透过那些鲜红的窗口,
会看见许多影子般的怪物
伴着不和谐的旋律飘游,
45 同时,像一条湍急的小河,
从那道苍白阴森的宫门,
可怕的一群不断地穿过,
不见笑颜——只闻笑声。

(曹明伦　译)

【点评】

这首诗歌收录于坡的短篇小说《厄舍府的倒塌》(*The Fall of House of Usher*),1839年发表。诗歌前半部分语调轻松、明快、愉悦,后半部分压抑、低沉,令人不寒而栗。这座宫殿坐落于最绿的山谷之间,庄严、美丽,犹如人间仙境、世外桃源。宫殿外旗幡飘扬、微风拂过、芳香四溢;里面莺歌燕舞,丝竹琴瑟之声不绝于耳。让人不禁心驰神往,欲一睹其芳颜。然而好景不长,思想的国王遭到了邪恶之魔的屠戮,昔日金碧辉煌的宫殿也日渐衰败,徒留一丝模糊的记忆。游客到此,看到的是魅影重重,听到的是刺耳恐怖的旋律,还有一群只闻其声、不见其人的精灵们进进出出,这种阴森恐怖的场景让游客不禁瑟瑟发抖、毛骨悚然。此诗中一个典型的意象就是被拟人化的宫殿。诗人用"fair""stately"来描述它的美丽,用"reared its head"来形容它的巍峨,屋顶飘扬的"banners yellow, glorious, golden"如同美女飘逸的金发。在第三诗节中,"two luminous windows"暗指人的两只眼睛,第六诗节中人的眼睛变成了"red-litten windows",被鬼魂萦绕的宫殿窗户由原本的"明亮"变为"鲜红",更加突出了恶魔邪恶的双眼。

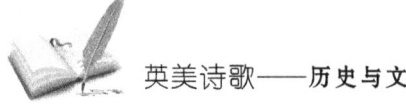

被珠宝点缀的宫殿大门宛如人之口，进进出出的"echo"变成了人之言语、溢美之词。整座宫殿象征着人的头颅，穿越宫殿之门，我们能了解里面发生的一切；正如同通过人之口，能知晓心灵深处的隐秘一般。

（二十六）"Alone"

Edagr Allan Poe

1　From childhood's hour I have not been

　　As others were—I have not seen

　　As others saw—I could not bring

　　My passions from a common spring—

5　From the same source I have not taken

　　My sorrow—I could not awaken

　　My heart to joy at the same tone—

　　And all I lov'd—I lov'd alone—

　　Then—in my childhood—in the dawn

10　Of a most stormy life—was drawn

　　From ev'ry depth of good and ill

　　The mystery which binds me still—

　　From the torrent, or the fountain—

　　From the red cliff of the mountain—

15　From the sun that' round me roll'd

　　In its autumn tint of gold—

　　From the lightning in the sky

　　As it pass'd me flying by—

　　From the thunder, and the storm—

第十章　浪漫主义时期诗歌

20　And the cloud that took the form

　　（When the rest of Heaven was blue）

　　Of a demon in my view—

【译文】
孤独

爱德加·爱伦·坡

1　从童年时起我就一直与别人

　　不一样——我看待世间的事情

　　与众不同——我从来就不能

　　从一个寻常的春天获得激情——

5　我从不曾从这同一个源泉

　　得到忧伤——我也不能呼唤

　　我的心为这同一韵调开怀——

　　而我爱的一切——我独自去爱——

　　于是——在我的童年——在我的

10　风雨人生的黎明——我获得，

　　从每一种善良与邪恶的深处，

　　那种神秘，它仍然把我束缚——

　　从湍湍急流，或粼粼飞泉——

　　从山顶那血红的峭壁之巅——

15　从那轮绕着我旋转的太阳

　　当沐浴着它秋日里的金光——

　　从横空闪动的银线飞火

　　当它从我身旁一闪而过——

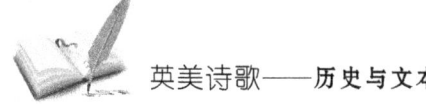

从狂风暴雨，从霹雳雷霆——
20　从在我眼里千变万化的积云
　　（当整个天空一片湛蓝）
　　它变成魔鬼在我眼前——

（曹明伦　译）

【点评】

　　此诗发表于 1875 年。根据坡的手稿，此诗应写于 1829 年，但生前不曾发表。这是一首 22 行诗，共 11 个对句，每两行押韵，韵脚各不相同，语气低沉、忧伤。全诗可分为两部分，从内容上看，前 11 句描述的是诗人自童年时就具有的孤独的、与众不同的一种内心体验和感受。他的激情与忧伤、喜悦与爱恋，都是那么的特立独行，与世界格格不入；后半部分则解释了外部世界中的神秘力量是让他产生孤独的重要原因。当他还是个孩子的时候，这种既神秘又神奇的力量就在他心里生根、发芽，直至成年。这种怪异的约束他的力量可以说是无处不在。在激流中，在喷泉上、在峭壁之巅，你都能发现它的身影。无论天空是艳阳高照、云海层叠还是星光闪烁，无论是狂风暴雨或是电闪雷鸣，你都会与它不期而遇。这时的它，如同魔鬼一般，攫取了诗人丰满的心灵，只剩下难以排遣的孤独。从叙述方式上看，前半部分诗人对自己的喜怒哀乐平铺直叙、娓娓道来；后半部分则气势磅礴，设置悬念，然而对于待解谜团，却不予理会，有意犹未尽之感。本诗借助大量的修辞手法、细腻的心理描写来增强诗歌的韵律，如暗喻、首语重复法（"From childhood's hour" "From the same source" "From the torrent" "From the red" "From the sun"）、顶真（"And all I lov'd—I lov'd alone—"）、拟人（"As it pass'd me flying by—"）等。

第十一章　现代主义诗歌

1912 年是美国诗歌史上的重要的一年。这一年，女诗人哈利特·门罗（Harriet Monroe）创办小杂志《诗刊》，为有志于革新诗歌的诗人提供出版园地，开始了又一次反叛运动——现代主义诗歌运动。也是在 1912 年，庞德（Pound）和英国诗人休姆（Hume）等提出意象派诗歌的三条原则：用精确的语言直接描绘主现或客观的事物；使用简练的语言、取消一切无助于表达的词语；节奏依附于音乐性词语的顺序而不是按照节拍来安排。庞德的主张得到艾米·洛厄尔（Amy Lowell）、希尔达·杜利特（Hilda Dalit）、威廉·卡洛斯·威廉姆斯（William Carlos Williams）等诗人的支持。1914 年庞德编辑出版意象派诗人的诗集，扩大了新诗运动的影响。作为新诗运动领军人物的庞德，不仅要求美国作家日新月异，形成新的"文艺复兴"和文学"大觉醒"，并且为试验革新提出各种理论主张和原则，介绍英国、法国和其他任何地方的诗歌信息。他大力推荐艾略特（Eliot）、弗罗斯特（Frost）等人的作品，甚至帮助艾略特修改他的《荒原》。与此同时，他也身体力行地把自己的理论原则运用到创作中，例如，视觉独特、个性鲜明的意象诗歌《地铁车站》；被一些评论家称为"现代派诗歌巨作"、内容庞杂、包罗万象的《诗章》等。另一位住在英国的新诗运动领袖是艾略

特,他在《荒原》中运用大量的文学典故、神话学、联想等写作手法,完成了一部既具思想内涵,又具意境想象的诗篇。这首诗结构松散、节奏奔放、语言多变,成为诗人们效仿的对象,但他的诗歌理论并不能被生活在美国的诗人完全接受。威廉姆斯不主张大量引经据典、强调修辞,但也不因循守旧。他的诗歌如《佩特森》等受惠特曼的诗歌影响较大,内容简洁、语言平实、不拘泥于形式,摆脱了传统诗歌的束缚。

这一时期的诗歌百花齐放、流派纷呈,充分体现美国诗歌多样化的特点。在中西部有坚持惠特曼的传统、反映劳动人民思想感情的芝加哥诗人;在新英格兰地区主要有弗罗斯特和罗宾逊(Robinson)。他们虽受到新诗歌运动的影响,但只是有选择地接受其中的一些理论原则。弗罗斯特的诗歌形式传统,主题多涉及俗人小事、自然景物,语言朴素、简洁、不矫揉造作,但寓意深刻,读来意犹未尽、发人深思。

一、Poem Reading

(一) In a Station of the Metro

Ezra Pound

The apparition of these faces in the crowd;
Petals on a wet, black bough.

美国现代主义文学开始于第一次世界大战前后,在诗歌领域中则涌现出了以埃兹拉·庞德(Ezra Pound, 1885—1972)、休姆(T. E. Hulme, 1883—1917),艾米·洛厄尔(H. D. Amy Lowell)、弗林特(F. S. Flint)、威廉·卡洛斯·威廉姆斯(William Carlos Williams)、劳伦斯(E. H. Lawrence)等为代表的意象派诗人。什么是现代文学? 庞德认为,"现代"的内涵是"创新"("to make it new")。作为第一波现代派诗人,

第十一章 现代主义诗歌

意象派就是从"创新"的角度入手进行了一番诗歌领域里的革命。意象派诗歌的发展包含三个阶段：第一个阶段（1908—1909）以休姆为代表，奠定了诗歌的理论基础；第二个阶段（1912—1914）以庞德为代表，这一时期是意象派诗歌的主要发展阶段；第三个阶段（1914—1917）诗歌的领导人物换成了艾米·洛厄尔，这一阶段的意象派诗歌被庞德斥之为艾米主义"Amyism"。

虽然早在1914年庞德就宣称和意象派诗歌决裂，转而投入到"漩涡主义文学"（Vorticism）之中，但是综观整个意象派诗歌的发展历程，庞德无疑是整个流派最重要的代表作家，而诗歌 In a Station of the Metro 更成为意象派最重要的代表诗歌。庞德等诗人提出了意象派诗歌的三原则更成为整个流派的创作标准。三原则分别涉及了诗歌的意象、语言和音律。首先，诗歌应该呈现客观事物本身，同时避免各种符号和象征的应用；其次，语言要清楚简洁，应该避免对呈现事物无用的单词；最后，韵律上应该避免传统的五步抑扬格，而使用更具现代意义的自由诗体，注重诗歌的节奏美。在庞德看来，好的诗歌能够等同于（equation）它所描述的事物，与此同时，还能激发读者的所感所想，与作者产生共鸣。这些苛刻的创作要求看来很难实现，但却在庞德的代表诗歌 In a Station of the Metro 中得到了比较好的呈现。

该诗最早于1913年发表在 Poetry 杂志上，而后在1917年再次被选入 Pound 的诗歌集 Lustra 中，又在1926年入选诗集 Personae: The Collected Poems of Ezra Pound。1912年，诗人在巴黎火车站下车后，立即被拥挤的人群所淹没，一张张"美丽"的脸庞映入眼帘。这一幕激发了诗人的创作欲望，但是令人沮丧的是，他却发现很难找到能准确地表达自己所见所感的语言。对于最初写下的30行诗文，庞德并不满意。六个月后又写下了另一首较短的诗，庞德最终还是销毁了文稿。直到一年之后，诗人才最终写成了这首由14个单词组成的诗歌。从诗歌创作的过程可以看出庞德遵守了意象派诗歌的创作原则,用最简练的语言勾勒出了诗人当时的所见所感,将巴黎火车站那鲜明的一幕生动地呈现到了读者面前。正如诗人自己所说:"我找的并不是单词,而是诗歌与场景之间的平衡,这不是用语言或是用点点色彩达到的平衡。"

初读起来, In a Station of the Metro 确实因为它的与众不同使读者眼前一亮。除了仅仅包含了两行诗文 14 个单词之外,它也没有传统诗歌固定的押韵格式。更有甚者,整首诗不包含任何一个动词,忽略了句法学对于文字的束缚作用。在 1913 年最初的版本中,诗歌行文与之后的版本略有不同,诗人用冒号而不是分号结束了第一行诗文,而后在行文之间加入了空格:"The apparition of these faces in the crowd"。空格的加入使得语流出现了停顿,而这些停顿使得文字勾勒的画面更加鲜明生动。虽然诗歌没有规律的押韵格式,但是 14 个单词却和传统的十四行诗歌相呼应,而且第 1 行 8 个单词、第 2 行 6 个单词的安排也和十四行诗的结构相一致,充分显示出诗人的别具匠心。另外,诗歌在读音的处理上也非常巧妙,诗人在诗歌中安排了相互呼应的几个读音,例如第 1 行和第 2 行中的 /p/ 音和两行末尾的 / au / 音。除此之外,诗歌中也不乏其他长元音和 / e / 音的重复等,而这些也都加强了诗歌的音乐感和节奏美。

诗人在创作时旨在打破传统的束缚,因此诗歌的形式标新立异,而评论家也没有就诗歌所要表达的主题达成一致。诗歌分为两行,第 1 行为庞德在巴黎火车站所看到的人群中的一张张脸庞,第 2 行所描述的是雨后漆黑树枝上的花瓣,这一情景使得前一行诗文更加形象。最初版本中第一行诗文后面使用冒号,更加强调了人脸和花瓣之间的比喻关系,而将冒号改为分号之后,则在保持比喻关系的同时强调了人脸和花瓣之间的独立性,使得诗歌的叙述层次更加饱满。两行诗文包含了两种相对的关系,即人脸和花瓣、人群和树枝。黑色潮湿的树枝使得粉嫩的花瓣更加娇艳,拥挤的人群中闪动的脸颊则被衬托得更加生动。用美丽的花瓣比喻人脸,用人脸

第十一章　现代主义诗歌

来提喻人，人群中渺小的个体被赋予优雅和美丽。潮湿树枝上的花瓣虽然生动美丽，但是由于失去了生命供给最终只能枯败成泥，而人的生命又何尝不是这样？美丽和优雅、生动和鲜活只是转眼即逝的东西，等待人类的也只能是死亡。正因如此，"apparition"（中文意为"鬼魂"）一词的选用更显诗人用词的讲究，它既生活化地描绘出人群中闪动的脸庞，更蕴含了生命稍纵即逝的意思。

（二）Patterns

Amy Lowell

1　I walk down the garden paths,

　　And all the daffodils

　　Are blowing, and the bright blue squills.

　　I walk down the patterned garden paths

5　In my stiff, brocaded gown.

　　With my powdered hair and jewelled fan,

　　I too am a rare

　　Pattern. As I wander down

　　The garden paths.

10　My dress is richly figured,

　　And the train

　　Makes a pink and silver stain

　　On the gravel, and the thrift

　　Of the borders.

15　Just a plate of current fashion,

Tripping by in high-heeled, ribboned shoes.

Not a softness anywhere about me,

Only whale-bone and brocade.

And I sink on a seat in the shade

20 Of a lime tree. For my passion

Wars against the stiff brocade.

The daffodils and squills

Flutter in the breeze

As they please.

25 And I weep;

For the lime tree is in blossom

And one small flower has dropped upon my bosom.

And he splashing of waterdrops

In the marble fountain

30 Comes down the garden paths.

The dripping never stops.

Underneath my stiffened gown

Is the softness of a woman bathing in a marble basin,

A basin in the midst of hedges grown

35 So thick, she cannot see her lover hiding,

But she guesses he is near,

And the sliding of the water

Seems the stroking of a dear

Hand upon her.

40 What is Summer in a fine brocaded gown!

I should like to see it lying in a heap upon the ground.

All the pink and silver crumpled up on the ground.

I would be the pink and silver as I ran along the paths,

And he would stumble after,

45　Bewildered by my laughter.

I should see the sun flashing from his sword-hilt and the buckles on his shoes.

I would choose

To lead him in a maze along the patterned paths,

A bright and laughing maze for my heavy-booted lover,

50　Till he caught me in the shade,

And the buttons of his waistcoat bruised my body as he clasped me,

Aching, melting, unafraid.

With the shadows of the leaves and the sundrops,

And the plopping of the waterdrops,

55　All about us in the open afternoon

I am very like to swoon

With the weight of this brocade,

For the sun sifts through the shade.

Underneath the fallen blossom

60　In my bosom,

Is a letter I have hid.

It was brought to me this morning by a rider from the Duke.

　"Madam, we regret to inform you that Lord Hartwell

Died in action Thursday sen'night."

65　As I read it in the white, morning sunlight,

The letters squirmed like snakes.

"Any answer, Madam," said my footman.

"No," I told him.

"See that the messenger takes some refreshment.

70　No, no answer."

And I walked into the garden,

Up and down the patterned paths,

In my stiff, correct brocade.

The blue and yellow flowers stood up proudly in the sun,

75　Each one.

I stood upright too,

Held rigid to the pattern

By the stiffness of my gown.

Up and down I walked,

80　Up and down.

In a month he would have been my husband.

In a month, here, underneath this lime,

We would have broke the pattern;

He for me, and I for him,

85　He as Colonel, I as Lady,

On this shady seat.

He had a whim

That sunlight carried blessing.

And I answered, "It shall be as you have said."

90　Now he is dead.

第十一章 现代主义诗歌

  In Summer and in Winter I shall walk

  Up and down

  The patterned garden paths

  In my stiff, brocaded gown.

95 The squills and daffodils

  Will give place to pillared roses, and to asters, and to snow.

  I shall go

  Up and down,

  In my gown.

100 Gorgeously arrayed,

  Boned and stayed.

  And the softness of my body will be guarded from embrace

  By each button, hook, and lace.

  For the man who should loose me is dead,

105 Fighting with the Duke in Flanders,

  In a pattern called a war.

  Christ! What are patterns for?

  随着美国文学的进一步发展、美国民主意识的进一步觉醒，在19世纪末20世纪初的美国涌现出了一批女诗人。她们以女性独有的敏感写出了炙热的情感，诗文更是在充沛情感之下凸显了韵律之美。当时的代表女作家有艾米·洛厄尔（Amy Lowell, 1874—1925），露易丝·博根（Louise Bogan, 1897—1970），希尔达·杜丽特尔（Hilda Doolittle, 1886—1961）等。艾米·洛厄尔是20世纪初美国诗歌领域里的重要作家。在埃兹拉·庞德之后，她引领了另一波意象派诗歌（Imagism）的高潮。和庞德的绝对权威的家长思想不同，洛厄尔在秉持了意象派诗歌创作理念的同时，强调了诗人自己在诗歌创作和修改中的主动性。第一世界大战之后，洛厄尔逐渐被世人所淡忘。但是到了20世纪70年代，随着女权运动的兴起，洛厄尔再次被人记起，更被称为女权主义运动的先驱者。洛厄尔的诗歌贯彻了19世纪女性作家的写作传统，行文中既有男性作家的自信和阳刚，更有女性作家的善解人意和阴柔，成为美国诗歌领域别具一格的一道风景线。

在诗歌创作理念上，洛厄尔提出了一系列创新的观念。她反对严格的格律形式，认为诗歌应该是可以在公众场合被大声地念出来的。在1917年的文章 Poetry as Spoken Art 中，洛厄尔就提到："诗歌既是一种艺术，也是一种音乐"（"Poetry is as much as art to be heard as is music"）。因此，在洛厄尔的诗歌中，自由诗体（vers libre）成为主要的艺术表达形式。对于自由诗体，洛厄尔有着自己的理解。她认为，所谓自由诗体是建立在韵律之上的韵文形式，自由诗的韵文写作应该设定为可以被读者大声地、顺利地读出。她更将自己的诗歌称为"自由韵律散文"（polyphonic prose），诗歌中的韵律称为"无韵之韵"（unrhymed cadence）。作为一位处于世纪之交的诗人，洛厄尔开启了一个新的诗歌美学的时代。一方面，洛厄尔写作诗歌时，不受格律的限制，根据诗歌的主题信手拈来，将自由诗体的作用发挥到极致；另一方面，洛厄尔的诗歌大多是带有强烈情感的抒情诗歌，继承了前期女诗人的创作习惯。Patterns 一诗是现代读者最熟识的 Lowell 的诗歌之一，也是集中代表她的创作理念的重要作品之一。

Patterns 选自洛厄尔于1916年出版的诗集 Men, Woman and Ghost，是现代人阅读最广泛的洛厄尔诗歌之一。诗人在该诗中运用了自由诗体，不拘泥于诗歌节律的束缚，从第一人称的角度讲述了一位18世纪维多利亚时代女孩的遭遇。诗歌行文简单，长短句自由地结合，加之以散文体的叙述形式，使之成为洛厄尔"自由韵律散文"的重要代表之一。诗歌共包含了七个诗节，以叙述诗的形式讲述了少女的遭遇，其中现在、过去和将来三个时态相结合，让读者感受到了作者对于文字使用的得心应手。少女在美

第十一章　现代主义诗歌

丽的花园中散步，内心却无比地沉痛，因为她刚刚收到消息，自己的未婚夫在战争中阵亡。故事发生的场景主要有两个：一个是现实中开满水仙和海葱的花园，另一个是虚幻里少女的脑海。现实中的少女，尽管已经得知了未婚夫的噩耗，仍然强装镇定，唯一能透露出她的不安的是诗中多次提到的她在不停地走动（例如，第1行、第4行、第8～9行、第79～80行、第91～92行和第97～98行）。穿插在现实中的是少女对过去和未婚夫之间的恩爱与噩耗传来时的回忆，以及在最后一个诗节中提到的对未来被束缚于"模式"之中生活的无望想象。

　　第一个诗节提到了两种"模式"，即少女"入时"的装扮和模式化的花园小径，与之相对立的是花园里怒放的水仙和活泼的海葱。第二个诗节开始仔细地描述了少女的穿着打扮，尽管时髦（current fashion），少女却不禁感叹，所有的装束都硬邦邦的，没有一丝"柔软"（softness）和温暖。坐在菩提树下，少女泪眼婆娑地看到了正在盛开的水仙和海葱。菩提树也在开花，一朵小小的花落到了少女的胸口上。第三个诗节中的大理石喷泉源源不断地喷洒着水滴，象征着少女内心无法遏制的痛苦。她回忆起和恋人在丛林中嬉戏，回忆起恋人温柔的爱抚，更加痛恨起象征"模式"的礼服来。第四个诗节中少女继续回忆和恋人的追逐嬉戏和亲昵的行为。在追逐少女的过程中，未婚夫突然摔倒，而他身上沉重的装备（sword-hilt，buckles，the buttons of his waistcoat）都象征着战争对两人爱情的破坏。第五个诗节中少女回忆了噩耗传来时的情景，在"模式"的规范下，少女并没有惊慌失措，反而强装镇定地先安排好了信使的招待。唯一透露出她不安心态的是她不停地徘徊在花园的小径上。第六个诗节少女直抒心意，感叹当时两人的约定，而如今残酷的现实是"他已经死了"（第90行，"Now he is dead"）。最后一个诗节中，少女想象自己的未来，也必定会徘徊在这样一个"模式化"的生活之中。在诗歌的最后，她大声地疾呼："模式到底有何用？"（第107行，"What are patterns for？"）

诗歌中应用了大量象征手法，少女硬邦邦的锦缎礼服（stiff brocade gown）在行文中成为其模式化生活的主要象征。在叙述中，少女多次提到在这种僵硬之中根本无法感受到自己身体的"柔软"。如果"僵硬"指的是模式化的生活，那么"柔软"自然指的是符合少女个人特点的个性化的生活。另外，在行文中多次出现的水仙和海葱，自由地生长、快乐地存活，是少女或者诗人眼中突破"模式"、追寻个性的重要象征。联想起洛厄尔在生活中的我行我素、在情感上与女演员阿达·德怀尔·拉塞尔（Ada Dwyer Russell）的纠缠（洛厄尔另一首代表诗歌 *Two Speaker Together* 便是为拉塞尔而作），诗人在该诗中所要强调的主题不言而喻。另外，尽管诗歌没有固定的押韵格式，但是却不断地出现两行之间、隔行之间的押韵，在自由诗体的模式中出现不规则的押韵，给读者以诗歌虽然"自由"，却受到韵律压抑的印象。如果自由诗体代表了"个性"，押韵模式则成为"模式"的代表，这样诗歌在形式上也强调了"个性"想要突破"模式"的主题。

（三）The Great Figure

William Carlos Williams

1　Among the rain

　　and lights

　　I saw the figure 5

　　in gold

5　on a red

　　firetruck

　　moving

　　tense

　　unheeded

第十一章 现代主义诗歌

10   to gong clangs

     siren howls

     and wheels rumbling

     through the dark city.

  威廉·卡洛斯·威廉姆斯（1883—1963）是美国20世纪现代主义文学的重要代表作家。威廉姆斯在宾夕法尼亚大学医学院毕业后，便成了一名儿科的医生。在从事医学职业的空闲，他尝试进行文学创作，在现代派诗歌领域中取得了瞩目的成就。综观美国现代文学史，史蒂文·华莱士（Steven Wallace）和威廉姆斯是少有的两个仅在工作闲暇时进行文学创作，并取得世人认可的诗人。威廉姆斯早期受到庞德的影响，接受了美国意象派诗歌的创作理念。随着自己诗歌创作的逐渐成熟，诗人开始表达与庞德不同的艺术观念，而他的作品逐渐区别于意象派诗歌。虽然在文学生涯开始之时威廉姆斯始终在艾略特和庞德巨大光环的阴影下生存，他逐步开始并确立了自己独特的诗歌理念。1962年，凭借 *Pictures from Brueghel and Other Poems* 一诗，威廉姆斯获得了普利策图书奖。在后来的五部诗集 *Paterson* 中诗人更开始大胆地尝试新的创作技巧，并逐步得到了评论家的认可，影响到罗伯特·洛威尔（Robert Lowell），艾伦·金斯堡（Allen Ginsberg）等众多美国诗人。

  不同于秉持欧洲文学传统的庞德，威廉姆斯主张将美国本土意识融入文学创作之中，提倡用具有美国特色的文学形式和声音进行文学表达。威廉姆斯创作了"三拍诗行"（triadic-line poetry），即将一行诗分成三行渐进的诗文，这三行诗文组成一个三音步的诗节。威廉姆斯认为，这种诗行更加符合美语的节奏，也能更好地平衡诗歌的形式和"自由诗体"之间的关系。例如，他的诗歌《麻雀》中就含有"三拍诗行"：

  "Practical to the end

it is the poem

of his existence"

作为美国现代文学的代表诗人,威廉姆斯认为作家在进行创作的时候,应该突破传统的束缚,使作品具有"陌生化"(defamiliarization)的特色。在 *Prologue to Kora in Hell* 中,诗人讲到:"将两个看似联系不大的事物放在一起,会产生读者难以预料到的破坏性的效果。"正是在这种创作理念的指导下,威廉姆斯的作品总是能够独树一帜,让读者眼前一亮。

The Great Figure 节选自威廉姆斯在1921年出版的诗集 *Sour Grapes*,诗歌比较集中地体现了诗人的艺术创作理念。威廉姆斯在自传中谈到了诗歌创作的灵感来源。一个炎热的七月,在回家的路上诗人想去拜访住在第15大街的朋友马斯登(Marsden)。当他到达朋友门前的时候,正好听到了急促的铃声和呼啸而过的救护车的声音。转身的刹那,诗人看到了红色救护车上印刷的大大的金色的数字"5"。这一意象使诗人灵感迸发,随即掏出笔来写下了这首诗。从诗歌创作的过程来看,*The Great Figure* 在很大的程度上受到了意象派诗歌理论的影响。除此之外,诗歌里也含有威廉姆斯特有的诗歌创作特色。

根据诗人自述,由于"figure"含有"人物"和"数字"两层含义,读者看到诗歌题目,自然会联想起——"大人物",只有在读完全诗之后才意识到"figure"就是指的它的本意——"数字"。这在威廉姆斯看来,就是一个"陌生化"单词的过程。诗文的前三行是一个"三拍诗行",指出在雨中、路灯之下,诗人看到了数字"5"。因此,诗歌伊始,读者便随着诗人看到了以雨水和路灯为背景下的大大的数字"5"。如此突出意象和意象派诗人的创作理念是一致的。而后,诗人运用了两个色彩,第4行中的"gold"指的是数字"5"的颜色,而第5行中的"red"指的是印有数字"5"的救护车的颜色。诗歌的第7,8,9行,每行用了一个形容词,描述了数字"5"和救护车在不经意间急速地驶过。从第10行开始,

第十一章 现代主义诗歌

"clangs""howls""rumbling"营造出了一种使读者振聋发聩的嘈杂声。诗歌的最后,救护车带着金色的数字"5"消失在黑暗的城市之中。

综观诗歌的整体结构,诗人巧妙地利用了诗文的长短使其看上去像一个数字"5"。更别具匠心的是,诗歌以三个形容词"moving""tense""unheeded"为分界点,前半部分集中在视觉效果上,而后半部分则集中于听觉效果上。灰蒙蒙的雨水中透着点点的灯光,红色的救护车上面印有鲜明的金色的数字"5",伴随着急切的铃声呼啸而过。色彩对比鲜明,声音效果突出,而在这所有的色彩和声音效果之中,凸显的则是一个大大的金黄的数字"5"。更让读者惊喜的是,数字"5"在模糊的背景下并不是静止的,而是急速地运动着,这更使诗歌具有了未来主义(futurism)所宣称的"一切都在运动,一切都在变迁"的内涵。威廉姆斯的创作理念和手法既和意象派相关联,又具有自己的本色特征。

(四)The Road Not Taken

Robert Frost

1 Two roads diverged in a yellow wood,
  And sorry I could not travel both
  And be one traveler, long I stood
  And looked down one as far as I could
5 To where it bent in the undergrowth;

  Then took the other, as just as fair,
  And having perhaps the better claim,
  Because it was grassy and wanted wear;
  Though as for that the passing there

10 Had worn them really about the same.

And both that morning equally lay
In leaves no step had trodden black.
Oh, I kept the first for another day!
Yet knowing how way leads to way,
15 I doubted if I should ever come back.

I shall be telling this with a sigh
Somewhere ages and ages hence:
Two roads diverged in a wood, and I—
I took the one less traveled by,
20 And that has made all the difference.

在意象派诗歌占主流的年代里，美国文坛仍然有一部分诗人坚持传统的诗歌写作技巧，他们也在现代主义诗歌大潮中分得一杯羹，开辟了另一片天地。罗伯特·弗里斯特（Robert Frost, 1874—1963）就是这样一位诗人，他用最简单的日常用语描述自然，用以隐喻人类精神世界。弗罗斯特的诗歌在20世纪20年代被广泛阅读，而他也被读者誉为"新英格兰诗人"及美国的"民族诗人"，更被称为"非官方的桂冠诗人"（the unofficial Poet Laureate）。因为诗歌作品广受好评，弗罗斯特一生获得了四次普利策图书奖，而他的诗歌创作理念影响了后来的许多诗人。

尽管在诗歌创作中遵循传统的诗歌韵律、节奏和形式，但是弗罗斯特却被公认是一位现代主义诗人，这主要体现在三个方面。首先，弗罗斯特的诗歌大量地应用日常生活语言，将诗性思考和大白话联系在一起，对当代的生活进行了深度的思考。其次，诗人的诗歌大多是对现代人生活困境

第十一章 现代主义诗歌

的思考，如他的代表作品之一《修墙》（Mending Wall），就是对现代社会人与人之间距离的哲学思考。最后，弗罗斯特的诗歌处处是悖论，貌似简单的诗歌其实另有所指，正如杰恩·帕里尼（Jay Parini）所说，他的诗歌在不停地"解构自我"（"deconstruct themselves"）。诗人曾经把诗歌称为"混乱迷惑中的片刻驻足"（"momentary stay against confusion"），对诗歌的这一定性正反映了诗人作品中的现代性。

The Road Not Taken 是集中体现诗人创作理念的诗歌作品之一。该诗最初发表于诗人的诗歌集 *Mountain Interval*，是诗集的开篇之作，并通篇用斜体写成。诗人将 *The Road Not Taken* 放于如此显眼的位置，似乎在折射自己的诗歌创作之旅。在成为诗人之前，弗里斯特做过很多不同的工作，他在新罕布什尔州做过农夫、在学校当过老师，更有过流浪汉的生活，而最终他选择成为一名诗人。因此，*The Road Not Taken* 可以看作他对自己选择诗歌创作生涯的思考和艺术沉淀。诗歌发表初期，因为最后一个诗节中的诗句"I took the one less traveled by"，诗歌的题目曾被错误地印刷为 *The Road Less Traveled By*，殊不知这与诗人最初的创作理念背道而驰。

该诗包含了四个诗节，每个诗行用四步抑扬格写成。但是，区别于传统的四步抑扬格诗行包含八个音节，*The Road Not Taken* 每个诗行包含了九个音节。这一点体现了诗人的别具匠心，继承传统却并不拘泥于传统。诗歌采用了叙述诗的形式，第一个诗节中诗人介绍了自己面前的两条岔路，他徘徊犹豫（"long I stood"），仔细斟酌（"looked down one as far as I could"），可就是拿不定主意究竟该走哪条路。第二个诗节中诗人做出了选择（"took the other"）并说明了理由：虽然两条路看来差不多，但他选择的那条路芳草萋萋、十分幽静，更加吸引人一些。但第二个诗节的后两句却又交代：两条路其实都少有行人经过。诗人在第三个诗节中说到，虽然选择了另一条路（"the other"），但是他决定改天去尝试走第一条路。随后的诗行里，却又承认前路茫茫、并无归期，诗人也怀疑是否有机会尝试新的路径。在第四个诗节中,诗人想象着未来在诉说选择道路之时,面对"另一条路"的无限可能,只能一声叹息。这一诗节的第3,4行,用了一个"跨行连续"(enjambment),出现了断句"I——/I",更再现了当时选择之难。

  初读该诗,读者会被回荡在诗文之中的"个性"(individualism)所打动:走自己的路,让别人说去吧。诗人未受客观环境的影响,按照自己的心愿选择了"另一条路",个性十足。正是该诗表面彰显自由、个性的主题,吸引了电影《死亡诗社》(*Dead Poets Society*)的编导,使其成为电影中的重要诗歌之一。此外,诗歌的另一主题是"选择"。站在岔路口,诗人不得不选择一条路继续前行。而人生即是如此,面对选择、做出选择,还要对选择的后果负责。在选择中,人既发挥了主动性,又承担起了责任。这一点和美国超验主义者艾默生所宣扬的自立、自主、自恃是一致的,也是弗罗斯特被誉为美国民族诗人的重要原因。

  谈到 *The Road Not Taken* 的主题,诗人曾经强调:"不要被字面意思所蒙骗。"言外之意,尽管诗文简单易懂,但其含义却深刻细致。细读之下,就会发现诗文的字里行间在不断地解构自我。第一个诗节中的诗人面对两条岔路彷徨无措,但他在第二个诗节就指出两条路其实区别不大(第6行,"just as fair";第10行,"about the same")。第三个诗节中本身就包含了一个自相矛盾的观点:诗人宣称改天要尝试第一条路,可是紧接着却坦白不可能再做一次尝试。第四个诗节中的关键词是"诉说"(第16行,"telling")。诗人想象当自己年老的时候,给儿孙们讲述做过的选择,这种选择使得他的生活变得截然不同。然而,诗文中,在"诉说"之后紧跟着的词组"一声叹息"("with a sigh")却又暴露了诗人做出选择之后遗憾的心情。所以第四个诗节的含义也在自我解构中变得暧昧不清,或许诗人对儿孙们所讲述的仅仅是一个谎言。综观整首诗歌,诗人对选择时的心情以及做出选择之后的态度并没有一个清晰的交代,而诗歌的题目《未选择的路》使作者的态度更加模糊不清。因此,尽管诗歌使用了松散的四

第十一章 现代主义诗歌

步抑扬格,但由于诗人在字里行间渗透了解构的思想,所以 *The Road Not Taken* 很明显是一首充满现代主义元素的诗歌。

二、Further Reading

(一)A Girl

Ezra Pound

1　The tree has entered my hands,
　　The sap has ascended my arms,
　　The tree has grown in my breast—
　　Downward,
5　The branches grow out of me, like arms.

　　Tree you are,
　　Moss you are,
　　You are violets with wind above them.
　　A child— so high—you are,
10　And all this is folly to the world.

【译文】

女郎

埃兹拉·庞德

1　树植入我的双手,
　　树液渗进我的双臂,

树在我的心里生长，

下垂的

5　树枝宛如臂膀出自我的身上。

你是树，

你是苔，

你是随风摇曳的紫罗兰，

你是一个高贵的孩子。

10　这真是蠢话连篇。

（邹　颉　译）

【点评】

　　这是庞德的一首爱情诗，很可能是为他早年的恋人希尔达·杜丽特尔所作。希尔达·杜丽特尔和庞德，威廉姆斯是大学同学，H.D. 的笔名也是庞德所取。

　　庞德的这首诗体现了意象派诗歌的主要特征。意象派诗歌主张还原静态的、特色鲜明的意象，并着力表达人面对意象的瞬时感受、所受到的心灵震撼，不添加任何主观性的评论，让读者本人去感知、品味、想象，使人、诗合一。这首诗有两个诗节，在第一节中，诗中没有明喻，只用了两个意象——树和我，以树来表现少女的形象，将树和少女糅合在一起，写树的同时其实是在写少女。表面上来看，写的是树：树植入手中 / 树液渗进臂膀 / 树在心中生长 / 树枝从身上长出。实际上，作者所要表达的是"我"与少女的关系——相识、相知、相恋、相融，感情逐步加深，最后两人几乎合二为一、不分彼此、你中有我、我中有你，达到一种让人迷醉、向往的爱情境界。树和我是两个意象的叠加，把树和我这两个貌似毫无联系的、没有交集的意象叠加在一起，并去除了句法上的关联和说明，不带动词，全凭人的感官去感受、体验，能达到一种突兀、震撼、出奇制胜的效果。

第十一章　现代主义诗歌

诗的第二节直言你就是树，又增加了青苔、紫罗兰等意象。总之，女郎应该是高贵的、圣洁的，是美的化身。这些意象的叠加让读者有了驰骋想象的空间。一系列的"you are"增加了诗的节奏感，促进了情感的抒发和意境的创造。

（二）A Pact

Ezra Pound

1　I make a pact with you, Walt Whitman—
　　I have detested you long enough.
　　I come to you as a grown child
　　Who has had a pig-headed father;
5　I am old enough now to make friends.
　　It was you that broke the new wood,
　　Now is a time for carving.
　　We have one sap and one root—
　　Let there be commerce between us.

【译文】

合约

埃兹拉·庞德

1　沃尔特·惠特曼，我与你有约在先——
　　我以前一直把你讨厌。
　　我现在向你走近，
　　因为长大的孩子已离开愚蠢的父亲；

5　我已长大成人，能交友择朋。
　　是你砍下了新木，
　　现在已适合雕刻。
　　我们合一种树汁，合一条根。
10　愿你我之间存有流通和交易。

（李正栓　译）

【点评】

　　直到20世纪初，惠特曼在美国学术界的地位仍旧是毁誉参半，虽然惠特曼在美国诗歌方面做出了开创性的贡献，但他的自由体诗文和过分积极乐观让庞德十分反感。随着时间的流逝，庞德不得不承认惠特曼在诗歌形式和题材上的革新以及对后人的影响。就是在这种背景下，庞德写下《合约》，这首诗表达了庞德对于诗歌创新的态度，并以坦诚的语气回忆了他对惠特曼由不理解到理解的一个过程。诗歌的开篇直抒心意，承认过去的偏见，肯定惠特曼在诗歌领域的成就。其中的一句"是你砍下了新木"暗示了惠特曼在诗歌形式方面革新，因为他使自由体诗变成了一种重要的诗歌形式。但是，仍有一些方面有待探索，诗中的"现在已适合雕刻"暗示出了庞德要对诗歌进行新的改革创新。庞德承认与惠特曼是同一条根，有共同的树液，但是他决不愿意拘泥于前人，而要勇敢进取。庞德希望通过交流向惠特曼学习，能够达到他们之间的和解，把惠特曼开创的局面推向新的高峰。由此来看，《合约》一诗在表达主题思想时采用了传统的诗歌形式，并非"为意象而意象"。

（三）Salutation

Ezra Pound

1　O generation of the thoroughly smug

第十一章　现代主义诗歌

    and thoroughly uncomfortable,

    I have seen fishermen picnicking in the sun,

    I have seen them with untidy families,

5 I have seen their smiles full of teeth

    and heard ungainly laughter.

    And I am happier than you are,

    And they were happier than I am;

    And the fish swim in the lake

10 and do not even own clothing.

【译文】

敬礼

埃兹拉·庞德

1 噢，洋洋得意

    却极不舒服的一代

    我见过渔夫们在阳光下野餐，

    我见过他们和邋遢的家人一起，

5 我见过他们微笑时露出满口的牙齿，

    听见过他们粗俗的笑声。

    而我比你们快乐，

    但他们又比我快乐；

    就像鱼儿在湖里游泳

10 甚至从不着衣裙。

(李正栓　译)

【点评】

这首小诗可视为是庞德告别拘泥约束的传统、追求朴实无华的创作风格的佳作，形神兼备、言简意赅。"敬礼"原意是一种仪式动作——举手敬礼，在这里用作诗歌题目，既庄重又形象，使得作者想要表达的主题思想也带有几分圣洁的仪式感。题目"敬礼"使用的是双关语，一是表示"辞别"，诗人打算摒弃那些传统的诗歌形式，也就是向那些拘泥于形式、不思创新、自以为是的一代诗人告别；二是表示"向……致敬"，表面看来，诗人向往鱼儿自由自在的生活状态，没有任何羁绊、无所顾忌，并对它们的这种生活方式充满敬意。实际上，诗人真正要表达的是他所提倡、推崇的诗歌写作境界：创作诗歌时，诗人也应该如鱼儿在水中游泳一般，自由、不加任何矫饰、浑然天成，但又不失优美洒脱。对题目的这两种解读也可反映在诗人对待渔民的态度上：渔民们行为动作粗鄙、着装不雅，这让我望而生畏，与之告别；可他们那种乐观向上、自由洒脱的生活方式又让我肃然起敬，心生向往。总之，这首诗语言通俗、题目含蓄、诗意丰富深刻，很能体现庞德的创作主张。

（四）Wind and Silver

Amy Lowell

1   Greatly shining,

    The Autumn moon floats in the thin sky;

    And the fish-ponds shake their backs and

    Flash their dragon scales

5   As she passed over them.

第十一章 现代主义诗歌

【译文】

风和银

艾米·洛威尔

1　闪着银光

　　秋月在清淡的天幕中漂浮；

　　当它在上面经过时

　　鱼塘摇晃着脊背

5　龙鳞闪烁。

（李新德　译）

【点评】

　　中国的古典诗歌引起了当时意象派诗人的极大关注，如同庞德一样，洛威尔不仅翻译中国诗，还模仿中国诗歌进行再创作，她和弗洛伦斯·惠洛克·艾斯科（Florence Wheelock Ayscough）合作，共同翻译了160多首中国古诗，大部分是李白的诗歌，在英语世界掀起了一股欣赏中国古诗的热潮。《风与银》就是深受中国诗风影响的一首。在此诗中，诗人的主观情感和描述的客观景物达到了完美的结合，情景交融，呈现给读者一幅秋天的夜景图。另外，读这首小诗，含蓄隽永，语言凝练、简洁，没有华丽的辞藻，却使读者脑海中呈现出一幅天水一色、光与影交相辉映，静中有动、动中有静、动静结合的景色，画面感极强。

　　在这首小诗中，诗人使用鱼的意象来表示波光粼粼的水面。水面在风的吹拂下，泛起波浪，犹如鱼儿摇晃着脊背在水中畅游。鱼池洒满月光，犹如鱼背上的鱼鳞闪闪发亮，呈现出一片宁静、祥和的气氛，给读者以无限遐思。诗中的"风"和"银"，是指秋风和银白色的月光。全诗没有一个"风"字，却让读者感到风无处不在。皎洁的秋月与水光潋滟的鱼塘一上一下，交相辉映。在天高云淡的夜幕下，淡淡的秋风、幽幽的月光、波动的涟漪,让读者置身于一种如诗如画的梦幻之中。全诗从秋月写到秋风,由秋风激起的涟漪再到鱼鳞般闪亮的池塘,诗人通过重重叠加的意象,静谧的池塘赫然变成了"摇动脊背""龙鳞闪闪发亮"的鱼,巧妙地写出静夜中活跃的动态,把月光笼罩下的秋夜之美表现得淋漓尽致,给人以清幽飘逸的美感享受。

(五) Falling Snow

Amy Lowell

1　The snow whispers around me

　　And my wooden clogs

　　Leave holes behind me in the snow.

　　But no one will pass this way

5　Seeking my footsteps,

　　And when the temple bell rings again

　　They will be covered and gone.

【译文】
落雪

艾米·洛威尔

1　雪花在我耳畔低语

　　我的木屐在身后的雪地上

　　留下一个个印迹。

　　但没人会沿这条路

5　来寻找我的脚印,

第十一章 现代主义诗歌

当寺庙的钟声再次响起

那些足迹将会被覆盖、淹没。

（李新德 译）

【点评】

  这首短诗为洛威尔《汉风组诗》中的一首，此组诗富有中国古典诗歌的神韵。漫天飞舞的大雪、孤独的旅人、深深浅浅的脚印、远方寺庙的钟声，人的视觉、听觉、感觉被这一连串的意象包围着、冲击着，这也构成了全诗的基调：清冷、萧瑟、孤寂、悠远。"雪地脚印"是一个隐喻，暗含了洛威尔在尘世的足迹。钟声过后，"脚印"被覆盖，表达了洛威尔的人生思索：人生一世，昙花一现，只是一匆匆过客，大可不必在意是否名垂千秋。洛威尔的这首模仿中国诗的诗作突破了单纯呈现意象的局限，将人的情感表达与感官体验结合在一起，形成一种笼罩全诗的情愫，达到了寓情于景、情景交融的境界。

（六）The Red Wheelbarrow

William Carlos Williams

1 so much depends

  upon

  a red wheel

  barrow

5 glazed with rain

  water

  beside the white

  chickens

【译文】

红色手推车

威廉·卡洛斯·威廉姆斯

1 那么多东西
  仰仗

  这辆红色的
  手推车运送

5 雨水浇得它
  浑身溜滑

  旁边有
  几只白鸡

（彭 宇 译）

【点评】

　　威廉姆斯受惠特曼的影响，在美国诗歌创作方面，坚持"本土化""民族化"原则，目的是挖掘美国题材诗歌的美学价值。为了表现现代美国人的思想和生活，他坚持不懈地进行具有美国特色的乡土诗试验。这种诗以日常生活为题材，语言简朴、清新、直接；只写具体事物，不谈思想、不雕琢、不引经据典。The Red Wheelbarrow 就是威廉姆斯最具有代表性的一首小诗，也是他的成名作。

　　这首小诗选自威廉姆斯于1923年出版的 Spring and All。通过对手推车、雨水、小鸡一系列意象的描写，呈现在读者面前的是雨后农家小院既清新亮丽、又活泼闲逸的日常生活画面。其中，红色的车、白色的鸡形成了鲜明的色彩对比，勾勒出了一幅色彩艳丽、动静结合的景象，而亮晶晶的雨水又增加了画面的清新质感。通过这幅动静结合的画面，读者不仅视觉上得到美的享受，还能够感觉到诗人观察事物的独特眼光，体会到诗人清新、隽永的语言魅力。诗中没有比喻、象征等手法，也没有诗人的复杂思绪，只在开篇表示了一下惊喜的心情，然而却有一种单纯的画面美，令人回味无穷。

诗的节奏也非常独特，诗人将句子多处断开并且跨行，全诗呈现短小精巧的四小节，正是这种断断续续的节奏感，使人们无法一下子把它读完，从而最大限度地留住读者的目光，充分发挥了每个字词的作用，增加了回味的空间，给人带来愉悦的感受。

（七）Spring and All

William Carlos Williams

1 By the road to the contagious hospital
  under the surge of the blue
  mottled clouds driven from the
  northeast—a cold wind. Beyond, the
5 waste of broad, muddy fields
  brown with dried weeds, standing and fallen

  patches of standing water
  the scattering of tall trees

  All along the road the reddish
10 purplish, forked, upstanding, twiggy
  stuff of bushes and small trees

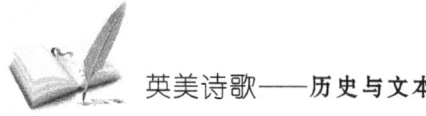

```
        with dead, brown leaves under them

        leafless vines—


        Lifeless in appearance, sluggish

15      dazed spring approaches—


        They enter the new world naked

        cold, uncertain of all

        save that they enter. All about them

        the cold, familiar wind—


20      Now the grass, tomorrow

        the stiff curl of wildcarrot leaf

        One by one objects are defined—

        it quickens: clarity, outline of leaf


        But now the stark dignity of

25      entrance — Still, the profound change

        has come upon them: rooted, they

        grip down and begin to awaken
```

【译文】

春天和一切

威廉·卡洛斯·威廉姆斯

1   去传染病院的路上

第十一章　现代主义诗歌

冷风——从东北方向
赶来蓝斑点点的汹涌层云。
远处，
5　一片泥泞的荒野
野草枯黄，有立有伏

一潭潭的死水
偶见几丛大树

沿路尽是灌木
10　小树，半紫半红
枝丫丛丛纠结
下面是枯黄的叶子
无叶的藤——

看来毫无生命，倦怠不堪
15　而莽撞的春天来临——

他们赤裸地进入新世界
全身冰凉，什么都不明白
只知道他们在进入春天。而周围
依然是熟悉的寒风——
20　瞧这些草，明天
野胡萝卜那坚挺的卷叶
一片一片清清楚楚——
它使叶子的轮廓越来越清晰

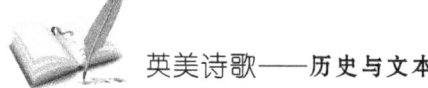

可是在此刻,进入春天
25 依然那么艰难——然而深沉的变化
已经来到:它们扎住的根
往下紧攫,开始醒来

(赵毅衡 译)

【点评】

题目虽然是 *Spring and All*,但威廉姆斯没有直接描述春天生机勃勃的景象,而是细致入微地描述了冬去春来场景中几个视觉意象。先是从上到下:天空、云彩、风、荒田、死水;再由远及近:树、灌木、藤蔓、小草;然后视线继续下移,一直延伸到黑色的土壤中,想象着"扎住的根,往下紧攫"。开篇提到的传染病医院,给人一种凝重、肃杀的印象,使全诗笼罩上了一层阴暗色彩。然后是寒冷的东北风、泥泞的田野、死水、枯木,无不让人觉得冬天的肆虐、春天的艰难。在这早春荒凉的描述之下,细读此诗,读者仿佛也能够感受到春天的脚步。貌似毫无生机的大自然,其实在悄悄地发生着巨大的变化:枝头上的萌芽,扎根于大地的根系,又让人燃起了对美好未来的向往。

威廉姆斯受意象派影响较深,但当认识到意象派诗歌在表达方面的局限性之后,他的诗歌内容由对客观事物的单纯描写转向借物抒情,内心情感表达也开始在诗歌中占据一席之地。在本诗的最开始,眼前这片荒凉、毫无生机的自然景色显然让诗人感到绝望、消极,但威廉姆斯敏锐的目光和乐观的心态很快就使他透过这片荒原寻觅到新生命的踪迹。这首诗从客观描写景物出发,抒发了诗人自己的内心感受、主客观结合自然、描写细致,而且蕴含着一种哲理:凡是新事物的诞生都得经历一个痛苦的过程。该诗中,诗人也对世人寄予希望:不管世事如何,我们要像那些不畏严寒的植物一样:萌芽、扎根、成长、不畏险阻,最终获得新的生命。它暗示了诗的诞生、人的精神的复活和生命的周而复始。

（八）This Is Just to Say

William Carlos Williams

1   I have eaten
    the plums
    that were in
    the icebox

5   and which
    you were probably
    saving
    for breakfast

    Forgive me
10 they were delicious
    so sweet
    and so cold

【译文】
也就是说

威廉·卡洛斯·威廉姆斯

1   我吃掉了
    那些李子

他们原本放在

冰箱里

5 这些

可能是你准备

早餐要吃的美食

原谅我

真好吃

10 真甜

真凉

（李正栓 译）

【点评】

　　威廉姆斯的诗受到意象派的影响，又在此基础上有所拓展，常被其他诗人所忽略的一些日常生活小事，貌似无足轻重，但经诗人威廉姆斯娓娓道来，顿觉兴趣盎然。*The Red Wheelbarrow* 和 *This is Just to Say* 就是很好的例子。*This is Just to Say* 类似于一封道歉信，读来深情款款。诗人因为抵御不了美味的诱惑，吃掉了爱人储藏起来的李子，却又为自己的行为感到不安、歉意。抵御不了诱惑是人的弱点，而这诱惑又是深爱着的人的喜爱之物，此诗反映了诗人想吃李子、自觉又不应该吃的矛盾的心理状态。前两个诗节叙述客观事件，最后一个诗节表达主观感受：一方面请求原谅；另一方面表达了感官体验。精彩之处为最后两行："so sweet" 给出了偷吃李子的理由，"so cold" 与 "so sweet" 句式一致，与之前的 "icebox" 相呼应，言简意赅，给人以紧凑感，反而让读者觉得偷吃李子不仅不应受责备，倒有几分可爱之处。威廉姆斯在诗中大量运用日常用语，音律和节奏也具备了后现代诗歌的一些风格特征。

第十一章 现代主义诗歌

（九）Mending Wall

Robert Frost

1   Something there is that doesn't love a wall,
    That sends the frozen-ground-swell under it,
    And spills the upper boulders in the sun;
    And makes gaps even two can pass abreast.
5   The work of hunters is another thing:
    I have come after them and made repair
    Where they have left not one stone on a stone,
    But they would have the rabbit out of hiding,
    To please the yelping dogs. The gaps I mean,
10 No one has seen them made or heard them made,
    But at spring mending-time we find them there.
    I let my neighbor know beyond the hill;
    And on a day we meet to walk the line
    And set the wall between us once again.
15 We keep the wall between us as we go.
    To each the boulders that have fallen to each.
    And some are loaves and some so nearly balls
    We have to use a spell to make them balance:
    "Stay where you are until our backs are turned!"
20 We wear our fingers rough with handling them.
    Oh, just another kind of outdoor game,
    One on a side. It comes to little more:

There where it is we do not need the wall:

He is all pine and I am apple orchard.

25 My apple trees will never get across

And eat the cones under his pines, I tell him.

He only says, "Good fences make good neighbors."

Spring is the mischief in me, and I wonder

If I could put a notion in his head:

30 "Why do they make good neighbors? Isn't it

Where there are cows? But here there are no cows.

Before I built a wall I'd ask to know

What I was walling in or walling out,

And to whom I was like to give offense.

35 Something there is that doesn't love a wall,

That wants it down." I could say "Elves" to him,

But it's not elves exactly and I'd rather

He said it for himself. I see him there

Bringing a stone grasped firmly by the top

40 In each hand, like an old-stone savage armed.

He moves in darkness as it seems to me,

Not of woods only and the shade of trees.

He will not go behind his father's saying,

And he likes having thought of it so well

45 He says again, "Good fences make good neighbors."

第十一章　现代主义诗歌

【译文】

补墙

罗伯特·弗罗斯特

1　有一样东西它不喜欢墙，

　　冻胀了墙下的基础土壤，

　　太阳一晒，墙上石块跌落在两旁；

　　墙体开裂，双人并肩而过像穿堂。

5　猎人的行为则是另一番景象：

　　要紧随其后修补不停地忙，

　　他们拆掉石块却不放回原位上，

　　而是把兔子赶出让它们难躲藏，

　　惹得猎狗叫汪汪。我所说的裂缝

10　没有谁见过其开裂听过其声响，

　　但到春天来修补，眼前已是百孔千疮。

　　我通知了山那边的邻居街坊，

　　约好了一天沿着墙巡查一趟，

　　重新垒起我们之间的这堵墙。

15　我们沿着墙各自走在各一方，

　　将各自一侧的石块收拾妥当。

　　有些石块成块状，有些近乎于球状，

　　我们不得不口念咒语确保其稳当：

　　"请待在那儿不要晃，等我们折回来查访！"

20　我们搬弄石块，手指被磨得粗糙无光。

　　啊，这种户外游戏只不过别于它样，

　　玩家各站一方。这让我若有所想：

  我们在这里并不需要修建这堵墙：
  那边种松木这边种苹果树隔墙相望。
25 我的苹果树永远不会越过这一屏障：
  跑到他松树下去把松果尝，我对他讲。
  他只好说："好篱笆会促成好街坊。"
  春天让我好心伤，我想知道
  我是否能让他这样去思量：
30 好篱笆何以能促成好街坊？难道说
  这是养牛的地方？但这纯粹是说谎。

  以前修建这堵墙，我就该好好想一想
  我要把什么东西来设防，
  我是否有冒犯谁的地方？
35 有样东西它的确不喜欢墙，
  就像妖鬼想让它倒塌一样，我这样讲。
  但准确地说这不是妖鬼，我宁愿
  他自己说出来是什么名堂。我见他
  用双手将石块上端牢牢抓住不放，
40 就像石器时代武装的野蛮人一样。
  我认为他似乎已坠入黑暗感到迷茫，
  这黑暗不只是来自树林和树的影像。
  他不去琢磨父辈曾如何对他讲，
  倒是认为父辈所说的话非常棒，
45 他接着又说："好篱笆会促成好街坊。"

第十一章 现代主义诗歌

【点评】

这首 45 行的 *Mending Wall* 因其中的一句关于邻里关系的经典话语"好篱笆会促成好街坊"("Good fences make good neighbors")而声名远扬。初读该诗,展现在我们面前的是两个农人修墙的画面。当然,诗的意义远不止于此,该诗真正所要表达的是关于"修墙"的自相矛盾的观点。

"There where it is we do not need the wall""Good fences make good neighbors"里的"篱笆"既有其字面意义,又有其象征意义。在该诗中,篱笆是隔开诗人的果园和邻居松林的一道不必要的有形障碍,毕竟苹果树不会自己跑去品尝松果。就其象征意义而言,是指隔开人与人之间关系的那道无形屏障。在诗的第 1 行和第 35 行,诗人重复了同样的一句话"Something there is that doesn't love a wall",这里的"东西",可以指"大自然",也可指那些"精灵、妖鬼",同时,也可指诗中的"我","我"讨厌这堵墙,实物的墙无益于保护我们的财产,无形的墙又阻碍了人与人之间的沟通、交往。较之邻居教条般的"Good fences make good neighbors",我对篱笆的思考"Something there is that doesn't love a wall""What I was walling in or walling out"凸显了我"宽容""大度""友善"的处世原则。出于希望人们之间能够友好往来的愿望,我反对墙的存在,要求推翻这堵墙;但我的邻人却固执先辈的教训,希望保持墙的存在。诗人把这种因循守旧、不懂得变通的人比作旧石器时代的野人,他们的愚昧无知如同处于原始黑暗的森林之中。但些许的讽刺之后,又略带苦涩,因为我的邻人和我的目的一致啊,都是出于"睦邻"的愿望。此外,诗中的"我"是不希望墙存在的,但每逢春季,又习惯性地邀上邻居一同修墙,也反映了我内心的纠结。大而言之,身处现代社会的"我们",受到许多规章、规则的约束,这堵"墙"在一定程度上阻碍了我们思维的跳跃,但这又是维持正常的社会秩序所必需的,这种生活的纠结也反映了现代文明的困境。

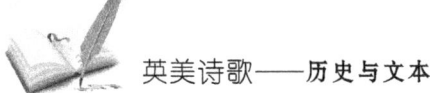

（十）Stopping by Woods on a Snowy Evening

Robert Frost

  1 Whose woods these are I think I know.
      His house is in the village though;
      He will not see me stopping here
      To watch his woods fill up with snow.
  5 My little horse must think it queer
      To stop without a farmhouse near
      Between the woods and frozen lake
      The darkest evening of the year.

      He gives his harness bells a shake
10 To ask if there is some mistake.
      The only other sound's the sweep
      Of easy wind and downy flake.

      The woods are lovely, dark, and deep.
      But I have promises to keep,
15 And miles to go before I sleep—
      And miles to go before I sleep.

第十一章 现代主义诗歌

【译文】

雪夜林畔小驻

罗伯特·弗罗斯特

1 想来我认识这座森林,
  林主的庄宅就在邻村;
  却不会见我在此驻马,
  看他林中积雪的美景。

5 我的小马一定颇惊讶,
  四望不见有什么农家,
  偏是一年最暗的黄昏,
  寒林和冰湖之间停下。
  它摇一摇身上的串铃,
10 问我这地方该不该停。
  此外只有轻风拂雪片,
  再也听不见其他声音。

  森林又暗又深真可羡,
  但我还要守一些诺言,
15 还要赶多少路才安眠,
  还要赶多少路才安眠。

(余光中 译)

【点评】

  弗罗斯特被称之为"工业化时代的田园诗人",清新自然的田园风光和闲暇惬意的乡村生活令他无限向往。他选择的诗歌主题通常是新英格兰的田园生活，被称为"新英格兰的农民诗人"。但他同时又是一位哲理诗人，大自然不过是他探索生活意义、表现大自然永恒进程的工具。*Stopping by Woods on a Snowy Evening* 是弗罗斯特最著名的一首短诗，也反映他心目中的人与自然的关系：大自然有其神秘的一面，但社会责任要大于自然。

诗人雪夜乘坐马车经过一片树林，不禁被雪花飘飘、神秘幽暗的树林所吸引，驻足欣赏，久久不愿离去。诗歌中的冬夜雪景，树林、路人、白雪、小马，构成了一幅宁静淡雅的水墨画。

此诗中，弗罗斯特借景抒情，表达自己对人生的思考。诗中的树林代表了大自然，村庄暗示了人类社会，赴约代表了对人类的责任和义务。在诗的前三节，诗人叙述自己来到树林，似乎被神秘、荒凉的自然风景所吸引，心中充满了困惑，陷入了沉思：走还是不走？就人生而言：是要回到纷纷扰扰的人类社会，完成自己未尽的义务；还是就此遁世、止步不前？在更为宽泛的人生意义上而言，诗人行程中不得不面对的孤寂和困惑也正是人生旅途中需要直面的冲突和抉择。

最后一节是本诗的高潮部分。银装素裹的树林此时显得"迷人""幽暗""深邃"，充满了诱惑力，不禁让人流连忘返，但它又神秘莫测，充满了未知。诗人很快回到现实中来，想起了他的"承诺"。这也反映了他对自然的态度：努力保持思想、感情与大自然的平衡，但又不唯大自然是从。此诗中的"承诺"，不仅仅是指单纯意义的约会，还包含对社会、对家庭的责任，甚至是对生命的承诺。诗的最后两句是重复的，第一句"miles to go before I sleep"可理解成字面意义"还有几里路才能达到我住宿的地方"，第二句暗示了诗人对自己的沉思有了答案，反映了他对社会的担当，"事业未竟，人生还要一直走下去"。弗罗斯特的这首诗描述的是宜人、宁静的田园风光，节奏明快、语言朴实，写出了心中的疑惑和担当。来自社会、逃离社会、回归社会，这是他内心的纠结历程，也是他个人生活的写照：竭力寻求既不脱离社会又保持自己个性的途径。

第十一章 现代主义诗歌

全诗语言平淡质朴、节奏舒缓流畅、格律工整。全诗有四个诗节,每节 4 行,每一行都是很规律的四音步抑扬格,运用连锁环抱韵,即押 aaba bbcb ccdc dddd 的韵式,给人以和谐感。

(十一) Fire and Ice

Robert Frost

1 Some say the world will end in fire,
  Some say in ice.
  From what I've tasted of desire
  I hold with those who favor fire.
5 But if it had to perish twice,
  I think I know enough of hate
  To say that for destruction ice
  Is also great
  And would suffice.

【译文】

火与冰

罗伯特·弗罗斯特

1 有人说世界将毁于烈火,
  有人说毁于冰。
  我对于欲望体味得够多,
  所以我赞同这意见:毁于火。
5 但如果世界须两次沉沦,

那么对憎恨我懂得深切,
我会说,论破坏力量,冰
也同样酷烈,
足能胜任。

(屠 岸 译)

【点评】

20世纪初,人类经历了第一次世界大战,最初的战争狂热过后,人类的信仰发生了动摇。一些知识分子开始对战争进行反思,抨击人类社会的种种卑劣行为。弗罗斯特也对人类的前途充满忧虑,但又苦于找不到出路,他的悲观情绪也反映了西方知识分子对战争的排斥和厌恶。反观战争根源:人类的贪欲和仇恨。恰在此时,一些"科学家"关于人类社会灭亡的预言也甚嚣尘上。一些人认为:人类将被太阳炙烤而亡;还有些人认为冰河世纪将会重返地球,人类将被冻僵而亡。在这种形势下,弗罗斯特写此诗阐述观点。当然,此诗中的"火"与"冰"还有更深的象征意义。"火"是人类贪欲的象征,"冰"是人类仇恨的象征,火和冰虽不能相提并论,但贪欲和仇恨却不是咫尺天涯。人类欲望若无法得到满足,会导致仇恨,燃起战火,其破坏程度不亚于冰与火对人类的毁灭。弗罗斯特在此诗中表达了他对人类前途命运的深深担忧。冰与火是对立的两个极端,但结果都是一样坏,如果人类不加以遏制贪欲、消除仇恨,世界将会被毁灭两次,这是弗罗斯特发出的正告。该诗用凝练的语言,富有哲理性的、冷峻的话语表现出了弗罗斯特对人生和世界的观察,也凸显了诗人高度的社会责任感。

(十二) After Apple-Picking

Robert Frost

1   My long two-pointed ladder's sticking through a tree
       Toward heaven still,

And there's a barrel that I didn't fill

Beside it, and there may be two or three

5 Apples I didn't pick upon some bough.

But I am done with apple-picking now.

Essence of winter sleep is on the night,

The scent of apples: I am drowsing off.

I cannot rub the strangeness from my sight

10 I got from looking through a pane of glass

I skimmed this morning from the drinking trough

And held against the world of hoary grass.

It melted, and I let it fall and break.

But I was well

15 Upon my way to sleep before it fell,

And I could tell

What form my dreaming was about to take.

Magnified apples appear and disappear,

Stem end and blossom end,

20 And every fleck of russet showing clear.

My instep arch not only keeps the ache,

It keeps the pressure of a ladder—round.

I feel the ladder sway as the boughs bend.

And I keep hearing from the cellar bin

25 The rumbling sound

Of load on load of apples coming in.

For I have had too much

Of apple—picking: I am overtired

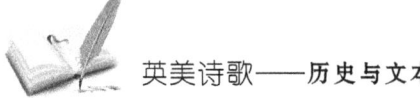

Of the great harvest I myself desired.
30　There were ten thousand thousand fruit to touch,
Cherish in hand, lift down, and not let fall.
For all
That struck the earth,
No matter if not bruised or spiked with stubble,
35　Went surely to the cider—apple heap
As of no worth.
One can see what will trouble
This sleep of mine, whatever sleep it is.
Were he not gone,
40　The woodchuck could say whether it's like his
Long sleep, as I describe its coming on,
Or just some human sleep.

【译文】
摘罢苹果

　　　　　　罗伯特·弗罗斯特

1　长梯穿过树顶，竖起两个尖端
　　刺向沉静的天穹。
　　梯子脚下，有一只木桶，
　　我还没给装满，也许
5　还有两三个苹果留在枝头
　　我还没摘下。不过这会儿，
　　我算是把摘苹果这活干完了。

夜晚在散发着冬眠的气息
——那扑鼻的苹果香；

10　我是在打瞌睡啦。
我揉揉眼睛，
却揉不掉眼前的奇怪——
这怪景象来自今天早晨，
我从饮水槽里揭起一层冰——

15　像一块窗玻璃，隔窗望向
一个草枯霜重的世界。
冰融了，我由它掉下，碎掉。
可是它还没落地，我早就
睡意蒙眬，快掉进了睡乡。

20　我还说得出，我的梦
会是怎么样一个形状。
膨胀得好大的苹果，忽隐忽现，
一头是梗枝，一头是花儿，
红褐色的斑点，全看得清。

25　好酸疼呐，我的脚底板。
可还得使劲吃住梯子档的分量，
我感到那梯子
随着弯倒的树枝，在摇晃。
耳边只听得不断的隆隆声——

30　一桶又一桶苹果往地窖里送。
摘这么些苹果，
尽够我受了；我本是盼望
来个大丰收，可这会儿已累坏了，

有千千万万的苹果你得去碰,

35 得轻轻地去拿,轻轻地去放。
不能往地上掉。只要一掉地,
即使没碰伤,也没叫草梗扎破,
也只好全都堆在一边,去做苹果酒,
算是不值一钱。

40 你看吧,打扰我睡一觉的是什么,
且不提这算不算睡一觉。
如果土拨鼠没有走开,
听我讲睡梦怎样来到我身边,
那它就可以说,

45 这跟它的冬眠倒有些像,
或者说,这不过是人类的冬眠。

(方　平　译)

【点评】

　　这是诗人早期所作的一首田园抒情诗,叙述主人公在一天采摘苹果的辛劳后的感想,充满对于人生和梦想的暗喻与哲思。在该诗中,苹果象征梦想,季节象征生命,而睡眠象征了死亡。该诗常被视作诗人对自己创作历程和处境的写照,即诗人通过辛苦创作取得了巨大成就后,又仍继续被名利所困扰。同时,诗中最后一行出现的"人类"一词,表明该诗映射了世界中的芸芸众生:每个人在生命中对梦想的追求如同采摘苹果的过程,一旦得到苹果,即实现了梦想后,人们反而因尚未采到的苹果产生巨大的失落感,又因一心呵护成果所得而患得患失。诗中与人类的行为形成鲜明对比的是土拨鼠:当农民们极力寻求丰收的时候,土拨鼠已经依靠提前存储的能量进入了安逸的冬眠。

第十一章 现代主义诗歌

（十三）Birches

Robert Frost

1 When I see birches bend to left and right
   Across the lines of straighter darker trees,
   I like to think some boy's been swinging them.
   But swinging doesn't bend them down to stay
5 As ice-storms do. Often you must have seen them
   Loaded with ice a sunny winter morning
   After a rain. They click upon themselves
   As the breeze rises, and turn many-colored
   As the stir cracks and crazes their enamel.
10 Soon the sun's warmth makes them shed crystal shells,
   Shattering and avalanching on the snow-crust——
   Such heaps of broken glass to sweep away
   You'd think the inner dome of heaven had fallen.
   They are dragged to the withered bracken by the load,
15 And they seem not to break; though once they are bowed
   So low for long, they never right themselves:
   You may see their trunks arching in the woods
   Years afterwards, trailing their leaves on the ground
   Like girls on hands and knees that throw their hair
20 Before them over their heads to dry in the sun.
   But I was going to say when Truth broke in
   With all her matter-of-fact about the ice-storm

I should prefer to have some boy bend them

As he went out and in to fetch the cows—

25 Some boy too far from town to learn baseball,

Whose only play was what he found himself,

Summer or winter, and could play alone.

One by one he subdued his father's trees

By riding them down over and over again

30 Until he took the stiffness out of them,

And not one but hung limp, not one was left

For him to conquer. He learned all there was

To learn about not launching out too soon

And so not carrying the tree away

35 Clear to the ground. He always kept his poise

To the top branches, climbing carefully

With the same pains you use to fill a cup

Up to the brim, and even above the brim.

Then he flung outward, feet first, with a swish,

40 Kicking his way down through the air to the ground.

So was I once myself a swinger of birches.

And so I dream of going back to be.

It's when I'm weary of considerations,

And life is too much like a pathless wood

45 Where your face burns and tickles with the cobwebs

Broken across it, and one eye is weeping

From a twig's having lashed across it open.

I'd like to get away from earth awhile

第十一章 现代主义诗歌

  And then come back to it and begin over.

50 May no fate willfully misunderstand me

  And half grant what I wish and snatch me away

  Not to return. Earth's the right place for love:

  I don't know where it's likely to go better.

  I'd like to go by climbing a birch tree,

55 And climb black branches up a snow-white trunk

  Toward heaven, till the tree could bear no more,

  But dipped its top and set me down again.

  That would be good both going and coming back.

  One could do worse than be a swinger of birches.

【译文】

白桦树

罗伯特·弗罗斯特

1 挺直、黑黑的树排列成行，只见

  白桦树却弯下身子，向左，也向右，

  我总以为有个孩子把白桦树"荡"弯了

  可是"荡"一下不会叫它们一躬到底

5 再也起不来。这可是冰干的事。

  下过一场冬雨，第二天，太阳出来，

  你准会看到白桦树上结满了冰。

  一阵风吹起，树枝就咯喇喇响，

  闪射出五彩缤纷，这一颤动使冰块坼裂成瓷瓶上的无数细纹。

10 阳光的温暖接着使那水晶的硬壳

从树枝上崩落，一齐倾泻在雪地上——
这么一大堆碎玻璃尽够你打扫，
你还以为是天顶的华盖塌了下来。
压不起那么些重量的树枝，硬是给按下去，直到贴近那贴地的枯草，
15 但并没折断；虽然压得这么低、这么久
那枝条再也抬不起头来。
几年后你会在森林里看到那些白桦树
弯曲着树身，树叶在地面上拖扫，
好像趴在地上的女孩子把一头长发
20 兜过头去，好让太阳把头发晒干。
方才我说到了哪里？是那雨后的冰柱
岔开了我的话头——我原是想说：
我宁可以为是个放牛的农家孩子
来回走过的时候把白桦弄弯了。
25 这孩子，离城太远，没人教棒球，
他只能自个儿想出玩意儿来玩，
自个儿跟自个儿玩，不管夏天冬天，
他一株一株地征服他父亲的树，
一次又一次地把它们骑在胯下，
30 直到把树的倔强劲儿完全制服：
一株又一株都垂头丧气地低下来——
直到他再没有用武之地。他学会了
所有的技巧：不立刻腾身跳出去，
免得一下子把树干扳到了地面。
35 他始终稳住身子，不摇不晃地，
直到那高高的顶枝上——小心翼翼地

第十一章 现代主义诗歌

往上爬，那全神贯注的样儿，就像

把一杯水倒满，满到了杯口，甚至满过了边缘。

然后，纵身一跳，他两脚先伸出去，在空中乱踢乱舞，

40 于是飕的一声，降落到地面。

当年，我自己也是"荡桦树"的能手，

现在还梦想着再去荡一回白桦树，

那是每逢我厌倦于操心世事，

而人生太像一片没有小径的森林，

45 在里面摸索，一头撞在蛛网上，

只感到脸上又热辣、又痒痒；

忽然，一根嫩枝迎面打来，那一枝给打中了的眼睛疼得直掉泪。

我真想暂时离开人世一会儿，

然后再回来，重新干它一番。

50 可是，别来个命运之神，故意曲解我，

只成全我愿望的一半，把我卷了走，一去不返。

你要爱，就扔不开人世。

我想不出还有哪儿是更好的去处。

我真想去爬白桦树，

55 沿着雪白的树干爬上乌黑的树枝，

爬向那天心，直到树身再支撑不住，

树梢碰着地，把我放下来。

去去又回来，那该有多好。

比"荡桦树"更没有意思的事，可有的是。

（方　平　译）

【点评】

该诗是一首遣词简单但意味悠远的无韵诗,运用清新的语言和新奇的隐喻揭示了对人生现实的思考。Frost 有名言"A poem begins in delight and ends in wisdom",而《白桦树》即为这样的一首诗。贯穿全诗的一大隐喻为"天空"与"地面",即秋千摇摆的两个方向,前者为理想世界,而后者为现实世界。

在全诗的开始,诗人看到弯垂的白桦树,便想象是因为有个孩子在白桦树上荡秋千而把树"荡"弯了,而不是被现实的冰霜压弯;而在诗的结尾,诗人转而承认尽管这世上的现实有诸多不尽如人意之处,但我们找不到更好的去处了。于是他从想象中荡秋千孩子的一去一回中得启示:纵使人可以暂时逃离现实一段时间,但没人可以彻底地将自己同现实永远地剥离,只有在幻想与现实之间找到平衡,才能充满信心地更好生活。

第十二章　当代诗歌

第二次世界大战是现代与当代的分界线，但在美国诗歌方面，并不是那么泾渭分明，诗歌有其延续性的一面。战前那一代诗人像史蒂文斯（Stevens）、卡明斯（Cummings）等还健在，笔耕不辍，他们的诗歌创作理论和风格仍旧影响着后来的诗人，被他们视为典范并加以模仿。"中间派"诗人大都按照战前就已确立的风格在写作，只是侧重点不同而已，在诗歌理论和原则方面并没有太大的突破，这是第二次世界大战后美国诗歌延续性的又一个表现。理查德·威尔伯（Richard Wilbur）、伊丽莎白·毕肖普（Elizabeth Bishop）是当时美国诗歌领域比较有影响力的人物。

20世纪40年代末50年代初是美国的麦卡锡时代，当权者的反动政策催生了"垮掉派"的诞生。他们的代表性诗歌《嚎叫》（*Howl*），风格奇特、内容惊人，轰动了整个诗歌界。他们认为好诗的标准就是写你的真切感受、体会到的东西，不加粉饰、原汁原味。作为一个诗派，他们重新发扬了惠特曼的传统，把诗歌从象牙塔拉回街头巷尾。"垮掉派"中最有影响的诗人是艾伦·金斯堡（Alan Ginsberg），他的第一本书《嚎叫以及其他》（*Howl and other*）奠定了他叛逆青年精神领袖的地位。金斯堡的诗歌气势磅礴、感情充沛、直抒胸臆，开启了美国当代诗坛的新时代。

一、Poem Reading

（一）Anecdote of the Jar

Wallace Stevens

1 I placed a jar in Tennessee,
   And round it was, upon a hill.
   It made the slovenly wilderness
   Surround that hill.

5 The wilderness rose up to it,
   And sprawled around, no longer wild.
   The jar was round upon the ground
   And tall and of a port in air.

10 It took dominion every where.
   The jar was gray and bare.
   It did not give of bird or bush,
   Like nothing else in Tennessee.

从20世纪前期开始，美国诗坛充盈着现代主义诗歌的气息，现代主义诗人们为了突出诗歌中的现代主义元素纷纷摩拳擦掌，华莱士·史蒂文斯（Wallace Stevens，1879—1955）即属于这些诗人群体中的一员。与艾略特探讨现代人颓废的精神世界不一样，与庞德集中探讨现代诗歌技巧也不同，更不同于弗罗斯特借助于自然媒介和传统诗歌技巧表达现代主题，史蒂文斯在他的诗歌作品中从哲学层面思考了现实与想象力、现实与艺术、诗人

第十二章 当代诗歌

的社会角色等问题。

史蒂文斯在美国众多诗人中独树一帜,除了诗歌作品中的哲学思考之外,他还有两个特别之处。一是,他属于"大器晚成"型的诗人,在第一部诗集 *Harmonium* 发表时他已经44岁,而直到晚年诗歌作品才被大众接受。二是,史蒂文斯是一位"兼职"诗人,在毕业于纽约法学院之后他成为了一名律师,因此他的诗歌都是在业余时间创作的。但是,这些都不影响史蒂文斯成为一位成功的诗人。他的诗集 *Collected Poems* 为他赢得了普利策图书奖,美国诗歌基金会(the Poetry Foundation)宣称,"从20世纪50年代开始,史蒂文斯就成为美国当代最伟大的诗人之一,他周密的哲学思考深深地影响了其他的作家。"

Anecdote of the Jar 是史蒂文斯的代表诗歌作品之一,其中蕴含了诗人主要的哲学思想。史蒂文斯于1918年在田纳西州伊丽莎白顿镇写下该诗。诗歌初次发表于1919年,其后被收录在史蒂文斯于1923年出版的第一部诗集 *Harmonium* 之中。由于其象征性的抽象语言,针对 *Anecdote of the Jar* 的具体主题含义,评论家众说纷纭。有的评论家从新批评论的角度出发,认为这是一首关于诗歌写作和艺术创作的诗歌;有的评论家从后结构主义出发,提出诗歌中包含了大量时间和语言上后结构主义性质的断裂;有的评论家从女权主义出发,认为诗歌中的罐子和荒野分别代表了现实中的男性和女性,谈论的主要是两性之间的关系;还有评论家从文化批评论的角度出发,从诗歌中寻找到了工业霸权主义的气息;而更有评论家从史蒂文斯诗歌中兼容了美国和欧洲两种文化的特点,认为这是一首基于济慈《希腊古瓮颂》(*Ode to Ancient Greek Urns*)谈论两种文化关系的诗歌。

诗歌由无韵体写成,分为三个诗节,第一行和最后一行诗文均以"Tennesse"结尾,首尾呼应。在一个诗节中,诗人在田纳西州的一个山坡上放了一个罐子,在罐子的对比下山坡周围的景色变成了"无边散漫的荒野"("slovenly wilderness")。第二个诗节写到了罐子和荒野的互动,

罐子使荒野带上了文明的气息，荒野在罐子的媒介下得以呼吸到清新的空气。第三个诗节围绕罐子展开，罐子的文明入侵浸染着荒野，罐子本身是灰暗粗糙的，它也不会生殖繁衍，但却是田纳西州独一无二的那只罐子。通读全诗，罐子和荒野很明显另有深层次的哲学象征，结合史蒂文斯作品中的哲学思想，下面将从两个方面的含义来讨论罐子和荒野的象征。

一方面，诗人很可能是想借用罐子和荒野两个形象来谈论想象力（imagination）和现实（reality）之间的关系。在史蒂文斯的哲学体系中，真正的现实（nature）是不可认识的，而所谓现实（reality）其实是经由诗人的想象力加工而成的"主观现实"（subjective reality）。这样的现实被史蒂文斯称为"超级虚构"（supreme fiction），诗人的责任就是将这种经由想象力加工的超级虚构呈现给读者。换句话说，诗歌就是超级虚构的（"Poetry is the supreme fiction"）。诗歌中，如果罐子代表了诗人的想象力，而荒野代表了现实的话，两者的互动正说明了主观世界和现实世界之间互惠互利的关系。诗文中第1行中"Tennessee"指的是真正的现实，而罐子或者艺术的介入，一方面凸显了自然的荒芜（"wild""wilderness"），另一方面却使荒野变得井然有序（"no longer wild"）。罐子介入之后的现实，即是想象力加工之后的艺术作品，它来源于自然，却不同于自然。没有想象力，自然是冷漠的、不相关的；而想象力的介入，让自然变成了人类可以认识的有序的现实。因此，对于自然来说，想象力就是那个将它释放的罐子（"a port in air"）。与此同时，诗人也意识到了想象力对自然的依存关系。最后一个诗节指出，虽然想象力浸染着荒野，但它本身却是灰白无力的，它不同于田纳西州其他的物体，必须依存于自然而存在着。

另一方面，诗中的罐子和荒野的关系也可以暗喻人类（humanity）和自然（nature）的关系。没有人类的介入，自然只能是冷漠的存在；人类的介入让自然变得井然有序，体现出人文关怀的一面。诗人在诗中利用不同的动词表达了两者关系之中的主动者和被动者。如果罐子暗喻了人类，

第十二章 当代诗歌

而荒野暗喻了自然界，那么诗文第 1 行中的 "placed"，第 3 行中的 "made" 施动者都是人类，即人类主动地介入了自然界。而自然也体现了主动性，第 5 行中的 "rose up" 和第 6 行的 "sprawled" 主动者又成了荒野，即自然因人类的介入而变得井然有序。"round" 一词在文中出现了两次，第一诗节中 "round" 和介词 "upon" 相对应，第二个诗节中 "round" 和 "ground" 对应。"round" 一词意为"圆的"，颇有后天人为的意思，和紧随其后的 "upon" 和 "ground" 对应，更突出了人性和自然的对立。第三个诗节提出，虽然人类在两者关系之中是较主动者，但脱离自然之外的人类却是灰白无力的，与此同时，自然始终保持着自己的独立性。

（二）Crusoe in England

Elizabeth Bishop

1　A new volcano has erupted,

　　the papers say, and last week I was reading

　　where some ship saw an island being born:

　　at first a breath of steam, ten miles away;

5　and then a black fleck—basalt, probably—

　　rose in the mate's binoculars

　　and caught on the horizon like a fly.

　　They named it. But my poor old island's still

　　un-rediscovered, un-renamable.

10　None of the books has ever got it right.

　　Well, I had fifty-two

　　miserable, small volcanoes I could climb

with a few slithery strides—

volcanoes dead as ash heaps.

15 I used to sit on the edge of the highest one

and count the others standing up,

naked and leaden, with their heads blown off.

I'd think that if they were the size

I thought volcanoes should be, then I had

20 become a giant;

and if I had become a giant,

I couldn't bear to think what size

the goats and turtles were,

or the gulls, or the overlapping rollers

25 —a glittering hexagon of rollers

closing and closing in, but never quite,

glittering and glittering, though the sky

was mostly overcast.

My island seemed to be

30 a sort of cloud-dump. All the hemisphere's

left-over clouds arrived and hung

above the craters—their parched throats

were hot to touch.

Was that why it rained so much?

35 And why sometimes the whole place hissed?

The turtles lumbered by, high-domed,

hissing like teakettles.

(And I'd have given years, or taken a few,

for any sort of kettle, of course.)

40   The folds of lava, running out to sea,

would hiss. I'd turn. And then they'd prove

to be more turtles.

The beaches were all lava, variegated,

black, red, and white, and gray;

45   the marbled colors made a fine display.

And I had waterspouts. Oh,

half a dozen at a time, far out,

they'd come and go, advancing and retreating,

their heads in cloud, their feet in moving patches

50   of scuffed-up white.

Glass chimneys, flexible, attenuated,

sacerdotal beings of glass ... I watched

the water spiral up in them like smoke.

Beautiful, yes, but not much company.

55   I often gave way to self-pity.

"Do I deserve this? I suppose I must.

I wouldn't be here otherwise. Was there

a moment when I actually chose this?

I don't remember, but there could have been."

60   What's wrong about self-pity, anyway?

With my legs dangling down familiarly

over a crater's edge, I told myself

"Pity should begin at home." So the more

pity I felt, the more I felt at home.

65　The sun set in the sea; the same odd sun

rose from the sea,

and there was one of it and one of me.

The island had one kind of everything:

one tree snail, a bright violet-blue

70　with a thin shell, crept over everything,

over the one variety of tree,

a sooty, scrub affair.

Snail shells lay under these in drifts

and, at a distance,

75　you'd swear that they were beds of irises.

There was one kind of berry, a dark red.

I tried it, one by one, and hours apart.

Sub-acid, and not bad, no ill effects;

and so I made home-brew. I'd drink

80　the awful, fizzy, stinging stuff

that went straight to my head

and play my home-made flute

（I think it had the weirdest scale on earth）

and, dizzy, whoop and dance among the goats.

85　Home-made, home-made! But aren't we all?

I felt a deep affection for

the smallest of my island industries.

No, not exactly, since the smallest was

a miserable philosophy.

90 Because I didn't know enough.

Why didn't I know enough of something?

Greek drama or astronomy? The books

I'd read were full of blanks;

the poems—well, I tried

95 reciting to my iris-beds,

　"They flash upon that inward eye,

which is the bliss..." The bliss of what?

One of the first things that I did

when I got back was look it up.

100 The island smelled of goat and guano.

The goats were white, so were the gulls,

and both too tame, or else they thought

I was a goat, too, or a gull.

Baa, baa, baa and shriek, shriek, shriek,

105 baa ... shriek ... baa ... I still can't shake

them from my ears; they're hurting now.

The questioning shrieks, the equivocal replies

over a ground of hissing rain

and hissing, ambulating turtles

110 got on my nerves.

When all the gulls flew up at once, they sounded

  like a big tree in a strong wind, its leaves.

  I'd shut my eyes and think about a tree,

  an oak, say, with real shade, somewhere.

115 I'd heard of cattle getting island-sick.

  I thought the goats were.

  One billy-goat would stand on the volcano

  I'd christened Mont d'Espoir or Mount Despair

  （I'd time enough to play with names）,

120 and bleat and bleat, and sniff the air.

  I'd grab his beard and look at him.

  His pupils, horizontal, narrowed up

  and expressed nothing, or a little malice.

  I got so tired of the very colors!

125 One day I dyed a baby goat bright red

  with my red berries, just to see

  something a little different.

  And then his mother wouldn't recognize him.

  Dreams were the worst. Of course I dreamed of food

130 and love, but they were pleasant rather

  than otherwise. But then I'd dream of things

  like slitting a baby's throat, mistaking it

  for a baby goat. I'd have

  nightmares of other islands

135 stretching away from mine, infinities

  of islands, islands spawning islands,

like frogs'eggs turning into polliwogs

of islands, knowing that I had to live

on each and every one, eventually,

140   for ages, registering their flora,

their fauna, their geography.

Just when I thought I couldn't stand it

another minute longer, Friday came.

（Accounts of that have everything all wrong.）

145   Friday was nice.

Friday was nice, and we were friends.

If only he had been a woman!

I wanted to propagate my kind,

and so did he, I think, poor boy.

150   He'd pet the baby goats sometimes,

and race with them, or carry one around.

—Pretty to watch; he had a pretty body.

And then one day they came and took us off.

Now I live here, another island,

155   that doesn't seem like one, but who decides?

My blood was full of them; my brain

bred islands. But that archipelago

has petered out. I'm old.

I'm bored, too, drinking my real tea,

160　surrounded by uninteresting lumber.
　　　The knife there on the shelf—
　　　it reeked of meaning, like a crucifix.
　　　It lived. How many years did I
　　　beg it, implore it, not to break?
165　I knew each nick and scratch by heart,
　　　the bluish blade, the broken tip,
　　　the lines of wood-grain on the handle ...
　　　Now it won't look at me at all.
　　　The living soul has dribbled away.
170　My eyes rest on it and pass on.

　　　The local museum's asked me to
　　　leave everything to them:
　　　the flute, the knife, the shrivelled shoes,
　　　my shedding goatskin trousers
175　（moths have got in the fur）,
　　　the parasol that took me such a time
　　　remembering the way the ribs should go.
　　　It still will work but, folded up,
　　　looks like a plucked and skinny fowl.
180　How can anyone want such things?
　　　—And Friday, my dear Friday, died of measles
　　　seventeen years ago come March.

当现代主义成为美国文学界的主流，艺术家们从开始的无所适从，到

第十二章　当代诗歌

后来跟随不同流派的所谓现代派主张，再到后来在作品中融入不同的现代主义元素。伊丽莎白·毕肖普（Elizabeth Bishop，1911—1979）是早期成熟的现代主义诗人之一，她曾经是美国桂冠诗人，在1956年获得了普利策奖，1970年获得了美国图书奖，1976年又荣获了诺斯达特国际文学奖（Neustadt International Prize for Literature）。虽然毕肖普并不是一位多产的作家，但是她的作品融合了意象派、立体主义（cubism）、精神分析学（psychoanalysis）、女性主义等具有标志性的现代主义理念，独树一帜又极具现代性。

诗歌 Crusoe in England 选自毕肖普出版于1976年的诗歌集 Geography III。虽然该诗集是诗人在世时出版的最后一部作品，但却主要反映了她在20世纪30年代时的一些思考。1934年，毕肖普曾经在马萨诸塞州的卡蒂杭克小岛上居住了几周。她的房东伍瑟努尔（Wuthenaur）是一位生活极其节俭的人，受房东这一形象的启发，毕肖普想要写一首关于追忆拮据生活的诗歌。这首诗歌就是1976年问世的 Crusoe in England，它是诗人所创作的最长的一首诗歌，也是最能体现诗人创作理念的一部作品。诗歌一共182行，采用了叙述诗的方式，由主人公克鲁索讲述了自己曾经在荒岛生存的故事。

诗歌采用了第一人称的视角进行叙述。第1~8行是个引子，克鲁索读报纸看到了一座火山喷发的消息，由此想到了自己曾经的荒岛经历，并开始回忆。从第8~153行，克鲁索讲述了在荒岛的生活。跟随着记忆，克鲁索描述了一个充满迷幻色彩的世界。那里有52座火山，而他经常坐在最高的火山口上，双腿悬垂在火山口外，看着其他正在喷发的火山，幻想自己是一个巨人（第15~21行）。那里有色彩斑斓的山羊、海龟和海鸥，也有不断涌向岸边的层层巨浪（第22~28行）。时而也能看到海上龙卷风，像柔软的玻璃烟囱，美丽但却孤独（第46~54行）。那里也是一个充满了奇幻色彩的各种喧嚣的集合地。山羊的咩咩声，海鸥的尖叫声，来回走动的乌龟发出细微的响声，伴随着密集的细雨嘶嘶的声音，这些声音混杂

在一起，仿佛是暴风之中摇摆的一棵参天巨树（第104～112行）。在荒岛上生活的克鲁索会在夜晚做各种各样的梦，他会梦到文明世界的美食和爱恋，也会梦到不断增多的岛屿（第129～141行）。弗赖迪的出现让克鲁索有了朋友的陪伴，而在这之后荒岛的生活戛然而止，克鲁索和弗赖迪一起被带回了文明世界。第153行诗文将克鲁索从回忆带回了现实，当初在荒岛上生活的用具，如简陋的刀子、残破的遮阳伞、破损的鞋子和裤子，都收藏到了当地的博物馆里，而好朋友弗赖迪也在十七年前死于麻疹。

  这首长诗是毕肖普的一首挽歌，写给已经过世的弗赖迪，也是写给埋藏在记忆深处的荒岛生活。与传统挽歌不同的是，它使用了自由诗体和叙述诗的形式，除了怀念哀悼的情绪之外，更表达了诗人对于现实世界的想法和观点。诗歌混杂了许多现代主义理念，例如意象诗歌元素、超现实主义等。整首诗读下来，读者的脑海中会对一个意象印象深刻，即坐在火山口，惬意地纵览其他火山的克鲁索，而这很明显是受到了当时流行的意象派诗歌的影响。当描写荒岛上充斥的声音时，毕肖普更是启用了超现实主义，利用"暴风中的参天大树"这个形象让各种嘈杂的声音充斥在读者的耳边。另外，该诗中还蕴含了"自白派诗歌"（the Confessional Poetry）的元素。和自白派诗歌代表人物罗伯特·洛威尔（Robert Lowell，1917—1977）交往过从甚密，潜移默化之中毕肖普也受到了影响。诗歌之中文明世界和荒岛生活形成了鲜明的对比，Bishop把荒岛称为"my poor old island"（第8行），暗含了想要寻找能够自由追逐爱恋的理想之地。诗人在诗中说到，"每样事物都有一样，而我也只有一个"（第67行，"there was one of it and one of me"），在荒岛上喝的是自制的饮料（"home-brew"），吹的是自制的笛子（"home-made"），这些只言片语都突出了诗人宣扬个性的自我情感的理想之地。

  诗文中充满了大量的文学典故和引喻。诗歌改编自丹尼尔·迪福（Daniel Defoe，1660—1731）的小说 *Robinson Crusoe*，尽管取材于迪福的

第十二章 当代诗歌

小说人物和情节，但是和之前那个追求理性、闪现着启蒙之光的克鲁索不同，毕肖普的克鲁索成为集中了现代人，特别是作者自己，对生活顾虑和思考的代言人。而诗歌中的经典形象——坐在火山口巨人一般的克鲁索，让读者很容易联想到乔纳森·斯威夫特（Jonathan Swift, 1667—1745）的小说 Gulliver's Traveles 里面小人国和巨人国的故事。另外，这一形象与约翰·济慈的诗歌 Hyperion 里面巨人泰坦（Titans）的特点也有重合。诗文的第 96～97 行"They flash upon that inward eye/which is the bliss ..."直接引用了华兹华斯的诗歌 The Daffodil 的诗句。诗文中的只言片语都可能让读者联想起它背后的文学典故和人物。第 55～62 行中，克鲁索提到了"自怜"（"self-pity"）的问题，对于生存意义的疑惑以及对人生的选择让克鲁索与赫尔曼·梅尔维尔（Herman Melville）笔下的以赛玛利（Ishmael）的形象相重合。

作为现代主义诗人毕肖普的代表作品，Crusoe in England 充满了现代主义中流行的时髦主题。首先，"能指"与"所指"的脱节，语言和现实世界的分离，成为诗歌的重要主题之一。在现代主义理念中，语言对现实起到更多的解构而非建构的作用。语言的这种不足性是诗人想要突出的一个重点。例如，当提到了曾经居住的小岛，克鲁索回忆到"None of the books has ever got it right"（第 10 行）；说到弗赖迪，他又指出："Accounts of that have everything all wrong"（第 144 行）。这两句话都指出，书中的记载都和他的经历脱节，语言并未真实地反映现实世界。第 96～97 行，克鲁索引用了华兹华斯的诗句，但有趣的是他却只记住了诗文的一部分，并许诺回家之后第一件事情就是查清楚整句诗文。隐藏在字里行间的意思是，因为语言不能完全客观地反映现实世界，所以它并不是那么重要。克鲁索可以随意地命名不同的火山（第 118 行），说明了语言的随意性。而紧随其后，克鲁索讲到一个经历，即将小羊羔用浆果涂成红色之后，母羊竟认不出小羊羔来。如果说颜色是可改变的，附着在客观事物外表的语言

更是可随意改变的。

  其次，诗歌的另一主题是寻找女性自己的发声地。毕肖普曾经否认自己是女权主义者，并多次在诗歌中以男性的身份出现。但不可否认的是，她的诗歌透漏出一丝讯息，即为女性寻找一个可以自由发声的世界。有学者指出，诗歌包含了两个世界的对立，即荒岛所代表的内心世界和英格兰所代表的现实世界，诗人借助叙述者表达了对实现内心真实世界的期盼。第129～141行中，克鲁索谈到了梦境。除了美梦之外，他更提到了误杀婴儿和岛屿自身繁殖的噩梦。如果荒岛代表了可望而不可即的梦想世界，那么在荒岛上生活享受美食和爱恋的同时，却受到了来自外在世界的压力，正是这种压力导致了噩梦的发生。可以说，她借助克鲁索的叙述表达了内心渴望一个可以自由爱恋的天堂。

  另外，该诗还包含了最原始的生态思想。荒岛代表了自然界，英格兰则代表了文明世界。克鲁索在诗中表达出对荒岛生活的怀念和眷恋，更是一种最原始最懵懂的生态思想。在最后一个诗节中（第171～182行），克鲁索把在荒岛上使用的笛子、刀子等捐赠给了当地博物馆。然而，失去了这些器具使用的环境，连克鲁索都自问："How can anyone want such things?"（第180行）。一方面突出了两个世界之间的对立，另一方面也表达了他对荒岛生活的怀念。作为挽歌，弗赖迪在诗文的最后两行出现：早在十七年前，弗赖迪已经死于麻疹。弗赖迪来自荒岛，是自然最直接的代表，他死于文明世界的疾病，因此这又是一次两个世界的较量。

（三）Howl—For Carl Solomon

Allen Ginsberg

I

1 I saw the best minds of my generation destroyed by madness, starving

第十二章　当代诗歌

  hysterical naked,

2 dragging themselves through the negro streets at dawn looking for an angry fix,

3 angel-headed hipsters burning for the ancient heavenly connection to the starry dynamo in the machinery of night,

4 who poverty and tatters and hollow-eyed and high sat up smoking in the supernatural darkness of cold-water flats floating across the tops of cities contemplating jazz,

5 who bared their brains to Heaven under the El and saw ……

6 who passed through universities with radiant cool eyes hallucinating Arkansas and Blake—light tragedy among the scholars of war,

7 who were expelled from the academies for crazy & publishing obscene odes on the windows of the skull,

8 who cowered in unshaven rooms in underwear, burning their money in wastebaskets and listening to the Terror through the wall,

9 who got busted in their pubic beards returning through Laredo with a belt of marijuana for New York,

10 who ate fire in paint hotels or drank turpentine in Paradise Alley, death, or purgatoried their torsos night after night

  ……

11 who broke down crying in white gymnasiums naked and trembling before the machinery of other skeletons,

12 who bit detectives in the neck and shrieked with delight in policecars for committing no crime but their own wild cooking pederasty and intoxication,

13 who howled on their knees in the subway and were dragged off the roof waving genitals and manuscripts,

14　who let themselves be fucked in the ass by saintly motorcyclists, and screamed with joy,

15　who blew and were blown by those human seraphim, the sailors, caresses of Atlantic and Caribbean love,

16　who balled in the morning in the evenings in rose gardens and the grass of public parks and cemeteries scattering their semen freely to whomever come who may,

17　who hiccuped endlessly trying to giggle but wound up with a sob behind a partition in a Turkish Bath when the blond & naked angel came to pierce them with a sword,

18　who lost their loveboys to the three old shrews of fate the one eyed shrew of the heterosexual dollar the one eyed shrew that winks out of the womb and the one eyed shrew that does nothing but sit on her ass and snip the intellectual golden threads of the craftsman's loom,

19　who copulated ecstatic and insatiate with a bottle of beer a sweetheart a package of cigarettes a candle and fell off the bed, and continued along the floor and down the hall and ended fainting on the wall with a vision of ultimate cunt and come eluding the last gyzym of consciousness,

20　who sweetened the snatches of a million girls trembling in the sunset, and were red eyed in the morning but prepared to sweeten the snatch of the sun rise, flashing buttocks under barns and naked in the lake,

　　……

II

1　What sphinx of cement and aluminum bashed open their skulls and ate up their brains and imagination?

第十二章 当代诗歌

2　Moloch! Solitude! Filth! Ugliness! Ashcans and unobtainable dollars! Children screaming under the stairways! Boys sobbing in armies! Old men weeping in the parks!

3　Moloch! Moloch! Nightmare of Moloch! Moloch the loveless! Mental Moloch! Moloch the heavy judger of men!

4　Moloch the incomprehensible prison! Moloch the crossbone soulless jailhouse and Congress of sorrows! Moloch whose buildings are judgment! Moloch the vast stone of war! Moloch the stunned governments!

5　Moloch whose mind is pure machinery! Moloch whose blood is running money! Moloch whose fingers are ten armies! Moloch whose breast is a cannibal dynamo! Moloch whose ear is a smoking tomb!

6　Moloch whose eyes are a thousand blind windows! Moloch whose skyscrapers stand in the long streets like endless Jehovahs! Moloch whose factories dream and croak in the fog! Moloch whose smoke-stacks and antennae crown the cities!

7　Moloch whose love is endless oil and stone! Moloch whose soul is electricity and banks! Moloch whose poverty is the specter of genius! Moloch whose fate is a cloud of sexless hydrogen! Moloch whose name is the Mind!

8　Moloch in whom I sit lonely! Moloch in whom I dream Angels! Crazy in Moloch! Cocksucker in Moloch! Lacklove and manless in Moloch!

9　Moloch who entered my soul early! Moloch in whom I am a consciousness without a body! Moloch who frightened me out of my natural ecstasy! Moloch whom I abandon! Wake up in Moloch! Light streaming out of the sky!

10　Moloch! Moloch! Robot apartments! invisible suburbs! skeleton treasuries! blind capitals! demonic industries! spectral nations! invincible madhouses! granite cocks! monstrous bombs!

11　They broke their backs lifting Moloch to Heaven! Pavements, trees, radios, tons! lifting the city to Heaven which exists and is everywhere about us!

12　Visions! omens! hallucinations! miracles! ecstasies! gone down the American river!

13　Dreams! adorations! illuminations! religions! the whole boatload of sensitive bullshit!

14　Breakthroughs! over the river! flips and crucifixions! gone down the flood! Highs! Epiphanies! Despairs! Ten years' animal screams and suicides! Minds! New loves! Mad generation! down on the rocks of Time!

15　Real holy laughter in the river! They saw it all! the wild eyes! the holy yells! They bade farewell! They jumped off the roof! to solitude! waving! carrying flowers! Down to the river! into the street!

III

1　Carl Solomon! I'm with you in Rockland

　　where you're madder than I am

2　I'm with you in Rockland

　　where you must feel very strange

3　I'm with you in Rockland

　　where you imitate the shade of my mother

4　I'm with you in Rockland

　　where you've murdered your twelve secretaries

5　I'm with you in Rockland

　　where you laugh at this invisible humor

6　I'm with you in Rockland

第十二章 当代诗歌

where we are great writers on the same dreadful typewriter

7   I'm with you in Rockland

where your condition has become serious and is reported on the radio

8   I'm with you in Rockland

where the faculties of the skull no longer admit the worms of the senses

9   I'm with you in Rockland

where you drink the tea of the breasts of the spinsters of Utica

10   I'm with you in Rockland

where you pun on the bodies of your nurses the harpies of the Bronx

11   I'm with you in Rockland

where you scream in a straightjacket that you're losing the game of the actual pingpong of the abyss

12   I'm with you in Rockland

where you bang on the catatonic piano the soul is innocent and immortal it should never die ungodly in an armed madhouse

13   I'm with you in Rockland

where fifty more shocks will never return your soul to its body again from its pilgrimage to a cross in the void

14   I'm with you in Rockland

where you accuse your doctors of insanity and plot the Hebrew socialist revolution against the fascist national Golgotha

15   I'm with you in Rockland

where you will split the heavens of Long Island and resurrect your living human Jesus from the superhuman tomb

16   I'm with you in Rockland

where there are twentyfive thousand mad comrades all together singing the final stanzas of the Internationale

17 I'm with you in Rockland

where we hug and kiss the United States under our bedsheets the United States that coughs all night and won't let us sleep

18 I'm with you in Rockland

where we wake up electrified out of the coma by our own souls' airplanes roaring over the roof they've come to drop angelic bombs the hospital illuminates itself imaginary walls collapse O skinny legions run outside O starry-spangled shock of mercy the eternal war is here O victory forget your underwear we're free

19 I'm with you in Rockland

in my dreams you walk dripping from a sea-journey on the highway across America in tears to the door of my cottage in the Western night

San Francisco, 1955—1956

第二次世界大战以及其后的美苏冷战，阻断了之前美国文学的现代主义进程。文学家不再拘泥于细致处的文字游戏，而将对时局的态度和观点写入了作品之中，他们或劝谏、或讽刺、或冷嘲、或呐喊。整个美国出现了一种反主流文化、反主流文学的趋势，这种趋势到20世纪60年代后期更发展成为反文化运动（counterculture movement）。"垮掉一代"（Beat Generation）是这场声势浩大的反主流文化的重要组成部分。战争以及冷战否定了之前所有的价值观和信念，"垮掉一代"对美国政府提出了疑问，他们反对盲目信从、反对政治压迫以及流行的物质主义，这是一场文学运动，同样也是一场社会运动。激进的情绪下，他们表现出对现有意识形态的敌意，倡导一种反传统的审美观和价值观。艾伦·金斯堡

第十二章 当代诗歌

(Allen Ginsberg, 1926—1997)、杰克·凯鲁亚克(Jack Kerouac, 1922—1969)、威廉·巴勒斯(William Burroughs, 1914—1997)是"垮掉一代"的代表作家。其中,凯鲁亚克和巴勒斯分别以 On the Road 和 Naked Lunch 在小说领域取得了极大的成功,而金斯堡则在诗歌领域成为"垮掉一代"作家的首席代言人。

金斯堡是出生在美国新泽西州的犹太人,父亲的古板以及母亲的疯癫都对他后来的艺术创作产生了极大的影响。1954年,金斯堡从纽约来到圣弗朗西斯科,成为"圣弗朗西斯科诗歌复兴"(San Francisco Poetry Renaissance)运动兴起的中坚力量。1955年,在"Six Poets at the Six Gallery"诗歌朗诵会上,金斯堡因朗诵了作品 Howl 而一举成名。他成为"垮掉一代"最重要的代言人,而 Howl 则是"垮掉一代"最重要的代表作品之一。由于迎合了时代的需求,"垮掉一代"作品迅速得到人们的推崇。学者安·查特斯(Ann Charters)认为,在这一运动中金斯堡的地位是不可质疑的,在当时与金斯堡的友谊甚至成为是否隶属这一群体的判断标准。"垮掉一代"作品从最初的边缘化文学,逐渐被人们所接受和推崇,后来演变为主流文化的组成部分。1974年,金斯堡获得了国家图书奖,在提名演讲中他明确表示,作为一场文学运动,"垮掉一代"已经终结。

金斯堡于1954年开始写作 Howl,1955年完成后在"Six poets at the Six Gallery"朗诵,由于其获得了立时的成功,Howl and Other Poems 在1956年由城市之光书店(City Lights Books)出版。该诗一经出版便广受争议,有评论家称诗歌语言粗俗,简直就像是色情作品,其出版商 Ferlinghetti 更是被告上了法庭。之后 Howl 逐渐被读者所接受,如今成为与艾略特的 Waste Land 相并列的重要的现代主义诗歌作品。受老师威廉·卡洛斯·威廉姆斯的影响,金斯堡在创作诗歌初期曾经想采用三行诗的形式(tridac form)。但在创作和修改的过程中,他却发现了一种更适合自己的诗歌形式,即用一口气能够读完的长句子作诗句,所有的句子都有一个共同的首词(a

-561-

long line based on breath organized by a fixed base）。诗歌的最初版本只包含了 Part Ⅰ和 Part Ⅲ，之后又扩充了 Part Ⅱ以及后来的脚注。

金斯堡的艺术创作风格受到不同时代作家的影响，而这种风格集中体现在诗歌 Howl 中。金斯堡多次提到了"布莱克幻象"，即在阅读布莱克诗歌的时候听到了布莱克，甚至上帝的声音。由此金斯堡推断，整个宇宙之中的事物是互相关联的（interconnectedness of the universe），人因此带有神性，这和艾默生的超验主义思想有异曲同工之处。诗人在诗歌中释放自我，将最本真的思想展示给读者，Howl 所展现的正是诗人的这种情怀。金斯堡还受到了浪漫主义时期的诗人惠特曼的影响。两位诗人都反对恣意妄为的征服，主张关注国家的未来，并宣扬个性的自由。Howl 的第一句（"I saw"）让读者联想起了惠特曼充满了爱国主义情怀的诗歌 I Hear America Singing，其中的"I"又与惠特曼的代表作品 Song of Myself 紧密相连，都赞美了一个为自我而骄傲的艺术家。另外，凯鲁亚克"自发性写作"（spontaneous prose）的理念也对金斯堡在 Howl 中使用长句子的写作风格有影响。

选文中的 Howl 包括了 Part Ⅰ的节选和 Part Ⅱ、Part Ⅲ的全部。第一部分是整首诗歌的重点所在，占据了大约三分之二的篇幅，详细列举了诗人身边"垮掉一代"的遭遇。开头的前三句诗文直截了当地指出了该部分的重点和主题。诗人作为一个旁观者看到了"垮掉一代"的悲惨遭遇。他们被疯狂摧毁、热切地渴望着救赎（第 1 行，"destroyed by madness, starving hysterical naked"）。其中的"疯狂"颇有"众人皆醉我独醒"的意味，看似疯狂实则理智地在旁观，而救赎的重要方式（也是主要的方式）则是通过艺术创作。因此，第 2 行中他们寻求毒品，第 3 行中他们渴求艺术的灵感，都是源自救赎。从第 4 行开始，每句诗文都以"who"作为首词，分别描述了不同的受难者。例如，第 6 行重述了金斯堡自己的"布莱克幻象"的经历，第 7 行中在窗户上写下亵渎言语而被开除的是大学时期

第十二章 当代诗歌

的金斯堡，而第8行中烧掉钱币的人是另一"垮掉一代"的代表卢西·恩卡尔（Lucien Carr），等等。正如金斯堡所说，这些诗文是"为像羔羊一样迷失的美国青年所唱的挽歌"。选文中的第11～20行详细地描述了"垮掉一代"的糜烂生活。其中第12，13行的疯狂行径属于比尔·坎纳斯特拉（Bill Cannastra），第19行描写的是生活腐糜的尼尔·卡萨迪（Neal Cassady）。这一段中加入了"pederasty""intoxication""cunt""ass"等粗俗的字眼。正是因为这些元素的介入使得 Howl 自问世之日便广受争议。

Part II建立在首词"Moloch"的基础上，摩洛是《圣经·利未记》闪米族的神，他索要的祭祀品都是生命鲜活的孩子。根据金斯堡的叙述，Part II围绕着摩洛展开，作为一个象征它侵蚀并烦扰着Part I提到的羔羊一般的年轻人，即年轻人痛苦的源泉正是摩洛。前3句诗文引入摩洛。第1句开门见山地指出一个用钢筋混凝土构成的怪兽，专食年轻人的头脑和想象力。它的威力无穷，"孩子们在楼梯下的尖叫！小伙子们在军队里抽泣！老人们在公园里哭泣！"（第2句）。第3句诗文指出了这个怪兽正是摩洛。第4～7句诗文描述了摩洛无处不在、无所不能的特点，它化身为监狱、战争、政治，甚至是充斥在身边的工业文明。第8～9句诗文把摩洛和诗人自己联系起来：诗人深受摩洛的折磨，无时无刻梦想着救赎的天使。第10～15句均是由短促的词语组成，让读者感受"垮掉一代"所受折磨和压力的同时，渴望和他们一起找到一个突破口。金斯堡曾经谈到，第7段的最后一句"Moloch whose name is the Mind!"是整首诗歌的关键句。这句话很明显来自布莱克的诗歌《伦敦》，其中有"Mind forg'd manacles"的诗句。金斯堡在这里是想指出，痛苦来源于思想，正是因为年轻人认识到了社会存在的问题，才会产生压抑愤懑的情绪。

和Part II压抑的情绪不同，Part III肯定并赞美了"垮掉一代"。金斯堡指出，Part III建立在重复的句子"I'm with you in Rockland"之上，整个部分成金字塔的形状，由逐渐变长的句子组成。这一部分的诉说对象是卡

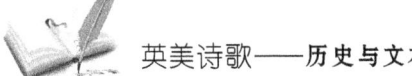

英美诗歌——历史与文本

尔·所罗门（Carl Solomon），金斯堡也将整首诗歌献给了他。1949年，金斯堡在哥伦比亚长老会疯人院（Columbia Presbyterian Psychological Institute）看望母亲时遇到了卡尔·所罗门。由于坚信达达主义已经彻底失败，所罗门主动住进疯人院，并要求做脑叶切除手术，在所罗门看来这和自杀没有什么区别。尽管院方拒绝了这一要求，他却经受了电击、穿紧身衣等非人的对待。金斯堡在所罗门身上看到了"垮掉一代"共有的精神和特质，并将他放置在诗歌的中心位置。贯穿于Part Ⅲ的"我跟你在一起"（"I'm with you"）将整个"垮掉一代"团结到了一起，将诗歌带来的情绪推到了最高点，振奋了年轻人，鼓励他们像凤凰涅槃一般勇敢、坦荡地面对现实。

二、Further Reading

（一）The Snow Man

Wallace Stevens

1   One must have a mind of winter
     To regard the frost and the boughs
     Of the pine-trees crusted with snow.

     And have been cold a long time
5   To behold the junipers shagged with ice,
     The spruces rough in the distant glitter

     Of the January sun; and not to think
     Of any misery in the sound of the wind,

In the sound of a few leaves,

10　Which is the sound of the land,

　　Full of the same wind

　　That is blowing in the same bare place

　　For the listener, who listens in the snow,

　　And, nothing himself, beholds,

15　Nothing that is not there and the nothing that is.

【译文】
雪人

　　　　　　华莱士·史蒂文斯

1　人必须用冬天的心境

　　去注视冰霜和覆着白雪的

　　松树的枝丫；

　　必须冻过很久

5　才能看到挂满冰的刺柏，

　　和远处一月的阳光里

　　粗糙的云杉；才能不因为风声

　　以及这片土地上

　　叶子的声音，想到

10　任何悲惨的际遇，

　　同样的风在同样

荒凉的地方，也为倾听者

而吹，他在雪中倾听，

完全不是他自己，看见

15　一切，以及一切存在中的空无。

（灵　石　译）

【点评】

　　该诗作为史蒂文斯最为著名的诗篇之一，曾多次被编选入集。诗人认为若想生活中不误入歧途，就需要面对精神与情感上的考验。只有拥有冬天的心境，才能真正地看到冬天，即不将荒凉与寒冷理解为标志着人类苦痛的意象，风声也不再代表着人类的悲叹和哭泣。在冬天的心境中，人在看见"一切"的同时，也看到"一切存在中的空无"。一位评论家称：该诗假定了两种读者，一种将自己的内心情感折射到诗中的意象，在风声中听到苦痛悲凉；而另一种则能收纳自己所有油然而生的无端情感，听到的仅仅是风声。对于诗人来说，可以永恒地延续下去的关于想象力与现实间关系的主题在本诗中彰显了极致的张力。所谓现实是否就是无想象力之人看到的世界？如是，那么所谓想象力又是否就是无法面对现实之人心中的世界？如果真相是这样的，那么真相注定也是苦难的。但或许，诗中不曾在风中听到苦痛的雪人，也像其他倾听者一样将情感投射和转移到诗中情境了。又或许雪人看见一切存在中的空无正是因为它本身即为空无的存在。正是因为自我的空无，才会见无所见、闻无所闻，与世间万物融为一体。而这种空无，也许就代表了宇宙的真实。就现实与想象力之间的关系，史蒂文斯认为，想象具有整合一切现实的能力，它作用于人的感官，使现实发生变化。因此，人必须要像那位雪人一样，摒弃感情，去观看雪景，这样就不会联想到人世间的悲凉，从而领悟到宇宙的真谛。

（二）The Idea of Order at Key West

Wallace Stevens

1   She sang beyond the genius of the sea.
      The water never formed to mind or voice,
      Like a body wholly body, fluttering
      Its empty sleeves; and yet its mimic motion
5   Made constant cry, caused constantly a cry,
      That was not ours although we understood,
      Inhuman, of the veritable ocean.

      The sea was not a mask. No more was she.
      The song and water were not medleyed sound
10 Even if what she sang was what she heard,
      Since what she sang was uttered word by word.
      It may be that in all her phrases stirred
      The grinding water and the gasping wind;
      But it was she and not the sea we heard.

15 For she was the maker of the song she sang.
      The ever-hooded, tragic-gestured sea
      Was merely a place by which she walked to sing.
      Whose spirit is this? we said, because we knew
      It was the spirit that we sought and knew
20 That we should ask this often as she sang.

If it was only the dark voice of the sea

That rose, or even colored by many waves;

If it was only the outer voice of the sky

And cloud, of the sunken coral water-walled,

25   However clear, it would have been deep air,

The heaving speech of air, a summer sound

Repeated in a summer without end

And sound alone. But it was more than that,

More even than her voice, and ours, among

30   The meaningless plungings of water and the wind,

Theatrical distances, bronze shadows heaped

On high horizons, mountainous atmospheres

Of sky and sea.

It was her voice that made

35   The sky acutest at its vanishing.

She measured to the hour its solitude.

She was the single artificer of the world

In which she sang. And when she sang, the sea,

Whatever self it had, became the self

40   That was her song, for she was the maker. Then we,

As we beheld her striding there alone,

Knew that there never was a world for her

Except the one she sang and, singing, made.

Ramon Fernandez, tell me, if you know,

45   Why, when the singing ended and we turned

Toward the town, tell why the glassy lights,

The lights in the fishing boats at anchor there,

As the night descended, tilting in the air,

Mastered the night and portioned out the sea,

50　Fixing emblazoned zones and firey poles,

Arranging, deepening, enchanting night.

Oh! Blessed rage for order, pale Ramon,

The maker's rage to order words of the sea,

Words of fragrant portals, dimly-starred,

55　And of ourselves and of our origins,

In ghostlier demarcations, keener sounds.

【译文】
基韦斯特的秩序观

华莱士·史蒂文斯

1　她的歌唱超越了大海的天赋。

水永远不会塑造出大脑或声音，

像一个全然是身体的身体，摆动着

它的空袖；而它模仿的运动

5　发出不断的叫喊，引发不断的叫喊，

那不是我们的，尽管我们能够理解，

它是非人的叫喊，属于名副其实的海洋。

海不是面具。她更不是。

歌声和水不是混杂的声音
10 尽管她所唱的就是她听到的，
尽管她的歌词清晰可辨。
也许在她全部的词句中
有水的碾磨和风的喘息；
但是我们听到的是她，而不是海。

15 她就是自己歌曲的作者。
蒙着头巾，姿态悲惨的海
不过是她前来歌唱的场所。
这是谁的精魂？我们问，因为我们知道
那就是我们一直寻找的精魂，并且知道
20 当她歌唱时我们应当经常这么发问。

如果那只是大海的黑暗之声
升起，被滚滚波涛染上色彩；
如果那只是天和云，被水囚禁的
珊瑚礁的遥远之声，
25 无论多么清晰，它都是空气，
低沉回荡的言辞，是夏季之声
在一个没有尽头的夏季不断重复
独自回响。可它不仅如此，
甚至多过她的声音，我们的声音
30 在水和风无意义的投入之中，
戏剧性的远方，青铜的阴影堆积在
高高的地平线上，天和海

第十二章　当代诗歌

　　显出山岳般的气氛。

　　正是她的声音
35　使天空的消逝变得最为清晰。
　　她测量时辰的孤独。
　　她是世界唯一的创造者
　　她在里面歌唱。当她歌唱，大海，
　　无论拥有怎样的自我，都变成
40　她的歌唱本身，因为她是创造者。而我们，
　　目睹她在那里独自游荡，
　　知道从来没有为她准备的世界
　　除了她歌唱的世界，和歌声创造的世界。

　　罗曼·费南德兹，告诉我，如果你知道，
45　为什么，当歌声休止，我们
　　便返回城里，告诉我，为什么
　　那些停泊的渔舟的灯火，
　　当黑夜降临，倾斜在空中，
　　掌管了夜，分割了大海，
50　划定纹章灿烂的区域和火红的标杆，
　　安排，加深，迷惑着夜晚。

　　哦！苍白的罗曼，为秩序而发出神圣的愤怒，
　　创造者为安排大海之词，星光黯淡，
　　芳香的门户之词而发出的愤怒，
55　以更为可怕的划分，更为敏锐的声响

为我们自己和我们的起源安排词句。

（马永波　译）

【点评】

《基韦斯特的秩序观》是史蒂文斯的早期代表作之一，也是公认的晦涩难懂的作品。这首诗创作于1934年，当时的美国正处于经济大萧条时期，工人失业、农产品价格下跌、很多人濒临破产，社会问题严重，整个社会动荡不安，毫无社会秩序可言。在该诗中，"我"沿着基韦斯特（Key West）海滩漫步，被一名面向大海唱歌的女子的歌声所吸引。在歌声中"我"开始思考人生和美，特别是思考歌声美的灵魂与自己的生活之间的联系。歌声消失后，在返回途中"我"对生活有了感悟。在诗歌创作过程中，与威廉姆斯等其他现代派诗人强调实物意象相比，史蒂文斯还注重了哲学思辨和抽象思维。如同史蒂文斯的其他作品，该诗描述的是"我"的心理活动，探究的是思维过程、感知能力以及想象力。

The Idea of Order at Key West 共有七个诗节，两种声音贯穿整首诗篇。一个是大海的风浪声，另一个是女歌者的歌声。诗的前两节对大海和歌者发出的声音做了比较，强调女歌者的声音充满了想象力和创造性，有一股巨大的、奇妙的力量。第三、四、五节意在探索歌声美妙的原因，并将歌声与天空、大海作比较，突出这些事物的无趣和不稳定的特点，反衬女歌者歌声的穿透力和驾驭能力。正是这充满想象力的神奇歌声，能够净化我们的精神世界，万物更新，最终建立一种诗人向往的新秩序。最后两节叙述了"我"返回镇上的感受。

该诗探讨了现实与想象力、艺术家与自然界的关系。诗人认为缺乏想象力的世界是混乱的、毫无生机的。艺术家的作品源于自然，自然界也亟待由充满想象力的艺术品来装扮。正是这种所谓源于生活又高于生活的艺术，我们才能创造一个世界新秩序。就诗歌而言，它不仅仅是作为艺术家的诗人的表达，也是现实和想象力的结合。

（三）The Emperor of Ice Cream

Wallace Stevens

1   Call the roller of big cigars,

    The muscular one, and bid him whip

    In kitchen cups concupiscent curds.

    Let the wenches dawdle in such dress

5   As they are used to wear, and let the boys

    Bring flowers in last month's newspapers.

    Let be be finale of seem.

    The only emperor is the emperor of ice-cream.

    Take from the dresser of deal.

10 Lacking the three glass knobs, that sheet

    On which she embroidered fantails once

    And spread it so as to cover her face.

    If her horny feet protrude, they come

    To show how cold she is, and dumb.

15 Let the lamp affix its beam.

    The only emperor is the emperor of ice-cream.

【译文】

冰激凌大帝

华莱士·史蒂文斯

1   让那卷大雪茄的人，那雄健的人

过来，让他去厨房

弄几杯诱人的冰激凌，

让少女穿上惯常的服装

5 来悠闲鬼混，让男孩们

用上个月的旧报纸把花儿包装好送来，

让看起来像的东西成为实实在在的东西。

唯一的王是冰激凌大帝。

从缺三个玻璃把手的妆台

10 取出那床单，

在上面她曾刺绣扇尾鸽图案

铺开它，盖住她的脸。

如果她角状双脚伸出单子外，它们

是显示她尸骨已寒，再也不能说话，

让那盏灯光亮闪闪。

唯一的王是冰激凌大帝。

（李正栓　韩志华　译）

【点评】

史蒂文斯的作品主题总是游走在两个极端——现实与想象力之间。他认为现实世界混乱不堪，人的想象力，也指艺术品的创作，能够改变现状，建立一个崭新的世界。但该诗却摒弃了以前的现实与想象力关系主题，展现在读者面前的是一个冷酷但平实的现实问题——妇人之死。

本诗谈论的是死亡主题，诗中的激凌淋象征了令人迷醉却短暂的感官享受，大帝指代的是统治的力量。题目暗示了这样一个现实——短暂的感官享受是人生的统治力量。

本诗分为两节。在第一节中，叙述人讲述了这样一个场景：在雪茄厂工作的男人在厨房搅拌冰激凌，女孩子穿着平时的衣服，男孩子用过期的报纸包着鲜花，一切都是那么随意，毫无参加葬礼的庄重感。第二节直接描述了葬礼的场景：残缺的梳妆台、绣着代表性爱的扇尾鸽的破旧的床单、死者脚上厚厚的老茧。通过第一节的葬礼场景和第二节真实的死亡场景的再现，作者暗示了这样一个事实：死亡就是死亡，无一例外、无法回避。在这两个诗节末尾，作者着重指出"唯一的王是冰激凌大帝"。冰激凌冰冷爽口，能给我们带来愉悦的感受，是我们生活的一部分；死亡虽然残酷，但亦是构成我们生活的一部分。该诗既体现了死亡，也强调了感官享受对于我们生活的重要性，意在提醒人们要用现实的一切来结束幻想。人生短暂，犹如品尝冰激凌，得到的只是片刻的感官之乐，很快就会化为乌有。

（四）The Fish

Elizabeth Bishop

1 I caught a tremendous fish
    and held him beside the boat
    half out of water, with my hook
    fast in a corner of his mouth.
5 He didn't fight.
    He hadn't fought at all.
    He hung a grunting weight,
    battered and venerable
    and homely. Here and there
10 his brown skin hung in strips
    like ancient wallpaper,
    and its pattern of darker brown

was like wallpaper:
shapes like full-blown roses
15 stained and lost through age.
He was speckled with barnacles,
fine rosettes of lime,
and infested
with tiny white sea-lice,
20 and underneath two or three
rags of green weed hung down.
While his gills were breathing in
the terrible oxygen
—the frightening gills,
25 fresh and crisp with blood,
that can cut so badly—
I thought of the coarse white flesh
packed in like feathers,
the big bones and the little bones,
30 the dramatic reds and blacks
of his shiny entrails,
and the pink swim-bladder
like a big peony.
I looked into his eyes
35 which were far larger than mine
but shallower, and yellowed,
the irises backed and packed
with tarnished tinfoil

seen through the lenses

40 of old scratched isinglass.

They shifted a little, but not

to return my stare.

—It was more like the tipping

of an object toward the light.

45 I admired his sullen face,

the mechanism of his jaw,

and then I saw

that from his lower lip

—if you could call it a lip—

50 grim, wet, and weaponlike,

hung five old pieces of fish-line,

or four and a wire leader

with the swivel still attached,

with all their five big hooks

55 grown firmly in his mouth.

A green line, frayed at the end

where he broke it, two heavier lines,

and a fine black thread

still crimped from the strain and snap

60 when it broke and he got away.

Like medals with their ribbons

frayed and wavering,

a five-haired beard of wisdom

trailing from his aching jaw.

65 　I stared and stared

　　and victory filled up

　　the little rented boat,

　　from the pool of bilge

　　where oil had spread a rainbow

70 　around the rusted engine

　　to the bailer rusted orange,

　　the sun-cracked thwarts,

　　the oarlocks on their strings,

　　the gunnels—until everything

75 　was rainbow, rainbow, rainbow!

　　And I let the fish go.

【译文】

鱼

伊丽莎白·毕肖普

1　我捉到一条很大的鱼
　　把他系在了船边
　　半露出水面，我的鱼钩
　　牢牢挂住他的嘴角

5　他没有反抗。
　　他一点也没有反抗。
　　他挂着，一个咕噜作响的重物，
　　憔悴而庄重，
　　并不好看。浑身上下，

10　有着带条纹的褐色皮肤
　　就像古老的墙纸，
　　而他深褐色的图案
　　也像是墙纸：
　　形状像盛开的玫瑰
15　由于岁月褪色和消失。
　　他的身上带着斑点和藤壶，
　　精美的石灰玫瑰花饰物，
　　滋生着
　　细小的白色海虱，
20　在下面两到三根
　　破碎绿草挂着。
　　同时他的腮吸进着
　　混浊的氧气
　　——令人害怕的腮，
25　鲜嫩而带有血丝，
　　可以深深地刺入——
　　我想到粗糙的白肉
　　像羽毛一样充填着，
　　大骨头和小骨头，
30　他发亮内脏的
　　引人注目的红色和黑色，
　　而粉红色的鱼鳔
　　像一朵大大的牡丹。
　　我观察他的眼睛
35　比起我的要大上许多

但更浅，并且发黄，

虹膜收缩就像包着

失去光泽的锡纸

透过有着旧日划痕的

40　鱼胶的镜头可以看到。

它们微微动了一下，但并不

回应我的注视。

——更像一个物体

朝着光倾斜着。

45　我欣赏他阴郁的脸，

他的下颚的结构，

随后我看见

从他的下唇

——如果你能够称之为唇

50　严酷，湿润，像兵器一样，

挂着五根旧日的渔线，

或是四根渔线和一个

仍然带着转节的线头，

所有的五个大钓钩

55　牢牢长在他的嘴里。

一根绿线，根部已经磨损

他从那拉断它，两根更粗的线

和一根黑色的细线

仍然卷曲着，由于用力的拉扯

60　在拉断钓线逃跑的时候。

像戴着勋章上的绶带

第十二章　当代诗歌

　　散开并飘动着，

　　五根智慧的胡须

　　拖在他痛苦的下颚。

65　我注视又注视

　　胜利填满了

　　这条租来的小船，

　　从舱底的积水中

　　油迹展出一道彩虹

70　在生锈的引擎周围

　　直到锈成橘色的水斗、

　　太阳晒裂的坐板，

　　排成一串的船桨，

　　船舷——直到每件东西

75　成为彩虹，彩虹，彩虹！

　　而我放了那条鱼。

【点评】

　　在诗坛，毕肖普和摩尔以善于观察而闻名。1939年1月，毕肖普在给摩尔的信件里，讲述了她写《鱼》这首诗的缘由："前天，我意外地钓到一条鹦嘴鱼。它们是可爱的鱼——是彩虹色的，每个鳞片都有银边，一张公牛似的嘴巴像绿松石；眼睛很大，带有野性，眼球也是青绿色的，它们的样子很滑稽。"

　　在该诗中，诗人对鱼的细致入微的描述可谓出神入化。诗人如生物学家那般观察着、审视着这条鱼，又如思想家般沉思着、猜测着、遐想着，语言质朴、平实，语气客观、冷静。先是鱼身、眼睛、下颚，甚至对海草和寄生物都做了详细的描述，在诗人真实、精细的刻画中，此时的鱼仿佛

有了灵性、尊严,蒙上了一层梦幻色彩,达到了一种超现实的效果,使原本单调、缺乏诗意的主题生动了许多,产生了一种难以抗拒的魅力。诗人眼中的鱼饱经沧桑,有着阴郁的脸,勋章绶带般的胡须,俨然如战功赫赫、威严无比的英雄一般,既让人同情,又让人油然而生敬意。接着诗人描述了小船中的积水,此时幻化成一道彩虹,诗人的情感也从这空灵的色彩中得到了升华:人的一生也如鱼的一生,充满艰难坎坷,但是我们应该和鱼一样百折不弯、不屈不挠,与命运抗争。这种心灵上的顿悟打消了诗人对这条鱼的占有欲,结局顺理成章:鱼被放掉了。细细读来,诗人对鱼有种惺惺相惜的感觉,鱼仿佛成了毕肖普的化身,代表了她内心深处最隐秘的情感,鱼的痛苦即是她的痛苦、鱼的创伤即是她的创伤、鱼的坚韧即是她的坚韧。最后她把鱼放了,在某种程度上而言,也是还自己以自由。

(五) Sestina

Elizabeth Bishop

1 September rain falls on the house.
   In the failing light, the old grandmother
   sits in the kitchen with the child
   beside the Little Marvel Stove,
5 reading the jokes from the almanac,
   laughing and talking to hide her tears.

   She thinks that her equinoctial tears
   and the rain that beats on the roof of the house
   were both foretold by the almanac,
10 but only known to a grandmother.

第十二章 当代诗歌

The iron kettle sings on the stove.
She cuts some bread and says to the child,

It's time for tea now; but the child
is watching the teakettle's small hard tears
15 dance like mad on the hot black stove,
the way the rain must dance on the house.
Tidying up, the old grandmother
hangs up the clever almanac

on its string. Birdlike, the almanac
20 hovers half open above the child,
hovers above the old grandmother
and her teacups full of dark brown tears.
She shivers and says she thinks the house
feels chilly, and puts more wood in the stove.
25 It was to be, says the Marvel Stove.
I know what I know, says the almanac.
With crayons the child draws a rigid house
and a winding pathway. Then the child
puts in a man with buttons like tears
30 and shows it proudly to the grandmother.

But secretly, while the grandmother
busies herself about the stove,
the little moons fall down like tears

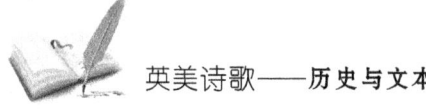

   from between the pages of the almanac

35 into the flower bed the child

   has carefully placed in the front of the house.

   Time to plant tears, says the almanac.

   The grandmother sings to the marvelous stove

   and the child draws another inscrutable house.

【译文】
六节诗

伊丽莎白·毕肖普

1 九月的雨落在房子上。
  黯淡的光线中，老祖母
  和孩子一同坐在
  厨房小巧的火炉边，
5 她们读着历书上的笑话，
  有说有笑，掩饰泪水。

  老祖母想着击打屋顶的雨水
  和自己昼夜之交时的眼泪
  都已被历书预言，
10 但仅为她一人知晓。
  铁壶唱着歌 坐着暖炉。
  她切下一些面包，告诉孩子，

该用下午茶了；可那孩子
在看着火炉上铁壶浑浊的眼泪
15 如屋顶上滂沱的雨水，
在乌黑滚烫的火炉上疯狂起舞。
收拾停当，老祖母
把聪明的历书挂于

绳子上。它像鸟儿一样
20 在孩子的头上，在老祖母
的头上，半张着翅膀，
而深棕色的泪水溢满了茶杯。
她瑟缩着说屋子有点儿冷
并将更多的木柴投入炉中。
25 火炉说："是时候了。"
历书说："我知道我所知道的。"
孩子用炭笔画了一幢歪歪扭扭的房子
和一条凌乱的走廊。然后
又添上一个小人儿：一排纽扣
30 好似一串眼泪，他骄傲地拿给祖母看。

然而，祖母在火炉边
忙忙碌碌，
微小的月亮如同眼泪
从历书敞开的书页间
35 神秘地落入孩子在屋前
精心布置的花床。

"该种植眼泪了",历书说。

祖母对着奇妙的火炉歌唱

而孩子画下了另一幢隐秘的房屋。

(吴德安 译)

【点评】

本诗用诗体 Sestina 来命名,Sestina 是一种结构复杂、严谨的诗体,共六节,每节6行,再加3行做结尾,共39行诗。六节诗的诗句可长可短,但是第一诗节决定了其余诸节,因为这种诗体是通过第一诗节中的诗句尾词在其余诗节中进行错综重复来营造效果的。在该诗中,第一诗节诗行的尾词为 "house" "grandmother" "child" "stove" "almanac" "tears",其余五节也都是以这6个词为诗行的结尾,只不过顺序不同而已。

在 The Fish 中,一条司空见惯的鱼,通过毕肖普精致、准确的描述,读者在佩服毕肖普奇特的观察力和客观想象力的同时,也产生了一种"鱼非鱼"的感觉,这种写作中的陌生化手法在诗歌 Sestina 中也被再次运用。该诗的主题是家。家庭应该是人们最熟悉、最敞开心扉的、充满笑声的温暖港湾,但毕肖普笔下的祖孙俩的家却是神秘的、充满忧伤和泪水的辛酸之地。

毕肖普的童年十分不幸,八个月时,父亲去世,母亲悲伤至极、精神崩溃,她的生活只能辗转在外祖父母和姨妈家。这种流离、孤独、缺乏沟通的生活在该诗中有所反映。细读该诗,悲伤无处不在,充斥着整个家的,除了泪水还是泪水。雨水、壶水、茶水、纽扣、月光,在内心凄苦的祖孙眼里,都幻化成苦涩的泪水,不动声色地诉说着不幸。现实中的房屋大雨滂沱,孩子画中的房屋神秘莫测,这也表达了作者的一种对未来生活的美好愿望,摆脱泪水涟涟的苦难,希冀一个不平凡的("marvelous")明天。

（六）The Armadillo

For Robert Lowell

Elizabeth Bishop

1   This is the time of year
    when almost every night
    the frail, illegal fire balloons appear.
    Climbing the mountain height,

5   rising toward a saint
    still honored in these parts,
    the paper chambers flush and fill with light
    that comes and goes, like hearts.

    Once up against the sky it's hard
10 to tell them from the stars—
    planets, that is—the tinted ones:
    Venus going down, or Mars,
    or the pale green one. With a wind,
    they flare and falter, wobble and toss;
15 but if it's still they steer between
    the kite sticks of the Southern Cross,

    receding, dwindling, solemnly
    and steadily forsaking us,

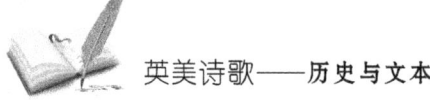

or, in the downdraft from a peak,
20   suddenly turning dangerous.

Last night another big one fell.
It splattered like an egg of fire
against the cliff behind the house.
The flame ran down. We saw the pair

25   of owls who nest there flying up
and up, their whirling black-and-white
stained bright pink underneath, until
they shrieked up out of sight.

The ancient owls' nest must have burned.
30   Hastily, all alone,
a glistening armadillo left the scene,
rose-flecked, head down, tail down,

and then a baby rabbit jumped out,
short-eared, to our surprise.
35   So soft!—a handful of intangible ash
with fixed, ignited eyes.

Too pretty, dreamlike mimicry!
O falling fire and piercing cry
and panic, and a weak mailed fist

40 clenched ignorant against the sky!

【译文】

犰狳

——给罗伯特·洛威尔

     伊丽莎白·毕肖普

1 年年这个时候

  几乎每夜都出现

  那些脆弱的，非法的热气球。

  爬到山顶的高度，

5 升向在这一带

  依然崇敬的一位圣人，

  气球纸壁发红，里面的光

  时亮时暗，像颗颗跳动的心。

  一旦升上天空，就很难

10 把它们与星星区分——

  它们是行星——有颜色的星

  下沉的金星，或是火星。

  或是那淡绿色的星。风一吹来，

  它们就燃烧、倾覆、翻滚、跌闪；

15 但无风时它们会航行在

  南十字那风筝架子中间，

  稳步地离我们而去，庄严地，
  渐渐退远，渐渐暗淡，
  也有可能，在山顶往下吹的风中
20 突然出现危险。

  昨天夜里，又一个大气球跌下。
  它撞上屋后的山岩
  喷溅开来，好像火蛋
  火焰往下窜，我们看见

25 一对营巢于此的猫头鹰飞起来
  翻飞着，时黑时白，
  肚子下映着红色，直到
  它们尖叫着飞出视野。

  这古老的鹰巢肯定已遭火焚。
30 一只皮色光亮的犰狳逃离大火，
  匆匆忙忙，孑然一身，
  斑斑红色，头垂着，尾也垂着。
  然后，一只短耳朵的幼兔
  蹦了出来，把我们吓了一跳。
35 多么柔软！——捧模糊的灰
  一双眼像有火在烧。

  太可爱了，这梦的模拟品！
  哦，坠落的火，刺耳的叫声

第十二章 当代诗歌

和恐怖,那孱弱的披甲的拳头

40　不明真情地对着天空挥动!

(赵毅衡　译)

【点评】

在圣约翰日,有放飞热气球的传统,该诗描述的就是当时里约热内卢的狂欢景象。这首诗出版于1965年,正是从此诗中得到灵感,罗伯特·洛威尔写出名诗 *Skunk Hour*。洛威尔评论说,他从这首诗中学会了如何驾驭诗歌、怎样才能收放自如,并对毕肖普不着痕迹的描写表示赞叹。该诗开篇叙述了这一美轮美奂的烟火盛宴,飘渺升入空中,可称得上气势磅礴。但热气球的破裂对动物而言,却是一场灾难,从猫头鹰、小兔子,甚至有着厚厚盔甲的犰狳也毫无反抗之力,不得不仓皇逃窜。作者通过这一美丽又残酷的事件,使读者意识到非法放飞的热气球造成的一片混乱景象,并对这种事故中丧生的无辜动物表示了同情,也抨击了人类这一不负责任的行为。作者通过对诗节构成和叙事力量的运用,气球的火焰之美与生物的怜弱之美得到了同等的体现,能给人以更多道德感的共鸣。

(七) At the Fish Houses

Elizabeth Bishop

1　Although it is a cold evening,

　　down by one of the fishhouses

　　an old man sits netting,

　　his net, in the gloaming almost invisible,

5　a dark purple-brown,

　　and his shuttle worn and polished.

　　The air smells so strong of codfish

it makes one's nose run and one's eyes water.

The five fishhouses have steeply peaked roofs

10 and narrow, cleated gangplanks slant up

to storerooms in the gables

for the wheelbarrows to be pushed up and down on.

All is silver: the heavy surface of the sea,

swelling slowly as if considering spilling over,

15 is opaque, but the silver of the benches,

the lobster pots, and masts, scattered

among the wild jagged rocks,

is of an apparent translucence

like the small old buildings with an emerald moss

20 growing on their shoreward walls.

The big fish tubs are completely lined

with layers of beautiful herring scales

and the wheelbarrows are similarly plastered

with creamy iridescent coats of mail,

25 with small iridescent flies crawling on them.

Up on the little slope behind the houses,

set in the sparse bright sprinkle of grass,

is an ancient wooden capstan,

cracked, with two long bleached handles

30 and some melancholy stains, like dried blood,

where the ironwork has rusted.

The old man accepts a Lucky Strike.

He was a friend of my grandfather.

第十二章　当代诗歌

　　We talk of the decline in the population
35　and of codfish and herring
　　while he waits for a herring boat to come in.
　　There are sequins on his vest and on his thumb.
　　He has scraped the scales, the principal beauty,
　　from unnumbered fish with that black old knife,
40　the blade of which is almost worn away.

　　Down at the water's edge, at the place
　　where they haul up the boats, up the long ramp
　　descending into the water, thin silver
　　tree trunks are laid horizontally
45　across the gray stones, down and down
　　at intervals of four or five feet.

　　Cold dark deep and absolutely clear,
　　element bearable to no mortal,
　　to fish and to seals ... One seal particularly
50　I have seen here evening after evening.
　　He was curious about me. He was interested in music;
　　like me a believer in total immersion,
　　so I used to sing him Baptist hymns.
　　I also sang *A Mighty Fortress Is Our God*.
55　He stood up in the water and regarded me
　　steadily, moving his head a little.
　　Then he would disappear, then suddenly emerge

almost in the same spot, with a sort of shrug

as if it were against his better judgment.

60 Cold dark deep and absolutely clear,

the clear gray icy water ... Back, behind us,

the dignified tall firs begin.

Bluish, associating with their shadows,

a million Christmas trees stand

65 waiting for Christmas. The water seems suspended

above the rounded gray and blue-gray stones.

I have seen it over and over, the same sea, the same,

slightly, indifferently swinging above the stones,

icily free above the stones,

70 above the stones and then the world.

If you should dip your hand in,

your wrist would ache immediately,

your bones would begin to ache and your hand would burn

as if the water were a transmutation of fire

75 that feeds on stones and burns with a dark gray flame.

If you tasted it, it would first taste bitter,

then briny, then surely burn your tongue.

It is like what we imagine knowledge to be:

dark, salt, clear, moving, utterly free,

80 drawn from the cold hard mouth

of the world, derived from the rocky breasts

forever, flowing and drawn, and since

our knowledge is historical, flowing, and flown.

第十二章 当代诗歌

【译文】

在鱼房

伊丽莎白·毕肖普

1   虽然那是一个寒冷的黄昏
    在一间鱼房里仍有一个
    老人在织网,
    他的网是暗紫褐色的,
5   在薄暮中几乎看不见,
    他的梭子磨损得锃亮。
    空气有一股浓烈的鳕鱼味
    让人淌鼻涕淌眼泪。
    五间鱼房都有尖尖的屋顶,
10 狭窄、嵌有防滑板的步桥斜斜
    伸向那些三角墙里的仓库
    让手推车可以上上下下。
    全是一片银白色:海沉重的表面,
    缓慢地膨胀,仿佛正在考虑溢出,
15 是一片模糊,但长凳、龙虾笼
    和桅杆的银白色却散开
    在嶙峋参差的乱石间,
    是一种清晰的半透明
    犹如古旧的小楼,近岸的围墙
20 爬满翠绿色苔藓。
    大鱼桶悉数排列着
    一层层美丽的鲱鱼鳞片,

手推车也同样厚厚地披裹着
柔滑的彩虹色铠甲,
25　身上爬满彩虹色苍蝇。
鱼屋背后的小斜坡上
放置在零星稀疏的明亮青草中
是一个古旧的木质绞盘,
破裂,有两个漂白了的长把手
30　和一些忧郁的斑点,像干了的血,
绞盘上有铁的部分已经生锈。
老人接受一根"好彩"烟。
他是我祖父的朋友。
我们谈到人口的减少,
35　以及鳕鱼和鲱鱼,
他正在等候一艘鲱鱼船进港。
他的背心和大拇指上都有金属饰品。
他已经用那把旧黑刀削掉了无数的鱼
身上的鳞片,那最重要的美,
40　刀身几乎已经磨损尽了。

在水边,在他们
把船拉上来的地方,在那条
深入水里的长长坡道上,银色的
细瘦树干横放在
45　灰色石头上,每隔四五英尺
就下一个坡度

冷、暗、深和绝对的清晰，

对生物、对鱼和海豹都难以

忍受的自然环境……尤其是一只海豹，

50　我在这里一个又一个黄昏都见到他。

他对我感到好奇。他对音乐感兴趣；

像我这个全身受过浸礼的人，

因此我经常给他唱浸礼歌。

我还唱《强大的堡垒是我们的上帝》。

55　他伫立在水中镇静地

望着我，摇一摇他的头。

然后他就消失了，然后又突然出现

在几乎同一个地方，耸了耸肩

好像这与他更好的判断不符。

60　冷、暗、深和绝对的清晰，

清晰的灰色冻水……回来，在我们背后，

那些高贵的无花果树开始出现。

淡蓝的，伴着重重叠叠的影子，

一百万棵圣诞树伫立着

65　等待圣诞节。水似乎悬挂在

那些灰色和蓝灰色的圆石上。

我一次又一次见到它，一样的海，一样，

轻轻地，淡漠地摇荡在那些石头之上，

冰冷冷自由地在那些石头之上，

70　在那些石头之上，然后是世界之上。

如果你把手插进去，

你的手腕立即就会发痛，

你的骨头会开始发痛，你的手会灼烧
仿佛水是火的化身
75　吃的是石头，燃起暗灰色的火焰。
如果你品尝，它首先会是苦的，
然后是咸的，然后便要烧你的舌了。
它就如我们想象中的知识那样：
暗、咸、清晰、动人、绝对自由，
80　从世界那又冷又硬的口中
从岩石般的胸膛里
拉出来，流动和扭曲，又由于
我们的知识是历史的，于是流动，和涨起。

（黄灿然　译）

【点评】

毕肖普的 *At the Fish Houses* 描写了人类文化与自然之间的神秘联系，给人以视觉上的层次感。她的诗，犹如徐徐展开的一幅画卷：暮色四合，冷清的鱼舍，编织渔网的老人，和老人聊天的"我"，泛着银色的鱼房设施，有灵性的海豹，神秘、膨胀的大海，置身其中，萧瑟、凄凉之感油然而生。让人不得不惊叹于她敏锐的目光和细腻、逼真的描写，而这一切的一切又是那么不动声色。

本幅画中最浓墨重彩的一笔当属老人和"我"的交流。仿佛远古时代的背景下，饱经沧桑的老人谈论着渔村的变迁，语气凝重。画中的"我"静静地听着、冷静地观察着，若有所思。"我"目光所及——鱼房、步枪、仓库、长凳、绞盘处，述说着时光的流逝。冷、暗、深、清晰的、蠢蠢欲动的大海，昭示着神秘。这样一幅动静结合的画面让人产生无限遐思。诗中的老人代表了经验的、世俗的世界，海豹则代表了未知和超验世界，它和"我"的互动不容忽视。海豹对我的好奇,对音乐的兴趣,对赞美诗的不置可否,人类般地耸肩动作,这种人与动物之间的奇特的、和谐的交流,让诗人从与自然的接触进入到一种顿悟式的沉思。人类必须面对生存环境如此不堪的现实:人口减少、鱼类数量下降、海水苦、咸等给人类全身带来疼痛。但是人类没有丧失信心,他们在期盼着,犹如期待着乘着渔船归来的渔民。该诗显示出毕肖普诗歌特有的客观、准确、传神的描述特点。诗中的"我"先以"隐匿之眼"冷静观察,再将"神秘发现"加以暗示,最终将诗人对生活的领悟含蓄说出,完成了诗歌的升华。

(八) A Supermarket in California

Allen Ginsberg

1 What thoughts I have of you tonight, Walt Whitman, for I walked down the sidestreets under the trees with a headache self-conscious looking at the full moon.

2 In my hungry fatigue, and shopping for images, I went into the neon fruit supermarket, dreaming of your enumerations!

3 What peaches and what penumbras! Whole families shopping at night! Aisles full of husbands!Wives in the avocados, babies in the tomatoes!— and you, Garcia Lorca, what were you doing down by the watermelons?

4 I saw you, Walt Whitman, childless, lonely old grubber, poking among the meats in the refrigerator and eyeing the grocery boys.

5 I heard you asking questions of each: Who killed the pork chops? What price bananas? Are you my Angel?

6 I wandered in and out of the brilliant stacks of cans following you, and

followed in my imagination by the store detective.

7   We strode down the open corridors together in our solitary fancy tasting artichokes, possessing every frozen delicacy, and never passing the cashier.

8   Where are we going, Walt Whitman? The doors close in an hour. Which way does your beard point tonight?

9   (I touch your book and dream of our odyssey in the supermarket and feel absurd.)

10   Will we walk all night through solitary streets? The trees add shade to shade, lights out in the houses, we'll both be lonely.

11   Will we stroll dreaming of the lost America of love past blue automobiles in driveways, home to our silent cottage?

12   Ah, dear father, graybeard, lonely old courage-teacher, what America did you have when Charon quit poling his ferry and you got out on a smoking bank and stood watching the boat disappear on the black waters of Lethe?

【译文】

加州超级市场

艾伦·金斯堡

1   今夜你令我浮想联翩，沃尔特·惠特曼。当我走在绿树如茵的街道注视着满月承受着自我意识的头疼时。

2   饿殍般的疲惫驱使我，出发去购买幻象，我冲进霓虹闪耀的水果超级市场，想象着你诗中列举的意象！

3   那桃子！那半影！全家出动购物的夜晚！塞满了丈夫们的走廊！鳄梨中的妻子，番茄中的孩子！——而你，加西亚·洛尔迦，你在

第十二章 当代诗歌

西瓜里做什么?

4 我看到了你,沃尔特·惠特曼,膝下无子,老朽孤独的劳动者,边瞟着店里的伙计,边在冰箱里的冻肉间挑挑拣拣。

5 我听见你提出一个又一个的问题:谁谋杀了猪排?谁给香蕉定价?你是我的天使么?

6 我跟随你在璀璨的罐头山间漫步,被想象中的超市密探尾随。

7 我们大步走在宽敞的走廊向着品尝着各自想象中的洋蓟,占有每一份冷冻食品,却没有经过那收款台。

8 我们去哪儿啊,沃尔特·惠特曼?大门将于一小时后关闭。你的胡须今夜指向何方?

9 (我抚摸着你的书幻想着我们在超级市场里的漫游倍感尴尬。)

10 我们能在孤寂的街道上走一整夜吗?在那树影憧憧、万家灯火中,我们都会感到孤独。

11 我们能梦游在失落的美国在曾经的爱开着蓝色的车沿着大道,回到寂静的故乡么?

12 啊,亲爱的先父,白胡子的贤者,年迈而孤独的勇气导师,当卡戎不再摇桨你站在雾气萦绕的岸边注视着船消失于遗忘之河时你拥有的美国是什么模样?

(惠 明 译)

【点评】

　　囊中空空的金斯堡饥寒交迫,只好来到超市"望梅止渴",这首诗就讲述了他在加州某个水果超市的经历和遐想。透过想象,诗人向读者展现了一幅色彩绚丽、如梦如幻的水果超市的画面:各色各样的水果、五光十色的罐头,以及正在选购食品的大人、孩子。在琳琅满目的商品中,金斯堡联想到美国精神的象征——惠特曼。幻想中的惠特曼和梦幻般的水果超市在诗中交替出现，暗含了现实生活中不可或缺的物质世界和精神生活，也反衬了美国当时物质丰富、精神匮乏的社会现实。在这首诗的后半部，金斯堡透过"the lost America of love"再次点明了全诗的主题。惠特曼写过许多歌颂当时的美国、歌颂人间友爱的诗篇，是勤奋、乐观、积极进取的美国精神的代表。但是到了金斯堡的时代，物质生活是前进了，但精神生活极度空虚，这也使得金斯堡对这种高度商业化的美国的前景并不像惠特曼时期那样乐观。另外，诗的最后一段更加深化了主题。惠特曼死后的亡灵渡过忘川河时，金斯堡问道："你心中的美国将是何等模样"？此问题将诗人的忧伤、愤懑和失望表露无遗。此诗婉约朦胧，情绪舒缓，细读之下不难发现诗人的忧伤与失望。他以跳跃性想象的方式和象征手法表达了自己渴望超越物质世界的羁绊，对到达理想的精神彼岸的向往，抒发了诗人对于逝去的美国精神的怀念和无法到达彼岸的忧伤，充分表达了"垮掉一代"对当时美国现实的愤懑和失望。

参考文献

[1] 毕小君.英美诗歌概论[M].北京:知识产权出版社,2009.

[2] 常耀信.美国文学简史[M].3版.天津:南开大学出版社,2009.

[3] 陈才宇.英美诗歌名篇选读[M].杭州:浙江大学出版社,2007.

[4] 董素华.英语名诗欣赏[M].延吉:延边人民出版社,2003.

[5] 辜正坤.英文名篇鉴赏金库·诗歌卷[M].天津:天津人民出版社,2000.

[6] 郭嘉.英美诗歌精品赏析[M].天津:南开大学出版社,2009.

[7] 郭群英.英国文学新编[M].北京:外语教学与研究出版社,2009.

[8] 何功杰.英美名诗品读[M].上海:上海交通大学出版社,2002.

[9] 侯维瑞.英国文学通史[M].上海:上海外语教育出版社,1999.

[10] 胡家峦.英美诗歌名篇详注[M].北京:中国人民大学出版社,2008.

[11] 胡开杰.诗艺:美国现当代诗歌赏析[M].上海:复旦大学出版社,2005.

[12] 黄家修.英美诗歌鉴赏[M].武汉:武汉大学出版社,2009.

[13] 黄源深,周立人.外国文学欣赏与批评[M].上海:上海外语教育出版社,2003.

［14］ 黄宗英.英美诗歌名篇选读［M］.北京：高等教育出版社，2007.

［15］ 黄宗英.抒情史诗论［M］.北京：北京大学出版社，2003.

［16］ 姜涛.美国诗歌赏析［M］.北京：新华出版社，2006.

［17］ 李赋宁,何其莘.英国中古时期文学史［M］.北京：外语教学与研究出版社，2006.

［18］ 李正栓,陈岩.美国诗歌研究［M］.北京：北京大学出版社，2007.

［19］ 李正栓,申玉革.英美诗歌教程［M］.北京：北京师范大学出版社，2014.

［20］ 李正栓.英国文艺复兴时期诗歌研究［M］.保定：河北大学出版社，2006.

［21］ 刘炳善,罗益民.英国文学选读［M］.郑州：河南人民出版社，2006.

［22］ 刘炳善.英国文学简史：新增订本［M］.郑州：河南人民出版社，2007.

［23］ 刘岩.美国诗歌导读［M］.北京：北京语言文化大学出版社，2000.

［24］ 刘守兰.英美名诗解读［M］.上海：上海外语教育出版社，2006.

［25］ 陆如刚.英语诗歌欣赏［M］.北京：外语教学与研究出版社，2007.

［26］ 罗选民.英美文学赏析教程［M］.北京：清华大学出版社，2002.

［27］ 罗益民.莎士比亚十四行诗名篇详注［M］.北京：中国人民大学出版社，2010.

［28］ 彭予.二十世纪美国诗歌：从庞德到罗伯特·布莱［M］.开封：河南大学出版社，1995.

［29］ 钱清.美国文学名著精选［M］.北京：商务印书馆，2005.

[30] 钱青.英国19世纪文学史[M].北京：外语教学与研究出版社，2006.

[31] 陶洁.美国诗歌选读[M].北京：北京大学出版社，2008.

[32] 陶洁.20世纪美国文学选读[M].北京：北京大学出版社，2006.

[33] 王守仁，方杰.英国文学简史[M].上海：上海外语教育出版社，2006.

[34] 王守仁，何宁.20世纪英国文学史[M].北京：北京大学出版社，2006.

[35] 王守仁.英国文学选读[M].北京：高等教育出版社，2001.

[36] 王佐良，何其莘.英国文艺复兴时期文学史[M].北京：外语教学与研究出版社，1996.

[37] 王佐良，李赋宁.英国文学名篇选注[M].北京：商务印书馆，1999.

[38] 王佐良，周珏良.英国二十世纪文学史[M].北京：外语教学与研究出版社，1994.

[39] 王佐良.英国诗选[M].上海：上海译文出版社，1993.

[40] 吴定柏.美国文学欣赏[M].上海：上海外语教育出版社，2002.

[41] 吴景荣，刘意青.英国十八世纪文学史[M].北京：外语教学与研究出版社，2000.

[42] 吴伟仁.英国文学史及选读[M].北京：外语教学与研究出版社，2010.

[43] 谢群，陈立华.英语诗歌阅读与欣赏教程[M].北京：北京理工大学出版社，2013.

[44] 杨金才，于建华.英美诗歌：作品与评论[M].上海：上海外语教育出版社，2008.

[45] 杨仁敬.20世纪美国文学史[M].青岛：青岛出版社，1999.

[46] 袁洪庚,卢雨菁,杜丽丽.英诗及诗学文选[M].北京:北京大学出版社,2008.

[47] 袁若娟.美国现代诗歌精选评析[M].开封:河南大学出版社,2006.

[48] 张剑,赵冬,王文丽.英美诗歌选读[M].北京:外语教学与研究出版社,2008.

[49] 张金霞.英语诗歌导读[M].保定:河北大学出版社,2008.

[50] 张礼龙.20世纪英美诗歌导读[M].厦门:厦门大学出版社,2008.

[51] 张曙光.从现代主义到后现代主义:二十世纪美国诗歌[M].哈尔滨:黑龙江大学出版社,2007.

[52] 张致祥.西方引语宝典[M].北京:商务印书馆,2001.

[53] 莎士比亚全集[M].朱生豪,等译.北京:人民文学出版社,1995.

[54] 德拉布尔.牛津英国文学词典[M]6版.北京:外语教学与研究出版社,2005.

[55] 狄更生.狄更生诗歌精选[M].王晋华,译.太原:北岳文艺出版社,2010.

[56] 柯恩斯.英国诗歌:从多恩到马维尔[M].上海:上海外语教育出版社,2001.

[57] 朗费罗.朗费罗诗歌精选[M].王晋华,译.太原:北岳文艺出版社,2012.

[58] 罗扎基斯,杨惠中.怎样赏析诗歌[M].上海:上海译文出版社,2005.

[59] 尼古拉斯·H.纳尔逊.英国经典诗歌阅读与欣赏:从多恩到彭斯[M].北京:中国人民大学出版社,2009.

[60] 威廉姆·华兹华斯.华兹华斯诗选(英汉对照)[M].杨德豫,译.北

京:外语教学与研究出版社,2012.

[61] 沃伦.理解诗歌[M].4版.北京:外语教学与研究出版社,2004.

[62] 沃尔特·惠特曼.草叶集[M].代秦,译.合肥:安徽人民出版社,2012.

[63] 沃尔特·惠特曼.惠特曼诗歌精选[M].李视歧,译.太原:北岳文艺出版社,2012.

[64] ADAMS M H. The norton anthology of English literature [M]. New York: W. W.& Company Inc,1986.

[65] BROOKS C,ROBERT P W. Understanding poetry [M]. Beijing: Foreign Language Teaching and Research Press, 2009.

[66] COTTESMAN B. The norton anthology of American literature [M]. New York: W.W.&Company Inc.,1986.

[67] DRABBLE M. The Oxford Companion to English Literature [M]. 5th ed. Oxford: Oxford University Press & Beijing: Foreign Languages Teaching and Research Press, 1998.

[68] PARINI J,BRETT C. The Columbia history of American poetry [M]. Beijing: Foreign Language Teaching and Research Press, 2005.

[69] PECK J,MARTIN C. A brief history of English literature [M].北京:高等教育出版社,2010.

[70] RAFFEL B T. Beowulf [M]. New York: Penguin Group (USA) Inc., 2008.